May you enjoy this tale about my
Grandpa Shaw in the Civil War.

Waldron Murriel McFeller

LEATHER
AND
SOUL

A Civil War Odyssey

From Bondage to Freedom —
A Passage of Body and Soul

Waldron Murrill McLellon

Butternut Press, Publishers

Published by Butternut Press, Publishers
    1913 Winnebago Trail
    Fern Park, Florida 32730-3015
    Phone/Fax (407) 339-9244
    Orders (800) 444-2524

Dedication

To the African Americans of the Old
South at the time of the Civil War and
their unrelenting quest for freedom.

Acknowledgment

My thanks to Enola May Lilly, May Lee Boulds, and Naomi McLellon, for their readings, encouragement, and helpful comments as the tale developed.

CHAPTER 1

Granny Mandy

November 1, 1864. Columbia, S.C. Temperature 72\57, rain, clearing by late afternoon, with scattered clouds and light breezes after the storm. Moon half full, waxing, rising in early evening.

Droplets of sweat rolled down the sides of his chest from his leaking armpits, his prone, quivering body strung tight. Cascading drops tickled his skin and increased his nervous shaking as he peered apprehensively into the gloom. His sweat added to the damp soaking his clothes from the forest floor. The ground seep wet his elbows and turned his pants legs into soggy messes.

"Do you see 'im, Hannibal?" Claude's voice was barely audible. Shivers ran along his spine and the hairs raised on his neck as he lay there waiting for the slave to answer.

"Yassah, Massa Claude." Hannibal grasped Claude's arm and pointed to a dark mass. "He right dere by de sweet gum tree, right like he say he do when I give 'im de note and de gol' coins. Lookin' de other way too."

Claude squinted his eyes in the dim light, almost black dark, with the moon not due up for an hour and the scudding clouds blanking some of the stars. Earth mists were rising from the warm rain in the afternoon.

Dim gloom blurred into a forest of trees until a black shape at the edge of the growth moved and grunted. An eye sees nothing still in blackness, only movement. The telltale error drew Claude's eyes to the sentry. Should be the right time, he thought. He turned to Hannibal and leaned over to whisper quietly in his ear.

"Sneak along down the crick, quiet-like, and see if he moves. If he don't, get way beyond 'im. Then call up a hooty owl and I'll come on easy and slow."

"Yassah, Massa Claude. A hooty owl. Yassah." His servant's stolid answer and stealthy retreat surprised the planter. Hannibal's movements as he stole away seemed all rather casual, almost as if he didn't realize the great danger. The Negro disappeared into the darkness of the steep, brushy bank, avoiding the water. His sinuous, creeping gait and careful path left not a trace of sound.

Claude kept his eyes on the sentry, afraid a sudden noise would draw fire. His thin but muscular frame was pressed tight against the forest duff. Sweat stained his shirt and he shivered constantly in the cool, damp air. The rolled blanket over his shoulder gave him no comfort and the little crawlers of the ground added to his miseries. He cursed under his breath at the ant bites, condemned to endure the torment, since there was no way to escape.

A few tree frogs were faintly peeping, adding to the rustle of the leaves in the light breeze. It was amazing to him that some of the tiny creatures still were out. But the weather had stayed hot and dry through late October, after a heavy, early frost on two mornings. The warm rain from the south had the hardy ones peeping still, before the fall cold drove them into hibernation. All the noise was just enough clatter to shield his movements, Claude thought. He shifted down closer to the low waterfall over an escarpment of a hard bottom ledge, easy for crossing. The ends were bordered by willow bushes, dense growths that provided a shadowy hideaway thicket while he waited.

The water in Gills Creek gurgled and splashed as it fell over the obstructions in the falls and riffles. Rising ground was a godsend, for the creek added another dimension to their escape. It was wadeable even beyond the escarpment, he knew, with a hard bottom everywhere except in the slow, wide bends, and not too difficult to get through. The guards had had them cutting willow brush all along its length. The pliable withes were used for weaving baskets, and for mats for paths and roads in the camp. Even the imprisoned officers had been forced to labor, though Hannibal had done much of his master's work. Claude's broken shoulder still ached. Must have been two damn miles up to the saddle that we stripped, he told himself. Blisters all over his hands! But Hannibal had never complained and had tried to shield him from the hardest tasks.

Bubbling of the creek water, with its musical sounds, was a benefit added to hiding their scent trail if they needed to take to the channel. Those damned dogs had caused the capture of the last three prisoners. It was foremost in his memory - dogs to hunt men. Only Johnny Reb would do that. Just the thought sickened him.

The sentry scratched and groaned. Claude silently laughed while he watched the man claw at his back, his dark shape contorting and squirming. Gray-backs, those pesky body lice, had no respect for rank or position. He could feel them biting in his hairy patches. Couldn't get free of the little buggers. Not even with a bath. But his anxiety increased as he suffered the hurts and waited on Hannibal's call. Where was that damned Negro?

An eternity later, when the starlit blackness finally was fading due to the moonlight flooding above the eastern horizon, he heard the "Who, who, who," of the hooty owl off to the south. The sentry grew still as stone until the call was repeated, then went back to his scratching.

Breaking quickly but silently out of his willow cover, Claude aimed for the entry Hannibal had used to penetrate the thicket. He found a well-trodden game trail and marveled that the body servant had known it was there. But then, Hannibal was a superior Negro. He had picked Hannibal to serve him when he volunteered in '62, mostly because of the slave's familiarity with horses. His wife, Letty, had tearfully objected. Him thirty five and with a family and plantations, traipsing off to war with the 7th Ohio Cavalry. And taking their strongest houseman, the youngest one but his most loyal servant. His belief in the Union had compelled him to go, with a new body servant named after one of the great, conquering generals of all time. But he still hadn't been successful in converting all the patois of the slave to his better English.

Claude's small cooking pot clanked when he passed the blackberry bushes on the slope, thick there in the open space at the creek that was accessible to the sun. Their wait-a-bit thorns would catch everything not successful in detouring though, particularly his woolen uniform trousers, tattered as they were from a year in Confederate jails. He struggled to free the offending thorns. Clicking of the rifle lock alerted Claude to the sentry's cocked rifle and imminent challenge.

"Who goes there?"

Claude snorted and stamped his foot, imitating a buck deer in rut. He struck his horn knife handle against the pot rim, then rattled the bushes before he stole on into the brush. Pausing, he saw the sentry ground his rifle and go back to his tree trunk. The gloom melded them both into a solid black mass. But the soldier's muttered remarks carried in the stillness.

"Fool deer. Jest come on over y'ear and we'uns 'll have good meat t'night."

With the sentry quieted, the planter eased on into the thicket and found good footing on the trail. A mile of the creek went by, his cautious stalk eating up the minutes. Gills Creek was alternately pooled and riffled, with a few small falls due to stumps and snags, along with bordering clumps of pines that added to the beauty of the land. The night lightened as the time passed, with the weather clearing and the silvery rays of moonlight starting to diffuse through the trees. Mist grew thicker in the sharp-banked draw, rising above the creek bed as the air cooled. Rain drops plopped from the trees, shattering down from the rustling leaves and twigs. The damp forest carried invitation along with menace, but the wet floor, with its scented, matted leaf burden, made for quiet steps.

Claude had planned his escape carefully to start with ascendancy of the moon from the first quarter into full glory. Moonlight would give him fine going during the first nights of rapid travel. Fast marches were needed to separate him and Hannibal quickly from the prison work camp northeast of Columbia and the Broad River. Past escapees caught by the dogs had emphasized the need to move far away from the Columbia militia, and into the covering forests of the mountains extending to the North Carolina-Georgia line, if he were to have a chance of escape.

Captain Kelly O'Reilly had waved his blood-stained, bandaged stump of an arm when Claude approached him for help, the amputation a recent souvenir of a minie ball when recaptured. He'd never again fight for New York's Irish Brigade. But his advice to help his friend escape and again take up the cudgel was blunt and specific; in character, the planter thought, as he listened.

"Now Claude," O'Reilly said, quietly serious. "The Johnny Rebs have a passel o' dogs. They're bear and coon hunters, man, used to the dark. Get yer ass away from here and into the Broad if ye expect to escape." He puffed on his pipe and thought for a moment, his added wisdom short and cogent. "Keep clear of the railroad. They's too many guards. Hide yer tracks in water 'til ye shake 'em, then move west into the mountains. Strike across to Dalton from the Chattooga."

"I'll do it Kelly, and many thanks. Work's about done here. Got to head out quick, before they move us back over to Camp Sorghum. Less chance from there."

"Yer right. Their guards shoot anybody passin' the deadline, so ye'd better git now."

Claude nodded in agreement. "About that map of yours," he said. "Could you draw it for me?"

"Gladly. Johnny took me copy but not me mind. Gimme the pencil and paper." Kelly hesitated a moment, his brow furrowed, then drew the map quickly with vigorous, incisive strokes.

Claude had the map, sketched by Kelly but improved by the hidden store of campaign memories of the other prisoners. Gills Creek was a prominent feature and ran up past the prison work camp, northeast of Columbia. The stream snaked south through the timbered, rounded hills, joining the Congaree River below the western junction of the latter with the Broad and the Saluda. He intended to circle

the city and make the Broad before daylight, then swim it
and den up under a snag until dark. But he knew from
Kelly's escape that he had to get away from the creek early,
for the dogs would head right for the water's edge to pick up
the scent.

Crack! Crack! Crack! The volley of rifle fire down the
valley took him unawares. Fear drove him into the cover,
prone and terrified. His heart raced when he heard shrill
shouts and trembling shivers consumed him as he spread-
eagled closely against the earth. Crashing sounds thundered through the dimly lit blackness. A thud followed by
curses came from a fallen man ahead to his right, tripped in
the maze of brush and vines. The thrashing medley that
followed told him several persons were running up the hill
on the other side of the creek. Their shouts, "Thar he goes!"
and "Come on, boys, we'll git 'im!" dismayed Claude. Was it
Hannibal they were after?

As soon as the charging men cleared the far ridge, the
sounds grew fainter. Strung like a bowstring, Claude waited
while the chase drew away from him, not daring to move.
Two more shots rang through the forest, then the yelling
and thrashing noises died out completely. The night sounds
of the forest picked up when peeping of the frogs resumed.
Their tranquility told him he could continue his quiet stalk
down the creek trail.

Claude felt his way along a small shelf where the valley
widened. His step was cautious while he listened and
peered into the gloom, but he still did not see the slave. Fear
was giving way to exasperation when he reached a sharp
bend. The creek was running in several channels at a
massive pileup of large trees, windfalls into the creekbed.
Water splashed and mist rose at the partial dam. The high
velocity caused by the restriction had eroded the hillside
into a steep cutbank to his left. It was overhung by a great
tangle and with no beach, forced him to cross the creek. He
had just felt his way along a huge tree trunk spanning the
water when he thought he smelled the slave. A massive,
overturned stump with its forest of roots rose before him in
the bottom. The clump was black as coal in the gloom of the
surrounding thicket.

A disembodied, "Hist," issued from the clump as he approached it.

Claude stopped in his tracks at the whispered warning. His right hand slid his bowie knife from his belt sheath as he melted silently into the brush. The evasion stimulated another call from the blackness.

"Massa Claude?"

A feeling of relief surged over the anxious planter at Hannibal's familiar voice, irritated though he was by the delay.

"Where you been, boy?" Claude said sharply. "I thought they'd got you! How come you came down so far?" His cutting tone didn't seem to faze Hannibal when the slave materialized from the blowdown.

The servant's white teeth shined in the moonlight as his calm voice reassured Claude. "Dey was some men wid rifles up dere. I cut behint 'em and th'owed some rocks inter de little patch of canes in de swampy place, den went runnin' off." He laughed scornfully. "Dey fired an' come atter me but dose ol' boys can't shoot."

"You're not hit?"

"No, Massa, but dose balls sho' do whistle when dey go by. Last I seed, dose rebs was thrashin' 'roun' in de brake, cussin', clean over ter de bottom behint de next ridge. I doubled back. Dey don' never fin' dis boy." Hannibal rolled on the ground, laughing and holding his sides after he told of the rebs' discomfiture.

Claude's throat clogged at any further recrimination. He felt humiliated that he had been so impatient. Not only had Hannibal protected him but the slave had drawn off the Confederate patrol and freed the way for his easy descent along the creek. His respect grew for the man, beyond the slave's simple loyalty and obedience and the brute strength of the animal. Hannibal had carried him from the battlefield at Rogersville almost a year before to the day, then placed him in the field wagon of the Confederates and never left his side. He had tended Claude's wounds and fed him, always helpful. And now the escape. Perhaps Hannibal no longer simply was a slave to be ordered about, but was he now worthy of respect and attention? And did the slave have a plan of his own? The thoughts troubled him.

Hannibal rose and waited, still chuckling. "Where yo' gwine now, Massa?" he asked, when the planter started down the trail. Claude returned to his side when the man delayed, mad enough to hide him. The darkness hid the planter's angry face but not his growl.

"Now you come along, dammit. We need to skedaddle over to the Broad and cross before first light, so we can't waste any more time here." He tugged at the sleeve of the resisting servant. "I'm goin' on down the crick a little farther, then swing west along the cross trail 'til we strike the Monticello road. Kelly said there was a good ford up the Broad past Crane Creek that the rebs don't guard."

"Bettah t'go by de school road, Massa. Good cover dere."

"But its longer and lots of people. We'll be sighted for sure." Claude's restless tenseness showed in his worried tone.

Hannibal stood in his tracks, stubborn but patient with the injured cavalry officer, sure enough of his position to disagree. "It be only a small piece ter de road ter de school, Massa. I'se got frens dere. Ol' Granny Mandy, she fix us up an' he'p. She got frens all 'roun'."

Claude pondered the idea, rejecting his alternatives one by one. Hannibal must have a girl near the college over by Smith Creek, he thought. The servant had hinted to him of a beautiful Hester, young, and at Granny's. But it struck him as Hannibal waited, and as he recalled his Greenbottom days, that the slaves always would help one another and that old Grannys were the most helpful of all. He had observed that. Making up his mind, the officer surrendered to his servant's plan and motioned him to lead. "Well, let's get on then," he said. " We can't let daylight catch us off the river.

Mandy scooted around in her splint chair. High-pitched complaints sounded from its arthritic joints as she wracked the seat, not much different from her screech, "Hester? Whar be yuh, gal?"

"Out here, Granny," came the girl's reply.   The old

woman sat in the caned chair in front of the cabin's fireplace. Leaping flames lighted up a leathery, seamed face, its burnished ebony cracking from age. Gray hair going white peeped from under her tight bandanna and a flowing skirt and apron covered all but the toes exposed to the intense heat. Firelight gleamed off the cabin windows and lighted the large loom at the other end. Little else occupied the dirt floor, two small beds along the walls and a leaning table holding some wooden bowls and utensils the only furnishings. Jars stood under the table and at places around the walls, out of the way of the occupants, and large baskets full of yarn balls were heaped in a pile in a back corner. Pots and mounds of clothes clustered on pegs around the cabin walls and a ladder rose to the darkness of a loft. A pot hung from a crane above the crackling fire. Vapors from its simmering brew added to the stuffy air of the cabin.

Granny Mandy grew impatient when the girl did not appear. She hit her stick against the table leg and screeched in a reedy voice, "Hester, whar you hidin'? You out dere wid dat no-count Jed?" At a rustle but no reply, the old woman drummed her stick against her chair. "Git on inyere right dis minute!"

Hinges creaked when the rough plank door swung open into the cabin. A young girl with a lissome, slender figure entered and closed the door against the chill, her charms little hidden by a bulky homespun dress and shawl. Her light-brown face was like a thundercloud as she flounced over toward the chair and petulantly spat out, "What you want, Granny? Can't a body be sparked jest a' bit? Way you take on, I jest goin' ter de bad. An' Jed, he's a good boy."

"Good fer nothin', you mean," Granny said scornfully. "He jist trash, lookin' ter fill yer belly. You run 'im off!" The old lady brandished her stick. "I flail you an' him too, I ketch yuh in de bresh. Dat nigger ain't no good."

The girl went over to the fireplace and stirred the pot with a wooden paddle. Satisfied, she sat down on the stone seat built at the face of the chimney on each side.

"Dose walnut hulls 'bout boiled long 'nough, Granny?" she asked. "Dye purty black."

"Leave 'em be," the old woman said. "Needs plenty fer de cloth termorrer." She sniffed and smacked her lips. "Dish up de stew. I'se hungry."

Pulling an iron pot from the warming alcove in the fireplace wall, the obedient girl took two wooden bowls and spoons from the table and filled the bowls full. Rising vapors added a savory aroma to the cabin and the lure of spices sharpened their hunger. They ate in silence, then rested before the fire after Hester cleaned the utensils and put the pot back. Both were dozing when the knock and call came.

"Granny? You dere, Granny? It's me, Hannibal."

The old lady struggled out of her torpor induced by a full belly and warm fire. Hester's face lit up and she jumped from her seat. She straightened her dress, then went over to a small cracked mirror on the cabin wall and primped before it. Their silence led to a furious pounding.

"Granny!" the voice boomed. "You dere?"

"Open de do', Hester, an' let 'im in." Granny's peremptory orders followed the hustling girl as she trotted to the door. "Den take de dye pot off de crane. Put it out in de seep ter cool."

The old lady pried herself up off the chair and faced the entrance, leaning on her cane while Hester opened the door. Dried up and wrinkled though Granny was, she stood regally in the rude cabin, a matriarch in her castle.

Hannibal crossed the floor to Granny, then bowed to her as he took her hand. His obsequies were prolonged, the imperious old woman finally pushing him away. But as he withdrew he reached into his kit pack and took out two bright bandannas and shook out their colorful folds. Claude had taken a stance at one side, appraising the cabin and its two women while Hannibal greeted Granny. Revelation of Hannibal's stash amazed him and left him wondering what the slave had traded for the treasures. The prison camp underground was full of loot, stolen items brought in clandestinely by the servants. And Hannibal always had had an eye for charming women, Claude knew, ever since he had bought the Negro.

Hester waited motionless after moving the dye pot, her eyes fixed on the waving bandannas. Granny was the first to break the penetrating silence.

"What you want, Hannibal?"

"We here, Granny, like I tol' yuh last week. Dishere Massa Claude. He a Linckum sojer. He needs he'p ter get back ter Georgia, up ter Dalton." Hannibal held out the bright colored bandannas and waved them. They shimmered in the firelight as the slave offered his tribute to seduce the women. "He brung a little present fer you an' Hester."

Granny's searching gaze shifted to the planter. The old woman measured him silently, letting him stand there without a greeting, while Hester looked greedily at the bright patterns. Claude stared back at the stately old woman, so typical of the many ancient mammies he had seen. Tough and strong, no, imperial, he thought, and very loyal to a family or a friend. Just the kind to help. He was about to speak, but refrained while he submitted to her piercing inspection and waited for her to accept him. Finally she nodded to Claude and he, accepting the dignity of her manner, bowed back in respect.

The gift broke the stiffness of the reception. Hannibal held out the bandannas to Hester and asked, "You wants one?"

Hester's pleased cry resounded in the cabin. Ignoring her granny's "Wait!", she seized the brighter one and wrapped it around her head. Its color immediately added brilliance to the flush of her cheeks. Hester tucked in its ends and ran to the mirror. She uttered a gasp of delight at her reflection. "Oh, Granny," she said, "it's so purty. Kin I keep it?"

"Yes, chile," the old woman gently replied. "It yer colors, awright." Granny offered the other bandanna to the eager girl. "Tek de udder too," she said. "I'se too old fer dat kin' o' purty."

Her eyes shifted from Hester and locked with those of the planter. He stared unflinchingly until she accepted his burden. "We he'p de gent'man," she finally said, her simple utterance speaking volumes.

Claude's heart skipped a beat at that. He looked about the rude cabin with its meager possessions. Practically nothing, but Granny and Hester would help him to escape.

Even while knowing that slaves who assisted Union run-aways were flogged or worse, the Negroes still persevered. The rebs had made an example of several at the camp. They beat them and killed a few afterwards, a sickening sight added to their severe punishment of the captured escapees. But the spirit of freedom was too strong to stamp out and freedom won - but at a dear price.

Granny broke into his thoughts with her commands to Hester. "Gal, go fetch Jed. An' Bub, too. We need 'em bof, come full moonlight." The girl went out without a sound, while Granny ignored Claude and spoke to Hannibal. The Negro jumped at her peremptory tone and pointed cane. "Boy, fotch de dye pot jist outen de do'." He shuffled off while she called after him. "Be keerful!" she warned, "it still be hot."

She tapped the cane on the stone hearth on his return with the pot. Hannibal obediently set it down in front of the fire and stood quietly waiting on her next task.

Claude was mystified. "What's going on?" he asked. He moved over to the fireplace. "What's that for?"

"Hesh," Granny said. She shook her stick at him. "I'se gwine save yer skin. You do what I says."

The old woman beckoned to Hannibal and issued crisp instructions. "Spread de blanket on de floor. Den you," she said, pointing her cane at Claude, "tek off yer clo'es an' git on de blanket."

Intimidated by the ancient mammy, the planter stripped down, but only to his trapdoor johns. He started to protest but the old woman was not to be denied.

"Hesh," she screeched impatiently. "Tek it all off, you hear, an' git on de blanket. Boots too," she added, when he delayed. "You tinks I ain't seed white folks, atter birthin' all Miz Ashley's chil'ren an' nussin' 'em? An' me wid six boys?" She brandished her stick at him and Claude shucked the underwear. Naked, he shivered in the cool air and sought the fire.

Hannibal had spread the blanket on the dirt floor as near to the hearth as it would fit. Claude sat down on it and faced the flames. He watched the wrinkled Negro woman, wondering what she would do next. Granny Mandy pulled her possibles bag around where it hung on the back of the chair. Rummaging past several projecting knitting needles, she took out a pair of scissors and snipped with them a few times. Then she hobbled over to him and began cropping his curly, dark hair as close as the scissors would cut.

Claude shied away and protested. "Why're you doing this?"

The old Negro whacked him on the back with her stick. "You hesh!" she ordered. She hit him again when he moved a bit and continued grumbling. "I'se gwine mek yer into a real slave, black. Den we seed if we can't git yuh by de rebs." She kept up the snipping as she talked. "Hester an' Hannibal go 'long wid yuh an' talk. You play dumb, iffen she run inter de pickets."

Her activity finally made sense to Claude and he entered willingly into the transformation. As soon as Granny had snipped his hair and beard, Hannibal shaved him bare. When the dye pot was set on the blanket, he and the slave applied the warm, walnut extract liberally, his color turning very dark from head to toe. His skin was drawing and itching while the dye stained him, but he knew it would make him a rich, chocolate brown. The planter dried off in front of the fire, close to it to make the dye set as soon as possible.

He was naked, warming himself at the hearth, when Hester and two young men came into the cabin. A faint aroma of skunk invaded the room, but Granny ignored it and fixed her gaze on the wide-eyed girl.

"Hester, git outen de do'," she said. Defiant, the girl stood her ground while she inspected the bare planter. Granny shushed her budding protest. "Ain't nothin' here fer you ter see. I'se call fer yuh when de gent'man git dress'."

The girl tossed her head angrily and went out into the night. Protesting squeaks sounded when she slammed down on the bench by the cabin wall. Her muttering came through the door. "He ain't no different from Miz Ashley's chil'ren. How come I can't come in?"

"You stay dere 'til I'se ready," Granny called out. "It don' hurt yuh none ter not look at de gent'mans."

The old woman went back to checking the color on Claude. "Dat be 'nough," she told Hannibal, after he patched a few light spots. "Dat let de gent'man pass, 'long's he don' wash."

She seized the back of her chair for support, then pointed her cane at a hanging string of gourds and said, "Tek one o' dose an' fill it wid dye ter tek wid yer. Dey's cobs fer a stopper in de jar under de table. Dat way, you kin fix de spots dat wear off de gent'man fo' you git ter de Yankees." Granny stowed the scissors in her bag while Hannibal transferred the dye.

"I'se Jed an' dishere's Bub," the larger Negro said, when Claude spoke to them. They lounged over by the table, unobtrusive and quiet. Granny had neither greeted them nor given any instructions. That they were fearful of the old woman could be seen in their rolling eyes and wary glances.

Granny's directions were quick and dictatorial when she spoke. "Bring all de clo'es from de pegs, Jed, an' put 'em on de stones by de fire ter warm."

Jed went off like a shot. He gathered and carried a big armful of the items and flung them on the hearth. His second trip was interrupted by Granny.

"An' git de gum boots from de loft. Dey have ter do fer de gent'man."

While Jed emptied all the pegs and then climbed the ladder to the loft, Claude turned his body before the hot fire and the warm chimney rocks and soaked up the heat. He waited, uncertain, while the rustling continued overhead. His amazement increased when Granny imperiously turned to Bub. The Negro shrank back from her ill-concealed contempt.

"You bring de skunk oil an' de skin?" she asked. Rather than answer, Bub held up a small ceramic jug with a cob at the end. He pulled out the stopper and the cabin air became redolent with skunk. From his stance by the fire, Claude could see Bub's smile broaden as the odor discomfited the old woman. She instantly spewed out a command.

"Stop dat!" Bub hastily restoppered the jug and drew back from her menacing stick. "You knows I don' want no skunk inyere. Set de jug down on de hearth."

Bub obediently followed her instructions. But he never spoke and watched warily until Jed came back down the ladder.

"Here de boots," Jed said, when he returned from the loft. He tossed the short boots and a sturdy leather thong onto the pile. "Found a good rawhide harness strip fer his pants."

"Dere dey be, Massa Claude," Granny said. She gestured to the pile of clothes and gum boots. "Put on plenty ter pertec' 'gainst de damp an' col'. Tek a passel o' days ter git ter Dalton."

Claude inspected the pile with distaste. Probably full of bugs, he thought. But he had no choice if he wanted to escape the area as a slave. Overcoming his reluctance, he sorted out a shirt and ragged pants and donned them. Their light weight made him conscious of their scanty thickness, the pieces worn threadbare. Granny tapped her cane on some dirty trousers.

"Tek dis pair pants," she said. "I mek 'em fum de wool years ago. Dey keep yuh warm. You put on 'nother shirt too. Ain't no under clo'es in disyere cabin."

When he started to take off the first pants, she whacked him again. "Wear 'em bof, Massa, an' de shirts too. An' dat heavy coat dere. It come down ter yer knees. You ain't got no blanket no more. Need plenty ter keep yuh warm."

He finally was fitted out to her satisfaction, even down to a battered hat with holes. Probably one from the plantation owner, he thought, for it was a wide-brimmed felt. Originally gray, it had acquired a sweat stained band and dirt color from much exposure. But the boots were bothersome, made for a field hand with big, splayed toes. Try as he might, when he clumped across the cabin, his feet still slid around in them.

Granny sensed his discomfort. She rummaged in her bag and came up with a pair of long wool stockings. "I'se been mekin' deze fer Marse Pickens," she said. "He Miz Ashley's man. But he up ter Virginny right now an' you kin tek 'em. If de boots gib yer trouble, stuff 'em wid grasses."

Claude looked at himself in the mirror when the costuming was finished. Only his knife remained from the original uniform. The face staring back at him was certainly dark enough, but the gray eyes were a bother. His broken nose from running his sled into a tree as a child gave him a passable set of features, he reasoned. With him playing dumb, just grunting, and Hannibal doing the talking, he just might pass. The planter's spirits lifted as he inspected his camouflage. Satisfied, he turned from the mirror and faced the old woman.

He smiled as he said, "It looks good, Granny, and I thank you. When I can, I'll be back to help you, as you've helped me."

Granny waved her stick and shook her head in deprecation. "Ain't no bother, Massa. I'se happy ter he'p 'scapes dodge de rebs. Now we got ter do de rest ter get yuh free." Her screeching call to Hester brought the girl running into the cabin.

"Feed de gent'man an' Hannibal," she said. "We sen' 'em off wid full bellies." Granny's next commands were to Jed and Bub, while the girl stirred the pot and filled two bowls with aromatic stew.

"Tek all de gent'man's clo'es in a bundle. An' de blanket. Roll up de blanket, Bub, so de hair don' fall out. Den you both go down ter de crick an' cut across to de upper island in de Broad, dere 'bove de Saluda. You unnerstan'?"

"Why, Granny?" Bub's question bubbled out in a squeaky, high-pitched voice. His puzzled face evidenced his lack of understanding as he knelt beside the blanket.

"Ter drag a trail to de ribber," Granny said disgustedly. "Pull de blanket and clo'es so dey flop on de groun' an' in de bresh. Leave plenty tracks 'cross de railroad an' de old canal. Dose houn' dogs, dey foller de trail right down de bank ter de water."

"Den what we do, Granny?" Jed asked.

"Tie de gent'man's pants, shirt, an' boots on a dry log and set it adrift. When de rebs fin' it, dey tinks de man drown."

Bub shifted uneasily while finishing up the blanketroll. "What 'bout de blanket, Granny?"

She waved her cane in his worried face and said, "Wash out de hair an' wring it out. Den bring it back here ter me." Her face grew stormy as she fixed her eyes on his and threatened him. "If you don', I put de hex on bof o' yuh. Now git!"

The two picked up their bundles and darted out, intent on their mission. When the sound of their footsteps died away, the old woman settled down in her chair with a groan. A small smile crossed her face as the fugitives sat at her feet and noisily wolfed the stew. Claude scraped his second bowl clean, but refused another helping and passed the piece of gourd back to Hester. He belched comfortably into his covering hand and stretched before the warmth of the fire, then sighed contentedly, now warm and fed. A big yawn presaged sleep.

Granny grinned mischievously. A sparkle lighted up her eyes as she broke into the planter's reverie. "Tasty, be it?"

"Yes, Granny," Claude answered. "What is it?"

"Skunk. Bub bring it dis afternoon. Bury de skin off fum de cabin."

Claude almost threw up. But the meat had been good and his belly felt better than it had in months. He pushed back the queasy feeling.

Sensing his unease, Granny reassured him. "It good meat, Massa. Ain't no beef ner hog no more. De rebs took 'em all. An' coon an' possum skeerce." She laughed triumphantly. "When de dogs come an' de man ask do I seed yer, dey fooled by de skunk."

Claude nodded and yawned repeatedly. His eyes felt heavy, but his urgent need kept him awake. "What next, Granny?"

"Sleep. When de moon full up, it be time ter git. Hester tek you bof ter de ribber." The old lady shuffled around in her seat like a hen on her nest. She watched him closely as he and Hannibal stretched out on the warm hearth and snored away, instantly asleep.

CHAPTER 2

Athey Minns

November 2, 1864. Harbisons, Broad River, S.C. Temperature 64\37, fog in early morning, sunny with scattered clouds. Moon waxing toward full, rising in midevening.

T The wooden pail reverberated from the splashing of the forceful stream. Awakened by the racket, Kelly sat up on his pallet, yawning and wiping the sleep from his eyes. Moonlight cast a silvery glow outside the crude barracks of the prison camp and a faint breeze carried the damp of the river fog through the window openings. But enough light shined through the haze for Kelly to see Frank at the waste bucket, his belly binding loose while he relieved himself.

Kelly stood up and stretched to undo the cricks in his back and shoulders, then ambled over to the pail. He waited patiently at one side for his turn, uninterested in the other sleepers, but couldn't help glancing at a pallet farther up the row. It was bulky from stuffing provided by the prisoners, he knew, with Claude and Hannibal probably long gone from the camp's vicinity. When Frank stepped aside, hitching up his pants, Kelly moved toward the pail, meanwhile whispering his friend.

"What's the time, Frank?" His low undertone not only was to avoid waking the dormant men, but also to not alert the guard nearby.

"Near three, I reckon, from the moon. Still maybe four hours at least to full daylight." Frank swore softly. "Can't tell, exactly. That Johnny took my watch yestiday, damn his hide. It was give to me by m'wife."

"Tough," Kelly said. He shrugged his shoulders. "You know that Atkins is a whoring thief. Corporal Bladin told me he gives it all to his girls down there below Gervais Street." He glanced down and adjusted his stream. "Bladin's all right. He helped me last time Atkins was on the prod."

"Well, at least the bastard didn't get Claude's gold," Frank said. "Claude had Hannibal keep it and that Negro wouldn't tell nobody nothin' 'bout Claude. He really loves that man."

"Do you know why?" Kelly launched into his tale when Frank shook his head. "About ten year ago, Claude come on Hannibal's owner on the road. Hannibal was just a boy. Their wagon had a broke wheel and the bastard was floggin' Hannibal with a whip for driving into a hole."

"Hannibal tell you this?"

"Yep. He said his back was streaming red. Claude knocked the man down and pulled his pistol on 'im. Bought Hannibal on the spot and treated his back. From then on Hannibal's been his man."

"Where was this?"

Kelly adjusted his clothes and stepped away from the bucket. "Up by Staunton in Virginny. Anybody tries to hurt Claude got Hannibal to reckon with."

"You s'pose they're up on the Broad by now?"

"Don't know. But if anybody can get Claude past the Johnnies it'll be Hannibal. He's one smart Negro."

The trail on the flood plain to the river ended in a crumbly, caving rim. Slippery small cobbles, lubricated by the liquid clay, forced Jed and Bub to cling to the willows as they descended the bank at the river's edge. Claude's clothes and blanket dragged in the dirt and brush and and the Negroes' shoes left scrapes that couldn't be missed. When they stood in the eddy of the cold, shallow water, Jed paused and looked about.

The bank was infested with brush, and sharp serrations in the earth and stones of the slope held interspersed

sycamores, willows and oaks. Great root masses projected
at places from collapsed cut banks. The rushing water,
though low, splashed in midriver, where large boulders
lurked and split the flow. Jed knew the quiet edge below the
old canal like his own cabin, from years of trotlining. The
shallow water at the bank continued downstream for miles,
though hard walking from the hidden cobbles on the bottom. They still could be tread, even if slippery from the mud.
His many falls as he fished were well remembered. But
before their wade downstream, a search was needed for a
float for Claude's clothes.

"Need a good big piece o' drift, Bub," Jed said. "You sees
any?'

Bub was standing knee-deep in the chilly water, and
the bright moonlight gave his body no added warmth. He
shivered and protested. "It col', Jed. Why don' we jist th'ow
de clo'es in de ribber an' git?"

"Granny hex us, dat's why. Dat ol' woman got de second
sight. She knows what we do."

"Ain' no way she do dat."

Jed doubled up his fist and waved it under Bub's nose.
"You gits yer ass up de ribber and fin' us a log. I'se lookin'
down." When Bub hesitated Jed punched his friend in the
shoulder and muttered a menacing, "Git!"

The smaller Bub shrank from the danger and waded
upstream while Jed turned down and searched along the
bank. In only a minute or two Jed heard Bub's splashing
return and soft call. The broken stern of a skiff surprised
him when he reached his friend.

"Must o' come down in dat last big water," Bub said. He
pushed the small remnant of a boat into the eddy. It rode up
high, well above the surface. The transom seat provided a
perfect place for Claude's possessions.

The two loaded the clothes into the skiff, but Bub
hesitated when he came to the leather boots. Holding onto
the transom, he picked them up and held the pair aloft.

"Now you looky here, Jed," he said. "Dese boots too
good ter gib ter de ribber er dose Minns."

Jed grabbed Bub's arm and twisted it until the captive
winced. "Put 'em back," he said insistently. His painful grip

forced the smaller man's hold to loosen. Jed finally over-powered the struggling Bub and stripped the boots from his hand. "Like I'se tol' yer, Granny git atter yuh if you do dis." But Bub seized the boots as soon as he was freed and ran up onto the bank.

"I keep de boots," he said, and pulled his knife. "If you tell Granny, I cut yuh bad. Here or den, it don' matter."

Jed shrugged. He pushed the skiff-end out into the current and waded out to waist-deep to make sure it took to the main river flow. Jed watched it float rapidly downstream for a few moments, then returned to the shallow bottom and picked up the blanket roll from its rest on a willow stob. He rinsed out the blanket in the moving water and called to Bub on the bank.

"Come on down, Bub. Ain't gwine tell Granny. We wring out de blanket and git on down de ribber."

It took only a moment for the two to twist the roll to a damp state. Jed threw the blanket over his shoulder and commenced his wade down the river.

Bub hesitated, complaining about the cold. "We freeze in dishere col' water. Why can't we git back up de bank?"

"Got ter keep de dogs fooled. Want dem ter think de sojer went 'cross de ribber." Jed shook his fist when Bub delayed at the edge of the water. "Move yo' ass, boy," he ordered. "It only 'bout a mile down ter de bridge. Den we hole up wid Bertha dere 'til we kin git back ter Granny's."

Hours later, only the gurgle of the river and its mists remained to greet the sunrise.

"Git up! Git up!" Granny's prodding stick roused Claude and Hannibal upright, their yawns belying wakefulness. "It 'most time ter go," the old Negress added.

Claude warmed himself at the fireplace, its stones soothingly hot, though the fire was burned down to coals. A vagrant thought urged him to stay longer within the comfort of the cabin, but the bright moonlight of the window told him it was time to move. Hester was quietly searching the jars and bags at the walls, then placing items on the table. The pile grew until she called to Hannibal to take stock of their supplies. The big Negro rubbed his hands once more before the fire, then ambled over to the table.

"Flint an' steel, parched corn, rawhides - he intoned a small list of urgencies for their trip. "You ain't got no sulfur matches?" he asked. Hester took down a small jar from a shelf and opened it.

"De flints an' steel hatter do," Granny said, softly voicing her disapproval. "Put de jar back, Hester. We keep de matches."

When Claude joined them at the table, the old woman examined him critically, her searching eyes turning up a defect. She picked up his hand and said, "Got ter mek more changes, Massa. Need yer gol' ring an' den you daub de dye on de finger. Can't have de light spot."

"Why?" Claude asked, combatively. "I been wearing that ring for near twenty years. Can't get it off."

"Ain't no slave got ring like dat," Granny said. "Use de grease. It come loose." Claude was fingering the ring, turning it unsuccessfully, when she spoke to the girl. "Hester, give de gent'mans a gob o' de bear fat."

Pulling by Hannibal removed the ring from the slippery finger, but the metal took along a strip of skin. The astringent dye soon clotted the bleeding. Granny fondled the gold, then put it in a crack in a wall log and plastered it over with mud made from the dirt floor and her spittle.

"Dere," she said. "It be safe 'til you come back fer it. Now gimme de belt an' buckle too. Slaves use de rawhide."

Claude was irritated and lashed out at the imperious old woman. "Dammit, Granny, I need a belt to hold up these heavy pants, not some damned thong."

She brushed aside his protest with a wave and a disapproving shake of her head. "Use de rawhide like de rest of de slaves," she said. Her voice sharpened into an order when he didn't move. "Tek off de belt!"

"Granny right, Massa," Hannibal said, explaining. "Ain't no slave got fancy buckle like dat. Leave de belt wid Granny."

The exchange left Claude with a narrow rawhide thong biting into his belly, not like the wide comfortable belt that rode well on his hip bones. He took the silver buckle from the belt and handed it and the strap to Granny. Her first act was to toss the leather roll into the fire.

"Ain't nobody gwine fin' dat when de Minns come," she said.

Claude's thoughts finally crystallized into understanding with his belated realization of the help and concern of the old woman. When the Minnses came, those feared man hunters, she and Hester would be helpless, subject to all the indignities of the brutes. Kelly's tales of the beatings and rough treatment of the Negroes during his escape attempt finally made sense. He felt ashamed of his protests and thinking to reward the old woman, he gave her the buckle.

"You keep the buckle and sell it, Granny. It's silver and worth eight dollars, U.S. It'll help you and Hester."

Fury twisted the old woman's face into a wrinkled, black tornado and her words spilled out in bitter denunciation. "You tinks I'se doin' dis fer money, Massa?" Granny shook her head emphatically in denial and spat, her tone contemptuous. "Reckened you was a better man." She stalked around to her chair and flounced down in it, then tapped her cane on the stones of the fireplace while she mumbled to herself. After toying with the buckle, she threw it into the fire, where the belt was rapidly being consumed.

"It ain't right, Massa." Hannibal's aggrieved face reproached Claude. "Granny an' Hester run de 'scape railroad fer both niggers an' Linckum sojers. Dey don' do it fer money."

Humiliated by the slaves, the planter was in turmoil. He went over to the chair and seized the old woman's wrinkled, black hand. Its soft skin had a grayish cast and shined in the light of the fire. Granny pulled back, but he held her hand firmly. Caressing the smooth parchment, he bent over and kissed her wrinkled cheek. His voice was soft and apologetic.

"It's sorry I am, Granny, that I fussed you and Hester. You're a good woman and I'm grateful. You remind me of my Mammy Rose. When I was a little boy, I used to do things to bedevil her and she always was forgiving. So I beg your forgiveness just like I did with her."

Granny's severe cast softened. She turned to him with a twinkle in her eye and her leathery hand caressed his face. "It ain' no bother, boy," she said gently. "You boys air all alike. Devils. But I reckoned you'd see us fer what we air.

We'uns air people, jist like you, an' tryin' ter he'p. An' you didn't."

Claude wiggled about like a chastised small child, ashamed and silent. His emotion brought a sigh and a shrug and another apology, this time from his heart. "You're right, Granny, and it mortally troubles me. But I meant no offense." He gave her a strong hug. "Please, Granny," he pleaded. "Keep the buckle and sell it. You can use a little money."

In the calm of conciliation, the old woman beckoned to the girl and said, "Hester, bring yer writin' fixins."

Hester produced an old, dilapidated lap desk from another shelf, this one hidden behind the loom. At Claude's amazed grunt and inquiring face, she said, "Miz Ashley taught her younguns ter read and write. She teached me too." Defensively, she added, "She give me de desk an' some paper ter practice with."

"You plays dumb on de trip, Massa," Granny said. "Let Hannibal do de jawin'. He tell 'em you can't talk since you was birthed. You don' do nothin' but grunt."

Claude's heart leaped at her judgment, the same as his. The reasoning made sense. Hannibal was intelligent and completely loyal to him. And he, as a white man, had no reason to question being told to be quiet, for he would condemn himself if he spoke. He couldn't begin to imitate the patois of the slaves. But why the writing desk?

Granny's shrewdness amazed Claude when she revealed the next part of the escape plan. "You need de paper ter fox de rebs. Ain't no niggers go runnin' 'round dis country by deyself 'thout a paper. You got a fren 'roun' close?"

"Pinckney Middleton down on the Cooper," Claude replied. "Osprey's Landing is just out of Charleston. Pinck was the one who arranged for the gold coins I used on the guards."

"Write de pass from him. He yer massa. Make it fer Hannibal ter tek him an' you ter de gol' mines in Jawga."

"The ones near Dahlonega?" Claude asked.

"Dat right. I'se over dere way back. My man dig in de mine fer Marse Pickens when we was young."

Claude selected a sheet of paper from the writing desk and applied himself to the forgery with alacrity. His mind concentrated mightily on imitating the flowing handwriting of his friend as he produced well-remembered loops and swirls. It took only a few minutes to compose the pass. He started to hand it to Hannibal for safekeeping but the old woman objected.

"Read it, Massa."

Claude held the document up to the firelight and read it off:

October 12, 1864

To Whom It May Concern:

This pass will identify my crew boss, Hannibal, and my mulatto, Claude, a mute and a stableboy. These two Negroes are traveling to Dahlonega, Georgia, under my instructions, to work in my gold mine, located between there and Ellijay. This is at the direction of President Davis, who has asked me for as much gold production as possible.

I request all concerned to assist these two Negroes. I will pay any expenses incurred for their upkeep or transportation on proper notice.

Pinckney L. Middleton
Osprey's Landing on the Cooper

October 12, 1864

Countersigned:

Renwick Lowndes, Colonel, Commanding, Charleston District, Army of the Confederate States of America.

by

Huger W. Young
Captain, CSA
Adjutant

"Dat soun' good," Granny said. "Ain' no rebs dare not he'p. Now gimme de paper."

Claude handed over the sheet. Granny went down on her knees on the cabin floor. He protested when she rubbed it in the dirt and smeared it a bit with her fingers, but she ignored him. Folding it into a fourway crease, she handed it to Hannibal, then explained.

"Can't be like new, Massa. Hannibal here got dirty fingers. Paper got ter be ol'."

Claude stood in wonderment of the old woman. He considered himself to be an educated and experienced man, seasoned in fierce battle with the rebs, but her sage advice and minute, detailed preparation savaged the tales of the happy, carefree children that slaves were supposed to be. But his experience as a plantation owner had revealed many to him who were shrewd and astute as well as being fine craftsman. When he considered the past, though, he had to admit that Granny was the best, a master tactician in the war with the rebs.

Hannibal was impatient, eager to leave. With all of Hester's items in his possibles sack, he fidgeted, then blurted out, "Time ter go. De moon gittin' past de prime an' mawnin' comin' on soon."

Granny called out for Hester, who had gone outside. "Where be yuh, gal?"

Hester was straightening her dress when she rushed into the cabin. "I'se here, Granny," she said.

"Take de gent'mans an' Hannibal by de ol' trail down to de ribber. Watch close when you cross de Monticello Trace an' den de tracks, ——, you unnerstan'?"

"Yes, Granny," the girl replied. But she flipped her skirt and tossed her head and her face showed her irritation. "Ain't you 'member I done do dis all dose past times? Why you tell me now?"

"Cause yer flighty, gal. Now you sneak past de pickets dere at Coomer's, den take 'em ter de ribber near Harbisons." Her voice sharpened. "You hear?"

At the girl's nod and continued injured grimace, Granny added some wisdom for the attentive Hannibal. "Dey's a john-boat hid under a blowdown dere. Hester know de place. Tek it an' go straight across de ribber den up 'bout half-mile. Hide de boat in de big drift dere from de spring flood fo' de wah. We get de boat back directly fer de next 'scape. You kin sleep in de logjam dere 'til atternoon."

"Den what?" Hannibal asked.

"Head fer de Meillins' place 'roun' Little Mountain. Joshua, de fiel' han' dere, he he'p yuh. You kin leave de Massa in de woods 'til you fin' Joshua." She paused a moment, ruminating, while they peered at her. "I'se ain't 'spectin' no trouble, if yer keerful."

Hannibal looked at Claude to see if he were ready to go, but then moved about restlessly when the planter nodded. The Negro dropped his head and shuffled his feet in little patterns in the dirt floor. When he did not depart, the planter pushed on him impatiently.

"We have to travel, Hannibal, and fast, if we're to make the river."

"Knows it, Massa. But dey's somethin' else here ter be settled fust."

Granny intent eyes followed the big man as he procrastinated. She looked at him sharply, then her face softened and broke into a smile when he stole a glance at Hester. "What's wrong, Hannibal?" she asked.

"Granny, be Hester spoke fer?"

"You want 'er, Hannibal?"

Hester perked up as her name and future were discussed. She preened a little, a young girl, but one who knew that she was pursued by many as desirable and beautiful.

Hannibal was titillated by Hester's showing off and hastened to the commitment. "Sho' do, Granny. If you gives her, I come back atter dis war an' git 'er. Can't be too long. Dose rebs 'bout whupped."

"She be here, Hannibal," Granny said happily. "Yer better'n dat Jed er Bub she been flirten' wid. You come back an' she be waitin'."

Hester stood silently while her future was settled. Her tempting smile invited Hannibal and he moved to her side and placed an arm about her waist. Turning up her face and kissing him on the cheek, she accepted his intentions. "I be waitin', Hannibal," she whispered. Hannibal's arm tightened in anticipation but Granny, sensing their desire, brought the moment crashing to earth.

She waved her stick and cried, "Git on wid yer. Time ter move, while de moon be up."

Hannibal slung his possibles sack over his shoulder and filed out into the night. Claude hugged Granny, then he and Hester hurried after him.

It was breaking daylight when Hester led the pair through a heavy stand of horseweeds near the river. She chose her path carefully and cautioned them to be quiet, and to be careful not to break the brittle stalks. A low-hugging mist was thick at the ground, with visibility only yards. They had had no trouble on the trails, receiving only one challenge when they passed the railroad, which Hester quieted with a faint tinkle of a cowbell. Creeping clear to the water's edge, Hester and the runaways were shielded from detection by the mists and the heavy growth of drying stalks. Claude inspected the slow current and the surface slick, a pooling above the riffle they could hear farther down. It would be easy paddling and Hannibal in the stern could do most of the work to save his master's shoulder.

When Hannibal grasped her hand and drew her to the water's edge, Hester pointed to the other side, dim now in the paling sky. A great slash in the tree line could be seen above the thick surface fog. "Aim right fer de gash an' paddle real quiet-like," she said. "Mist so thick, nobody see yuh goin' 'cross."

"What den," Hannibal asked. "Same as Granny said?"

"Sho' nuff," replied Hester. "When you git across, go up de ribber 'bout half-mile. Dey's a big drift dere. Hide de boat in de little gut below de pile o' logs. Dey's plenty o' cover. Den you go on up de drift ter de other side an' hide. Put out a little skunk ter drive off de dogs or men."

Claude was casting about, looking for the hideout. "Where's the boat, Hester?" he asked.

Hester led them a few steps to a small rivulet grown over with dense willow and briars. She lifted a willow branch hiding a small split in the brook. "It hid in de little tunnel dere in de thicket. Hannibal got ter crawl in ter git it."

It took only a moment to retrieve the skiff from the tangle, a narrow john-boat with two rough paddles. Hannibal told Claude to take the bow paddle and the planter entered the craft. He staggered when it wobbled, the narrow beam making it more like an unstable canoe. Little knocking sounds reverberated when his boots struck the boards and splashes rolled out over the water surface from the rocking of the hull. To Claude they seemed loud enough to alert any passing reb and shivers of fear ran up and down his back.

"Don' worry, Massa," Hester said. "It git yer 'cross de ribber. But you gotta be keerful an' quiet." Her extra caution produced another admonishment. "Don' want no noise, so be easy wid de paddle."

Chills ran over him when he faced the river and contemplated the crossing in an increasing light, even though good mists still covered the surface. Claude waited impatiently while Hannibal took his leave of the girl. His annoyance grew as the slave delayed and the lightening sky became ever more bright. Turning cautiously as the boat rocked, his slight movement almost tipped over the narrow vessel. But his alarm changed to anger when he found the slave in tight embrace. Hannibal was hugging Hester, whispering in her ear, oblivious to the increasing danger of detection. Furious, Claude hissed at the man, "Hannibal! Get in the boat! Hester told you she'd be waitin'."

The big black man sighed. He reluctantly released the girl's slight, rounded form but held onto her hands. "Be back, Hester," he said, "so don' you go traipsin' with dat Jed er Bub."

"I be waitin," she replied, and held up her lips for a parting kiss. "An' may de good Lord pertec' yuh both." She waved her farewells until the boat disappeared into the mists.

By full daylight the two fugitives had passed the river and hidden the boat in a small cove under the projecting logs of the drift. They climbed over the jumble, its great jam the result of a massive flood. All the small limbs were gone, but the projecting stobs gave good purchase as they worked along the trunks, gradually moving up-river. The obstruction thinned when they reached the end of the big web of fallen trees. A flat extended above the logjam, covered the ever present horseweed. Willows were interspers any approach by an intruder could only be made with great difficulty. The loud rattle of breaking horseweed would prevent surprise.

Claude inspected their position with approval. It was an impregnable place for the two runaways, the natural alarm system and tangle allowing them enough warning, and a difficult path preventing encroachment from behind. Aches and tiredness flooded over him and exhaustion made his eyelids droop. But Hannibal appeared as strong and alert as ever. He bustled about in his search for a quiet, soft bed in the tangle of logs.

"Here de place, Massa," he said, finally satisfied. The servant straddled a three foot log and pointed down under it. Claude moved over to the trunk and looked into the cavity below. It was a small tunnel under the pile, the bottom paved with dry sticks, dead branches fallen off the trees.

"You git on down dere," Hannibal told the planter. "I put out de skunk over here on de side next ter de meadow. Ol' dog er man come 'long tinks de skunk here. Not want ter fool wid him. Go right on by." The slave chuckled. "Massa, dey don' want no trouble wid no skunk."

Claude was almost asleep when he smelled the skunk and heard Hannibal join him on the stick bed.

The bugle call and guards' oaths roused all the prisoners out into the damp morning. Peeping over the eastern forest, the sun bored through the faint mists from the river. A loud bell at the gate announced the arrival of the Commandant and relief detail. Prisoners gathered in groups in front of their crude shelters. Sleep still stained their faces when the guards came among the separate messes to call the roll. Sergeant Atkins started on his list with Corporal Bladin looking on. The alphabetic roll went swiftly as the prisoners answered, until the late letters brought the inevitable confrontation.

"Ryan?"

"Here."

"Shaw?" Atkins waited for the answer but only silence prevailed. The prisoners were extremely quiet, readying for the storm.

"Shaw? Answer, God damn it." Atkins stalked over to the ranks, swearing at them. "Where's Shaw, you damned Yankee pigs."

The prisoners milled about a moment to confuse the Sergeant. Then Kelly O'Reilly replied. "I think he went down to the sinks. The loose bowels been givin' him fits lately."

Atkins called up his Corporal. "Go get Shaw, Bladin, if he's there."

"Right Sergeant." Bladin ran off down the sidehill slope to the sinks, which were located at the lowest extremity of the camp, while Atkins continued with the roll. The affirmatives blended into a smooth set of query and answer.

Bladin had not returned by the time the roll was complete. The Sergeant stomped about impatiently as the minutes passed and his florid face grew red with anger. Atkins' bulbous nose was veined from drink, and his corpulence hinted at more than the reduced rations of the militia. Kelly and all the others knew he feasted on the best, obtained with the money and jewelry extorted from the prisoners, while they ate cornbread and molasses and an occasional piece of meat. Atkins' restlessness finally drove him into the crude hut of Shaw's companions.

"I'll see Shaw's bunk," he said. "Which one is it, Captain?" Prodding O'Reilly with his rifle, he herded the reluctant officer along the beds. Kelly took him to his own pallet, where Atkins dismembered the meager bedding.

Kelly cautiously glanced about and fixed his eyes on Claude's pallet. To his immense relief, it was flat. Some of the pine fronds of the night were bound up into a broom and the rest were scattered about in individual pieces.

Atkins' suspicious gaze roamed the hut, taking in the disordered bedding and the fronds. "Why you got all those pine branches, O'Reilly?"

"It's for the scent, Sergeant. We smell pretty high and the resin is sweet."

Sniffing and unsatisfied, Atkins left the hut and went toward the headquarters at the gate.

Corporal Bladin arrived moments later. His furrowed face mirrored his anxiety. "Lieutenant Shaw, he come back? He ain't down to the sinks."

"Nope, he ain't here," Kelly said, as spokesman for the mess. When Bladin looked about uncertainly, Kelly pointed down the line of huts. "The Sergeant went off to the gate."

Three hours passed before the guards completed their search and reported to the Commandant. Major Jones sat in the rude chair behind his desk in the headquarters shack, Sergeant Atkins and the officers of the camp paraded at attention before him. Blunt in his instructions and exuding authority after leading men and experiencing several wounds in battle, the twenty five year old Commandant was irritable and direct.

"The entire camp been searched?"

"Yessir, Major," his deputy replied. "We checked every mess and the early details. He's not in the camp." The officer stood at rigid attention, waiting on the Major's orders.

"He's escaped then," Jones said, disgustedly. "Anybody have a guess how he did it?" At their silence, he shook his head resignedly. "Well, no matter now. Got to get him back. Gives the others bad ideas." He leaned back in his chair and scratched an itch, his face thoughtful. "We can't have even one escape among the 200 odd we got. Bad example for the rest." He paused. "And the other Yankees at Sorghum when we move in a few weeks."

The officers mumbled approval when he announced their course of action. "Sergeant, go get Athey Minns and his dog. Fetch him in to see me soon as you return. That woodsman brought back the last three right quick and he'll get Shaw too."

Atkins saluted and turned smartly on his heel. He hurried out, his footfalls rapidly fading.

"Any further questions?" Jones asked. Headshakes by his staff brought a quick "Dismissed."

The large cabin sat on the side slope and dominated the cleared area, its outbuildings sprawled closeby. A thin, blue tendril of smoke trailed from the stone chimney of the house when Atkins came up. He smelled the fire as he approached, its acrid aroma permeating all the downdrafts along the meadow. Built during the Indian troubles decades earlier,

Minns had never improved his cabin, a fort with slits instead of windows. Talk at the camp was that he was a dangerous man. Even though he knew Minns, the Sergeant felt the menace. His hair rose on his neck as he hallooed and approached the projecting porch. Quiet was broken by a pack of motley dogs running out of the woods at the side, barking and aggressive. Atkins stopped and raised his rifle, ready to protect his person.

"Blue! Sing! Song! The rest of ye, git! Git on back!" At the command of Minns, who had stepped out of the door, the dogs raced off, except for one that stood there and wagged its tail. The Sergeant knew the dog from an earlier chase and tossed it a bit of pone.

Minns laughed. "Ol' Blue 'members yuh, Sergeant. He never fergit that grub you give him afore." Athey Minns towered over the fat Sergeant from his position on the porch. Tall, whipcord gaunt but solidly muscled, Minns' sharp, high cheekbones and dark, slick hair attested to his Cherokee blood. His grayish beard covered the lower part of a jagged scar, one that rose up through his missing left eye, closed and sunken. Moccasins set him apart from the settler and the plow, and no corn grew on his homestead. He was a hunter of hides, meat and men, and whiskey stiller, and little given to speech.

Atkins broke the uncomfortable silence. "Major needs yuh, Athey." Minns stared down at the Sergeant, skewering the man with his contemptuous tone. "'nother one done 'scaped?"

"Yep. Lieutenant from Ohio named Shaw. Major wants yuh to come down with yer dogs an' find him."

"Jared! Jeremy!" At Athey's shout, kids came tumbling out of the door behind him and two large boys approached from the sheds by the spring above the cabin. The dogs ran around barking, caught up in the excitement, but trailed the boys to their stance by Atkins.

"How's she runnin', boys," Minns said.

"Fine, Pa, Jared replied. "The mash, it's ready to do all the 'stillin'."

"How long to finish?"

"Reckon rest o' t'day, Pa."

Minns nodded. "Then that does it, Sergeant," he said,

and dismissed the man with a wave. "I be in to the camp termorrer, come daylight."

Recalling the Major's blunt instructions and fearing failure, Atkins plaintively protested. "Major says to come right now, Athey."

Minns' scar flamed red at the order. His face clouded and he took a step toward Atkins, who half- raised his rifle. At Athey's wave, Old Blue was on the Sergeant like a shot and chewed on his arm. Jared seized the rifle as the soldier struggled, then took a stance to one side and pointed the weapon at the Sergeant. Athey's quick command brought Old Blue to heel, but his attack left the soldier staggering and cowed. Atkins cringed in front of the cabin. He rubbed his aching arm and swore at the lot of them. But the woodsman's descent from the porch and close approach scared the Sergeant into silence, his shivers warning of disaster.

Minns thrust his face up close to Atkins' and repeated his decision. "Now you tell the Major I be there termorrer. You hear that?"

"He ain't goin'a be happy, you puttin' him off that way." Atkins whining, woeful voice matched the anxiety in his face. "He don' want no 'scapes, an' that Shaw'll have two days start afore you even come in."

Minns made a slighting gesture, again dismissing the man. "Git on back to the Major." he said. "We'll ketch the bastard jest like we done all the others. I ain't goin'a leave off runnin' the shine t'day." Scorn added to the combative timbre of his voice. "You tell the Major that." But then he temporized, adding, "He likes his dram an' I'll bring you both a gourd termorrer."

Motioning to Jared, Minns ignored the Sergeant and went back into the cabin. The youth tossed Atkins the rifle. "Git!" he said contemptuously, and turned away.

The big boy went back up toward the sheds with his brother and left the Sergeant alone with the circling dogs. Atkins backed off with his rifle ready until the hounds lost interest, then turned and ran down the slope to the trees. He was sweating from the exercise and fear, and went forward to his meeting with the Major at a slow pace.

An hour later, suffering from the Major's furious outburst at Minns' intransigence, Atkins was consoled by the thoughts of receiving a gourd of whiskey. It would lead him to the oblivion he so desperately wished. But he still smarted from the Major's curses when he was dismissed.

The pale sun lay low in the west when Hannibal stirred and rose off the pallet of sticks. Claude sat and watched the grace of the slave, his coming alive, his feral stretching when Hannibal imitated a great feline. Claude admired the brute strength displayed and felt gratitude that the Negro's loyalty to him was unquestioned. In a time when slaves were deserting their masters, particularly after the Proclamation, Hannibal had remained at his side without complaint. And, he remembered, even had risked his life on the battlefield to save Claude when he was wounded.

"It's almost time to get on," Claude said. He held out a palm full of parched corn to the slave, dividing his meager store. "Granny said the rebs don't patrol up here, except in the morning. We need to head up the river to Meillins' place like she told us."

"'fo' we go, Massa, we get us each a staff. Dishere's a good place. Down wood nice an' hard."

"Why?" Claude asked, mystified.

"Need walkin' staff. An' sharpen upper end inter spear. Ain't got no weapons 'cept knives. Spears he'p, huntin' er fightin'."

A short search produced two stout hickory rods, remnants from the flood waters. The two men cut them to about six feet and sharpened the small ends. Claude hefted his and twirled it in his hand. He felt of its substantial weight and imagined the use of the point. It was a comforting weapon to add to his knife.

Descending from the log jam, the fugitives struck out toward the sun and soon passed from the thickets of the river flats. A mile of hilly, forest travel took them to a rutted road. It led off parallel to the river, a slash through dense woods with no fields in evidence. Claude inspected the road from his hiding place in a clump of sumacs, the bright red flowers and leaves a secure blanket of color, beautiful and very good cover. Hannibal lay in the forest mulch behind him. His dark skin and clothes blended with the bark of the stately hardwoods. The two were invisible to any passersby as long as still.

Dusk had almost fallen before Claude moved. His voice was very soft, almost a whisper. "Don't seem like there's no traffic on this road, Hannibal. You go circle around down there and look at the tracks. See if anything looks recent. Talk low and sneak quiet."

"Yassa, Massa." The slave eased into the big trees at the rear and backed away silently. Once clear, he made a wide detour through the open glades to throw off anyone if he were accosted, then entered the road. Bending over the loose surface, he inspected it closely as he sauntered along back toward Claude's hideout. He stopped at the side there as if to relieve himself.

"Horses 'long here dis mawnin', Massa." Hannibal's low rumble carried easily in the dusk. "Ain' nobody since. Ain' no wagon since last rain."

Claude eased down the slight bank with its open southwest exposure that had caused the luxuriant sumac grove. He spoke into the slave's ear so that the sound would not carry. "We'd better get on up the road then. Another ten miles maybe before the big snag that marks the turnoff to Meillins. Granny said we couldn't miss it."

"Dis chile sashay ahead, Massa. You stay bout hundert foot back. Dat way de rebs can't ketch both o' us."

The slave's concern and forethought touched Claude. He patted the man on the back and shook his head. "No, Hannibal," he whispered, "we travel together. Remember, we have the paper."

The servant pushed ahead of Claude, his face determined. "I leads, Massa. Nobody gonna ketch yuh, if I'se in front."

No matter how hard he tried, Hannibal's voice came out in a low boom. Claude despaired of their chances if they ever got in a tight. His "Whisper, Hannibal," brought a nod, then the slave was off to the west on the trace.

Stars twinkled and the big dipper pointed to the North Star when full dark fell. But the faint starlight and the gloom of the high trees bounding the open trace made it easy to follow. The two hustled along, but cautiously, as their steps ate up the miles. Bright, silvery rays from the glowing moon in the east told them that it was late evening when they stopped for the night, planning to wait until it was lighter. The fugitives had passed by Chapin's turnoff a half-hour back, recognized from the fork and the crude sign. Hester's and Granny's directions had brought them without fail, and in a quiet section of the country, with few people.

They had just gone off the trace into the woods when the clink of harness and hoofbeats resounded up the road. Men were talking and the amount of noise told Claude that it was a substantial patrol. The leading rider reined in opposite them and held up his hand to halt the other horsemen.

"Sergeant?" he called out.

"Yessir?" came the instant answer. "This's a likely bench. Good water in the creek we just passed and the ground's high and dry. Dismount the men. We'll camp here tonight."

"Yessir."

The Sergeant's commands congregated the patrol at the stopping point. Claude listened wistfully to the familiar orders and the commotion. He pictured the activity when a picket string was established along the edge of the road where the horses could crop a little grass. The men rattled the leaves as they moved about, looking for campsites after tending to the horses. When some drifted toward the fugitives, Claude grabbed Hannibal's arm and urged him away.

"Let's go," he whispered.

The Negro resisted and pulled away. "Can't, Massa," he said. "Done looked. Dey's a big draw jist over dere. Can't git down 'thout noise."

"Well you ease along the bank and I'll follow."

The two cautiously prowled the sharp edge of the collapsed cutbank of the draw, searching for a place to slide down. Claude's heart raced as the patrol spread out and each man sought a good place for his bed. The troopers were crowding the fugitives when Hannibal pulled the planter under a large windfall. Claude smelled the pungent odor of the cedar and knew it was a huge tree, recently fallen. They burrowed deep into the mass of green needles, thick as only a cedar can be. Their hope of escape dangled in the wind, dependent on the sharpness of the patrol and their own silence.

CHAPTER 3

Lieutenant Hartsill

---

*November 3, 1864. Little Mountain, S.C.
Temperature 65\32. Calm with light mists
in morning, patchy frost in clear areas,
high cirrus clouds, wind building during the
day. Moon waxing, rising before 11 P.M.*

The hunters halted at the stockade gate. "Ring the bell, Jared," Minns said.

A disembodied shout, "You leave the bell to us!" stopped them only for a moment. The protesting sentry rushed from the shadows of the wall with his rifle at ready port but Minns brushed him aside. A malevolent glance from the woodsman cowed the man into a wary silence. The sentry took a fighting stance nearby, his position quickly reinforced by his partner.

Jared's first peal of the bell reverberated softly across the slope. "Loud, boy, bang it," Minns said, prodding his son. "I tol' that Sergeant I'd be here fust light an' they ain't even stirrin'. Hit that bell hard!"

The next strike boomed out. Minns had ignored the soldiers and waited right at the gate with his two boys. He stamped about impatiently while Old Blue investigated the vapors and left his marker on a post.

Jared rang the bell continuously, even though the sentries swore at him. But the two men shifted uneasily when they eyed Minns. They shrank from the menace of the hunter and did not call for the Corporal of the Guard.

Barely light, the east showed the promise of sunrise and a fair, clear day. It was a fine, cool morning, damp with the mists and dew, just right for the dog and Athey Minns didn't intend to miss the best tracking time. Later, when the grass dried, the scent wouldn't be so bold.

Strident tones from the bell finally brought the Major running. Jones hobbled on his bad leg and fumbled at his jacket buttons as he hurried along. His cavalry saber flopped about his short legs, an ungainly sight.

Athey laughed when the officer came up to the gate. His laugh changed to a chuckle as he admonished the man. "Ye'll stick yerself with that if you ain't keerful, Major."

Jones ignored Minns and halted before the gate guard while he still was adjusting his uniform. One last button snapped into place and then his temper took over. "What the hell's happening?" he said, angrily. He passed over the man's hesitant reply. Fuming as he glanced about, he castigated the Corporal of the Guard, who had emerged from the headquarters building in similar undress, then grumbled bitterly at the lot of them. "I don't see no God damned fire."

"It's Minns, sir, him an' his two sons," one of the sentries volunteered. "They rang the bell. They wouldn't stop."

"Yer damn right, Major," Minns said forcefully. "I sent word by Atkins I'd be here, come daybreak. Well, here I be."

"God damn it, Athey! Did you need to make such a racket? Got the whole damned camp stirred up." A veritable din arose across the pole stockade. The prisoners were protesting and the guards ordering them to shut up.

Minns ignored the melee. "Got any pieces of Shaw's belongings?" he asked. "Shoes er pants, maybe?" He spat a brown stream and hitched up his pants. "We wanta git along, on up the trail. The damp got Old Blue interested."

The big bluetick hound was circling around the men while he explored every scent. His snuffling intakes carried loudly in the damp air. They all watched in silence, mesmerized while the dog worked. Old Blue knew a hunt was underway and was eager to get started.

"Whar's the Lieutenant's possibles, Major?" Athey's impatient tone brooked no argument. "Can't start 'thout Old Blue gets a good scent."

It was Atkins who responded, from his position on the porch of the nearby headquarters building. He had come out in his pants and sock feet when the commotion began. Yawning and scratching, he bellowed out a reply.

"I got 'em in here, Major. Ever'thin' he left."

"Well, fetch 'em, man," Jones yelled. "They ain't doin' us no good up there."

The Sergeant carried out Claude's meager possessions, a ragged pair of pants, blanket and towel, and threw them down in the dust for Old Blue to survey. The dog's nose investigated each piece while he pawed at the items to turn them about, savoring every intricacy of odor so as to imprint them thoroughly. When he was satisfied, he took off in a wide circle, casting about for the trail while Minns struck his bargain with the Major.

"Same as last, Major?" Minns asked.

"Agreed. Four wool blankets an' fifty bushels of corn. An' I get back ten gallons of whiskey from your stillin'."

"Done. You want him 'live er dead?"

"Alive if possible. Don't shoot 'im 'less you have to. But the nigger he's got with 'im, do whatever you want."

A nod of Minns's head sealed the bargain. Then he motioned to Jared, who gave a gourd each to the Major and Atkins.

"Hyar's the gourds I promised," Minns said. "It's been run through a charcoal barrel an's fair tastin'." He looked questioningly at the Major. "You got anythin' more to say?" At the shake of Jones' head, Minns shifted his rifle into a right-hand carry, ready for rapid trailing.

Old Blue was already out of sight in the forest north of the camp. Minns hallooed and shouted encouragements. His sons picked up Claude's possessions, then followed their father as they trotted off in a lope that would eat up the miles. The men at the gate heard the dog strike while the Minnses were still assaying the first ridge. Old Blue's yelping yodel rang over the hills. His excited, harmonic bugling confirmed a hot trail and presaged a fast recapture.

"Hester?" When the girl didn't answer, Granny shuffled around in the chair to sight her. Hester was primping before the looking glass. Dissatisfied, she stripped the first and tied the brighter bandanna around her head. Then she cocked her head and smiled and postured while she adjusted the folds of bright cloth. Granny rapped her stick impatiently on the hearth stones. Her sharp, "Hester, you answer me," brought a slow response.

"You recken he really wants me, Granny?"

"If I don't save yer hide, you ain't gwine know," the ancient warned. "You gotter git 'way fum here fer de next day."

A hound dog coursed the hills at a far distance, its bugling faint but clear. Granny listened intently, waiting for the tones she had heard before. A distinctive series of notes spurred her into action.

"It's dem Minns an' Old Blue," she said. "You git on up ter Miz Ashley's an' bed down wid Ruth in her cabin." She shook her stick at the girl while she added to her warning. "You hide tight, you hear? Keep out o' sight 'less Miz Ashley want yuh. An' you don' know nothin'."

The girl nodded and her face twisted in fear. "I don' tell 'em 'bout de sojer, Granny."

The dog's bugling grew louder. A shivering-fit ran over Hester's body. She had been there once before when the Minnses came in. Mistreatment of Granny had not scared her so much as the covetous glances and crude remarks of the boys. But Minns had taken them away on that chase without causing harm, the escapee being of more reward than the savaging of a female Negro. Jared's burning glance when he promised he'd be back had transfixed her. It had riveted her feet to the dirt floor. Almost fainting, she had feared not for life but for Granny and herself. The Minns boys had taken several of the slaves in the past for brutality and pleasure and she shook with fear as she hurried with her departure. Slipping around in the cabin, she seized a blanket and a few possessions, then ran out of the door and disappeared into the forest on her circle to the other quarters.

Granny stirred the stew first, then refreshed the skunk odor from a small gourd hanging from a peg. Next, she hobbled to the stool at the loom and began the task of threading the yarn ends through the hettles. Its interminable detail occupied her fingers and her mind while she waited for the visit of the Minnses.

The cavalry Sergeant strode rapidly along the edge of the cutbank in the grayness of early morning, his passage quiet in the soft burden of moist leaves and needles. A dense forest mat lay thick all over the bench. His troopers had had a restful night stretched out on the cushioned mounds assembled from the abundant debris. But with his gut griping from the greens he had eaten the day before, the Sergeant did not tarry among his men. His need was urgent, one to be satisfied quickly before the stirring troop and the commands of the Lieutenant demanded his attentions. He accosted the last sentry as a matter of form, however, stoically challenging to see if the man was alert. The Sergeant hurried on in his noiseless glide down the slope, an increasingly demanding need driving his search as he sought a secluded spot for his now critical morning ritual. His gut griped him cruelly as he passed a thick cedar top. Its three foot trunk and high root fan attested to centuries of growth before the recent storm toppled the giant tree. Fifty feet past was all he could manage. But it was a good place and he was well screened. He undid his pants and squatted, purging himself of his discomfort.

The massive cedar log attracted his attention when he slowly ambled back. The Sergeant had worked in his father's sawmill before the fighting and a three foot cedar was a thing of beauty. With a large log, the wood came out blazing red and streaked in grain. Its planks polished to perfection and were full of the oils preventing decay or moths. The tree's size compelled him to estimate the footage. "Reckon it'd go a thousand board feet o' red heart-wood," he mused aloud, reverently patting the log. "Sure a shame fer it to be lyin' here."

He was sitting on the log with his memories when a small sound in the pungent cedar top startled him into a taut alertness. The damp breeze from the east carried a penetrating odor from the thicket, one he easily recognized. The Sergeant fumbled at his belt for his pistol as he ran back up the hill and spread the alarm.

"Corporal of the Guard!" he shouted.

"Yo-o," came the call.

"I want two men here with rifles. On the double."

The small camp exploded in pandemonium as the troopers vaulted from their blankets and struggled with clothes and their gear. Several men with carbines pounded down the slope toward the Sergeant. He circled the cedar with rifles while he waited on the Lieutenant.

Claude and Hannibal were fairly trapped and the two burrowed deeper into the needles to stay hidden. Claude's heart pounded and his breaths came in short, gasping tries while he attempted to remain absolutely silent. He could feel the slave's fear from Hannibal's leg quivering where they touched. The big Negro grasped his hickory staff and slid the point along the ground ahead of him. Claude restrained him with a quiet nudge, the two still invisible to the troopers though the daylight was coming on. His thought was to stay quiet unless they were forced out of the thick cover.

"What's happening, Sergeant?"

Their Lieutenant's quiet voice calmed the men, who had been speculating on the hidden fugitives.

"Somebody thar in the cedar, sir," the Sergeant said. "Made a noise and I can smell 'im. Probably another runaway."

"Well, root him out."

At that the Sergeant fired a shot into the cedar and shouted at the hideaways, "Show yerself, or we'll volley the bresh."

"We's comin', we's comin'," Hannibal called, but he delayed, instead, and glanced uncertainly at Claude.

"Come on out," the Sergeant ordered, when no one appeared. "What'r you damned niggers waitin' fer?" His irritation grew when no cedar fronds moved. Pointing his revolver, he loudly warned, "I'll count to three, then we'll fire." He waited a few seconds, then started his count. "One!"

At Claude's poke in the back, Hannibal crawled out from under the green fronds and stood erect. He leaned on his staff and bowed subserviently in front of the assembled guns. Claude scurried out and halted behind him, mimicking Hannibal's bent shoulders and downcast gaze. Bits of leaves and needles covered them like chaff in a wheat threshing and their bodies' rank odor offended him. A flush of humiliation colored his brown cheeks. Claude's rage consumed him while he bowed to the Confederates. Him, a Union officer, and bowing to those rebs. But he controlled his passion and peeked at the Lieutenant, who had paced out in front of the Sergeant.

The officer's tone was harsh and overbearing. "What are you doing in that cedar?"

"We scairt, Massa," Hannibal said, his voice quavering. "When you'uns come up last evenin', we skedaddled bes' place we fin'. Dat thicket warm las' night."

Hannibal bobbed up and down as he spoke and Claude kept his hunched over stance, even while he occasionally stole a glance at the soldiers. The thin, hatchet face of the Lieutenant, with it's small goatee, exuded distrust and a scowl. Claude's skin crawled when his fear overcame his curiosity.

"Whose niggers are you?" the Lieutenant asked. "You runaways?"

"No sah, Massa," Hannibal replied. He volunteered only meager information, the slaves common habit when they feared retribution for some unforeseen wrong. But his respectful tone struck the right chord with the Lieutenant.

"Well what are you, then?"

"We gwine ter de gol' mines up to Jawga, Massa. Fer Massa Middleton down ter Osprey's Landin'."

The Lieutenant's jaw dropped in amazement. "Pinckney? Pinckney Middleton?"

"Yassah, Massa," Hannibal asserted in a forceful voice. "He give us de paper ter tell who we is."

Hannibal fished in his pocket and brought out the much folded, dirty sheet from Granny's. The Lieutenant snatched it and quickly scanned the certificate. Claude chuckled to himself at the sight of the slack-jawed face and the officer's obvious befuddlement when he finished with the sheet. Pleasure erased all his own feelings of rage and fear. The subterfuge of the wily Granny when she helped them spread balm over his spirit.

"Well, I never!" the Lieutenant exclaimed, after a hasty perusal. "Pinckney sent you here alone? Hard to believe he'd trust you that much."

"It de trute, Massa. Massa Pinckney tol' us ter skedaddle fas'. He need dat gol'. We come bes' we kin." Hannibal bobbed up and down in servile submission. "Massa Pinckney treat us good. Ain't no runaways."

The Lieutenant fidgeted, not completely convinced. But the note from his friend was clear. He read it again. The handwriting was not too good, but then, Pinckney's wound had changed that. The officer's intuitive caution, mandated by a lifetime of experiences and tales by his forebears, counseled further investigation. A shrewd belief in the conniving nature of the slaves to confound white owners drove him on.

"How'd you come here?"

"Ketched a barge up de Cooper 'bout ter Moncks Corners. Den been walkin', mostly." Hannibal paused and scratched his head. "Ketched one wagon ride down by Wateree. Sojers don' let us on de railroad cars so we mostly walkin'. We git dere directly."

The Lieutenant hesitated, sure he was missing something. An indefinable doubt clouded his mind, fed by the glib answers of the slave. How many times had he seen the guile and heard the evasions of Negroes on his father's plantation? Many, he concluded, and suddenly spoke to Claude.

"You have anything to say?"

Claude grunted and pointed to his face. He mouthed some unintelligible, rasping gurgles, interrupted by Hannibal.

"He can't talk, Massa. He done been borned like dat. Maybe de po' whites' blood in 'im. Got de twisted tongue. But he good han'."

The Lieutenant gave up and accepted the note and their answers. But he cautioned the two when he handed the paper back to Hannibal. "I'll be down in Charleston next week on leave. If Pinckney tells me any different while I'm there, I'll hunt you down when I'm back, flog both of you and send you back in chains."

"Ain't no trouble, Massa," Hannibal assured him. "We tell de trute." Claude grunted and bobbed his head up and down.

The Lieutenant's order doomed them to servitude. "Sergeant, put these men to work 'til we leave. No reason to cut firewood as long as they're here." He chuckled and added, "Old Pinck owes me that much. He lost that last poker game we played and hasn't paid up yet."

Claude and Hannibal spent an hour of hard labor before the patrol finished its morning feed and saddled the horses, ready to leave. The sun was up above the horizon, burning off the morning mists. Quail were calling when the troop prepared to mount. Gobbles of turkeys echoed through the big trees covering the hill, enticing calls from a flock scattered about the slope lying toward the Broad.

"Care to try fer a turkey afore we go, sir?" The Sergeant had reported ready to mount up but had left a few men at the trees. He smacked his lips and said, "Mighty fine eatin'. Better'n the fatback an' deermeat we got yestiday."

The Lieutenant shook his head. "No, Sergeant, mount 'em up. Got to move on down the river. No time for any more huntin'."

The officer called Claude and Hannibal to him, to a stand by his stirrup where he could overlook them. He stabbed with his gloved finger when he ordered them on. "You niggers hustle on over to Georgia soon as you can. Don't you dawdle, you hear me?"

The two bobbed and bowed and Hannibal assured the Lieutenant of their resolve. Rather than anger at debasing himself before the Confederate, Claude's thoughts were on the hunger that gnawed at his belly. He still scented the meat and pone they had seen in the trooper's meals and the juices flowing in his mouth added to the rumblings in his stomach. Claude tugged at Hannibal's sleeve, then grunted and pointed to his mouth.

Hannibal caught hold of the officer's stirrup as the reb

waited on his mounted troop to form up. The Lieutenant had eased the reins and his horse seized the opportunity to crop a tuft of grass.

"Kin we have some meat an' pone, Massa?" Hannibal asked. "We powerful hongry."

"Let go, you black bastard," the Lieutenant shouted. He struck Hannibal hard with a whip and his horse pranced away under a tightened rein. A moment later, again under control of himself and his mount, the officer reconsidered. "Well, I guess for old Pinck."

"Sergeant!" he said loudly.

"Sir?"

"Give these nigras a chunk of that deer and some of the pone."

A remnant forequarter of venison and a few pieces of cornbread hit the ground when the Sergeant threw them down from the packhorse. The display of contempt sickened Claude. Feeding them like chickens or dogs, throwing the food on the ground for them to scavenge up. His rekindled anger at the Confederates made him more determined. If we get out of this he thought, I'll kill as many of them as I can. They'll get no mercy from me.

When the patrol cantered away, with its thudding hoofbeats and jingling harness, the Lieutenant stayed behind for one last piece of instructions. "You're near Chapin's Corners," he said. "Go on up the road by Stockman's place. It's the first branch to the left past Little Mountain. He'll feed you." He absently stroked his goatee and fingered it into a sharp point. "Keep on to Newberry after that. You can't miss it." He watched their nodding heads in vigilant silence, then pointed west. "This road'll take you clear through to Anderson and Georgia. Now I'm tellin' Pinckney you're going to hustle and you'd damn well better or I'll hide you when I get back."

At his grim stare, the two fugitives nodded in abject subservience and Hannibal mouthed, "We git dar, Massa. Yas sah!"

The fugitives hurried to the fires with the meat when the cavalryman's hoofbeats faded and laid strips directly on the coals. Claude's fears cut the searing short. They ate the

partially roasted strips and pone. Surfeit left a few scraps for
their pockets and a long drink at the creek prepared them
for the hike to Little Mountain. Its beacon rose in the west
and called them on to Stockman's and the road to freedom.

Old Blue pushed his head slowly past the unlatched
door of the cabin. The trail searched out by his nose led out
of the damp and into the warmth radiating from the fire. He
sniffed and snuffled in the dirt and drew back, wary of
entering. Inner imprints recalled the blows of Minns at his
cabin when he assayed the entrance there. But the man-
scent was too strong and the old woman too silent. Blue's
head gradually invaded the room as he eased around the
door. His treeing instinct drove him on and the hot scent
overcame his caution. The old dog rushed into the cabin and
danced about, barking wildly at Granny.
    She struck at his rush with her cane and cried, "Shet
up." Granny rose from her stool when he did not quit under
the threats. "I knows how ter quiet yer," she mumbled. The
old woman fended off the jumping, barking dog as she
hobbled to the table.
    Granny broke off a piece of cornbread from the sheet on
the smooth boards and tossed it to the dog. Blue instantly
gulped down the unexpected manna. Granny's morsel
silenced him and he wagged his tail. The old dog grinned up
at her and begged, expectantly, then dropped his haunches
to the floor. Another chip of bread won over the immobilized
hound. Old Blue was flopped down by Granny's chair being
petted when Minns and his boys arrived at the cabin.
    "Blue!" Minns' yell galvanized the dog into erect, quiv-
ering attention. "Git!" the woodsman bellowed. He waved
his rifle and the dog raced from the cabin.
    Minns and Granny heard him strike again, almost
instantly after he darted through the open door. His bugle
resonated through the woods as the man hunter moved to
confront the old woman. She sat quietly, her stick at her
side, her dark, wrinkled face impassive while he leaned on
his rifle. Minns' cold, searching gaze, implacable, tested the
mettle of the unyielding old woman. How many times had he
entered her cabin, always trying to subdue her? But her

spirit had defeated him in the past and he knew it would be well-nigh impossible to make her yield on Claude's escape. The two enemies were facing each other, knights readying for the joust, when Jared stuck his head in the door.

"What you want us to do, Pa?"

"Run Old Blue all around the place. See's you kin find where those two went."

Jared and Jeremy encouraged the dog through the surrounding brush. Barking of the hound added to the thrashing sounds of the boys as they circled the cabin and searched the surroundings. The noise receded as they gradually worked farther west.

Athey Minns turned his attention away from Granny and poked into the corners of the cabin. Not satisfied, he crowded into the space behind the loom and upset some baskets of yarn. The hunter grumbled to himself, then climbed the ladder to the loft, his slow step by step rise and alert listening symbols of his caution. Minns took no chances; he pointed a pistol ahead of him when he risked a first, peeping glimpse above the pole ceiling. He was breathing rapidly when he rose through the opening and disappeared into the blackness of the loft in one long, flowing effort. Rummaging sounds filled the cabin, along with creaks, and debris sifted down from the ceiling. Granny chortled when she heard the trap snap and Minns' curse. He slid sinuously out the loft like a startled snake, his left hand bleeding from the teeth of the steel trap that mangled his fingers.

"You damned ol' bitch," Minns cried out. "Help me git thisyere thing off my hand."

"Can't, Massa. Ain't got de strength no mo' ter spring bek de trap."

Minns cursed, then ran out of the door and yelled for Jared. Granny's face crinkled into a broad grin at her victory over the man hunter. She rocked back and forth in her seat and cackled when he was gone, and beat her cane against the fireplace hearth. But her good humor gave way to deadly intent while she listened for Minns' return. Pounding sounds outside and his continued calls for Jared vouched for his preoccupation with his hand. Granny left her chair and stole over to Minns' rifle. The hunter, hurting, had left it leaning against the cabin wall when he rushed out. Her chance to damage the man hunter excited her, but she hesitated before touching the weapon.

Shouts for Jared filled the air between Minns' curses. The distress of the injured man while he pried at the strong trap added to her resolve. When Jared answered, but from a distance, she seized the rifle and commenced her work. Minns' boys and Blue had come back up and were releasing the trap when she finished plugging the touch hole with a bit of clay, forcing it in tight with a needle. A large glob of clay and yarn well down in the barrel completed the sabotage. Granny was back in her chair when Minns re-entered the cabin.

"You damned ol' bitch!" he screamed. He threw the trap down in front of the chair. "Why the hell's that in the loft?" His left hand still dripped blood. The red drops congealed into small, dusty globules on the dirt floor.

Granny laughed. "Reckon you got inter de trap fer dat coon been stealing our corn. Jed set dat trap nigh onter a month ago." She cackled away and hoorawed Minns. "We done caught de big he coon I recken."

Her glee infuriated the hunter. Minns grabbed her by the neck with his bleeding hand and jerked her out of the chair. Red blood stained Granny's dress while he held her squirming body and slapped her face repeatedly on both sides. Then he lifted her until her feet about cleared the floor. Minns shook the old woman and swung her violently about while his blows continued. "I'll choke the life outen yuh," he threatened. "You he'ped those two escape, damn yuh, an' set the trap fer me."

Fury possessed him for a few minutes while he abused the old woman. She fought back, kicking and clawing, and flailed at him with her cane. But her struggles were growing weaker and life was slipping out of Granny when Jared grabbed Minns' hands and Jeremy pulled him away.

"Don' learn nothin', Pa, if you kill her," Jared cautioned. "We want to git as much outen her as we can. Can't do nothin' if she's dead."

The pinioned hunter cursed, and trembled, and fought his sons. They defeated him, holding him firm until he grappled with himself and subdued his raging hate. Granny had gasped and sputtered, her breath a wheezing whistle until she regained her strength. She struggled up with her cane, very erect, her dignity unshattered and still defiant. When at last she could speak, her icy voice, rather than a furious tirade, surprised Minns. He was used to shouts and curses and clawing females, not rigid, regal ones.

"Murder me, would yuh, Athey Minns," she said. Granny's slow, strangling croak attested to his violence. She had insulted him grievously, also, by omitting Massa in the address. "You ain't nothin' but white trash," she added, presenting her final epithet.

The hunter paled at Granny's denigration. Then his cheeks flushed red with anger at the gravity of the old slave's insolence and transgression. Infuriated, he shook free of his sons and pulled his knife. Jared seized Minns' knife-hand and Jeremy closed on the other side.

"We got to git on, Pa," Jared said. "You kin allus come back an' deal with the likes o' her."

Thwarted by his sons, Minns sheathed his blade and looked at his injured hand. "Any whiskey in the cabin?" he asked.

Granny coughed and sputtered, then pointed to a jar with her cane. Jared brought over a large dipper of the liquor. Minns cursed as its rank smell permeated the cabin. He plunged his hand into the whiskey and stirred it around while Jared cut off a piece of a dress hanging from a peg. Wrapped, the hand was useable but unhandy. Minns felt it and grimaced before he picked up his rifle and tried his grip.

"You awright now, Pa?" Jared asked.

He had started for the door but Athey called him back. "Got more questions, boy," he said. His scar bulged, reddening again, but his voice was very low and calmly determined.

"Now Granny, they was here, warn't they?" Her angry, silent gaze spurred Minns to raise his fist, its threat opposed instantly by Granny's cane.

"I feed 'em de skunk stew," she admitted, grudgingly, "den dey head on down to'ard de ribber."

"There was a skunk, Pa," Jared said. "Jeremy an' me found the skin buried out in the trees. An' you kin smell that skunk in here." He wrinkled his nose in disgust. "Pretty pore eatin'."

"Gooder'n you know, boy," Granny said. "It better'n no meat a'tall."

Minns' scowl silenced his son. "What else, Granny?" he asked, "you tell us quick." He prodded her with his wrapped fist, drawing in return an instant blow from her stick.

The hunter pulled his pistol and threatened the old slave. But her spirit challenged him in her flashing eyes and a grim set to her jaw offered no surrender. He waited, the two staring in a test of wills. Granny crumpled when he put the pistol muzzle between her eyes. The old woman sagged and started crying. She wailed about her sore neck and begged him not to hurt her any more. Granny's guile and her plan produced Minns' false trail.

"He aimed fer de ribber," she said. "He got some fren down ter Cha'leston." She sobbed and snuffled and blew her nose, and wiped away her tears with a rag. "He gwine try mek de ribber an' float down. Den over ter de city an' ketch de ships."

The hunter, suspicioning another ruse by the slave, called to his son, who had joined Jeremy and Blue outside.

"Jared!"

"Yes, Pa," answered the boy. He stuck his head in the door.

"Cast about. See if they's new tracks to the Broad er the Congaree. Put Old Blue on it. She says they went back down to'ards the river."

Granny eyes gleamed and her snuffling stopped. Her lips briefly showed a slight smile of triumph. She and Minns glared at each other, neither speaking while the rustle of the dog and boys receded. Their concentration broke when the dog struck and went tearing off towards the Broad. Jared and Jeremy followed, hallooing. The sounds of the chase were fading when Minns gave Granny a final slap on the face and staggered her.

"I be back," he said. Granny's hate and hushed curse followed him when he turned abruptly and left the cabin.

The Minnses reached the Broad by sundown, sliding down the bank where Jed and Bub had taken to the water.

"They put in here, Pa," Jared said. The boy had squatted by the tracks in the mud opposite the upper island and was testing their dryness.

"Yep," Minns said.

He inspected the evidence closely and patted Old Blue. But the hot, rangy dog slipped from his grasp and took to the water. Blue flopped in the shallows and lapped up a drink, then splashed about and cooled himself. His exit from the river was just as sudden. Minns was laughing at the old hound when he showered them all with drops from his shuddering purge of water from his coat.

Minns wiped off his beard and swore. "Old Blue gonna make sure we all git a bath."

"We gonna stay here t'night, Pa?" Jared asked.

"No, boy," Minns replied. An' it's too late ter git across ternight. We'll go back up an' camp in the trees on the bench. Cross at first light. We'll git those two termorrer."

The sun lay low in the western sky, so low that its yellow rays shined obliquely through the forest. The glinting light struck the clearing where the road forked, a suspended dusty haze and indentations evidence of recent passage of a wagon. Bordering plants were yellowish from the coating, a film covering all the stalks and leaves. Dust particles streamed from the travelers, and puffs rose at each step that disturbed the slightly damp surface.

Hannibal stopped at the fork and examined the tracks. "Recken dishere's 'bout where Stockman's turns off," he said. "You recken we orter go dere, Claude? Ain't stoppin' at Meillen's like Granny tol' us?"

Claude shook his head and kept them slowly westing on the main road. He trod slowly, cautiously, his hearing attuned to the forest sounds. But even as he listened, he thought of his relation to the Negro. He was happy that Hannibal finally had eliminated the subservient "Massa." Claude had repeatedly cautioned the Negro about it in the hours of lonely travel, instructions that broke the habits of a lifetime. Survival depended on their passing as slaves and the big servant needed to use all of his wits as well as the camouflage of equality. Only some emergency might inadvertently bring out the "Massa," Claude now was sure. It would doom them. Detection would bring floggings and imprisonment or worse.

Dust rose about them in little spurts as they walked, and added to their discomfort. The road toward Newberry passed through a sand clay that pulverized under the traffic. Fine particles from the passing of heavy wagons during the long, dry fall billowed up when disturbed, even though the light rains had crusted the top. Hannibal sneezed incessantly, incapable of holding back the great explosions caused by the aggravating suspension. When they came to the next rivulet, both men wetted their bandannas and tied them around their faces to ward off the the irritant.   Near sunset, Claude figured they were within five miles of Newberry and looked for a suitable place for a night hideout, one to shield them until the moon was well up. He had surveyed the rolling hills as they traveled. The road on the ridge line offered many ravines running down toward the river, most with water and choked with heavy growth. They stopped at a likely place, a dense thicket where a slide in a ravine had created a tangle of downed trees. Hannibal aimed his staff at the many skewed trunks.

"Dat good place, Claude," he said. "Gotta be cover wid dose oaks an' cedars. We go down dere?"

A flurry of hoofbeats and gunshots up the trail toward Newberry drove them off the road. The startled fugitives charged through the bordering briers and went to ground in the tangle, shielded by a heavy patch of honeysuckle and sassafras bushes. Approaching dusk covered the two dark, prone figures with its protective shades as they endured the clawing thorns. The hoofbeats grew nearer, muffled in the soft dirt of the road, while the fugitives hugged the ground and imitated downed logs.

"Quiet," Claude whispered, when Hannibal moved slightly. The servant was sliding himself toward the woods. His scrapes and the clattering brier stems seemed to Claude to reverberate through the still forest. But Hannibal's faint rattling mingled with the chirps of roosting birds settling in for the night. A lone turkey gobbled in the distance, and a flicker flitted by. The hoofbeats grew louder; their pounding thuds silenced the birds, and interrupted the forest's peace.

A flashing dark shape with a burr on top rose over the western slope, a small ridge at right angles to the road. Outlined in the western glow, Claude could see a hunched figure on the horse, indistinct in the gloom. The tattoo increased until the horse flashed by their hideout. A piercing shriek rang out when the mount fell at the washout. The fugitives had passed the ditch across the road a hundred yards back, a legacy of the great storm of September. Its cutbanks had been faired into ruts by wagon traffic and some spade work but it was a treacherous place for a galloping horse. And this horse had fallen.

"Come on, Hannibal," Claude whispered. "Sounded like a woman. She may need help."

He started out of the hideaway like a jumped rabbit and ran blindly toward the horse. It had fallen with a thud but was back up and snorting as it pranced about. A crumpled figure lay unmoving when he reached the ditch. Hannibal caught the horse and gentled it while Claude tended to the fallen rider.

When he stretched the crumpled figure out on its back, he was shocked that the attack had been on a young woman. His loathing increased when he saw the fairness of her face and her dark hair that had spread out from under her bonnet. The woman was unconscious but breathing easily and Claude could feel no blood when he checked her head. He patted her hands and fanned her cheeks in an attempt to revive her.

Shouts up the trail and another gunshot preceded sounds of running men. "It must be some of those damned deserters," Claude said. "Those bastards'd steal anything. Got no respect for anyone."

"We got ter git, Claude," Hannibal said. "Dey comin' purty fast."

He fidgeted nervously while Claude vigorously fanned the unconscious woman. The Negro's alarm transferred to the horse which stamped and neighed, then pulled him around by the reins. Hannibal whispered soft "steady boy" commands and patted the neck of the trembling beast until it stood quietly.

The din up the road grew louder as the pack of men drew closer. Claude was sure now that the men running toward the fugitives were deserters or guerillas, for the swarm was certainly a lawless group to attack a woman. Robbing, pillaging, such men were outlaws to Confederates and Union alike. And this could only be one of the bands that sprang up in the anarchy of the closing days of the rebellion.

"Tie the reins on the saddle and run the horse on down the road," Claude ordered.

The leathers secure, Hannibal switched the horse violently and the animal pounded off. Cries of the approaching men increased when they heard the renewed hoofbeats. Their closeness, even in the obscuring dusk, was acute and frightening.

Claude, unable to rapidly hoist the slack weight of the woman with his weakened shoulder, turned to Hannibal for help. "Pick her up, quick," he said. "Get into the bushes and hide."

The powerful Negro tossed the woman over his shoulder like a sack of grain and noiselessly picked his way down the hill into the ravine. Claude followed but slid on some of the exposed clay at the bottom of the wash. Pain wracked him from the strike on his injured side, but his fear drove him to follow the slave on into concealment. The trio were well off the road and hidden under a downed tree when the guerrillas reached the washout.

"She done fell hyar," a black figure shouted. "Bring one o' them torches."

Milling men at the washout sorted out the accident. A cry from the road below started them again. "She run on," was the shout. "She can't be too far."

The pack resumed its chase, wolves after plunder.

Chapter 4

Old Blue

November 4, 1864. Newberry, S.C. Temperature 61\33, drizzle or light rain starting after midnight. Light mists in early morning, cloudy and cool. Winds to ten MPH, waxing moon obscured. A rainy, gray night, clearing after early morning showers.

"It col', Massa." Hannibal tried to whisper, but his croak and cough exposed his discomfort. He shifted around on the hard-packed clay, its surface but thinly clad with pine needles. The unyielding bed offered little comfort.

Claude looked over the sleeping woman before replying. Even in the darkness her white face shined, a tiny, pale oval that he could see up close. Her figure was inert, still unconscious. The planter's exploration revealed that she had thrown off some of the pine fronds used as a covering. After repairing the protective, warming layer, he turned to the slave.

"Don't you ever use Massa again, dammit! You hear me!" Claude's intense voice was reinforced by his hard grasp of Hannibal's arm. "We got to do like we agreed. Now you call me Claude, you hear."

"Yas sah!" the slave replied emphatically. "Claude?"

"What now?"

"Kin I have a swig o' yer whiskey? Dat kin he'p me. I'se col'."

Hannibal's cough contrasted to the reassuring night sounds. His hacking, explosive discharges could give away their hiding place in the dense stand of small pines, saplings perhaps two heads high. A burn many years past had left a fertile slope for reforesting. Profuse seed had produced a thicket of growth, ideal for concealment and camping. The tops were so dense and intertwined that the drizzle had not wet the ground, but the cold, damp air was penetrating to the bone. Even with his thick clothes, Claude felt himself shivering.

The planter pulled a silver flask from his coat, the spirits a parting gift from Kelly. The Irishman had laughed when he handed it over, along with a joke about Minns' whiskey or his bullet killing them. Raw whiskey from the stiller was a sure cure for a congested throat and the prisoners were a ready market for the whiskey. Downing a swig, the planter passed the flask to Hannibal who took a long pull from the vessel.

Gurgling gulps were followed by a "Dat's good" from the slave. He wiped his mouth on his sleeve and handed back the flask for pocketing by the planter.

"What we do now, Claude? Dishere rain done make it bad fer travelin'." Hannibal's voice sounded better and his coughing had subsided.

"Come daylight, we'll circle on west. Got to keep away from the trace though."

"How's de lady?"

"Still sleepin'. She probably belongs in Newberry and we'll get her to somebody. Now cover yourself and sleep."

Three mounds of fronds protected them as the fine raindrops gradually percolated down through the pines and started wetting the ground. Claude lay there, his plans for a rapid passage west in ruins, thwarted by the woman. But what else could he have done, he thought. She would have been taken by the rabble for robbery and worse. He drifted in and out of sleep as the hours wore on, worried by the fugitives' impasse with an unconscious woman on their hands. And the damp cold prevented any comfort. Shivering brought into his reverie an intense longing for the feather bed at Greenbottom, so different from the thin pine-needle mat. Letty would be snuggled there, her warm stove ready for his chilled body. And more. His sighs in the cold forest were mostly from self-pity rather than lack of comfort. Willing himself to sleep again but unable to drift off, he shivered and waited while the long night wore on. Compelled by a colder wind, a hard, driving shower saturated the pines in the early morning. Their dripping needles flung droplets on his face. But scattered moonlight and scudding clouds following the front hinted at a better day. It would be damp and bitter but at least dry, small consolation for the weary travelers.

Morning mists and the peeping sun found Athey Minns and his sons across the Broad onto the midchannel island. The low, marshy edge where they went ashore was soft, fertile ground for the keen nose of Old Blue. Starting at the upstream end, populated with its fine stand of oaks and hickories, their search concentrated on the great pile of drift at the point of the island, the residue of the most recent flooding. Its trunks and stobs presented a labyrinth of hiding places and the Minnses had caught two prisoners there in earlier chases. Old Blue wiggled through the wreckage, encouraged by the shouts of Athey and the two boys.

An hour of probing yielded nothing but sweat and growling bellies. Some handy drift provided a good, dry seat for a welcome rest. They ate their pone and bacon in silence and tossed a few remnants to Blue. The old dog lay before them and wagged his tail. His lolling tongue dripped from the exhausting search.

"Guess they ain't in the tangle, boys," Athey said, once he had finished his meager breakfast. He pulled from a flask, then washed the whiskey down with a few handfuls of cold water from the river.

Impatient as always, Jared had been the first to rise from his perch on the downed log. He hitched up his pants and cradled his rifle. "We'd best be on down the river, Pa," he said. "Member we took the last two there in that little flat across the Congaree, where the Saluda makes the big sweep when it joins? If they crossed there we'll find tracks."

Athey ignored the boy. He started the dog and headed

down the island, with his sons well out on his flanks in a skirmish line. "Keep sharp," he yelled. "Watch for their tracks."

A veteran campaigner, a champion hunting dog, Old Blue coursed ahead of them. He swept from one side of the advancing hunters to the other in a weaving pattern, one to cut any trail. His shuffling gait covered three times the ground of the searchers. Sniffing the odorous breezes and snuffling at bushes and tracks, the old hound's talented nose sorted the scents as he sought the one true key to Claude. Silent when they reached the downstream point, the four bunched at the last sycamore. Its tangled roots suffered from the current. Undermined, the tree would likely be the next casualty of high water.

"They ain't been on the island, Pa." Jared said. "Old Blue done find them if they had."

"Let's git on 'cross the river, boys," Minns responded. He took off at a lope for their skiff.

The beach was bare when they put in at the point below the entering Saluda, after threading through all the rocks and islands. Clear and fast, the Congaree's currents had carried them well downstream of their goal. Mud on the soggy bank seeped through their moccasins when they beached the boat. The boys dragged the vessel over the slick clay to the line of bushes and tied it to a sapling. Minns had run on up the bank and left the work to his sons. He had called the dog to his stand on dry ground and sent Old Blue ahead, up the river.

Jared protested. "They ain't goin'a be upstream, Pa. It's 'most certain they went down the river."

"Why, boy?" Minns asked.

"Ain't nothin' up the Saluda but hard goin'. If they steal a skiff, they kin float the river clean down to the Santee. Then they's on to the coast an' Cha'leston like you said Granny told you."

Minns spat in disgust. "Didn't believe that ol' nigger. She jest tellin' lies. Those city folks don' cotton to no Yankee officers."

Jared's earnest face gave Minns pause when the boy explained. "When you sold that Kelly the whiskey the last time, I overheard 'em whisperin'. Said Lieutenant Shaw had a friend in Cha'leston. 'member they paid you a gold piece? It was the Lieutenant's."

Minns took out his exasperation in his castigation of the boy. "Why the hell didn't you tell me that before, God damn it! We could'a been on down the river instid o' on the island."

Jared shied away from Minns' blow toward his head and ignored the curse. "Didn't think it mattered at the time and jest now recollected it."

The information instantly changed the hunter's search. The Congaree was a large river, entering the Santee River at the junction with the Wateree near Fort Motte. It passed through high ground in its western reaches, rolling terrain of pines and hardwoods, then entered areas of bordering swamps not far below Columbia. Its lower reaches penetrated immense swamps with hardwoods and cypress, impossible to pierce on foot for a search. If he intended to catch the fugitives he would need to do so within the first ten miles below the city, before they could steal a boat. Minns, with long experience at hunting men, knew that his delay to still his whiskey had not hurt the search. Usually little distance was covered the first day by an escapee because of extreme caution and fear of recapture or being shot. He recalled the dozen or so he had caught within five miles of the prison camp, immobilized by the fear of going on. So he probably was fairly close to them, he thought.

"Jeremy?" he said.

"Yes, Pa?" The usually silent, obedient boy looked up at Minns expectantly.

"Take the skiff 'cross the river an' scout down 'long the bank. Keep in hollering distance, boy. Might need the boat."

Jeremy nodded and knelt to tighten a leather legging before heading back across the river. Minns looked on approvingly at his stalwart younger son and what passed for a smile twisted his ruined face. He clapped the boy on the shoulder when Jeremy picked up his rifle from its stand against a bush.

"Keerful boy," he said. "Keep yer eyes peeled." He rolled his chaw and spit, then rearranged the tobacco to suit his jaw. "Me an' Jared an' Old Blue'll stick to the road side down as far as Wolf's Landin'. They's probably on this bank. Nowhere else to steal a boat after the swamp starts."

The two parties split in their grim search and headed down the river. At his gesture, Old Blue and Jared bounded ahead of Minns and searched the flanks. By early afternoon, the hunters' slow chase had reached an eddy two miles above the landing. Jeremy had hallooed across the river to them now and then, and had reported no contact. Resting on a down log, Jared's eyes searched the river as Athey chewed his cud and spat. They were silent while the hunter faced the dilemma. What had happened to the fugitives? He was deep in thought when Old Blue and Jared went for a drink at a clear seep at the river's edge.

"Oooah! Oooah!" The dog's strike startled them all when his full throated bugle rang out across the water. Jeremy began hallooing and yelling questions. It was but a few steps for Minns. He ran down to the edge with his rifle ready, but found only the boy and dog. Jared had grasped the scruff of Blue's neck and was pulling him away from a bundle caught in some willows dragging in the water. A few hard slaps drove off the dog. Blue barked safely from the bank while Jared seized the packet and tossed it onto a dry place. His slash cut the binding and the pants, shirt and coat came free, the Union uniform a telltale of the escapees.

"It ain't right," Minns said, a few moments later. They had spread out the clothes on the grass above the bank. Old Blue had kept his distance. But he sneaked in for a sniff, then circled and barked, "Treed." Minns' puzzled face clouded and wrinkled as he inspected the sparse display.

"Ain't no boots, no blanket. If they swum the river, there orta be two blankets, an' boots. An' they ain't nothin' here from the slave."

"Could be they was lookin' to leave us a false trail, Pa," Jared said. "Jest like that ol' coon we got last week. When they doubled back at Granny's, could'a been that Granny sent Jed with their clothes to throw us off."

Minns nodded. "Yer right, boy. That ol' black bitch done fooled us afore. We better git back up the river to talk to the Major, then take the horses an' swing west. That Lieutenant's smarter'n I reckened."

Dark was chasing the last afterglow of the sun when the tired travelers arrived back at the prison camp. The sentry's stout ring of the bell called the Major to the opened gate.

"What the hell happened?" Jones asked. The officer's amazed eyes took in the dirt covered men, mud caked and bedraggled. "Where's Shaw?"

"We turned over in the river and had to crawl out," Minns said testily. He ignored the important question.

"Well, I never!" The Major stifled a laugh. "Where's Shaw?"

Minns' two boys and Old Blue flopped down on the ground while Minns swung a pack from his shoulder and rummaged in it. The hunter faced the officer and tossed Shaw's clothes into the dirt in front of Jones' boots, his disgust evident. "He done outfoxed us," he said, his scar reddening. "Sent his clothes downriver while he done struck out to the west." At the Major's incredulous look, Minns stared at him unflinchingly. "Don' you worry none," he said. "We'll git the bastard. Me an' the boys are headin' out at dawn on the horses."

Jones sniggered. "Don't tell me you got one smarter'n you boys," he said derisively. "Must be that slave Hannibal that Shaw owns. My Jacob tells me the niggers say he's downright invisible in the woods."

Minns bristled at the insult. The scar on his burning, murderous face bulged and turned red and his whole being radiated menace, a threat that made Jones, a veteran of many fights, step back. But Minns would not let him escape. His eye locked intimidatingly with the Major's. He had captured Jones' spirit by the time he made his blood vow. Minns had trouble speaking, so intense was his fury, but he slowly got it out in little, rasping bites. "We'll fetch im back, you bastard. An' kill that uppity slave too. Jest you pay up when we bring 'im in."

Minns huffily refused the Major's offer of a drink. He called up his sons and dog and stalked away.

Jones wiped sweat from his face when the hunter was gone. He wanted to laugh but his shaking and thought of Minns' anger left him unsteady. "Need a drink," he told himself, and headed for his quarters.

The old slave stirred the pot on the crane, her wobbly frame supported by the ever-present stick in her left hand. Granny Mandy spooned out a small sample and tasted the soup. "Need mo' salt," she said aloud, though alone in the cabin. "Could use some o' dat hot pepper too. Still don' taste like much."

Hobbling to a shelf next to the fireplace, she took down three small crocks and rummaged in each. She shredded the bits of herbs extracted, added them to a handful of salt, and tossed the mixture into the pot. Tiny bits missing the boiling soup flamed in the fire, and added slight glints to the orange from the salt grains. The next spoonful satisfied Granny. Her cut and try recipe yielded a pungent odor that permeated the cabin. She had swung out the crane and was reaching for her bowl when Bub entered the door. The enticing aroma pulled him right to the pot, a moth drawn not to the flame but to the soup. Jed followed closely on his heels.

"Dat smell good!" Bub exclaimed and reached for the spoon.

Granny hit his hand with her stick and drove him away from the fire. "Stay away from de pot," she said. "You git some soup atter Jed tells me what happen."

"We took de clothes down ter de ribber like you asked, Granny." Jed's plaintive tone and wry face protested her blow to his friend. "We drug 'em all thoo de bushes an' mud at de ribber bank. Ain't no way Old Blue miss dat scent."

The young man inched in closer to the fireplace. He shivered as he rubbed his hands together and warmed himself. Granny looked suspiciously at the pair and blocked Jed's way to the pot. He eyed her warily, but the old woman was silent when he edged in near the opposite corner from the crane. Bub had followed Jed and crowded close to the fire, while he mumbled about the cold. Granny sniffed and made a face when the heat from the fire started their clothes steaming. The vapors permeated the cabin with a faint odor of skunk. Jed and Bub were unbuttoning their outer coats before Granny chose to speak.

"Recken you got caught in de rains last night?" Her grim, uncompromising visage and piercing gaze sent Jed into a long tale.

"We went up ter Bertha's atter puttin' de stuff inter de ribber," he said, in conclusion, "but she don' let us in. Said we stink like skunk. We had ter sleep out." Jed shivered and moved closer to the fire with his hands palmed toward the blazing billets. His tone turned plaintive as he begged. "It col' out dere, Granny. Can't we have some soup now?"

"Whar's de blanket? Don' see it an' I tol' yuh ter save it."

"Hid it in de big holler beech down by de crick. De one wid de hole way offen de groun'. Leave it dere 'til de fuss done."

Granny nodded. "Ah," she said, "dat good."

Satisfied, she stirred the soup with a big ladle and readied her own dish. "Bring two more bowls from de table," she said. "Spoons too," she called out, when both went hurrying off.

With their bellies full of soup and corncake that Granny pulled from a griddle on the hot ashes on the hearth, Jed and Bub sighed and belched contentedly. Happiness returned with warmth and a good feed and they joshed each other while they relaxed and baked in the heat. They were sitting on the floor with their backs to the fire when Granny noticed Bub's feet. His pants had hiked up on his legs, bent as he was in his hunched over squat. The black Union boots stood out, their fine texture and high tops hardly representative of the slave. And they would smell of Claude to Old Blue's sensitive nose.

It was more than the old woman could bear. She berated Bub and beat him about the head. He scrambled to his feet, protesting, while the stick rose and fell.

Bub threw up his hands and grabbed the stick. His strong grip easily restrained the old woman. "Why you hit me, Granny?" he said. "I ain't done nothin." His aggrieved tone and denial stimulated a flood of invective from Granny.

"You dumb nigger," she said scornfully. "I tol' yer ter git rid o' all de clothes. An' here you bring de boots right back ter dis cabin. Old Blue track yer rightchere. Ain't you got no sense?"

"Too good ter throw away, Granny," Jed said, in defense of his friend.

"Warm too," Bub added. "Better'n my ol' wore out shoes. Dey allus pinchin' my feet."

The old woman struggled with the small but powerful youth. She cried out in exasperation at her failure to wrest the stick from his hands. He held her easily and her tears and anger mounted at her inability to control the headstrong young man.

"Gimme dem boots," Granny cried. "Lemme have 'em. I burn 'em right now. You kin have de old man's other boots in de loft."

"I ain't a'gwine do it, Granny." Bub spoke softly but firmly, his face poked against hers. "Might as well quit yer cryin'."

Exhausted in body and spirit, Granny stood quietly when he released her and handed her the stick. Resolve turned her face into a calm but stern mask when she spat out her ultimatum.

"Gimme de boots er git out, both o' yuh. Dey ain't gwine bring us nothin' but trouble."

"Ain't gwine do it, Granny," Bub said. "Dey's too good ter th'ow away."

The old woman raised her stick at Bub's obstinate refusal. It wavered between the two defiant young men, rising and falling as Granny vacillated, but it never once touched their hands lifted in defense. Finally, Granny pointed it at the door like a rapier and ordered, "Git out! Git!"

She was dozing in her chair before the fire, hours after their silent departure, when faint hoofbeats awakened her. "Dose Minns come soon," she murmured. "De Lord pertec' me." Granny placed her hands in a vee over her heart and bowed her head.

Hoofbeats of several horses pounded along the college trace but went on past, going off to the west at a gallop. A grateful sigh filled the lonely cabin as the beats faded. Granny pulled her shawl closer about her shoulders and re-settled herself in the chair before the comforting fire.

Daylight revealed a clearing sky and bright sunrays

that glanced into the glade where Claude and the others rested. When he rose from the heap of pine fronds and shook the bits from his clothes and hair, his first thought was for the injured woman. She had not stirred, but, though still unconscious from her fall, was breathing normally. Her rosy cheeks reassured him, colored as they were by the cool air. The sleeping, smooth face was composed, untroubled. The planter adjusted the fronds to cover her fully while he pondered his dilemma. What to do with an unconscious woman was not part of his escape plan. But he would not abandon her and determined, as he gazed on the tranquil face, that they would deliver her to Newberry.

Hannibal's bed was empty when Claude left the woman's side. His probing hand found it cold to the touch. The slave had slipped away in the dark with no warning while the planter had finally slept in the oblivion brought on by exhaustion.

The sun was well up before the slave returned. Claude had probed his pockets for crumbs in the interlude but found only a few leftover kernels of parched corn and a little pone. It had been a sparse breakfast and washing it down with cold water from the rivulet nearby hadn't helped his growling gut or his temper.

"Where the hell you been, Hannibal?" he said.

"Cast over toward de Broad an' west a mile er two," the servant said cheerfully. "Lookin' ter see if it be easier goin'."

"Was it?"

"Yassah, Claude. Dey's a woods road just dere behint de second ridge. Aims to'ard Newberry an' ain't traveled. No tracks but deers."

Omission of the "Massa" pleased Claude. He had thought the Negro would have more trouble falling into the first name habit. But the servant's intelligence and quick witted actions in the escape had belied Claude's previous notions of the slave's inferiority. And his thinking ahead and scouting out that back trail was a real stroke of enterprise. The planter's belly rumbled again and reminded him of his hunger. He hiked up his sagging pants. Their large size enveloped his shrunken middle and needed two tucks under the rawhide thong.

Claude patted his stomach and asked, "You got any more pone left? My belly's achin' for some food."

"Better'n dat, Claude." The Negro smiled and hitched the sack around on its strap. The officer's eyes widened when the slave brought out a rabbit and held it up by the hind legs.

Hannibal chuckled. "Ketched him sittin' in a patch of sage grass down de slope. De stick do de rest."

Claude's mouth watered expectantly at such a munificent prize. He had clubbed rabbits in the snows when they couldn't run fast but catching them sitting was another matter. It took sharp eyes and a silent approach, though he knew a setting rabbit would stay quietly in its nest while a dog or hunter went right by. Camouflaged by its color and statuesque quiet in cover, its safety lay in invisibility.

Hannibal glanced at the woman lying so quietly. "How de lady doin'?" he asked.

The planter dragged his thoughts away from the coming pleasures of a savory rabbit and shrugged his shoulders. "Can't tell," he said. "She's still unconscious. But we can't wait. We got to get on west."

The slight breeze drifted the remaining mists toward the Broad and the rustle of the trees warned them of the carry of any smoke or noise. Chirps and rustles in the forest proved they were alone, the forest animals their best protection against surprise. The two stood there while Claude decided their direction. Hannibal waited in respectful silence until the planter moved.

"Let's go," Claude said.

He threw the pine fronds from the sleeping woman and loosely tied her wrists together. Her body was limp and her head lolled when he picked her up. Claude headed off through the trees to the north, taking the path of Hannibal's return. The slave ran alongside and protested.

"Lemme tote 'er, Claude. You hurt yer shoulder agin."

The planter shook his head and said, "I'll carry her first."

Claude strode on resolutely, though his shoulder twinged at every step. Hannibal assumed his lead position and selected a path through the forest. Though he picked his way, it still was irregular ground and the planter, burdened, struggled to keep up. His load became ever more intolerable until it finally overwhelmed him. Claude was puffing hard and sweating heavily when he stopped for a blow and laid the woman on a soft bed of leaves.

"Wait up," he called out.

Hannibal dropped back and joined him. "Want me to take 'er, Claude?"

"No," the planter replied. "But next time go on slow, she's pretty heavy."

He walked away a few steps and squatted behind some bushes. Hannibal was fanning the woman's face when he returned.

"She ain't knowin' we's here, Claude," he said.

"Well, we'll get her to Newberry. We'd best lug her over toward the trail you mentioned, so you head for there."

"Sho' kin," the servant said. "Tain't fur, but de groun' hard walkin'. We git dere directly."

"When we're farther from the road we'll make a fire," Claude said. "Won't take long to cook that rabbit. Need to get over the ridge though, with the wind to the north, so any smoke'll blow into the swamp."

An hour's slow travel saw them through the small ravine with its thickets and onto higher ground as they angled northwest over the next ridge. Claude threaded his way slowly with cautious steps. With her head exposed, he took care not to bump the woman against any trees or bushes. Her sleeping face remained rosy, and her dark auburn hair gradually escaped from the bonnet, traces flying in the wind. A loud sneeze shocked him into a halt. Squirming and moans and the girl's heavy weight forced Claude to his knees. He laid her down on the forest mat with a welcome sigh. The sleeper pawed at her nose and pulled at the loose strands of hair.

"Tickling her, I reckon," Claude said, as Hannibal knelt with him.

"Don' see 'er comin' 'round," the Negro responded. "She done sleepin' sound."

"Spell me, Hannibal, but be careful of 'er." The planter rose and led off on the next hike.

The powerful Negro picked up the unconscious woman as if she were a feather and headed off. From their stop, he bent his way further west into the deep forest. Claude strode on ahead of the burdened servant, his object to weave through the largest trees where the brush was least developed. It was a fair hike before their way was blocked by a large blowdown area. Remnant trunks and tops meshed across their path in an impenetrable abatis. Claude paused for a another rest.

"Where's the trail to Newberry?" he asked, once Hannibal came even with him. "You said the trail ran over here past the ridge."

"It be 'round de blowdowns on de nawth side, Claude. Can't git thoo here. Got ter go 'roun'."

A fine, clear area faced them at a massive fallen oak, backed by a large fan of roots. It was a natural abatis, a protected place with much dry, down wood, perfect for their fire. Claude poked about for a level, cushioned place to put the woman while they ate. He scraped up a soft mat of leaves and worked quickly to shape it, then gave way to Hannibal.

"Right pretty lady," the Negro observed, as he placed her carefully on the leaf bed. "Make some gent'man a fine wife."

The woman moaned and moved her head slightly, then stretched out to full length on her back. Her arms worked and she tried to escape the ties restraining her wrists but the feeble effort receded into a renewed limpness.

Bending over, Claude patted her cheeks gently and said, "Miss! Can you hear me, Miss?" When she did not respond, he shook her lightly with a sharp, "Wake up! Wake up!"

Only lassitude and silence answered, her face again composed. Claude's face fell, his hopes dashed. He thought of the hours slipping by while he and the servant were tied to the dead weight of the insensible woman. They needed to get rid of her soon or the risk of capture would be great. Minns' reputation for bringing back prisoners had even impressed O'Reilly. His friend's comments drifted through Claude's consciousness, a reminder to get on down the road.

"That Minns is a devil," Kelly had said. "He don't just like to bring in prisoners, he likes to shoot 'em. An' he don't fail or miss. Looky here at my arm." Kelly had waved the stump at him again. "He brought back all the last ten an' ever'one had a bullet wound, mostly maiming. So Claude, git as far on up the Broad as soon as you can."

The thought decided the planter and incited him to action. He scouted up a few small twigs and some sticks, then fished some cedar bark from the underside of a fallen trunk. Clustering of the bark and twigs in a cleared firepit prepared the mass for Hannibal's flint and steel.

"I'll clean the rabbit while you build the fire," Claude said.

The servant squatted down obediently and struck a spark at the cedar tinder. Claude picked up the rabbit and took it away from the camp. A few moments later, he was back with the stripped, gutted carcass. He had saved the liver, heart and kidneys for use as well. Blood dripped from his hands when he placed the rabbit on a piece of bark. A few short steps carried him back to a small seep down the slope. Its swampy, thickly grassed drain trickled into a delightfully clear pool shaded by a spreading oak. The trunk of the sheltering tree inclined out over the pool and the sloping ground. Protected, the sparkling water was bordered with green moss and floating water cress. Its coolness so refreshed Claude that he took a potfull up to the camp to give sips to their patient and to wash her face.

A few minutes of blowing and fanning by Hannibal produced a tiny blaze, fed to a larger size by dry branches. The flame was clean with little smoke, since the windfall tangle provided select dry stove wood from long dead branches under the trunks. Splitting the rabbit in two, the fugitives spitted the pieces and placed them right in the flames to roast the meat in as little time as possible. Hannibal set the sticks solidly. His powerful hands thrust them deep into the soft ground while Claude took the pot over to the recumbent figure.

"You recken she wake t'day," the servant asked, when he joined them.

"Can't say." The planter was bathing the woman's face

with the cold water after holding the pan to her lips for a tiny drink. That she had swallowed a few sips had been gratifying. He kept hoping she would wake.

"We got ter be rid o' her soon's we kin, Claude. She keepin' us from gittin' on up ter Jawga."

The planter's irritation boiled up out of his exhaustion. "I know that!" he said. "But we just can't leave her. We'll find someone to give her to over by Newberry. Should make most of the way today."

Juices falling into the fire sputtered and added their aroma to the clearing. The cooking meat attracted the two men closer as their hunger drew them away from the patient. As soon as the organ meat looked done they split it and gulped it down, the burning and half-done taste ignored. The rabbit went soon after. Famished, their need drove them to tear at the hot meat even though not quite roasted. But the urgency to leave Minns far behind demanded that they not tarry. A long drink at the pool finished the simple but satisfying meal.

"I'll get the fire, Hannibal," Claude said. He poured water on it and carried up another potfull before the last wisps died. One more pot satisfied him on destruction of the flames and scent. "No sense leaving any kind of trail," he said, as he scattered the wet ashes and threw leaves over the site.

The Negro picked up the woman and circled the fallen tree. Obediently, Claude led off to the west on the game trail Hannibal had pointed out, a split in the brush with many deer tracks. He skirted the big blowdown to avoid the rash of blackberries and other clutching bushes. His lead soon took them to a cleared area, an old field no longer worked. It was but a few steps to the main forest trail to the west. A close look confirmed Hannibal's judgement. The weedy trail showed only wild animal tracks.

By late afternoon they were exhausted from lugging the heavy, limp sack of the unconscious woman. It was impossible to carry her without immense strain, though the old trail made for easy going. Their burden was increased by a big clutch of chinkapin chestnuts that filled all of Claude's pockets and made Hannibal's possibles sack bulge. A soft carpet of moss and Hannibal's wheezing decided them on a rest. He laid the woman on the shady, mossgrown ground and smoothed the hair out of her face. She slept on, while he sank down on an adjacent log and wiped the sweat from his brow, and voiced the fears of both.

"We ain't close ter de town yet, Claude. Got ter rest ternight. I'se done in."

Claude squatted beside his friend. Fatigue lines showed in Hannibal's face. He could feel the aches in his own legs and damaged shoulder. The servant had carried the woman twice as much as he and he was ready for rest. A cooling wind caused him to shiver, its bite sharper now that the sun was low. They needed to seek shelter before the dark caught them, but no thicket showed anywhere close.

"We'll go on up to the next high ground," Claude said, "then look for a place to camp. I'll carry 'er this time."

Hannibal's tiredness was evident in his lack of protest. No more insistence on spelling the planter or protecting his shoulder. Hannibal adjusted the sling of the possibles sack and picked up the spear, then started up the trail ahead of the others.

The saddle carried the trail through a small cleared area, evidence of a long abandoned homestead. Perhaps fifty acres were grown up in lush grass and the meadow was bordered by sections of a rotting rail fence. To the south Claude glimpsed the almost hidden remnants of a log cabin, the chimney and part of the roof intact. A few withered blossoms in a garden bed near the trail were evidence of the touch of some long ago woman. But it was a wild place now, just the hideout they needed to recuperate. And the thicket of medium sized, intensely green pines encroaching around the sides of the cabin helped to enclose it and to make it less visible except directly in front on the trail.

Hannibal already was entering as Claude came up. He reappeared almost immediately with a broad smile, then ran down to help with the woman and to relieve Claude's tired, aching arms.

"It's purty dry, Claude," he said, as he carried the woman into the cabin. "An' de fireplace good. We kin roast dose ches'nuts ternight."

Flames sparkled in the fireplace a few minutes later. The woman lay in a rude bed along one wall, close enough to feel the warmth. Claude was sorting out the chestnuts for puncturing when Hannibal came back from a scout around the small clearing. The servant held several golden apples and pawpaws in his hands and placed them down next to the nuts.

"Dey's a big ol' apple tree out by de fence," he said, "jist full o' apples. De deers been eaten 'em on de groun'." He picked up a big pawpaw and turned it around in his hands. Its yellow and green skin shined in the firelight as he showed it to Claude. "Pawpaws growed up out dere in de flat whar dey had de pasture. Best place fer pawpaws. Frost done make 'em sweet." He peeled the fruit and took a bite. Streams of juice ran down his chin as he announced his verdict. "Dishere's a good place."

Roasted chestnuts and the pawpaws provided a filling if not a satisfying meal. Cold water from the spring out back washed it all down but they still felt empty. Lack of flesh and fat kept their stomachs lean and their cravings led inevitably to thoughts of succulent meats.

Hannibal picked up his staff and tested its point. "Recken we might take a deer, Claude?" he asked.

"How?"

"Wid de spear. Kin wait in de tall grass out near de tree. Mebbe dey be atter de apples ternight."

It was black dark when the deer finally came into the clearing. Claude could hear them snorting and rustling in the surrounding bushes but they wouldn't approach the apple tree. He gave it up, driven not by hunger but by his shivering and the intolerably cold wind.

"We're too rank for 'em," he said softly. "They'll never get close."

Though disappointed in the hunt, Claude eagerly returned to the welcome heat of the cabin. Hannibal carried in an armload of sticks when he entered and replenished the fire. Its cheery light and warmth relaxed them and added to their sense of safety, and, at the same time, compounded the drowsiness brought on by exhaustion. They drifted off to sleep in beds of fragrant pine boughs with their feet to the fire.

A chair squeaked inside the cabin as Minns rose from his seat and called out to his son. "Got them rifles cleaned yet, Jeremy?"

Athey's spur stirred the boy to faster work. He was standing the third rifle against the cabin wall when the hunter softly padded out onto the porch.

"Them rifles clean an' reloaded?" Minns asked. When his son bent to pick up some scraps, he added sharply, "Answer me, boy!"

"Yes, Pa," Jeremy said. "But I got somethin' out'n yer rifle barrel jest now you orta see."

Jeremy held up some strands of yarn covered with clay. The mess was still slippery from the water and stained the boy's fingers.

Athey took the mass and studied it closely. His jaw set when he realized what it was. Recollection of the trap at Granny's and his bleeding fingers confirmed his suspicion.

"What is it, Pa?" Jeremy asked.

"That old bitch, Granny, done stuffed it in the barrel when we were thar. It'd killed me had I fired that ball."

Minns picked up the rifle and cocked it, then aimed it into the woods and pulled the trigger. Only the cap fired, the rifle remaining silent. The hunter swore and looked closely at the lock.

"She done plugged the flash hole in the nipple too," he said. His voice turned brittle as his gorge rose, and his scar bulged and reddened. He spat and cursed. "That's one smart old nigger. If Mista Perkin's don' mind, I'm goin'a kill that old bitch."

Jeremy shook his head and objected. "You'll have to pay fer her, Pa. Beatin's good enough."

The hunter busied himself in cleaning out the nipple. A probe cleared the dirt plug and a new attempt fired the rifle. When Athey reloaded it and tried again, the weapon worked perfectly.

Minns tossed the rifle back to Jeremy and passed the rest of the work to him. "Swab the bore, boy, and reload 'er. Then come on in and git some sleep. We'll settle with Granny when we git thar termorrow."

CHAPTER 5

Aunt Lucy

November 5, 1864. Newberry, South Carolina. Temperature 58\31. Blowing and cold, cloudy to the west with high haze. Moon waxing, approaching full, rising about midnight.

At the screams, Claude bounded fearfully into the center of the cabin from his rest by the fire. He looked about wildly, the eerie howling raising the hair on the back of his neck. He shivered in fright and sweated as he crouched there with his knife drawn, and tried to orient himself to the threat. Moonlight sifting into the cabin told him it was well after midnight. The empty bunk was proof that the woman was gone and that the banshee screams outside likely were her panicked hysterics.

Hannibal rushed past him and disappeared through the cabin door. Claude's fright receded at the sight of the servant and he sheathed his knife and followed. The woman was running away from the cabin, her form ethereal in the diffuse, silvery light of the nearly full moon. But her long dress dragged and hampered her progress. It caught on all the growth of the untended farmstead. They overtook her easily in the wet, tall meadow grass, rimed with ice in spots. The planter enveloped the shuddering figure with his arms and pinioned the struggling woman while Hannibal tried to quiet her.

"It awright, Missy. You safe from de tramps. Me an' Claude pertec' yuh. We keep 'em from gittin' yuh."

Screams and protests filled their ears. She kicked the planter on the shin and stamped on his foot. "Let me go, you brutes. I'll have you flogged."

Claude swung her off the ground and tried to evade her wild kicking and attempts to bite. Her hands grasped at his arms and tore the cloth in her frenzy. The maddened woman wrestled with him, her strength testing the limits of his still sore shoulder. She was about to escape from his weakened grip when Hannibal seized her.

The servant fell to his knees and clasped her flailing legs in a tight grip. She struggled and tore at the men but the two of them finally subdued the crazed girl.

"Claude an' me put yer down if you promise not to run," Hannibal said soothingly. Their tight grasp and his calming tone quieted the last struggles but not her wailing. "Me an' Claude, we don' hurt yuh. We saved yuh from dose white trash on de trail."

Screams gave way to sobs as the moment lengthened. Claude felt her trembling reduce to shivers, then her body relaxed. But he held the girl's hands firmly when Hannibal released her and stepped aside. Her tear-stained, drawn face looked up at the bigger men, her fright apparent to them.

"Carried yuh from de post road all yestiday, Missy," Hannibal said. His soft voice was comforting and submissive. "We on de path ter Newberry now ter take yuh home. You from de town, ain't yuh?"

"I'm Melody Newberry. My father's president of the Lutheran Christian Academy for Females."

"We git yer home, Miz Melody," Hannibal said, reassuringly. "Soon's de sun's up. Done brung you dis far an' we's gonna take you ter de town safe."

The frightened girl pulled away from Claude when he nodded and grunted. "What's wrong with him?" she asked.

"He done been born dumb, Miz Melody. Can't talk. Jist grunts."

"Good worker though," he added, as he glanced slyly at

Claude.

The planter could see the grin and the servant enjoying his mild ascendancy to leadership. An irritated flush ran over him and his frown stopped any further talk until they re-entered the cabin.

"Why this is the old Jenkins place," Melody exclaimed, when she saw the fireplace. Her interest had immediately shifted from the raiders once they were in the cabin.

"My daddy used to bring me out here to get apples when I was a little girl. I remember the step in the stone. Miz Jenkins used to give me cider."

"What happened ter dem?" Hannibal asked.

"Mister Jenkins was killed in sixty two up in Tennessee. Miz Jenkins moved to Columbia to get work. She had three chil'ren to feed."

The story resembled so many others that Claude had heard in his years before capture. Families, north and south, destroyed by the war. All the fine, strong men gone, killed either by the belching cannons and rifles or the galloping diseases.

Melody peered speculatively at the two Negroes and went to the doorway. The moonlight was strong and bright and the trail through the trees was easily visible. A heavy growth of pines lined the sides of the road like fence palings.

"We're not more than two miles from the school," she said. "We can see good enough. Will you take me home now?"

"Dis de right trace, Miss Melody?"

"Yes. It's the old road that goes down to Hughey's Ferry, there where the wagons used to cross the Broad to the Monticello trace. It's not used now. There's a new place to get over now, Ashford's Ferry, up by Strother's."

A hesitation and tucking up of her hair were followed by fluffing of her skirts. She was oblivious to Hannibal and Claude while she made her meager toilet. "Did you really save me from those ruffians?" she asked, once the rearranging satisfied her.

"Miz Melody, yore hoss done throwed yuh. You's lyin' dere knocked out. We take yuh outen de road quick an' dey went poundin' by. Atter de hoss, I recken."

Hannibal's simple narrative brought a sigh from Melody and a tear ran down her cheek.

"They've been trying to steal Red all along. He was a grand horse."

"It don' matter, Miss Melody. You safe. Dat's de main thing. Now we git yuh ter Newberry."

The girl fidgeted and glanced about. "Well, I need to wash my face first and fix up a bit. I must be a sight."

"Dere's a spring at de back o' de cabin," Hannibal said. "We wait fer yuh."

Claude was apprehensive when she hurried around the corner of the cabin. She'll most likely bolt, he thought, even though we brought her this far and haven't hurt her. Her shrewd, sneaked glances at them bothered him. She was a sharp woman, he concluded, suspicious and alert, untrusting. And she had convinced the open and helpful Hannibal of her sincerity. But she was ready to turn the tables on them if she could, he believed. Meanwhile she'd go along. He was surprised when she came sauntering back, still shaking out the wrinkles of her great skirt. Her tears were off a clean, pale face and her hair was completely straightened and pinned back tight against her head.

While the girl was gone, Claude whispered to Hannibal about the small derringer they had found in a secret pocket of her waistband. They had not taken it, not robbing the woman, but the planter wanted the dangerous piece out of her hands.

"Miz Melody, we need de little gun you tote," Hannibal said. "Might run inter trouble on de way."

"No! I carry it for myself!" The girl felt swiftly for the weapon. She grasped its hard outline and cartridge box firmly in her hand and backed away, suspicious. Her brow furrowed as her face clouded with doubt, and she clutched the hidden pocket even more tightly.

"We need it, Missy," Hannibal insisted. "If dose thieves come back, you ain't gonna shoot. But Claude will. He good shot. Hunt game fer Massa Middleton all de time."

Claude extended his hand and further exhortation by Hannibal conquered her doubts. But she delivered the derringer, powder and balls into Claude's palm slowly and with obvious reluctance. He checked the load and cap and placed the weapon and ammunition case in his pocket before turning to the trace.

The party went up the road with care, the robbers uppermost in Claude's mind. He led the way with his hand on the pistol. Hannibal and Melody followed silently. It took almost an hour for them to arrive at the edge of Newberry. It was incomprehensible to the officer that no pickets challenged. He had used the duff on the trail, wet with dew, to muffle his steps but the three were clearly visible in the moonlight. They crouched there in some cover while Claude surveyed the silent street and widely scattered houses.

As if reading Claude's mind, Hannibal questioned the girl. "Any sojers 'roun', Miz Melody?"

"No. All the ones here went off toward Atlanta a week ago. There's supposed to be another big battle. Are you afraid of soldiers?"

"Me an' Claude on de way ter de gol' mines in Jawga. Dig gol' for Massa Davis. But dem sojers allus make us stop an' do chores. Don' hold no truck with sojers."

"Well, why are you traveling alone?"

Hannibal pulled out his paper and offered it to her. "Got paper from Massa Middleton in Cha'leston. Tells us ter go ter Jawga an' dig gol'. We on de way." He paused, reflective, then sighed. "Sojers allus trouble. Mek us work. Can't go ter Jawga like Massa Middleton tell us."

The girl looked at them doubtfully, hesitating, but then took over the directions into the small town. "We'll just walk down the street a short way, then I'll be home." Her face broke into a smile. "Home," she repeated with jubilation. "I never realized how wonderful it was."

Claude's doubts gnawed at him, misgivings that undermined his confidence. It was as if small worms were wiggling in his mind, loathsome creatures that were gradually destroying whatever faith he had in the girl. It struck him as remarkable that never once had she thanked them for being rescued from the ruffians. Her casual, friendly cooperation appeared contrived, a charade that veneered over her deeper emotions and plans. Was she going to have them captured? Would she be the one to end their journey?

A girl they had saved from death or worse? The niggling questions tore at him as he reluctantly followed her along the street. She halted before a large brick building a few blocks to the west.

"That's the academy," Melody said. "Our house is just next door."

The house was a sleeping giant and no light showed in its windows. Only silence and moonlight embraced the massive structure. The great white dwelling stood well away from the school building, a castle with a broad porch that clasped it on three sides. Moonlight glinted off the slates of a conical roof above a circular corner-tower, a shaft whose bulge extended down to the porch. Large windows, many open, ventilated the floors, though the night was cold. White pillars added to the symmetry and beauty of the facade, and splint chairs and a swing gleamed in the moonlight, their cushions comforts for fine afternoons. Tall, mature trees shaded the yard and added to the restfulness of the porch.

Melody stopped at the edge of the brick walk and scrutinized the two Negroes who faced her in the moonlight, respectful and subservient. Their ragged clothes and dirty, smelly persons were not in keeping with any idea of honor. Or suggestive of the faithful way they had served her and carried her safely home. A shadow of distaste crossed her face. Now secure, now back in her sheltered, autocratic world, she was again the haughty lady when she spoke. Her brusk voice both commanded and exuded authority.

"Go around to the carriage house," she said. "There's a hayloft you can sleep in. I'll have Aunt Lucy bring you some food."

Claude recognized the subtle change, the condescension in the girl's voice, the oppression. His gorge rose at the imperious way she stood there, and viewed them with disgust now that she was safe. Melody angered him even further when she wrinkled her nose and sniffed audibly at their rank odor, the sweat of days on the trail.

"Miz Melody?" Hannibal interrupted her start up the walk to the porch.

The girl stamped her foot when she turned, and muttered some remark under her breath. Her tone with them turned sharp, irritated, complaining. "Well, what do you want now?"

"You won't tell nobody other'n yer family we here? Don' want no sojers ter take us. We got ter git on over ter Jawga."

"No. I'll see you on your way. And when you leave here, you should go on over to Cross Hill. The road up the Saluda is easier."

It was as good a promise as they would get, Claude thought. He whispered to Hannibal when they were in the carriage house that they would use another route. Gloom settled on him from his lack of trust in the woman as he waited, unwilling to sleep.

Dim crack of dawn found Minns and his sons back at the stockade. The Army was issuing them food and powder, the latter a supplement to their own lead rifle balls, which were cast to fit. Major Jones joked with Minns while the quartermaster sergeant measured out the supplies, but his overture to ease the past day's tension did little to mollify the hunter. Minns was withdrawn, uncommunicative, stolidly uninterested in anything except preparations for the journey. Their horses stood quietly at the hitchrack before the headquarters, fattened and ready for a hard chase. In the cool air, little clouds of steam issued from the breaths of horse and man alike. Heavy coats and coonskin hats warmed the Minnses as they moved about, skins the first choice of the woodsmen, not much different from the animals they hunted. The saddlebags bulged when the sergeant carried them out to the horses. He tossed them up behind the cantles and secured the lashings, then reported to the Major. The hunters ignored the soldiers as they checked their cinches and weapons. Minns was preparing to mount when the Jones' curiosity overcame him.

"Where first, Athey?" he asked.

Minns was very formal. "To see that Granny Mandy, Major. She done he'ped those two. I plan to thrash it outen her where they went."

His bile rose at the memory of the plugged rifle. "She stuck clay an' yarn down my barrel."

"No!" the Major exclaimed. "Didn't ruin it?" He reached for Minns' weapon. The hunter relented at the officer's interest and handed him the rifle. Jones examined its lock and nipple and cocked the weapon a few times.

Minns looked on with a grim smile. "Never fired the rifle," he said. "It war a good thing we fell inter the river. When Jeremy reloaded, he cleaned it out. That Granny triflin' with my rifle really riles me. Goin'a beat 'er good."

The Major looked up in surprise at the long speech, so unusual for the taciturn hunter and so unexpected after their disagreement. His warning was blunt.

"Don't kill the old witch. Old man Pickens'll have your hide. That nigger raised him."

Minns' pained voice ridiculed the obvious. "I know that," he said, "but it don' keep me from wringin' her scrawny neck."

The Major handed back the gleaming weapon after turning it over and over and aiming at a tree. "Pretty small bore for huntin'," he said.

"Straighter shootin' with the small ball and long barrel," Minns retorted. His scornful assessment continued. "You soldiers think you need a minie ball er fifty caliber. Tain't so."

He swung up into his saddle, then clucked to his horse and kneed the animal. His boys fell in behind him. When the Minnses rode off, the Major turned to his Sergeant. The man was shaking his head, his doleful face full of foreboding.

"What's wrong, Sergeant?"

"I was raised round here, Major. Old man Pickens sets a powerful store by Granny. They kill Granny Mandy and he'll hang 'em all."

The pone was rich and the milk cool from its storage in the spring. Bub stretched before the smoky cabin fire, his boots out for his listeners to ogle while he gulped down his simple breakfast. Aunty Florinda took more cake from the fire and handed it to him until he was full. He was wiping his mouth on his sleeve and belching when Ezell sidled over.

"Whar'd you git dose boots?" Ezell asked.

The Negro's envy delighted Bub, the two long competitors and veterans of many fights as they grew up. They struck sparks at every meeting. The slaves said that one would end up dead some day. But today Bub puffed up and bragged.

"Offen a Union officer, dat's where."

He ignored Granny's earlier admonition to keep quiet, and his crowing over Ezell added to the damage.

"We done he'ped a Union officer ter 'scape de camp. He gib me dese boots."

"Hesh, Bub!" Aunty Florinda's warning failed to halt the impetuous youth. The elderly Negress left her stool and hobbled toward him while his mouth babbled on.

"Me an' Jed done he'ped him."

At that admission, Florinda threw her chicory coffee into Bub's face.

"Why you do dat, Aunty?" Bub aggrieved look challenged her while he wiped off the coffee.

"You knows de rules of de 'scape road, Bub. You don' tell nothin' ter nobody not in de chain. So why yer blabbin'?"

Bub's gaze fell before Aunty's recriminations. He could not answer nor meet the fierce eyes of the woman, his memory of Granny's grim instructions reinforced by Aunty Florinda's rebuke. When Ezell stole from the cabin, Bub did not notice, his attention distracted by continuing invective from the old Negress.

The horse moved in its stall, nervous at the scent of the intruders. Hannibal and Claude had long since taken stock of the carriage house. The planter circled it outside at first arrival, then studied the large forest encroaching on the pasture to the west, a likely escape route. They investigated the interior up and down after they entered. Sweet-scented hay in the loft offered comfort, as Melody suggested. Its soft bedding was enticing. Hannibal threw himself down in cured grass and pulled clumps of hay over his body. A moment of wiggling followed, then a sigh of comfort.

"Soft, Claude. Dishere'll be a good place ter sleep. Warm too."

But the steep ladder worried the planter. They'd be trapped there if any troops came, he thought. His unease drove him to action. "Get up," he whispered. "I don't trust that girl. She's goin'a try to get us captured."

Hannibal disbelief spilled out. "Dat purty gal? I tinks she treat us good atter we save her from de white trash."

"No. We'll leave soon. She's bound to harm us."

As if to confirm Claude's thoughts, a door slammed in the front of the house. A half scream and lighted lamps had been followed by a commotion and loud voices after Melody had entered. While they inspected the barn, wailing and angry tones, too vague to understand, had disturbed the night. They were capped off by the thunderclap of the door. Claude slid hurriedly down the ladder rails, polished smooth from long use, and ran out of the barn door. He took a stand behind a large tree at the side of the yard and was just in time to see a man hurry along the street. The dark shape carried a rifle in his hand, and was shouting and crying out in alarm.

To the planter's surprise, a Negro woman came slinking out of the kitchen at the same time. But her steps angled toward the barn, not the house. The separated kitchen was attached to the mansion by a walkway, a structure that created good shadows. Their cover shielded the stealthy movements of the woman until she was in the protection of some bushes. Hannibal and Claude met her at the barn door and drew her inside.

"You got ter git away right quick!" she burst out. "Marse Newberry gone fer de militia boys."

She pressed two packages in their hands. "Here's some vittles. Corn bread, catfish, an' cold greens to take wid yuh."

The scent of the food overwhelmed the hungry men. They wolfed the tasty greens first, then tore at the fish and corn bread. Hannibal, his mouth stuffed full, responded to Claude's nudge.

"How long, Aunt Lucy?"

"How you knows my name?" the woman asked. Her suspicious face wrinkled, and her worried frown added to the uncertainty of the meeting.

"Miss Melody tol' us. She 'llowed not ter tell nobody 'bout us." Hannibal's confusion and aggrieved tone expressed his hurt.

"She's jist a liar. Been lyin' all de time, since she was a little gal. Can't trust her, no way. Had me licked more'n oncet lying 'bout me." Aunt Lucy's impassioned diatribe switched to their predicament.

"You git movin' right now," she urged, "fo' de militia boys come."

"Miz Melody tol' us all de sojers done gone," Hannibal replied.

"Dat's right. But Marse Newberry's brudder, Micah, been livin' wid him since de Yankees shot 'im. He hate de Yankees and de niggers too. Marse Micah gathered up 'bout dozen boys ter be de militia. Dey got shotguns 'n de like. He drills 'em an' dey be atter yuh right soon."

Hannibal persisted in his interrogation of the cook. "She tol' us ter go ter Cross Hill. Dat be right?"

"She was lyin' agin. Nothin' but trouble dere. You aim nawth. Pass by Laurens' place an' look fer Silas and Aunt Rachel. Dey he'p yuh."

Lucy reached into pockets on her apron and brought out a few irregular lumps, easily recognizable in the moonlight. She pressed them into their hands and said, "Take dese sweet taters wid yuh too. Dey right good dis year."

Shouts down the street alerted them to the oncoming militia. Aunt Lucy glanced fearfully out the door, then clapped Claude on the back and whispered, "Git, an' fast!" before she picked up her skirts and ran toward the kitchen.

Dawn was barely adding to the diffuse moonlight when they stuffed the remaining food into their pockets and licked their greasy fingers. The fugitives angled away from the barn along the pasture fence rails and aimed for the thick forest to the west. Its dense stand beckoned, their refuge and concealment guaranteed unless the militia brought dogs with them.

They were a quarter mile away, just into the cover, when a commotion at the barn drew them back. Claude's curiosity overcame his caution and he edged to the border of the woods. A glance down the slope revealed running figures with torches surrounding the structure. A man with a rifle was shouting and gesticulating and directing the boys. The group bunched in the yard when the search was unsuccessful.

It dismayed Claude that the group had assembled so rapidly and that the leader was so decisive. While he watched, the man looked toward the forest, the only escape route with cover, and pointed to it. The militia group fell silent, then started toward the trees in a scattered skirmish line. It was time to run. Each militiaman carried a weapon and Claude knew they would be shot. Laying hands on Miss Melody had been a cardinal sin, something never tolerated with a Negro man, even though they had saved her life or worse. That was a hanging offense to a lynch mob. Except here the boys had guns.

He and Hannibal ran for their lives. Terror produced panic and a sprint rather than a slow, marathon run. The fast pace quickly exhausted their stamina as they pounded through the forest. A half- mile of dodging trees, thorns and deadfalls took them to the edge of a small, open glade, the shouts of their pursuers behind them.

The seep had been there for millenia, a tiny spring that watered the ground in the partial shade. Its lubricant converted the surface into a soggy, yielding gruel on top of the soft, underlying clay, perfect bedding for the even, green moss that spread over the spot. Hannibal hit the slick in full stride. His fall carried a large section of moss with him when he scarred the soft surface. Crash! His leg struck a dry snag when he hit and skidded under it. The sharp spike tore through the clothing and savaged Hannibal's shin.

Claude ran to him. "You hurt?" he asked.

"Don' b'lieve so, Claude." The servant sat up and worked on his entangled pants.

Claude bent over the fallen man and helped him free himself from the stob. It had run clear through the pants on his lower right leg and was standing out on the other side. The planter was relieved that no blood was showing. But when Hannibal tested his footing with a few steps, he was unable to bear down hard without a groan. He limped and favored the leg when they resumed their flight.

Shouts echoed through the trees and far down the line a dog gave tongue. The planter shivered and Hannibal hurried his tortured pace. When a gunshot resounded near the dog, the animal's baying became frantic, but grew fainter as it receded in the distance.

"Dey done put out a deer, Claude," Hannibal said.

"Right," the planter replied. He stopped and listened to the yodeling for a moment. "It's traveling fast. It'll take off some of 'em but that Newberry'll probably bring the rest along after us." Claude shivered and nervously glanced about. "We got to hurry," he said. "Can you make it?"

Hannibal nodded with a weak, "Sho' kin." He hastened after the planter when the guide headed out. But he was limping badly now, unable to keep up any motion other than a walk. His staff served to lift him when the sore leg came down but the end left telltale punctures and scrapes in the forest duff. Claude dropped back and walked beside the Negro, to steer him and to help him over the down limbs or brushy places. Hannibal paused at a large blowdown. He faced the great tangle with resignation on his face.

"You leave me, Massa," he said. "I kin hide here. You save yerself."

"They'll kill yuh, Hannibal." Claude's temper added to his anxiety. "And no more Massa, you hear."

He spoke with an intensity that surprised him. The servant had offered to lay down his life to draw off the pursuers. Somehow, the old biblical ethic flashed unbidden into his mind. How often had he heard about "no greater love than to lay down his life for a friend." Claude had never felt such friendship for a slave before. His affection grew for the struggling man and his resolve led to but one conclusion.

"We go together, Hannibal," he said. "We need to find a place to hide and hole up for a day 'til your leg is better."

Another few minutes of difficult travel took them to a second tangle, a relic of the storm earlier in the fall. They hid there in a small, natural hut made by several pine tops falling on a root fan. Minutes later a step rattled the dry leaves of the forest. When he peeped out from a flanking post at the side of the tangle, with Hannibal up the slope in the thickest part, Claude saw a large, well-set-up boy approach in the early morning light. The hunter was armed with a short barreled halfstock rifle, a flintlock carried chest high.

The youth advanced cautiously, bent over and intent on the ground. Claude's heart sank as the boy tracked their scrapes in the surface, keenly alert and implacable in his pursuit.

Calls from the distant men halted the boy's advance, his head up while he listened to the other searchers. From the faintness of the shouts, the trio had strayed far from the pursuit by the militia. The boy hallooed once, but, receiving no answer, resumed his inspection of the trail.

It was the wind that betrayed them. A little shift in the breeze striking against his head, and rattling of the leaves, reminded Claude of his peril. He watched the oncoming boy in dismay, realizing that the wisps were directly from them to the hunter. Leaves were rustling but the fugitives' scent would overcome any noisy distraction. The boy sniffed and tensed when he approached their cover. He stopped and raised his weapon and his body transformed from the alert tracker to the man hunter, strung for action. A vagary of the wind decided him, for he instantly cocked his rifle and took a fighting stance a few yards from the natural hut.

"Come outen there!" he nervously ordered. "I smell fish, an' you too."

"I'se comin', Massa." Hannibal rattled the brush when he thrust himself through the fallen tops and his shape gradually issued into view. He leaned heavily on his staff, and hobbled and hopped some as if sorely wounded. Advancing on the off side, his approach drove the boy toward Claude when the man hunter backed up.

"Who air ye?" the boy asked, then halted again with his rifle pointed at the Negro.

"Hannibal, Massa. On de way ter Marse Middleton's gol' mines in Jawga." He commenced bobbing and his voice whined subserviently. "Ain't hurtin' nothin'."

"You laid hands on Miss Melody, 'ccordin' to her talk. Reverend Newberry's brother told us. He said we'd hang yuh. But I've a mind to kill yuh right here fer that."

The rifle wavered and settled on the Negro's chest. But the boy hesitated and his face worked. His nervousness was apparent to the planter, a boy who faced his first kill, difficult to do. It was the sudden set of his jaw, the killing resolve, that decided Claude, determined to prevent the murder of his friend.

Claude rattled the bushes violently to distract the boy, then launched himself across the short space between them. His spear caught the hunter in his clothing at the side as the youth spun toward his attacker. Claude's thrust missed the boy's body but deflected the rifle, which discharged harmlessly into the air. The youth clubbed his rifle and struck the staff out of Claude's hand. But the stunning impact of his great blow dislodged both weapons and they fell into the leaves. The disarmed boy, facing two men, did not back off as Claude expected. Though barehanded and only a youth, he was strong and courageous, a courage now multiplied by fear. He cursed and grappled with the planter.

The boy cried out in anger when he seized Claude and threw him to the ground, then fell on top. The two rolled over and over as they thrashed about wildly and the cursing youth beat the planter in the face and about the body. His blows and the strain were telling as he gradually overcame the weakened man. Hannibal hobbled about with his spear aimed but the entangled, rapidly moving fighters left him no clear target. Claude was near fainting from pain in his shoulder when he finally freed his knife. Struggling atop the youth, his arm rose and fell and buried the blade in the boy's breast. The body beneath him shuddered but the youth's hold did not relax. A throaty gurgling and a rush of blood from the victim's mouth followed a second thrust. His knife dripped blood when the planter jumped away from the body. Horrified, Claude knelt, gasping for breath, as a great shiver ran through the prone shape. He could not take his eyes away from the sight until the boy's eyes set.

Claude quivered and jerked, then retched. Sour bile gagged him, its distasteful gruel a relic of Aunt Lucy's greasy food. Unable to control his shaking, he sought the servant for support. He cried and trembled as he held onto Hannibal.

"I didn't want to kill 'im, Hannibal," he repeated over and over. "He's just a boy."

The Negro held the planter and comforted him, patting him on the back. His resigned voice quietly summed up the fate of black and white in the south. "He kill yuh, Claude, and' me too. You hear' 'im. Miz Melody done lie agin when she 'ccuse us o' mistreatin' 'er."

"Better hide 'im, Claude," Hannibal observed matter-of-factly, when the planter stepped away. But the servant leaned on his staff and offered no help.

Tears coursed down Claude's cheeks when he faced the body. He grasped it with distaste and avoided looking at the bloody head and accusing face. Using the slope, he rolled the inert burden under the overhanging pine branches, well out of sight. The great gout and splashes of drying blood mocked his effort at concealment, but the body was not visible.

Bloody from the battle, Claude washed his knife and hands at a rill nearby, and cleaned off the spatters on his clothes. With the horror behind him, it was time to move on. He picked up the rifle and the boy's pouch and powder horn and led off. Hannibal forced a swinging gait with his gimpy leg as the fugitives rapidly moved west. They halted a mile beyond in a small draw and gulped down the rest of the cooked food; after, the planter reloaded the rifle. Antique though it was, the weapon added to his confidence. This time they buried the remnants of their meal and their waste under the duff to hide the scent. Two hours later, Claude stopped at a trickling, musical creek. They waded up it for a mile and denned up under a dense, small pine. It shielded a soft mat of needles and was hemmed in by thick clusters of brush. It was with a sigh of relief that Hannibal sank to the matting and favored his stretched-out leg. But Claude drank at the creek and splashed his head in a pool before joining the servant nearby on the mat of needles.

"Let's see that leg," he said.

The planter reached for the injured member while Hannibal lay prone. He still was blowing from the hard walk. Claude split the pants leg. Its stripping revealed a debarked shin with skinned flesh that oozed a stream of gummy serum. A great bruise swelled the muscles but the bone was intact.

"You'll be all right," Claude said confidently. He bathed the wound with cool water from the creek. The servant winced at the hurt, but was silent even when the planter sloshed whiskey over the wound and bound it up with his bandanna.

Sleep came quickly to the exhausted men, sleep that erased Claude's turmoil, sleep in a nest that was sheltered from the cool wind by the brush, sleep in a hidden place where they were reassured by the watchdog forest sounds.

Hoofbeats drawing to a halt before the cabin and the blowing of the horses alerted Granny to her visitors. Snug in her chair on that chilly day, her projecting legs and feet baked in the heat of the comforting fire. She did not stir when the door crashed back against the cabin wall. When Minns and Jeremy entered, she confronted the angry hunters with a composed being and sought to disarm them.

"What you want dis time?" she asked, calmly. "Why you back here?"

Minns strode purposefully toward her and shouted, "You lying ol' bitch!" He tossed his rifle to Jeremy, then grabbed Granny by the neck and hauled her up out of the chair. "You he'ped that officer an' his slave to 'scape. An' plugged my rifle."

Strangling, unable to say anything, Granny kicked and struck at her tormentor. Minns held her tight and beat her about the head and body with his other hand. He sought to subdue her, but the old Negress continued her anguished squawks and gasps when she was able to struggle loose. The hunter stepped back and struck her with his riding crop just as Jared dragged Hester into the cabin. Old Blue followed and crouched beside the loom, intent on the pair as the boy whacked the struggling girl a few times to gentle her.

"Found 'er comin' down the trail from the Pickens' house," Jared said.

"Hold 'er tight, boy." Minns voice was brittle with the hate of the poor white for the slave. "I'm goin'a see if Granny kin stand to have Hester's back stripped." He called to Jeremy who guarded the door. "Bring in the big whip, boy."

His younger son reappeared quickly with a six foot leather, the end serrated into strips.

"Don' let 'em do it, Granny," Hester pleaded. But Granny's protests and Hester's struggles were unavailing.

Minns' boys bound her wrists tightly to the loom. They stripped the top of her dress all the way down to her waist while Athey shook out the whip.

Tears coursed down Granny's withered black cheeks. Hester's scream after the first blow and the welts popping out forced her surrender.

"Stop it!" she croaked. "I tells yer, Minns. But I spit on yuh. Yer nothin' but white trash."

Her dribble missed but infuriated the man. The hunter struck twice more and Hester's screams filled the hut. Welts sprang up all over her back and a trickle of blood glinted red in the firelight. Her unconsciousness reduced the cabin to silence while Minns waited on his answer.

"Dey gone ober ter de Congaree ter float down ter Cha'leston. De sojer got frens dere."

The false trail exacerbated Minns' fury. Grasping the old woman by the throat, he shook her again, then threw her into the chair.

"It ain't right! They went up river, didn't they?"

He got no answer. Granny's silence infuriated the hunter. He threw the whip to Jared and said, "Beat that Hester some more. Maybe this old nigger'll be beggin' to tell me the truth."

Hester moaned when the whip struck and the muscles on her back quivered. Granny capitulated when blood flowed red from the welts. But she lied once more about the fugitives' path.

"Dey gone up to'ard Monticello. Dey gwine cross de Broad 'bove dere an' strike up by de Spartan's place. Dey hopes ter git nawth from dere inter de mountains."

The Minnses were on the trace past the college, striking across country to cut the Monticello road, when Ezell hailed them.

"Massa Minns, suh?"

Minns' "Whoa, Whoa," came as he sawed on the reins and pulled up sharp. Old Blue's hackles rose while he circled about and barked treed. The hunters grouped their horses and surrounded the Negro. Ezell's frightened face shifted back and forth between the men and the menacing dog. Minns crowded him with his horse and backed the youth against Jared's mount.

"Whose nigger are you?" the hunter asked.

"I'se Ezell Pickens sah. Headin' ter de camp ter tell 'em 'bout Bub an' de boots. But I knowed yer huntin' de Linckum sojer, so I tells you."

"Well, git on with it!"

"Bub's at Aunty Florinda's wid a pair o' boots from de Yankee. He he'p 'em 'scape."

"Where's Bub now?"

"Still dere. Aunty Florinda's one o' Miz Ashley's niggers. Dey over here close by in de cabins."

"Swing up behind Jared," Minns ordered. "We'll get 'im quick."

But Bud was nowhere to be found when the party invaded Aunty Florinda's cabin.

CHAPTER 6

Beulah

November 6, 1864. Ninety Six, S.C. Temperature 56\29. Gray, leaden sky, moon obscured. Possible scattered sleet and snow in early morning, turning to intermittent clouds and possible drizzles during the day. Freezing by nightfall. Winds to 15 knots during the daylight hours.

They had moved in the late afternoon of the day before, too frozen to remain under the pine trees. The damp cold had seeped into their bones as they slept. Shivering discomfort had awakened them from the oblivion of exhausted sleep and the intolerable cold had driven them on. Claude broke trail as the fugitives cast through the forest toward the northwest in their search for better cover. Hannibal hobbled along on his injured leg, his staff braced at the awkward places. The fugitives crossed several abandoned fields but did not have the good fortune to encounter a hut until late. It was a decrepit cattle pen with a shed roof, the split poplar timbers mortised neatly together, evidence of fine work years before to make a weather shelter for stock. Surrounded by brush on its small bench, the grown-up field long reclaimed by nature, the pen was well shielded from both man and weather.

Hannibal took down some of the fence rails while Claude started a fire. He placed it so that the heat would radiate into the most protected corner. With a little gunpowder on the tinder to strike a bigger spark, the bark and twigs caught easily, then built into a crackling fire when smaller pieces were added. The Negro spoked a set of rails into the flames. He would feed their points toward the coals as they gradually were consumed.

The fugitives were settled in the corner, basking in the heat, when Claude's stomach rumbled loudly. Hannibal rummaged in his possibles sack and brought out a sweet potato. He cut it in half and handed one to planter.

"Need water first," Claude said.

"It's jist down the slope. Nice pool from a spring dere comin' outen de bank."

Only a few feet across, the pool sparkled when the two faced it, so beautiful with its frosting of ice and the needles and leaves on the banks. Shade from the forest on that bitter eve kept the tiny glade cold, its frozen leaves brittle and echoing when they crunched under the men's tread. Holly trees bordered one side with thick, green leaves and bright red berries. Crouched like any animal, the two drank deeply of the pure water. Its cold was piercing but refreshing.

"Mighty purty place," Hannibal observed, when they again were upright.

"Yes, and those holly trees bring back memories."

They communed together in that quiet temple of reflection, the forest at peace. Only the mists and sighs of the cold wind through the trees disturbed their thoughts. Even the forest birds were silent. Long since sheltered in thick brush, their habits protected them from the coming cold night. The charm of the moment and elegance of the pool mesmerized the fugitives, each unwilling to break the spell. Claude's reverie of past Thanksgiving and Christmas seasons culminated in a deep, mournful sigh.

"What's wrong, Claude?" Hannibal said.

"Just thinking of Greenbottom. Letty'll have the house decorated pretty soon for the holidays coming up. Plenty to eat. Warm. Nobody trying to shoot us."

"Don't you worry, Claude. We gonna make it."

The optimism of the servant stirred the planter. His spirits lifted as he shook off his foreboding and turned away from the lovely spring. "You're right," he said. "And we can't be hanging around here long. We'll strike out at first light.

Now let's go roast those taters and some more chestnuts and get warm.

The rime was about melted by the middle of the next morning, though the wind was still cold. Its chilling dampness struck through their clothes when they cut the road to Laurens. The trace lay about two miles to the north of their shelter and headed up to the northwest through large, dense timber. No travelers were in sight when they entered it and bent over its surface. Heavy use had left deep ruts and horse tracks, with skim ice in a few muddy dents. But even though the way seemed peaceful, the fugitives paced cautiously, alert to any warning by the birds.

Hannibal turned over some solid, cold droppings with his staff. "No horses by since yestiday." he said. "No steam a'tall."

The planter nodded absently. He was listening more than observing, conscious of the forest birds in full cry. An ass-up circled a nearby oak. The small bird's picking dropped shreds of bark that struck with faint rattles at the base of the tree. Farther from the road, a woodpecker drummed a hollow trunk. Its furious pecking blows reverberated through the forest. A flicker crossed ahead of them in its looping soars, the white on its back flashing. It called as soon as it lit on a dead stob, and scared the chickadees and nuthatches on the beech nearby. "KuheKuheKuheKuhe...," it screamed. It and the smaller birds were telling them, "No danger here."

A full hour of slow, cautious travel had passed when they heard the creaking of a wagon and the hoofbeats of horses. The road turned to the north and they secreted themselves at the bend and waited for the oncoming travelers. Clinks and groans from protesting joints and axles preceded the arrival of an ancient flatbed wagon. The decrepit vehicle was driven by a Negro bundled up against the cold. A high mound of turnips and sweet potatoes topped the sideboards. Such an enormous load had burdened the wagon to protest, as the screeches of its joints confirmed.

When it was closeby, Hannibal jumped into the trace

and waved his arms and shouted, "Hold up!"

"Whoa, dere!" The man on the wagon sawed on the reins and hauled the horses to a stop just short of the servant. The animals stood patiently, blowing and stamping.

"Who you?" the driver asked. Fear was evident in his trembling hands and lined visage. His hand crept toward a whip that stuck out of a holder next to the seat.

"Stop dat!" Hannibal ordered. "I'se Hannibal. Ain't gonna hurt yuh none. Jist want ter ask 'bout de Laurens road."

The old man slumped in his seat, his head bowed. White showed through holes in a battered hat and his sagging frame was evidence of the decrepitude of advanced age. He was a fitting companion for the wagon, Claude thought. While Hannibal jawed with the man, he crept out to the rear, his rifle ready, intent on any following traffic. A few short steps took him past the bend and into an empty road. Reassured, he returned to the front of the wagon and re-joined Hannibal. The driver shook violently, visibly frightened when the planter appeared with the rifle.

"He ain't 'bout ter shoot yuh," Hannibal said. "He jist like me, on de way ter Jawga. Now who you?"

"I'se Albee. What fer he got de rifle? Ain't no slave got gun."

"Shoot game, dat's why. An' pertec' us. Ol' Massa down ter Cha'leston give us dat ter use on de way." The lies rolled easily off Hannibal's lips. Albee was tranquil, but his mien was not trusting as he absorbed the tale.

"How come yer on de Laurens road?" he asked.

"Aunt Lucy down ter Newberry's tol' us ter go by Laurens an' ter see Silas an' Aunt Rachel. She say dey pass us thoo ter Jawga 'thout no trouble wid de rebs."

Albee perked up. His troubled face gave way to a broad, toothless smile. But his excitement at their message was followed by a firm warning.

"Knows Aunt Lucy. She sold by Massa Laurens ter Marse Sallers 'bout ten year back, den ter Marse Newberry. You can't do like she say jist now." Albee waved his arms at them and his weak voice grew more shrill as his agitation increased. "Rebs coming thoo dere some, gwine ter 'lanta fer more big fights."

"Kin we go 'nother way?" Hannibal asked.

"Best you head south ter Ninety Six," Albee said. "Ain't much fuss 'roun' dat town. Den on ter Greenwood's. Road safer dat way jist now. Aunty Jenny and Paul dere he'p yuh."

Claude's gratitude compelled him to reach for the old man's hand and shake it. The planter grunted and nodded his thanks.

"He got no tongue?" Albee asked. But he didn't draw back from the Claude's fawning.

"Born dumb," Hannibal replied. "Can't talk."

Hannibal glanced at the load of vegetables. He beckoned to Claude and the two walked along the wagon bed. They filled their pockets with potatoes and a few turnips.

Albee called back to them. "Tek a good bait. Dey's mo' comin' down de road ter C'lumbia fum Marse Laurens."

When they returned opposite the seat he gave them an unexpected gift, a chunk of cured bacon. Their protestations at the magnificent offering, one that deprived him of much-needed, scarce meat, could not sway the old slave. He waved away their thanks, even as he continued his advice. Albee counseled caution and invoked his faith in support.

"You boys be keerful an' you 'scape. De good Lawd be wid yuh."

Hannibal's worry showed, and his question acknowledged it. "You be awright if de rebs ketch up?"

Albee's old, wrinkled face turned grim and his lips creased tight. "Don' yer worry," he said. "I don' never tells."

When the fugitives had backed away from the wagon, Albee waved farewell and drove off. His straight back and dignity were reinforced by a cracked voice singing spirituals.

Claude sighed in regret as the old slave left with his creaking wagon. It struck him deep, twisted his soul, that another fine man, a Negro, had helped them unselfishly on their travel through the wilderness. He thought of the underground with respect, almost love, the slaves risking all to save him, and to relieve the tragedy of the infamous burden of the white man and the Negro. It was at that moment that he perceived that Negroes could be persons,

just like him. Granny Mandy's challenge intruded into his
thoughts. Were they just like him? Doubts about bondage
began to slowly crystallize and the heresy that slavery was
wrong could not be expunged. The idea of freedom for the
slaves transfixed him. Should he help all of his former
slaves, particularly Hannibal? The Bible story of Saul of
Tarsus came to mind, and Saul's stroke that converted him
to Jesus. Its message always had penetrated to his soul
when the Preacher had thundered away in the pulpit about
giving one's self to God. Was he to experience the same type
of elemental change?

Claude's absorption within was shattered by a "Hist!"
from Hannibal. When he shifted his attention to the Negro,
he found Hannibal with his head up, intent on the back
trace.

"More comin', Claude. Best we git on."

Without waiting for the planter, Hannibal struck south
into the big woods. He swung his injured leg wide in his
labored travel, its weakened support complemented by his
thrusting staff. Claude followed close behind him. A hundred yards of determined running cloaked them with invisibility. With safety assured, they went on at a hurried walk
to get farther away from the road though harness sounds
and clip-clops of the small, passing troop faded out quickly.
After a pause to drink at a forest spring, the fugitives took
their bearings and aimed for Ninety Six.

Minns and his sons caught Bub in a cabin on Two
Notch Road, the slave's escape toward Camden delayed by
a coy vixen. Jared and Jeremy dragged him out of the loft
naked, his clothes trailing from his hands. Claude's boots
came flying out behind him, thrown by the girl who peeped
from the crack at the cabin's door. Her long, braided hair
streamed and she held her clothes before her breast. The
door slammed behind Bub, a crack of doom not lost on the
frightened man.

Bub quailed as he stood before the grim hunter.
"Huccome you wan' me?" he asked in a frightened voice.

It was Old Blue that drew his attention. The hound
growled and pointed the Negro like a partridge. His body and

tail were rigid, intimidating. Minns prodded the boots with the end of his rifle and turned them over and over. His face flushed red while he inspected them. The hunter's silence and the menacing dog unnerved the slave, who groveled before the man.

"I'se ain't done nothin!" he exclaimed. He trembled as he begged. "Lemme put on my clothes, Massa."

When none of the Minnses answered, Bub chanced the temper of the dog and suited his action to his words. He hurriedly donned his shirt and hauled up his pants. It was his reach for the boots that provoked an enraged bellow from Minns.

"Leave 'em thar!" He raised his rifle and threatened the trembling man. "Nigger like you ain't deservin' o' no fancy boots."

"Most likely the Yankee's, Pa," Jared said. He picked up the pair and inspected the tops and soles. "Pretty fancy leather. Nothin' fer a no'count nigger."

Bub shivered in the cold wind. Unsettled and apprehensive, his unease stimulated his body and supplemented the heat from his earlier encounter with the girl. He sweated heavily, a sweat both of fear and exertion. Large drops beaded his face and ran down his cheeks. But he protested and resisted strenuously when the two boys moved to pinion him. Pitiless, they wrestled him into submission and tied his arms behind his back, then hobbled him like a horse.

"He won't go nowhere, Pa," Jared said. He stepped aside while Jeremy made a final pull at the lashings.

Old Blue sniffed and growled, his tail and hackles up when he circled the Negro. Bub froze into an ebony statue as he tried not to alarm the threatening hound. The slave's eyes rolled and his head twisted to follow the dog as the hound made its inspection, then came to a halt by Jared. Old Blue crouched at Minns' command but fixed his eyes on the man, ready to attack.

"Don' like the houn', do yuh boy?" The man hunter chuckled. "Think I'll jest let him at yuh, jest like an old bar in the woods."

"No! No!" Bub's scream dribbled off into sobs. "Don' let

'im hurt me, Massa!"

Minns turned hard as flint and his sharp tongue flayed the Negro. "Tell me quick, boy, 'bout the Yankee. Truth, now. If ye don't, it's the whip fer yuh, then Old Blue."

"Don' know nothin', Massa. Seed de man 'long de crick an' traded fer de boots. Don' know no mo'."

Bubs lying infuriated Minns. "Strip him boys," he said wrathfully, "and tie 'im to the sapling there. We'll see if the whip don't change his story."

The deed was quickly done. Jared and Jeremy tore off Bub's shirt and pants before they tethered the terrified youth. He hung from the trunk with his back bare, exposed to the full force of the whip. And he blubbered and begged neverendingly as he tried to escape the lash.

Minns prodded the slave in the back with the butt of his whip. "Tell us the truth, boy," he said.

When Bub just blubbered, the hunter laid on a dozen lashes with his leather whip. The welts and cuts added torment to a back already scarred. Bub pulled against his bonds and begged for mercy. But he told nothing to the waiting woodsman. Minns cursed and scraped the leather across the cuts. It drew a howl from the flinching slave and a smile from the hunter.

"You been whipped lots, ain't yuh, boy. You want more?"

Minns' whip cut the air as he flexed and cracked it before the Negro. Bub eyed the whistling leather and shuddered.

"You recken we won't give you more?" Minns asked. "Tell me the truth 'bout the Yankee."

When he raised the whip to strike, Bub screamed, "No! No! I tells."

Minns cut him once to spur on the crying man. Bub winced but remained silent until the cursing Minns delivered several slashing blows. The whip broke him down at last and he blurted out the truth.

"Granny done mek us drag de Yankee clo'es ter de Broad an' set 'em floatin'. Ceptin' I'se don' want ter th'ow away dose good boots. So I teks 'em. Dat de truth, Massa."

The slave flinched and blood spurted when the hunter

again cut him with the whip. "Where's the Yankee headed?" Minns asked.

"Nawth, Massa." Bub sobbed out the rest. "Dey gone nawth up de Broad, ter Chester, maybe over ter de Spartans town, atter Granny fed 'em dat stew. I take 'er de skunk an' bury de skin."

Bub's lies prompted a suspicious glance from Minns and protests from his sons.

"He's run west fer sure, Pa," Jared said. "Granny told us he was headin' up to Spartans, but that don't make sense, nor t'other either."

He was joined by Jeremy. "Ain't none of them other prisoners escaped that went nawth, Pa. Those two got to move over to the Yankees in Tennessee or Georgia. Too many o' our boys in Carolina."

"Yer right, boys," Minns said. "Those niggers are all lyin'. He ain't runnin' nawth er to no Spartans. We'll jest git on up the Broad a ways and then cut over west to the Saluda. If that Yankee an' his slave been along either, we'll cut their trail."

Jared motioned toward the cabin. "We got time fer the gal, Pa, 'fore we go?"

"Leave her be. She be here when you git back. Then she can pleasure you all yuh want."

Minns contemptuously poked Bub with the whiphandle. The slave was hanging from the lashings, semiconscious. Minns rolled the Negro around and kicked him hard in the crotch. Then he coiled the whip and mounted his horse. His sons and Old Blue fell in behind him when he wheeled his horse into Two Notch Road.

The girl rushed from the cabin and cut down the bloody slave when Minns no longer threatened. Later in the morning he was enduring the sympathetic cluckings of Granny, her treatment interspersed with castigations for exposing them all to danger from the rapacious and vindictive hunter.

The Greenwood-Abbeville-Laurens Road led on to Atlanta after passing Athens, Georgia, a major artery through the Carolinas. Its intersection with the old Cherokee Path, leading northwest to Keowee, was occupied that day by a detachment of irregulars from Ninety Six, old men and boys mostly armed with sporting weapons. Raw as the weather was that morning, the detachment had pickets out, their enfilade aimed at intercepting the thieving, clandestine traffic that had sprung up, wolves that preyed on the edges of the South's dissolution and expected collapse. Passing all legitimate travelers, the pickets lay in wait in their holes, their ambush a spray of infantry works camouflaged and concealed against the unwary, two men on each of the four roads.

"Got any 'baccy left, Lem?" Ezra said. His whisper carried easily in the cool air.

"Jest the hand we picked offen that wagon the other day," Lem replied. "Ain't much o' it left."

He tossed the leaf to Ezra who stuffed part in his mouth and passed the remnant back. The two longtime friends huddled in their pits, two slashes to the north of the Path. Ezra was shivering from the cold and damp from the sleet during the night and loudly protested his misery.

"It be damned cold, Lem. I'm 'bout froze up. You reckon yer Grandaddy Walton have some hot stew when we git off?"

"Probably. But he ain't got much meat. Those Virginny boys 'bout cleaned him out. Best we go down ter Aunty Beulah's. You know she allus saves somethin' fer us."

The two lapsed into silence as they waited for their relief. Chewing tobacco gave small comfort to their hunger. Their shrunken bellies growled and ached as the morning advanced. When the two replacement pickets arrived, the weather was lightening but still offered a cutting, cold wind. Lem led out as they headed east toward Ninety Six.

Her anger had abated but Granny Mandy still was put out at Bub's indiscretion. She slapped on a gob of grease and rubbed it around. But her rough treatment stung the injured man as much as it soothed his hurts. "Why you tell dat Minns where Hannibal an' de gent'mans go?" she said.

"I don' tells 'im de trute, Granny," Bub said, defensively. "Tol' 'im dey head nawth 'long de ribber." He moved painfully on the bed while his back received another treatment of bear grease from the old woman's exploring fingers.

Jed held the warm pot as he knelt nearby.

Granny ruminated aloud while rubbing in more grease. "Dey sure ter run dose hawses west an' aim up de Saluda atter dey check de Whitmire trace. Gotter get de word up ribber dat Athey Minns be out. Dat Minns boun' ter kill 'em if he ketch 'em."

"I go, Granny," Jed volunteered.

"Take keer, Jed." Granny wagged her forefinger at him. "Git ter Zeke first, up past Harbisons. Axe 'im ter run de word 'long de line right pert dat Athey Minns be out wid 'is boys."

Jed set the pot on the dirt beside the bunk. He placed his hands on his friend's head and reassured the prone man. "Granny tek right good keer o' yuh, Bub. I'se gwine kill dat Minns fer yuh. He done beat us too much." He girded up his belt when he stood. Its shifting brought a knife into view. The old woman halted him when he started for the door.

"You leave dat Minns ter de white folks," she said. "Dey hang yuh if you kills 'im. Jist git de word upcountry an' come right bek." When he did not answer, her harsh voice cut him. "You heah me, Jed?"

His cold face turned to a storm cloud, his words defiant as he resisted her. "I pass de message. But I git a chance at dat Minns er his boys I kills 'em all."

His threat silenced Granny. She plucked a gob of grease from the pot and resumed the kneading of Bub's back. Jed pulled his hat down tight and darted from the cabin.

Hester returned to the cabin at noon. She was bubbling over with her news. Granny warmed her hands at the fire, their skin softened by the penetrating grease. She rotated on her stick to face the girl.

"Miz Ashley goin' up ter Greenwood ter see her mammy," Hester said. "Her mama done take sick but she ain't bad."

"Huccome you knows dat?"

"Listen' at de do'. She's figuring on visitin' an' den go on over ter Due West ter see her frens at de college while she's upcountry."

The old lady tottered slightly and Hester ran to assist.

Granny seized the back of her chair for support, then sat down heavily. Her old chair's splints groaned at the impact. Hester bent over her and straightened Granny's bandanna. The girl tucked in a few stray wisps and stroked her lovingly. Granny's head bowed a moment, then she once again was the forceful matriarch.

"Kin you go wid her?" Granny asked, her eyes sharp and piercing. "You kin git word ter Paul an' Aunt Jenny at her mama's. An' Granny Owdoms. She at Due West."

Hester's grin and her dancing joy gave away the secret. "Miz Ashley takin' me 'long ter he'p. Her new maid, Cleo, feelin' poorly."

She circled the cabin like a whirlwind. Her meager belongings hardly filled her possibles sack as she prepared for travel.

"When you leavin'?" Granny asked. The old woman sat stolidly in her chair, but her keen eyes missed nothing in the girl's preparations.

"Soon's I'se back ter de big house," Hester told her. She kissed Granny's withered cheek and hugged her as soon as she completed her tasks. "I'se ready to git now, Granny," she said.

The old woman nodded. "Member, you see Paul an' Aunt Jenny. An' don' fergit Granny Owdoms. Tell 'em ter he'p the gent'mans up de line an' dat Minns be out. He kill any slave he fin' 'scapin', jist like de gent'mans an' Hannibal, so dey's got ter be keerful."

Hannibal and Claude swam a Saluda pool west of Chappell's, a stealthy, if chilly, fording that avoided the busy Confederate traffic at the regular crossing. Beyond, the fugitives crept through the cover of the woods and paralleled the trace to Ninety Six. The gloomy, patchy sky had clouded over solidly again. Daylight in their trying afternoon was growing dimmer when they split from the broad road and headed west on a grassy path up the river.

"Ain't been nobody 'long here since way back," Hannibal said. He pushed some bushes aside, adding, "Right growed up."

"I'm glad of that," the planter replied. "The other was

powerful worrisome." He glanced about at the shielding forest. "Spect that road we left is the new one. Probably this is the old road. Maybe we'll find another abandoned cabin up the way."

They hiked in silence, Hannibal's limp less pronounced, though he skipped now and then and labored to get over the down logs across the path. At a draft in an open place, he shuddered and held up a wet finger to test the wind.

"Gittin' col' agin, Claude," he said. "Got ter fine a place purty quick ter hole up. Need a fire ternight, looks like."

The planter nodded and kept up a fast walk, but with the rifle ready in the crook of his arm. A few miles passed before they glimpsed a light ahead through the crisp night air, well after sundown. Claude halted and shifted the rifle to a point position.

"We'll sneak up quiet and slow," he whispered to Hannibal. "Soon's we get close, you go around to'ard the door. See what's goin' on."

The slave wagged his head and the two eased cautiously up the trail until they were about thirty yards from the cabin. It was a one room log shack, set off to itself but with railings nearby. Wood smoke from its small chimney hung all over the heavily treed bottom. Added to the pungent odor was the smell of roasting meat. Claude's mouth watered at the opportunity, his craving reinforced by the rumbling in his empty middle. The bacon and potatoes at noon had long since disappeared from his belly in the afternoon's cold, strenuous hike.

At the planter's signal, Hannibal circled the cabin. His dark form disappeared silently in the gloom of the trees and dying light. Claude waited with his thumb on the rifle's lock, ready to cock and fire the piece at a moment's notice. He was heated and perspiring, a fact that amazed him when he reflected on all his past combats. "Never changes," he whispered to himself, realizing the cause. "Man just naturally gets scared."

The servant came back in a few minutes. He materialized out of the darkness, unannounced and frightening, and before Claude realized he was there. It nettled the planter, for a raider could have killed him with the same approach. Hannibal placed his hand on Claude's arm before the planter could raise a fuss, and leaned over close to his ear.

"Jist a mammy dere, Claude," he said softly. "We kin eat some'a dat meat."

The planter quietly set out his plan. "I'll hunker down in front of the cabin with the rifle while you go up to the door. Once you're in safe, I'll come in."

Hannibal squeezed Claude's arm and shuffled toward the cabin. He rustled the leaves and bushes and called out loudly as Claude shifted his position. The planter was kneeling with the rifle pointed when the servant knocked on the door and hallooed out his greetings.

Silence at first was followed by a tremulous, "Who dere?"

"I'se Hannibal," he said forcefully. "Lemme in. Ain't gonna hurt you none. I'se from Granny Mandy down ter Columbia."

Claude's heart jumped at the shrewd move by the servant. Granny probably was known all over that section for her work with escaped slaves. If anything would open the door, invoking Granny Mandy's name should be the key.

The door cracked a mite, then was thrown open by a huge Negro woman, shiny black in the firelight. But she blocked the entrance with her bulk. Her size and the hatchet in her hand offered pause to Hannibal, who drew back from the menace.

"Ain't meanin' no trouble, woman," he said. But he retreated a step even as he spoke and raised his arms in defense. When she did not back off, Hannibal adopted a plaintive, injured tone. "Jist need some'a dat meat and de fire. I'se hongry an' it col'."

"You knows Granny Mandy?" the Negress asked.

"Sho' do. She sent us up de ribber ter Joshua at Little Mountain. But Aunt Lucy at Newberry's done passed us on ter here."

All the familiar names cleared the woman's bulk from the opening. Hannibal strode in close behind her and beckoned to Claude when he passed the door jamb. The planter uncocked his rifle and entered the cabin.

"Who he?" the Negro woman asked. She half raised her hatchet at them while backing toward the fire.

"Claude," Hannibal replied. "Can't talk. Borned dat way. But he good shot an' he'p pertec' us on de way."

Claude had commenced inspecting the cabin as soon as he entered. His eyes roved, darting from one possible danger spot to another. But he saw only a small space and the bulky woman. With no loft, they were as safe as the surrounding country, he knew, only vulnerable to roaming patrols or marauders. The hot meat took his mind off danger and he and Hannibal drifted over to the hearth. A large roast punctured by a spit rested at the side of the fire, its drippings caught in a small crock set underneath.

The woman turned the iron spit and stuck the meat with a knife, then basted it with some fatback. Juice bubbled out and splashed down into the crock. At Hannibal's sharp intake of breath and smacked lips, the woman smiled, a relaxed welcome set off by her black skin and white teeth.

"Like some meat, would yer?" she said.

"Sho' nuff," Hannibal replied. "An' we need ter know yer name ter thank yuh."

"I'se Beulah."

The woman swung out the iron and brought the meat to a point over the hearth. She pulled a long knife from a shelf in the fireplace and sharpened it with a few swipes at a stone. Then she sliced off several large pieces and put them on two trenchers. The simple meal was improved with two blocks of johnnycake and some drippings dipped from the crock.

Claude and Hannibal ravenously attacked the hot food. The first serving disappeared in minutes and a second was downed as quickly. Beulah sliced as much meat as they could swallow. She smiled in delight when they set aside their trenchers and belched.

"Liked it, did yuh?" she asked.

"Sho' nuff, Beulah," Hannibal answered.

He continued to erupt as his stomach gurgled and he expelled gas. Claude grunted and bobbed his head in satisfaction. Beulah beamed when he wiped his mouth with his sleeve and patted his stomach.

The large bait of hot food and heat from the fire soon made Claude nod, ready to sleep. It alarmed him, for the deer meat had to have come from some man, the woman not being able to hunt the animal. He hoped Hannibal would be cautious enough to ask and pointed to his rifle and then to the meat with puzzlement on his face. His servant immediately grasped the connection.

"Where you git de deer meat an' de fat, Beulah?" he asked.

"Got fren over de Saluda near Cross's," she replied. "He fetch me de meat fer my pleasurin' 'im. I'se good at dat."

Her matter of fact statement amused Claude, but Hannibal's next question revealed the shrewdness of the servant.

"Why you outchere all by yerself? Whose nigger are yuh?"

"Miz Joanna run me off soon's Marse Sallers off ter de wah," she said simply. She laughed after a pause and a sly glance at Claude. "He like my pleasurin' better'n her. Say she got icicles 'tween her legs."

The common sense answer tickled the planter, but he was mystified that the slave wasn't sold. As if to echo his thoughts, Hannibal said, "Don' sell yuh?"

"She try." Her face turned doleful. "Can't have no more chil'ren. Nobody want dis ol' slave. So I'se got ter make it bes' I kin in dishere cabin."

When their faces turned troubled, she tried to allay their doubts. "De big hog pen uster be 'tween here an' de ribber. Dishere cabin's fer de boy tendin' 'em. Marse Sallers move it outen here, long way from de big house 'cause it smell too bad. But nobody use de path no mo' wid all de hogs gone."

"Anybody visitin' ternight?" Hannibal asked.

Her plump sides shook as she laughed heartily. "Don' you worry, Hannibal. Ain't nobody come ternight."

The two fugitives settled down before the fire after a trip outdoors. Full bellies, lassitude, and the heat opiate lulled them into a deep sleep. They were yawning and reluctant when Beulah woke them before dawn. She fed the two to capacity while warning of the militia block at the Greenwood crossroads. Firelight shined through the open door and lit the stoop when they took their leave from the helpful Negress. Claude grasped her hands but his emotion forced him into a great bearhug of thanks.

"Go 'long wid yuh," she said. Her smile was his reward, along with her blessing. "May de good Lord pertec' you bof in yer 'scape."

CHAPTER 7

Aunty Jenny

November 7, 1864. Greenwood, S.C. Temperature 64\33. Clearing but damp and cool, with strong, gusty winds. Mostly overcast through the day, partial clearing at night. Moon almost full but partly obscured, rising about an hour and a half after midnight.

Winds chilled Minns and his sons as they rode toward Newberry in late morning, their search to the north fruitless. A sweep across the country at Alston's and Krohn's plantations had turned up nothing, the individual Negroes uncommunicative and the crews quiet. Athey's informers among the men had not responded to enticements; even Jared's former female conquests were unable to bring him any news of the fugitives.

"They done gone to the west, Pa," Jared said, when they left the Whitmire Road and he caught up with his father. "Probably up to'ard Lauren's or over to Ninety Six."

Minns nodded and said, "Moving purty fast, I expect." He shifted his chaw and spit at a puddle in the road. "We'll git on into Newberry an' ask the Reverend. Ain't more'n five mile." He wiped some brown dribble from his mouth with the back of his hand and kicked his horse into a faster pace. "He'll know," Minns said. "That man's got good friends 'mong the niggers."

The horses covered the rolling ground quickly, the trace a well traveled and easy path. Old Blue moved along it effortlessly, his trailing days long practice for hunting fugitive or beast. When they cantered through a small creek he lay down in it and rolled over in the flowing water, cooling his body and protruding tongue. He came out running at Athey's whistle and raced to his place beside the horse.

"Old Blue takin' it pretty good, Pa," Jeremy said. Usually the quiet one, he had interrupted his chewing on a piece of jerky. After tearing at the tough meat, he tossed the end to the trotting dog.

Athey chortled when the hound jumped and caught the meat on the fly. One gulp and Blue resumed his easy lope. "He ain't but eight year old yet," he said. Orta last 'nother four er five years."

Blue's bark alerted them to a fence and outlying house. A few choruses responded from within the village. One feisty dog ran toward them and faced Blue in a stiff-legged standoff. The two followed the horses up the street after convivial sniffs and lowered hackles. Minns halted at the school building and went in to visit Reverend Newberry while the two boys stretched.

"They were through here, Athey," the preacher said, in answer to Minns' query.

But the Reverend was vague and reticent about the incident. His description of the harassment of Melody neglected to tell of the fugitives' part in rescuing her from the bandits, but dwelled instead on the Negroes handling of his daughter. His aggrieved tone provoked the hunter and aroused Minns' ire. He swore and begged the preacher's pardon at the same time.

"Sorry, Reverend," Minns said, after his blasphemous outburst, "but my tongue's not as fine as your'n."

The preacher waved off the apology. "No matter," he said. "These are troubling times."

Minns face wrinkled in bewilderment. "You said they was two niggers come by. Warn't one a white man?"

"No, two Negroes. That's who came in. But Melody said one had blue-gray eyes and was not too dark. He couldn't speak. Dumb from birth."

Minns exploded in a whoop of exultation. "That's the Yankee!" Granny's strategy burst upon him like a flash of light. "That Granny had a pot o' hot walnut dye in the cabin when we first come on her. You know how it smells, Reverend. Bitter. She hoped the skunk would cover it."

"What on earth are you talking about?"

"Granny Mandy down to Pickens' place done dyed the Yankee black. So Miz Melody saw two niggers. But the dumb one's the Yankee officer."

"Well, I swan!" the Reverend exclaimed.

"Did you hear their names?" Minns asked.

"Hannibal was the talkin' one. The other was called Claude, according to Melody."

"It's them all right!"

The hunter's face crinkled in jubilation and he uttered a short laugh. Restlessness drove him up out of his chair. He hacked and spit several times while he paced back and forth and pondered the startling information. Feline in his unbounded energy, Minns suddenly stopped and smacked his hands together, then leaned over the desk. His puzzled, grim face intimidated the preacher, who shrank before him.

"How come you didn't git a chance at 'em with yer militia boys?" Minns asked. "Seems like you should'a got 'em."

"We thought we had them cornered in the hayloft at the carriage house but they took off to the woods."

The Reverend rose and pushed a spittoon closer toward his guest and tapped the container noisily with his foot. He winced at the next splash. It left brown stains on his office rug and added to the damage from Minns' poor aim. "That Aunty Lucy warned them," he said, "before my brother Micah could get out the militia boys. I strapped her good."

Minns wagged his head in agreement. "Only thing to do with a nigger." He shot out another brown stream, no more successful than the others.

It's splat was enough to convince the Reverend to hurry Minns out to the barn. The preacher was puffing at the fast pace when Minns stopped at the corral fence abutting the structure and leaned on the top rail. His survey of the pasture and tree line took but a moment.

"Took off over there, did they?"

"Yes," Newberry said, "and Micah went after them with

a skirmish line and dogs. But those fool hounds put out a deer right away and headed north."

"Lost 'em, did they?"

"Yes; the militia split. Everybody straggled in later except one boy. He's still gone." The preacher's worry showed. "We've been praying for him and hope he's just strayed. Micah and some of the boys are out there now looking for him."

"He's dead, Reverend. Those men done kilt him."

"If that's so, I'll pray for his soul and that we find his body for a decent burial."

Gloom cast a shadow over the preacher's face. Minns didn't make statements lightly. His reputation as a man hunter made the death a virtual certainty. The Reverend's preoccupation with the killing took him away from the moment. His melancholy reflections were accompanied by a deep silence broken only by his mournful sighs. Minns interrupted his thoughts.

"What else can you tell me, Reverend?" the hunter asked.

"Melody told them to go to Cross Hill. They were asking about getting to Georgia. They're going there to dig gold for a Middleton in Charleston.

"Lyin', jest like all the niggers. That Yankee's smarter'n I reckened."

Minns stepped out briskly toward the front of the house with the Reverend in sharp pursuit. "Got to move on, Reverend," the hunter threw out over his shoulder. "We'll ketch up with 'em t'day."

He and the boys were mounting up before the preacher recalled the rifle. "Athey?"

Minns held his horse on a tight rein. He leaned over toward the man when he saw the preacher's worried frown. "What is it, Reverend? What's troublin' yuh?"

"That boy had a rifle, an old flintlock."

"The Yankee's got it now," Minns replied with finality. "He done kilt the boy and took that rifle. We'll fetch it back after we take 'em both."

Kicking the horses in their sides, the three headed out the road toward Chappell's.

"We'll go up the Cross Hill Road a ways at Chappell's,"
Minns told his sons, "then ride on to Ninety Six if nobody
seen 'em."

It took three hours of cautious travel for Hannibal and
Claude to advance five miles up the river above Beulah's.
They had stayed close to the trace, sliding into the woods
when the bird calls faltered. Their wary flight had taken
them over the thickly timbered, rolling ground at a slow
pace, fear of capture sharpening their senses and adding to
their caution when they passed farms and open fields.
Beulah's warning of the pickets continually intruded into
their senses. The slightest unusual forest sound was cause
for alarm and a retreat to a thicket.

A large, serrated revetment faced them after they forded
a rushing creek. The works scared them and they broke for
cover, the mounds and dents too regular and frightening to
be other than infantry diggings. Claude slunk along the
grown-up emplacements while Hannibal circled to meet
him on the other side at the trace.

"Old revetments from the Revolution," Claude said,
when Hannibal rejoined him. "Nothin' showin' any new
shovel work. And there's trees growin' in 'em."

The Negro nodded. "Ain't see no fresh dirt, Claude, de
way I come. Dey's nobody 'roun'."

A mile on took them into deep woods, their rolling
contours broken by good ravines and seeps.

Crash! Breaking, splintering wood and a brown flash
through the trees panicked the fugitives. They instantly ran
off the trace and were aiming for a down tree when a rifle
roared close upon them. A whoop of triumph sounded and
stopped the bird calls in the forest.

"Got him, Ezra!" a voice yelled. "That buck'll feed us
good t'day."

The fugitives were running hard, headed for the sheltering deadfall, when a rifleman stepped out from behind a
tree before them and shouted, "Halt!"

His menacing rifle and bayonet, not ten feet away,
brought them up short.

"Don' try it, nigger," he warned, when Claude made as

if to raise his flintlock. "Git yer hands in the air. Quick now!" He pointed his rifle at Claude and the latter dropped his weapon and elevated his arms. The rifle muzzle moved in a small arc as the man covered first one fugitive, then the other. He moved nervously about, glancing toward the deer kill, then backed off a few steps.

"Lem! Lem! Git'cheer quick!" The rifle waved as the man shouted for his companion, his nervousness and agitation reflected in a high pitched, scratchy voice and shuffling feet.

"What'cher want, Ezra? Whyn't you git on over here an' he'p me with this deer?"

"I done caught two niggers," Ezra screamed. "He'p me!"

Crashing through the brush, Lem joined the group at a run. His rifle picked up the guard from another side.

"Well, now, looky here," he said.

Lem inspected the prisoners while Ezra remained at the ready. It was apparent to the fugitives that Lem controlled the other man and they watched him warily. He gradually circled the two prisoners as his sharp scrutiny took in their decrepit appearance, and Claude's flintlock and Hannibal's staff. The servant leaned on the shaft heavily and stood quietly with his eyes turned downward in submission. Claude belatedly assumed a deferential posture. His soul rebelled at being prisoners of the rebs again, and not regulars either from their rustic clothes.

"Whose niggers air yuh?" Lem asked. "Ain't never seed yuh 'roun' these parts." His contemptuous tone was reinforced by a brown stream spat at Hannibal's shoes.

"I'se Hannibal, sah. Dishere's Claude." Hannibal reached toward his pocket. His hand froze when he was threatened by Lem's rising rifle and Ezra aiming his piece.

"Don' do that, boy," Ezra warned. He aligned his rifle barrel with Hannibal's chest, the weapon at point blank range. "Don' want no knife comin' outen that coat."

Hannibal bobbed his body up and down in submission. "Yassah, Massa. Ain't got nothin' in dere 'ceptin' de paper, sah." His whining voice expressed the humility of the slave.

"What paper, boy?" Lem faced the Negro just off the muzzle of his rifle, his doubt evident in his tone and frown.

"De one gib me by Marse Middleton down ter Osprey's

Landin'. Takes me an' Claude here ter Jawga."

Lem impatiently waved his rifle barrel. "Well, lemme have it, boy."

The militiaman seized the paper when Hannibal fished it out of his pocket. Unfolding the document, he inspected it, then handed it to Ezra.

"Kin you read it?" he asked.

Ezra puzzled over the writing a few minutes, laboriously repeating a few words. Claude was disgusted with his fate. A pair of filthy, uneducated Johnnies holding them at gunpoint. Easier to shoot their prisoners than to take them in to the crossroads, if the two took a mind to it. His throat grew dry and shivers and chills ran along his backbone from the fear that consumed him while he contemplated his imminent death. Sneaking furtive glances, he debated escape routes. His derringer was in his side pocket and his knife was in his boot. The militiamen weren't too far away. A sudden pistol shot and a rush could overwhelm them if Hannibal joined in. He was about to make a break when Ezra handed back the paper. Lem put it in his pocket and backed off with his rifle at the ready.

"We take 'em to the Capt'n," he said. "He'll figure what to do with 'em."

"How 'bout the deer?" Ezra asked.

"They kin finish the guttin' an' carry it to camp fer us."

Lem prodded Hannibal with his rifle and the two herded the fugitives to the deer carcass.

"Needs knife, Massa," Hannibal explained, when the militiaman berated him for not starting the dressing out.

Lem's disbelieving face wrinkled with doubt. "You mean you ain't even got a knife?"

"No sah, jist razor." Hannibal hauled out his straight razor and showed it, but made no attempt to cut the deer skin. "Tain't no good fer skinnin'." He tossed the razor to Ezra when the latter beckoned and raised his weapon.

Lem pulled his bowie knife and pitched it down in front of the Negro. Hannibal soon finished the dressing out and piled up the innards. He sorted the edible parts while Ezra and Lem leaned against a tree and lazed away at gossip. Their inattention robbed them of desirable food. Hannibal's

eyes gleamed and he glanced surreptitiously at the militiamen. He signaled Claude with a little shake of his head and
motioned toward the liver. The planter moved to his other
side and shielded him from their view. The Negro sliced a
chunk off the liver and shoved it in his pocket. The rest of
the internal edibles went into the deer stomach, emptied to
serve as a bag.

"We done, sah," Hannibal said. He held up the bloody
knife and his dripping hands when he called to them. "Got
ter wash off at de little crick, Massa, fo' we goes. An' I'se in
powerful need of a drink."

Lem nodded and motioned them toward the water. "Git
on to the crick an' make it quick. Gimme back my knife
when yuh come back." His after thought rang after them.
"Make sure it's clean, you hear?"

Under his alert guard, they slid down the creek bank
nearby and splashed in the stream. After returning to the
carcass, the fugitives picked up the small spike buck, with
Hannibal shouldering the deer and Claude the stomach.

Lem pointed out a faint trail diverging from the trace.
"Strike on over to the west," he said. The path penetrated the
massive stand of oaks and poplars, the virgin timber so
dense its tops shielded out the light-seeking brush.

The fugitives led off with Lem behind them. Ezra
followed in the rear. Both militiamen's rifles were ready for
action, Claude noted. Lem had his bayonet fixed and
prodded Claude once when he stumbled, swearing at the
planter's clumsiness. The men were alert and the planter
could find no way to escape in those open glades. They'd be
easy shots, he thought, just like the deer. Use of his
derringer would have to wait on a better time, a slackness
when the militiamen weren't so vigilant.

A split in the trail at a large creek stopped them, but
Ezra sent Hannibal on with a curse and a prod. "Take the left
fork," he said. "We'll cut the Greenwood Road in not more'n
three mile. The Capt'n'll say what to do with yuh when we
git thar." He laughed uproariously. "Probably shoot yuh jest
like the last three 'scaped niggers we caught."

"Jest ain't no trail up here, Pa." Jared's plaintive tone

strengthened into conviction. "I tol' yuh we orta go on over
to Ninety Six right off. That ol' nigger lied to us."

"We'll light and calculate a minute while we spell the
horses," his father replied. Minns swung down from his
mount and tied the reins to a sapling.

The party was up the Saluda almost to Cross Hill.
Minns had visited a few small plantations on the way and
had halted every traveler. It had been a fruitless search. No
trace had been found of the runaways, though the old Negro
they had stopped with the wagon load of potatoes outside
Newberry had insisted the fugitives were headed that way.
Albee delayed them for a half-hour while they worried him
about the Yankee officer. Exasperated, they had strapped
him until his back bled when he evaded their questions. The
old slave's bull-headed resistance incited Minns into a fury.
Repeated beatings weakened Albee until he was almost
near death. His head lolled and he sagged in the lashings on
the wagon wheel when he gasped out the fugitives' plans to
go to Cross Hill. He was bleeding and unconscious when
Jared cut him loose and he slumped to the ground. Minns
kicked the old slave before he mounted and cantered off,
with his boys and his dog behind him.

It was the quiet Jeremy who decided Minns during their
pause. "They're bound to go to Greenwood, Pa," he said,
"then strike fer Belton's and Calhoun's plantation on the old
Cherokee Path. Lots o' slaves through there that'll he'p 'em."

Minns' jaw worked and he spat. He did not move from
his relaxed sprawl against a fallen shagbark hickory, con-
templating his plans in silence while the others left him
alone. His head fell over as he dozed off. A snore was followed
by choking sounds. Instantly on his hands and knees, he
hawked and spat out his chaw. He coughed and struggled
for air while his boys pounded on his back. A minute of
asthmatic wheezing subsided into steady breathing.

"Damned chaw 'bout done me in that time, boys," he
said with a rueful smile.

"You ain't keerful, Pa," Jared said, accusingly, "yer
goin'a choke one o' these days." His finger waggled before
Minns' eyes. "Ma done tol' you a thousand times."

Minns waved him away. The hunter rinsed out his

mouth from his canteen. After a long drink and a satisfied belch, he sat down again and sucked away on a weed stem. Old Blue flopped by his master's leg while they rested, back from exploring the nearby trees. His protruding tongue dripped saliva from his running searches. Scratched behind the ears, the old dog stretched out reflexively and waited for more. But his comfort gave way to action when Minns rose to his feet and prodded him into a hunt. At Minns' urging shouts, Old Blue circled the party and yelped. His tail wagged furiously as he snuffled and searched for a scent.

"What you think, Jared?" the hunter asked.

"Member we caught that prisoner all the way to Due West last year, Pa? Those slaves don' he'p nobody but runaways."

"Yer right, boy," Minns said. "That Cross Hill tale from Miz Melody an' Old Albee jest a false trail. We best git on back to the crossin' at Chappell's. Ain't no good place to ford right near." He grasped his saddle horn and swung up into his seat, then shifted his rifle to his left-arm carry. "After we cross the river we'll head to Ninety Six. The militia up thar'll have somethin.'"

"Captain Griscom orta know, Pa," Jared said. He reined his horse around, with Blue at its heels. "Old Ruffin done he'ped us afore."

"Git up!" Minns said, and kicked his horse into a trot. The animal's hooves carved out moist clods from the trail as they headed for Chappell's.

The black coach came to a halt before the portico with a flourish of commands and announcements, its liveried Negro driver following the protocol of embellishing the importance of the visitor's arrival. The huge white manor house fronted on the river and the salt marshes beyond. A broad, sloping green lawn with boxwood maze stretched all the way down to the water and its landing. Storied bald-cypress trees rose above the reeds in a small swamp upriver of the projecting wharf, one of the spreading tops home to an osprey's massive nest. Tall magnolia and maple trees set off the lawn, their size evidence of the ancient permanence of the plantation house. Off to the side rested an arboretum overgrown with vines, and a white pillared summer house kept vigil on a knoll overlooking the grounds. Osprey's Landing on the Cooper had served the Middleton family for generations, an old, pillared monument to success and luxurious living.

Footmen surrounded the coupe when it drew to a stop on the fine gravel surface. One sturdy young slave was positioned at the step to help the passenger debark. Lieutenant Arch Hartsill waved him away and bounded up the wide marble steps to the porch and the waiting couple. Pinckney Middleton and his sister Rose stepped toward him with pleased smiles.

"Welcome, Arch," Middleton said, feelingly. The planter's cane helped his balance when they grasped hands. Their firm, pumping handshake and simple greeting renewed a long friendship, and cooperation of their families.

"It's really good to be here, Pinck," Hartsill replied.

"And to have you visit," the planter said. "How are things over toward Atlanta? I hear Sherman's settling in. He going to stay the winter?"

"You hush, Pinckney," Rose said. The young woman grasped her brother's arm and pushed him aside. She took a step toward the officer and turned up her face invitingly. "Don't I get a welcome too, Arch, before you men talk of war?"

The Lieutenant hugged her tight and kissed Rose's blushing cheeks. "You know you're always first in my thoughts, Rose, even before old Pinck, here."

"Landsakes, I'd never know that. Pinck's been talkin' all day 'bout winnin' back that debt he owes you. Said you'd be here to play poker soon's you got straight over on Jim Island."

Hartsill laughed. "Maybe so," he said. Then his face turned somber as he stared into her eyes. "How's James?"

"Still with General Lee up to Virginia." A shadow crossed her face. "He was wounded at Petersburg. I pray for him every night."

"And I too. If I couldn't have you as my bride it's good it was James. He's a fine man."

Rose shivered in a sudden gust of wind. She adjusted her shawl and brushed the hair from her face. The ends of her curls escaped and flew wildly about. "Well do come on in," she said. "It's chilly standin' out here on this windy old porch." Linking his arm, she steered him towards the door, with Pinckney hobbling behind. Rose clutched Hartsill tight and bubbled over with gladness and laughter. "Aunty Emmaline's been cookin' all mornin', Arch, gettin' ready. She's been flighty, orderin' the girls about. She always set a big store by you. Said I should've married you instead of James."

Hartsill bowed his head to the girl. He smiled as his voice caressed her. "It'd have been my happiest day, Rose. But James is a good man. And we'll always be friends." He laughed and said, "Now let me go give Aunty Emmaline a squeeze."

Rose and Arch left Pinckney and went off to the kitchen from the front hall. The disabled planter hobbled to his padded chair in the parlor. His wound still drained and the pillowed seat eased the hurt.

The afternoon was languorous after a munificent meal. Aunty Emmaline had fussed over Arch, and insured he had the best. She brought in his apple cobbler herself, its spicy crust topped with the heavy cream that he liked so well.

They were back in the Middleton parlor, with Pinckney taking out the cards for some Twenty One, when the Lieutenant recalled Hannibal and Claude.

"Say Pinck," he said, "I saw those two niggers you sent to your Georgia gold mines. I didn't even know you had any."

"What slaves? What mines?"

"Hannibal and the mute. We ran onto them west of Columbia. They had your note."

When his host stared silently at him, openmouthed and obviously perplexed, the Lieutenant reverted to his legal training. He fired off questions like the prosecutor he had been before the war.

"Don't you have gold mines in Georgia?"

"No! Never!"

"Didn't you send two niggers to Georgia?"

"No! Never!"

The conclusion was obvious to both of them. The two fugitives had shown him forged papers! Hartsill swore at the subterfuge and colored at his embarrassment. The illicit document was a diversion, part of an escape plan through the underground slave net the Southerners had heard so much about but the Confederacy had been unable to suppress.

"You reckon you can catch 'em, Arch?" Middleton asked. "We can't have nigras doin' that."

"Well, I'll be up to Anderson next week, back with my unit." The Lieutenant paced the room, his angry face a warning to the planter not to interrupt. "Those bastards lied to me, made me look the fool. I'll catch 'em probably at Calhoun's or a little west. They can't have got much past the Toccoa Falls by then."

"Then what, Arch?"

"Hang 'em right off. And any I find helping 'em."

The trip was going well. Miz Pickens' rockaway was making good progress on the trace to Ninety Six from their overnight stop with the Gilberts. Their host's manor on Big Creek had impressed Hester, along with the fifty slaves busy around the plantation. She had been attentive to Miz Ashley and her young daughter, but had visited the slave row as soon as she could slip away at dinnertime. Granny Liza's cabin was smoky, in part from the curl from the old woman's pipe but mostly from the poorly drawing fireplace. Hester coughed when she stood before the fat bulk, a massive woman whose flowing dress and body folds spilled over the sides of the chair.

"Heard anythin' o' two 'scaped slaves, Granny?" Hester asked.

The girl's deferential tone and bow were taken in by two shrewd, piggy eyes buried in a mass of fat. Granny's leathery, bloated face remained unchanged, her puffed cheeks burnished into a gleaming brown by the firelight. A rough corncob pipe stuck out to one side of her bulging lips. Silent as they eyed each other, the old woman's gross body never moved. She let Hester stand there and wait. Two puffs went by, with no sign of recognition marring the silence.

"Granny Mandy tells me you knows, if anyone," the girl volunteered.

"Granny kerec'," Liza said. "Why you need it?"

"Granny tol' me ter see Aunty Jenny an' Paul up ter Greenwood's. We goin'a be dere termorrer. Gotta he'p dose 'scape."

"Boy come runnin' in dis atternoon wid de news from Beulah up onter de ribber. Dose two be ter Greenwood's same time's you folks 'less de militia git 'em."

Hester had been unable to budge the old slave into any other comments as the evening waned into a dark, overcast night. The silent Granny sat there immobile, puffing on her pipe. Hester finally was driven out of the smoky cabin by its irritating fumes. Her coughing disappeared while she slept away the night in the Pickens' daughter's bedroom.

She got up early, packing the child's things and ready to leave when the party started for Ninety Six that morning. But it had been a slow departure. Long farewells followed a leisurely breakfast, even though Miz Ashley was anxious, and repeatedly dwelled on the illness of her mother. Her lamentations had not foreshortened the protocol of hospitality.

Hester was half asleep in the front seat of the buggy, her travel less comfortable than the cushioned and covered back, when the driver waved to a branch in the trace and called out, "Dere's de split ter Ninety Six, Miz Ashley. We be ter Greenwood's afore dark."

"Thank you, Eli," the woman replied.

In the cool, dreary afternoon the travelers drew their shawls and coats more closely about them. Miz Ashley tucked a blanket over the sleeping child. She did not rest but endured the rocking and groaning of the carriage. Miles flew by rapidly and they drew near Greenwood as the light faded. They passed the crossroads pickets with no difficulty. Impressed by the handsome coach, the men touched their caps deferentially to the regal Miz Ashley. Eli delivered them safely to their destination. He arrived just before sundown and brought the coach to a stop with a flourish. Red rays poked through the clouds when the travelers halted in the circular drive, the sky's fleece above driven and contorted by the cool westerly winds. Gusts picked at every loose fold and crevice as the passengers alighted before the manor house of the Epworth's. Hester shivered in the cold and clutched her meager clothes tighter to her body.

"Mighty col' here, Miz Ashley," she said.

"Won't be once we're inside," the woman told her. "You and Eli see to things." Leaving them, she and her daughter entered the house.

Situated on a knoll just out of town, the Epworth mansion commanded a fine view of the Academy. Hester smelled the wood smoke from the slave cabins off to one side. It created a drifting haze that easily identified their location. But with Miz Ashley's demands, it was after seven before she reached Aunt Jenny. The tall, thin old woman sent a small child playing at her feet to call in Paul and his runner, Owdoms. A skinny but supple boy of about fourteen led the pair into the cabin. But once inside, Owdoms kept behind the larger, dark skinned Negro. He responded quickly to each of the man's commands, whether for a coal to light his pipe or to bring in some wood. Aunty Jenny and Paul took two old rickety chairs and the elderly woman motioned Hester to a third. Aunty's pockmarked face was placid as she waited on the girl's question.

"Seen two 'scaped men, Aunty?" Hester asked.

"How you know 'bout dem?"

"Granny Mandy down ter Pickens sent me ter ask."

"Dey's named Hannibal an' Claude. Dat right?"

Hester nodded. Her hands flew to her breast as she gasped, "Dey's safe?"

Aunty Jenny shook her head. "Caught by de militia t'day. Dey been out cuttin' wood. Militia tinks dey b'long ter a Massa Middleton down ter Cha'leston an' on de way ter Jawga. Gwine git some work outen 'em fo' dey go."

"Claude be a Linckum sojer. Granny say ter he'p 'em both 'scape."

The two Negro men started at the news but Aunty Jenny kept on with her knitting. Her gauntness reflected in the shadows of her cheeks, accentuated by the flickering flames. Hester shuddered at the death's head vision. As if to confirm her premonition, the old woman coughed and bright red blood stained the cloth she rushed to her lips.

"Got de lung fever, Hester," she explained. "Gwine die. But still time ter he'p de Linckum sojer."

Her paroxysm of coughing resumed but disappeared after a drink from a gourd. The penetrating odor of strong whiskey filled the cabin.

"Owneys way I'se kin keep goin'." she said, wiping her mouth with the cloth. Paul and Owdoms waited quietly as she gathered her strength.

"We he'p de Linckum sojer," Aunty Jenny said. "An' Hannibal."

"How?" Hester asked.

"Paul git him free atter midnight. He know how. Owdoms dere, he my grandson," she added, smiling at the boy. "He take 'em ter his other granny, Granny Owdoms at Due West. Got way ter 'scape from dere."

Hannibal and Claude were tied to a tree, their bodies in the deep sleep of complete exhaustion. A slight scrape and pull at his pantsleg woke Claude, prone in a line of slaves bound together, hobbled much like horses. He jostled Hannibal, his hand over the slave's mouth to stifle any sound. A darker shadow slid past them on the ground. Its silence and stealthy movements did not disturb the guard at the fire about ten yards away, nor the militiamen prone around it. Claude could see the man gazing into the fire, a sure mistake, unable to pick up any movement in the black night. As if to help, the picket nodded. His head bobbed down then jerked back up in startled wakefulness. But his slackness indicated a tiredness no different from the slaves.

A knife blade flashed briefly in the firelight and the visitor's pull at their bindings set them free. A tug at Claude's sleeve gave him direction and led him in behind the figure that slid out into the trees. He crept along silently fearful, feeling his way among the twigs and debris of the forest. Hannibal followed him slowly on hands and knees. Fifty yards of wary crawling delivered the men to a declivity, a sharp bank forested in pines. They slid down the slick slope and gathered together at the bottom.

"Gwine go faster here," the guide whispered. "Got good

needle cover." He silenced Hannibal's question with a firm, "Quiet!"

The man strode through the pines at a fast pace. Only a whisper came from the thick needle mat, and not a cry of alarm arose from the sleeping camp. Their guide's aim was unerring and rapidly increased the distance from the picket. They were beyond the next ridge and on a smooth trail when a slim figure stepped from the bushes ahead. Claude pulled his derringer from his pocket, his heart quickening, but was reassured by the guide's raised hand greeting the other. When they bunched, their rescuer rapidly delivered an explanation and their instructions.

"Owdoms take yuh to Granny's," he said. "He smart boy." His rising hand stifled Hannibal's open mouth. "He done dis lots. You jist go 'long quiet an' follow Owdoms."

Their Negro savior melted into the brush before they could thank him. Owdoms beckoned to the fugitives to follow. He half-loped along the path, his pace challenging them to keep up.

CHAPTER 8

Jared and Jeremy

November 8, 1864. Due West, S.C. Temperature 70\36, sunny and cool, with scattered clouds and strong winds during the day. Moon full, rising about 3 A.M.

Long after midnight, Owdoms led the fugitives to the main trace to Due West. Clanks and harness rustling kept them back from the road, hidden in the bordering brush and silent observers of the rebs. A Confederate troop movement raised tiny spurts of dust from the surface when shuffling feet penetrated the top crusting to a few remaining dry spots below. The fine dirt coated bushes and men alike, the soldiers a ghostly, gray army that passed in a mist of reflected moonlight. Shifting gusts of winds created small, swirling dustdevils. The tired plodding of the troops was broken by sneezing and curses but unrelieved by talk. Little by little the line of men oozed by, its interminable length occasionally broken by the rattle of passing batteries and cavalry. Claude's absorption with the long train of Confederates disappeared when Owdoms grasped his wrist.

"Gotter go 'nother way," the boy whispered.

He beckoned to Hannibal and strode away rapidly, even though the dim light made for hard going. The guide slanted to the west into the deep woods. Their way impeded by the faint light and dense forest, the three stumbled on, following Owdoms closely while he wended his steps between giant trunks. The boy avoided the creek bottoms with their washed places and soft spots. He felt his way along an intercepting ridge which gradually bent around to the south. Its broad top grew sharper and narrowed into a hogback within a mile. At the spine, an impassable slide forced them to the shadows of the south slope, its forest more open and inviting. The boy paused at the edge of the immense sag in the earth, a slide burdened with sticks of fallen trees that crossed into a mat on its unstable surface. Their trunks were gray slivers in the pale moonlight that faded and flashed in the river of scudding clouds. Overhead, branches of the trees whipped and shivered in the easterly winds, winds that brought the cold home to the weary travelers.

Hannibal's brusk tone bludgeoned the youth. "You losted?"

"Can't seem ter fin' de way," Owdoms admitted. "De troops done druv us back. We got ter get back ter Massa Verdery's 'stead o' Granny's."

"Where dat?"

"West o' Greenwood. David dere he'p. Massa Verdery preacher at de school."

The boy straddled a fallen log and rested, more from indecision than exhaustion, to Claude's notion. He and Hannibal waited impassively, but the rest did no good. Owdoms' thin body shook and he descended into panic. His fright at the tragic turn degenerated into sobs. Hannibal comforted him with a giant hug and Claude patted his back.

"I'se been losted, boy," Hannibal said. "An' Claude," he paused and chuckled, "he done led us wrong twicet back dere 'roun' de ribber. So don' you fret."

"Ain't never had no trouble a'fo'," Owdoms gasped out. His agitation increased and he jumped away and looked wildly about. "Dey ketch us, dey hang us! Got ter fin' David!"

Splat! Hannibal's hard slap jerked the boy's head around and tears started from his eyes. Grasping Owdoms' arms, Hannibal shook him violently. His rough handling reduced the youth to a quivering, crying child.

"Now you shet yer mouf," the big Negro said forcefully,

"an' we conjure what ter do. Moanin' don' he'p none."

He shook the boy again while Owdoms sniffled and wrestled against the tight hold. Panic won. The youth struggled wildly to escape and cried out, "But I don' know which way ter go."

As if to answer his question, a cowbell tinkled far to the east, followed by another that clanked in a dull off-tone. Owdoms started and jerked free of Hannibal's grasp. "Dat de milk cows down to Massa Verdery's." he said, his voice unsteady. "De cracked bell be on Cubby."

"You knows de trail now?" Hannibal asked.

"Sho' do," Owdoms replied. His confident voice and and relaxed posture reassured the fugitives. "We jist strike down de slope to de next crick, den 'round de little hill wid de big shagbarks an' we be at de Hodges trace. Ain't hard goin'. Tek us right ter David."

The night was late when they reached the edge of the Verdery outbuildings. Hannibal and Claude hid in the shadows of the south wall of the barn, prone in a heavy growth of fig bushes and weeds. Owdoms returned with David only a short wait later. The tall, elderly slave led them back into the forest, his crabbed gait hinting at an old injury. Gangling and thin he might be but his movements were quick and sure, and his path led unerringly to his target. False dawn found them at a slant tunnel on the north slope of the hill bordering the pasture, an old hideout dug long before.

"Don' you move nowhere," David cautioned them. "Dishere ol' place done fergot by most. Massa Arthur an' I dug it when he was small." He chuckled. "I'se de one dat dug; he jist give de orders. He uster hide from ol' Marse Verdery ter keep from gittin' lickin's."

"Take a look, Claude," Hannibal said.

The planter fell to his knees and pushed aside the obscuring brush. He swept away some spider webs, then crawled into the small opening and disappeared from sight. David and the servant listened patiently to the scuffling noises inside but Owdoms' curiosity drew him to the hole. A faint glow showed past him as he crouched and peeped in but Claude did not come out.

"De Reverend yer massa?" Hannibal asked.

David nodded. "Ol' Marse Verdery give me ter Massa Arthur 'bout fifty year back, when he was small. Took keer o' him ever since."

"Dry in dere?"

"Dat clay hard an' no water come thoo. You be fine. Probably plenty o' ol' bresh and some candle ends too. De grandsons used it mebbe twenty year back when dey was small. But nobody here fer years. "

Hannibal twitched his hand toward the inquisitive boy. "Owdoms gonna stay wid us?"

"No. I sends one'a my grandsons, Samuel, ter get yuh late afternoon. Sam take yuh ter Granny Owdoms over ter Due West. Owdoms here, he go home. You bof hide in dere an' wait."

Their negotiations were interrupted at the sight of Owdoms backing out of the opening. David called to the boy to follow and the two disappeared through the trees. A shadowy false dawn and moon revealed the faint mists in the protected lowland. Cattle bawled in the pasture and the off-tone cowbell led the herd's march toward the waiting barn.

Claude's re-emergent head was followed by a flailing to remove spiderwebs. His spitting and face scrubbing were accompanied by low curses. Once he cleared the opening, he shook himself and his clothes and fanned his hat to remove the dirt and twigs.

"Real dry in there," he reported, "but dirty. Not used in a long time, too, from all the spiderwebs. Some candle stubs on a little shelf. I lit one for us." A faint glow from the hole shined on their feet, little apparent in the moonlight.

"How, Claude? We ain't got no matches."

The planter laughed. "I stole some from Lem at the crossroads. His possibles sack was layin' right out while he went off to dump in the woods." He looked about. "Come on, Hannibal, let's get a drink quick before we den up."

The fugitives watered at the small stream at the edge of the pasture. With only sparse cover handy, they furtively dashed from bush to bush in their movements on the slope. The cave entrance received more attention. Hannibal inspected the sprays of limbs at the mouth. Dissatisfied and rumbling, he bent down and cracked two limbs with many twigs to thicken the screen. The addition made the hole virtually invisible. Claude admired the bushes growing over the opening, set by David according to his account, and the great profusion of fallen leaves. Together, they made the entire clump resemble a natural forest thicket.

"Looks good, Hannibal," he said. "Nobody should find us."

"Best we crawl on in an' sleep, Claude. Most likely hard march ternight ter git 'long ter Due West."

The small cave's few candle stubs joined other useful items in Hannibal's possibles sack. Claude took one for his pocket. An old brush bed lay at the inner end, much more recent than the early years described by David. Probably boys playing, the planter thought. But the sticks and leavings were old, thinly covered by dirt fallen from the ceiling of the cave, and no prints or boot scrapings were visible in the litter other than his own. The hideout had not been used in a very long time.

After wolfing the johnnycake David had given them, the fugitives nestled into the debris and slept the day away, warm in the protecting earth.

Minns braced the officer directly, his rifle across his saddle horn. "You seen anything o' two niggers passin' through?"

"Depends," Captain Starr replied.

The elderly militia officer's erect, soldierly bearing and uniform contrasted to the dirty, wedge- shaped tent behind him. Resting his stubbed left wrist on his pistol holster, his wary blue eyes appraised the visitors. At his wave, militiamen surrounded Minns and his sons. Their fighting stance left no doubt of an imminent hazard. Minns gentled his fractious horse when it reared. Its eyes rolled as it shied from a militiaman reaching for the bridle.

"Ain't no need fer that," Minns said.

The man hunter slouched in his saddle and propped the butt of his rifle on his thigh, its muzzle pointed to the midmorning sky with its fleeting clouds. Jared and Jeremy followed his mollifying example and offered no threat to the troops. But Old Blue cruised about, his hackles up. He and the other dogs of the camp crowded each other in a stiff-legged, growling standoff, until their challenges finally eased into circling and smelling. The hunter's sharp command cowed the dog into a slinking retirement behind Jared's mount. When the hound had retreated, Minns coldly eyed the officer.

"I be Athey Minns," he said, brusquely, "lookin' fer a 'scaped Yankee officer from Camp Sorghum." Minns waved a hand toward his sons. "These here's my boys."

The legend of the man hunter, his feats well known through South Carolina, electrified the men. They jostled each other and passed excited comments as they gathered in a tight group around their portly Captain. Intent faces and grounded arms replaced the earlier threat. Starr visibly relaxed and greeted the hunter with a smile as he stepped closer to Minns' horse.

"Ain't seen no officer, Minns. Just niggers tryin' to 'scape."

Athey ignored the Captain and looked about. "Whar's Griscom?" he asked. "I done dealt with Ruffin afore."

"Old Ruffin got hisself kilt last week," Starr replied. "Run onto a slave in the dark. The bastard had 'scaped from down to Gilberts an' had a knife." He paused a moment and said in afterthought. "I'm from Ninety Six like Ruffin. Name's Starr."

The hunter's scar bulged and tinged red. Minns shook his head and grimaced. "Ruffin was a good man," he said. "What'd you do with the bastard?"

"Hung 'im up, what else? Folks from Ninety Six mighty put out 'bout losing Ruffin an' some o' 'em come to he'p.'" Starr chuckled briefly, then laughed as his men broke into grins. "The men had a little fun with 'im, o'course, afore we swung that nigger."

"You got any others recent, Starr? Say last day er two?"

"Yep. An' we keep 'em busy. But some bastard slipped 'em a knife last night to cut the lashings an' all are gone. Most o' the boys are out roundin' 'em up. Got lots o' whippin' to do."

"The two men I want have a paper from a planter down at Cha'leston. Both black but one's a Yankee officer."

"That's them, Captain!" Lem shouted. The militiaman waved his rifle and pushed forward out of the cluster of men. "The ones me an' Ezra took in the bresh along the river."

Minns' horse spooked at the shout and the gesticulating soldier. It pranced back and halfway bucked as it tried to get free. The hunter pulled on the reins and muttered "Whoa, boy, whoa." But the nervous animal stamped and snorted and backed away. Minns patted its neck and calmed the beast into a quiet stand.

"They was here," Starr said. "The big one, Hannibal, he had the paper an' did the talkin'. The other was dumb."

"What'd you do with 'em?"

"Put 'em to work on the timber pile jest like all the rest. We're cuttin' timbers fer a new railroad trestle the Army wants to build."

"But you lost 'em last night?"

"Yep. Like I said, some bastard give the line a knife. I take all their razors soon as they come in. We had 'em all hobbled an' under guard but they slipped away."

The hunter spat and followed his disrespectful action with a contemptuous curse. His malevolent glance caused Starr to back off a few steps. The militia officer sought the flap of his holster with his mangled left arm, and eased up the leather for a ready draw by his right hand. Minns ignored the hostile gesture and resumed his questioning, but civilly, not insulting.

"Whar you think they might head?" he asked.

"Most likely up to'ard Belton. The slaves seem to run the 'scapes through there."

"You sure 'o that?" the hunter said, his face creased by doubt. "Hear tell the line most likely goes to Greenville er over by the Spartans' place."

"Ain't so. Belton mostly, then west, from the 'scapes we kilt 'long the way." Starr chuckled. "Even found one in a railroad car oncet. But most keep to the woods."

Minns turned away from Starr and stared at his sons. They answered his unspoken question with nods. The militia Captain's mouth dropped open in wonderment at the

mysterious communication as the three hunters blended
into one psychic being, one common mindset. A full minute
passed in their quiet communion while the militia grew
impatient. The men shuffled about and joked among themselves about the chances of finding the runaways. But their
banter slowly died away at the continuing silence of the
Minnses. Then, without another glance at the Captain and
his men, or a word of farewell, Minns and his boys spurred
away. Dirt sprayed in wide arcs from their horses' hooves,
damp traces from the old Indian path toward Belton. Old
Blue raced behind them, with the camp dogs in full cry as
the party left.

"Those 'scaped bastards gonna ketch it, Captain," Lem
said. Rumbles of agreement rose from the men crowded
around him, their eyes intent on the disappearing hunting
party.

"Yer right, Lem," Starr said. He rebuttoned the flap on
his holster and rested his stub on top. "That Minns even
scared me. But I was ready to pistol 'im if he took offense. He
ain't no man to cross an' that Yankee officer done give him
a good run." He laughed. "Riled him, I recken, to be played
a fool. He'll kill 'em both."

The mounted party halted in the late afternoon. Both
the Minns and the horses were dirty and slow-moving.
Foam flecked the wet necks of the animals. They blew and
flicked their tails when they were pulled up in front of a large
building. A sign on the side before the double doors announced the Academy to the approaching visitor.

Jared and Jeremy grasped their cradled rifles and
dismounted from their slouched seats in their saddles. The
boys stretched and sighed in relief and pulled at binding
irritants in their crotches. Blue dragged along behind the
horses. His tongue was hanging out and dripping when he
lay down in the dirt. The sun had fallen well toward the
horizon in that brisk, late afternoon, and the wind raised
small twirls of leaves from the loose surface.

"Gotta see Reverend Verdery, boys," Minns said. "Wait
here with the horses."

He had started for the school building when a door

slammed across the street. Minns attention shifted to the elderly gentleman in a black suit and frock coat who came down the steps of the facing, red-brick house. With four square walls set with stone quoins, along with a decorative cupola in the middle of the roof, its solid bulk exuded an air of permanence and comfort. A wide, shading porch held rocking chairs and a swing. The manse sat well back in a fine grove of trees, its genteel appearance attesting to the quality of the folk it housed. A barn lay beyond and an open pasture and cropped fields showed in the distance. Nearer by, a cock crowed lustily in the barnyard. The man coming from the house strolled toward them with a lame step but at a brisk pace, and he twirled his cane occasionally like a baton.

"Reverend Verdery?" Minns asked.

The stocky, alert walker paused and touched his hat. "I am, sir," he said. "And who are you?"

"I be Athey Minns. We atter a 'scaped Yankee officer an' his nigger." Minns worked his chaw and spit. "Been circlin' 'round the plantations all day afore headin' to'ard Belton. Ain't no trace. Any o' your people seen 'em?"

"Land's sakes," the Reverend exclaimed. "Captain Griscom was through here every few weeks huntin' runaways, God rest his soul. And now Starr. You mean you got some other ones you're after?"

"These two 'scaped from the camp down by Columbia. Not local niggers. I'm to bring 'em back."

"Well I haven't seen any Yankee officer, nor strange niggers either. But come on in an' you can ask for yourself. Nobody at the school is going to hide any Yankee."

Grilling by Minns failed to turn up any information from the staff or the Negro help. The latter were reticent and recoiled from the grim hunter, their impassive faces and subservient replies hiding any truth they possessed. It was a nettled Minns that strode back out to his waiting sons. His temper exploded into a "Git!" and a kick when Blue wagged his tail and ran toward him. The old dog shied from the expected blow and dodged behind Jared's mount. He flopped into a pile of leaves in the grass beside the street, his brown eyes alert.

Jared's incensed protest defended his dog but ended in a plaintive whine. "You ain't got no reason to fuss at Old Blue, Pa. He ain't done nothin'."

Minns brushed off his son's lament and shouted to Verdery, "You comin', Reverend?"

He pulled the reins of his horse from Jared's hand and vaulted into the saddle. His mount pranced away, but his move was just across the wide street to the hitching post in front of the residence. Jared and Jeremy were guarding its entrance when the Reverend hurried out of the school building and hustled across the street. He was puffing from the short run when he arrived at the front steps of the manse. Joining Minns, the two went into the house. The carved front door clattered when it shut behind them and muffled the talk inside.

"What is it, Arthur?" came a call from the back of the home.

"Escaped slaves again, pet, and a Yankee officer."

"Well, I never!"

The small, spry woman entered the front hall and looked in distaste at the rough hunter. She adjusted the spectacles resting on her nose, tiny ovals that gave her an owlish appearance, then inspected Minns more closely. A frown grew into open disgust as she wrinkled her nose and sniffed the stink permeating the air.

"Now don't you spit in here!" she said sharply. "And why don't you take a bath? Landsakes, Arthur, the people you drag in. It's a disgrace to us gentlefolk."

Minns' lips thinned into a tight line and his scar reddened, but he took the browbeating in silence. He shuffled his moccasins against the polished floor and leaned on his rifle, his Indian blood keeping his face impassive against the contempt of the nagging woman. But his tolerance, his silence and seeming unconcern set her off again. Her tirade resumed in a flood of derogations, even as she picked nervously at her habit, adjusting her shawl and hair. Verdery suffered her barbs patiently and did not answer his wife's irritable outburst. His resigned face told the hunter not to resist. The vituperation ceased as suddenly as it had begun.

"Well, what does he want?" she asked.

"This is Athey Minns, pet. You've heard of Mr. Minns. He's caught more runaways than anybody else in the state. He's famous."

"I don't care how famous he is," she said. Disgust clouded her face as she stared at Minns' working jaw. "So he catches slaves. But he'd better not spit on my floor!"

The excited woman paced about and wrung her hands. "Why can't things be like they used to? Killing people. Fighting this war. And for what?" A paroxysm of bitter crying consumed her. Verdery cuddled her in his arms. He murmured endearments and consoled her shuddering body and spirit.

"You must forgive my wife, Minns," he said, imploringly. The preacher stroked his wife's hair and lovingly patted her head. "She's high-strung and the war has taken her three grandsons. It's a sad time."

The hunter nodded, then scanned the hall. He stepped out onto the porch and spat out his chaw, then rinsed his mouth from his canteen. His gliding footsteps back into the hall were soft and quiet, and his forgiving smile was aimed at the now calmed woman.

"Recken I won't offend yer more, ma'am," he said, "an' I beg pardon fer the smell. Been chasin' mighty hard an' no time fer warshin'. Man huntin' ain't no easy work."

"Well, I know that," she replied, petulantly. "But how can we help?"

"Like to talk to yer hands, ma'am."

Turning toward the rear of the hall, she clapped her hands and called out, "David? Where are you, David?"

A sepulchral voice carried up through the floor. "Down de cellar, Miz Ida. Comin' right up." Shuffling sounds issued from an open door leading off the back of the long hall. David emerged a moment later with a bucket heaped high with potatoes. He halted and peered at them, his look uncertain.

"Set those down an' come here," Miz Verdery ordered.

David stepped lackadaisically along the hall and stopped before them. His slow, delaying gait contrasted to his brisk steps with the fugitives in the forest. Assuming a slightly bent over, submissive stance in deference to his mistress, he waited on her pleasure.

"This is Massa Minns," she said. "He's got some questions for you about some runaway slaves. Now you answer him, you hear?" Her autocratic tone brooked no argument. "And truthfully," she added. He bowed and nodded.

It was the same as at the school building. Minns' repeated questions to David and the assembled house servants produced denials and evasive looks from the sullen slaves. No amount of cajoling, or even threats from the temperamental tantrums of Miz Ida, could change their stories. When it was done, including Minns searing the field hands and scaring the children in the cabins, the hunter had to admit defeat in his search for the fugitives.

"They's lyin', Reverend," Minns said later as he stood by the hitching post. He went on checking the cinch on his mount. "They know somethin' but they ain't tellin'. I kin feel it. Those bastards er 'round close."

David idled on the porch, then clumped down the front steps, favoring his gimpy leg. He sidled over to the cluster of small children that gawked from the side of the street and stooped to comfort a small, crying girl. As he dallied with the group of children, his eavesdropping produced the information he desired.

"Where you going next, Minns," the Reverend asked.

"Over to'ards Abbeville, to check with some friends. Then strike fer Belton."

Minns mounted his horse and turned it to follow his boys. They already were trotting their mounts up the street, with Old Blue trailing close behind. Some of the children waved when Minns left and one small boy threw a clod at his horse. He shied the animal at the child and laughed when the little fellow ran to David. Reining his mount back into the street, he didn't glimpse the angry face of the Negro and the clenched fist.

Letty'll be fixin' to get the dinner on soon, Claude mused. He was sprawled in the cave, looking out toward the pasture, his face hidden by the bushes at the opening. The green pasture, not yet killed down by frost, reminded him of Greenbottom. His flight of longing took him back to those well loved acres. Far to the north in Virginia, his plantation lay in a broad, fertile valley with little rock, and was bounded by a deep, navigable river that coursed alongside the lower fields. Shaw's Landing was known to all the river traffic, along with his log rafting down to New Orleans. His plantation's fields would be sere this time of year, but Greenbottom was precious. Hunger for his family and his hearth rushed over him in a flash of unbearable desire.

If only the war could end. And the killing. And the slavery. He glanced over at Hannibal, still sound asleep. The Negro had saved his life and had protected him from want and hard labor in the prison camp. A rush of compassion and fondness for the man raced through his thoughts. Was he a friend or a slave? What was the difference between the Negro and the white? Claude pondered the question, uncertain in his answer, still not sure of the direction of his internal struggle. Lincoln had freed the slaves, but the old habits and attitudes died hard. The plantations could not be worked without massive labor. But did they have to be slaves?

He crawled out a little farther to observe the Verdery house, a full half a mile away. It and the school lay on the far side of the pasture and fields of the small, shallow valley, with the spires of the town beyond. A road bordering Verdery's place cattycornered across into another slight, intersecting hollow, around the slope holding the cave. The low, forested hill of their hideaway was a woodlot of massive old oaks and beeches. Claude always had liked the beeches, with their distinctive gray bark and light brown leaves hanging on in sprays in the fall. Rays from the low- hanging sun flashed through the trees and daubed spatter patterns on the forest duff. Bongs from a loud bell startled him, the set of four strikes coming from the tall school building.

"Must be four o'clock," he whispered to Hannibal, as he shook the man. "We probably'll be gettin' out of here soon."

Hannibal sat up and sleepily rubbed his eyes, then yawned and stretched. He joined the planter at the opening and peered out. "Mighty purty farm," he said, admiringly. "I'se git one fer me, someday, Claude."

Claude's reply froze in his mouth and his body stiffened

at the sight of the three riders who were coming into view on the quartering road that passed the school. A dog led a pack behind them. The animal's bodies were stretched and fluid as they raced in and out and chased each other. A chorus of barking, yelps and yodels attested to the great mix of mongrels. The riders moved silently but swiftly along the trace, with clods of dirt thrown up from the horses' rapidly striking hooves. It was evident the patrol was aiming for the nearby gash in the rounded hills and would pass close to the cave. Claude let his breath out in a rush. His heart pounded and shivers coursed over him.

"It's Minns and his boys and Old Blue," he gasped out.

"Yassah, Claude," Hannibal said. "An' he be atter us." Somehow, the big Negro's voice remained calm and confident. "He ain't a'gonna get us here, Claude. David see ter that."

The horses trotted on into the intersecting hollow and passed out of sight around the forested slope. But Blue dallied with the pack of mongrels. His animal friends rushed hither and yon in their now playful race. A shout echoed through the gentle, rounded hills and called Blue on. At the summons, the old dog broke off and trotted down the trace. He was worried by the village pack at first, but then the mongrels fell away one by one to straggle back toward the buildings.

Even with their watchfulness, the approaching boy took them by surprise. He had come along the gentle, timbered slope from the west, and his slow, hesitating approach delivered him close to the entrance before they heard rustling in the leaves. Claude pulled his derringer and withdrew slightly into the darkness of the cave, his arm extended for a quick shot. Hannibal crouched beside him, ready to spring on the intruder.

A low call sounded in the opening. "You dere, Hannibal? You dere?"

A fat, roundfaced boy of about twelve showed through the lattice of the protecting bush, his dark clothes well suited for a night of travel. He slid slowly around the bush and fell on his knees before the opening, then cast aside the screening branches. Startled by the waiting gun barrel, his frightened eyes rolled wildly when Hannibal seized him by the coat and dragged him into the cave, his hand over the boy's mouth.

"You from David, boy?" Hannibal asked. His grip pinned the squirming youth in the loose dirt. The boy nodded as he struggled and protested. His gurgles led to gasps when his mouth was freed. "Why you treat me dis way?" he protested. "I'se Sam. David my granddaddy."

"Jist bein' keerful, Sam," Hannibal answered. He brushed debris off the boy as he let him up. "Now what you got ter tell us?"

"Fust off I give you de fixin's, den talk." The boy produced a cloth packet from his possibles sack, its aroma welcome to the hungry men. Boiled sweet potatoes, pieces of fatback and pone disappeared quickly while Sam recited David's plan.

"We gwine ter de west ter cross de Due West trace. Army done quit marching dere. Dat Minns on de way ter Abbeville."

"How you know dat?" Hannibal's mumble came out through a mouth full of meat. Grease ran down his chin and dripped from his short beard. He wiped the back of his sleeve across his mouth before stuffing in another piece of potato. The tasty morsels occupied him and he and Claude were only half listening.

"Fo' dey left, Old Minns tol' Massa Verdery dey's ridin' ter Abbeville." Sam rummaged in his sack and hauled out a piece of greasy bacon. He chewed on it, mumbling through bites. The strip hung out of his mouth like a taffy pull as he talked. "Dey went out on de south road. Ain't no turnoffs fum it fer five mile, so you be safe de way we gwine."

Short work on the food finished the packet. Claude belched with pleasure, then scuttled to the cave entrance and grunted. He motioned to Hannibal and to the creek. The Negro nodded and led the way for a drink. Painted a deep orange, the round ball of the fading sun showed through the trees on the ridge to the west. A few rays lighted the village and the brick of the Verdery manse flashed blood-red in the dying light. Claude shuddered at the omen as he drank, a premonition of doom and death overcoming him.

Sam held out two sticks when they returned from the creek. "David sent yer staffs," he said. The boy handed them the two long, sharpened spears. "Dey's tobacco sticks, Hannibal, hickory, an' right tough. He tol' me ter tell yuh he ain't got no knife ter give."

Hannibal flexed the hickory and tested the point. "Dey do fine, Sam," he said. "We got Claude's gun too. Now which way we run?"

"Jist 'long de sidehill ter de next saddle den cross ter de ol' woods path. Ain't more'n two mile ter de Due West trace. We orta be at Granny Owdoms fo' de moon be up." He giggled. "Good ter travel in de dark. David says dey can't see us in de dark. Good ter be a nigger."

Sam started at a fast trot and quartered the gentle slope of the sidehill to the top of the western ridge. Claude was breathing hard by the time they had gone the first mile. Fat but fast, he thought, when the boy's pace belied his corpulence. They had turned west at the intersecting ridge, running easily in a forest of immense trunks and little understory, when the three struck the imprint of countless deer crossings. The depressed, broad track through the woods angled to the north, its indentation smooth and easy going. Sam stopped and examined the game trail, while Claude slumped down on a nearby log, hot and sweating.

"Don' see no other tracks but deers," the boy observed.

Hannibal bent over in close scrutiny and traced out a big, two pronged dent. "Big buck, dere," he said. He sniffed. "Kin smell de musk. "

Sam nodded and started north on the trail. "Come along behint me," he said. "We be at de Due West trace purty quick."

Minns and his sons had stopped out of view of the Verdery manse, behind the hill a half-mile past the turn of the road. The horses bunched while they watered at a small creek and Old Blue jumped into a nearby pool. The dog rolled in the water and lapped it up as it cooled his body. Minns summons brought him racing back along the bank. His tail wagged and his shaking frame showered the bushes while he waited on a handout. Blue caught the piece of jerky in midair, a rawhide-like strip too tough for the hunter to conquer. Flopping in the dusty road, the old dog tore at the spicy, dried beef and gulped it down bit by bit.

The hunter chuckled at the sight of Blue tearing at the tough meat, and said, "Old Blue ain't lost his git, Jared."

"No, Pa. He's a fine, old dog. We cross those niggers an' Blue'll put us on 'em."

"I got my idees on that. If they're goin' to Belton like Starr said, they got to pass Due West. That right?"

"Yes, Pa," Jared replied. "But we're aimin' fer Abbeville. We ain't goin'a be there."

Jeremy had taken the opportunity to water himself as well as his horse, and to fill his canteen before he offered an opinion. He was the quiet one, the thinker of the two brothers, used to resolving his questions before he made his infrequent suggestions. The impetuous Jared and reticent Jeremy added to the shrewd experience of the man hunter, a formidable combination able to outwit any slave in his escape attempt. They always got their man, albeit many times dead. But the planters wanted no escapes and dead by a Minns' hand was a fiercer deterrent than recapture and the whip. Just the idea of Minns on the trail struck terror in the slave community, and scared off all but the brave or the foolhardy.

"We orta double back around, Pa," Jeremy said, "an' circle to that crosstrail on the Due West road." He remounted his horse and turned it back along the rutted road toward Verdery's. "Member last year? We caught two o' them 'scapes right there.'

"Jeremy's right," Jared added. "Buried 'em too. Good hidin' fer an ambush." He shifted in his saddle and scratched his leg, then kneed his horse toward his brother's. "If they's goin' that way it's the place. Better'n Abbeville."

Minns paused, reflective, then reined his horse around with a few kicks and clucks. "Don't want those niggers at the the Reverend's to see us circlin'," he said. "They'll spread the alarm." He walked his mount toward town with his boys ranged beside him. "We jest cut across to the south a'ways, then loop past 'em. Not more'n three mile to that junction."

The party split off the road at a well-defined game trail.

Deer tracks led them back into the woods to the south. A bushy cross trail carried them on around the town and shielded their movements from the taletelling Negroes. Athey Minns and his boys were scattered along the Due West road by just before sundown. The red globe sank close to the horizon and the sky started turning from orange to blue as the day slowly faded into the approaching dusk. Minns placed his sons about twenty rods apart near the crosstrail and gathered their horses' bridles as his boys sought cover.

"Quiet!" the hunter cautioned each. "Goin'a lead the horses back aways an' tie 'em off. Old Blue stays with me. You see anythin', call the hooty owl an' t'others come runnin'. Those niggers ain't got no gun, so's ain't no fight if you jest stay back with yer rifles."

Blue followed when Minns led the animals down the road and disappeared around a bend. The boys' stands in the cooling breeze were lonely, full of noise. Branches of the trees whipped against each other and leaves swirled in little gusts. Jared missed the sounds at first, at his center position opposite the crosstrail that placed him at the best stand for intercepting the runaways. A shuffle and cautious movement in the bushes across the road attracted his gaze. His startled, nervous twitch intensified when the black face of a boy peered out. The latter was followed by a rotund body that eased into the road. Looking up and down the trail, the figure inspected the markings in the dirt of the trace, then beckoned to the bushes. A moment later, the fugitives he hunted confronted Jared's shaking body.

Caution fled his mind. Without thinking, he cocked and leveled his rifle and stepped out of the trees. "Hands up!" he shouted. "Pa! Jeremy!" Jared's scream echoed through the forest. "I done got 'em!"

Jeremy pounded down the road toward the silent Negroes but Minns did not appear. The shaking Jared advanced on the three fugitives with his weapon pointed at waist level. His rifle wavered from one to another as the two Yankee runaways separated widely and threatened a rush upon him. The youth's calamitous misjudgment in approaching the party turned into a precipitous failure when

Sam darted in toward the rifle and seized the barrel. It went off as the boy jerked Jared's weapon against his finger. Staggering back at the impact of the ball, the slave collapsed, moaning, and clutched his side.

It was too late for Jared to reload, to escape. He clubbed the rifle and struck at Hannibal. The slave tore it from his hands and took him by the throat, murderously shaking and choking him. Fury and fear turned Jared into a violent madman, too powerful for the Negro to hold. The boy's imprecations thundered out and his suppleness and heavy blows broke Hannibal's grasp and forced him to retreat. Bravely, the boy felt for his knife and closed the Negro. Two strong men, though the one was only a youth, entwined in mortal combat and rolled over and over on the ground. But the big Negro, even with his brute strength, had trouble subduing the screaming, crazed youth. Jared had just freed his knife when the cursing Jeremy ran up to the fight and pointed his weapon at the pair.

"Stop or I'll shoot yuh, you black bastard!" Jeremy danced around and poked his rifle barrel first toward the fighters, then toward Claude. He intimidated the planter but was unable to fire into the whirling figures.

At a lessening of the struggle Jeremy took aim. With the momentary distraction, Claude pulled his derringer and shot him through the body. The impact of the heavy ball deflected the discharge of the rifle. Plummeting to the earth, Jeremy's slack face and open eyes turned up to the early stars he would never see again. He shuddered into limpness as he lay on his back. A red stain spread on his shirt and a gout of blood dribbled from his mouth.

"Another boy," Claude whispered to himself as he stared at the crumpled, dead body. He shook his head and choked at the thought of the death about him. "How many more have I got to kill?"

Jared lay quiet in the dirt nearby. Hannibal was wrapping a rag around a bleeding hand. "Done choked him Claude," he said, "knocked him out." He finished the wrapping and tied it off with a knot pulled tight by his teeth and other hand. "He ain't dead," he said, when Claude bent over to inspect the boy.

"Well we won't kill him, that's for sure." Claude's belligerent voice brooked no argument. "Minns can find 'em. Don't know why he didn't get into the fight." At a moan from Sam, he hastily ran over to their unconscious guide. Blood showed on his hands when he inspected the boy's side. He glanced about nervously and said, "Let's take Sam and the weapons, and get the hell out o' here."

A quarter of an hour later, Minns came up with the horses. He galloped the last few rods when he saw Jared bent over the body. Swinging off in panic, he ran to the two and bent over his weeping son.

"Where you been, Pa?" The tearful boy held his younger brother's hand. His tormented face looked up accusingly into his father's drawn visage.

Minns' scar rapidly changed color, its red adding to the bleakness of his stare. "Dan got spooked by a fox jest as we went around the bend. Took me a' half hour to ketch him." He swore feelingly, but his tirade died into soft pathos as he placed his hand on his son's shoulder and patted it. "Jeremy never did get that hawse gentled right."

Without another word, Minns squatted by the body. He straightened the dead boy's flowing hair and brushed it back on the pallid brow. Jeremy's eyes reproached him. They stared at him unblinkingly, and so intently that he could not bear to watch and bowed his head. Old Blue stretched his lean frame, its taut muscles rigid as his nose sought the blood, the scent of the dead boy so different from the animals he hunted. His howl, a soul in torment searching for his lost master, rose eerily over the mourning family.

"What happened here, boy?" Minns low, ominous voice cut the air like a steel knife. Its harshness grated on Jared's sorrow.

"They come out from the trail, Pa, jest like we figured. An' I hollered. Jeremy come runnin' but you didn't." Jared's tears flowed and he wiped his eyes with his sleeves. Hawking and spitting, he patted Old Blue.

"They had a nigger boy with 'em. The boy run in an' grabbed my rifle and I shot 'im. But the big one wrestled me an' Jeremy couldn't shoot we was so mixed up, fightin'. T'other one shot Jeremy, the Yankee."

Gloom of night settled over the road and their huddled figures grew more indistinct in the gathering darkness that cloaked the dismal scene. Minns stirred when they no longer could distinguish the dead boy's face. "We'll load Jeremy on Dan an' take 'im to the Reverend. He'll likely read over 'im tomorrow."

Jared was in the saddle and leading Dan when Minns searched the site for the missing weapons. His mumbling imprecations revealed that futility. The hunter faced west before mounting, and stood erect, trembling. Little moans and curses spilled out of his twisted, scarred mouth. All the pent up fury and anguish at the death of his son erupted into a raised, clenched fist shaking at the western sky, and a shout of hate, a vow that changed his blood oath into a blood feud.

"I'll kill yuh, Shaw! You an' that nigger o' your'n."

CHAPTER 9

Granny Owdoms

November 9, 1864. Due West, S.C. Temperature 69\35. Possible scattered showers during the night and cool, with moderate winds. Moon just past full, rising three hours before sunup.

Cool as it rustled by, the night breeze invigorated and steadied them, burdened as they were with Sam. The ball had passed through the muscles on his left side, just under the shoulder. Claude suspected that the heavy slug also had broken a rib or two, since little grating sounds arose whenever the boy moved. Their rasping collisions were accompanied by Sam's woeful groans. Hannibal had bound up the wound after washing off the blood at the first stream. They had run for a mile after that before the boy collapsed, only half-conscious.

The fugitives unbound the bandage and fussed over the bullet wound. To Claude's satisfaction, it had closed and quit bleeding. But Sam screamed when they wrenched his side while rebandaging the ribs. He tossed about and wailed, "I hurts!"

"Knows it, Sam," Hannibal said. He stroked the boy's sweaty brow. "Gonna git you ter Granny Owdoms'. She make yuh well."

Claude picked up the injured boy. "I'll carry him awhile, Hannibal, then you can spell me."

"Den I goes fust," Hannibal said firmly and led off up the road at a slow step. The Negro kept about ten yards ahead, wary and far enough away to let the others make it to the woods if danger threatened. The reloaded guns converted them into a formidable party, equal to the Minnses if the hunters returned. Sam's head dangled in unconsciousness as the fugitives struggled on, their cautious progress toward Due West and Granny Owdoms dependent on brute strength, determination, and not a little luck.

Claude and Hannibal interchanged several times, each picking up the burden more reluctantly as the miles grew long and the night late. Faint moonlight finally suffused the countryside when they paused alongside a rail fence for another, needed rest. The cleared sky was a welcome relief from the brief, heavy shower that had plagued them earlier during a black- dark squall. Hannibal put down the boy and breathed a sigh of exhaustion.

"'bout wore out, Claude," he said. "Dishere boy gits heavier ever'time I carry him."

A small trickle of water glinted and gurgled along the road, cold to the planter's fingers. Hannibal disappeared into the grassed pasture, leaving Claude to tend to the mumbling and feverish boy. Sam lay prone on his back while the planter soothed him with gentle pats and a cold wet rag. Bent over as he was, the shadow down the road escaped his attention as it crept silently toward their resting place.

Protesting rails and a dim shape hurtling over the fence were followed by thuds of blows and thrashing figures in the weeds. The bodies rolled and wrestled with flailing arms, and curses split the quiet of the night. Springing to his feet in alarm, Claude ran to the fighting, his derringer ready. But the scuffle ceased abruptly when Hannibal rose to full height. His arms pressed a slight, squirming body against him.

Hannibal shook the small figure into submission. "Why you spyin' on us?" he asked.

A crying girl answered. "Runner tol' us ter look fer yuh. Granny Owdoms done sent me out hyar."

The fugitives were speechless. The tiny, sobbing girl

pulled loose from the unresisting Hannibal and bent over the trickle. She winced and swore as she splashed cold water on her face and probed gingerly at her cheeks.

"You hurt me bad," she sobbed. "My eye done swellin' closed a'ready an' my lip bleedin'." She bawled loudly and scooped up more water, crying out when it struck her face. The girl flayed the men with a torrent of unflattering maledictions; her scorn heaped ashes on their heads.

Claude reached out his hand, her slap an instant retaliation. "Don' you touch me!" she shouted. Falling to her knees beside the rivulet, she cupped up more cold water, then immersed her face in the pooling for a moment.

"Claude jist wanta he'p," Hannibal said, apologetically. "What's yer name?" When she continued sobbing, he knelt beside the crouched girl. His arms encircled her in another peace feeler until she pulled away with a curse. But the big Negro persisted in his attempt to make amends. He patted her back with his big hand as she blubbered and shook and daubed at her face. Then he drew her erect with her head against him.

Hannibal's voice was gentle as he cradled her. "What's yer name, chile?"

"Lillie," the girl replied. Her sobs gave way to sniffles. "Granny sent me ter bring yuh to 'er. Tain't but 'nother mile er so."

"Den we better git on," Hannibal said and released her. The big man picked up the guns and cradled them. "You carry Sam, Claude," he said. Hannibal took the lead and went on up the road with the weapons. The girl hesitated and looked fearfully at the burdened planter.

"He dead?" she asked.

The planter grunted and shook his head. Waving at her impatiently to go on ahead, he took to the trace. The girl ran to Hannibal and skipped along beside him to match his rapid pace.

Claude was gasping and his arms were leaden when they reached the slave cabin. He laid Sam on the rude pallet Granny Owdoms pointed to when they entered. Her hands stroked Lillie's face, her stormy visage a presage to the invective they expected.

"What you do ter Lillie?" she demanded. "Why you beat 'er?"

"Dat gal snuck up on us in de dark," Hannibal replied. "I tinks she ain't up ter no good." He squirmed under Granny's angry gaze and epithets and again apologized. "I'se sorry fer it an' tol' her."

Hannibal leaned the rifles against the cabin wall and gestured toward the planter. "Dishere's Claude. I'se Hannibal."

"Know who you be," Granny replied, disdainfully. "Word come thoo from Granny Liza down ter Gilberts. She allus got de runners out. But you don' need ter beat Lillie."

"We been 'spectin' de Minns back agin'. Figured she was dem."

"De Minns all de way up here?" The old woman's brown, leathery face wrinkled and her bulky body shook. "Liza don' say nothin' 'bout dem."

"Claude kilt one last night and de rest 'roun'. We got ter git on. Leave Sam hyar so you kin he'p 'im. He shot by de Minns."

Granny's skirts rustled from her rapid movements. She pushed the girl away and beckoned to several little boys in a wide-eyed cluster near the cabin door. They came running at her wave and squeaky, demanding call. Picking out the largest, her pat and restraining hand demanded his full attention.

"Git ol' George, John. An' fetch 'im back here quick. Tell 'im ter be quiet, you hears?"

The skinny eight year old nodded and dashed out of the cabin. Abandoned, the rest of the children eased farther away from cold; their small bodies inched toward the smoky fireplace. Claude handed them a handful of chinkapins and Hannibal's offered pawpaws produced quick smiles.

"Dey was plenty in de meadow, Claude," the servant said. He shrugged apologetically and handed the planter two when Claude gave him a reproachful glance. "Had a big clutch in my possibles sack when Lillie come up. Fetched 'em along."

Claude gulped the soft, yellow meat and spit the shiny black seeds into the fire. Those fruit and another were finished quickly. His skins and those from the children sizzled in the flames and added to the fire's smoky texture.

Granny took off Sam's coat and shirt while they ate. The old woman's hands tenderly explored the wound. He groaned when she moved him and put her ear to his side. Sam was conscious and protesting as her probing fingers investigated his ribs.

"Hush," she said, reassuring him. "You ain't hurt so bad, Sam. I'se fix you up good, den hide yer 'til we kin gitcher back ter Verdery's.

With Claude looking on, Hannibal bent over the boy and patted his head. "He awright, Granny?" he asked.

"Not hurt bad 'tall. Jist'a little cut an' cracked ribs. He be fine."

"You look ter my han' too, Granny?" Hannibal held out the bandaged member. "It cut fightin' wid de Minns."

She inspected the deep gash in the heel of the palm, already sealed over and caked with blood.

"Soon's George gits here, I put a good chaw on it an' on Sam. Nothin' like de 'baccy an' yarbs ter draw out de pison. You be fine."

The old woman busied herself with the injured boy but groaned repeatedly as she stooped and moved at Sam's pallet. "Got de misery," she said, in answer to Hannibal's question. "Hard ter keep up in de col' time."

Lillie had washed and had bound a band around her forehead at the hairline when she returned to their sides. Her pleasant face had a bright scrubbed look, distorted by the swellings at the eye and mouth. But the girl no longer castigated the fugitives. Instead, she appraised Hannibal boldly and moved closer to him. The old woman stepped between them.

"She too young fer yuh, Hannibal," Granny said firmly. She shushed the girl's protest and shooed her away. "She ain't but 'bout twelve er thirteen. You leave 'er be."

"Mebbe she like a little present ter make up fer de beatin'."

Hannibal rummaged around in his possibles sack. He brought out a long string of flashing beads and tossed it to the girl. She squealed in delight and slipped it on over her head in a double loop. The flaming red brilliants richly accented the smooth brown skin of her neck.

She's a beautiful girl, Claude thought, wasted in a cabin like Granny's. His sharp inspection revealed the same crude comforts as at Granny Mandy's, only a few necessities provided by the owner for the hard working slaves, and no amenities. The dirt floor, compacted into a dense clay like brick, was uneven and damp, the fireplace smoky, the pallets barely livable, the furniture crude or broken, the cabins no better than the cow pens. Did he do the same? The thought progressed into a flash of shame. It had been some time since he had inspected his own slaves' cabins at Greenbottom. As other owners, he left all supervision to Campbell, his tough Scots overseer. The man was hard working, with his faithful slave driver, Samson, a Negro to be trusted, the driver big enough and ruthless enough to subdue any recalcitrant slave. But did the slaves get fair treatment? Did he get the most yield from their labor? His conscience nagged him and a small voice wormed its way into the morality of his actions. "Do unto others —," popped into his mind unbidden, staggering him with its implications. His shaken faith again was blossoming into the idea of freedom for all his slaves when Hannibal tugged at his arm.

"Claude! Dey's somebody comin'."

The two men seized their rifles and faced the door, the weapons cocked and ready.

"Ain't no cause, Hannibal," Granny said. She listened a moment. "It's jist George. Hear de clumpin'? He got de bad leg."

George entered the cabin door with John preceding him. The boy cried out in alarm and ran behind Granny when he saw the leveled guns. Pulling him around, the old woman gave him a hug and a pat.

"Ain't no need ter be 'fraid, boy. Dey don' hurt yuh, ner George."

The latter trembled at the muzzles of the rifles, which pointed menacingly at his middle.

"Put down de guns!" Granny ordered. She stepped over to Hannibal and struck him in the back. "Dishere's George, come ter he'p."

She groaned when she again knelt at Sam's pallet. "Over here, George," she called out. "Need yer big chaw."

George clumped to the pallet and obligingly disgorged a great wad of juicy tobacco into her waiting hand. His short leg and built up shoe, heavy and ugly, swung widely when he walked, and produced a rolling motion in his body.

Not much use, Claude thought, when he also saw the wretched back with its small hump. A man disabled since birth, one an owner couldn't sell, forced to use him at whatever tasks could be found around the barn or shops. He had one such slave at Greenbottom, a pitiful sight, a man that Campbell kept away from the house.

"Com'ere!" Granny's call to Hannibal and beckoning hand gathered them both at the pallet. Sam was sitting up, a brown-stained bandage stuck tight against his wound. Granny held out a juicy, brown mass of chewed tobacco, topped by a mat of soaked, shredded herbs. She slapped the copious wad on Hannibal's cut hand and smeared it to cover, then bound it up tight. "It draw any pison right out," she said. "Ain't no more trouble wid dat. Now I feeds yuh fo' you go."

The fugitives ate of the meager cabin fare, ill-cooked bacon that dripped grease on the cornbread on the hearth. While they worried the fat meat, Granny explored their escape path with George. Claude kept an attentive ear as he chewed the rancid, odorous bacon. It was barely acceptable, but his hunger forced his gullet to accept the greasy, unwelcome prize. Poorly fed and uneasy, his conscious thoughts rebelled at his fate and its dependence on the two slaves. But their intelligent casting and discarding of ideas and shrewd observations on the rebs improved his flagging confidence.

"Hide 'em here t'day," Granny finally concluded. "Put 'em in dat old root cellar off de spring house, de one de big house don' use no mo'. Dey keep out o' sight jist like de rest o' de 'scapes."

George mumbled his approval. "I'se taken de wagon o' taters termorrer, Granny. Inter de Army dere at Belton. Dey kin hide under de load."

"Dat's de bestes way," Granny said. "Dey ride wid yer. The old woman chuckled. "De Minns not 'spec' dat. Dat Minns tinks he smart but we gwine lick 'im agin dis time."

"Where dey git off?"

The old woman's squeaky voice filled the cabin. "Drop 'em at de big thicket," she said, loudly. "Dey do fine fum dere."

Her dictatorial orders reminded Claude of Granny Mandy and his Granny Rose at Greenbottom. Those old Negro women ran things, he knew, whether it was the big house or the slave quarters. They ordered the men about and invariably were shrewder, surpassing even the overseers sometimes. And they had control of the children, the future of any plantation. His awed contemplation of the events unfolding bolstered his thoughts of escape, controlled as he was by the old woman. It was apparent that his future depended on her cunning and his faith in her.

Granny's shrill, "John?" interrupted the boy's attack on another pawpaw.

The small child scuttled to her side and grasped her hand. His cheeks smeared with streaks of fruit, he cocked his face up attentively as he waited on her instructions.

"You take dese two ter de old spring house and hide 'em," she said. He leaned against her and she stroked his head lovingly. "Gitten close on ter daybreak so you go 'long now."

Hannibal and Claude followed the boy when he started for the door. "Keep quiet an' watch close so nobody see yer," was her parting admonition.

John led them through a clump of trees, creeping on his knees the last way. The dewy leaves and dripping branches soaked their pants and added to their discomfort as they crawled toward the back of a large mansion with its outlying cookhouse. A hump in the ground faced them at the rear of the cookshack, deformed by a fallen in, sloping front. The boy pushed aside a rotted panel, then crawled into the blackness of a tunnel with Hannibal and Claude close behind. It was pitch black dark inside, but they found a small cave with its stone-walled pool of cold water.

"Massa done had 'nother spring house built t'other

side," John whispered. "It better. Dis one got stove in when he blowed out a big stump. You be safe here an' dey's plenty water." He put his hand on the mouth of each fugitive. "Quiet like Granny say." The boy disappeared into the tunnel before they could reply.

Sounds of the panel being pushed back into place and his hasty withdrawal rapidly faded away. Left alone, they were entombed in a silent, total darkness except for a small, grayer aperture in the ceiling. When the hole filtered in a meager daylight, they recognized a sleeping bench with some old rags and a remnant blanket, their home for the next day.

A pale, midmorning sun showed through the fleeting clouds and high haze as the party stood at the open grave. Rain in the night had muddied the ground, marked as it was by the footprints and shovel marks of the Minnses. Raindrops dripped from the sighing trees, a windy dirge for a solemn day. Gravestone sentinels, gray as their Confederate comrades, guarded the grove behind the church, their numerous ranks indicative of long settlement of the region. A spray of yellow-red slashes on the outer edge of the gathering marked the more recent burials of the surrounding war. The silent stones stood in mute testimony of man's final destination as the burial service commenced, its sad interment adding an unexpected arrival to their midst.

"You 'bout ready, Parson?" Minns asked.

"Any time, Athey," Verdery replied.

A rude pine box stood on crosspieces over the open grave, its boards exuding the resiny odor of uncured wood. A single spray of green pine fronds lay on the box and added its fragrance to the yeasty smells of the damp, wooded cemetery. The Reformed Baptist Church of Greenwood had received and converted its sinners but now would have another fallen member before its ministrations were possible.

Minns and Jared ran their hands over the box and lovingly caressed it. Reverend Verdery held his bible in readiness, already at the head of the grave. His wife waited at the side, impassive, resplendent in her coal-black burying dress. But Athey delayed and delayed while the Reverend coughed and then prayed aloud. Both Minnses held on to the casket as if unwilling to let Jeremy go into the ground.

"We got to do it, Athey!" Verdery's irritation rose at the long wait and the dripping trees. Drops cascaded onto his wife and his uncovered head as he spoke. Their splashes sharpened an already abrupt tone. "You can't bring him back, man. He needs to have a decent burial. And I must get back to the school and get my wife out of the damp."

"I knows that, Reverend," Athey said. "But I jest can't seem to let 'im go. Those Goddamned slaves gonna answer fer this."

"Athey!" Shocked at the blasphemy, the Reverend's anger exploded. "You quit that talk or we'll leave you to your own buryin'." His impatience and the cool wind added to his choler. "The Lord says, 'vengeance is mine,' and you shouldn't use his name in vain."

"Ain't in vain, Reverend," the hunter retorted, his scar bulging. "I'm goin'a be his instrument." He stepped aside from the coffin. "Finish the buryin', Reverend, so's I kin git on after those bastards an' kill 'em."

The service ended quickly in its simplicity, spurred on by a light shower and the Reverend's increasing annoyance. Droplets sprinkled them from the trees swaying in the wind. The spattering drops and sighing gusts added their melancholy benediction to the burial service. "I am the resurrection and the light —" and "Ashes to ashes, dust to dust," were interspersed between the simple eulogy and the prayers of the clergyman. He and his wife left quickly after handshakes. They were a few steps down the path when Athey called out, "Wait, Reverend!"

The hunter hurried up to them. "Done fergot, Reverend," he said. Fumbling in a leather pouch hung on his belt, he removed a heavy gold coin and handed it to the clergyman. A wigged portrait stood out on its face. "It's Spanish," Minns explained, when Verdery turned the coin over and over. "Worth 'bout twenty dollars U.S."

"But I don't want anything, Athey," the clergyman exclaimed.

He held out the piece, but his wife seized the coin and

clutched it tightly in her hand. Her frown at Verdery silenced him and her sharp voice accepted the gift. "We thank you, Mr. Minns. It is thoughtful of you."

"The Minns allus pay their debts, Ma'am, an' we owe you both fer the box an' the funeral." Addressing the clergyman, he continued. "You take the gold an' put up a stone fer Jeremy. Keep the rest fer yer good offices."

His departure was as abrupt as his run after them. Jared and Minns were filling in the grave when the Verderys reached their carriage at the church steps.

What they didn't see was Minns' rage after the mound had been tamped. With Jared and Old Blue by his side, he stood erect by the grave, his coppery-brown face darkened by grief. His explosion was short and bitter, a grim warrior confirming an implacable, coming vendetta.

"You was a good boy, Jeremy, too good to be put down by that no-good Yankee. I swear to you, boy, an' to the living God, I'll see 'im dead."

Hester hurried down the path from the big house and headed for the slave cabins. "I'se got ter fin' Granny Owdoms," she mumbled. "Best git back 'fore dinner time er Miz Ashley hide me good." Rounding the corner at the big clump of lilac bushes, she ran full tilt into Granny Owdoms. The old woman bounced to the ground with an "Oof!"

The girl murmured apologies as she helped the fallen figure rise and held her upright. "No reason ter knock yuh over Granny. I'se sorry but I'se in hurry ter fin' Granny Owdoms." Hester brushed dirt and leaves off the old slave and reclaimed Granny's walking stick. It steadied the old woman.

"What you want wid 'er?" Granny asked.

"Got message from Granny Mandy down ter Columbia."

The old woman looked at her suspiciously. "How you git here?"

"Miz Ashley come up ter Greenwood and den on ter Due West ter visit her frens here at de college. I'se her maid. She stay a while."

"You don' know Granny Owdoms?"

"No, an' I need ter see her bad." Hester leaned over and kept her voice low. "It be 'bout two 'scapes. One's a Linckum sojer."

The old pastor was taking his daily walk in the shaded streets. He cut across the neighborhood on common paths when it suited him, an elderly gentleman, widely known. Reverend Watts prayed a lot as he ambled along, prayed for the souls of his wife and his two sons in the soil of Virginia. Absentminded, the villagers called him, overhearing the soliloquies he repeated as he walked, his head bowed, and ignored their greetings. He was taking his usual shortcut through the garden of the manse of the college when he overheard the two Negroes on the other side of the dense lilacs. Curiosity converted him into an eavesdropper.

"Dey's a Linckum sojer loose?" Granny's face was inscrutable. She admitted nothing of her knowledge of the fugitives.

"His name be Shaw, an' Hannibal wid him," the girl replied. "Granny Mandy ask fer Granny Owdoms ter he'p an' I'se got ter tell 'er." Her nervous eyes were unable to be quiet. She glanced about uneasily, while her hands fluttered over her bandanna and her dress. "Miz Ashley be lookin' fer me, 'lessen I hurries back."

"I'se Owdoms. An' I'se heard o' de two 'scapes. Dey gittin' on."

The girl squealed and embraced her, and kissed the wrinkled old cheek. "Oh, Granny. Hannibal, he my man. I jist got ter keep 'im safe."

Pastor Watts had kept his stick and himself motionless through the conversation of the two women. His children dead in the fight for the South, the revelation of escapees nearby assaulted him like a thunderbolt.

He burst through the screening bushes and thrust his cane at them, his red, angry face adding to the menace of the rod. "You ungrateful nigger bitches," he shouted, ignoring all his religious teachings. "An' you, Granny. You're helpin' a damned Yankee to 'scape. A dammed Yankee like the ones that killed my boys!"

Unbridled, unreasoning fury removed his lifelong religious bonds, his teachings to turn the other cheek. He raised his cane against the women but Hester seized it before he could strike. She wrested it from his feeble, shaking hands, and threw it into the bushes, then placed herself between the bent, thin body of the pastor and the slave.

Granny's icy tone bathed Watts. "I done saved yer boys twicet when dey was growin' up. Can't he'p what de Yankees do."

"But do you have to aid a Yankee escape?" Watts plaintive, whining protest hung there between them, a trembling, old man and a defiant woman. "They killed my boys," he cried. Tears trickled down his cheeks and sobs wracked his slight frame.

"De good Lawd says ter he'p thy neighbor." Granny's quiet dignity and scripture penetrated the reverend's grief.

"'An eye for an eye,' also is in the good book," he retorted. "Can't I wish him dead?"

"No!" the old slave thundered.

Granny Owdoms grew in stature as she stiffened her back and straightened herself, stretching up to a full height. Her metamorphosis compelled Hester's attention, the girl's gaze riveted on the striking scene. The old woman's face turned placid. Her composure and peaceful mien were reassuring to Watts. He blew his nose into a large cloth and recovered his stick. But he was attentive to Granny and listened respectfully as she spoke. Her soft voice soothed him.

"I done listened ter yer sermons dese forty years er mo', Reverend. An' I he'ped raise yer boys, an' saved 'em fum de fever." He nodded as she added, "More'n oncet." Her voice sharpened as she sought the scriptures. "You allus say ter 'turn de other cheek,' an' 'ter do unto others as others would do unto you,' an' 'ter fergive.'"

"It's hard, Granny," Watts replied. "My boys are both gone." His tears started again.

"Killin' others don' bring 'em back, Reverend. Forgive de Yankees."

Watts faced her with streaming eyes and a stricken look. He left them to their escape plans and retreated rapidly back up the path.

"I send a boy ter watch 'im," Granny told Hester. "We know if he talk ter de sojers. But I'se tinks he jist prays."

"What about Hannibal and de Yankee?"

"Don' you worry yer head 'bout dem. Tell Granny Mandy I'se gwine see 'em safe on ter freedom."

"Hold up thar!" Minns shouted at the advancing riders.

The hunter cantered toward the small force of Confederate cavalrymen, perhaps a hundred yards away. Walking horses proceeded in single file on the narrow trace, a cut through sentinel pines, tall and denuded of branches except for the thick green tops. Banter assailed them as he and Jared approached, but not a few riders moved their carbines to cover him. The Sergeant leading the detail sawed at his reins and held up his arm. Bunching, the horses stopped at a wide place in the road. Creaking of saddle leather and blowing of the mounts added to the noise. Some troopers shifted in their seats and pointed rifles at the oncoming Minns but a few inattentive others unlimbered canteens.

"Who air ye?" the Sergeant yelled. His challenge to the advancing hunters and his suspicious look were reinforced by his hand undoing the flap on his pistol holster.

"Athey Minns and my son, Jared," the hunter bellowed back. Wet dirt caused by the showers scattered from the hooves striking the road, but dust from a few pockets in the underlying dry ground puffed up slightly around the horses legs. Winds whipped it into the air. Sifting particles added to the already dirty coloration of the men. Minns pulled up his mount in front of the troop.

"So you be Minns," Sergeant Irvine observed, and sat up straighter in his saddle. Rumbles and awed swearing went through the troop at identification of the man hunter. "Don't look 'tall like I pictured yuh from all those tales."

Minns dismissed the respectful glance with a gesture and a grimace. "Don' matter," he said. "Got business with you 'bout some 'scapes. Who'er you?"

"Irvine. We're patrollin' fer 'scapes and Yankees."

Old Blue lay stretched out on some pine needles at the side, his tongue hanging out.

"Purty nice bluetick," a trooper observed. "My Pa got a whole passel jist like 'im. Never give up on a trail."

"A redbone er a black an' tan's better," another argued. "They run the 'tick inter the ground."

The friendly dispute grew louder while Athey took a swig from the Sergeant's canteen. He swished water in his mouth and spat, then swallowed the next gulp before he passed the canteen to Jared. The hunter shifted around and idly surveyed the vehement troopers while the boy drank.

"You got some hunters there, Sergeant," Minns said. He laughed. "But they don' know nothin' 'bout man huntin'."

"Quiet in the ranks," Irvine roared, "so Minns can tell us what they're a'lookin' fer."

"It's a Yankee officer and' his slave Hannibal," Minns announced to the silenced group. "The officer dyed black an' playin' dumb. Has a paper sayin' they's Middleton niggers from down to Cha'leston way."

The Sergeant swore and slapped his hand down hard on his thigh. "I'll be God damned! Those air the ones Captain Starr had when we went through day 'fore yestiday. He showed us the paper. He was laughin' 'bout Middleton trustin' those sneaky bastards."

"They 'scaped from Starr an' are on the road."

"No!" The Sergeant cursed and spat. "I tol' 'im not to trust them niggers."

Restless squeaks came from rigs of the troopers as they shifted about in their seats. Their muttered support for the sergeant and maledictions against the fugitives added to the whine of the wind against the pines.

"Whar you headed?" Minns asked.

"Over to Elberton." Irvine sketched out his mission. "Then up the Savannah an' Tugaloo, watchin' the river crossin's. That bastard Sherman's strikin' out 'roun' 'lanta. We're told to look fer any flankin' raids."

The man hunter spit a brown stream at a stick. His thoughtful eyes returned to the Sergeant's, and his direct, searching gaze compelled Irvine's attention. "Keep yer eye peeled fer them 'scapes as well," he said. "You be crossin' their track somewheres 'long the rivers."

The Sergeant nodded and his troop muttered their

assent. "What you want us to do if we catch those bastards?"

"Hang 'em right off if you don't shoot 'em first." Minns raised up in his stirrups and pulled at a binding crease in his crotch, then shifted around in his saddle until he was satisfied. He spat a brown stream at a pine cone and said, "Oncet ye got 'em, send word to Major Jones at Camp Sorghum down to Columbia."

"We'll do that," the Sergeant replied. He raised his hand, ready for the troop to move out. His men came to attention and tightened their reins.

Minns blocked their way a moment longer. "Let the headquarters at Anderson know," he said. "We be workin' all the north side outen there."

The hunter spurred away at the Sergeant's wave and the two parties separated rapidly. Minns and Jared struck into the well spaced pines, their trackless path to the north aimed at cutting the road to Due West and Belton.

Hester darted into the street, chasing the small girl and her ball. The clearing weather in the late afternoon allowed the children to be out with their games, but each was well swathed against the cool air. Hester shivered in her thin shawl, poor protection against the gusty swirls of the wind. Busy with the children, she took no notice of the two horsemen who entered from a side street, nor the dog that trotted at Minns' side.

Jared gasped and pointed with his rifle barrel. "It's that Hester, Pa! The one from Granny Mandy's cabin."

"Well now, boy," Minns said. Uncertainty creased his face and his scar colored. "Wonder why that nigger wench's way up here?"

His mount turned down the street at his kneeing and small chirk and Old Blue perked up. The two horses plodded on so slowly that the advancing party did not alarm the playing children and their watchful slave girl. Old Blue trotted ahead in his usual search. His weaving took him right and left across the street as the party advanced. But when they neared and the ball bounced ahead of his sniffing nose, he seized it in his mouth and chased about.

Crying children surrounded Hester at Old Blue's intru-

sion. They wailed and ran after the hound and tried to catch
him. Consternation and indecision filled Hester's being.
The girl was torn between her charges and her fear of the
Minnses, their hated faces nigh on top of her. Frozen by
uncertainty, she stood by the side of the street, fixed in place
as a statue. Her paralysis riveted her feet to the ground
while the children fled and the horsemen paused beside
her.

"What you doin' here, nigger?" Minns asked.

When she didn't reply, the hunter walked his horse into
her body. Leaning over, he seized the girl by the bodice and
shook her violently. The cloth tore loose but he had enough
to restrain her. Minns' hiss struck her like a blow as he
repeated his question.

"What you doin' here? Where's them 'scapes?"

Minns' bearded face, with its brown tobacco stains that
descended at each side of his chin, grew even more menacing when she trembled and struggled to escape.

"Lemme go!" she screamed.

Caught up in the excitement of the treeing, Old Blue
circled and barked treed. He rushed toward the panicked
girl and bit her on the leg, then pulled back as he would with
a bear. Hester's screams increased and her struggles grew
more violent. The hunter hoisted her off the ground and
cuffed her into limpness and sobbing submission.

"Take her, Pa!" Jared yelled. His horse pranced around
under his tight rein, skittish from all the commotion. "We git
the truth outen her t'night. She won't say nothin' 'thout no
beatin' and here's not the place."

A door swung open on the porch of the manse. Miz
Ashley hurried across the porch, surrounded by crying
children. The sight of Hester's owner galvanized Minns into
a decision. He dragged the girl across the saddle in front of
him and galloped off, ignoring the protests of the angry
woman hastening down the steps. She and the children
were waving their arms and screaming when he and Jared
turned the corner out of sight, with Old Blue close behind.

CHAPTER 10

Old George

November 10, 1864. Belton, S.C. Tempera-
ture 70\45, cloudy with a slight possibility
of showers, and cool, gusty winds. Moon
just past full, rising about an hour before
dawn.

"John!" Granny Owdoms shook the boy into somno-
lence, then slapped his bottom hard when he
sleepily yawned and mumbled a complaint. "Wake
up, John."

The boy rubbed his eyes as he jumped up from his
pallet. He yawned and stretched, then scratched his crotch
and buttocks as he shuffled over to the hearth. The youth
warmed himself before the smoky fire, his thin pants and
shirt toasting hot against his skin. He held his bare feet up
to the flames, first one, then the other, while his grumbling
continued.

"It col', Granny," John complained. The young boy
rotated about and roasted himself as if on a spit.

The old Negress wrapped her arms around him in a big
hug. "Knows dat a'ready, chile," she said, sympathetically.
"But you got ter go git Hannibal an' Claude. Dey have ter
move on wid George fo' sunup. He be here right quick."

As if she were psychic, clumps could be heard approaching down the path to the cabin.

"Dere's George a'ready. Now git!" Granny pushed the

boy toward the door. He almost collided with George in his scrambling haste to leave the cabin.

A spate of hard running took him to the entrance to the old spring house. He had set the door aside when a hand reached out and seized his throat. Its painful squeeze choked off any sound as he was thrown on his belly and straddled by Hannibal. The servant stuck Jeremy's horn-handled bowie knife against the side of the struggling boy. Its prick and the fugitive's iron grip quickly subdued the small, skinny figure. Clamping his hand over the boy's mouth, Hannibal dragged him into the cavern.

"Who are yuh?" Hannibal whispered, while he and the planter muffled the child's protests and wrestled with his supple, wriggling body.

In answer, John bit Hannibal's fingers. The Negro jerked his hand away from the unrelenting teeth. He swore at the pain and slapped the boy hard in the face, then dipped his injured hand into the cold spring water.

"God damn it!" he growled. "I'se a mind ter beat yuh good! What yer name?""

"Jist John agin," the boy answered. "I brung yuh las' night. Why you hit me like dat?" The fugitives relaxed at his youthful, protesting voice and sniffling, his tears unnoticed in the darkness. Their figures were dim blobs that coalesced into a tight group in the blackness of the cavern.

Hannibal's deep rumble quietly reproached the boy. "It's so dark, you come sneakin' up on us an' we mebbe kills yuh. You allus wanta give some kind of call, child. Now what yuh want?"

"Come ter fetch yuh. George 'bout ready ter start up de road wid de wagon."

Their passage to Granny's cabin was marked by dripping trees. Prodded by wind, wet twigs and leaves shed the last vestiges of the showers during the night. No stars could be seen and the rising moon of their previous night's travel was invisible. The windy weather brought gusts and clashing tree branches, and the dark and noise effectively masked their hurrying figures. Claude shivered in his coat and wondered if anyone were about. His thoughts and pity shifted to the helpful boy. How the lightly clad John could keep warm, he didn't know. Only a shirt and pants clothed the youth, both torn in the struggle with the fugitives. The thought bothered him, another wound that nagged at his conscience and his recollections of his slaves at Greenbottom.

An open door at the cabin and welcoming firelight erased his unsettling doubts and the smell of hot bacon awakened his hunger. His stomach growled and cramped at the invitation. Sizzling sounds came from the hearth; overpowering odors drew them right to the fire. Granny welcomed the fugitives with a smile, her round cheeks and ample girth the beneficiary of countless strips of fatback. Spearing the strips of hot bacon with a metal rod, she dished up a shingle of the savory meat for each and topped it with a huge piece of johnnycake.

"Recken youse mighty hungry," she said, "atter a day in de springhouse."

"Sho' am," Hannibal replied. His annoyance exploded in his complaint. "Dat place mighty tryin', waitin' in de dark."

"It safe," was Granny's sharp rejoinder.

Her spear hovered over the sizzling meat, ready to add to their ration. Silent, the fugitives' dripping fingers and greasy lips were busy with the hot food. More pieces appeared on their trenchers as they wolfed down each helping and stuffed themselves until they were satisfied. Claude set aside his platter when he was full and started to thank the old woman but his words were cut off by an uncontrollable urge to belch. He covered his mouth in embarrassment as the rumbles bubbled up. Granny grinned broadly at his repeated eruptions.

"Liked it, did yer?"

"Sho' did, Granny," Claude said, and walked over to the water bucket. Dipping water after Claude had drunk, Hannibal complimented the old woman. "Dat mighty satisfyin', Granny. Any extry ter take wid us?"

"'bout used up all we git dis week. Ol' Massa purty mean 'bout de bacon and corn he pass out. Give a body lots o' sweet taters ter fill de belly."

Her laconic reply was accompanied by two boiled sweet potatoes to each man, stowed in their pockets for the future.

"You kin tek as many o' my wagon load as you kin tote," George added. "Dey's plenty and' de old massa don' miss 'em."

Claude hugged Granny and the boy after Hannibal's brief goodbye. The planter's last sight of them was of Granny's pleasant face and John chewing on his bacon strip.

George led the two to the wagon by a circuitous route. Black had given way to a gray, dripping dawn when they reached the back of the barn and climbed aboard the farm wagon. A trench left in the load was their resting place for the day, a confinement and restraint anticipated by a long drink at the cow trough and a visit to the bushes.

"Keep real quiet," George cautioned, when they again reboarded. "I stop dar at de big thicket 'bove de shoals, atter noonin'. You kin git 'roun' Belton easy fum dere. Granny a'ready sen' word fer Gabe ter be a'watchin' fer us, an' ter he'p yuh." He motioned toward the hole. "Inter de taters."

Once they were flat on the wagon bed he fitted some broad boards crosswise into notches in the sides. Claude inspected the coffin arrangement, his soul rebelling at the imprisonment. But the worn enclosure with its battered planks gave silent evidence to earlier, successful escapes. The strong cover would protect against the weight of the load and still leave him air to breathe. The fugitives submitted and lay quietly while the old Negro completed the camouflage. George shoveled potatoes from the great pile in the barn and mounded up an immense load above them, sealing them in. Splits and joints in the wood of the wagon gave them ventilation, but the dry dirt coating the tubers sifted down into the air and their clothes and added to their discomfort. Tickling dust forced a loud sneeze from the planter, an outburst that drew an instant admonition from George.

"Hesh! Don' mek no thumpin' er talkin'."

Creaks and groans from the wagon protested the heavy load when George drove from the barn. The fugitives could see the roadbed in the early morning light, their view restricted to the cracks in the flooring. Their bodies shuffled and jostled from side to side as the ruts passed. But they were helpless to assist George or to resist a challenge, their success dependent completely on George's shrewdness, and Granny's ingenuity.

"You understand your orders, Redding?"

"Yes sir, Colonel." Redding reeled off Colonel Hyatte's instructions. "Patrol to the East around Belton and on over to Simpson's ford. Then circle down to the lower ford, check the railroad, catch any escapees and deserters. Stay out four days and return all prisoners here."

Colonel Hyatte looked at the erect, young officer with a fatherly gaze, one reserved for the inexperienced. He added another piece of advice for the recently arrived boy, a youth turned prematurely into a man.

"Remember, Lieutenant, all those people are treacherous. Don't trust anything they say and keep 'em ironed. They'll kill you if they can."

"Yes sir!"

"Get movin', Lieutenant. Take ten men and Sergeant Gill. If that old scamp can't keep you all alive nobody can. He's been in a passel of skirmishes."

Saluting smartly, Redding rotated on his heel and strode away from the headquarters tent. It was separated from the long lines of the several camp streets of the militia stationed at Anderson. His saber flopped about his slender legs until he grasped it firmly, unused as he was to the weapon. The lounging Colonel pulled on his cigar and wafted smoke up toward the heavens. His aide drew close and commiserated with him when the senior officer sighed and his face saddened.

"Get younger every year, Colonel," the aide said.

"Yes, Rob, an' it's a pity. Redding's just sixteen, but he would come when his brother was killed. My cousin Nancy'll never forgive me if he's lost too." Hyatte shook his head in gloomy defeat, fatigue lines aging his youthful visage. He slapped his gloves against his leg to remove the dust, and his bitterness and resignation boiled over. "God damn it, Rob! We're killing all our good, young men with this damned war. It's time it's over."

"Can't say as I don't agree, Colonel, but Hood said to

keep on after the Yankees while he circled west and went into Tennessee. Hardee ordered the same. Guess we'll see some o' Sherman's boys soon."

Hyatte nodded absentmindedly. In mournful silence, he took one last, sad look toward the diminishing figure of Redding, now down at the picket line in the trees. Then his shoulders straightened up and he was again the soldier. He threw away the remnant of the cigar and turned for the tent.

"Well, lets get at that plannin'," he said, "to see how we can fox 'em if any come by."

Hester crawled to the bucket at the side of the hearth and took a dipper of water. Her greedy swallows were followed by a dash into her face and onto her head. She shivered when the cool water dripped down onto her crouched, naked body. Nearby the Minnses slept, the older man on the one bed of the slave cabin and Jared on the floor. Old Blue raised his head at the commotion and went over toward the fire, then pointed her like a bird. His suspicion showed in his rigid body and straightened tail. The dog's snuffling and low bark awakened Athey.

"Whar you goin'?" Minns asked. The hunter bounded out of bed and seized her arm, twisting it to one side. His tawny, coppery-brown body and corded muscles contrasted to the smooth, darker brown of the lissome girl. Lasciviousness and desire led to a sliding of his free hand over her rounded buttocks.

The girl wailed and pulled away against his restraining grasp. "Don' you hurt me no more," she begged. Hester wiggled about and tried to evade his nakedness, but was jerked remorselessly toward his aroused body. "You done beat me 'nough. I ain't got nothin' ter tell yuh."

"It ain't that I be a'wantin' right now." Athey threw her down on the bed and fell on her while Jared, awakened from his sleep, padded out the door.

Jared's naked body mirrored his father's boney, rangy build, but was shining white in the light when he returned to the cabin and warmed himself before the fire. He tossed on a couple of billets of dry oak and watched impassively as his father wrestled with the frantic girl.

Hester's cries grew strident, ascending to a scream as Athey clubbed her in the face. Repeated blows subdued her struggles and he violently consummated the forceful joining. When he flung himself off her, breathing hard, her conquered body lay and trembled, and her sobs gave way to a pitiful whimpering.

"You done, Pa?" Jared asked. "Kin I take 'nother turn at her? She's purty good."

When his father nodded and walked toward the fire, the husky boy covered the girl quickly. His coupling with the unresisting body proceeded apace. The conquered, whimpering girl was unable to resist either his blows or his thrusts.

The two hunters donned their buckskins quickly after the violations and gathered at the fire to roast a few strips of meat reclaimed from their saddlebags. A length of jerky occupied Old Blue as they ate and contemplated the now unconscious girl.

"What'er we goin'a do with 'er, Pa?" Jared said.

"Take 'er to the woods with us an' try agin," Minns replied. "If a little more beatin' won't fetch her 'round, we leave 'er there. Weather purty cold. She'll die quick."

"Her face's awful swole an' bloody now, Pa. An' she can't talk lyin' there plumb out o' her head. Why not jest leave 'er here?"

"Don' want those niggers to find her, the ones we throwed outen the cabin. They might bring her 'round. I don' want that."

The two hunters left the outskirts of Due West in the raw, damp cold of the early morning. Completely unconscious, Hester dangled over Minns' saddle, her nude body hanging limply on each side. Blows from the western style saddle horn added to her injuries as Minns galloped his horse along the road to Anderson. Five miles into the forest, the two veered far off the trail into a dense tangle of brush and overturned trees. Minns slid Hester down from the saddle and threw her limp body into an old stump hole, well hidden from the casual hunter. He tossed a few pieces of dead limbs over the opening, ill-covering for the inert girl.

"Ain't nobody ever find her," he told Jared, as he

remounted his horse. "Time to ride on to Anderson. See if the Army's heard any news o' them bastards."

Morning had progressed on toward noon and they were miles up the trail when a driving rainshower hit the area. Its cold water pelted down on the brown body. A shudder ran through Hester's muscles at the chill and her head raised slowly from the mud of the bank. She shook her head from side to side and moaned softly but the effort exhausted her and she sank back down into the mud. Continuing cold raindrops shocked her into revival, consciousness revealing her desperate straits. "Got ter git outen dishere hole," she mumbled. Sliding her hand slowly up the bank, she seized a small root and pulled with all of her faint strength. Her will to live forced her body to inch upward as she began her slow crawl to deliverance.

Escaped slaves had a camp in the big thicket on the Saluda River southeast of Belton. It flourished in the heavy growth that extended to the confluences of Broadmouth Creek and other tributaries with the river. Projecting into the peninsula the Saluda formed with the Reedy River, the thicket provided succor, a place to hide. A floating population of men, from light sons of planters to the coal black of African origin, fled first into, then out of camp, as the slave holders harassed them over the years. The slave labor force at the railroad junction at Belton protected the runaways, diverted food, and served as lookouts, and provided warning of raids. Though the camp's general whereabouts was known, the thicket along the river prevented the owners from driving the area with horses. Dogs could penetrate but the thought of going in afoot alienated the softer planters. Better to leave slave hunting to people like Athey Minns and their dogs. Occasionally a slave was retaken, with harsh penalties of flogging and ironing, but these captures were mostly from the edge of the hideaway.

The war had brought an increasing population to the thicket and some weapons. A regular traffic of escapees passed through to the federal forces. Union troops put the men to work at pay, a welcome contrast to the subservient role of the beleaguered slaves on plantations, so many sought sanctuary.

Austin had arrived at the river the day before, a man child from Granny Owdoms, a messenger seeking Gabe. His marathon run from Due West had taken the back paths through the woods, and had avoided and evaded the Confederate militia blockades and patrols. Coursing up the river from his first striking, he sought the camp until dark, but was forced finally to seek shelter for the night. He was shivering when he went to ground under thick brush, little protection from the chilling winds. Austin ate his sweet potatoes quickly, then covered himself with broken off pine fronds. Sleepless as the long blackness passed, the youth suffered the cold shower of the early morning.

He had just sallied from his hideout when a shadow leaped at him from behind. Gripped tight and held off the ground, his kicking incited punishing cuffs and curses from his captor. An arm choked off his rising scream.

"Who be yuh, boy?" The low growl brought on renewed kicking from the pinioned youth.

Austin could only gurgle as he strangled under the choke hold. Shaking him, his captor slacked the vise of his arms but still clasped the boy and prevented him from turning around. Austin was flailing about without success when an enormous black man stepped in front of the struggling pair and held a long bowie blade up to the boy's throat.

"Who be yuh? Ain't seed yer a'fo' in dese parts."

His threat scared the boy into rigidity. Austin's eyes followed the knife as it moved in and out, only answering when the question was repeated, this time in a more threatening tone.

"I'se Austin," he gasped. "Got message fer Gabe."

"What's it say, boy?

"Granny Owdoms tol' me ter tell only Gabe," the boy retorted, angrily. He renewed his struggling against the bearhug. "Now mek 'im put me down!"

Granny's name electrified the pair. The other man instantly cast Austin away and stepped back. With the confining arms gone, the boy whirled around and raised his fist. His blow halted in midair and he retreated a half-step at the sight of a short, but immensely bulky man, one with a light, tan complexion and the hooked, aquiline nose of a white man. His long, reddish hair was wavy at the sides, with the top hair drawn back tightly against his skull and fastened at the neck with a thong. But it was his distinctive, chiseled features that held Austin's attention. A sharp gasp exploded from the boy's open mouth.

"You looks jist like Massa Moss!"

"You's right, boy!" The man chortled and slapped Austin's shoulder lightly. "He my pappy." His laugh faded into a suspicious frown. "Where you see him? He from way down de ribber."

"Brung his boy ter de college at Due West last year an' was dere mo' later. 'member his hook nose and red hair."

"Dat my pappy an' brother, awright," the man bellowed. His sides shook with laughter. "But dey don' want me. I looks too much like dem. Ol' Missus make 'im sell me." The man's jollity as he heehawed infected the other two, their chuckling adding to the uproar.

"Need ter see Gabe," Austin reminded them, when the din subsided.

"I'se Gabe," the giant replied. "Dishere's my fren Rufus. Now what Granny want?"

Gabe's face turned serious and his mouth compressed into a crease. Rufus drew near, his banter replaced by a tight grasp on the boy's arm and his head in close. Austin recited Granny's instructions in a low voice that would not carry, while the others paid close attention.

"George be bringin' a Yankee officer thoo t'day in de tater wagon. He Claude. An' a 'scape he'pin' 'im named Hannibal. Gwine let 'em off at de regular place. Granny says you's ter send word ter Granny Esther at Calhoun's an' ter he'p 'em git 'round Belton an' over ter Esther."

"Yankee, huh?" Perplexity wrinkled Gabe's face. "How we hide his white skin?"

"Granny Mandy down ter Columbia done shaved him bare an' dyed 'im black wid walnut stain. Got ol' clo'es. He look jist like you an' me, Granny says."

"No!" Gabe exploded, then began chuckling.

Rufus laughed and clapped his hands together. His

roaring merriment rang through the forest. "We got us a white nigger, Gabe," he chortled. "Wonder how dat Yankee feel ter be a nigger?"

Nooning allowed a blow for the horses and rest for the men. Claude welcomed the relief from the battering of the lurching wagon, its motion stilled while the team picked a little grass from the side of the trail. But Hannibal cursed the long wait in the fugitives' tight hiding place. His quiet grumbling didn't seem to bother Old George, Claude thought bitterly. The driver rested a spell, talking aloud to his team as he ate his lunch. His raspy, coarse voice carried easily to the prisoners hidden under the load of potatoes.

"'nother ten mile ter de thicket, old hawse. Git plenty grass. Ain't no more stop short o' dar an' de creek crossin' a'fo' Belton."

He walked into the woods after a brief nap. Jingling of harness bells announced the old Negro's return as he slowly went along the rig and checked the leathers, rings and pins. The wagon shook when he climbed aboard and settled into his seat. George released the protesting brake and slapped the reins on the horses' backs. "Giddap!" he shouted. He chirked in encouragement as the animals strained against the harness and the wagon groaned its protests.

"Hold on thar!" a hoarse voice called out, intimidating in its intensity.

George sawed on the reins at the loud command and shouted "Whoa," to the horses. As the wagon lurched to a halt, a few potatoes plumped to the ground from the shaking of the sudden stop.

Running feet slapped down on the cemented earth of the nooning site, their thumps drawing nearer to the wagon. Only three or four men, Claude concluded. His heart beat rapidly and a fear chill caused a shudder. He forced his eye closer to the cracks in the wagon bed to stretch his limited view of the ground, but could see only one set of legs on his side. Hannibal pressed twice on his arm, his slit exposing the men on the other side. The two fugitives lay utterly silent and still while George's wits jousted with the three men.

"Whar you goin', you no-good nigger?" their challenger

asked. His insulting epithet was followed by a brown stream, spat into Claude's view.

"Yassah, Massa, yassah. Jist takin' dese taters ter de Army up ter Anderson. Dey from Massa Donald down by Due West. Ain't meanin' no harm, Massa. Dey Army taters."

The wagon rocked from the bowing and subservient motions that George was making with his body.

"Well, we be Army too, nigger. Recken we're due some o' them taters."

"Iffen you says so, Massa, you tek any taters you wants. I jist tote de rest ter de Army like Massa tol' me."

Deserters, Claude concluded. The dregs wandering on the edge of the war now that the Johnnies were about licked. Looking for whatever they could steal. He felt for his derringer and knife, and silently readied each. He could feel Hannibal slowly ease his bowie out of its sheath.

The men joked while they went along the wagon and selected potatoes, carelessly spilling others over the sideboards. Soon overloaded, they ignored the potatoes on the ground and left them to George to recover.

"You git plenty, Yancey?" another man asked the spokesman.

"Sack's purty heavy fer totin', I recken," Yancey replied. "But I'll jest take another bayonet full fer good measure.'

"God damn it Yancey, you allus was a hog."

"Recken ain't much chance ter get good feeds like these," Yancey loudly countered.

His companion's laugh receded as he headed for the trees with the third man. Yancey's shout rang out after them. "Best you take more. They's good taters."

The two ignored him, their laughter following his saunter along the wagon bed. Reaching the rear wheel, he stepped up on a spoke and balanced himself. Once set, he thrust his rifle toward the mound. Its bayonet penetrated a long file of potatoes until the blade was covered to the muzzle of the barrel.

Claude felt the sting when the point tore through his pants and stuck him in the right calf. He could not help the little jerk of agony from the sudden hurt, but his fear forced his leg back into rigidity as the flame of the wound pinking him coursed through his body. He wondered at the man with the bayonet, so close to compelling them to fight, a contest with them at great disadvantage.

George had shifted on the wagon seat and wrapped the reins around the brake handle when Yancey moved. He stood up and watched the outlaw closely while the man stepped on the wheel spokes and balanced himself against the side rail. The slave was shuffling his feet and prying on the brake lever when the bayonet thrust came, his rocking motion sending tremors through the wagon bed. The slight swaying covered any start by the fugitives that would have alerted the reb. George's shifting weight made the old wagon bed shake and creak in protest as he continued his diversion with the reins and brake.

"You got 'nough?" he asked.

"Plenty," Yancey replied. "Soon's I step down, pick up all them loose ones, then git on 'long the trail."

Yancey pried his bayonet up out of the mound and jumped back to the ground. He whistled and waved to his friends, then picked up his sack and marched off with his rifle shouldered, parading its potato trophy. Ribald, derisive comments greeted him when he rejoined his companions. But each took a potato when Yancey offered his bayonet booty. The outlaws were peeling the potatoes when they disappeared into the forest.

Once their sounds faded, George hopped off the wagon in agile steps that belied his appearance of disability. He scurried about, picking up the fallen potatoes and tossing them onto the load. All during his scavenging, he talked aloud as if to himself, and issued instructions to the travelers.

"Keep quiet 'bout dis. We be on de road ter de thicket directly an' stop dar."

He was after some potatoes under the wagon when the red drops struck him on his hand. Continuing to toss potatoes from under the wagon, he spoke directly to the cracks.

"Youse awright, Hannibal?"

"Claude got stuck in de leg. Bleedin' real good. I'se he'pin' him wid de wrappin's. He gonna need doctorin'."

"Can't stop a'fo' de thicket. Have Gabe dere ter he'p 'im. We go fast as dishere ol' wore out team travel."

Ignoring the rest of the fallen potatoes, George mounted the wagon seat and started the team. He spurred on the horses with a stream of profanity and his whip. The oxhide's snap as the frayed end cracked at the horses's ears did little and the heavy load kept their progress to a fast walk.

No one was waiting at the thicket when George stopped the team. It was coming on dusk when he pulled off the road, the daylight closed down early from the lowering clouds. A great clump of small trees and honeysuckle at the edge hid the wagon from any passersby. Their progress had been slow, what with the heavy rutting of the softened road and the mounded load. The tired animals blew and switched their tails as they rested. George hopped down from the seat and moved along the bed to the rear wheels. He was up on the back part of the load in an instant and threw off enough potatoes that the fugitives could crawl out of the gash in the mound.

Two exceedingly dirty figures emerged, their clothes and heads covered with the earth from the potatoes. In the half light, streaked by a slight drizzle of mist, they resembled their background, forest animals fleeing from the hunter. Claude hobbled about and favored his leg as he stretched.

"You awright, Claude?" George asked.

Claude grunted and nodded assent. He brushed off the loose dirt and shook himself like a dog. Dust cascaded from his clothes, then the hat as he beat it against his thigh. George bent to check the bandage on the planter's leg when Claude sat down on a nearby log, then rebound it with a gob of tobacco from his quid. The old slave's face bore a troubled frown when he finished.

"Bad cut," he said, gloomily, "but de 'baccy he'p."

Hannibal reassured the wagoneer. "He be awright, George. Cut bled out good."

The big Negro took the time to clean off the two rifles and check their locks. Satisfied at last, he leaned the weapons against the log and covered the locks and muzzles against the mist.

After a bit, George looked about, his unease evident. "Don' know where Gabe be. He been 'roun' here ever'time a'fo'."

"We in de right place?" Hannibal asked.

"Rightchere ever'time." George pointed to a slight break in the bushes on the down slope. "De ribber over dere 'bout mile er so an' de deer go right thoo dar. Gabe allus come like de deer."

"Mebbe he got took?" Hannibal's question hung between them for a moment until the wagoneer shook his head in disagreement.

"Nobody ketch Gabe." George's pride and confidence strengthened the timbre of his voice. "Gabe knows de woods jist like de deers. Not even Minns ketch him an' Minns try ha'd 'bout two year back."

Hannibal's questions continued while Claude listened from his seat on the log. "Minns chased Gabe?"

"Sho' did," George said. He chuckled as he recalled Minns' failure. "His Massa had Minns up wid 'is dogs. But dey nebber ketch Gabe. Mek ol' Minns mad. Nebber seed a man cuss so loud when he come by my Massa's."

"Gabe livin' here since?"

"He stay in de thicket ter he'p 'scapes. Got Rufus wid him too. Dey strong. An' dey kills ter pertec' yuh."

Waiting finally became unendurable for the fugitives. Their seats on the log gave way to pacing and frequent peeks toward the road. Hannibal's decision was not long in coming.

"Got ter go, George. Git ketched, we stay here."

Hannibal sorted through his sack in preparation for leaving and checked the strap. The boiled potatoes had long since been gulped down, along with a swig from the wagoneer's hidden whiskey flask. George brought over a large armload of potatoes from the wagon. The old man burdened down their sacks to overflowing.

"Some fer Gabe," he said, when they protested at the amount.

Hannibal's possibles sack bulged with bumps when he picked it up and hefted the weight, then swung it easily into place with the strap. He tapped George on the shoulder. "If we be goin' inter de brakes," he said, "how we find Gabe?"

George was watching Claude instead. The planter's pained face twisted in agony when he shouldered his sack. He stood mostly on one foot and leaned heavily on his rifle. The slave knelt and rechecked the chaw against the wound. His rough tightening forced a groan from the fugitive. Claude jerked his leg away and hobbled to the side.

The wagoneer grimaced and shook his head in dismay. "Git Claude ter Gabe soon as you kin, Hannibal. He know de roots fer de tonic 'gainst de blood pison."

"I do dat. Where we run now?"

"Tek de trail ter de ribber an' move up 'long it. 'bout mile nawth, dey's a dugout cave at de big downed poplar. It hid under de top. Gabe fin' you dar if I don' ketch 'im fust."

With a wave of farewell the two cut into the forest, the deer trail easy to follow. Claude limped at the rear, his rifle trailed to avoid the bushes. He thrust the stock against the ground now and then to support him through a tough place. Dense growth along the river was penetrated by a well defined trail. It wove through the tangle, the bushes closing above at times, forming a tunnel where the fugitives occasionally had to bend over or crawl. Well matted with duff, the path left no sign of their passage.

Only a dog could put us out, Claude thought, as he crawled through one narrow bend. The river gurgled at the side, its water invisible in the increasing darkness. But the poplar was easy to identify when they came to it. A bush over the cave entrance hid them when it was pulled back into place after their entry.

"Good place here, Claude," Hannibal observed, invisible in the dark. "Some tow sacks layin' in de back ter cover wid."

Claude's leg was swelled around the wound and fiery to the touch when he felt of it and the pain ran up to his thigh. A thirst consumed him and the leg's heat added to his discomfort. Foreboding overcame fear and drove him from the cave, his exit protested by the servant.

"Stay here, Claude! Gabe fin' us."

Claude brushed away Hannibal's restraining hand. "I

got to go to the river," he insisted. "This wound needs to be washed off. And I'm burning up."

The two eased down the bank to the water once the path had been passed. Removing the bandage and saving the chaw, Claude stuck his leg in the cold water. Its cooling balm rapidly eased the pain. He washed the wound with care, turning out the edges to remove dirt. With the leg clean and well soaked, he bound the poultice tight and trusted once again to the curing power of the tobacco. A full belly of potatoes and cold water readied him for the night in the cave.

Hannibal shivered as they climbed the bank. "Gonna be cold, Claude," he said.

The planter sniffed the wind and clutched his coat tighter about him. "Probably sleet or snow the way things feel. Damp. But not freezin' yet."

The cave's inviting recess was warm compared to the chill of the night and the cold, dank breeze that blew along the river. They huddled together with the sacks over them, waiting on Gabe.

CHAPTER 11

Aunty Emma

November 11, 1864. Belton, S.C. Tempera-
ture 63\32, possible sleet or light snow in
early morning, followed by clearing and
cold. Northwest winds to 15 knots. Moon
rising just before dawn, no moon at night.

Her knees crusted over with dirt and dried blood, Hester crept from under the pile of leaves she had amassed to protect her during the raw, stormy night. Glinting skim ice edged the puddles around her. The crisped, outer leaves covering the massive mound where she had denned up, first soggy from the night's mists, then frozen into thin sheets, crackled and tinkled as they were thrown off and shattered. The whole world about her glistened in the sunrise of the new day, limbs and remnant, hanging leaves glazed with a gleaming curtain of ice. A white forest of spectral arms reached for the sky, beautiful, but an icebox of danger to her nude body. She shivered and hugged herself and ran her hands over her quivering skin, its surface a dirty mess from her half-conscious crawl of the previous day. Swinging her arms for warmth, she labored up the gentle, wooded slope and headed away from the sun.

"Got ter fin' a road an' git he'p," she sobbed.

Hester's cry came out involuntarily as she grasped saplings and bushes to help her in her staggering travel. Her face swollen from the beatings and half frozen from the cold, she almost fell into a small, brushy ravine, headed by a small spring and pool. Kneeling, she bathed her face, but flinched at the shock of the cold liquid. The girl persisted, groaning and wincing when the freezing water struck. A slow flushing cleaned off the mud and dirt coating her body and her knees, a purification that recreated the graceful, though damaged, goddess of before. When she stood, clean and awake, she headed west at a run.

The sun was well up when a road appeared from nowhere. Her leap from the concealing bushes took her into a trace with many prints of wagon wheels and hooves. Hester paused in fear, her head raised, sniffing like a hunted buck. An odor of wood smoke hung in the air, carried to her on the morning breeze, but no cabins were visible. The cotton fields to the west were barren, stripped of their bolls, but the dried up stalks were still decorated with small white tufts. While she listened, the blows of a axe resounded to the north. Running down the road a short way, the girl saw a double cabin with a dog trot. The low structure sat back in the trees, shielded from the dust of the road by its separation. To one side was a frozen garden with killed plants and a few rows of green turnip tops. It was bordered by a pole barn and corral that fronted the working space behind the house. A tall, wiry axman hacked energetically as she warily approached, keeping to the cover until nearby. He grunted as the axe rose and fell. The farmer was splitting billets of wood on top of the block and tossing them onto a growing pile. Smoke trailed from the cabin chimney, its sharp, biting odor and sinuous curls a beacon to the half-frozen, shivering girl.

But Hester eased around the opening in the forest instead of rushing in to seek the warmth of the hearth, an injured animal suspicious of the settler, unwilling to face another danger.

"Sho' he's one o' dem po' whites," she muttered, while he finished cleaving a small billet. "Can't tell if he's got a woman er not."

She was about to accost the man when he set the axe into the block. The farmer picked up an armload of wood chunks and went toward the cabin. A woman's voice berated him as he knocked his feet on the doorjamb to remove dirt before entering. After the door slammed, the fretful squall of a small child added to the crescendo within.

"Halloo de house! Halloo de house!" Hester's loud cry when she ran for the step was followed by scuffling sounds inside the cabin. Its plank door opened quickly, a shotgun barrel preceding the face of the man. His contorted frown deepened when the naked girl stopped before him. Sudden fright rooted her feet to the ground as she inspected the injured face, its left side wrecked by a massive scar. Shivering need won out over panic. "He'p me," she pleaded. "I'se freezin'."

His jaw dropped in amazement as she waited, his gaping mouth an open cave of silence. Irritated complaints inside the cabin were followed by a fat, youthful face that appeared over his shoulder. The woman stuck out her head and craned her neck for a better view, her blonde hair flying in the breeze. But to the girl's dismay, she simply stared in surprise. Their frozen silence was broken by another, weaker whimper from Hester. "He'p me! I'se freezin'!"

At the girl's piteous cry, the buxom woman pushed the man aside and drew Hester into the cabin, taking her right to the fireplace. "You poor thing," she murmured. She enfolded the naked, shivering body in her arms and pushed it closer to the fire. The girl sobbed, finally breaking down, her weeping face next to the warm bosom. The housewife wrapped Hester in the shawl about her shoulders and called to the man, "Pete! Get my other dress from the peg."

"Now Gert, you don' want to give 'er yer dress."

His protest cowed by her spouting mouth, he brought the woolen garment to the pair. Gert slapped his face when he leered at Hester's rounded, smooth figure.

"Git, Pete," she said hotly. Furious with his lecherous glances, she shoved him away. "You jest turn around. The girl's hurt an' don' need no man droolin' over 'er."

"Ain't seed nothin' so purty in a long time, Gert. She's a wonder to look on."

"Well she's done got enough o' men right now. You kin see somebody beat 'er bad." Her scorn heaped ashes on the head of Pete and men who maltreated women.

"You men kin take purty girls like this an' pleasure with 'em any time you want. It jest ain't right." She looked at him sharply, resentful of his attention to the girl. "You got me an' don' need no other. I don' hear no frettin' 'bout yer bed, so you leave this girl alone. She don' need no more trouble."

A fast shift and the dress went on over Hester's head and settled on her shoulders. Its voluminous bulk hung like a tent on the slenderer recipient. Her benefactor drew in the waist with a bright, braided belt, a cinch whose color added to the flowers embroidered on the cotton at the bosom and hemline. Gert drew back the girl's long hair and added a rawhide thong at the back, completing a rapid conversion.

"Lawd, child," the woman said, as she clucked away in sympathy. "You'd be right purty if you warn't so beat up. Who done it?"

"Them Minns," Hester spat out contemptuously. "Den lef' me fer dead."

"The man hunters?" Pete asked. "They 'round here?"

Hester nodded. Her mouth worked but nothing but sobs emerged to accompany the tears trickling down her cheeks.

Pete's excitement and curiosity propelled him back to Hester's side. His rough hand brushed his wife away despite her vehement protests. He seized the slave's arm and pulled her close. She shrank back, her face mirroring her terror. Hester was unable to escape the grasp and the questioning face, and was unready for more inquisition.

The housewife beat on his back repeatedly with her fist. "Leave 'er be, Pete!" she shouted.

But the man, intent, paid no attention to the blows. A sudden wail from the infant called Gert to a swinging bundle. Picking up the baby, she walked and rocked it and crooned a lullaby.

Pete had Hester cornered at the rock wall of the fireplace, her body pressed tightly against the stones. "Whose nigger are yuh?" he asked.

"Miz Ashley Pickens, from down ter Columbia, at de college." The girl broke into sobs as her eyes overflowed and streams cascaded down her bruised cheeks.

Pete let go of her as if he had seized a hot iron. He

backed up a step, his next question much more respectful.

"She the wife of Captain Pickens, the one that led the charge at Chattanooga?"

Hester nodded, her eyes gushing tears. "He's up in Virginny jist now."

"He he'ped yuh when you was shot, Pete." Gert's quiet interjection carried the weight of authority and added to the man's pause.

"Yer right," he replied. "An' I'll he'p him now. I'll take 'er back."

He turned to the girl and asked, "You got a name?"

"Hester," she replied.

"Where was yuh took?"

"Due West. Miz Ashley visitin' her kin dere. Heard dose Minns was huntin' some 'scapes. Dey run onter me in de street whilst I'se wid de chil'ren. Took me an' pleasured demselves all dey wanted." Hester left out her complicity in the escape of the fugitives. Her tears and sobs riveted the poor whites' attention. "Dey thowed me in a mudhole in de woods when I'se 'bout dead." Sobbing and tearful, her choked voice added, "Dey left me dere ter freeze."

Gert fussed all during the recital, muttering threats and curses against the Minnses and men in general. She put down the infant and comforted the girl again, then left Hester at the fire while she searched through a wardrobe at the back of the room. Her energetic ministrations turned up two pieces of deerskin, adequate for makeshift moccasins when she bound them around Hester's feet. The shawl over the girl's head and shoulders completed a defense against the cold and equipped her to leave.

Gert nudged her husband after a close inspection. "Hitch up yer team, Pete," she said forcefully. "This girl ain't goin'a walk to Due West, not in this freeze."

Under his wife's urging, Pete headed outside. He harnessed and led his team out of the pole barn in short order. The horses' breath steamed in the cold, morning air but they worked willingly even as they shivered. It took only a few minutes for Pete to move the wagon to a stop by the cabin and to re-enter. At the cold blast of air, Gert started Hester for the door, but the girl delayed and looked longingly at the johnnycake on the pan at the hearth.

Gert struck her forehead with her hand. "Laws a' me," she said. "I clean fergot. You ain't had nothin' to eat, have yuh?"

"Not since day fo' yestiday," Hester answered. "A piece o' dat pone would be powerful welcome."

Gert handed Hester a gourd dish to carry the aromatic food, then broke off a good bait of corncake and tossed on some bacon. The girl was gnawing at a strip of meat when the kindly woman helped her climb up to the wagon seat, her gourd carefully protected. Gert waited at the front wheel while Pete checked the harness. The vehicle rocked when he climbed aboard and settled into the seat. Releasing the brake, he took up the reins for the double team.

"Hold a minute, Pete," Gert said. Hester stared down at the woman and continued on the food while Gert paused uncertainly. Only the girl's chewing and horse sounds intruded until Gert's face set and she added, humbly, "If it ain't too much to ask, Hester, send the clothes back with Pete."

"I'll do dat, Miz Gert, an' I'se grateful fer de he'p." Hester's words came out of a stuffed mouth, her hunger exceeding her humility and thanks. "An' I tells Granny Owdoms 'bout yer kindness. She have de men try ter he'p yer man if dey kin." She bent over and whispered so Pete could not hear. "On de sly, you unnerstan', so de Massa don' fin' out."

Gert smiled at the conspirator and nodded. She waited in the breezy morning as they drove away, her blonde hair still loose and blowing in the wind. The farm wife's exuberance knew no bounds when she threw her arms wide and danced a jig, then whooped with joy. "That girl was a godsend!" Gert hugged herself in jubilation as she shouted out more good news. "If the slaves help us, maybe we kin git enough to buy that big Chapman piece." Chuckling after her lonely soliloquy, the lucky absurdity tickled her into laughter until the tears came. "All these years we been trying," she sobbed, "and it was those Godawful Minns that done it."

The five miles to Due West passed quickly for the

travelers. Sight of Hester's bruised face brought tears to
Granny Owdoms' eyes, followed by a grim tightness about
her jaw, her anger evidenced by her tense body and silent
ministrations. Miz Ashley, notified of the girl's return,
visited the slave cabin in shocked silence. Her face paled
and her body went rigid at the story of the Minnses'
brutality. Only a single comment came from her drawn face
and tightened lips when she faced the fact of the injury to
Hester's person, and the violation to her right of ownership
and the services of her maid.

"I'll have Captain Pickens speak to Minns." Its crisp
message and her bearing presaged ill for the man hunter.
Her face softened when she patted the girl's head. "Granny'll
make you well. Come back to me tomorrow."

Pete waited before the crackling fire and warmed himself before facing the return trip. His rough clothes contrasted to those of the well-dressed woman and he kept
himself in the background, not uttering a word. But his
isolation was not to be as she sought him out.

"You and your wife helped Hester?"

"Yessum, Miz Ashley." Pete's nodding head and obsequious manner testified to the wide gulf between them, the
plantation owner and the poor white. "Gert done loan her
the shawl an' dress an' feed her. She was purty pore and
'bout froze when she come onter our cabin."

"Well, I thank you for the help. Your wife'll get her
things back. I'll see to that and send her some others
besides. A kindness like that by a body deserves reward."

Her tone settled the issue and dismissed him at the
same time. He was walking away from the fire when she
called out to him.

"Do you own land?"

"Yessum, a small piece." His open but puzzled face
mirrored his mystification.

"I'll send a hand to help you with the spring clearing
and plowing, three months."

Pete's pleasure at the magnificent gift exploded into a
repeated "Thank you, Ma'am!" and genuflections. He could
hardly contain himself as he danced along the path to the
barnyard and his team. "We goin'a make it this year," he told

the trees. His glee subsided into worry and doubt by the time he reached his wagon. "Her word gotta be good," he muttered, consoling himself. "A fine lady like that don' lie."

A Negro boy greeted him at the wagon. "I'se Joel," he said.

"What you want?"

"Granny Owdoms done sent me ter go wid yer. I'se sees if I kin fin' Hester's clothes in de woods. She had some right good things."

Pete nodded and motioned to the seat. "Hop on up thar quick. I got to move." They creaked out of the yard on the way to his place.

Back at the cabin, Granny took down the bear grease pot and kneaded the warm, soothing lotion into Hester's bruised back. The girl groaned as the old woman's fingers pressed and rubbed the welted skin.

"It still hurt bad, Granny," she wailed.

"Don' take long ter heal with dishere grease, girl. It's powerful soothin'. Keep near de heat an' you be better fast."

"Those damned Minns need whippin'," the girl said angrily. But her temper gave way to groans when Granny struck a sore spot.

"Dey git dere comeuppance directly, chile. Joel gone ter tell Gabe an' Hannibal 'bout yer beatin's an' de Minns' pleasurin'. Dey kill dose Minns soon's dey git de chance."

Thump! Thump! The knock on the poplar log came well after the sun was up, just as George had told them. Water droplets dripped from the trees and struck with little spattering rustles on the damp duff. A few bits of ice crashed down amid them. The early, melting thaw gladdened Claude's heart. A rapid change from the freeze presaged a good day to follow and the chirping of small birds in the forest argued against danger. But rattling leaves along the massive log alerted them to a slow, cautious sneak of the intruder. Fearful, Claude drew his derringer and Hannibal unsheathed his knife. Rustling at the den's entrance was followed by a tanned face and bushy, red-bearded head that poked through the entrance hole to the cave. The intruder's eyes opened wide and his cheeks paled at the sight of the derringer muzzle at the end of his nose.

"Ain't no call fer dat," the man complained, drawing back with a gasp. "I'se Rufus, here ter take you ter Gabe."

"Jist keerful," Hannibal replied. "No rebs hereabouts?"

"None. Dey don't come down ter de thicket 'thout they come in big bunches."

The two fugitives crawled from the hole and stretched, then checked their weapons before leaning the rifles against the big log.

"Got some meat an' corn fer yuh," Rufus said. "Reckened ye'd be hungry."

He handed them some parched corn and strips of meat from his possibles sack. They wolfed the food while going down to the river for a drink. Dunking of their heads and a visit to the bushes finished their morning ablutions. But Claude delayed and soaked his sore leg in the cold water until the wound was clean, while Hannibal crouched nearby. Then he hopped up and shook the injured member before reclaiming the bandage and tobacco from its storage on a log, ready for rewrapping.

"Ain't lookin' good, Claude," Hannibal said. He felt of the dripping leg, which was puffy and red at the wound.

"It's sore all right," Claude admitted, softly so Rufus couldn't hear. His glance confirmed that the big redhead was on up the trail. "Don't know how, but I'll walk it, hurt or no." He winced at the pain when Hannibal slapped on the remains of the tobacco and wrapped the bandage tightly against the wound. Hobbling up the bank to the log to retrieve his rifle, Claude faced the speculative gaze of Rufus.

"Got a bad leg, have yuh?" the redhead asked.

"Botherin' me some," Claude said, "but I'll make it."

"He got stuck wid de point o' a reb bayonet yestiday," Hannibal interjected. He interposed himself between the two men. "Claude need somethin' more'n 'baccy ter keep out de blood pisonin'."

"Gabe give 'im de tonic but we best git 'im ter Granny Esther over to Calhoun's. She good on any miseries." Rufus glanced around the campsite. "You ready?"

Hannibal looked expectantly at Rufus while the fugitives picked up and cradled their weapons. "Got any more o' dat deer meat?" he asked. Smacking his lips, he added, "It mighty tasty."

The blocky redhead felt around in his sack and drew forth a few more remnants of meat. He brushed off the residue from other possibles and handed them the dried-up strips. "Got de hungries, have yuh? We ain't had more'n deer fer a long time now. Ain't no fat much but dey's right good cooked wid spice."

Rufus headed up the river through the thickest tangle, the two fugitives following at a walk. His caution kept them at a very slow pace, his wary progress much like the deer he fed on. Claude's leg cramped and pained but he persisted against the growing discomfort and his inability to depend on his leg's strength. His calf throbbed painfully by the time they broke out into a clearing. It was just before noon and the cooking fire and pot were welcome sights. Exhausted by the short but tiring hike, Claude sank down on a large log, his leg stretched out toward the fire. He saw two figures coming toward him, two giant Negroes weaving in and out together, before he fell off the log in a faint.

A splash of cold water revived him. Sputtering and spitting water, he jumped to his feet and cursed Hannibal and Gabe. "Why'd you do that, God dammit?" Claude shook off the droplets while he wiped the water from his slight beard. "Did you have to gimme a bath?"

"You been lying' dere las' few minutes, Claude," Hannibal replied patiently. The servant's soft reply soothed the planter.

He looked at them wonderingly. "I been out that long?"

"Yep," Gabe said, "but you ain't said nothin'. Hannibal tol' me 'bout yer bein' a Linckum sojer an' playin' dumb. I don' tell nobody, not Rufus ner 'nother, Aunty ner Luke. You jist keep on quiet like."

"Rufus already knows," Claude said. He put a forefinger to his lips. "Keep it from the others."

"Sho nuff," Gabe replied.

Claude groaned when he assayed a few steps. "I'm wore out," he said. "An' this leg hurtin' right bad. Need a good feed and a long sleep before we move on. You got a better hidin' place, Gabe, besides this?"

"Hut in de bresh an' Aunty Emma ter cook de stew. We

feed yuh good, den put you bof dere til termorrer."

"What then?" Claude's tired body settled again onto the log.

"I talk ter Rufus 'bout dat." Gabe paced about before them, his face wrinkled in concentration. "Got de idea we kin gitcher by dem rebs wid a coffle. We got de irons."

"Need big bunch fer dat," Hannibal observed. "Can't have jist me an' Claude."

Gabe brushed aside the difficulty. "Use some o' de other boys hereabouts. Dey's plenty ter he'p."

"But you need a white man fer de coffle." Hannibal's objection brought a laugh from Gabe.

"Ain't you seen dat Rufus? He look like de overseer an' he kin talk jist like 'im. An' Luke, he was a slave driver. We kin fool 'em all."

Claude's stomach revolted at the idea of being shackled by the neck in a coffle. He never had used that method of transporting slaves but had seen the results many times. It revolted him, the barbaric neck collars chained together in file, with the open sores on the slaves from the metal edges grinding into their skin. The slaves had to shuffle forward in unison while chained, all the time trying to prevent sudden hurts from the unyielding clamps. But he was at the mercy of these helpful fugitives from the plantations and listened raptly as Gabe and Hannibal planned the maneuver. They would go right through the rebs, first to Calhoun's then to Georgia.

"Kin take yuh over by Toccoa Falls er Clarke's," Gabe said, in conclusion. He drew a map in the dirt in front of the fugitives and pointed out the salient geography, adding, "Den we move de coffle ter Demorest's springs. Granny Ella send yuh on west."

The planning done, the giant guided them to a small hut well hidden in the thicket along the river. He shook his head when Claude limped badly in climbing a set of deadfalls that guarded the cabin's secluded location. The planter wondered about its safety though, since the smoke trail was very visible. It would be easy to find he thought. As if reading his mind, Gabe reassured him.

"Nobody mess wid us, Claude. We run away if dey come

an' dey ain't never ketched us yet. Dey give up tryin' atter we kill two er three."

Gabe bent to feel the planter's injured leg after they entered the cabin and Aunty Emma greeted them. "Yore leg gwine stand it, Claude?" he asked.

The planter nodded but the aching pain in his calf made him wince and hobble about, all the time wondering if he would be able to walk farther.

Aunty Emma's shrewd, old eyes took in the problem for a full minute before she took charge. Her angular, spare frame settled onto the stone hearth near the pots set for warming. Tucking in her gray hair flying below her bandanna, she reached out two bony hands and patted her apron.

"Put yer leg 'cross my lap, boy."

Claude lay on his back in the dirt, his boot stripped and his pant's leg split up the side. The healer handled the wound gently, first washing away the mess of the tobacco. Ragged edges of the injury flared out without sealing together and reddened swelling bulged the skin edges.

"Got some 'fection dere, Hannibal," she said. "Could be de blood pisonin' comin' on. I give him de purge but better ter put de hot iron to de gash. It mostly best fer de stabs."

Her blows shook Claude. Blood poisoning! And after the escape, to be hot ironed! He shivered in fear of the burning of the iron, but steeled himself against the sizzling and stink. His mind flashed back to the slave ironed at Greenbottom when his foot was torn off. He had watched the wretch scream himself into unconsciousness. But ironing had cured the hurt and the man had healed up quickly.

"Drink dis," Aunty Emma ordered. She held out a draught from one of the pots on the hearth. It steamed in its gourd dipper, an herb tea with a dirty-brown oily look and noxious odor that offered little attraction to the patient.

When he turned his head away in disgust, the healer seized his nose and poured the concoction into his rapidly opened mouth. Claude gagged at the foul taste, but held tight by Aunty and Hannibal, he swallowed it down. He came up off the floor when they released him and spit out the leavings. His protesting growls intermingled with gurgling swallows as he reluctantly finished off the last of the medicine in Aunty's gourd dipper.

"Got ter treat yuh jist like a little boy," Aunty Emma said, smiling. Her satisfaction at the success of the dosing brought a grudging laugh from Claude. "My chil'ren and Miz Pearl's uster do de same thin'," she added.

Aunty giggled at the planter's discomfiture while he hacked and coughed and cleared his throat, then wiped the dribblings from his unshaven face. Claude laughed with her and Hannibal chuckled as he held out a dipper of clear water.

"Wash de yarbs down quick," the Negro said, "an' dey don' taste so bad."

Claude eyed the fireplace irons in trepidation while he finished the dipper. His worst fears were realized when Aunty took down a straight iron poker from the hanger and put its tip in the coals. She left it to heat and called to Gabe.

"Need Luke an' Amos here, Gabe. 'bout ready wid de hot iron."

The four Negroes, strapping, muscular figures, seized the planter when she was ready and held him flat on the dirt floor. He could see the hot iron, its orange, glowing end tested by the spit of the woman, droplets that exploded from the intense heat before they struck the rod. His eyes riveted on its path as she bent above his leg. Try as he might, he could not turn away from the oncoming gleaming tip. Claude bit down on the stick Hannibal had forced into his mouth and steeled himself not to cry out when the rod struck the wound. But the searing flame of the hurt coursed through his body, overpowering in its demands. A low moan turned into a scream and his body arched against the restraint before he fell back, limply unconscious.

"He done right good," Aunty Emma observed. The old woman hung the poker back on its hook and returned to the unconscious man. She hoisted up the leg and turned it to the light. Then she crushed a large mass of soaked herbs against the cauterized wound and held it tight. Covering the poultice with a gob of hot, salty pork fat, she wound a fresh binding snugly around the leg with practiced skill.

"Put 'im in de bed dere," she ordered, as soon as the

bandaging was finished. "Dose yarbs done mek 'im sleep 'til night. Den we feed him an' termorrer he likely be ready ter go in de coffle."

Gabe led the others outside after they had settled the sleeping planter. He paused at a nearby squared log that was surrounded by shavings and sat at its center. The other men grouped around him on the convenient seat. Gabe spit and picked up a stick to whittle on before he spoke.

"We got ter lead 'em 'way from de two of yuh, Hannibal. Kin use Luke an' Amos here fer it."

"How you plan ter do dat, Gabe?"

"Kin send Luke an' Amos up nawth to'ards Greenville. Dey stop at Pelzer's an' let de word git out dey's Claude an' Hannibal. Dey ain't known up dere."

Luke and Amos nodded in agreement, their impassive faces quiet. Luke puffed on his pipe and Amos wrestled a large chaw in his cheek.

"But you said Luke's needed fer de coffle." Hannibal's reminder produced an immediate change in Gabe's plan.

"Well, den, I let Amos be Hannibal, and I git Charlie, his half-brother, ter be Claude."

"Charlie don' look like no nigger?"

Gabe shook his head emphatically. "No way," he said in denial. "Dey mama half-Injun an' some white. Charlie's pappy a free issue. Charlie kin pass anytime." He went on in his description of the decoy. "He brown, 'bout like Claude, but mebbe lighter. An' he won't talk none, act dumb, jist like Claude. Dat all right, ain't it, Amos?"

"Sho' nuff, Gabe." The placid Amos continued his chewing, a brown stream of spit occasionally relieving his full mouth. Residue dribbled down at the sides of his mouth and stained his grayish beard.

The plans were soon made and Amos and his brother instructed about their subversive journey. Gabe coached them carefully, drilling in the nuances of diversion and the falsehoods needed. Hannibal listened to the great detail without comment. The devious plan satisfied him that the giant slave was an overpowering master at fooling the planters.

"Whcre dey go atter Pelzer's?" Hannibal's doubts resurfaced in his wrinkled frown.

Gabe had just finished repeated cautions to the brothers to identify themselves at the Pelzers' slave row. Being open about their escape while asking for food would be tantamount to telling Minns, for gossip would expose them. He soothed Hannibal's fears.

"On up de road to'ards Greenville, den dey cross de Reedy Ribber. Stop at Simpson's an' do de same as at Pelzer's. Den dey be jist like de fox an' double back ter Woodruff's Tavern atter dey sidle on nawth a'ways. Come back in fo', five days. By den you an' Claude inter Jawja."

"Won't Minns be suspicionin' a trick?"

"Dey's many a 'scape gone ter de underground railroad in de mountains an' he been dere a'fo'. Some o' dose hill folks don' hol' wid ownin' slaves. Dey he'p us wid 'scapes."

Amos and his brother soon were gone, their sacks fleshed out with a good bait of food from Aunty Emma. And they carried the fugitives' rifles, the weapons surrendered over Hannibal's protests and at Gabe's insistence.

"They's got to have 'em," Gabe had told Hannibal during their heated argument. He had been adamant when he claimed the weapons. "De Minns knows you's armed, so's de rifles got ter go 'long."

Hannibal had grudgingly given in. After the two Negroes were out of sight, he returned to the hearth and accepted Aunty's offered bowl and spoon. His belly stuffed full with the fragrant stew, he surrendered to the fatigue of their wearing chase and snored away the hours in a corner of the cabin.

Minns' temper steamed at the empty road and their futile search. The Confederate cavalry patrol was out of sight after their unrewarding visit. He could still hear the jingling and creaks of the leathers when he yanked on the bit. His cruelty brought a protesting buck from his horse. Kicking at its sides, he cantered northeast on the road to Greenville. His son joined him abreast and Old Blue panted to keep up.

"Ain't no need to be fussed, Pa," Jared said.

Minns swore. "That God damned Lieutenant ain't even

dry behint the ears. He don' know nothin'. They ain't goin'a find that Yankee jest ridin' the roads."

His scorn of Redding and his patrol goaded him into renewed cursing. Jared let the tirade run down before he ventured a mollifying sequel.

"They'll drive 'em into us, Pa, if we jest keep to the east. I think they's goin' to the mountains 'tween Greenville an' the Spartan's crossroads."

"Jest like that one last year?"

"Yes, Pa."

Minns' face grew thoughtful and he slowed his mount to a walk. His quiet reflection extended into a mile of travel, Jared keeping his silence while his father sorted out the possibilities.

A cross trail to the east toward the Saluda brought the party to a halt. Old Blue splashed into a nearby trickle and lapped up its cooling water. The two riders dismounted and stretched in relief, then watered themselves and their horses.

"We'll git on over to the other side o' the Reedy River," Minns announced, while they knelt and filled their canteens. "You called it right, boy. They's probably goin' to the mountains."

Chapter 12

Rufus

November 12, 1864. Anderson, S.C. Temperature 65\33, clear and cold, with scattered clouds. Light northwest winds to ten knots during the day. Daytime moon.

Wind sighed in the trees as the soft light of early morning filtered through the smoky mists that drifted in the open window of the rude cabin. Claude woke with a start, his senses alert to an unusual cry. Its tremulous, wavering warble resonated through the mists and the forest's music, a disembodied wailing like a lost soul. He shivered, then laughed when he belatedly recognized the call. Leaves rustled and water drops from the trees plopped as they struck the ground. All whispered peace to the planter, his ears attuned to the menace or safety of the forest. The screech owl's quavers re-echoed in the woods. Its interruption took his mind off the hurt in his right calf, throbbing now from the hot ironing and its flaming pain. He rose from his bed in the gray dark and sought the doorway, instantly conscious of stirring shapes in a corner of the cabin. Aunty and Hannibal materialized by his side and propped him erect when he haltingly took a step, swaying and dizzy.

"You awright Claude?" Hannibal asked.

"Just dizzy from bein' out," he said, unthinkingly. His

mind did not react to his revealing lapse into speech. "How long I been asleep?"

Aunty's eyes gleamed and she took in a sharp breath. "Nigh onter a day, BOY," she replied. The old woman grunted as she emphasized the epithet of the white man for the Negro. "Sees you kin talk too."

The irony of her words was not lost on Claude. The derogatory "Boy" denoted any male Negro, confining him always to nothingness, to no status or influence. He surely was one of them, he thought, black and in their company and power, hunted like an animal. His hurt disappeared in the fading black of the cabin, black that hid the shame visited on the humble hut and all its occupants, but not the heart and humanity of help by the slaves. All black, him, Hannibal, Aunty, and the night. And Gabe and the others who helped him. His guilt at the thought of the demeaning servitude overpowered his pain. Remorse piled on the guilt added to his resolve to help the slaves if he were lucky enough to survive.

"God help me," he prayed aloud.

"He most sure ter do dat." Aunty's instant response buoyed the planter.

Hannibal's left arm gripped around Claude's body. He held the planter erect, while he clutched the injured man's right arm. A vise of rigid muscles prevented Claude from falling. Aunty stood at his other side, silent and intent. Her hands brushed back her hair and straightened her voluminous skirt while she waited. "You needs me ter he'p?" she asked.

"No," Claude replied, "I can make it." He shook loose of Hannibal's embrace and stepped forward. "I got to go outside to the necessaries."

Claude assayed the few paces to the door with growing confidence as his head cleared and his balance returned. Though his leg ached, he faced the new day with anticipation, his resolve to escape and to change his relation with the slaves crystallizing into firm dedication.

Even after his purging, his gut growled loudly on his return to the cabin, and pains in his middle convulsed and wracked him. Its upset added to the aching protests of hunger pangs. An aroma of stew attracted him to the fire, where Aunty ladled from a pot on the crane.

She handed a full bowl to Claude. "Recken you kin swaller dis down," she said. When he smelled it and smiled, she added, "Dey's mo' if yer want."

The steaming bowl and a spoon occupied his full attention. Corncake and the stew disappeared rapidly into his busy mouth.

Hannibal already had scraped his bowl and held it out for another dab. Aunty filled it mechanically, her dipper adding to Claude's bowl also. The two fugitives sat on stools before the fire, the planter with his leg close to the heat while they filled up. Once the edge was off his hunger, Claude stirred his stew with the spoon and picked out chunks of vegetables and meat to savor.

"Gabe be here directly," Aunty said. She set the ladle aside and expanded on the giant's plan. "He got ter pull de coffle tergether, an' Rufus an' de hawse fer de overseer."

"Horse?" Claude asked. "Where can you get a horse?"

"Two head o' our'n hid out wid a fren. He don' hold wid de rebs, er slavin'. He he'ped us right much."

"They in good shape?"

Aunty laughed. "Allus 'cept de one youse eatin' right now."

Claude's wonder stopped his spoon in midrise and Hannibal paused and looked at his bowl.

"Ain't nothin' wrong wid hawse," Aunty protested. "Go on wid yer eatin'. Dis one lamed a leg so we changed from deer meat yestiday. De hawse been feedin' good an' mighty fat. Not like de deer."

The reason for the skim of grease and the globs of fat meat amid the vegetables was immediately clear. But the stew, with its turnips, onions and potatoes, was spicy and tasty, even if horse. He had relished the skunk stew at Granny Mandy's and now horse at Aunty's. Claude laughed, recalling the fine table at Greenbottom, then thought of the days ahead through Georgia. Before he was at Dalton, maybe he'd even have to eat dog, what with the poor state of the country. The idea sobered him, but he faced the hardship of the rest of his journey with composure and returned to the task of filling his belly.

"When Gabe comin'?" Hannibal asked.

"He an' de others be here a'fo' midmornin'." Aunty stirred the pot and swung the crane into the fireplace recess before sitting on the hearth with her own bowl. "Ain't no reason ter start fo' then. You got ter git up ter de Anderson road quiet-like. Gabe put yer in fo' Anderson. Den he march de coffle right thoo de rebs dere on de Calhoun road. Git dere 'bout de time dey's all eatin' supper."

Claude was mystified. "Why so late?" he asked.

"Dey ain't so rousty den."

"No!" Claude exclaimed.

The planter's amazed cry tickled the old woman. Her face crinkled up and her sides shook in glee as she broke into laughter.

"Rufus done it twice dis spring wid slave 'scapes," she told him, between chuckles. "He good at overseer. De rebs ain't smart when dey eatin'."

The two men filled themselves to bursting with their helpings before going out to the sitting log. Claude stretched his leg out straight and wiggled his toes. Even when extended, its ache added to his woes, and there seemed to be no comfortable way he could bend or straighten it. His continuing limp bothered him and the pain reached up to his rump.

Hannibal's knelt by the leg and felt its heat. "You gonna be able ter make it, Claude?"

"I'll do it somehow." The planter patted his thigh and moved the leg to one side. He grimaced when a shaft of hurt ran through him.

"Could stay here a few days, 'til dat leg some better."

Claude shook his head, his face full of worry wrinkles. "Can't do it, Hannibal," he said. He waved his arm toward the east. "That Minns is just right over there, not far away." He smiled sheepishly and glanced about as if embarrassed by his next disclosure. "I dreamed about him last night and can feel him somehow. If we stop, he'll catch us."

The big slave nodded and sighed, his mournful glance taking in the leg. "De second sight mighty powerful. If he here we need ter move. But dat leg mighty sick."

Aunty joined them in their wait for Gabe. She checked the wound while Claude and Hannibal looked on in apprehension. The burn was ugly, its crusty gash surrounded by blisters. A few small red streaks radiated from the break in the swollen skin. She clucked in dismay when her gentle probings brought winces from the planter.

"You got ter git on up ter Granny Esther at Calhoun's, Claude. She de onliest one can he'p yuh."

Aunty's anxious face transmitted a foreboding to the planter, a feeling of mortality and doom. She again felt of the edges of the wound, his sharp intake of breath and a groan stifled by sheer will. Her new wrapping with a fresh mass of boiled herbs added to his dread but another dipper of her medicine brought relief from the worst pain in a few minutes.

"I'll make it, Aunty," Claude said loudly, as if buoying up his own spirits. He smiled wanly when he rose to assay a few steps. "You must have given me somethin' that works. It don' hurt as bad."

The planter stomped about in desperate trial, thrusting his right foot down hard while the others inspected him intently. He was able to walk without too much limp when he deliberately forced himself into a brisk activity. His confidence restored, he smiled at them and resumed his seat.

"I'm ready to start soon's Gabe comes," he said.

"He be here d'rectly." Aunty knelt and stitched at the split in the pants leg. "He have Joel wid him fum down ter Granny Owdoms."

"Who he?" Hannibal asked.

"'nother o' Granny's runner boys. He carry messages all de time. He brung word fum Granny 'bout yer Hester."

The woman's face grew solemn, her grim, turned down mouth and furrowed brow alarming them. She put away the needle and stood before the log, her hands on her hips. But her silence gradually gave way to trembling and tears.

"What happened to Hester?" Claude asked. He rose from the log and grasped the crying woman's arm. The planter shook her while she twisted her apron in her hands and a stream of tears wet her cheeks. "What happened?"

"Dose Minns take 'er an' beat 'er bad. Dey pleasure demselves an' lef her in de woods fer dead."

Hannibal swore and jumped up as Aunty bawled. He was trembling when he picked up a large piece of downed branch and beat furiously on a nearby tree. His raging attack splintered the stick into small pieces but the violent release did not satisfy his anger. Enraged, unable to be still, he strode about shouting, "I kill dose Minns!"

"Is Hester all right?" Claude said worriedly.

"She be well d'rectly," Aunty replied, as she wiped her eyes. "Got beatin' but she safe wid Granny an' Miz Pickens. Dose Minns got ter answer ter Marse Pickens, 'cording ter Joel. Miz Pickens right put out."

Claude's gorge rose at the revolting news and the desecration of the female slave. His words were brittle and hard to get out through his anger. "Those bastards'll answer to me an' Hannibal. They won't be alive to see Pickens."

"Yer right, Claude," Hannibal added. His hands convulsed into knotty balls as he paced before them. "I kill 'em bof myself."

"Gwine git de chance, bof o' yuh," Aunty Emma said. "Joel say de Minns gwine chase yuh clean ter Dalton."

The old Negress left them to their rage and wait, and passed back into the hut.

"Your people seen anything of escaped slaves, Miz Pelzer?"

Lieutenant Redding was halfway up the steps of the mansion, his hat doffed. The stylishly but shabbily dressed imperial lady facing him clutched the shawl around her shoulders. Erect on the porch, her elevation and bearing commanded the respect due good breeding and status. A Negro butler waited near the door behind her, his faded black suit of fashionable cut and fine material. She ignored Redding's question for the moment, and rose to the demands of southern hospitality.

"Will you come in Lieutenant?"

Redding bowed. "No Ma'am," he replied. "That's mighty neighborly of you but we have to get on."

Miz Pelzer nodded. "Reckon there's no time for visits

anymore." Her bitter tone graded into defeat. "We used to have such grand times here and at the parties up in Williamston. Now it's just war, war, war and killin'. I wish you men would end it and Tom could come home."

A deep quiet fell over all of them, her gloom preventing Redding or the patrol from intruding into her silence. The troopers gawked at the pillars and portico while they sat their horses in the circular turnaround in front of the steps. Grown up grounds showed the neglect due to absence of the owner, off to the wars, and the worn habits of the woman and butler were ample evidence of decay in the fortunes of the plantation. Leathery rubs and creaks of the harness broke the stillness as the troopers shifted in their saddles. With the relaxation, two of the horses reached for a mouthful of green grass that peeped between some of the boxwoods.

"Miz Milly?" The old butler bobbed his white head and moved a few steps to his mistress's side.

"What is it, Joseph?"

"Dey was two strange niggers down't de cabins las' night. One named Hannibal. De other don' talk. Ophelia tol' me dis mawnin'."

"Why didn't you tell me this before?" Miz Pelzer made as if to strike the slave, her petulant, angry voice rebuking him.

Joseph bowed and bobbed before her in abject supplication while he made amends. "Don' want no trouble, Miz Milly. I'se jist keep quiet like."

"Well, are they still there?"

"No Ma'am. Dey was gone fo' fust light 'ccordin' ter Ophelia. Filled der bellies an' lit out."

Redding grasped his hanging saber with his left hand and swiftly mounted the steps to the portico. He aimed right for the slave and confronted Joseph as his men reined their horses. The excitement of the information infected the troopers with restlessness and an urge to be off on the chase, and the horses sensed the change. And even as the riders gentled their restless mounts, they fixed their attentions on the old slave and his message.

"Which way'd they head, old man?" Redding's intent face was thrust forward, ignoring Miz Pelzer as he intimidated the slave.

"Dey's goin'a try fer Simpson's ford, den cut nawth past de Spartan's crossin' ter 'scape, 'ccording ter Ophelia."

"You sure of that?"

"It's what Hannibal tol' Granny down ter de cabins when she fed 'em. Ophelia dere ter git some yarbs an' she saw de two o' 'em. Dey recken she gone but she listen at de do'."

Redding ran down the steps and swiftly mounted his horse. He swung it around with a flourish and eased it into his position at the head of the patrol. Flanked by his Sergeant, he swept his hat off in a final courtly bow and took his farewell of the woman.

"Your servant, Ma'am. I thank you for the hospitality."

"Good luck, Lieutenant. I hope you catch those niggers."

She was berating Joseph in a loud voice as they galloped out the lane and headed up the road that would lead to Simpson's ford.

Minns and Jared halted their horses at the river crossing, their mounts sucking up the water. Old Blue's protruding tongue dripped from the hot run following the horses. He jumped in splashingly and submerged for his usual bath, then came back toward shore. The old hound lolled in the shallows of the cold river as he lapped at the water and cooled off. Its current swirled about him on the sandy bar of his immersion.

Jared chortled at Blue's swim. "Old Blue gittin' baptized agin, Pa. Funny how he likes the water. Flops in ever'time we hit a place."

"We been goin' purty fast, boy. He gits powerful hot runnin' an' that tongue o' his'n don't keep him cool. The water gits him ready fer another run."

Minns dismounted and tried his cinch. Then he walked around with the reins in his hand, leading his horse as he inspected the tracks at the ford. The loose dirt was a jumble of wagon wheel imprints and hoof marks but no pair of footprints. Handing off his horse to Jared, his search widened to a large circle around the ford while the boy led the horses to a stand of grass. The mounts cropped the feed and ignored the boy squatted nearby. Jared left the search to his father. But Blue charged out of the shallows to join Minns. He shook off the water first, his vigorous shower wetting the shying horses. The wagging tail and snuffling of the hound as Minns encouraged him stimulated the hunter into a more intense inspection. Minns was bent almost double as if sniffing the ground at the last. Finally, finding nothing, he penetrated the open stand of willows and poplars in search of a trail. The dog gave up before the hunter and circled back to the ford. He ran to Jared with his tail wagging when the boy held out a stick of jerky.

Jared shook his shoulders resignedly as he watched his father. "Come on in, Pa," he finally shouted. "They ain't been here."

The hunter ignored him and loped through the trees in an ever-widening arc. It took two more circuits to satisfy him before he rejoined Jared. His son waited while Minns stood in silence and surveyed the crossing and the swift river. Only his chewing and spitting broke his quiet contemplation.

"They jest got to cross here," he finally said, his irritation showing. "Warn't nothin' over past the Reedy an' this be the main trail. An' the niggers hereabouts likely he'p 'em."

"Couldn't they a'got ahead o' us?"

Minns shook his head. "No way, boy. They's walkin' an' we got the horses."

Athey squatted at a sandy place and drew a map in a smoothed section. The two Minns were scratching and revising, intent on their plans, when Blue scampered up the trail to an old deadfall. Suddenly his head came up and his nose sniffed after a faint scent. Crash! The deer flashed its white tail when it jumped and ran. Its high bounds carried it directly into the forest. Old Blue's melodious cry rang through the trees as he struck and chased. The hot trail pulled him on, a tether of musk tying him to the deer.

"Blue! Blue! Come back you damn fool!"

Athey's shouts carried after the diminishing bugle of the pursuing dog. It was evident that the deer was moving rapidly across country away from them.

"That fool deer's a traveler," Jared said. He cradled his

rifle and caught up the reins of his horse. The youth shook his head in disgust as he prepared to mount. "Got to move, Pa. Old Blue's goin' fast."

"Yer right," Minns said. "We git Old Blue off that buck quick, boy, or he'll be clear on east o' the Reedy agin. Never find 'im."

Minns swung into his saddle and galloped up the trail with Jared in hot pursuit.

Departure of the hunters left the ford untended. Two furtive figures from the bushes across and downriver quickly occupied it. They held their rifles and kits above their heads while they waded the waist-high, swirling water, its gritty bottom providing a firm foothold. The men passed the worst place braced together to keep from falling in the drag of the powerful current.

"We cross fo' dey's others hereabouts," Amos said. His brother nodded and clasped his arm even more tightly.

Amos waded downstream before leaving the water at a brushy place. His brother followed close behind with his rifle held high. Mud from roiling in the shallows disappeared in the downstream current, the ford again clear and unmarked. The two men kept to the leafy mats as they sought higher ground and a hideout. They stripped and wrung out the water in a dense copse, then reloaded the two Minns' rifles Gabe had insisted on over Hannibal's objections.

"We rest a bit here," Amos said. "Den slope on up de trace to'ard de Spartan's crossroad like Gabe tol' us, fo' cuttin' back ter Woodruff's Tavern."

His brother nodded and lay flat on the ground with his rifle propped against a sapling. Their snores soon resounded among the trees.

Gabe and Rufus straightened the coffle of twenty, sturdy Negroes into a line of sorts, the men silent in the deep woods adjacent to the Anderson road. Luke and another outrider were up and down the road to warn of any traffic, particularly patrols. Claude was impressed with the way Gabe handled the coffle as it formed. The giant Negro issued crisp orders and treated the movement in a strictly military manner. His whispered compliments, hidden from the other slaves, brought a pleased grin from the giant.

"Went in de war fer 'bout two years wid ol' Massa, 'til he killed at Gettysburg. Learn right much 'bout de sojerin'."

"The men you've got. They all escapes?"

"Yes, Claude. An' dey's good fighters. Each got a knife an' a small gun hid out. We been armin' ever'time we catch a secesh. We fire at 'em if anybody stop us, den we run."

"If its the Minns, I want a shot at Athey. And let Hannibal kill the other one."

"Hester's beatin' fussed you right much, did it? Aunty told me de two o' yer was bad put out."

"We're goin'a kill 'em, and that's a fact."

Gabe switched his attention to the yoking. His sorting of the collars and chain quickly resulted in a line of shackles for the men.

"How will you handle the chains?" Claude asked as the work went on. "Everybody yoked together with these damned neck collars. Can't get at anyone that way."

"Easy, Claude. We done file de catch down 'til it spring loose wid a hard pull. Watch."

Gabe took up one of the collars and locked it. With a powerful twist of his hands, it immediately released. Claude tried another. It sprang open easily in his tight grip but remained closed while on his neck.

The planter stepped into the line behind Hannibal while Gabe and Rufus finished yoking the men by the neck. The long coffle of slaves whispered and joked while the ironing went on. A few sharpening stones appeared and almost all men pulled out their knives and guns to examine them before facing the journey. Claude wondered at their attire. Some were shoeless, others hatless and in rags, all on the briskly cold day.

"Why aren't they better fixed with outfits?" Claude whispered to Rufus. He adjusted his collar with a bit of insulating cloth as he listened to the overseer.

"Slaves in coffles down here don't get much, Claude. They're sold off with nothin', so we keep our coffles just like the planters. It's not right but we get 'em to freedom this way. These boys'll help you an' Hannibal on into Georgia."

"You've changed your speaking, haven't you?"

Rufus laughed. "I can talk right like the white folks when I want. It helps get us past the rebs."

"Where'd you learn?"

"I grew up with my brother. Old Massa gave me to him. Went to school with him when he was a little boy. Listened close and learned to read. Read all his books. I can write and cipher too."

"Well, if I make it back to Virginia, there's a job waitin' for you there. I have plenty of work. Not as a slave either but as a free man on wages. You and Gabe and Luke."

"I might do that, Claude."

His serious face and nodding head were diverted by a wave and a low hail from Gabe.

"Boys on de trace callin'. De road's clear bof ways. It's time ter git on."

Rufus swung up into his saddle and sat erect, much like a cavalryman. His spirited horse pranced and minced away until it obeyed its rider's reining and commands. The mount's rig bore a brace of saddle holsters ahead of its rider's legs. A shotgun hung at the side, suspended by a thong. Rufus carried his rifle across his lap before him. He was a veritable arsenal with all the weapons. Added to the firearms was a coiled whip over the horn. His slicker and blanket roll covered two saddle bags at the cantle. Try as he might, Claude could see no difference between him and dozens of overseers he had known. Or trooper, if the clothes were changed.

The coffle swung out into the road and shuffled along toward Anderson. Luke, with his whip and prod, walked at the side of the column and Rufus rode at the head. Jingling of the chains was interrupted by curses as the slaves stumbled at a bad place or their iron harness pinched them. But the miles passed as the sun arched overhead. They intercepted more traffic as the line approached the broad, rolling land by Anderson, one dotted with white tents and huts of greater magnitude. Cooking fires smoked everywhere and knots of men gathered around each. A few bars from harmonicas carried to the travelers when they were stopped by the pickets.

A Sergeant strolled over from a fire after they reached the road junction. "Got'cher a good bunch there," he said. The Sergeant of the Guard walked along the line and appraised the stopped men. "Where you headed?"

"Through Calhoun's," Rufus said calmly. "Then on to Demorest's. He's over past Toccoa Falls, near the springs above Hughesville." His reply was laconic, and interrupted puffs on his stogy.

The overseer reined his horse to face the moving man, his rifle grasped tightly in his right hand. The six armed soldiers at the crossing continued their lax stance, observers of this one of many coffles. But each of the slaves placed a hand in a pocket or inside a covering, ready for action.

Claude peeped from under the broad brim of his hat, his derringer in his sweaty grip, ready for cocking and firing. He chose a man to fire at in case of detection, his target unknowing of his fate.

The Sergeant approached two large Negroes and inspected them closely. He punched them in their chests and felt their arm muscles. Then he pried open their jaws and looked at their teeth before stepping back.

"Purty nice bunch o' fiel' hands," he observed. "Stink like they been workin'. Whose niggers were they?"

"Old man Demorest bought these niggers two weeks ago from Mr. Gilbert down on the Saluda."

"Heard o' Gilbert. Breeds purty fine hands. You from there?"

"Demorest hired me away from Gilbert to bring 'em up to Georgia." Rufus paused and blew out a cloud of smoke. "Pays good, too, —, better'n Gilbert." More smoke puffs drifted away. "I want to hurry 'em along but they're pretty slow."

"Have yer slave driver give those bucks a little o' the whip. That allus moved the ones we had on our place over by Marion."

Rufus nodded. "Need to do that," he said. He walked his horse closer to the group of soldiers at the junction. "All right to move on? We need to hustle on up the road. Want to make Calhoun's tomorrow."

"All clear an' good luck to yuh."

The Sergeant motioned his men out of the road. Creeping like a caterpillar, the coffle passed slowly on, with Luke snapping his whip across the backs of the men. They were down the road fifty yards or more when the Sergeant shouted a parting shot.

"Keep those chains tight. Don' trust those black bastards."

Rufus waved back and urged the men on in a low voice. Their pace quickened at his signal. A long mile of shuffling steps delivered them back into a dense forest, where cover could be found in an instant. The march crawled along the Calhoun road, progressing even into the night. At half-dark, Rufus took the coffle off the road a mile and forted up, his pickets a precaution against an accidental patrol.

When the group was free of the chains, Hannibal knelt beside the recumbent planter and helped him with his bad leg. "How you doin', Claude?" he asked, when the planter groaned.

"I'm makin' it but this leg's pretty sore and swelled."

Claude lay on the ground while a roaring fire was built. He inched over to it so that the wound could be inspected in its light. The gash had turned ugly, the swelling obvious and the skin reddish at the edges and too tender to touch. Hannibal heated a large stone and wrapped it in a piece of clothing. Its warmth next to the wound soothed the pain. Claude drifted off into a troubled sleep, once he had eaten of the deer meat Rufus handed him and drunk the smelly herb potion Aunty had given Hannibal.

Redding pointed his saber and shouted, "Charge!"

The cry echoed over the slight slope when the patrol came out of the trees onto the meadow. Lieutenant Redding led the group with his saber flashing and his horse at a dead run. Sergeant Gill followed at the head of the galloping troopers. Caught out in the open, two rough figures ran for the brushy, steep bank and hillock that headed the weedy space.

Jared peeped out from the obscuring bushes. "Recken they's the two we're lookin' fer, Pa?"

"Can't say, boy. Too fur yet. We'll jest hunker down here

and see what goes on."

The hunter's horses were hid in the thick brakes behind them, tied off tight. Minns and Jared sought convenient deadfalls overgrown by dense honeysuckle. They slid their rifles over the edges and covered the running men, now about one hundred yards away.

Yelping of the troopers disturbed Old Blue. He pranced about, his tail up, resisting Minns' command to lie quiet. The hunter restrained the dog, but his grasp on the struggling body kept him from observing the action in the meadow.

"They's goin'a fire, Pa," Jared whispered.

"Who, boy?"

Crack! Crack! Two rifle shots rang out over the slopes of the rolling hills surrounding them. The resounding pows carried clear and sharp in the cool air.

Minns let go of the dog and switched his attention to the field. He was just in time to see the two lead riders fall from their horses, which veered off wildly. The following men split. Some chased the horses while the others gathered around the fallen. The two Negroes ran on toward the hidden Minnses, seeking the brush, their path almost directly toward where the hunters were hid out.

"Right in here," Amos called to his brother.

He pounded into the small game trail and was knocked flat by Minns, his unconscious form covered by Minns' rifle. Taken at gun point by Jared, his brother threw down his weapon and faced the youth. Jared promptly kicked him in the crotch and savagely thrust the butt of his rifle into the slave's stomach as he doubled up. The Negro fell to the ground vomiting and cramped over, his hands clutching his groin. Groans and cries of pain were interspersed with pleas for mercy from the half-restored Amos.

"Don' hurt me no mo', Massa. Don' hurt me."

Minns picked up the two weapons while Jared kept his rifle on the moaning prisoners. Athey's face flushed during the inspection of the Negroes' rifles and his scar bulged into a red streak. His increasing choler culminated in a string of oaths, a furious outburst that changed into an icy hate as he contemplated the captives. His voice was low and malignant when he spoke to Jared. "The bastards got your's an'

Jeremy's rifles, boy."

Minns kicked the two men upright and swore at them, then led their horses and marched the two prisoners into the meadow. The hunters headed directly for the patrol. Vengeful men quickly surrounded the marchers, the troopers' oaths and threats aimed at the Negroes but including the Minnses.

"I be Athey Minns," the hunter shouted. "You back off. These niggers belong to me."

"They done kilt the Lieutenant," a trooper yelled back.

"And crippled Sergeant Gill," a second added. He pointed his carbine at the prisoners only to be threatened by a pistol held by the hunter.

"We'll deal with 'em directly," Minns said. "Let's see to yore Sergeant."

The party walked through the rank grass, its brown and green mat not cropped in years and sprouting cedar seedlings. Minns found Gill sitting up, his left forearm bandaged and bloody spatters all over his uniform. Nearby, Redding lay on his back, a red, spreading stain centered on his shirtfront. His sightless blue eyes stared at the sky and his mouth hung open, a slobbery hole from which his tongue protruded like a bloody sausage. Jared gazed fixedly at the dead man as if mesmerized but Minns passed the body with no more than a glance.

"Howdy, Gill," Minns said. The hunter's laconic greeting penetrated the dulled consciousness behind a white face and the shock that peered from the Sergeant's eyes. Surprise jolted Gill back into full alertness.

"You back here agin, Athey? What'cha still doin' in these parts?"

"Huntin' those 'scapes we talked 'bout yestiday with the Lieutenant." He looked at Redding's body. "Seems like he ain't gonna hunt no more."

Gill nodded and winced and clutched his arm.

Minns pointed to his captives. "These two 'ppear to be the ones I want. They got my rifles they took when they kilt Jeremy down to'ard Due West. Like I said to the Lieutenant, I been chasin' 'em ever since they 'scaped near Columbia 'bout two weeks back."

Gill's pain-wracked face was slack again and uncomprehending. "Why're they way up here?"

"One's the Yankee Lieutenant we talked 'bout. He's headin' back nawth. The other'n's his slave."

"But they's both black, man!"

Minns' temper flared as he chastised the Sergeant. "Warn't you listen'n yestiday when me an' the Lieutenant had our set-to? One's dyed with walnut stain. We find out which one back at yer camp." He glanced at the body. "I 'spect we better git yer Lieutenant to Anderson."

The Sergeant groaned and held his arm. "The Colonel'll tear my head off."

"Why?"

"Lieutenant Redding there was his kin. I warn't s'posed to let him git kilt."

The hunter shrugged. "Can't he'p what comes. It war his time."

The group loaded the Lieutenant's body on his horse and tied his legs securely under its belly. The captive slaves rode double behind troopers, threatened constantly by the other men. Progress was slow and the horses skittish, one runaway bringing a bang on the head for a trooper, knocked senseless by a limb. He was loaded across his saddle, unconscious. The unlucky patrol retreated sluggishly to the Anderson camp and safety.

Hannibal shook the snoring overseer. "Wake up, Rufus," he said softly. "Wake up."

"Yo, Hannibal," Rufus said, and instantly rolled out of his blanket. He sat up, alert, a pistol in his hand. "You hear somethin'?"

"It's Claude, Rufus. He mumblin' and tossin'."

The two men found the planter only semiconscious and hot with fever. He had torn off his coat and shirt, his upper body exposed. The overseer commenced removing the rest of the planter's clothes.

"We'll strip 'im to keep 'im cold an' the fever down, then carry him in a litter in the mornin'."

Hannibal wiped the sweat from the planter's dotted brow and fanned his face and chest. Claude was muttering

about Letty and the children as Rufus finished the disrob-
ing.

"You'll git back ter 'em, Claude," the servant said. The
planter's hot hand clutched at his and held it tightly. The
strong grasp dropped off slackly when the injured man
drifted into unconsciousness and silence.

CHAPTER 13

Granny Esther

---

*November 13, 1864. Calhoun's Plantation,
Pickens County, S.C. Temperature 61\41,
cloudy and damp, with possible showers.
Light winds to ten knots. Moon waning,
setting about two hours after sundown.*

Claude's fever abated in the night but left him limp
and light-headed. He went in and out of lucid peri-
ods, murmuring to Hannibal and Rufus when he
was conscious and burning up when not.

Hannibal inspected his friend's leg in the early morning
light while the other slaves built up the fires. Rufus joined
him when the big Negro uttered a sigh of dismay. "He ain't
gonna be able ter walk," Hannibal said fearfully.

Rufus's optimistic judgement reassured the servant.
"Looks better'n it did," he said. The overseer squeezed the
leg a little, and elicited a complaining groan from Claude. A
slight stink swirled up from the liquid that oozed out of the
wound. "See the pus runnin'?" Rufus said. "That little stab
was deeper'n Aunty Emma thought. She didn't get the iron
in far enough. But I think Granny Esther can cure that
quick-like."

"She got de yarbs an' de medicine touch?"

"And the knives. One o' the men passin' by Calhoun's
picked up a kit."

"Where?"

"Off some dead Yankee doctor at Stone's River. He was soldierin' with his master. Master got killed an' he snuck back to Carolina with a wagon loaded with Yankee possibles. Granny bought it for a side o' hog meat."

Hannibal pulled the planter off the ground, wrestling with the limp body. "We best git Claude up," he said, "an' walk him around a mite."

The two hoisted the naked planter upright and supported him on a half-way walk across the thick mat of pine needles. Dense tops covered them and blocked out the sky. Claude shivered in the damp breeze and muttered unintelligibly. But he suddenly came completely awake and shook off their grasp. He swayed but remained on his feet.

"What the hell you doin' to me?" he asked.

"Tryin' ter gitcher back on yer feet an' walkin'," Hannibal replied. "You been out de hull night."

When Claude swayed, the Negro grabbed his arms and held him erect. Rufus paced alongside at his left as the planter tentatively took a small step.

With the Negroes bracing him, the three padded down a gentle slope to a nearby creek. Its current burbled along, alternately in riffles and pools. Claude stumbled on the graveled clay at the edge and held onto the willow bushes to keep from falling. He threw himself into the stream and lay prone in a cold pool, splashing the water over his face and head. It was his first bath in two weeks and the frigid water cleansed his body and his mind as he bounced up and down on the bottom and surged the flow over him. He washed out the wound with the cooling water, its clear, swirling flood a balm to the hot, sensitive leg. When he stood on the mat again, dripping from the bath, he tested the leg.

"I don't think I can walk, Rufus, but it feels less tight. Not swole so much."

"We're goin'a carry you in a litter to Calhoun's," Rufus said, decisively. "Then Granny Esther'll fix that leg."

He looked over the planter in the growing light and Hannibal walked around him. Claude twisted his neck and his body, following the men. His face wore a puzzled frown.

"What's the matter?" he asked.

Hannibal chuckled. "You got ter dab on de walnut

stain, Claude. De white showin' in some parts an' dat sweatin' done give yuh a speckled face."

Rufus guffawed and slapped his leg. "Damn if you don't look just like a dominecker chicken. Ceptin' you ain't so black."

A quick treatment with the bottle supplied by Granny Mandy fixed the fading spots and added to Claude's darkness in the face. His greasy sweating during the night had all been washed off in the cold brook and he felt refreshed. With his blackness restored, the stinking, dirty clothes, infested with their population of graybacks, recreated the slave. He was a Negro in color and clothes, he thought, as he stood there, anticipating a hard day. His sidling glances at Hannibal and Rufus while they helped him created a dilemma in his mind. Did he now understand them he wondered?

"I can try to walk," he said. He stepped off a few paces but would have fallen if a tree had not been handy.

Rufus shook his head and grasped the planter's arm. "You'll take the litter 'til we see Granny Esther at Calhoun's." He was insistent when Claude hesitated. "It's not more'n ten or fifteen mile."

Claude's continued protests were drowned out by Rufus and Hannibal. "Litter been ready, Claude," Rufus insisted. "Hannibal'll carry one end for a start. The men'll take turns."

"What about my talkin'? They all heard me. How can I play dumb again?"

Rufus' face tightened and his lips compressed into a cruel seam. He dropped back into the dialect of the Negro, his calm conviction making his words even more impressive. "Gabe done told 'em yer a Linckum sojer. He tol' 'em dey's not ter tell nobody 'bout yuh er he kill 'em. Dey's scairt o' dat nigger. Dey don' talk." He added his own warning. "An' I kills 'em if he don't. Dey know dat too."

"You jist be quiet from here on, Claude," Hannibal said. His order was reinforced with a pat and a reassuring grin. "You be awright."

"Granny Esther good with the medicine?" Claude asked. "This leg is still hurtin' right pert."

"She'll lance that place to make it drain out clean," Rufus said. "And she'll hide you both for a couple of days whils't she doctors yuh. Granny mostly heals. She don't lose nobody much."

The coffle started in a mist after a simple meal of pone and half-scorched bacon. Claude's eyes inspected the sky as he rode in the litter. Attempts to turn his head or rise up for conversation had broken the stride of the litter bearers. He finally lay prone after their curses cowed him and subdued his urge to see the road ahead. Swinging of the litter lulled the wounded man as the bearers paced in unison. He dozed and covered his face from the drizzly sky as the miles dropped slowly behind. The smooth trace and care of his bearers produced few jolts to his sore leg.

A hail from the sentries called the Colonel to his tent flap.

"It's the Lieutenant," a sentry shouted. "He's been kilt!"

Hyatte rushed through the flap and stood in the noon damp, rain no longer plaguing the camp. The patrol was walking their horses up the slight slope to the headquarters tents. One body hung over a saddle, its officer's regalia painfully visible. Two other men showed white bandages. A pair of civilians were riding double and two buckskin clad men with rifles across their saddles followed the train of troopers.

Sergeant Gill came to a halt before the Colonel and a man led Redding's horse to a position beside him. "Dismount!" Gill shouted, after they had gathered. Several troopers surrounded the dead man's mount at his further command.

Four men gently unloaded Redding's body and laid it out at attention in front of the silent Colonel. The eyes and mouth were open on the white face of the corpse, its unyielding gaze disconcerting to the officer. Hyatte's eyes fixed on the large red stain on the shirt front as he went down on his knees before the body. The men uncovered when he masked the face with a cloth, then bowed his head and murmured a short prayer. Covering the wound with the flaps of the uniform coat, his spring up to full height had the coiled rage of a madman. He wrung his hands together as he strode back and forth and vented his anger on the Sergeant.

"God damn it, Gill! I told you to take good care of 'im. And you bring him back dead."

"Can't help it, Colonel. He went chargin' off after these two niggers. They had rifles an' shot 'im dead. I was right behint 'im an' they shot me too. Not much," he added, "jest a cut on the arm."

Troopers dragged Amos and his brother forward at the Colonel's roar. They cringed before him, on their knees as they waited on their fate, a sure hanging for killing a white man.

"Whose niggers are they?"

"Won't say, Colonel," Gill answered. The Sergeant ignored Minns' identification in the report. "Claim to be named Hannibal an' Claude. Ceptin' Claude don' talk. He's dumb."

The Colonel walked around the two Negroes while the troopers waited. He looked at the captives distastefully and kicked them a few times. "Escapes, are they?"

"From down to Columbia, Colonel," Minns said. He had dismounted and approached the group while the Colonel raged at Gill.

The Colonel glared at the man hunter. "And who might you be?"

"Athey Minns and my son, Jared."

"So what's your business here, Minns?"

"Major Jones down to the prison at Columbia sent us to capture these two. The dumb one's a Yankee officer dyed black with walnut stain."

"No! You mean a Yankee did the shootin'?"

"Him an' his slave Hannibal, the one that talks. I tol' Gill but he won't listen." Minns wrestled his chaw and spat. "We been chasin 'em nigh onter two weeks. They kilt my son Jeremy down near Due West." The hunter's raw tone turned ominous. "I'm goin'a kill 'em both."

The Colonel's face blanched white, then flushed red as he trembled. He could not speak from the rage that choked him. Gill and the troopers and hangers-on held their breath, only harness and bowel sounds of the horses disturbing the fearful quiet.

The two kneeling men commenced humming a hymm. Its words followed, as they sought divine grace and salvation.

Athey cried out triumphantly and prodded the kneeling slaves. "They both talk! They's the ones, an' I want 'em."

"You'll get nothin'," the Colonel replied, his voice strangling and thick with emotion. "But you and your boy can help with the hangin'."

The assembled men watched silently, some turning away, as Hyatte's trembling increased. He made an attempt to speak but emotion overcame him; then he balled his fists and struck one against the other as he shook uncontrollably in his collapse. He seemed unable to be still; both his body and his face were wracking within, and his feet shuffled about in an uncontrollable dance. Finally he broke and tears flowed down his cheeks, tears accompanied by great, gasping sobs and moans. The release ended the spasms in moments as his military training reasserted itself. When he dried his eyes and straightened up, he again was a soldier, a cold, grim, merciless soldier.

"Adjutant!" he bawled out in a hoarse voice.

"Yes sir!" came the instant reply.

"Get my order book and camp desk."

The Adjutant entered the tent for the objects, his commands to the men handling the camp desk crisp and quickly executed. In five minutes the Colonel was seated behind the desk with the slaves bowed before him. The drumhead trial proceeded apace, with Gill's troopers and the Minnses rapidly presenting the evidence against the prisoners. But one mystery remained.

"The one's a Yankee officer, you say?" The Colonel had been unable to elicit any information from the prisoners except their names. His doubting question brought Minns forward.

"Yes, Colonel. Hannibal's the slave. Other's the Yankee."

"Don't look like a white man to me."

His disbelieving thought was banished by sight of Arch

Hartsill hurrying into the arena before the Colonel. The commander bounded out of his chair and received Hartsill's hand with pleasure, but with a sad, mournful smile.

"You back already, Arch?"

"Yes, Colonel, and I hustled over here when I heard the news. You got the men who killed Redding?"

"Those ones there," Hyatte said, pointing. "Minns here claims they're escapes from the pen at Columbia and that one's a Yankee officer. Claims Hannibal is his slave. But it don't seem right."

Hartsill looked over the prisoners, his intent search while he walked around them stilling the comments of the surrounding crowd. His verdict sealed their doom.

"I met Hannibal and the Yankee down on the Saluda below Little Mountain, back ten days ago. They fooled me then. Shaw was dyed black. They had a paper from Pinckney Middleton down to Osprey's Landing. Pinck told me last week that it was a forgery. But these aren't the men I saw. So you got two escaped slaves leading you on a wild goose chase."

Minns leaped forward. His scar was flaming red when he spoke. "That's why Old Blue didn't tree 'em, Colonel."

"Old Blue?"

Minns waved his rifle at the hound that was investigating the site. "Old Blue didn't bugle when we caught 'em. They ain't the men I want."

"So who are they?"

"Runaways in the thicket. The two here done hid out Shaw an' Hannibal down in the thicket. They might still be there."

Implications of the use of the slave hideout, and arrangement of a diversionary escape by the prisoners to draw attention from the Yankee, were not lost on the Colonel. But his orders were about the immediate punishment of the slaves and not the thicket. Hyatte ignored the waiting Minns.

He beckoned to his Sergeant and called out, "Gill!"

"Sir?" the Sergeant said. He drew himself up to full attention and his troopers lined up behind him.

"Take the two prisoners down to the creek. Scrub the

both of 'em hard to make sure those niggers ain't white. If one is bring 'em back. If not, take 'em to the big oak. Each gets two hundred lashes and lay 'em on hard. When you're done we'll hang 'em." Hyatte's vindictive gaze fastened on the trembling men who knelt before him. He had trouble speaking, his throat and body tensed. "I want to be there to see the last of the lashes, and the hangin', so you send word when you're ready and wait 'til I'm there. You hear me?"

"Yes sir!"

"What about me?" Minns demanded.

"You can watch," the Colonel replied. "Or try your hand at the whip if you've a mind."

"But I think we orta clean out the thicket. Mebbe the Yankee's still there."

"God damn it, Minns, he's long gone, and you know it." The Colonel's waving hand and twisted lips thrust off the suggestion and indicated the meeting was at an end. His dismissal was ignored by the hunter.

"If you don' go," Minns said scornfully, "Jared an' me'll hunt 'em by oursel'es." His tone turned sharp, casting insults. "The trail leads from the thicket an' you know it. So send some o' these lazy troopers after 'em. From the looks'a things, they ain't doin' nothin'."

Minns' brown tobacco stream lit in the vicinity of the Colonel's boots. His contemptuous remarks and spit elicited angry looks from the assembled hangers-on. They closed about him in an ominous group. The hunter drew his pistol and his knife and faced the Colonel. Jared dropped their horses' reins and stepped off to one side of the men. He cocked and raised his rifle and backed up his father.

"Call 'em off, Colonel," the hunter said in a soft voice. "I don' want'a kill yuh but I'm a mite put out right now."

"Back off, boys." Hyatte's command and raised hand stopped his muttering troopers, some of whom had readied their rifles. "Go on, now, and help Sergeant Gill with the niggers."

The Colonel made a conciliatory gesture to Minns. "You can put down those guns, Minns. Ain't no need to fight."

Gill started off when Minns sheathed his weapons and Jared relaxed. The troopers slowly followed, taking the two prisoners with them. Down the slope a ways, they whooped about the whippings and hustled the Negroes toward the creek. One ran beside them and kicked the captives as the troopers dragged the violently resisting men along the ground.

Minns had sheathed his weapons, but his whipcord alertness did not leave him. He and the Colonel stared at each other, a test of wills that pitted the bereaved, beaten officer against the vindictiveness and bloody past of the cruel man hunter.

Hartsill stepped into the breech. "Let me take Company "A" to the thicket, Colonel."

Hyatte nodded thoughtfully. "What are you proposin', Arch?"

"We'll clean it out for good," Hartsill replied. "That damned thicket's been nothin' but a nest o' vipers ever since we've been here. Always trouble."

"I know that!" The Colonel's testy impatience flared when Hartsill failed to continue. "What are you plannin' to do about it?"

"Drive and burn the whole place, and kill everybody we catch. It's the only way to get those niggers in line and to cut off their den. And if we cut Shaw's trail, I'll send a detachment after him."

"How long to do it?"

"Four days at most, leaving today as soon as we're ready. We'll swing around to the north to fox 'em, then surround the place quick."

"Be careful, Arch. This damned war's about over. Don't get yourself killed like poor Redding."

"They'll not get me, Colonel, nor any of my men. We'll kill 'em all."

Minns interrupted them. "Mind if me an' Jared go along, Lieutenant?"

"It's fine with me, Minns," Hartsill said, "but you stay out of our way." Turning from Minns, Hartsill remained by the Colonel, who began shivering violently. The younger man held him erect for a moment while the officer passed a personal watershed. Then Hyatte knelt by his fallen kinsman, his sobs embarrassing the waiting men. But his face was peaceful when he rose and wiped away the tears. He held out his hand to Athey.

"Minns, I'm sorry about your boy and that Yankee. If we can take him we will." Minns gripped the officer's hand hard, the two sealing a pact as the officer's face grew grim and he spat out his venom. "If we catch him, he'll hang!"

Rufus stopped his horse at Three and Twenty Creek, south of Pendleton, and called out to Luke.

"Run 'em into the creek and water the lot. We'll get on directly, after they's rested some."

While the overseer dismounted and pulled out a cheroot, the slaves put the litter down in a protected spot out of the wind. Claude sat up on the thin cloth and doubled up his knee. Unwrapping the bandage on the wound, he ignored the slaves' headlong rush for the stream as he inspected the injury. The men splashed boisterously in the clear, cold water and jollied each other. They bathed their heads in the creek and gulped its refreshing liquid and some dunked their bodies. Hannibal was dragged along by his neck collar, even as he protested about his friend. He gave up in the creek and eased his thirst, then washed off the sweat of the hard march.

Rufus puffed on his cigar after giving Claude a drink from his canteen. He watched unconcernedly while the slaves frolicked and his horse cropped small tufts of grass by the trace. The woods came down close to the creek crossing, no fields leaving an open space. He leaned against a large oak, blackened charcoal of many campfires near its roots testifying to the shelter it had given travelers. His smoke and a stretch were rudely interrupted by a laconic voice.

"Ain't you gonna shackle the sick one?"

Rufus's spring and crouch turned him leftward, face to face with the visitor. He aimed his cocked pistol at the tattered figure cradling a rifle, hesitant now as it emerged from the shadows of a nearby gigantic sycamore. The man wore remnants of Confederate gray, but so shabby as to be nothing but a caricature of a soldier. His head was uncovered and his matted hair and beard left only a small dirty face peering out.

"Ain't no need to git yer dander up," the man said. His doleful expression did not change but his eyes glinted in anger and his command was clear and very loud. "If he shoots me boys, kill 'em all."

Rufus looked about uncertainly. No other men were visible but it had not escaped him that the man held a fine Mississippi rifle, a small bore, percussion weapon, much prized by mountain hunters. A bowie carried in the belt and a tomahawk in a loop added to his assessment of a dangerous threat. Rufus shuffled about and his nervous twitch increased when a rustle near the trees drew his attention. Two long rifle barrels slid into view, aimed at his middle, with eyes glinting along each. The overseer hurriedly backed down and reholstered his pistol in one swift motion. But he kept his hand hooked into his belt close by, ready for instant action while he mollified the man.

"Can't be too careful in these parts," he said, "since old Sherman started raidin' ever'where over in Georgia an' Tennessee."

"He ain't close," the mountaineer replied. "Where you goin' with the niggers?"

"To Demorest's over in Georgia. Stoppin' at Calhoun's first."

"You got any pone er corn? We been eatin' lots o' deer but no bread."

"I can fix that. How many men you want for?"

"Need 'nuff fer me an' two more."

Rufus' call to Luke and brief instructions set the driver to rummaging in the pouches of the pack horse. The stranger walked along the litter and bent over to sniff at the wound in Claude's leg.

"A mite o' mortification there. Git it fixed right quick er he's a goner." He rose before Rufus, his question spilling out.

"Whyn't you jest kill 'im. He don' look to be much fer a buck."

"Can't," Rufus said and shook his head. "Old Man Demorest'd skin me. Claude saved two o' his chil'ren down at Due West. House burnt where they was visitin'. An'

Claude's good with the leathers. Saddle an' harness maker."
The lies rolled off Rufus's tongue, and his leisurely, intermittent puffs from the stogy added to a relaxion of tension
between the two men.

The bushy head of the mountain man nodded in
agreement. "They's hard to come by these days, sho' 'nuff.
Take 'im inter Granny Esther's cabin when ye're at Calhoun's.
She cure him right up. That old conjurer got all kinds'a
tricks."

Luke's sack of corn burdened the robber when he
hefted it onto his shoulder. His generous, parting advice
added to their wariness.

"'bout three mile up yonder they's maybe two, three
nigger 'scapes hidin' out. Up by the big oak stob near the
church crossin'. You can't miss it." He counted on his
fingers a moment. "We done kilt four, five of 'em in the last
month but they's allus more come in. Be keerful o' yer pack
horse er they's likely ter drive it off. If you git on ter
Calhoun's 'fore dark, you most likely won't have no trouble."

The mountaineer disappeared into the tangle with his
tribute, the thick growth concealing him and his companions. Their rustle in the underbrush died out rapidly and
left Rufus and Luke to the silent coffle. The slaves picked up
Claude's litter and started up the trace without any encouragement. But Rufus rummaged in his saddle bags and
pulled out a brace of small pistols. He handed them to Luke
and cautioned the driver.

"I'll keep the pack horse reined up, Luke. If they come
in, let 'em git close. You kill two an' I'll get the rest with the
shotgun."

Luke nodded and hastened to the tail of the coffle. He
shook out and snapped his whip and shouted at the slaves
to hustle along. Any observer would have missed the sham,
the whip end always cracking but never touching the flesh
of the victim. But the slaves howled in pain and added to the
illusion of a coffle. With Rufus and the pack horse in the
lead, the miles rolled by steadily, if slowly, under the weight
of the litter and the confinement of the collars and chain.
After two stops to ease Claude, one at sleepy Pendleton, late
afternoon found the shuffling, clinking line approaching

the slave cabins at Calhoun's. Rufus went up to the manse
to make his obsequies to the Mistress, while the coffle
stopped at the line of cabins far down the slope from the big
house. Luke hurriedly sought out Granny's cabin and
pushed the door open.

"Granny Esther?" he called out into the darkened
interior.

A screech of chair joints answered, then the woman in
it. "Dishere's me," she said. The bent, wrinkled crone stared
at him through pungent tobacco smoke, so old her skin was
a soft, dark-brown parchment stretched over a bony skull,
a dome balding on top, with little wisps of white hair. Luke
was about to speak when she faced back to the flames and
spit. The brown stream from the snuff ball bulging under
her lip sizzled in the fire close to her chair on the hearth. A
curl of smoke rose from the pipe in her hand, and added its
rank aroma to the smell of onions and assafetida. Over in a
wall bunk, a tiny, lone child coughed and moaned. The
cabin sides were pegged to hold several beds and a big bed
rested in the center.

Granny slid her chair back around toward him and
looked suspiciously at Luke. "Ain't knowed you a'fo', boy.
Who er yuh?"

"I'se Luke, here wid a coffle wid Rufus."

"Rufus here?" she said. Her face lighted up and she
gave a pleased laugh. "De Good Lord be praised! Ain't seed
'im since de spring plantin'. He out dere?"

"Up talkin' ter de Mistress 'bout de stop. Need he'p,
Granny."

A cough from the child interrupted. Granny waved her
hand at Luke and shushed him into silence. The old woman
rose from her chair and placed her pipe on a nearby table.
Joints squeaked when she leaned on it, protests of the
rickety furniture and decrepit state of the interior complementing the appearance of extreme age of woman and
cabin. Esther hobbled over to the child, but her stick barely
balanced an otherwise unsteady step. Luke started forward
to help, but the old woman brushed him aside.

"Leave me be! I'se plenty strong. Jist got a mite o' de
staggers."

Her arrival at the bed coincided with more coughing and complaints from the sick youngster. Granny took down a gourd that hung from a peg over the bed. Pouring a cupful of liquid from its neck, she forced it down the throat of the wailing invalid. Her thin arms enfolded the crying boy and clasped him to her meager bosom. A few crooning lullabies and her rocking restored his quiet. The child slept quickly, only to be placed in the bunk and covered completely, his blanket tucked in tight. Hobbling back to her chair, Granny put her forefinger to her lips and cautioned Luke to keep quiet.

"Dishere's de sick house," she said in a low voice. "He be awright, jist a tech o' de croup. De medicine make 'im sleep and de onion clear de throat. He sweat out de fever in two, three days."

Luke finally found the courage to interrupt. "Got a sick man in de coffle," he said.

"What de trouble?"

"Bayonet in 'is leg de other day from de rebs. Ain't deep but it festered some. Aunty Emma hot ironed it down in de thicket but de cut still runnin'."

Granny's contempt burst out. "Dat Emma ain't got no sense 'bout doctorin'."

The old woman's scornful glance at Luke cowed him into silence as she started for the door. Her thin frame moved quickly, if in a weaving track, on her jerky, staggering exit. He followed her out the door, but easily slipped ahead to the litter on the dirt runway before the line of cabins. They knelt together, but Granny elbowed him away as her long, bony fingers stripped the bandage from Claude's wound. Squeezing and kneading around the gash brought pus oozing out and complaining grunts from the planter.

Granny slapped his face. "Shet up," she said disgustedly, "it ain't dat bad." She looked up at Luke, questioning him. "He don' talk?"

"No, Granny, Claude, he dumb. Hannibal, his fren, he do de talkin'. He dere."

Luke pointed to the big slave, still bound up in the coffle's chains. Hannibal was straining to get close but the press of the other men kept him away from the litter.

"Git Hannibal outen 'is chains," the old woman or-dered. "Want 'em bof in de cabin."

Luke didn't move. Instead, his worried face swiveled about to search the surroundings. "Ain't gwine cause no trouble?"

She pressed his arm and reassured him. "Ain't no white folks 'bout. Git 'em in dere."

Granny's orders produced quick action by the coffle. The slaves forced open the loose locks on the collars to free themselves, then carted Claude into the shelter and laid him on the main bed. Granny's practiced hands refelt the heat of the wound once Claude was settled in the cabin. She pointed her cane at a large, brown chest, but only after her inspection and a few sniffs at the wound.

"Fetch de box," she said imperiously.

Luke and another man hefted the multidrawered chest. Calling for two more, the four lifted the heavy weight and set it beside the large bed. The wood and fine lines of the medical kit had once been polished but were covered with knicks and scratches.

"Lieutenant dat owned it kilt at Stone's River," Granny told them. She traced out the faded, painted name and the large U.S. marking. "It be full o' doctorin' tools."

Their astonished gasps when she opened the top amused Claude, propped up on his elbows on the shuck mattress. Inside was a bewildering array of surgical tools, saws, knives, scissors, retractors, all for the doctor to practice his craft.

Luke held up a long, thin blade for the admiration of his helpers. "Dat some knife," he said. But Granny slapped his hand down and took the blade away from him.

"Dose fer doctorin', not carvin' up nobody in a fight, er fer whittlin'. Now you leave 'em be!"

Granny turned her attention to Claude's leg and pulled it to the side of the bunk. He groaned but shifted his body to make the cut accessible to her, steeling himself for the worst. The old woman picked around in the tray of instru-ments and brought forth a wide but short, curved blade on a long handle. With a dexterity he did not expect, she made a quick slash to the bottom of the wound, not deep but one that penetrated the most reddened flesh. A small amount of pus boiled out as he gritted his teeth and groaned again from the pain. Granny's face gleamed in triumph as she spread the sides to drain the wound. Her knife picked a few black strands out of the yellowish pus.

"Dat de trouble," she said. She held out the blade with its cargo. "De thread from de pants down in de flesh. We clean dose all out and you be fine."

Rummaging around under one of the bunks, she brought out a clay jug. The onlookers smacked their lips and their eyes gleamed at the sight of the jug and the aroma of raw whiskey when its plug was pulled.

"Dishere's fer doctorin'," Granny said coldly. "Ain't none here fer no coffle." At their disappointed glances, she chuckled and relented. "Ask Rufus," she said. "He kin git yer some upribber."

Granny poured a liberal dose in a dipper and forced the liquor on Claude. The planter gasped and choked at its burning passage. Agonized, asthmatic sounds welled out from the air whistling through his constricted throat.

"What the hell is that stuff?" he croaked.

The old woman grinned. "Jist stilling usin' plenty o' bee honey. De honey make it powerful good." She poured herself a dose and tossed it down without a quiver. After another small draft, she smacked her lips and returned to the wound.

Kneading and washing with water were followed by Granny's whiskey rinse. She took in a large mouthful, then put her toothless gums about the wound and forced the liquid in and out, alternately sucking and expelling the liquor. Its burning stream cleaned the very depths of the incision and the wound, and continued until Claude was nigh onto senseless from the pain. Granny released his leg finally and spit out the whiskey remnants.

"Onliest way ter clean out de pison," she told him. "It heal right quick now, once'st I put de sugar to it."

Sweat ran down Claude's brow and he trembled from the throbbing pain in the leg. Waves of heat ran over him, fevers that alternated with shivers. His distress subsided a bit as he watched her other treatment.

Granny aimed her cane at a glazed clay cylinder under the rickety table. "Fetch dat big crock, Luke," she said. The driver jumped at her firm tone and flashing eyes. "Keep de cover on," she warned. "Don' want no dirt in de honey. An' none o' yuh stealin' none, nohow."

Prying off the lid, Granny fished about in the crock with a long-handled wooden spoon. She recovered a heavy glob of sugared honey, long past the runny stage, then stuffed the wound full of the sticky, granular mass, and forced it down into the inner recesses. When the entire wound was covered with a heaped coating of sugar, she bound it loosely to the leg with a clean bandanna.

"Sugar allus heal, Claude," she told him. "It keep out de pison. Now we doctor yuh on de inside."

With the wound dressed, the old woman tossed a deft combination of shredded herbs into some hot water from a steaming pan. Her stirring and steeping leached out a dark, stinking tonic. Claude wrinkled his nose in disgust and turned his head away from the offered dipper.

Granny would have none of it. "Now you drink dis er I have Luke an' de boys pour it down yer guzzle."

Her grim, determined stare cowed him into acquiescence. His open mouth received the draft with a grimace but down it went, followed by a flush with water. The old woman grinned when the dose was gulped and swallowed. She patted his shoulder and comforted him.

"It clean yer blood an' mek yuh sleep. We fix a good place ter hide yuh, an' Hannibal too. T'others git on inter de empty cabins at the end o' de street. Dat where Mistress send de coffles."

"How long?" Hannibal asked. He bent over the bed and hoisted Claude's leg into a more comfortable position.

"Figure two days, de leg be better. Den you bof kin go on wid de coffle. You stays wid Claude."

She ordered the rest of the slaves out of the cabin, and sent them down to the row of huts in Luke's charge. But unwilling to leave, they milled around in front of Granny's cabin and insisted on some of the honey and whiskey. Luke shouted angrily at the unruly men and cursed them to restore order, unsuccessful in his attempt. But when the old conjurer's malignant face and raised cane appeared and she threatened them with a hex, they went off with the chains, subdued to murmuring and dark looks.

Claude's belly growled once his pain subsided, and reminded him of his need. His mouth watered at the smell of a stewpot. "We's hungry, Granny," he said.

The toothless old crone cackled when he broke his silence. She looked at him with a droll expression but said nothing as she stirred the pot. Steam rose from it as she worked. Its irresistible aroma drew Hannibal closer and sharpened Claude's desire. Granny laughed and dropped some batter on a hot iron plate, the corncake sizzling as it browned. With the food about ready she said, "I fix dat empty belly, Claude, fo' Hannibal take you ter de crypt. We keeps you safe dere. Ain't gwine hunt fer sojers in a buryin' place. An' ain't tell nobody you kin talk."

His startled, apprehensive look amused her. "I knows you's a Linckum sojer," she said. "Granny Owdoms done send word long back. We he'p, jist like all de rest."

She reached for a dipper and bowls while he and Hannibal whispered together. Granny fed the two fugitives large gourds of stew with corncake, then some clabber and honey and a gourd of milk. His full belly added to Claude's malaise and he quickly succumbed into a deep sleep.

Full dark had fallen before Hannibal and the limp planter were safely ensconced in the Calhoun mausoleum, about a half-mile west of the manse. The family cemetery was on a high knoll that overlooked the river bottom, its eminence wooded with oak and hickory trees. A few graves surrounded the large stone and brick crypt. Hannibal discovered a huge mound of corn shucks in a corner away from the door, plenty for bedding and covering in the cool air. Granny also had sent a ragged quilt for Claude.

"Needs ter rest," she had told Hannibal before he toted Claude out of the cabin. "You keep de man warm."

"What'cher do next, Granny?"

"I be up ter see 'im fo' daylight atter talkin' ter Rufus. We feed yuh but you keep hid an' quiet. Unnerstand?"

Hannibal nodded. "How I know where ter go?" His plaintive cry brought a cackle from Granny.

"You jist foller Sissie dere at de do'. She know de place an' how ter git in. She don' tell nobody 'bout'cher." She called to the alert little girl who had joined them. "Tek 'em by de bushy path, chile, so dey can't be seen."

It had been an easy tote, even with the limp planter. Hannibal arranged his friend's cover before he burrowed into the shucks for a warm night's sleep.

A candle flickered on the camp desk, bothered by the breeze entering the opened tent flap to his back. The Colonel picked up the white sheet before him, its regimental logo at the top an impressive decoration. The page was unmarked by pen after an hour of staring. He lounged there smoking a cigar, one of the package from Arch. Redolent smoke wafted out to the pacing sentries along the officer's row, the Cuban's perfume so different from the acrid scent of the coarse leaves of their hands of tobacco.

"Midnight," he murmured, after a glance at his watch. "I just got to get at it." He sighed and picked up the pen. A stifled sob broke the stillness as he bent his head over the repositioned paper.

In camp
Anderson, S.C.
November 14, 1864

My Dear Suffering Cousin:

I write with a most intense agony, the dagger's blow in my breast bringing tears. The vipers of the Union have struck us again, may their souls rot in hell.

It is most painful for me to report to you the death of Edward, your second and most devoted son. Oh, how sorrow fills my heart, its sadness overflowing from our family loss of so many fine, young men, and now the fairest of them all! Such a gentle boy, one attuned to books and the cloth, not war. But if I am so stricken, how must you suffer, my dearest cousin, what with all your sons fallen on the field of honor? I cannot hold and soothe you, being so far distant, but my prayers go out to you and up to our Lord above, the

Father who forgives, consoles, comforts. May He have mercy on you and give you peace.

Your loving son was killed carrying out his duty as a soldier. He led his men into battle, in the fore as a brave man should. Dear Edward was shot down by a Unionist, receiving a ball through the heart and suffering no pain. The cowardly skulker who killed him was trying to get to the federal lines, but was taken and given the rope. Two others escaped, including a despicable Yankee officer. I have sent Arch Hartsill to pursue them, to the ends of the earth if necessary, and to kill the villains and all others who helped the Yankee. Those vile people must be exterminated!

When the action was over, his men brought Edward's body back with honor. We will bury him in the cemetery at Anderson tomorrow, giving him the rich, religious service he so respected. The Reverend Eggleston has agreed to preach and to read over our dear departed.

I cannot write further, it is such a blow to my heart. May the Lord protect you in your grief.

With sorrow, your loving cousin,

George A. Hyatte

A last tendril of smoke rose from the cigar stub on the edge of the desk. It played into the staring eyes of the mesmerized man, his gaze transfixed by the paper and its message. Slowly, the entire frame of the Colonel collapsed into itself as he shrank from the horrifying passages. Dropping his head onto the desk he wept, his tears blotting the neatly inked page.

CHAPTER 14

Goldie Hawkins

November 14, 1864. Calhoun's Plantation, S.C. Temperature 69\40, fair and sunny with a cool wind. Mild westerlies. Moon waning, setting about two hours after full dark.

Wind sighed in the hardwoods around the mausoleum and rattled the thick layer of fallen leaves. A protesting scrape at the metal door woke them in the dark before dawn. Claude was up with his pistol ready when a small figure called out from lightened crack, gray compared to the blackness of the crypt.

"Hannibal? It Sissie."

The small girl entered the opening, preceded by a mouth-watering smell of bacon and pone. Claude's ravenous hunger drove him to a dish held out by the child. He eagerly seized the handle of the bowl and picked pieces off the pile of hot food before he held it out to Hannibal. Claude was cramming bits into his mouth when the big servant grunted beside him and wolfed down the offering. The dish emptied quickly under their fierce assault. Scraping with the pone shined the wood as their bread soaked up the last grease. A gourd of milk completed their simple meal, followed by a few satisfied belches that rumbled in the crypt. Sissie was framed in the gloom of the opened door, all three figures black wraiths in the dim starlight, when Granny's soft and distinctive whisper broke the silence.

"Liked it, did yuh?"

"Mighty tasty, Granny," the planter replied. He searched the gloom, unable to see the old slave. "We're mighty grateful."

Hannibal grunted and made licking noises as he cleaned his fingers of grease, then wiped his mouth with the back of his hand. He murmured to Claude before he disappeared through the door and on down the hill. His rapid steps added little noise to that of swirling leaves.

"Hannibal be back soon as he's straight with his bowels," Claude explained. "Got the cramps some an' the flux."

"I fix dat," Granny said. "Few draps o' tonic an' some clay stop it right quick." The old woman jerked at the sleeve of the figure standing behind her chair. "Fetch me inside, Luke, den close de do'."

The silent Luke dutifully picked up the elderly, shrunken woman in her chair and carried them inside the crypt. The door shut easily on quiet hinges, a fact not lost on the planter.

"How come the hinges don't squeak? They ought to be full o' rust."

"We oils 'em regular," Granny said. She chuckled, then laughed outright. "Mistress don' know we hides de 'scapes in de family buryin' place. She right mad if she fin' out."

The old woman fumbled in her clothes, the rustling and her mumbling finally ceasing. Her peremptory command split the darkness. "Luke, bring de pine knot. Needs de light."

Blackness concealed the scratch of a match but its brief flame lit up Granny's fingers and revealed Luke holding a resin knot on a stick. He pointed the splintered end at the old slave and her fire. The resin caught immediately from the match's brightness and the torch flared up, a good light that cast shadows in the crypt. Sulfur from the match and acrid smoke from the resin caught at Claude's nose. He sneezed uncontrollably, unable to subdue the irritation until he moved farther from the light.

"Can't have dat, boy," Granny said in reproof. "Got ter

look at de leg."

The old woman beckoned him to her chair, with its hanging sack of nostrums. His steps were firm, but with a small limp. Lying down flat on the cold stone floor, he placed his leg in her lap.

She bent over the wound, once it was unwrapped, and gently fingered its edges. Little, pleased exclamations burst out as she inspected it. Granny's voice was confident when she cheerily delivered her opinion. "It sho' be better, Claude. It still painin' yer?"

"Not as much, Granny. And I can walk all right for a few steps." Claude sat up and inspected his calf. It was back to normal size. The skin had almost regained its old, healthy appearance, with the heat out and little reddening left of the colored swelling of the day before. He shook his head as he got to his feet and hopped about. "Not dizzy either. Don't have no fever now."

"It's de cleanin' wid de whiskey, den de sugar, boy, 'long wid de blood tonic. Work 'bout ever'time. But you needs one more day o' restin' an' feedin' a'fo' you go back on de road. So you hides right'chere fer de day."

After she had added gooey sugar to the wound and rewrapped his leg, Granny dosed Claude with more tonic. He opened his mouth willingly this time to receive the noxious draft. But he gagged when he found it no more palatable than before. She chuckled while he hawked to clear his throat and spit out the foul tasting residue.

"It good fer yuh, boy. Take some water; it he'p."

Luke unshipped the shoulder strap of a bladder full of water and held out the vessel for Claude's rinsing. The planter swallowed a huge gulp, then hung the strap on a wall projection near Granny's chair.

Hannibal had re-entered the door during Claude's doctoring, sliding into the light like a great, slinking cat. Granny rummaged in her bag and produced an assortment of powders and shreds which she mixed with water in a bowl made from a gourd. A black liquid from a glass bottle finished off the dose. She stirred it rapidly with her forefinger and held out the potion to Hannibal.

"Tek it boy," she ordered. Her sharp voice cut the night

when he hesitated. "Right now! Dreen it!"

Hannibal still looked askance at the draft. His nose wrinkled and his lips squeezed together tightly as he shook his head in refusal.

"God damn it, Hannibal, drink the tonic!" Claude's peremptory order infuriated the servant.

Hannibal spun around, his hands clenched when he stepped toward the planter. "Don' you tell me what ter do, Claude. I don' want no fixin'."

Claude shrank away from the menace, amazed at the slave's belligerence. Here was a new Hannibal, one of equality, ready to challenge his domination of the Negro. Its implication exploded into his mind like a thunderbolt, a recognition that always after they no longer would be master and slave but equal, sharing partners, deferring to each other's opinions.

Granny's quiet wisdom settled their fuss and brought peace to the crypt. "Leave Claude be, Hannibal," she said gently. "He right." But her stern order brooked no delay when she again offered the medicine. "You tek dishere tonic. It cure yer flux."

Hannibal sipped, grumbling at the taste, then emptied the bowl with reluctance. Granny sloshed in a little water to rinse the container and handed it over for his last draining gulp.

"Good fer yuh, boy," she said, when he downed it. "Stop de flux right quick. Now guzzle some water. Wash it down good."

She motioned to the bladder and his greedy mouth half-emptied it before he sighed and rehung the strap. Her firm commands demanded their full attention, the domineering old matriarch their savior and not to be trifled with.

"You stay here all t'day an' sleep an' git strong. We tek yuh outen here termorrer, early."

"How you feed us?" Hannibal asked.

"Git some vittles ter yuh easy. Sissie brings 'em fer de day but you stay hid inside."

Hannibal held up his foot to the light. "Need new boots, Granny. Bof Claude and me." He rotated his foot. The side of the shoe was split from the sole and his skin showed through.

Granny shook her head, doubt showing in her lined face. "Don' know. Had shoemaker fo' most o' de han's run off ter de nawth. I'se look in de shop."

Claude thought of the large number of hands the big plantation would require. Surely there had to be an overseer, maybe also an assistant. It worried him that Granny had not mentioned them. The fugitives were sure to be discovered if some alert white men were about the place.

"Got any white men here?" he asked. "They's bound to find us, Granny, if an overseer's about."

The old woman sighed and shook her head in dissent, then launched into a tale of woe. "All de men er gone. Massa an' his boys in de wah. Two been kilt." She paused. "Ain' no slaves much ter manage. Dey mostly all run off up ter de nawth atter Linckum freed 'em, 'ceptin' fer de ol' folks in de cabins."

Granny pulled the little girl close and Sissie melted against her. "I'se too ol' ter run an' Sissie here, she ain't got no folks but me. Onliest others de ol' ones in de big house." She wiped her eyes and gave a little sob. "Can't make no crops 'ceptin' fer food. Missus ain't no Calhoun or dey kin. She Hawkins, de overseer's wife. Army come got him too."

Her bitter tone and doleful face shocked Claude. The overseer's wife in the big house? It was unheard of. His disgust and curses prompted Granny to elaborate.

"Old Missus died atter de second son got kilt. Jist pined away. Warn't no gals. Cunnel an' de rest o' 'is boys rode off ter kill de Yankees. Tol' Hawkins ter keep up de house an' crops bes' he could. Army took 'im right atter. He fightin' up in Virginny jist like de rest."

"But what about the Mistress?"

"Ol' Miz Hawkins jist white trash from over 'round Green's place. She move right in de big house an' put on airs. She terrible bad wid de beatin's. Make us call her Missus."

"You don't use her first name?"

Granny spat and made a strangling sound of disgust. "Her fust name Goldie but I ain't gwine call her Miz Goldie. Ain't fittin'. Miz Hawkins bad 'nuff."

A whole plantation gone to ruin, Claude thought, the owner away and a ruthless white trash in charge. No crops except for food. Impossible to plant and make cotton or any other salable goods without the hands to work the acres. It was a revelation like a flash of light, a foretelling of his future. His mind switched instantly to Greenbottom. He wouldn't be able to continue his cropping there; his labor would disappear in the same way. It was the river that would save him, rafting logs to New Orleans, a steamboat and trading, things he was good at besides farming. He knew he faced the apocalypse, that his days as a big planter were done, ended in a crypt in South Carolina, buried there just as the hopes and dreams and men of the South.

"Take me back, Luke." Granny's command broke the silence of the group, its members engrossed in their own dilemmas. Luke picked up the chair and Granny and headed for the door. Hannibal grasped his arm and stopped him.

"Fo' you leave, Granny, I'se ask 'bout de fishin'." Hannibal's face shined in the light, the fat from the bacon glistening about his mouth.

Granny perked up in her chair. Her eyes sparkled as she faced the big slave. "What you thinkin'?"

"Dat ol' ribber down dere in de bottom. Could be I gits some cats in de bank, grabblin' ternight. Still ain't too col'. De han's ketch any?"

"Allus' git fish in de past, Hannibal. Right good holes. But all de men gone dat do dat, er de seinin'."

Hannibal nodded. "If Luke take me ternight," he said, "I sees what I kin git. Done grabblin' ever since I'se a little boy."

"He's good at it, Granny," Claude added. "He got big fish lots o' times up in Virginia."

Granny smacked her lips and settled the arrangements. "Luke come fer yuh atter full dark. Fish mighty good wid de pone." She waggled her finger at them. "Put out de torch atter we leaves. Both o' yer git plenty rest and stay here."

The three visitors passed out into the dark night. Only a small shaft of light shined from the cracked doorway.

Claude quickly made a stop outside then put out the blazing knot. The tomb was dark and silent when he and Hannibal fell asleep, their full bellies comforting them.

"Dat Miz Ashley done 'ccuse me agin," Hester said, dejectedly.

"O' what, chile?" Granny Owdoms asked.

The old Negro granny hovered sympathetically over the crying girl. Hester sprawled in a chair, her hands covering her head. The ancient's gentle fingers massaged a bump on the girl's cheekbone, still not healed from the abuse of the Minnses. But the maid moved the old woman's hand to the top of her skull, where Granny found a rising swelling.

Hester blurted out the story between sniffles. "Stealin' her ol' red beads, dat's what. I ain't seed 'em, Granny. Had ter be one o' de other gals. But Miz Ashley, she allus watch me sharp, an' she hit me wid de brush." She winced and complained when Granny struck a sore place. "It hurt!"

The girl broke into tears again, her sobs and shuddering body taken into Granny's close embrace. The old woman patted her back and soothed her.

"Don' take on so. De white folks, dey allus tinks we de big thieves. Dey jist can't recken no other way. De nigger works and de white folks gits de pretties. Dey b'long ter us fer de labor but de white folks don' take kindly ter us wear'n nothin' purty."

"But I don' think she mind," Hester burst out. "She got a whole box full o' beads an' I works hard fer 'er."

"Ain't make no difference, chile." Resignation clouded the old servant's voice and her innate cheerfulness descended into pathos and a bitter judgement. "Miz Ashley don' give yuh nothin'."

The girl's stormy face hardened in the firelight of the cabin. Her body tensed into a vibrant whole, strung tight for action. "I'se goin'a run," she said. "Goin' ter Hannibal. He treat me right."

Hester pulled away from Granny and jumped up like a released spring. The aroused girl paced before the fire, her imprecations damming her mistress into hell-fires.

Granny's gentle voice soothed her. "Ain't he'pin' none,

yer th'owin' a fit." When the tirade did not subside, the old slave tried another tack. "If yer gwine run, you need a plan ter git away. I he'ps wid dat.'

Hester's temper tantrum subsided as fast as it rose, once Granny's advice had penetrated the cloud of her distress. The girl looked imploringly at the old woman and sought her hand. "Will you he'p, Granny?" she asked. She wiped off her tears and said, anxiously, "An' George too?".

Granny squeezed her hand reassuringly. "Sho' 'nuff," she replied.

With their heads together, after the women were joined by George with his ever present chaw, the three plotters mapped out Hester's escape. She was hidden in the wagon George took out of the barnyard that afternoon, her escape aided by a bag of food and a sharp knife, gifts from Granny. The old slave prayed for the girl when Hester left the hut, her eyes teary as she watched the departure of another of a long stream of runaways she had helped to freedom.

"O' Lord. He'p de chile ter de promised lan'.

Granny's tears flowed and she collapsed into her chair before the fire. Soothing prayer gave way to a soft chant taught to her by her friend, Millie, years before.

"Massa sleeps in the feather bed,
Nigger sleeps on the floor;
When we get to heaven
There'll be no slaves no more."

"Let me live ter see de freedom, Lord," Granny prayed. "But particular, dat chile, Hester. Tek her safe ter Hannibal an' Claude, up to dat free lan'."

"What she want me fo'?" Granny Esther asked.

Her suspicious, belligerent reply reinforced the bullying power her imperious stance projected. As if an intimidating presence were not enough, her unyielding stare braced the old man facing her in the cabin. He was in the livery of the house servants, his white hair evidence of long service. The frail old slave shifted nervously before her and the shine of his boots disappeared under a coating of dust stirred up from the dirt floor.

"Well, Moses, what she want?" Granny said sharply.

The ancient placed her hand on the head of the bent figure and patted him like a child. Her suddenly soft voice reassured him. "Don' want no trouble wid you. We growed up t'gether. Member how we played when we was chil'ren?"

His head lifted and his crinkled face laughed. "Good times den, Esther, when de Calhouns here." His face clouded. "Gone now. Dose peoples livin' in de big house since de war ain't like de Calhouns, er dey kin here after Massa John died. Dey mean. Warn't right dat overseer movin' in whilst de Cunnel and de boys gone ter de war." He shook his white head and dolefully repeated his message. "Missus want yuh."

"Why she do dat?"

"She done heard from dat trouble maker, Iris, dat you got 'scapes hid out. You know dat Iris. She hate yuh bad. An' she like snake, bite yuh when she can."

Granny grunted. "Don' fancy it dat I'se kept her from Big John. He gone ter be free, th'outen her, an' good riddance." She spat disgustedly. Her temper rose as she stood fixedly in the cabin, with Moses waiting silently nearby. Boiling over, her string of oaths split the quiet. Sissie sat quietly on the hearth, bright eyed and attentive, as she absorbed Granny's lesson in plantation intrigue.

Moses fidgeted uneasily when the old woman made no effort to leave. Finally unable to delay further, he clasped one of her hands and beckoned with his head. "Come quick, Granny," he urged, his voice quavering. "She powerful mad."

Luke delivered Granny and her ever-present companion, Sissie, to the circular drive in front of the mansion in a few minutes. He was puffing hard from lugging the old woman and her chair up the hill. The slope's steep incline had rutted from the heavy storms in September and picking his way with a shifting weight had burdened even the robust Luke. Granny faced the porch while she waited on the Mistress, with Luke and Sissie behind her. Her's and Sissie's shawls were wrapped tight against the cool, westerly wind that blew in over the bottom lands. But Luke was not so warm and shivered and muttered, protesting the wait. When their Mistress at last appeared, she swept out onto the porch with Moses and Iris behind her, followed by two small children. Granny kept very still, her head bowed in submission until a sharp query forced her to face the probing eyes and lean, pointed face of the overseer's wife.

"What's this I hear about your hiding some escaped slaves?"

"Tain't so," Granny burst out. "Dat Iris jist lyin'."

Granny's spirited rejoinder infuriated her Mistress. As the woman's temper rose, she unconsciously fell into the idiom of the slave that she had learned in her childhood. "Don' you talk ter me like dat!" She shook her fist. "I'se have yuh whupped. Now you tells me de trute. You got 'scapes hid out?"

"Dey's one in de cabins," Iris broke in. "I'se heard it from de coffle." Her malignant smile at Granny lorded it over the old woman.

Granny rose out of her chair in protest and threatened Iris with her stick. "Tain't so," she shouted. "Yer nothin' but a nigger bitch."

Hawkins ignored the old woman and turned on Iris with a furious attack. "How come you're in the cabins with those niggers? You're s'pposed to stay with me."

The woman struck at Iris with a short whip which was hanging from her belt. Her flailing arm laid on fast, heavy blows. Iris threw up her arms and howled as the split end of the leather cut through her dress. She cowered and shielded her head while the blows fell, until the burden became too much and she ran from the porch.

Granny's laughter pealed out and she chortled to Luke and Sissie. "Looky at de sneakin' liar run."

Her glee lasted only a few seconds. The enraged Hawkins stormed from the porch and beat Granny about the head and shoulders with the leather scourge as she castigated her.

"Don' you laugh, you worthless ol' nigger. I'se give it ter you too."

She flogged Granny until Luke stepped between them. The Negro received cuts on his cheek from the whip-end thongs but seized the braided leather and yanked it from her. Screaming, Hawkins ran back a few steps. When she turned around she held a Navy Colt pointed at Luke. Its leveled barrel scared them all into immobility as her choked voice stumbled in and out of the idiom of her childhood.

"Now you beat dat old woman good," she ordered. "If ye don', I shoot yer both right'cher." Her thumb cocked the hammer in an instant. Its rasp was loud and threatening, a fearful sound demanding instant obedience.

"Don' cross de missus, Luke," Granny said. She grabbed the end of the whip hanging from his hand and yanked on it. "I'se tek de beatin'."

The old slave rose from her chair and staggered a few paces to a grassy spot. She fell into the mat of leaves from the large trees in the yard and lay prone. Sissie ran over and settled down beside her, nestling in close. Granny covered the child with her arm and shawl and hid her completely. Hawkins stepped closer and waved the revolver between Luke and Granny. "Beat 'er good," she commanded. "An' give that chile a few licks."

Luke, indecisive, glanced first at the implacable Hawkins, then at the two prone figures, hesitating between the loathsome task and the menace of the leveled gun. Its barrel aligned with his head as the bullying woman took careful aim. His peril ended with Granny's anguished scream.

"Hit us, Luke! Don' let 'er kill yuh."

The whip rose and fell, but with all of Luke's skill at evasion. Its tip snapped as close to the figures as he could manage without hurting them. His deceit incited another tirade from Hawkins and a shot past his ear.

"Lay it on, boy, or yer a dead man. Don' want no slackin' when I tell yuh ter do somethin'."

A flurry of blows rained down on Granny and the child. The two under the shawls screamed and wept loudly as the whipend fluffed and split their clothes. Their squirming and cries of pain brought a cruel smile to the face of the watching woman. She lowered the pistol at last and walked back up the porch steps. Luke threw down the whip as soon as Hawkins turned her back and knelt to help Granny and Sissie.

"We be awright, Luke," Granny whispered. She sat up

as she quietly reassured him. "De shawls heavy. De whip
don' hurt."

She was back in the chair, sobbing, when Hawkins
faced about. Granny daubed at a small cut on her face and
smeared the blood to look like a torrent, then cried out as if
in terrible anguish.

"You done hurt me bad," she wailed. "An' Sissie."
Granny took the child into her lap while whispering to her
to howl. Sissie threw her arms about and shrieked as if in
terror.

The attentive Hawkins smiled in satisfaction at the din.
Her sharp tongue cut up Granny as she pursued information on the fugitives. "You goin'a tell me 'bout the 'scapes
you got hid or I got ter whip yuh agin?"

Granny spat between them, contempt in her contorted
face. Her silence and gleaming eyes were answer enough.

Hawkins cocked the pistol and pointed it at the old
woman. Sissie screamed and hid her head in Granny's lap,
quaking and crying. The ancient old Negress patted and
soothed the child into silence, then straightened up in her
chair. She locked eyes with Hawkins, uncowed as she faced
her death with dignity and fortitude. But the pistol again
went back into the waistband of the mistress, its charge
unused as she called to her house servant.

"Moses!"

"Yessum?" The old slave shuffled to her side, his bent
frame bowing up and down.

"We got one horse left, ain't we?"

"Yessum. In de small pasture next to de barn. Ol' Molly
'bout broke down though. She more'n twenty year ol' an' not
much."

"Well, we'll just have to use 'er. Mr. Rufus won't he'p.
He's got to take his coffle west."

"Yessum. What you want wid Molly?"

"Goin'a send a note to Colonel Hyatte, down to Anderson 'bout the 'scapes. He'll ketch 'em. Can't have no rousty
niggers wandering through." Her tone turned peremptory.
"Find Iris an' get her ter he'p you saddle Molly."

Moses protested. "Dat girl can't go, Miz Hawkins."

"She's got to," Hawkins replied. Her firm voice took on

an icy-sharp edge as she intimidated the old Negro servant.

"Iris kin ride. I saw 'er myself." Shaking her fist at him, she said, "She'll either do it or I'll hide her back myself. Now git."

Two hours later, Rufus hailed down Iris on the road to Anderson. He read the note from Hawkins, then lighted it from the end of his thick cigar and let the paper burn to ashes before he rode away. Cowed by the threats of the bulky, fearsome man, Iris meekly followed him back to Calhoun's, where the two travelers reported to Granny at her cabin. The ancient slave scrooched her chair around to face them, leaving the warmth of the fire on her back.

Rufus ignored Iris' curses and thrust the resisting girl forward once they were inside. His violent smack on her buttocks propelled her to a stand before Granny's chair. Iris sagged and began to cry as she rubbed her stinging rump.

"What I do now?" she wailed. "Miz Hawkins gwine kill me fer not takin' de note."

"You tell 'er you give de note ter de Cunnel," Granny said.

Iris sniffled and heatedly protested. "She know I'se lyin', Granny, an' beat me agin. I ain't gwine do it." She crossed her arms, defiantly facing the old woman and mouthing oaths. Her anger tempered when Rufus grabbed her by the neck and choked her. She was gagging and gasping for breath before he let her break free.

His blazing eyes stared her down and his bushy red beard rose and fell as he threatened her. "You do what Granny tells yuh, er I'll beat yuh 'til you's dead."

Iris nodded and choked back her sobs. She wiped away her tears and waited submissively in front of the old woman. But her sniffling persisted as she eyed Rufus. Fearful, she shrank from his closeness and the strong presence that overpowered her will.

The girl started when Granny grasped her hand, and then sought the safety of the old woman's side. "Rufus put up Old Molly," Granny told her. "You go on down ter de coffle. Sport wid de boys 'til atter dark. Den go back inter de big house an' tell yer missus 'bout de note."

Iris perked up at the mention of the coffle. A smile came

back to her face and she began primping, first wiping off her tears and smoothing her face. She fixed her hair a bit, then straightened her dress and adjusted her bandanna. With her good humor restored, she and Rufus left the cabin.

When their voices had died away, Sissie crept out of her hiding place behind some sacks and large clay jugs at the side of the cabin. Granny took the child to her bosom and comforted her trembling body.

"Ain' nothin' ter be scairt of, chile. Dat ol' woman up dere in de big house don' hurt yuh no more." Granny's voice hardened with hate. "She gwine git herself kilt when de Yankees come. When we's free, we kill 'er."

Hartsill rode along the scattered line of dismounted men, the two Minns following him at the rear. Old Blue's tongue hung nearly to the ground as he loped behind them. The warm sun of the late afternoon and a fast run had burdened the old dog and his tongue dripped a river of saliva. But Blue never quit on a trail and his sniffs constantly searched the vapors for Claude's telltale odor. When they came to a small brook he slid down the cutbank and jumped in, the riders clearing the hurdle at a bound. Rolling over in the cold water and lapping up some mouthfuls, Blue dallied in the rushing brook and refreshed himself. Minns roar fetched him out in a single bound. His rhythmic shudders showered away the water before he raced to overtake the riders. Blue's preoccupation with the stream, and the westerly wind, made his nose fail him when the party rode by the Negroes' hiding place.

"Right pert hound," Gabe observed to Aunty Emma.

She nodded. The two crouched downwind, in a willow patch along the small creek. But Emma shrank further into the dense growth when the dog passed their clump. Once he was gone, she moved the willow fronds slightly where she peered out.

"Dishere's a good place," she said in a low voice. "Kin watch de rebs easy from here."

Gabe put his hand on her arm and squeezed. He kept very quiet, his tense face alert to the danger. His rifle barrel pointed out through the willow branches, ahead and capable of instant firing. The giant's huge belt knife was sheathed but Emma clutched her long corn knife.

It was a fine perch for the Negroes to observe the military formation. The troopers deployed into an expanding, single line of men, then formed a pincers in the open forest above the start of the thicket along the river. Their circle widened and slowly moved forward as Gabe and Emma spied on the line.

"Austin's a' good boy, Gabe, ter come back an' warn us." Aunty Emma's muttered aside barely carried to the hidden man.

"Dat grapevine from de han's at de railroad work jist fine," Gabe whispered. "Dose rebs can't do nothin' we don' know fust."

The dismounted troopers stole quietly through the woods, converging on the dense part that contained Emma's cabin and the campsite. When they had passed the two slaves, Gabe and Aunty waited until the noise died out. Darting from one clump of bushes to another in short bursts, they moved to the northwest, directly away from the skirmish line.

Over to the east Minns argued with the Lieutenant.

"You ain't goin'a ketch none o' them bastards this way, Hartsill." Minns sat his horse in front of the trooper's and blocked his movement.

The Lieutenant unsheathed his saber, its metallic shriek on exiting the scabbard grating on the tension between the two antagonists. Hartsill raised it over his head when Minns didn't move. His ominous voice was very low and even.

"I'll give you just five seconds to clear out, Minns. You ain't been nothin' but a grumbling ass the whole day. I don't need you here no more."

"Watch out, Pa," Jared shouted, and reined his mount to the trooper's side. He cocked his rifle and stuck it up close to the Lieutenant's body, then leaned over toward the man. "You hit my Pa," he said fiercely, "an' I'll kill yuh right here."

Hartsill weighed the choices, his face alternately white and crimson as he met the youth's glaring stare. Reason won. He lowered his saber and Minns backed his horse. The hunter looked at the trooper in a pitying fashion.

"You dumb bastard," he said. "You can't pull no s'prise on those niggers. They know yer comin' in. Yer goin'a git some men kilt if they's any niggers left in the thicket."

The hunter's scorn infuriated Hartsill. In his frenzy, the man of old southern family gentility regressed into the colloquial language of the hunter. "Git!" he raged. "Git, afore I hang yuh both."

Minns and Jared cut across country, but stopped south of Gabe's thicket. Old Blue cast about at the halt and ended up at a slight crevice by an adjacent log. His snuffling nose explored it thoroughly, his interest increasing as he pawed at the deep end. With his tail wagging, he commenced a frantic spate of loud barking and digging.

Jared's laugh pealed out in the open woods. "Old fool after another o' them chipmunks, Pa," he said. "He can't keep from chasin' those things ever'time they squeak at 'im."

Minns chuckled. "It's good fer 'im. Keeps his nose goin'."

"Where to now, Pa?"

"We head on 'round the thicket and over to Anderson. Hartsill's gotta come in t'morrow. He ain't gonna find much here. Those slaves er all gone." Minns stuffed some fresh leaf into his mouth and worked his new chaw into a wad. "We'll find out what he did, then go on to the west. Shaw's gotta be someplace close."

Minns wheeled his horse and picked a way through a tall stand of pines interspersed in the hardwood forest. Thick needles left a soft covering, so their horses moved along silently through the cathedral of giant, smooth trunks. They had gone only a mile when Old Blue struck. His melodic yodel and fast run signaled a hot trail, but he soon quit. Blue's furious "treed" barking guided them to his side. The dog ran from one end to the other of a hollow log. He was pawing into the hole and growling when the riders pulled up.

The Minnses dismounted, Jared holding the horses while Athey cocked his rifle and warily approached the hole. The hunter stayed about five feet away. Cautious, he lined up his rifle barrel with the poplar trunk as he bent over to sight into the blackness of the cavity.

"Keerful, Pa," Jared said. He moved off to one side and readied his rifle. "Might be one o' them bears. Plenty o' mast through here an' not too cold."

The hunter kicked the fractious old dog from in front of the opening. "Git, Blue," he said. Blue retreated to a spot behind Minns, his hackles up. His barking subsided into fearsome growls as Minns knelt and looked up the length of the hole.

"It's a damned nigger," he said disgustedly, and poked at the hole with his gun barrel. It set Blue to barking again, the dog dancing about the log.

"Come on outen there, boy," Minns ordered, "afore I shoot yuh."

A youthful Negro inched out of the narrow trunk at Minns' grim threat, his wooly head and body covered with decayed wood. Austin protested plaintively as he shied away from Blue and stood with his hands up.

"I'se ain't done nothin', Massa. Jist on de way ter Belton."

"Then why you hidin' in the log?" Minns asked, his skepticism evident. He prodded the boy with his rifle barrel while Blue sniffed at the Negro's heels.

Austin ignored Minns and shrank from the dog, his eyes following the animal's bared teeth and growls. His feet shuffled away from the hound's threatening mouth as he tried to avoid an attack.

"Answer me boy," Minns said. He jabbed Austin hard in the ribs. The impact of the iron barrel crumpled Austin inward. He clutched his side as he doubled up and cried out in pain and fear.

"I'se sceert o' de houn'," Austin said. "He come a'runnin' an' I sceert he bite."

Minns laughed and kicked at Blue again, keeping the dog away. "He won't hurt yuh," he said.

"He looks like a nigger I seen down to Due West, Pa," Jared said. "'bout when we found Hester."

Minns' frame stiffened at the thought. He inspected the

captured slave closely, searching the trembling boy's teary eyes with a cold stare. When Austin's eyes fell and he turned to run, Minns knocked him down with a sweep of his rifle butt.

"Don't do that, boy," he warned, "I shoot yuh dead." His ominous threat made no impression on the semiconscious boy, whose quivering body lay in the forest duff.

"He's up here to warn Shaw an' Hannibal, Pa," Jared said.

Minns paused and leaned on his rifle while he studied the downed slave. Jared walked the horses to a bush and tied off the reins, then took a firing stance at one side with his rifle ready for action.

Minns finally broke his silent contemplation of the now cowering Austin. "Yer right, boy," he said. "He couldn't look me in the eye." The hunter fingered the whip tied to his saddle, then took down the leather. "We beat it out o' 'im. Find where they's gone."

A scattering of rifle shots and rebel yells far behind them absorbed their attention. Minns laughed. "I tol' that dumb Hartsill. Those niggers er gone an' this boy's likely the reason." He snapped the whip. "With a little o' this leather, we orta git it outen 'im."

The next few minutes carried the sounds of a few more faint shots and a smoke column showed above a break in the trees. It drifted off toward the east, hanging just above the forest.

Jared pointed with his rifle. "They burned the camps, I recken."

The hunter spat, derisive of the effort. "Warn't much up there. Those niggers move 'round all the time an' they's more to the south in the bresh at the big fork in the rivers."

Minns turned back to the slave and kicked the sitting Austin until he was upright. The boy held his head, his hands discolored by a trickle of blood that seeped through his fingers. Austin's eyes wandered back and forth between the two grim hunters as tears coursed down his cheeks.

"Don' hurt me," he sobbed. "I don' know nothin'."

Their whip and knives and a few kicks to the groin soon reduced him to a quivering jelly, ready to tell anything to prevent further pain. The beaten boy's confession came out through choking sobs.

"Claude an' Hannibal gone west ter Anderson in a coffle wid Rufus. Dey's headin' fer 'lanta an' de Yankee lines. De coffle hide de 'scapes."

Minns sheathed his knife and reached for his rifle. Picking it up from its rest against the log, he vaulted into the saddle of his mount, his action followed swiftly by Jared.

"What you goin'a do with the nigger, Pa?" Jared asked, as he reined his horse around.

Minns extended his arm with the rifle barrel steady as iron. At the shot his horse reared. The hunter gentled the mount back to a stand and reloaded apace when the animal was still. Austin's body jerked once or twice on the ground and lay relaxed. His eyes stared and his tongue hung out at the side. A little bloody seep dribbled out of the canted mouth and stained the brown needles cradling his head.

"He won't cause no more trouble," Minns said. He chirked to his horse and kneed it around to the west. The two riders threaded through the big trees of the forest, aiming for Anderson.

Crack! . . . . Crack!

At the shots Aunty Emma went down in a heap, her figure unmoving ahead of him. Gabe didn't wait, the ball that tore his muscles ample reason to run like a deer. He doubled back south, holding his side as he dodged through the forest. Behind him, Rebel yells of triumph resounded but their sounds grew fainter as he ran. Miles downcountry, the giant slowed when his lungs burned to bursting and his legs grew wobbly. Staggering and sliding into a brushy ravine, he collapsed beside a small trickle of water, senseless from the wound and the run.

A hooty owl's tremolo awoke him in the early dark. When he felt of his side, he found a gash from the ball, one that had sliced the skin and muscles but did not penetrate his ribs. Gabe washed the wound clean, unable to bind it up. He crept stealthily along the creek to a thick place by a downed log and crawled into it for shelter. The den was warm, with lush, dry grasses for covering and bushes to break the wind. Succumbing to his wound and exhaustion from the marathon run, he slept away the night.

CHAPTER 15

Sissie

---

*November 15, 1864. Calhoun's Plantation,
S.C. Temperature 71\39, fair and sunny,
with scattered clouds. Mild westerly winds.
Moon half full, waning, setting about three
hours after full dark.*

Sissie woke the fugitives before cockscrow. The dark
quiet of the night was giving way to the chirps of birds
heralding the new morn. Stars shined in full force
when the men left the crypt, their heavenly sparkles reborn
each time after a few scudding clouds erased their faint
glow. A never-ending procession of the fluffy masses passed
slowly above, and the clear air and twinkling stars presaged
a fine day. Hannibal stretched and took a few deep breaths.

"Gonna be good, Claude, ter git on de trail agin."

The planter savored the clean air and cool breeze.
"You're right," he said. He walked around a moment and
tested his leg. "I feel like hiking now. This leg's about in
shape."

Claude stomped about, then accelerated his movement
into a few hops and jigs. He skipped around the perimeter
of the crypt, stopping only when Sissie caught at his arm.
The planter grasped the child's hand and stood with her
before the door of the vault. He gazed affectionately at the
massive structure and chuckled.

"Didn't think I'd sleep in one of these so early," he said.

His ironic good humor evoked a rumble from Hannibal. "Got ter wait 'til yer dead, Claude. You's promised a long time yet."

A few minutes travel in the sparkling night took them well down the trail to the quarters. Hannibal sniffed the swirling breeze on his way to Granny's, intent on a vagrant scent. Overlying the damp odor of woods, a fragrant message from the bottoms and cabins pulled them along the hillside. When they approached the row, the aroma of fried fish was unmistakable. Sissie and Claude followed the half-running Negro, their steps aimed toward the spark of light at Granny's and the smell of food. Hannibal already was wolfing down fish and pone from a trencher when they entered the cabin.

Granny Esther greeted them from the hearth. "Some good fish hyar, Claude. Hannibal do hisself proud grabblin'." She was on her knees before a skillet resting on some separated coals, her sweat-stained face reflecting the hot glow of the fire.

The planter went over and hugged the old woman. He caressed her sparse hair and planted a kiss on her cheek. His gratitude spilled over into a second embrace and a whispered thanks as he nibbled at her ear and side of her neck. "Leg's goin'a be just fine, Granny, thanks to you."

She shied away and shook her fork at him, but a pleased grin revealed her delight, and her toothless gums. "Go 'long wid'yer, Claude," she said. "You treat me jist like my man when I'se young. But de sweet talk mighty pleasurin'."

Claude fell to his knees before the feast. He sniffed at the frying fish and his stomach rumbled as the smell of the juicy feed took hold. Sections of fish popped and drops of grease flamed in the coals. He reached for some of the corncake on a flat next to the skillet but Granny cracked his knuckles with her fork.

"Stop dat!" Her reproof and blow drove him back. He massaged his stinging, singed hand and eased back beside her. The ancient's voice softened as she turned the fish. "It not done. I'se give yuh a piece when it ready."

He leaned forward to sniff again, his hunger evident as

he wet his lips. "Smells mighty good, Granny," he said.

Pieces of fish coated with meal were coloring into a golden brown as they spattered grease and crackled away in the large skillet. The sheet of pone baked on a separate flat of metal. Granny turned the fish and flipped the pone, expertly keeping it on the grill. When she was satisfied she called to Sissie.

"Git Claude a board, chile, an' one fer yerself."

Sissie brought the planter a board for his breakfast, then held out her own shingle with her tiny hands. Granny served her first. The silent child retreated with her prize to her hiding place behind the jars and sacks.

Claude's pile of fish and pone teetered in a high pyramid. He sat before the fire and eagerly attacked its bulk with his knife and fingers. No fancy fixings, he thought, but the food was good and the simple tools served his table needs. Granny picked up a small slab of fish, its flaky whiteness disappearing bit by bit as she gummed it. A crumbly piece of pone followed. She was turning a new set of strips in the skillet when Hannibal came for a second helping.

Daylight was seeping through cracks in the door as the night receded. The dim gray of the early morning added to the light from the cabin fire. The glow of its flames reflected off Hannibal's greasy cheeks when he held out his trencher, his first load exhausted. The Negro's question diverted Claude's attention from his food.

"Rufus an' de coffle gone, Granny?"

"Dey done left more'n hour ago," she replied. "Rufus heard de troopers might be a'comin'. He wait fer yuh 'cross de ribber on de big hill. It by de west trace dat passes de ol' Injun town dar at Seneca." She poked at a piece of fish, then wiped her sweating face with her apron. "Can't miss whar de creek fork. Go up de holler by de big cedar."

"De rebs 'bout?" Claude fell into the idiom unconsciously, his usual precise English suffering from the prolonged run with the slaves.

"Dey down ter Anderson, Claude. But dey's bound ter come by Calhoun's. Allus does." Granny turned the fish and the pone, and dished up the rest of the hot pieces when she was satisfied with the browning. She waved her fork at them. "You bof eat dese an' git."

They gulped down the sizzling helpings, swallowing some clabber and cold water to relieve their scorched gullets. Claude belched repeatedly when he stood, his involuntary explosions covered by his hand while he muttered an excuse. Granny giggled and grinned with pleasure. She shuffled back and forth on her knees while she cooked the last few pieces of fish and corncake and set them aside. Sweat dropped from the end of her nose as the fireplace heat took its toll.

"Seem like you feed right good," she said, at the break in her labors. "Now you hustle an' I prays fer yuh." At Claude's questioning look, she guessed his mind. "We don' tell de rebs nothin'."

"You want ter look at Claude's leg fust?" Hannibal asked. "He heal'd awright, Granny?"

Hannibal replaced the loads in their pistols while she treated the planter. Claude lay prone in the dirt and put his leg across her lap for unwrapping and inspection. The old slave's gentle fingers stroked the edges of the wound, gradually exploring while she watched him intently. As her touch increased its pressure, the planter groaned and moved his leg away from her.

Granny Esther mumbled to herself and her face clouded momentarily. Then she patted him on the thigh and slid the leg back into her lap, saying, "Still tetches you some, do it?"

"Not too much, Granny," Claude replied. "I'll make it."

The old woman smiled and uttered little sounds of satisfaction. She cleaned the wound with water before adding more sugared honey, then bound up the injury with a fresh cloth. Granny gazed at him speculatively when she pushed the leg off her lap.

"Do de jig," she ordered.

Claude danced nimbly about the cabin, though slight aches ran through his leg. But he felt better as he stretched the muscles, his confidence lifted as well as his agility. Standing only on the hurt leg, he bent his knee and then rose to full height, a severe test of its strength. He was smiling when he retained his balance and stood erect again.

"You fixed it, Granny," he said happily. "It don't hurt

much an' it's strong. Hannibal and I'll make it to Dalton with Rufus' help. An' I thank yuh."

The enormity of her gift overwhelmed Claude as he paid homage. He felt ashamed somehow in the presence of the gentle, unstinting good-will of the old woman. Generous good-will though he was a planter and she a slave. Her imposing presence and his debt humbled him when he contemplated the danger of his wound and his rapid recovery. A weak, old Negro woman faced him, placid, at peace, an ancient slave with practically nothing but a sharp mind and the will to help, willing to risk all in the face of being killed for befriending him, a Yankee. A loving, caring granny who had enfolded him, the stranger, into her circle of affection and charity, protection and help. "I was a stranger and ye took me in." The scripture flew unbidden into his mind, another thundering message from Jesus, much used in the pulpits near Greenbottom. It reverberated through his conscious thought, hammered at his pride, and his need for forgiveness. Humbled before Granny's majesty and her Christian humanity, he sank to his knees before her chair, and hugged her and kissed her cheeks while he muttered repeated thanks.

The old slave pushed him away, protesting, but her eyes glistened with tears. "Ain't no need, Claude," she said. "I he'ps yuh jist like all de rest, ter git ter freedom. You hurry on like I say."

He shook his head and demurred. "We don't leave before seein' Sissie."

Granny's repeated calls awakened the little girl. Sissie slowly eased out into the firelight, her belly distended from all the fish and pone. She rubbed the sleep from her eyes, yawning, and sought Granny's arms. Uncaring about their thanks, Sissie napped in Granny's lap as the men approached her.

Hannibal and Claude knelt before the chair of the Negro Madonna and child, goddesses in the rude comforts of the slave cabin. Claude could not but recall other scriptures as he worshipped there, but the phrase "And a little child shall lead them," vanquished all others. He patted the head of the sleeping child and stroked her body and spindly

arms, overcome with emotion, unable to express his gratitude and love. But Hannibal's simple eloquence surpassed
the educated man at his side.

The Negro looked down on the two, his great, callused
palms hovering over them in blessing as his hands made
little stroking motions. His face turned to the sky when he
intoned his prayer. "Lawd, Granny an' Sissie yore chil'ren
fum de manger. But dis place de wilderness, Lawd, an' dey
sufferin'. Keep dem safe 'til I'se git back ter free 'em."

Granny was dozing in her chair before the fire, with
Sissie asleep in her arms, when they left the cabin and stole
away.

By late morning the fugitives were hiking up the creek
past the great cedar tree that Granny had described. A
straggling detachment of rebs crossing the Seneca River
had delayed their escape. They pressed their bodies to the
ground in a dense growth of cane grass along the river bank
until the rear guards cleared the area. As Granny had
predicted, it was easy to ford the hazard at a shallow,
secluded place downstream where the river widened into a
riffle. The crossing fronted on a natural gully that led them
into forested hills, easy to penetrate.

Claude's leg loosened with every step and its wound's
aches rapidly passed out of his consciousness. The fugitives
climbed toward the summit of the hill at the cedar, leaving
the creek in its meander around to the river. Crackling
leaves from the drying of the winds crunched under their
steps in spite of their care. The alarm put out a deer ahead
of them. The spike buck bounded away, its white flag flying
as it slipped through the trees.

Bang!

Hannibal and Claude threw themselves to the ground
at the loud rifle shot around the slope. Its sharp, clear tone
carried distinctly through the forest. Alarmed, they scurried into a cluster of honeysuckle vines and brush to seek
a hiding place, penetrating the dense growth rapidly as they
headed away from the kill. When they suddenly broke out
onto a path, Claude and the Negro ran downhill, only to be
tripped and thrown at the first turn by a grapevine stretched
across the trail. Their misfortune was followed instantly by

an attack of brown bodies that hurtled in from the side. The attackers smothered the fugitives under an avalanche of power, and covered their mouths with hard grips. When their struggling bodies were turned over by their captors, Claude found Luke astride his chest. The slave's cocked derringer rested on the planter's chin.

"You jist be still," the driver warned. "We got Rufus up de trail watchin' dat deerhunter. He be back shortly."

Claude gurgled and struggled until the hand left his mouth. "I'll be quiet," he pledged. "Now let me up."

The men turned him loose at Luke's whisper and the slave driver helped him to his feet and brushed the dirt from his back. Claude swore and waved him off, his face still red with anger. He rubbed his wrists and shook out his tangled clothes, relieved to be free. But he found himself trembling and sweating as he tried to recover his composure. Oily sweat ran down his face and more wet his armpits and added to his stink.

Nearby, another group had Hannibal pinioned, but uncertainly at best, Claude saw. The entwined mass was flopping around, its upheavals forced by the powerful Negro's frantic struggles. Hannibal's angry face puffed from his exertions and his raging mouth spat out a stream of oaths and threats as his captors struck him repeatedly. When he tried to bite a muscular arm, one of the slaves put a stick across his mouth and pulled on the bit to throttle off the noise and the menace. Blood dripped from the Negro's mashed tongue and lips as the bit took hold.

Claude ran to the melee and pulled at the slaves, throwing one aside as he swore at them and protested to Luke. The driver ambled over slowly, his triumphant grin progressing into a chuckle. He studied Hannibal's jerking body and ignored Claude until the planter pulled his pistol. Luke looked around, questioningly, when the metallic cocking of the piece carried over the noises of the fight. Claude stuck the muzzle in the driver's side, his grim face right against the Negro's cheek.

"Now you let 'im go," he ordered.

Luke stared at the planter without fear. His eyes gleamed while a sneer wrinkled his face and his animosity spilled out. "Hannibal done need ter be knocked down. He too uppity with us niggers, an' us tryin' ter save him from de rebs. He need de beatin', so we give it ter 'im."

Claude jammed the pistol barrel in again, hard against the ribs. Luke cried out in anguish from the thrusting metal and clutched his side. He recoiled from the blow but the planter's fist followed the slave's body to keep the barrel at point-blank range.

Forcing the slave to give ground, the implacable officer jabbed again and hissed, "Turn 'im loose!"

Impending doom converted the driver's frightened grimace into a gasp and servility. "I'se do it, Massa. Jist don' kill me."

Luke's frantic cries and his kicks at the men bought Hannibal's freedom. The driver helped the big man up from the ground while the others ignored him. Then he sought out and retrieved Hannibal's hat and slapped it against his leg. Dust drifted away and settled as he handed the covering back to the Negro and tried to make amends.

"Don' mean yer no harm Hannibal. Rufus tol' us ter be keerful an' we don' know yuh when you run on us sudden."

Hannibal brushed off the clutter from the forest floor and straightened his clothes. His silence made his murderous stare all the more dangerous. Luke fidgeted under the threat and protested his innocence. The servant silenced him with an impatient gesture.

"I'se heard yer uppity talk. You bother me agin, I kill yuh."

Pow!

The shot close on to their cluster drove them all into cover. A moment of terror and frantic activity delivered Claude into a hiding place with Hannibal, concealed in a natural clump of bushes lying down the slope. The other men were nowhere to be seen when he peeped out. Thick growth obscured all of the coffle's secreted bodies. Rufus soon appeared on the trail up the hill. He strode openly, a small deer over his shoulder and a second, strange rifle grasped in his hand. Breaking out of the understory brush, the rest of the coffle surrounded him and seized the dropped deer. It was skinned and divided in moments, but several men fought over the liver until Luke violently reclaimed it.

Rufus was waiting for them when the more cautious Yankee crawled out on the trail below. Claude waved and hailed before hurrying up to the redhead. Luke's kicks and curses at the slaves ceased as Rufus and the fugitives came together. The driver quickly joined them with four strips of bloody liver. He handed one to each and began to gobble his.

"Eat," he said between bites. "Good meat." Luke's strip disappeared rapidly under the onslaught of his white teeth.

Claude held his dripping strip with distaste. His gorge rose at the bloody, raw liver, a sickening purplish-red even his hungry stomach rejected. But he often ate the organ at Greenbottom and assayed a small bite. Hannibal and Rufus salted theirs and offered him their salt bags. The two attacked their strips with vehemence, tearing off pieces of the rich meat. Claude salted his heavily and got it down, a filling meal, but one that left blood all over his mouth. He laughed at the sight of all the men alike. He was a slave just like they, he thought, hungry. And needing to escape just like they, hungry for freedom. Intense longing overcame him and he turned impatiently to Rufus.

"Where we goin' now?" he asked.

The Negro delayed a few moments until Luke walked back down toward the coffle. When the man was well separated, Rufus' low voice counseled caution. "Don't tell Luke," he said. His voice dropped almost to a whisper while he kept his eyes on the slave driver. Luke was out of earshot, jollying the men. "I'm takin' the coffle further west to the Tugaloo. Then you and Hannibal'll strike northwest and cross the rivers up above the falls there at Tallulah. You can take the extra rifle." He laughed. "That reb don't need it no more."

"Where then?"

"Come back down southwest to Clarke's; it's just a little town. Then over to the Mount Yonah village to the west. We're goin' past Jarrett's inn, the Traveler's Rest." Rufus thought a moment. "We'll ease on over to'ard the springs at Demorest's, then to Hughes' place. All our meanderin' should lead those Minns off your trail. After you're safe we'll split up and circle back 'round to the thicket."

"You know that country?"

"Sure do, Claude. My daddy took me an' my brother all through there, fishin'. The Tugaloo and the Chattoogy are good for trout.

Claude was incredulous. "That's hard to imagine," he said. "He up here just for fishing?"

Rufus laughed at the planter's disbelief. He stole a glance at Luke, who was still well down the slope, before replying in a normal tone. "He was doin' lots o' tradin' 'round there when we were boys. Stayed at Traveler's Rest, a mighty fine inn. We learnt the country good. If you go around, nobody'll expect that an' you can come back down easy. They's good trails an' passes but rocky, steep slopes." He grinned. "Country's fine for hidin'."

Doubt crept into the planter's voice. "How about the rivers? Can we get across?"

"It's easy if you pick a gravelly place. Just keep away from the big riffles and rocks. Drown you right quick in the slide."

The red-head ruminated a moment. "According to my daddy, they's lots o' families in North Georgia holds with the Union. They's mostly scairt quiet 'cause o' the militia."

"How do we find 'em?"

"Hannibal can mosy 'round most places with his ears open, while you hide and play dumb. The Dancys'll help. They're near Mount Yonah. It's a little, old town an' ever'body knows 'em."

Rufus kept up the advice until the coffle assembled and readjusted its collars and chains. Luke carried the new rifle when they struck out to the west and headed for the Tugaloo.

The flaming sun stood at midday when Hester approached the upper thicket. An acrid smell of burnt wood and brush rose from the blackened landscape. Fires smoldered in stumps and downed logs, creating spirals of gray smoke that drifted off under the light breeze. The girl had left George's wagon the evening before, nighting in the safe place he sent her to. His directions leading her to Gabe had brought her right to the cabin site.

A movement scared her as she gingerly worked up the blackened slope toward the chimney of the burnt cabin. The girl froze, then tensed like a deer ready for flight while her eyes swiveled about. Hester screamed when a weak voice called, "He'p! He'p!" and a pink and brown arm waved from behind a stump. Its skin was peeling and hanging. She held her nose against the stink and eased around the stump. A barely conscious, burnt Negro lay on his back in the ash. His ravaged, nude body shed skin in sheets and strips. Burns from the fire added to the insults of a bullet hole in the side of his breast and a cut on his thigh.

Hester could not bring herself to touch him, her squat before the wreckage compelled only by the pleadings of his swollen lips and his teary, tormented eyes. They followed her's despairingly and his open mouth croaked, "Water, Water."

She ran down to the creek nearby and brought back a shoe full of the cold liquid. He drank it eagerly and beckoned for more. When she had satisfied the poor wretch, he drifted into a somnolent state, resting quietly while she inspected the site.

Its burned cabin and forest left nothing of value for her to reclaim. Ash boiled up into her nostrils, acrid, fine flakes that caused her to cough and hold a cloth over her nose. Three dead men were scattered within her view, their bodies already bloating in the heat. The stink of the dead forced her back to the injured man. Her right hand protected by a piece of skirt she tore off, Hester reached gingerly for his arm and shook him into consciousness.

"Where's Hannibal an' Claude?" she asked.

His teary eyes focused on her only after repeated proddings, her question finally penetrating his shocked memory.

"Wid de coffle."

"Where dey go?" Hester struck him violently as the dying man slipped silently toward unconsciousness. "Tell me!" she screamed, her mouth at his ear. His odor repelled her but she seized the battered body with both hands and shook it in a panicked frenzy, abusing the man with blows and oaths as she sought an answer.

His eyes barely opened as "On ter Calhoun's" came out in a low whisper. As if the exertion had been too much, the slave eased back with a sigh, and his breath and life passed out together. His eyes half-opened and his mouth made a little "O" of darkness as the poor, ravaged body flattened against the earth.

Hester tossed down the piece of cloth and looked at her hands in distaste, then ran to the stream to wash off the shreds of burned flesh. She struck out to the north, her stride little affected by the squeak of her wet shoe. By late afternoon she was edging around the fields near a row of slave cabins, quarters with children playing around them. Tendrils of smoke from their chimneys beckoned, the quarters a place to feed the rumbles in her belly and to shelter against the cool night. She rested comfortably in a cabin by full dark, well hidden, while the other slaves planned her escape to Calhoun's.

Minns and Jared leaned against a tree by Colonel Hyatte's tent when Hartsill's patrol halted before the picket line. The Lieutenant's orders carried up to them as the group dismounted, then pulled two limp bodies off saddles. With his sergeant taking over the men, Hartsill strode up the slight slope toward the Colonel's tent. He dusted himself with his gloves as he walked, little puffs drifting off at each blow to his uniform. The late afternoon sun struck golden shafts through the trees, a fan of rays that added to the beauty of the setting. Hyatte dipped his head and slipped through the tent fly at his orderly's call, his erect, well groomed figure turned out in full military regalia. The Colonel donned a slouch hat with trailing feather and trimmed it rakishly to finish his uniforming. His stogy trailed smoke while he waited for Hartsill and his report.

The Lieutenant marched resolutely past the flagpole to parade before the Colonel. His bearing had straightened up as he paced, a very erect back and set face complementing his salute when he stopped at attention before Hyatte. Minns grinned at the pomp. His own slouch deepened into a more comfortable one as he listened to the officers.

"Well, Arch?" Hyatte asked.

"Burned one cabin and the upper thicket, Colonel. Killed four buck niggers we know of." Disappointment clouded Hartsill's face. "No sign of the Yankee Lieutenant or his nigger."

"You lost two men killed?"

Bitterness tinged the Lieutenant's reply. "The bastards we killed had guns. Held their fire and picked off two o' my men as we came in. We also got a woman. She must have been that Aunty Emma we heard of, the one that doctored 'em."

Hyatte digested the Lieutenant's report while he puffed away, shaking his head and standing absentmindedly in silence. Minns, restless, finally shifted and spat. His action interrupted the reverie of the Colonel and drew a distasteful glance of reproach. Hartsill had remained at attention until Hyatte, relaxing, offered him a cigar and waved him to the two camp chairs before the tent. The Colonel ignored the Minnses, who slouched nearby. Ensconced in the comfortable chairs, the two officers puffed at their smokes while Hyatte reported on the previous events at the camp. "The two we hanged told us Shaw and his nigger Hannibal got away in a coffle. Minns here captured one at the thicket that also said they went west toward Atlanta in a coffle."

Hartsill nodded and said absentmindedly, "Then they had to pass the crossroads here." The implications struck him suddenly and with force. He sat straight up in excitement and clapped his hands together, crying out exultantly, "We can get 'em, by God!"

"Already checked the guards, Arch," Hyatte said. He bit off a piece of cigar and spit it away. The listening Minns' brown stream joined the litter on the ground.

"Six coffles went through two days back, four toward Atlanta and two up to Calhoun's. Lots o' niggers movin' to do bridge work for us."

"But which one's got the Yankee?"

Hartsill's question was answered by Minns, the hanger-on. "Me an' Jared'll git on up to Calhoun's termorrer an' check the two. You chase the rest."

Hartsill swore at the hunter's interruption and jumped up from his chair. His neck swelled and his face turned red as it bloated with rage. But he was too angry to speak when he confronted Minns. The Colonel eased between them and backed Hartsill away.

"Minns makes sense, Arch," he said. "You take your patrol out to the west tomorrow. Leave Calhoun's to Minns."

Hyatte's strong grip held the Lieutenant but did not stop his mouth. Infuriated and struggling, Hartsill's baleful glances reinforced his cursing abuse of Minns. When the flare-up ended and Hyatte relaxed slightly, the Lieutenant shook off his Colonel's arm. He opened his mouth to speak but Hyatte silenced him with a scowl. Hartsill half-bowed to his commander and strode off down the slope, leaving Hyatte to face the aroused hunter. Minns' clenched hands and flaming scar warned the officer to conciliate the man.

"You must pardon Arch, Minns," Hyatte said, almost pleading. "He's hotheaded 'bout the Yankees. They killed most all his family."

The hunter's mood subtly shifted and tension went out of his tall body. He nodded his understanding as he and the Colonel gazed after the impetuous officer.

"I don' mind the Lieutenant, Colonel. He's jest fussed bad 'bout losin' kin." The scar bulged on Minns' cheek and his jaw set. "I kin feel that Yankee's close. One er t'other o' us is goin'a kill 'im!"

Hyatte's exasperated voice disagreed. "You bring him in, you hear. We want him for trial first."

"It ain't no Army matter no more, Colonel." Minns was respectful but firm. "It be personal fer me an' Jared. Hartsill too, I 'spect. The good book says, `an eye for an eye,' an' we're goin'a kill 'im if the Lieutenant don't do it fust."

The Colonel stared at the stony face of the hunter with its jagged scar, its reddened color a sign of the man's anger. Minns' hate surrounded him like a dark cloud, the hunter's implacable resolve impossible to change. The officer sighed in surrender. "Then do it quick, Minns. We can't have no Yankee running around loose, rousin' the niggers."

Sergeant Irvine halted his patrol at Walton's ford in midafternoon, the trail from it leading to Toccoa Falls and Clarkesville to the southwest. He paused for a moment and

inspected the banks, then the rippling surface of the Tugaloo
River crossing. Its shallowness was readily evident from the
fast current and the swirls in the riffle. Wooded slopes
behind them offered good cover and plenty of firewood. The
troopers dispersed up and downstream slightly, alert to any
danger. But only the gurgling river added to music of the
bird calls in the trees and the cawing of crows far off.

"This's a good place, boys," Irvine said. His "Dismount!"
was followed by creaking, leather sounds as he swung down
and stretched.

Troopers tumbled off their horses at his order and led
their mounts along to the river. They scrambled down the
slight bank to drink and to dip their heads in the cold
stream, the men and horses interspersed on the rocky
slope. Grousing banter rose as they came back up to a tiny
grassy spot. The Sergeant waited for them while he stuffed
his mouth with fresh leaf and his horse nibbled at the short
stubble.

"Don' know where Duncan an' his men be," he said. "He
was s'posed to stay 'til we relieved. Ever'body search the
area fer their camp."

The men scattered in twos and spread out into the
surrounding trees. A moment later a shout to the north
called the troopers to the spot. Old fires and tent marks
scarred the ground, evidence, with choppings and discards,
of a settled camp. But the two fresh graves with stick crosses
drew the silent throng together. The men nervously glanced
about, muttering, and gradually assumed a fighting alert.
Irvine's warning clustered them into a ring, their weapons
facing in all directions. They eased slowly back to the
tethered horses, shying at every shadow. Gulps and silence
replaced the banter of the advance.

"We goin'a strike west," Irvine told them. His decision
brought exclamations of relief from the nervous troopers
and a short laugh from the Sergeant.

"What next, Sarge?" a trooper asked.

"Check if any seen Duncan in the next few miles an'
round up some supplies. If he ain't nearby, we'll be back to
guard the ford." He took a last look around, then said,
"Mount up!"

Curses pilloried him as he headed down the trace and signalled for them to follow. Three hours later, with dusk hard on them, the patrol was back at the ford, its pickets hidden along a half-mile stretch of the river.

Sissie rested in Granny's lap after their simple supper, both of them full of the remaining fish. The dozing child held herself close to the old woman's bosom, Granny's dress clenched tight in her hands. The two Negroes warmed themselves before the fire while Granny stroked the little girl and crooned a lullaby. Her song changed to a little shriek of fear and her head swiveled around when the door squeaked open. But her tension turned into a grim stare when Iris came in out of the dark night. The girl sidled up to her chair, making little supplicating gestures and pleadings as she approached, submitting to the dominance of the imperious old woman. At Granny's permissive nod, the girl sat on the hearth and warmed her back.

"What you want, chile?" Granny asked, warily.

"Dat Rufus in de Missus' bed last night, Granny."

Iris' white teeth flashed and her laugh rang through the cabin. She grasped her thin shanks and rocked back and forth as she chortled, her face crinkled in glee.

"De Missus an' Rufus?"

Iris nodded. Granny's sudden jerk at the news startled the child. Sissie rubbed her eyes as she yawned and stretched. The old woman pushed the little girl off her lap and shooed the child toward her hiding place. The obedient Sissie disappeared behind the sacks and jars. Faint scrapings quieted when she resumed her bed.

When the noises stopped, Granny beckoned Iris in closer and put her forefinger to her lips. "Don' talk too loud," she said. "Don' want Sissie bothered. Now you tell me all 'bout dis."

"I'se come back ter de big house late," Iris said, "atter bein' wid de coffle." Her attention wandered back to the night's visit. "Dey good ter pleasure wid."

Granny's sharp retort prodded the coy girl. "You tell me 'bout Rufus an' de Missus!"

Iris hesitated, drawing out the tale in well-savored

excitement. "Moses git me soon's I in de house an' tol' me de Missus want me in de evenin'. She mad I not dere. It so late, I sidles up by 'er do' hopin' she done gone ter sleep."

"An'?" Granny struck impatiently at the girl with her stick.

Iris shied away and laughed. "De do' locked." She delayed again, giggling until the annoyed Granny prodded her in the ribs.

"What happen?"

"I listen at de do'," Iris said, snickering. "De ropes squeakin' in de bed. Hawkins done moanin' an' gaspin' an' cryin', 'Rufus! Rufus!'"

Granny's eyes gleamed and her triumphant face broke into a short laugh. "I'se knowed it. De second sight allus right."

"What dat, Granny?"

"Last night in de fire, I seed de Missus holdin' a nigger baby. Rufus done knocked 'er." She paused. "How long he in dere?"

"Most all night. I hid in de bend at de back stair. Rufus snuck out fo' fust light."

Granny's face clouded and her sunken cheeks tensed. "Reckened we kill 'er when we free," she said. "But de rebs 'bout done an' ol' man Hawkins be back soon. He kill 'er sure when she births a nigger chile."

"But she hate de niggers!" Iris burst out, forgetting about Sissie.

Granny laughed at the girl's confusion. "Dat Rufus pass fer white. She don' know he nigger an' she allus atter de menfolks." She spat into the fire and scornfully said, "You knows dat."

Iris nodded, deep in thought.

Granny chuckled and said, softly and with satisfaction, "Dis snake done bit 'er."

The two women stared at each other, their quiet broodings inscrutable, as each mulled over the enormity of the mistress taking an overseer to bed. A white overseer who really was a Negro. Iris broke the silence with a giggle. Granny followed, their infectious humor progressing into paroxysms of laughter. They continued long after their glee woke Sissie and she climbed back into Granny's lap.

Gabe staggered tiredly when he crept through the trees on the cemetery hill at Calhoun's. Lights in the row of cabins attracted him, slave quarters easily visible though the night was dark. He sneaked around the cabins and peered in the cracks and slits for windows. Gabe halted his search at Granny's cabin when he smelled the strong odor of fried fish and saw the old woman with the child in her lap.

The old Negress squealed in fright and bucked her chair around when the door crashed open. Her eyes widened at the sight of the giant Negro revealed by the firelight. He closed the door instantly and barred it. Granny shucked the child from her lap and seized her cane. The startled Sissie disappeared instantly into her hiding place.

"Who yer?" Granny asked tremulously, her stick raised.

"I'se Gabe, Granny, from de thicket over ter Belton. Dey done burned us out an' kilt Aunty Emma."

A shadow passed over the old woman's face as she absorbed the terrible blow. "Aunty Emma was a good woman," she said. "I prays fer her like de others." She inspected his hurts as he waited, then beckoned him to the fire saying, "Tetched you some too, seems like. I'se look at dat bloody place."

Her ministrations were followed by Gabe's downing of some pone and clabber. His sniffing nose investigated the rank odor of the fried fish while he gulped the clabber. "Any mo' dat fish I smells?"

Granny shook her head. "It all gone an' no other meat 'roun'. What'cher do now, Gabe?"

"Lookin' fer Rufus," he answered, between swallows. "We done run tergether at de thicket nigh onter two year. Got ter fin' him, an' de Yankee. Kin he'p 'em bof." His face saddened. "No mo' livin' in de thicket."

"Dey gone on west t'day," Granny said. "You wait here one day ter feed up an' I tells dey plans. You kin ketch 'em by de Tugaloo maybe."

"Do dat, Granny," he replied.

The old woman appraised his great size, looking him up and down as he tore at a piece of pone topped with honey.

"Dey kin use yuh, Gabe," she said. "You orta be named Samson, big as you is."

The slave nodded, his mouth busy with the last piece of the pone while Granny roused Sissie. Holding onto his great paw with her tiny hand, the little girl led him to the crypt, their passage unchallenged in the dark. He burrowed into the heap of shucks, warm and asleep by the time she swung the door closed.

Chapter 16

Colonel Hyatte

---

*November 16, 1864. Toccoa Falls, Georgia.
Temperature 67\42, partly cloudy and
damp, increasing threat of rain toward
evening. Light, westerly winds to 10 knots.
Moon waning in 4th quarter, setting about
four hours after sundown.*

The ball of the sun glowed weakly through a cloud
haze, its yellowish light adding little brightness to the
grayness of the damp morning. Heavy dew wet the
coffle and its camp, a site on the edge of the forest of oaks
and hickories, one sheltered from the wind and handy to
much downed wood needed for its fires. Little spirals of
smoke rose from the dying, overnight embers and floated
away on the wind. The glowing coals were soon replaced by
crackling flames when dry deadwood was added. The men
drifted back from their pause in the woods and visit to the
creek before roasting spitted hunks of pork, choice, fat meat
from a purloined hog. Drips from the juicy meat flamed in
the fires, the offerings retrieved as soon as hot and singed.
They were wolfed down by the hungry mouths, mixed
together with a few pieces of pone turned up from pockets.
Chinkapin chestnuts and wormy apples from a tree at a
nearby, abandoned cabin filled out the morning meal.
Belching after the hot, satisfying feed, smokers relaxed and
lighted pipes, while others refilled cheeks with chaws. It was
a resting time, one for joshing and jokes before the new stint

with the hated collars and chains.

Rufus and the fugitives cooked their meat with care, blackening the spitted lumps on the outside but leaving succulent centers. The pork's tantalizing odor and salted taste roused gushes of saliva in Claude's mouth as his strong teeth tore great chunks from the roasted meat while he filled his belly. He rotated his stick and bit off the last scraps of the hot, savory pieces, seeking every tantalizing fragment. A sigh of contentment escaped him as he wiped his mouth on his sleeve and stuck his stick back into the ground. Nuts and apples topped off the pork. Shifting before the warm fire, he lay back on his elbows and stared into the flames, his ruminations interspersed with rumbles from his belly. When Rufus tossed his empty skewer into the fire, its green sizzling roused Claude from his dozing reflections. Back in reality, he inspected his own stick, still hanging over the flames. A missed tidbit of hot meat remained. He picked off the remnant with the tip of his knife and sniffed it. The shred was a tasty morsel. Claude popped it into his mouth and noisily chewed the piece.

"Mighty good, Rufus," he said, once it was swallowed. He belched and wiped his lips with the back of his hand. "I'm full again and ready to go."

"How's your leg?"

"Tolerable. Mostly well." Claude rose to his feet and danced a jig, only a slight grimace on his face. He squatted back down with the others and held his hands to the fire, warming himself against the damp wind.

"You knowed Luke's gone?" Hannibal asked.

The planter looked about nervously at the servant's implied warning, then checked the gossiping slaves in the coffle. A tremor of fear ran over him when he realized that Luke was nowhere in sight. Hannibal inched over closer, while still chewing on his roasted meat. "He lef' las' night," he said.

Claude shivered and a chill ran down his spine. His query to the overseer confirmed the truth of Hannibal's news.

"Yep," Rufus said. "He took the extra rifle too. He'll try to kill Hannibal up the trail." The Negro's face darkened, a cloud passing over it. "He can hold a grudge bad. Allus has. Just hope he don't go to the Johnnies."

"He can't do dat," Hannibal said. "Dey kill 'im fer he'pin' us." The Negro spat a great gob of phlegm into the fire, its flames curling in protest. He thrust out his jaw and his lips twisted into a sneer. "He be a coward if he ain't got de rifle. I kill 'im, if he don' shoot me from de woods."

Rufus' bobbing head ratified the servant's assessment. "You might have to do that," he said.

The men warmed themselves until the sun rose into a fiery orb, clear of the damp morning mists. Once the moist air was drying under strong sunlight, Rufus called to the Negroes to recharge their pistols and then reform the coffle. But he lined them up and did the reshackling without Claude and Hannibal. Afterwards, the men lay close to the fires, laughing and smoking while Rufus squatted with the fugitives. The overseer scraped the dirt in front of their fire into a clear pane, then scratched a crude map with a stick while the fugitives waited on his instructions.

"Like I told yuh," Rufus said, "you ain't goin' with us. It's too dangerous." He stuck his pointer in the ground at the river he had outlined on the crude map. "We're about five miles from Walton's ford on the Tugaloo an'll be there in two hours o' marchin'. They's bound to be pickets. Allus were before, ever'time I come through with the 'scapes."

Hannibal's concern was not with the bypassed pickets and echoed Claude's. "What about Luke?" he asked.

The overseer's chuckle and satisfied smile reassured them. "Luke don't know you're goin' 'round. He thinks you're travelin' on with the coffle." He frowned. "That no-good nigger may be with the rebs at the ford or hid out waitin' for a shot. So you're goin' north to the Chattooga."

Claude gestured to the hills about them. "That country passable?" The sharp slopes and timbered places facing the fugitives promised unusually hard going. The creek bottom wasn't much better.

"Yes," Rufus said. "Go on up the creek." He pointed his stick at the stream and then put its tip at their location on the map. Once positioned, he drew a wiggly mark as he talked. "Cut through the gap here." His stick stopped and jabbed a hole in the sketch. "At the fork, you'll strike a good trace to the north. It ain't much used, according to Granny. You go far above Tallulah Falls an' the gorge. Can't get through there."

The Negro quickly described the tremendous gorge and the easier crossing of the Chattooga miles beyond, farther up where the river was smaller. But he warned them of the chutes. "Cross at the gravel bars or where they's small boulders. You get caught in one o' them chutes an' you'll drown."

"Where you want us ter go den?" Hannibal asked.

He stuck his own pointer into the map next to Rufus', which still was stopped at the Chattooga crossing. A silent observer, Claude had been listening intently, memorizing the overseer's trail wisdom. Rufus thought a moment, then swung the sharp end of his stick down to the southwest and gouged out a deep, circling scrape.

"They's good passage through the valleys if you make a wide swing across the west fork an' back down to Clarke's. They's not too many cabins. My daddy an' I fished up both the forks lots when I was a boy." He laughed, but then his face grew solemn, a flicker of pain crossing it. "With my brother too, the white one."

Claude felt his friend's agony, and he was his friend, he knew, even on brief acquaintance. One black brother, one white brother. The black brother had nothing, was not even an accepted man, though he exhibited a fine, physical appearance and was learned, with knowledge and manners. The cruelty of the hypocrisy of the South overcame him, the southern planters at once with their high and mighty society but willing to father children that they would sell without question. And he was one of them! Even though he had no slave children, his soul rebelled at being part of the practice, of looking aside, of not seeing. Slavery's barbarism struck into his soul as he listened to a slave, a fine man who was advising him, trying to save his life from the rebs and from Luke. His passion overcame him and his tight squeeze of Rufus' hand transferred his anguish, and pity, and outrage. As Claude's face contorted and his eyes grew misty, the slave's arm stole about his shoulders and squeezed him tight.

"It ain't no matter now, Claude," he said. "Can't do nothin' bout me bein' black an' him white. But you understand now, don't you?"

The planter could but nod, his strangling preventing speech. Hannibal held out his canteen and Claude dashed a spray into his face and took a swig. The two Negroes stared into the fire until Claude cleared his throat and spat. Holding out his hand to Rufus, he made his offer.

"You're a good man, Rufus, white or black, and my friend, an' you saved my life. Come to Greenbottom when the Johnnies are whipped and I'll help you just like Hannibal. You'll be a free man with land."

Rufus met Claude's intense stare, but he looked long before he took the proffered hand. The two gripped hard when he accepted. "I'll be there, Claude. But meantime we got to get you an' Hannibal up the river to the Chattooga.

The fugitives filled their canteens, then recharged their pistols against a failure from the damp. They were ready for flight when their possibles sacks had been sorted and stuffed with cooked pork and apples. At Rufus' shout, the coffle shuffled along the road to the Tugaloo crossing. He delayed, sitting his horse, erect and in command. A fine trooper, Claude thought, as he watched the confident man. Rufus chirked at his horse and kneed him around to the trail, but he held the mount at the camp site a moment longer.

"When you strike Clarke's," he said, "have Hannibal run down the shoemaker. He'll help yuh."

Hannibal tightened his belt and shouldered his possibles sack as the overseer galloped away. Rufus waved at them from the bend when he turned for a last look. In the silence, only the woods sounds resumed, the sound of peace and no threat. Hannibal led off into the deep woods of the rising creek bottom, the two travelers rapidly becoming invisible to observers on the trail.

Colonel Hyatte faced the two men, Hartsill with his scowl and Minns slouching in front of his horses. Old Blue snuffled around a nearby stump and finally lifted his leg to deposit his marker. He trotted back to Minns and flopped in the dirt, his head flat along the ground like an old trooper seizing his rest. But his searching brown eyes missed nothing. Down at the picket line, Hartsill's eight men formed their horses into a column. They mounted at Sergeant Gill's order, his loud instruction also alerting the Lieutenant.

"You ready to leave, Arch?" Hyatte asked.

"Sure am, Colonel. But I prefer to go north instead of toward Atlanta."

Hyatte's anger surfaced in an explosive reprimand, brutally delivered. "You'll check the coffles to the west as I ordered, Lieutenant. Now, are you ready or not?"

"Yes sir!" Hartsill assumed an even more rigid brace, his knuckles white on the scabbard held tight at his left side. His set jaw and stony eyes protested the order.

Hyatte sighed. "You have a job to do, Arch, as well as Minns." His voice softened. "You know your men can check the coffles to the west quicker than Minns. So after, if you don't find them, go on up the Tugaloo to the ford off Toccoa Falls. They'll be caught between you and Minns if they're goin' to the west."

"I got a feelin' they're at Calhoun's," Hartsill said. He pleaded his case, a lawyer to the last. His right hand forcefully punctuated his solicitations for a change in plan before he finished with his peroration. "Can't we all go north?" he asked.

"Goddamn it, Arch," Hyatte said angrily, "you carry out your orders. And keep me informed of what you find."

Hartsill started and his face flamed a beet red. He took deep breaths for a few seconds in an obvious internal struggle with his emotions. But his voice was under strict control when he responded. "Yes sir," he said, in icy disapproval. He turned hard on his heel and ran down the slope to the horses as if his life were at stake. His fierce commands to the troopers drifted up the slight incline, enveloping the Colonel and the hunter as the patrol departed at the gallop.

Minns cleared his throat and spit. He was laconic in his assessment. "He be driven, Colonel."

"True." Hyatte's bitter voice trembled as he wiped his

eyes. "And I too, since Redding was killed. They as much as did it."

"He your kin?"

"My cousin Nancy's boy. All her sons been killed by those damned Yankees." His voice rose in pitch and his face degraded into misery, then a devil's mask, the ruddy, blotched skin adding menace to his promise. "I'll kill as many as I can."

The hunter bobbed his head in agreement. "We start with that damned Shaw."

Hyatte paced around, swinging his arms and muttering, but his anger was soon spent. Standing again before the slouching hunter, he offered a cigar and pulled out another for himself. Minns ran the cheroot along under his nose, with loud sniffs usually reserved for juicy, roasting meat. He spat out his chaw and rinsed his mouth from his canteen before he bit the end off the cigar. A coal from the nearby campfire and a few puffs begat a cloud of smoke and a sigh of pleasure.

"It be mighty good, Colonel, an' I thank yuh."

Hyatte motioned Minns to a chair and puffed away from his casual sprawl in the other. Clouds of gray haze surrounded the two men as they smoked in silence and in private thought. Minns waited, drawing on the fine tobacco, his pleasure evident in his smoke rings and puffs.

"I want you to get that Yankee, Minns," Hyatte said, finally breaking the stillness. "Arch is right. He went to Calhoun's probably. If you don't find him at Calhoun's quarters an' get there soon enough, try to trap him and the slave at the Tugaloo. Sergeant Irvine's already there, guardin' the ford on the west trace."

"Irvine?' Minns said in surprise. "Why I run onter him down by Greenwood. Must have been six-seven days ago. Said he was headin' fer Elberton, then up the Tugaloo."

Hyatte expelled a cloud of graying smoke and flipped the ash off his cigar. "Had word from 'im this morning. He's on Walton's ford. He'll be there while Arch sweeps behind and you come across from Calhoun's. Should pinch that Yankee between you." His face grew solemn and his lips compressed into a thin line. "If he gets past, run him down."

"I'll do that anyway," the hunter replied. "Fer Jeremy."

The two ruminated as they smoked, each with his own thoughts. Jared's stamping about and Old Blue's exploration of more trees, his snuffling loudly audible, woke Hyatte from his reverie. He bounced up out of his chair, laughing at the old dog.

"He's got a lot o' water in him, Minns. 'bout treated everything in sight." He studied the bluetick for a moment. "Good lookin' hunter," he said. "Just like some we used to have at home. Best hound yet on a trail."

Athey smiled, his scar twisting grotesquely, and called to Blue. The hound rushed up to be patted and scratched by the two men. His tail wagged furiously and his body wiggled as he sought their favors. Blue and the cigars cemented a bond of respect and understanding. Minns gave in to the officer when he and Jared were mounted and ready for the trail.

"If we kin take him alive," he told Hyatte, "I'll fetch him to yuh. But I get to haul on the rope. He kilt my son as well as Redding."

Hyatte slowly puffed away, his "Agreed," and wave sealing the bargain.

Firelight gleamed in the cabin at the Norris plantation and outlined the two figures in its yellow glow. "You looks awright, Hester," Granny May said cheerfully.

Her shuffling figure circled the girl as her fingers straightened a few folds in a bulky black dress. Its ample tucks and voluminous, sweeping bottom were gray with the dust of the cabin. A huge bonnet covered Hester's head, leaving only her face peeping out. Her shoes stirred up even more fine grit when she stamped impatiently on the dirt floor. The old granny ignored the girl's insults and her complaints as Hester picked at the dress and fluffed out the skirt. But Granny's patience deserted her when the tirade continued. She shook Hester violently and chastised her with a hard slap on her bottom. "Be quiet!" she ordered. "So de dress an' de shoes big. I'se fat an' ol' an' you's jist a slip o' a girl. But we git yer ter Calhoun's in it."

Hester pouted. "Don' see why I has ter wear dis rag. It

like bein' in a big, ol' blanket wrap 'roun' me. Don' fit nohow."

Granny slapped her face hard and said, "Shet up!" With the girl subdued, she made another adjustment to the bodice. "Miz Gwen gwine by Calhoun's t'day on de way ter de town dere at Clarke's. We put yer in de boot and tells 'er you's me. So you gotta wear de dress an' walk slow like me."

"Dis ol' Norris place ain' much," Hester countered scornfully, unable to be humble or silent. "I'se Miz Ashley's nigger, from de Pickens place down ter Columbia. Make dis ol' place look like nothin'."

Granny's huge bulk bumped the girl and drove her body against the rough timbers of the cabin wall. Her furious face butted against Hester's as she screeched, "Shet up, you no-good, uppity nigger!" The old woman's sausage-fat fingers twisted Hester's arm as she pinioned the girl and thrust against her repeatedly. Cries of pain bubbled out between gasps. The fat woman's bulk and great strength soon forced tears from Hester, and her abject surrender. Granny's heated instructions brooked no protest.

"You ack like me an' we git yer ter Calhoun's. I'se got gran'chilluns dere an' Miz Gwen kin', lemme visit some. So you ack right."

Soon outfitted with a cane and a knitting bag containing her clothes stuffed under the yarn and needles, Hester hobbled out to the waiting rockaway carriage. She was ensconced on a seat in the boot when Miz Gwen swept from the porticoed porch and entered the closed body of the vehicle. It swayed back and forth as the woman settled herself.

Miz Gwen tapped on the back panel and called out, "Is Granny in the boot?" Her knock and musical voice echoed through the curtained space for baggage and servants, a boxy appendage behind the seat compartment. Hester sat in its confining darkness with the small trunks of the owner.

"I'se here, Miz Gwen," the girl answered. Muffled by the layers of wood and cloth, her faint reply satisfied the woman. She started them on their journey with a crisp command to the driver.

The rockaway arrived at Calhoun's in late afternoon,

with Miz Gwen received stiffly but with deference by the overseer's wife. Hawkins' lifetime of poor-white status cowed her into fawning servility before the imperious mistress of Norris plantation. Fear forced the obsequious underling to bow to the visitor's treatment of her as a servant, and she followed the woman into the manse to do her bidding. Moses threw aside the cover of the boot as soon as they disappeared, the driver beside him to handle the trunks.

The old house servant's eyes widened when he saw Hester, not Granny May. "Who you?" he whispered.

She put her finger to her lips and shushed him. He and the driver helped her down. Hester groaned as she stretched and felt her back, then complained crossly about her aches and stiffness from bouncing in the cramped boot. Moses took her arm and walked her off to one side, with Hester using her cane and bent over like an old granny. When they were hidden from the house she straightened up.

"I'se Hester," she told him. "I'se lookin' fer my man, Hannibal."

Moses' jaw tightened and he swiveled his head and glanced around. His worried face and grasp on her arm alarmed her.

"Hannibal an' Claude done gone ter de west dis mawnin'," he said in a low voice. He pointed to the slave row along the side lane. "You git down ter Granny Esther's cabin, de one at de end. She he'p yuh."

Moses hurried back to the manse while Hester hobbled down to Granny Esther's, using her cane as Granny May had shown her. When she arrived at the door, she pushed it open and entered the cabin. Her action startled Sissie into flight to her hideaway, little scuttling sounds arising as the child burrowed in deep. But Granny raised her stick belligerently from her stance by her chair.

"What yer want?" she asked.

Granny Esther's suspicious glance and wary body lasted only long enough for the girl to explain. Once Hester was back in her ordinary clothes from the knitting bag, Granny fed her and soothed her fears about Hannibal. It was after full dark when Sissie took her to the crypt, a time of terror for Gabe. He grabbed Hester violently when she

entered the dim vault and choked off her rising scream. A
sputtering candle flickered and emitted a faint, smoky light.

"I'se Gabe," the giant said. Hester squirmed and tried
to get loose. But she was unable either to scream or to free
herself from the giant's tight grip, however hard she struggled.
"Be still," he told her. "I ain't gwine bother yer none. Granny
sendin' me on termorrer mornin'.

When the girl relaxed her body, Gabe let her go and
looked over the food that Sissie had fetched. Hester sought
his hand reaching for the pone and took it to her breast. She
pleaded for help when he paused, puzzled at the gesture.

"I'se Hester," she said. "Granny tol' me yer goin' ter fin'
Claude an' Hannibal. Wants ter travel wid yuh. Hannibal
my man."

The giant slave smiled and nodded. He pulled his hand
free and again reached for the food. Gabe's fingers tore at
the corncake in Sissie's package and folded a sheet over a
strip of bacon. He attacked the food ravenously, the sides of
his mouth dribbling bits of the crumbly bread. The hungry
Negro gestured to the great bed of shucks between gulps of
food and swigs from a hanging bladder, and told Hester to
sleep. She took the far corner when Sissie left and burrowed
in, hiding from the giant. But he left her there alone after his
meal and a visit to the woods. Gabe uttered a great sigh and
sank tiredly into the shucks. He snored away as the candle
flickered its last and black dark conquered the tomb.

Hoofbeats on the circular drive penetrated the Calhoun
manse and Moses' hearing an hour after the rockaway had
been driven to the horse barn. The old slave rushed to open
the door and step onto the porch. A small Negro boy ran up
to the horses when they stopped before the steps. He
reached for the reins but Minns shied his mount away from
the clutching hand. The hunter's swing with his quirt sent
the boy scuttling around the side of the building just as
Moses bowed from the edge of the porch.

"Miz Hawkins about?" Minns asked, wasting no time
with pleasantries.

"Yassah, Massa. Who be callin'?"

"Tell 'er Athey Minns an' Jared from Colonel Hyatte,

hunting some 'scapes."

Hawkins swept out onto the porch within seconds of Moses entry into the house. Trailed by the old slave, she hesitated on the edge of the planks, her eyes on the same level as Minns.

"The Colonel got my note about the escapes? You here 'cause of that?"

Minns' mouth dropped open, his flustered surprise disconcerting to the woman. She whipped him with a sharp tongue when he did not reply, her cutting voice striking the man hunter like a challenge.

"Are you deef? Speak up, man! Did you come because o' my note?"

Minns pulled on the horse's reins and jockeyed his mount around to a closer position to the steps. He leaned over toward Hawkins and jabbed his rifle barrel almost into her breast.

"Don't you talk to Athey Minns like that," he said, menacingly. "Maybe you kin flog yer slaves but I don' take no uppity talk from no women."

Hawkins shrank back, her face a combination of submission and desire. Her eyes roamed over the tall man with the striking, stern visage and rangy, yet muscular body, its tight buckskins highlighting the bulges she so loved. She picked up her skirts and descended two steps, then looked up to the hunter, her idiom soothing him as well as her inferior position on the flagstones.

"Don' mean to fuss yuh none, Athey. I jes' naturally figured you to be here 'cause o' my note to Hyatte."

"He never got no note," Minns said. He waved his rifle barrel at Jared and Old Blue, who was exploring a large, shagbark hickory in the front yard.

"Me an' Jared an' the dog yonder been chasin' a Yankee officer from down to Columbia. He'd be in the coffle that went through here. T'other over to Liberty don't have 'im."

"They's gone, Athey," Hawkins said. "Heard they had a 'scape with 'em an' sent a note to Hyatte." The woman fingered her small whip hanging from her belt and flicked it at Iris on the porch. The handsome Negro girl cringed and edged away. "Got to whip that Iris for not takin' it on to

Anderson."

Increasing clouds and cool air added to the uninviting prospect of heading west with the sun almost down. Minns' uncertainty transmitted itself to the woman, for she walked down to the horse and turned a welcoming smile up to the rider. She stood close to his leg, her bosom rising and falling as if in invitation.

"Too late to go t'night," Hawkins said. "You can use the overseer's place down the lane." She extended her whip hand and singled out the small house in the trees, on the slope above slave row. "Iris'll fetch hot water an' yer dinner." Her voice lowered to an inviting whisper the others could not hear. "Maybe you can come an' visit later?"

Athey nodded imperceptibly, his gleaming eye responding to her desire. "We accept, Ma'am, an' thank yuh." His loud reply echoed in the cool breeze and painted a further camouflage on the reason for his acceptance. "Kin we talk to you an' yer han's 'bout the 'scapes ternight? We be leavin' in the mawnin' an' need directions."

"Soon's Miz Norris retires after dinner," Hawkins said. "She's right tired. I'll send Moses to get you an' have Granny an' Iris here at the step. They's the onliest ones knows."

Minns inclined his head in a slight bow. "Thankee, Ma'am," he said. The hunter reined his horse around and kneed it as he started toward the lane and the overseer's cabin. Jared followed, with Old Blue cruising yet another tree before he trotted after the horses. Hawkins' shrill commands to her servants carried easily to the riders. Her scoldings blanketed Moses and the house Negroes alike.

Jared laughed. "Jest like a vixen, Pa. Plenty o' body but sharp teeth an' a lot o' bark."

"She be fine in bed ternight. I git you one too. See that Iris she's goin'a whip? She give you plenty o' pleasurin'."

A good wash and full bellies improved their tempers and camaraderie as they lounged in comfortable chairs before a warm fireplace. Stars winked in a black sky when a knock sounded and Minns followed Moses into the night. It was not much later, with Jared dozing, when Iris hesitantly crept into the cabin. The girl's coy wiles, successful with the coffle's men, proved unavailing with Jared. He was used to force and submission, not seduction. It took his blows to reduce the protesting, reluctant girl to a timid, fearfilled participant. Jared's exhaustion from the long days of chase compounded his weariness from the night's violent purges, purges foreshortened by his tiredness and his need to sleep. Iris soon was gone, her muttered curses unheard as Jared turned his back. The youth was oblivious and snoring when Minns returned to the cabin. Old Blue's tail thumped at the hunter's arrival, his head rising from his stretched-out sprawl before the coals of the fire and his eyes shining in the yellow light. Minns grinned and patted the old hound and scratched behind his ears. Blue sank back into his sleep with a sigh while Minns stripped and washed his sweaty body. The hunter chuckled as the dog's legs jerked and he uttered little yelps.

"Old Blue done dreamin' agin'," he muttered. He yawned and stretched. "Time I best git to sleep."

In a few minutes all three were filling the night with snorts and whistles.

The coffle was three-quarters across the Tugaloo ford when Sergeant Irvine ran down the strand and challenged.

"Ho there!" he shouted, as he waved to Rufus. "Bring yer men up the trail here and stop."

Rufus' horse was in belly-high water, unable to hurry. But the Negro spurred his mount ahead of the wading men, the gurgling water splashing about his boots as he passed the coffle's line. He kneed the horse and chirked to it on the slope leading to the road, then reined in the beast and turned it to face the Sergeant. As soon as he was in place, he formed up his coffle into a small group around them.

"Patrol!" Irvine's yell called in his troopers. He paled and his countenance turned anxious as he searched the faces of the slaves that surrounded him. Their utter quiet and vacuous glances created fear, a disquiet such that he screamed, "Patrol!", this time in panic. He tried to back off, his hand seeking his pistol holster as he edged away.

Most of the small detail of troopers ran down the slope, their carbines ready. But one lookout stayed at the break in the forest where the bank steepened and the big trees stopped. The advancing men closed in around the coffle to almost point-blank range, a few yards only. Edgy fingering of their weapons and nervous curses supported the penned-up Sergeant.

The two parties were bridling at each other, uncertain, when Luke's voice rang out from his stand at the treeline. "It's them!" he shouted.

Rufus forced instant action, yelling, "Kill 'em all!"

While he crowded the Sergeant with his horse he pulled a pistol from a saddle holster and shot Irvine in the face. Cracking reports sounded all along the coffle from the slaves' hidden pistols, interspersed by the heavier booms of the trooper's carbines. A shotgun spread havoc among three Negro escapees grouped in the coffle, blood and flesh spattering the men around them. All of the troopers were down in seconds, their bodies joining the three dead slaves. A few of the coffle moaned and held bloody places on their clothes, while the others methodically cut the throats of wounded troopers amid pleas for mercy. Up the bank, the lone cavalryman fired at Rufus. His ball whistled by, its aim offset by movement of the overseer's skittish horse. The man ran into the trees at the back without reloading, his retreat followed by the sound of rapid hoofbeats to the southwest. Rufus' horse pranced away from the carnage but the rider reined him in and sprang off to inspect the downed soldiers.

He kicked all the bodies before he was satisfied, then freed his men with a joyous shout. "Strike off the chains an' toss 'em into the river!"

Whoops of relief followed Rufus' cry. The happy men danced and ran on the bank when the last of the hated chains had splashed into the pool below the ford. A few gathered around the overseer, who was recharging his weapon. He gestured toward the forest.

"Get that Luke if you can," he said.

Half of the freed slaves snatched up and reloaded carbines. Running up the slope, they spread out in a skirmish line and passed rapidly into the forest after the driver. They came back in a few minutes, less one man, and joined the others. Their leader strode over to Rufus.

"Luke done kilt Ben," Judah said. His simple report,

confirmed by the others, attested to the tragedy of the single gunshot that echoed over the hills shortly after the chase began.

"You don' git 'im?"

"He runnin' too hard, Rufus, atter he shoot. Luke fas'. Ain't nobody ketch 'im runnin'."

Rufus absorbed Judah's simple logic, his shrug dismissing the matter. "We kill 'im when he comes in agin," he said. "He be layin' out som'ers up the way fer a shot at me. Hannibal too, if he can cut 'is trail."

The men rested and smoked while the overseer walked about and inspected the spread of bodies. Talk died out in the coffle, all their eyes following him when he scraped the moist dirt with his boot toe and bent and felt of its texture. But his deliberations were not to be hurried even as they waited and wondered. Rufus lit a stogy and puffed a moment more until he was settled in his mind. His next orders galvanized the slaves into frenzied motion.

"Take all the weapons an' anythin' else you want. Throw all the dead an' their traps in the river below the ford. The current'll carry 'em off."

Under Rufus' urging, the coffle converted itself into a heavily armed band in the hour it took to dispose of the bodies and to assemble all the weapons and food. Four wounded Negroes forded the river and headed for Calhoun's and Granny Esther's doctoring. They had been cautioned to stay hidden and to escape to Tennessee as soon as able. The other, healthy slaves erased evidence of the presence of Irvine and his men. Harness and saddles and the camp fixings were hidden in brush far downstream where the bank would flood in high water. The horses were driven off and scattered. A few scuffs to cover the bloodstains were followed by the coffle marching in and out of the water over the bloodied site. The tramping back and forth and the water slopped by the slaves soon removed the evidence of the action and their cleanup of the camp left only tent marks and cold campfires for future travelers. A motley crew faced the overseer when the men finished the camouflage, troopers' boots much in evidence as well as Confederate clothes and swords. He chuckled at the gang of slaves and their motley arms. Gun barrels stuck out in all directions like a hedgehog's quills and were just as menacing.

Rufus scented the air when the remaining dozen men gathered around him. "Smells like rain," he said, his eyes questioning. Nods and rumbles from the group agreed. "It git dis place washed out. Can't tell we been here."

"What we do now, Rufus," Judah asked. He had replaced Luke as the driver.

"Goin' on over 'roun' Demorest's place at the springs. We he'p Claude and' Hannibal atter they come on down ter Clarkes'. Kin cut de trail dere an' wait." His vernacular grew thicker. "When dey on de track ter de free lan', we goin'a kill as many o' dem rebs as we kin."

Judah shook his rifle in the air and cheered. His triumphant voice was seconded by shouts from the rest. "Dey kilt us," he said, when the tumult died. "We kill many's we kin a'fo' gwine ter de free lan'."

When they moved on, Rufus' bulky frame stepped out at the head of the column on the trail west, with Judah in advance as scout. Three pistols protruded from the overseer's belt and a shotgun slung from a thong added to the fearsomeness of his appearance. With his rifle in the crook of his left arm, he strode alertly along the trail, intent on the sounds of the forest. They would warn him of intruders ahead if Judah did not notice them.

Mists covered the mountain peaks when Claude and Hannibal approached the Chattooga. It had been a hard climb over rough ground, their path often deflected to avoid contact with the few settlers, or travelers sighted as the fugitives cruised through the thickly forested slopes and narrow valleys. Immense poplars and hardwoods carpeted the ground in the dense stands. Claude stopped at one yellow poplar giant that was a good seven feet in diameter. He felt of its bark and looked up the straight spike to the towering top, while Hannibal stooped to a nearby spring. The Negro splashed water in his face, then cupped up a drink from the pool overflowing to a seeping rill below.

"Timber here somethin' to behold," Claude said. His hand reverently patted the tree before he knelt to the cool water.

"Make plenty o' good timbers, Claude." The servant stepped back and looked up at the top. "Right straight. An' it go up dere 'bout halfway ter de good Lord, I recken."

Their brief stop refreshed the two fugitives, brisk strides taking them on down a feeder creek to the river. The shallow bottom was choked with little trees and roots, foot twisting obstacles that made for hard going. They struck the Chattooga on a high bank, its swirling waters below. Claude stopped a moment and tossed in a stick. It rode downstream at a fast clip.

"We'll head up above the next chute, Hannibal," he said. "Rufus told us right about this old river. It's fractious."

He led off, the servant following. They had passed a constriction between two large rocks when the river widened into a tumultuous rapids. In its haste, the water tumbled through a collection of rocks, some showing above the surface. Claude squatted and watched the flow falling over the edge of the chute. He pointed out the smooth, graceful curve and its tremendous power and warned Hannibal of its dangers.

"We don't want to get caught in that. See the big wave below? It can drown yuh right fast."

The servant shuddered, his face sweaty from fear. "I can't swim, Claude," he said.

"No need," Claude told him confidently. "We're goin' on up the river some to the head o' the riffle. Then we can cross fine."

A long section of soggy bottomland faced them, narrow, but with clear going between the trees. Their hike up the river to a better fording place took only about fifty paces. They stopped beside this stretch of shallower, rippling flow, a widening where the bank sloped into the water in a gentle grade. Downstream from more scattered, massive boulders that broke up the discharge into whirling torrents, this easier reach offered a possible entry and fordable depths in the fast current. Claude threw a few pebbles from the water's edge while they inspected the ford and he made his plans.

"See the old trunk jutting out there?" he said. When the

Negro hesitated, Claude tossed a small cobble at a large tree-trunk in the water. His missile landed alongside the massive timber, the stone's deep "plunk" and a rippling wave marking the objective. The mossy tree rested half-submerged, well below them, and was angled downstream from its stump on the far bank. Fast water swirled around the end in the river but the surface smoothed out upstream of the log.

"We head fer it?" Hannibal asked.

"Yep. We let the current help us. But first we got to check the bottom before we try."

Hannibal soon handed the planter a six foot, stout stick he had cut and stripped. Wading into the stream, Claude poked the pole into the water beyond him. It struck solid bottom at about knee-height. He stepped out a little farther and reached as far as he could toward the middle but found no difference in the depth. The rocky bottom continued and seemed like sound footing.

"We go together," he said, after he regained the bank. "Each with his staff," he insisted, holding out his left hand to the Negro. "Grip tight and use the pole to balance with."

The two waded into the stream, feeling ahead with their staffs as they edged out toward the center. When the water deepened, its rapid flow pressed against their legs with great force and dragged at their soaked pants. The fugitives staggered along in the turbulence of the crossing, slippery cobbles on the bottom making for treacherous footing. Claude and the servant wobbled and fought as the force increased. They had almost made it to the safety of the slower pooling above the log when Hannibal's fall over a submerged boulder stripped him from Claude's grasp. The planter swayed and stuck his staff in the bottom below him, wet by Hannibal's splashing but still upright as he struggled with the current.

Hannibal rolled over and over in the rapids, unable to gain his footing in the fast water, his shouts erupting whenever he surfaced. Claude watched in horror when he disappeared into the chute. His last glimpse of the man was his head surfacing in the pool below the big wave at the bottom. Tearing himself free from his paralysis, the planter fought his way to the protection of the log. He pulled himself quickly along it to the Georgia bottom, then ran downstream, water spraying from his shoes and pants.

"You'll be all right," Claude said, a short time later.

Hannibal lay on his belly, his head down the slope to the river. He gagged and retched, but more water than food spewed from his mouth and nose. The planter pounded hard on the servant's back as the Negro gasped and strangled, his labored search for air gradually becoming less strident. Claude helped him stand when he breathed without choking. But the Negro swayed dizzily and slumped back down onto the gravel. He struggled with his trembling, sitting with his head between his knees while deep breaths whistled in and out. Finally he gulped, then hawked and spit to expel the mucus. Hannibal's clear eyes reassured the planter when he met the latter's concerned stare.

Claude knelt beside him and patted his shoulder. "It's over, Hannibal. You feelin' better?"

The Negro bobbed his head up and down as he coughed and rid his windpipe of more mucus. When it was clear, he tossed his head violently, throwing a shower of droplets, and wiped the water off his face.

"'bout drowned, Claude," he said in a weak voice. He was trembling and sank back down after a half- hearted attempt to regain his feet. "You got me out?"

"You were half out already," the planter said, "with your head up the bank. I dragged you around and pounded out the water." He looked at the western hillsides with their heavy timber and valley between. "We're goin' on. Walkin' up that slope'll get the rest o' the water out o' yuh."

Hannibal got up and shucked his clothing, the wet pieces clinging and difficult to get off. The two men wrung them out to dampness. As soon as the Negro was redressed, they headed up the forested valley to the west. Drying his possibles sack and pistol would have to wait on a fire, so he slung them wet.

Late afternoon found them on a ridge overlooking a narrow valley. A haze of chimney smoke hung in the air in the northern end of the depression, the forest to the west apparently little broken by settlements. The next ridgeline carried a smooth, deep dent.

"Look at that," Claude said happily. "I figure the west branch Rufus talked about is beyond that saddle."

"Be hard goin' ter git dere," Hannibal said. He pulled at his crotch and the still damp clothes. "Dese ol' wet pants done rubbed me mighty sore."

"We'll likely find a cabin and can scare up some fixin's. Probably some grease'll do it."

Claude angled down the slope without waiting for the servant. Large trees interspersed with scattered brush offered a clear path with easy footing, and good concealment. A hard climb from the creek in the bottom delivered them to the western saddle, though not without its cost. They were puffing and sweating and ready for a rest. Hannibal shucked his clothes while Claude lay prone and inched to the edge of a steep, denuded overlook. The naked slave hobbled to his side when the planter shouted with joy.

"There's the west fork, Hannibal," he said with satisfaction.

A ribbon of water glinted in the valley below. No chimney smoke or road was visible in its heavy forest. Without fear of detection, the planter walked along the projecting ridge and appraised the best way down.

Hannibal's face wrinkled in pain as he spread his legs wide. "Can't cross ternight, Claude. I'se got de misery bad."

The planter inspected the rubbed skin and the sweating servant. "Keep your clothes off," he said. "We'll find somethin' to help that soon's we put in. Now let's get on down there."

He struck along the ridge until the sharp crest gave way to a slide, its slope well carpeted with leaves from the small growth covering it, and no hard rock showing. Striding rapidly down the steep slope using the saplings as handholds, they quickly entered open glades among giant trees, their passage to the river unimpeded. The bottom next to the river contained a profusion of small growth, a thicket at the edge of the slope forested with giant trunks.

Large chestnut trees proliferated at the toe of the bank that rose from the side of the bottom. As they went along the flat in search of a spring and a shelter for the night, Claude paused at a dense laurel patch. His fear rose when the forest sounds suddenly stilled. Anticipating the worst, he motioned for the servant to stay behind him and drew his pistol. A rapid grunting and scraping in the thicket added to his alarm, increased when the bushes shook from the intruder's passage. A furred, black face, sniffing and inquisitive, stuck itself almost into his body before he saw the bear. In reflex, he shot it between the eyes, its thrashing and groans resounding in the bottom. Hannibal dropped his clothes and pinioned the jerking hind legs, hanging on tight while he avoided the claws. The bear's death throes reduced to trembles as the blood poured from the head wound. Claude stabbed it in the throat when it weakened. The animal's struggle for life ended with feeble tremors and a rush of blood. As soon as the bear was still, the planter sat on the carcass and tried to calm himself. His legs shook uncontrollably and his body quivered.

"Scairt me bad, Hannibal," he said, wiping his brow of sweat. "Don't like no bear close up."

The servant felt the slick sides and thumped the round belly. "He plenty fat. Been feedin' on de chestnuts. We eat good ternight."

Butchering produced a huge pile of meat and fat, bound up in the welcome skin. Claude shouldered the burden when they moved on, while Hannibal carried a bag of the rich nuts. Their search ended at a blowdown of a sizeable oak. Its projecting root fan provided protection on one side that could be roofed over into a half-face lean-to. Flames from a comforting fire soon flickered in the gathering dusk, the sun's rays touching the tops but darkness falling in the valley. A hundred yards away, the river gurgled and splashed in musical whispers that carried faintly to their camp. Small birds chirped as they settled in for the night, their calls to each other a welcome sign of peace and no intruders.

With their clothes drying on sticks before the fire, the two naked men roasted bear meat and chestnuts. Grease dribbled down their chins as they stuffed themselves. The last of their whiskey topped off the meat and mellowed their fears, while belches reduced the pressure of gluttony on their distended bellies. They squatted in the heat, somnolent from exhaustion and contentment. When he was well warmed, Claude touched up his light spots with daubs of the walnut dye. Then he shook the gourd and listened to the sloshing. "Plenty more," he told himself as he stoppered the neck tightly and put the vessel back into his sack.

Meantime, his cooking pot simmered and bubbled, reducing bear fat to a light oil. Hannibal filled the whiskey flask with the fluid after the rendering. He had smeared on the first batch to cure his scrapes, and his thighs glistened with an oily sheen.

"Dishere grease good," he said, sighing contentedly. "It done made dat scrapin' better a'ready."

"You can do it again tomorrow 'fore we leave," Claude said. "Should cure you up good."

The planter stretched out flat and put his hands under his head as he shifted about. He cursed at the pain when a sharp root stuck him in the small of the back. The agony of the dent forced him up and to a seat on a nearby log. He rubbed his hurt place, grumbling, and felt his wounded leg. The calf barely pained him and was healing over with a healthy scab. He picked at the crust a little but it was hard and fixed tight.

"Fetch the oil," he said.

Hannibal rubbed the hot bear oil into the dent from the root, then into the wound, before rebinding the bandage lightly around Claude's leg. He set the pan aside, next to some coals, for his use later.

A slight swirl in the leaves and a sighing in the treetops took their attention away from their hurts. The thickening clouds and change in wind was warning enough. Claude sniffed the damp air and inspected the blowdown.

"May rain tonight," he told Hannibal. "We need a hut."

After testing the edge of his knife, he searched out a small, flat rock and splashed oil on it. A few minutes of honing sharpened the edge. He was not satisfied until the blade would shave hair from his arm. Hannibal's bowie took more work, with Claude idling contentedly by the fire until the Negro was done.

The nearby bottom, with much dead wood and thick, small growths, provided ample supplies to the fugitives. Their ready knives and strong hands stripped unneeded whips from saplings and downed wood. Leaning the shafts against the blowdown fan created a half-face hut in front of the fire. By full dark, a thick mat of pine branches covered the saplings, a dense roof of matted needles that would turn away any light rain. Encased in their warm, dry clothes, the fugitives spoked the fire with several long billets of seasoned wood and crawled in for the night.

Claude spread the bear skin over a springy layer of pine boughs. The bear's odor contrasted to the sharp, resiny scent of the green pine. He ran his hand over the coarse fur. "This skin'll do for a cover if we get cold," he said. "Fur not good yet, though."

Hannibal poked his head from the hut and glanced about nervously. "You recken any militia see our fire?" he asked. The Negro's unease and restlessness as he was settling in amused Claude, who pulled him back onto the skin.

"Get to sleep," he said. "We're too far into the hollow. We can sleep safe."

A light shower in the night was their only alarm. Awakened and yawning, Claude shoved the billets into the dying fire while the final drops fell. As it flamed up, he took a short walk into the woods, then resought the fragrant boughs. Only snores disturbed the glade until the sun was well up.

Chapter 17

Isaac

November 17, 1864. Clarkesville, Georgia.
Temperature 60\45, partly cloudy, slight
chance of showers. Southerly winds to 10
knots. Crescent moon waning, setting be-
fore 11 P.M.

Resin popped and sparks flew in the updraft of the hot, crackling fire that warmed the fugitives. They crowded close enough to scorch, its intense, welcome heat quickly drying the dampness of the night's showers. Claude stooped in front of several sticks angled over the blaze, then rotated them to expose raw sides of meat chunks to the intense heat. Sizzling of the roasting bear, the pieces interspersed with fat along the skewers, added to the sputtering of dripping grease as it struck the flames. A tantalizing aroma of hot meat permeated the camp and was wafted away on the mild breeze in the bottom.

Hannibal hung over the sticks, his knife out in anticipation. "Ain't ready yet, Claude?" he asked.

"A few minutes more," the planter replied. He rotated the skewers again and inspected the blackening chunks, then reached in close with his knife. A few fast swipes reclaimed a group of chestnuts from the hot ashes and divided them into two piles. He pushed one cluster over toward the Negro.

Hannibal picked up a hot nut, only to drop it with an

oath. He stuck his burned fingers in his mouth, muffling his continued grumbling.

Claude laughed as he turned the meat again. When satisfied, he pulled a stick and handed it to the Negro. Hannibal's knife and teeth busily demolished the chunks while Claude attacked his own skewered pieces.

The planter gnawed at a tough cut, its red, greasy juices all over his hands and spread around his mouth. It struck him funny and he laughed, an upwelling of good humor that spilled out over the camp. Here he was, no white table cloth or silver as in the Greenbottom dining room, gorging on his food like his hound dogs. No better than an animal. He was an animal, Claude surmised, as he finished the meat. A hunted animal, no better than the foxes he used to chase, chases where the bugling of the pursuing dogs thrilled him through the night. Now the hounds and hunters were after him. And he sat there in the dirt and gulped down half-roasted meat in his hands, anxious to escape. His withdrawal to Greenbottom brought brilliant pictures of the dining room to mind, the high ceiling with its crystal chandelier glinting, setting off the snowy white cloth. A silver platter or dish offered for his savoring enjoyment by the servant in livery, while Letty in her pretty gown sat at the end and his children learned their manners at their seats at the side. Flames of the fire reflected on his blank stare, mesmerized back to Greenbottom, when Hannibal violently shook him.

"Somebody out dere, Claude," he said.

Claude pulled his pistol in an instant and sought cover behind a nearby bush. The big Negro lay beside him, his knife ready. Soft footfalls and rustling bushes sounded in the trees of the bottom, the intruders effecting a stealthy approach from down river. Claude motioned the Negro to seek cover to the right and Hannibal obediently scuttled across to some screening brush. The planter crept back up the slope behind the root fan where he could peep out at the intruders and keep a clear line of fire.

A low, bass rumble alerted them to the threat in the forest. But as if to allay their fears, the hidden intruder coughed loudly and said, "Smells meat, I tells yuh."

"Well, we see who 'tis," another man replied. "Can't be no militia way outen here. They's probably jest like us."

The two voices carried clearly to the fugitives as they listened but the sounds of movement slowly died out as the men drew closer. Furtive, creeping noises and a muffled curse preceded the appearance of a Negro at the other edge of the root fan. His face stuck out of some bushes, framed like a picture. The smell of the roasting meat sizzling over the fire decided him. He rushed out and pulled a stick, biting at the hot meat and fat with relish. A tall, gaunt white man slowly followed and took a stand at the edge of the brush. He carried an axe, and each of the two men bore a small wooden cask on straps across his shoulders. The white man's head swivelled around as his eyes warily surveyed the camp, his body tensed. When no one appeared, the intruder stole silently across the opening to the fire and chose a skewer.

As soon as the two were together, eating the meat, Claude shouted "Hands up!" and stepped from his concealment. Hannibal ran out with his knife and closed the Negro from the other side. He placed the point against the ribs of the man and seized his arm.

The white man threw his arms in the air, his stick trailing from one fist. "Hold on," he pleaded. "We jest hungry. Ain't botherin' yuh none."

But the Negro ignored the knife at his side and kept tearing voraciously at the meat. Claude cursed and took deliberate aim at his head. When Hannibal pricked the man's skin with the knife, he winced and dropped the almost empty skewer. His injured whine protested the holdup as he slowly raised his arms.

"Don' hurt me," he said. "We hongry. An' we ain' done nothin'." He bobbed and bowed in supplication. "We jist choppin' bee trees. Ain't had no meat in three days. Jist honey an' corn."

Claude waved his derringer at the white man. "That right? You just wanderin'?"

The man nodded and replied, "I'm Isaac Caffey. He be Matt."

"Search 'em, Hannibal," Claude ordered, taking no

chances.

He leveled his pistol and aimed at Caffey while Hannibal ran his hands over Matt. The servant came up with a fearsome knife, a broken off saber that had been ground into a twelve inch blade. Hannibal threw Matt to the ground and threatened him into immobility, then went next to Caffey. But Matt didn't stay put even when menaced. He kept eying Claude's weapon while he slowly crawled over to the fire and resumed chewing on some meat. Hannibal's search of Caffey yielded a small knife and a flintlock pistol.

Claude's irritation with Matt's disobedience increased his ill-temper. "You live 'round here?" he asked, testily.

Caffey started at the planter's sharp impatience and his face flushed. "I don' answer no more questions to no damned nigger," he said indignantly.

Hannibal stuck his knife against the man's side and whispered in his ear. "He be a Yankee officer. I kills yuh if you don' do it."

The captive's face turned ashen. His searching gaze examined the erect posture and cold, chiseled features of the planter. Claude's light colored eyes and steady pistol decided him. He met the planter's gaze directly, without evasion, the truth evident in his face and his simple explanation.

"We live over the ridge," he said, pointing, "'bout three mile east o' Bates place." My folks hold with the Union. But my brothers an' me got put in the militia. Deserted first time I could." He shrugged his shoulders resignedly and his mouth drooped. "Been hidin' out with Matt ever since. Cuttin' bee trees fer my pa, last few days."

Claude relaxed his stance and lowered the derringer. He pocketed it and held the flintlock at his side. Motioning to the sticks spiking the remaining meat and the little pile of roasted chestnuts, he offered his hospitality, pitiful as it was.

"Eat and be welcome," he said. "We're headin' southwest an' maybe you can help us."

The fugitives feasted on honeycomb dipped from the barrels while Isaac and Matt filled up on bear meat and nuts. Replete with the meal, the four men squatted around the campfire while Caffey told them about the travel to Clarke's.

"Easy to cross the west fork 'bout a mile down. Wade it, but keerful o' the rocks, they's mighty slick. Then head fer the notch you kin see right to the west."

"How far, Isaac?" Claude asked.

"It's 'bout five mile o' rough goin' over to the Soquee. Foller it down 'bout eight or ten miles to Clarke's." He shook his head and finger in warning. "You be keerful there, Claude. The militia boys 'roun' the town right mean."

The two parties split up in an hour. Caffey and Matt headed to the north on their search, now burdened with a large chunk of bear. Hannibal carried a birch- bark bucket of honeycomb, firm in the cool air.

Isaac laughed when Claude fired the flintlock before parting and handed it to him empty. "Don' worry," he said. "We don' chase you and can't tell nobody. We's hid out too."

The door banged open under the kick of the boy. Two figures struggled on the threshold, while Old Blue squeezed around them and danced about, barking. The dog rushed in for a bite just as Jared swung the girl into the room. "Git in thar," he said, angrily. He thrust Hester away, then knocked her down when she leaped at him and tried to claw his face. She crawled away from his foot when he drew it back for a hard blow, her malevolent glances uncowed.

Hester sprawled on the floor of the overseer's cabin at Calhoun's with Jared standing over her and Old Blue growling from his crouch at her side. Minns' head had come up out of the soapy water in the washbasin when the commotion started. Droplets and soap bubbles flew as he toweled the remnants from his amazed face. He still dripped when he joined them and nudged the girl with his moccasin. Her slow slide away from him transmitted her fear. But her face, contorted with hate, carried a hidden menace.

"Whar'd you git 'er, Jared?" Minns asked.

"Sighted her comin' outen Granny Esther's cabin when I was scoutin' some vittles. Brought her 'long to yuh. Maybe she can add to what you got last night."

"Warn't nothin', boy. Those women ain't told me nothin'."

Jared bent over and cuffed Hester about the head while he questioned her. "What you got to say, gal? Why you here?"

The girl spat at them. "Don' know 'bout no 'scapes," she said. Her temper flared and her eyes gleamed. Hate coupled with fear in her, and the two, compounded, produced both a warning and an entreaty. "I'se Miz Gwen's nigger now, visitin'. She goin' on t'day, so you leave me 'lone."

Minns grasped her arm and jerked her up off the floor. He beat the girl with his open hand, slapping her head back and forth until she stopped her protests.

"Yer lyin'," he said. "Miz Norris ain't got no nigger like you. I seen 'em in the manse last night."

Hester slumped against his grip and her whimpers subsided into abject pleadings. "Don' hurt me agin," she wailed. Her tears flowed until the cuffings stopped.

Jared pulled her dress up to her head while Minns held the wriggling girl's hands. Hester's supple body resisted with all its strength but Minns easily restrained her while Jared continued his efforts to peel off her clothes. The hunter chuckled at the boy's haste. "Iris didn't give you 'nough last night?"

"Ain't none like Hester, Pa," Jared said. He stripped off the last of the slave's clothes and threw her on the nearby bed, then satisfied his passion in a fury of movement while his father watched.

Minns laughed at the sweating, supine boy lying on his back after the coupling. Jared's chest rose and fell while he rested and recovered. His bare middle and white legs contrasted to the gray cover of the shucks mattress. The two Minnses paid no attention to the girl while the youth relaxed. Her slide off the bed and insertion into her dress escaped their usual vigilance. But the girl didn't run. Instead, she stole spiteful, surreptitious glances at them as she stealthily reached for Jared's belt and knife lying next to the bed. Seizing the hilt, she withdrew the blade and lunged for the boy. Old Blue growled and launched himself at her as she struck. It was enough warning to save Jared. He rolled off the bed at the dog's growl and a glimpse of the screaming, hurtling girl. The knife missed his chest but stuck clear through his raised left hand, its blade jammed between the knuckle bones of the middle fingers.

"Git 'er, Blue!" he shouted.

The hound growled ferociously and ran after the fleeing girl, while Minns turned to his son. Blue howled when the edge of the swinging door struck his neck and pinched it against the jamb. The frantic Hester bounced it once and slammed the door closed when he pulled back. Old Blue jumped up against the confining timbers, scratching and barking. Unable to escape the cabin, his interest soon shifted to a rag rug before the fire, where heat from the the coals warmed his injured neck as he sprawled in comfort.

Jared sat erect in a rocking chair, his face drained of blood. He moaned and grasped his wrist near the knife while he bobbed back and forth in the squeaking rocker. The blade still penetrated the gristle of his hand, its point inches beyond the knuckles. Blood oozed from both sides and ran down the boy's fingers before dripping onto the floor.

Minns grabbed the hilt and jerked hard. The knife came free with a scraping noise as it cleared the bones. Jared screamed and collapsed in a dead faint, and his head fell back against the rocker. His savaged hand dropped beside the chair and sprayed blood as it fell. Bright red blood ran out of the wound in a steady stream and collected in a pool on the wood floor. Its size frightened Minns. He stormed out of the door and ran down the lane crying out, "Granny! Granny!"

Claude cautiously skirted the fence at the weedy, cultivated field. Its withered potato plants were matted on the ground amid sparse dry thistles and grass sprouts. He motioned to Hannibal in the trees, the big slave hanging back while the planter reconnoitered the farmstead. Timbers of a burned out cabin hung off a rock chimney, its site well separated from the remnants of the rail fence that enclosed the garden patch and farmyard. A water bucket rested on the top of the stone lining of a nearby well, the lever a skeleton shaft angled into the sky. A large creek swung a wide loop around the homestead, its waters sending out little wavelets as it curled around a forked snag in the bend

near the cabin. Claude circled the place, the house's aban-
donment recent from the charred smell of the timbers. He
waved to Hannibal, who loped in across the field. The Negro
stopped to dig near the fence and then brushed the dirt off
an unearthed potato. He held it up as the planter sauntered
towards him.

"Dey ain't dug de taters yet, Claude," he said.

"We'll take a sack," the planter replied. He fell on his
knees in a potato row and pried out tubers with his bowie.

The white potatoes were a welcome change from the
sweets of the past days. Eating them raw as they dug, they
filled their pockets and sack. Some bluetop turnips nearby
added tangy tubers to their noon meal as well as the greens
of the tops. Vegetables, together with roasted bear meat and
chestnuts, filled them to bursting. Big swigs of water topped
off the satisfying feast. A feeling of contentment suffused
Claude as he belched and sought a comfortable grass bed.
The lassitude accompanying his full belly seduced him into
a rest next to the chimney. Hannibal eased down beside
him, gnawing on yet another potato.

"What you recken happen here, Claude?" he asked.

"They were burned out on a raid." The planter pointed
at some bullet marks on the rocks and three graves, with
their yellow-clay coating barely mounded above the ground.
"See?" he said. "Probably the militia an' some family like
Isaac's. Could be just evening scores, too."

"Isaac tol' us ter go on down de creek when we struck
it. Dis de one?"

"Probably. We're far enough west and it's big, like he
said. Soon's we rest a mite, we head on down to Clarke's.
Can't be more'n ten, maybe fifteen mile."

Minns rampaged about Calhoun's in a fury that even
Hawkins feared. She avoided him and Jared after his
threats scared her into silence. His curses spewed out in a
never-ending stream while he searched the cabins and outbuildings one by one. Jared followed silently, his hand
bound up with Granny's potions and torn sheeting. They
had turned out all the slaves, but the cabins yielded
nothing. Minns still was fuming when they came to the

barn. Urging on Old Blue, he sent Jared around the side to stand guard with his rifle.

"Oooaah! Oooaah!" The dog struck and rushed into a pile of hay. He sniffed about and burrowed in, a squall and yelp coming from the heaving mound of fragrant grass. Minns raised his rifle, only to be deluged with chaff that erupted from the hurried exit of a maddened tom and Blue in full cry. Spitting down from a cross beam, the big tailed cat arched its back and offered defiance. Old Blue jumped about barking treed, but his excitement only infuriated the hunter.

"Git, Blue," he shouted. His curses filled the air when he missed with his first kick at the jumping hound. "Goddamn it, Blue, git! We don' want no Goddamn cat!"

Blue ignored his kicks until Minns rushed in and seized the dog's ruff, then cuffed him into submission while he dragged the animal out of the barn. The hunter's firm grasp choked off a few plaintive yelps from the struggling hound. Minns held him until he quit squirming, then petted the old dog and gentled him down.

"He ain't been onter Hester nowhere, Pa," Jared said. He rested his rifle in the crook of his left arm. His hand was covered by a white bandage below his fringed coat sleeve.

"We got to go beat that Granny," Minns growled. His scar reddened as his exasperation rose. "She knows ever'thin' 'bout those 'scapes an' that Hester." Emotion overcame him, strangling him such that he could hardly get out the threat. "I beat her 'til she tells, er I kill 'er."

Minns threw the dog away from him with a parting curse and a kick, then strode down the slope to Granny's cabin, his dark mood evident in his repeated curses and flaming scar. Jared and Blue hurried along behind, but the dog snuffled and digressed toward likely scents as they moved down the lane. The hunter didn't hesitate at the door of Granny's cabin. Thrusting it open with a crash, he leaped inside, his rifle ready. Hawkins faced him from a place before the fire, her body rigidly erect beside the ancient slave in her splint chair.

Minns ignored the overseers wife. "Git outen yer chair, Granny," he ordered.

"What'cher want, Athey Minns?" Hawkins asked. She stepped in front of the slave and put her hand to her belt, close to her whip and her pistol. Her hostile, combative stance and determined face brought his advance to a halt.

Minns' open mouth and confusion fell off into muttering while he gathered himself. Jared and Blue crowded into the cabin behind the hunter and explored the corners. Blue soon found the hiding place of the whimpering Sissie. The small girl rushed out of her concealment into the arms of the waiting Granny.

"Hesh, chile," Granny said. The old woman patted the clinging child and soothed her. "It be awright. He ain't gwine hurt yuh."

Hawkins flicked her little whip in front of the hunter. "I asked what you want, Athey."

His face mottled with the snap of the whip and his scar swelled and reddened with anger. Seizing the rawhide, he jerked it from her hand. "Goin'a whip that Granny 'til she tells us whar's Hester an' those 'scapes." His neck swelled with his passion and his tongue thickened when he tried again. "Goin'a whip 'er."

Minns gestured to Jared. He and the boy set their rifles against the wall and moved toward Granny's chair, pulling away the screaming child. Sissie scuttled into her hideaway, her sobs muffled by the cloths she pulled over her. The two hunters dragged the woman out into the dirt of the lane. Granny lay on her belly, her withered frame quiet, her eyes closed. When Minns applied the whip, her slight body quivered but her reedy voice told him nothing between his curses and demands about the escapes. He laid on blows until his arm tired, then he handed the small whip to Jared. The boy looked at the old slave prone before him, her clothes cut to ribbons, blood showing from some of the exposed brown skin. His indecision and a look of pity on his face earned him a blow and a curse from Minns.

"Whip her, Jared! Git to it."

Jared's resolve failed after a few weak strokes. "She ain't goin'a tell nothin', Pa. I don' want to hit 'er no more." He threw down the whip and went into the cabin, returning with the two rifles.

The hunter stood above the small, prone body, its cuts and stains showing. His raised arm was poised to strike when Granny commenced singing an ancient Negro chant, her voice faint but its message joyful and triumphant.

"An' Massa tink it day ob doom,
An' we ob jubilee,
We'll soon be free! We'll soon be free!
De Lord will call us home!"

Minns seized his rifle from his son. "I'll set yuh free, you old bitch," he said. His muzzle came around to line up with Granny while he cocked the piece.

Hawkins pulled her Navy Colt and stuck the barrel in Minns' face. "Hold on!" she said, scowling. Her hard challenge stopped him, especially when she wiggled the muzzle in front of his eyes. "Ain't nobody kills our niggers. Now you put down that rifle an' rustle. You an' yer boy ain't welcome here no more."

Jared helped Granny into the cabin while Hawkins and Minns glared at each other. The pistol barrel against his nose decided the hunter. Cursing, he uncocked his rifle and stalked off, followed by Jared and the dog. Hawkins watched them from the cabin door until they splashed their horses across the river on the way west.

The Tugaloo gurgled at Walton's ford, up an inch or so from rains in the mountains. Gill drew rein at the edge of the musical, roily water, its usually clear depths obscured by the recent runoff. His horse reached its head down and drank, slurping up the water, while the other riders halted beside him. Creaks and animal noises rose from the troop as the soldiers rested themselves and watered both man and beast. Gill and Hartsill stretched with the men and filled their canteens, their cautious, anxious eyes searching the ford and the trail across it.

The Sergeant scratched and spit and his troubled face sought Hartsill's. "The outriders didn't see nothin' o' 'em, Lieutenant, whilst we come up."

"They're bound to be close," Hartsill said. "Scatter out an' look for their camp soon's you're ready."

Alarmed shouts from troopers split the damp moun-

tain air in the search that followed. A gunshot from the
cache of saddles and harness had Hartsill and Gill racing to
the spot downstream, only to find another man reporting a
body on the bank below. The troop gathered about the
white, stiffened corpse. Its clothes were missing and a bullet
hole was centered in its chest.

"They done been ambushed, Lieutenant," Gill said. He
spit and shifted uneasily in his saddle while his eyes
searched the forest on both sides of the stream.

"Damn," Hartsill said, regretfully. "Got 'em all, looks
like. I counted eight saddles."

"No, Lieutenant," Gill replied. "Irvine had a squad with
him. One man got away." He thought for a moment. "Those
bushwhackers are on foot. They didn't take the horses."

"Means they're runaway slaves," Hartsill said. "Maybe
the coffle with the Yankee. White men would have stolen
everything."

The Sergeant hawked and spit, his mouth dribbling
remnants into the brown stains in his beard at each side.
"They's got to go over to'ard Toccoa Falls er Clarke's. The
ones we caught afore headed thereabouts, then up to'ard
Tennessee."

Hartsill simply nodded. He bowed his head a moment
for a prayer, then crisply issued his orders, swift and
decisive in his actions. Sending one man to alert Colonel
Hyatte, he detailed three troopers to the ford to bury the
dead man and establish a picket line. In an hour, he and Gill
led the remaining four men in pursuit of the coffle.

Rufus' coffle scattered along the game trail in a line, a
few paces separating each man as they loped along its
narrow track. It headed toward Clarkesville and paralleled
the main trace a mile distant. Rufus stopped at a feeder
stream to rest and drink. The men gathered together as he
idly walked downstream through the light brush and small
willow trees that hugged the bank. Judah trailed along
behind, his sharp gaze searching the forest and his rifle
ready. A deep pool with a magnificent, entering riffle attracted Rufus to its side, one bordered with a soft, needled
slope under massive pines. The Negro halted on the mat and

stood in statuesque, brooding silence, his head bowed in that idealic glade. Water rippled as it spilled around a submerged, mossy trunk, the log's bulk creating a slight dam where the flow from the pool resumed its noisy travel down the slope. The two Negroes held a silent communion at the pool, each with his own thoughts, their deep reflection disturbed only by the musical flow of the stream. Judah came alert when Rufus sighed and moved down to dip his fingers in the water. His gloom surfaced in a troubled face and a sad reflection.

"Me an' my pappy come all through here, Judah, when I'se a boy. Me an' my brother fished this creek an' the Tugaloo fo' goin' up on the Chattooga."

"Ketch any?"

"My pappy did," Rufus said. He smiled wryly. "Me an' my brother not much."

His red beard quivered and his eyes squinted, but his hand brushed quickly across them as if to erase his pain and memory. "Dem days done gone," he said. "I'se jest a 'scaped nigger." His tone grew bitter and he slumped in resignation. "Ralph, he own de home place soon as old Marster dead. An' I'se as white as him."

Rufus gazed long into the pool, its still surface peaceful between the noisy riffles. Judah waited quietly, his gaze intent on his friend yet alert to the hazards in the forest. Rufus' pathos finally gave way to determination. Shaking his shoulders and throwing back his flaming red head, he stretched upward and resolutely straightened his backbone, an erect, confident man in charge of his destiny. "Don' make no nevermind," he said. "Man got ter live his life best he can." Beckoning to Judah, Rufus strode back upstream along the creek to rejoin the others. Some snores added to banter and laughter as the men smoked and sprawled on the forest mat in their temporary camp. He roused them out with shouts and gentle kicks. "Let's git, men," he said. "We gotta make it past de falls t'day. Move on past Clarke's termorrer."

"What den, Rufus?" Judah asked.

Rufus held up his hand and motioned to the coffle to gather around. The men left their beds slowly and coalesced into a group. Some were gossiping and grumbling, some checked their weapons and a few chewed morsels from their sacks as they drifted close. When the overseer waited and made no move to leave, Judah repeated his question.

"We see Claude an' Hannibal safely through the rebs," Rufus told them, "when dey come down from de Chattooga. Den we kill rebs afore we head fer Tennessee. Got plenty powder an' ball in de pouch, an' lotsa whuppin's ter settle fer, so I ain't in no hurry fer de free lan'."

With curses and grim, assenting rumbles, the Negroes cast their lot with his. The escaped slaves gripped their rifles tightly; determination and hate inflamed their passions as they shifted, eager to be gone. Rufus led out, his ground covering lope matched by the others. Judah brought up the rear, falling back occasionally to listen for pursuers.

Red rays of the setting sun scattered between the scudding clouds, spikes of color that turned edges crimson with their glow. Smaller shafts penetrated the forest. Their dancing dots of light marched slowly along the duff as the afternoon advanced. The weary travelers labored on, Claude's shoulders sagging as an ache grew into sporadic stabbing pains. He shifted the weight of his coat and hunched up his injured shoulder to relieve it. With his wounded leg also aching, he was close to exhaustion from the prolonged walk. An inviting log seduced him. He sank down on it, a fine seat next to a swampy seep in the forest, and took off his hat and wiped the sweat from his brow.

"I need to rest some, Hannibal," he said. "This ground's rougher'n Rufus and Isaac told us. We musta missed that last trail o' Isaac's."

"We fetch up at Clarke's ternight, Claude, I look fer de shoemaker. But best we fin' a place ter keep warm fust. Gonna be col'."

Hannibal bent to the seep and dipped his head, then sucked up mouthfuls of water. His noisy sups stilled some nearby chirps. Satisfied, the Negro wiped his mouth on his sleeve and joined Claude on the log. Pulling out a piece of bear from his possibles sack, he brushed off the surface dirt and handed it to the planter.

"Eat, Claude," he said, "an' you feel better." Suiting his own action to his words, he fished out another dirty chunk and swiftly demolished it, then followed it with a potato.

Their simple meal was soon finished. Claude scooped up some water and washed off his sweaty face. He filled his canteen and splashed a good bit into his mouth. When he stood up, Hannibal chuckled, then burst out laughing.

"Needin' some dye, Claude," he said. "Yore face right speckled."

Claude touched up his color with the walnut dye with Hannibal's help. With the sun to guide them and the creek bed to follow, they headed off down the valley looking for Clarke's. A mile of travel took them into a broadening of the hollow. Its easier going broke out into a field, a man-made clearing glimpsed through the trees ahead. Wood smoke settled along the forest in the cooling air. Its pungent scent signalled them to increase their caution.

The blunt thuds of a chopping axe stopped them in their tracks, its location alerting them to a nearby house. They crept to the edge of the field, wiggling through the briars and honeysuckle along the fence. A man in homespun chopped not fifty yards distant. His broad back and long arms rose and fell as he split billets on a huge stump and tossed them onto a big pile. Evening shadows gathered as he worked, his labors interrupted at dusk by the squeak of an opened door. Light spilled out onto the stoop and outlined a buxom woman waving a spoon.

"Supper, Jake," she hollered.

The axman stuck his blade into the stump and picked up an armful of firewood to carry in as he went. As soon as the door closed, Hannibal scuttled for the corncrib next to the barn. The latter was a large, pole building that lay in the back of the farm yard, its high, projecting hayloft silhouetted against the sky. Claude's heart pumped when he joined the Negro, his alarm so great that he reflexively started for the barn and its warm hiding places.

Hannibal's iron grip on his arm drew him back, the Negro restraining him when he tried to break loose. The servant put his hand over Claude's mouth and whispered, "We steals us some corn fust, then I looks dere fo' we go in."

The planter collapsed exhaustedly against the poles of the crib. His tiredness kept him at its side while the Negro raided the corn and filled his sack. Sliding down against the bottom of the crib, Claude found a stone foundation, interspersed with holes to ventilate under the corn. The Negro had just pulled him erect again when a flurry of hoofbeats sounded down the lane leading to the house.

Hannibal's grip tightened on Claude's arm. "Got ter hide," he said excitedly.

The Negro cast wildly about while the hoofbeats grew thunderous and the cabin door opened. Jake rushed out with a rifle and faced down the lane. Light from the cabin splashed across the yard where the horses were pulling up. The planter grabbed the servant's trembling body and whispered into his ear.

"Under the corn crib. Quick!"

A fast, slithering entrance took them through the vents in the rock foundation and into the blackness under the floor of the crib. Claude ignored his few, hurtful scrapes and shaking hands as he readied his weapons. Little tremors ran along his back and the hair raised on his neck. He could hear Hannibal fumbling with his weapons and smelled the man's rank odor, an odor of fear and sweat, just like him. They rested on their bellies and peered out at the loud, milling rebs when satisfied with their arms. They were safe, Claude thought, with the crib above them and the night coming on. All they had to do was wait and then escape to the safety of the barn. Wait while Jake finished his shouting, passionate objection to the coming plunder of his corn. A dog trotted into view as the men harangued each other, a lean hound that had to have a good nose. Claude's heart flip-flopped in dismay. He pounded his fist against the ground and swore.

"Damn, Hannibal. They're goin'a catch us for sure this time. Can't get away if that dog comes sniffin' around."

Old Blue burrowed into a hole and furiously barked at its occupant. His tale wagged and his front paws threw back dirt in spurts as he alternately dug and then tried to stick his head farther down in the den. Jared grabbed his tail and pulled him back, then held the wriggling dog. Blue's head had dirt everywhere, crusted crumbs dropping off as he shook. Uncowed by the boy's cuffs, he dashed right back to his excavations when Jared loosened his grip. A few minutes more digging satisfied the dog, his dripping tongue and dirty body seeking the cold water of the creek nearby when he gave up the chase. With a yelp and a jump, he plunged in and indulged his habit, while the Minnses hunkered down on the bank and warmed themselves. When his bath was complete, the hound showered off the water and slumped down in front of the Minnses' fire, his eyes intent on the two men.

"Let's give it up, Pa," Jared said. He was chewing on a piece of bacon, and its greasy fat coated both his face and his good hand as he worried it with his teeth. Old Blue begged, his tail wagging as he stretched out toward the boy. Jared laughed and threw the remnant to the waiting dog, who caught it in the air. The boy washed his hand and face before he turned his attention to his bandage. He grimaced when he lightly squeezed the bound hand, then worked his fingers before tightening the cloth and holding his injured knuckles out to the welcome heat.

The older man stared into the fire, his cross-legged seat part of his Indian heritage. Jared left him be, his father's trance-like state of meditation well known to his family. Minns' immobility and the heat of the close fire made his face sweat copiously. Originally droplets, the oily exudate coalesced into large beads that ran down his cheeks and beard and dripped onto his pants. Minns was oblivious to the fire and to the wetting. He finally came out of his spell when his buckskins singed from the flames. The hunter slapped out a few sparks and swore violently at the scorching and the stink of the blackened leather.

"Goddamn it, boy," he said, "why didn't you wake me?"

"You know you don' want that, Pa," Jared replied. "How many times you beat us back at the cabin fer doin' that?"

"Only when you deserved it," Minns said pointedly. His face softened from the grimness of the implacable man hunter, one never quitting a blood trail. "So you want to turn back, do you? Don' want to git the man that kilt yer brother?"

Jared squirmed away, shying from the expected blow. "We ain't goin'a find 'em, Pa. Can't he'p it Jeremy got kilt."

Minns' face set in a cold mask. Its scar alternately flushed red and turned white as he trembled and struggled with his demon. Calm won, but it was the quiet of a brittle, messianic hatred that culminated in his oath. "Ain't no 'scapin' the chase no more, son. It be a blood feud. Blood got to be washed away by blood. We're chasin' that damned Shaw 'til we kill 'im."

CHAPTER 18

Jessie Mae

November 18, 1864. Cleveland, Georgia. Temperature 61\44, sunny and clear, turning cloudy by evening. Light breezes, shifting to westerlies. Crescent moon, waning, setting before midnight.

C laude and Hannibal had crept from under the corncrib as soon as the few men in the patrol had settled in for the night. The troopers lay in blanketrolls with their feet to the campfires, oblivious to the fugitives as the latter stole away. All of the cavalrymen had stayed close on to the farmer's house and rested in the shelter of the oaks surrounding the cabin. The rebs had built up their fires with billets from the raided woodpile after they first occupied Jake's yard. Relaxed and comfortable, the men laughed and joked as they cooked their meat and cornbread and played with the dog. Its hungry mouth gulped down all bits tossed to it, some caught in the air. At Jake's angry protest and their Sergeant's curses, a few spent time working the axe at the chopping block. But the rest just smoked and offered pungent slanders consigning the farmer to hell. Most men turned in early, a few pipe smokers holding out for yarning, but even they soon succumbed. The sleeping men filled the night with their snores. Not even a picket roamed a post, slack discipline, or a safe area, Claude thought, as he slunk away.

It had been easy to crawl to the barn past the screening blacksmith shed, with its banked charcoal bed and row of hanging tongs. The stable was a scented place with a large hayloft and a restless, stamping horse, disturbed at their smell and movement. Instead of burrowing into the hay, they had chosen a great mound of cornshucks in an empty, dry stall, a less likely target for the tines of a pitchfork in the morning. But they rose before the patrol, Claude's fears keeping him in a fretful state the entire night. He rolled Hannibal out before false dawn, ready to start for Clarke's, only to be pulled back into the barn by the Negro.

"Somebody comin'," Hannibal warned. "Git down."

Footfalls and a grumpy voice swearing at the soldiers materialized into a black shape with a lantern. Jake's sour face reflected in the light when he entered the barn. The farmer hitched up the horse to a light wagon as they watched, then led the rig to the corncrib where a few black shapes waited. A cow lowed in the pasture, its call diverting the settler. Jake left the horse and went for the cow with a rope- end in his hand. He took down the pole gate and drove the nondescript animal into the barn.

"God damned bastards," he swore. "Take all a man's corn jest cause some damned gineral on the march."

Jake tied off the cow at a post. He tossed some short feed into a wooden bucket while he grumbled, placed it before the cow, then wiped off the teats with a cloth. His three legged stool went down before the udder, his plop driving its pegs into the dirt floor. The farmer milked quickly while the cow worried the feed bucket. Her tongue made a medley of rasping sounds as she scraped up all the fermented grain. Splashes in the milk-pail grew into a plunging stream as the bucket filled and the cow was stripped, Jake's effortless milking completed in about five minutes. The farmer set the pail to one side and covered it with a cloth before he untied the animal. With the rope-end in one hand, he slapped her on the rump, then hurried her out into the pasture. The cow bawled and kicked her hooves when he twisted her tail and drove her through the pole gate. Jake headed for the wagon after replacing the rails, hurrying his steps at the sound of hard ears of corn striking the wagon bed. The wagon creaked when he mounted the wheel and held out his lantern. Its yellow light cast wide arcs on the growing load and on the ground.

"What the hell you need it all fer?" he angrily asked.

Jake's explosion and grasp of the Sergeant's arm infuriated the soldier. His face twisted as he jerked his arm free, then pulled and pointed his pistol at the enraged farmer.

"Git away er I shoot yuh," he said coldly. He cocked the piece and aligned the barrel with Jake's heart. "We's travelin' to Tennessee an' need it all. Ain't much up through them mountains."

Jake backed off instantly and put up his hands in surrender. He shrank from the threat and plaintively said, "I got my family to feed, man. Ain't you got no chil'ren?" But his ire rose at the silent Sergeant as the pillage continued. The trooper ignored him and his pleas while his men emptied the crib. Jake's fury finally overcame his fears and subjugation. He shook his fist at the man and complained. "You ain't got no call to ever'bit. Leave us be."

The Sergeant was unmoved. "Need it," he said. "Few o' us left here in nawth Georgia goin' on up to Tennessee. We's crossin' quick since ol' Sherman's left Atlanta, marchin' down through Georgia."

"Good riddance," Jake said scornfully, "but you don' have to steal it all." He fawned on the man, beseeching him in a piteous voice. "Need some corn fer my family, Sergeant. An' seed too fer the spring plantin'. Don' take it all."

The trooper holstered his revolver but ordered his men to continue loading. "Hood's circlin' west," he said, "then goin' up from Alabama." He shifted his chaw and spit. "The Army o' the Tennessee goin'a fight those Yankee bastards. They ain't doin' to Tennessee like Georgia. Word come that damned Sherman's burnin' ever'thin'."

The information struck Claude like a lightning bolt. He and Hannibal couldn't cut across the mountains directly to Dalton, not with scattered troops moving north on the main roads. With Sherman gone from Atlanta, they couldn't rejoin there either. He recalled the map Kelly and the other prisoners had made for them. They'd probably have to cut down south of Gaines' and then go northwest. He listened to the jabbing thrusts of the Sergeant and Jake as they argued over the corn, the soldier finally telling his men to leave a few bushels. The farmer drove the loaded wagon to the cabin, his lantern creating shadows for the men walking behind him.

Dawn broke as the patrol saddled up, ready to leave. A few men dawdled over fires, cooking bacon. Its smell floated to the fugitives in the barn, delicious odors that tantalized the famished planter. His juices flowed and his stomach rumbled, hunger his familiar companion. But Hannibal's pull at his sleeve and proffered piece of smelly bear meat gained the man only a shake of Claude's head and a look of disgust.

"I'll eat the chestnuts and a little honey," he said. "Got any left?"

The Negro handed over the almost empty bark bucket while Claude searched in his pockets and pulled out the last of his chestnuts. He cleaned out the remaining wax comb and honey, then tossed the bucket into the shucks. A few shelled nuts finished his meager meal. The remnants just aggravated his ravenous hunger, not helped by watching Hannibal wolf down the last of their cooked bear meat. Just the skin was left. Claude's hands explored the surface. It was drying nicely, even with only their light fleshing of the first night, and was not smelly. He threw it over his shoulder and looked out again, just in time to see Jake drive off with the wagon, followed by the foragers.

The two fugitives gravitated to the forgotten milk bucket once Jake was lost to view. They were stripping the cloth when a light sound behind them caused Claude to wheel and draw his pistol. A woman held a shotgun on them, a spray of shot from its huge muzzle capable of killing both. The planter hesitated and pocketed his derringer, holding his palms face out in surrender and friendship.

"We don't mean no harm, Ma'am," he said. "But we're powerful hungry an' could use some food. Your man forgot the milk."

"You don't sound like no nigger," she said nervously. "Who are yuh?"

Uncertainty on her face and a trembling body as she

questioned him were protected by the muzzle of the shotgun. Its great open eye wavered between the two men's
chests. The planter stood very still, with Hannibal frozen
beside him. Claude chose his words carefully as he gauged
the woman's temper. She wasn't militant, he thought, just
resigned to finding them on her property, almost as if it had
happened before. Her lack of anger decided him for the
truth.

"Lieutenant Claude Shaw, Ma'am, Seventh Ohio Cavalry. And this is Hannibal, my friend. We escaped down at
Columbia and are headin' for Dalton."

The shotgun barrel fell a little, not threatening them
directly as the woman relaxed, her relief evident to the
planter. "Why are yuh black?"

"Dyed with walnut," Claude said. "Made it easier to
escape."

She laughed, her chuckle progressing into great guf-
faws. "A black Yankee? God almighty, what'll I find next?"

Her paroxysm ended as suddenly as it began. Her jolly
face relaxed from the worry of the holdup and a talkative
mouth spilled out news as she shifted the shotgun to her left
hand.

"Lot o' 'scapes come through. My man's a rebel but I'm
from up to Tennessee. My folks don't hold with slavin' and
er fer the Union. So I help ever'one I can." She stepped
forward and held out her hand. "I'm Jessie Mae."

Claude seized the proffered hand, its grip firm and cool.
He gazed into a pair of steady, brown flecked eyes, Jessie
Mae's lined face and gray-streaked hair complementing a
dumpy, sack-enclosed figure. A shadow ran over her face
when she noticed his appraisal. Her hand rose absentmindedly to her hair and tucked in a few wisps before she
straightened her dress.

"Bring the milk," she said, "an' you'all come-on up to
the house. I'll get you some breakfast."

Her chatty talk filled them in on Hood's march to the
west while they attacked the bacon, eggs and pone. They
stuffed themselves with hot food until they bulged, meanwhile only half-listening to her tale of Hood's plans to go to
Tennessee. When Claude pushed back, replete, Jessie Mae

was cautioning them about the small units still trailing up to the mountains on the few passable roads. Hannibal cleaned up all the remnants while the planter visited and asked about the rebs who stole the corn.

"The patrol that was foragin' 'll leave off the corn at Clarke's," she told him. "'least that's what the Sergeant said. Then they's makin' a sweep over to'ard the Tugaloo. They'll cut south at Turner's place east o' Tiger, then go back down to Gaines'."

"Why?" Claude asked.

"Lookin' fer army stragglers, not you or any other that's runnin'. But it's best you go 'round the village to the west. Then get on over to'ard Mount Yonah afore you cut south."

She busied herself clearing the table as Claude pulled out the remnant of Kelly's map and spread it out flat. A glass of milk set before him took his attention off the paper. Draining the rich milk, he followed Jessie Mae's finger as it traced their journey after leaving Clarke's.

"You can't go on west past the Tesnatee River," she said. "The gold mines are thick 'round Dahlonega an' lots o' militia. Head south from Mount Yonah." She stabbed at the map with her forefinger, picking out the location of the mountain and its namesake community. "You can't miss that little town. The mountain's starin' down at yuh an' the river's to the west."

"Will the south road take us to Gaines?" Claude asked.

Jessie Mae bobbed her head. "Don't stop there though. Go on past to Blackshear's place. It's near Young's crossroads, east of the Chattahoochee. That's the onliest good way right now. Then cut back by Coal Mountain an' up to Nelson's Tavern."

His questions on the state of the roads and militia brought ready answers from the helpful woman, amplified later when they stood in the yard and she pointed to the hills around her.

"Clarke's is jest a mile down the lane where Jake headed. You need to cross the crick in the pasture, then skirt 'round the hill in the timber so's you's hid."

"Any trail there?" Claude asked.

Her directions were precise. "Aim west soon's you hit

the old wood's road. It's purty growed up but easy walkin'. But keep a sharp eye out fer the militia. They's not many 'round here but they kill all the 'scapes they catch."

"What's at Blackshear's place?"

"Hear tell of a Granny Pearl that helps folks. Jest talk from escapes comin' through. Lots o' folks movin' up from Atlanta since Sherman." She tucked in a wisp of blowing hair. "An' over near Coal Mountain is the preacher."

"Preacher?"

"The Right Reverend Rodney Duckworth." Jessie Mae laughed, her soft humorous chuckle progressing into full-throated bellows. "The Reverend's a legend," she said. "He's from England and gives the rebels hail columbia all the time about slaves. He'll help yuh."

"They haven't killed him?"

"Tried, but the good Lord pertects 'im. He hid out after last time. He comes back now an' then to preach hellfire and damnation if they don't repent."

"Well, how do we find him?"

"Jest head up the trail, north from Coal Mountain, if he ain't at the church. About a mile out start singing Rock of Ages. His men'll find yuh soon enough."

Jessie Mae looked about in the bright daylight. "You'd best be gone," she said, worriedly. "No tellin' who might be a'comin'." She hesitated a moment. "I'll get the word on west yer comin' through. We got ways," she added, in answer to his mystified face.

Claude handed her the bear skin. "For you, Jessie Mae. And our blessin'."

Tears filled her eyes as she received the gift. She ran into the house when they headed across the pasture. Hannibal shelled one of the dozen hard-boiled eggs she had given them before he was well into the forest, his appetite overcoming Claude's caution to save them for their midday meal. The shells sparkled on the forest floor where the Negro tossed them aside, their whiteness calling attention to Claude's footprints sunk deep into a seep in the trail.

Rufus stopped his men for nooning at an old campsite near Habersham's place, just south of Clarke's. Driven by the overseer and suffering from the hard travel, they all were tired and sweating, ready for a rest. The coffle halted in a sweet, grassy spot, their nooning by a small branch far from the road. The Negroes sighed with relief, jollying each other as they dispersed into the woods. They straggled in a short time later with filled canteens and armloads of small treelimbs. Resinous splinters from a piece of lightwood were passed around, starters used to kindle several campfires.

"Don't make but small fires," Rufus cautioned. "An' dry wood. Can't have no driftin' smoke bringin' on de rebs."

The Negroes busied themselves with strips of deer meat. Sliced thin, they roasted quickly on sticks held over the dancing flames. It was a noisy time, with men chewing on hot chestnuts and the meat and just gossiping. Some apples appeared, holdovers from another homestead's trees west of the Tugaloo. A few sweet potatoes were sliced raw to divide the small store. Judah and the overseer relaxed with the men and shared their food as well. Afterwards, Rufus paced back and forth before them and pulled out a cigar, while his band sprawled out on the well-littered grass.

Rufus held up the stogy and rotated it before he ran it along under his nose. All eyes were on the weed, some covetously, as he took a few sniffs and savored the aroma of the tobacco. Satisfied by the inspection, he bit off the end and lit the cigar, drawing in and exhaling a few puffs. A spiral of gray smoke rose from the glowing tip when it was well lit. It added to the mellow odor of the tobacco. When Rufus exhaled another puff, it was with a sigh of regret.

"It's my last one, boys," he told them, "so we'll share."

A little cheer arose from their pleased faces and a grayhead said, "Dat good, Rufus. We all 'ppreciate dat."

Passing the stogy to Judah, Rufus motioned to hand it on. The cigar made the rounds until it was a stub, the remnant tossed into one of the fires.

"What now, Rufus?" Judah asked.

All the men perked up and looked expectantly at the overseer. A few checked their weapons and one headed for the woods.

"You sidle on in ter Clarke's," Rufus said. "It's only maybe a mile ter de nawth." Rufus shook his forefinger at him. "Don' let nobody see yuh. Fin' de shoemaker an' see if he's heard from Claude an' where he's goin'. Den come on back."

Fires were down to coals when footfalls and a soft cry interrupted their hour's sleep, a refreshing rest seized while the men waited on Judah's return. The group gathered around him when he slid into camp.

"They's been to Jessie Mae's this mawnin'," Judah said, "jist nawth o' Clarke's." He paused and reached for his canteen, swilling down a draught.

"Well, where'd she send 'em?" Rufus asked impatiently.

Judah ignored the irritation and stoppered his canteen before replying. "Over ter Mount Yonah," he said, "'cause o' de rebs 'roun'. Den dey's gwine head on down south ter Blackshear's place fo' they cuts nawthwest to'ard Dalton."

"Why not nawth er west?"

"Gol' mines ter de west full o' people, an' rebs all over. Some o' de people er dose run outen 'lanta. De shoemaker say dey's militia an' bandits ever'where. Claude and Hannibal best chance ter de south."

Rufus fell into deep thought, his brow wrinkled as he pondered the news and its implications. The men whispered, chewing, spitting, smoking, but not disturbing his concentration while the coffle waited on his orders. Judah electrified them all with his added information.

"De Minns been seed on de way up nawth past Turner's. An' Rufus," he grasped the big redhead's arm, "dat Lieutenant Hartsill, de reb from Anderson, he pokin' about wid four er five men. Lookin' fer Claude."

"God damn!" Rufus said. A stream of profanity split the air until he calmed down. "The Minns and Hartsill?" he asked, incredulously. "You sure?" At Judah's nod, Rufus shook his head. "Claude's goin'a need he'p," he said, gloomily.

Judah sketched a map in some smoothed dirt, naming the places as he drew in the roads and villages. "We kin git on west easy," he said, "'thout nobody ketchin' us."

"How fur?" Judah asked.

"De shoemaker say ain't more'n ten mile ter Mount Yonah an' de road on south winds thoo some sharp valleys."

Rufus marked an X a mile or two below the village at Mount Yonah. "A line there cuts their trail," he said. "We wait fer 'em there."

By late afternoon they had fed and were in a widely spaced skirmish line. Their hideouts lay across the road and bordering hills, ready to intercept the fugitives.

The moon hadn't quite set when Gabe and Hester followed Sissie into the cabin, its heavy, plank door banging behind them. They had run hurriedly after the flying girl, hastening to answer Granny's summons. Sissie's gasps of fright and tears had urged them on the whole way. Granny lay on the floor, her body naked and her back covered with welts. The old woman raised her head when they entered and weakly beckoned them to her. But she cried out in anguish when Gabe started to lift her into her chair and waved him away. Hester picked up the crock of grease warming on the hearth and smeared its oil on the tortured skin. A groan answered her kneading, but Granny's little sobs silenced as the oil and heat worked their magic. Sitting up, the old woman reached for her chair. Gabe threw in some cloth for a seat and deposited the battered form in its accustomed place. Hester followed with a blanket to cover the old woman's nakedness.

Granny drew in a sharp breath, whimpering as she stretched. "Dat Minns 'bout beat me ter death," she said.

The girl trembled and glanced about, her terror evident to the ancient. Sissie ran to Granny's lap, crying and clutching her tightly. Granny folded her blanket over the child and patted her bottom as she crooned. Her lullaby stopped Sissie's sniffles and calmed Hester.

With quiet in the cabin, Granny said, "Minns gone. Miz Hawkins run him off, 'long wid 'is no-count boy an' dog. Dey gone ter Jawga."

She kept patting Sissie as the child clung to her, and spoke directly to Gabe. "Take keer o' Hester, Gabe. See she gits ter de free lan'. An' ter Hannibal."

He nodded and fell to his knees beside her chair. "I'se do it, Granny," he said forcefully. His powerful body tensed and his heavy muscles bulged through his clothes. The giant's scowl turned fierce and he trembled as he smote one fist into another. "I be lookin' fer dat Minns. If onliest I kin' git a'holt of 'im.'"

Granny placed her hand on his head and said a little prayer. "Oh, Lawd. Bring dese two safe ter de free lan'.'"

She sent them off into the dark with full bellies and a pouch of food, emptying her meager store to fill their needs. Hester left her after a kiss for her and Sissie. Gabe, the inarticulate giant, encased her with a bearhug until she groaned.

Overnight hiking in the many hours to sunrise took them far to the west, to a slope overlooking the Tugaloo ford. Gabe led the crawl to a hidden observation point screened with bushes. His nudge in her side and whisper warned her of the danger posed by the rebel picket. He pointed out the man on the other side of the stream, a soldier half-hidden behind a tree. The man's rifle rested on a small parapet, its bayonet toward the river.

"What we do now, Gabe?" she asked.

"We eat an' sleep in de thicket 'til dark, den we move."

She burst into tears and said, "But I'se got ter git on ter Hannibal."

The Negro shrugged his shoulders, then crawled into a thick pocket of bushes. He beckoned to her to follow while he scooted around and arranged a bed of leaves. She crept in with him, complaining of her aches from the long hike. Her good humor returned when he jollied her and handed her a piece of bacon. Hester's lassitude overwhelmed her as soon as she finished the bacon and filled her belly with Granny's sweet potatoes and pone. Her head dropped back and she lay flat on her back, slipping into the deep slumber of exhaustion.

They slept and ate the day away, sneaking out at times to observe the pickets. Dark brought a sliver of moon with its faint light and increased Hester's eagerness to be gone.

"We wait 'til de moon's down, Hester," Gabe said.

She did not argue with the Negro's refusal to move until ready, but rested, instead, in the bed of leaves, with his coat over her to keep her warm.

Luke had run like a deer to escape the coffle's wrath. He drifted west, uncertain, with no one like Rufus to tell him what to do. His steady gait covered the miles quickly and carried him into the general movement to the north. Buffeted by the militia units and the wanderers on the roads, both of which he avoided, he hiked on west. The traitor arrived at Clarke's in a ravenous state from over a day with nothing but a few nuts and apples picked up during the trip. An aroma of frying bacon was irresistible to the demands of his hungry stomach, and its lure erased his sense of caution. Luke sneaked along the side of the building in the settlement, seeking the kitchen, his concealment helped by a great mass of fig bushes. He was peering in a window next to the smoking chimney when the troopers across the street spied his head above the bushes and the glint of a rifle barrel.

"He's got a carbine, Lieutenant," one said. The man holding the officer's horse spat out his chaw and shifted his weapon to the ready. "Ain't no nigger s'posed ter have no gun."

"Where's Gill?" Hartsill asked.

"Here sir," came the instant reply. Gill hustled forward from his inspection of the horses and stood at attention before the officer.

Hartsill watched Luke a moment as the Negro peered through the window. "Get that nigger," he ordered, "and bring him here. Be careful men, he's armed."

Gill's pistol against Luke's head and crisp, "Hands Up!" took the hungry Negro by surprise. Three rifles covered him when he turned. Subservient bowing and bobbing accompanied his begging.

"Ain't done nothin', Massa. Jist hongry. Want some o' dat bacon."

"March!" Gill said. His prod with his pistol forced Luke into a quick step. The Sergeant had Luke and the captured rifle at the Lieutenant's side in a few seconds.

Hartsill's inspection of the rifle, turning it over and over, was interrupted by a cry from Gill. "It's one o' our guns, Lieutenant."

"Where'd you get it, boy?" Hartsill asked. His cold eye looked over the sights at Luke as soon as he cocked the piece.

"Kilt a 'scape nawth o' Anderson when I was wid a coffle gwine ter Calhoun's. He come on us wid de rifle."

Luke's monumental lie trapped him. His body shrank away from Hartsill and the Sergeant when Gill pulled his sword and stuck the point next to the Negro's body.

"That's the coffle with Shaw, Lieutenant," Gill said. His action and grim statement set the troop into an uproar. One loud voice rose above the rest.

"He's Luke, the one with us at the ford when they kilt our boys."

Hartsill beckoned to the trooper. "Is that right, Rogers?" he asked. "You're sure he's the one that came in to Irvine's patrol?"

"Yes sir!" the man answered. The slightly built trooper sidled forward out of the group, then advanced hesitantly to a point in front of the trembling captive. He stuck his carbine against Luke's chest and repeated his accusation. "He's the one. An' he lied 'bout 'em. Didn't tell us they was armed."

Hartsill uncocked his piece and handed it Rogers, Gill's sword enough to deter Luke from running. The other troopers grumbled and cursed and crowded about the slave.

"Where'd they go, nigger?" Gill asked. He prodded Luke with the sword point to reinforce his question.

When the slave didn't answer, Hartsill called for a whip. A few slashes with a leather reduced Luke to a supplicant for mercy. At another stinging blow, he surrendered and blurted out the coffle's plans.

"Rufus takin' de coffle on west ter he'p de Yankee an' Hannibal git ter Dalton. He leave 'em fo' dey at de gol' diggin's, den circle back ter de thicket.

Gill laughed. "Ain't no more thicket. We burnt it an' killed those black bastards."

Luke started at the news and turned his face pleadingly toward the officer. Hartsill's thin lips twisted in a sneer. He laughed at Luke's shock and open mouth, then the downcast expression and incoherent mumbling. Seizing the slave's head, he jerked it up and thrust his face almost against that of the frightened man.

"God damn it, nigger," he hissed, "where are they and where they headin'?"

"Dey's 'round here close, Massa. Dey's s'posed ter go by de springs near Demorest's, den on west. But dey hide lots. An' dey slow. Can't go fast. De Yankee got bad leg."

"Damn, Lieutenant," Gill said, exultantly, "we got 'em."

Troopers joined in with their curses and shouts, and celebrated the welcome news. Excitement stirred them into a restless milling. Some few picked up their horses' bridles, eager to mount.

Hartsill's verdict and action were swift and sure.

"Get a rope, Sergeant," he said, "and hang him from the oak there. Leave him hangin' for the others to see."

"I ain't he'p de Yankee, Massa," Luke said, trembling violently. He started crying, piteously beseeching Hartsill for mercy. "Don' Massa. Don' kill me, Massa."

Three troopers shut off Luke's sobs and protests with a tight noose, then hauled the line over a limb until he was off the ground. Luke clawed at his neck, blood flying from torn skin as he tried to get his fingers under the strangling loop. His eyes protruded and face turned purplish-black while the lack of air was shutting off his life. As soon as his kicks and twitches ceased, Gill fired a bullet into the hanged man's chest to finish the execution. The body swung back and forth when Hartsill led the patrol west toward Mount Yonah.

A man at an open door near the tree went unnoticed by the patrol, another Negro workman, eavesdropping while they savaged Luke. He turned back into his shop after the execution and whistled up his sons. A few moments later one lanky, young boy ran behind the houses of the settlement, headed west on his marathon. With a group of children playing along beside him, the other sauntered up the north lane that passed by Jessie's place.

Minns tied his horse to a sapling on the edge of the clearing but left the animal enough slack for it to crop grass during the rest. Old Blue ambled over and nuzzled Minns' leg when the hunter sat down on a nearby log. The hound stuck his face up to the man, begging, and received the automatic scratching behind his ears, his tail wagging in gratitude. Blue's long tongue hung down and dripped saliva from the hot, tiring run as Minns petted him.

"They ain't up here to'ard the mountains, Pa," Jared said. He unwrapped his injured hand as he sat nearby. "We been all over from Bates' to Wiley's an' jest nothin'. They's jest too many militia fer 'em to chance it."

Minns spit, his brown stream staining some dried wildflowers. "Yer hand feelin' better?" he asked.

"Tolerable," the boy answered. He held up the brown encrusted member and violently wiggled his fingers. A grimace escaped him when he inspected his hand. "Hurts some still but I been takin' the tonic Granny give me."

Minns nodded. "That old woman's good as a regular medicine doctor. You be well directly."

Jared rewrapped his injured hand after rubbing in some salve. He replaced the small container in his possibles sack, then recovered a large chunk of pone. Old Blue begged, his tail wagging, when Jared passed a piece to his father.

Minns spat out his chaw and rinsed his mouth before he chewed on the dry pone. The tasteless mush and uneaten piece joined the tobacco on the ground while the hunter cursed in disgust and cleared his mouth with water. But Old Blue eagerly gulped the discarded remnant.

"Got anymore o' the jerky, boy?" Minns asked. The hunter felt around in his own sack, without success. "That pone's mighty poor feedin' an' I ain't carryin' nothin'."

"All gone, Pa." Jared said. The boy's unhappiness boiled over and he issued a bitter challenge to Minns' unflagging pursuit. "We runnin' out o' vittles, Pa. We need to give it up, er stop an' rest up fer a day. Old Blue needs it too. Jest look at that dawg. He's downright gan't an' limpin' on that sore paw."

Minns squinted at the lowering sun. "Maybe got 'nough time to git clear down to Clarke's," he said, reflectively. "We see 'bout campin' there fer a day. Got to buy some fresh powder too. Don't want no more misfires like that shot at the deer this mawnin'.' "

Jared rummaged in the saddlebags and came up with a small piece of jerky he had hidden. Tossing it to Blue, he passed a sweet potato to Minns and sat down with another. He peeled it rapidly with his knife and chewed on slices. Old Blue sat up on his haunches and begged, the jerky long since down his gullet. The boy sliced off a chunk of the potato and tossed it to the old dog, who caught it in the air. He ran off a few steps and lay down, then crunched on the sweet potato as if it were a bone.

The three snored away for an hour after the meager meal, while the horses picked grass and rested. Neighs from the horses and hoofbeats of a passing group of riders scared them into their saddles in a bound. Jared yawned and stretched but Minns kept his rifle cocked and ready until the men were clear. The hunter didn't waste any more time.

"Let's mosey, boy," he said. He struck off south down the trace, Jared and the dog ambling along behind.

A round cobble, worn smooth from several millenia of water flow, turned the horse's hoof in a rocky creek a few miles above Clarke's. Minns' horse broke the stride of its canter and almost fell in the rushing riffle. The hunter dismounted in a second and led the limping horse to a grassy bank. He folded the right foreleg and pulled the hoof up between his thighs. Oaths split the air as he rattled the loose shoe and inspected the hoof.

"Damned stone done broke it, boy," he said disgustedly. "Ain't goin'a make it to Clarke's ternight."

Jared dismounted alongside and bent over. "Need a blacksmith, Pa?"

"We git one at Clarke's. But Blacky's hoof split some. Could be we gotta leave 'im."

"Can't we stay there awhile, Pa?" the boy asked, his voice hopeful.

"No, God damn it," Minns swore. "We go afoot if we have to. That Shaw ain't gittin' away."

The two hunters unsaddled the horses and picketed them on the grass. It took only a few minutes, and their camp fire flared up soon thereafter. Blue sought the blaze once he had come back from his nosing of the trees and roll in a nearby pool. The old dog inched in so close that his hair steamed from the heat. Crackling flames drove him farther away as he searched for a warm, comfortable place to lie down. His soaked, dirty coat gave off a stinking, sour odor. Sniffing in distaste, Jared moved upwind from the wet, smelly hound and sat down cross-legged. The boy's sweet potatoes and nuts from trees nearby made for another meager meal. But Old Blue eagerly crunched his potato into chunks, the sweet rapidly disappearing down his gullet. Silence followed the meal as each sought comfort. The dog sprawled with his back to the heat and snoozed. Minns and Jared stared into the leaping, yellow flames, an occasional sigh erupting from the boy. Athey's jaws worked and his spit hissed while he ignored his son and meditated in his trancelike communing. But the hunter soon lay back, asleep with his feet to the fire.

"Dey's a passel o' 'em, Claude," Hannibal whispered.

The Negro lay on the top of a bank in a clump of brush, his eyes fixed on the short, passing column on the trace. A little dust billowed up around the legs of the marching men, fine particles from a layer of dry earth under the damp surface of the trace. It surprised Claude. There had been a long, dry fall but he had thought the light rains during their journey had laid the dust. But even though there had been showers, the swinging and stamping feet pounded out a little flour-like earth in small, gray puffs. The dust coated the men and tendrils drifted with the wind even while their shoes picked up globs of sticky surface dirt. Coughs and curses from the column carried to the fugitives as the military movement delayed them.

"Where you figure we are, Claude?" Hannibal asked. His low whisper rumbled, even as the planter held his finger across his lips for silence.

Claude stuck his mouth close to the servant's ear. "We cut the river and had to come back to the bend in the trace. Got too far to the west, just like Jessie Mae said. Guess we must be a mile or so north o' the village at Mount Yonah." He watched the Confederates for a moment, appraising the troops. "They's a few o' those headin' up to Tennessee."

The planter's face wrinkled in pain and he grasped at his stomach. He rapidly slid back into the dense forest, his noiseless rise and careful steps taking him about fifty yards into the growth. Hannibal followed cautiously; he picked out his way and repeatedly glanced over his shoulder toward the trace as he retreated. But no shouts or alarms arose. Claude's pants were down by the time the Negro approached his stop. The planter was squatting, his brow sweating as he relieved himself of a yellow, spurting liquid.

"Still got de runs, Claude?" Hannibal asked sympathetically.

Claude's agonized strainings and purges were enough of an answer. The planter could think only of the pain in his gut and the need to stop the drain on his strength. Those damned greens yesterday and the grease of the breakfast, he thought. Not used to good food and it had savaged him. He shook when he stood up, and leaned against a tree while he tried to get his trembling and sweating under control. Hannibal was nowhere in sight.

The planter's body shook violently and weakness overcame him. He sank down against the tree and waited for the Negro to return. Hannibal's hands grasped a big clutch of bark and roots when his rustle nearby scared the sick man into drawing his derringer.

Claude's angry voice flailed at the Negro as he pocketed his piece. "Don't come up on me like that. I might'a shot yuh."

Hannibal held out the collection of plants for inspection. "Got de willow bark, blackberry root, dogwood bark, and a little sassafras root. Dey's good place ter hide over de ridge. We camp dere today an' go on termorrer. Make you de strong tea. It an' de hard eggs gonna cure yuh."

He led the struggling planter on the steep climb to the ridge line. Claude exhausted himself in pulling his weary body to the top of the slope. His near collapse and wracking gut convinced him it was time to rest. They slid down to a slight, protected bench hid behind the ridge, the back slope and heavy growth enough to hide their fire from any travelers. Several large draughts of Hannibal's bitter, brown tea stopped up Claude's gut by nightfall, the eggs split with the servant as they camped. They denned up against a down log for warmth, sleeping through the night under a thick covering of pine boughs.

CHAPTER 19

Judah

November 19, 1864. Blackshear Place, Georgia. Temperature 66\47. Mostly cloudy with a chance of showers. Breezy with westerly winds to 15 knots. Sliver crescent moon, waning, setting just before midnight.

"Y ou 'bout ready, Hester?" Gabe asked.

His shiny face reflected the wan light of the pale moon, its faintness bolstered by a few winking stars. The girl rose from her bed in the leaves, a rounded depression that would puzzle any passing deerhunter or dog.

"I'se ready, Gabe," she said, looking about uncertainly. "But it's fearful dark. Kin we make it?"

Gabe patted her back reassuringly. "Don' you worry, gal. I sees good in de woods an' dere's a big deer trail dat go right ter de ribber. Dat why we camp b'side it."

He gripped her arm and steered the girl to the trail. "We black too," he said, chuckling. "Ain't nobody see us."

Gabe led the way down the hillside to the Tugaloo, his steps slow and careful. Hester followed with her hand on his back. The river's musical chant carried through the bottom and covered up any slight sounds made by the fugitive Negroes. Once on the soft flat with its spongy leaf mold, Gabe crept upstream to the next riffle. It had the typical gurgle, running over the rounded rocks with falls and diversions, but did not appear especially deep. He took Hester by the hand after he tied her big skirt up around her waist, then cajoled the frightened girl into the rushing water. The two entered the ford with Hester upstream of his sturdy body. Gabe's left hand probed with a stout staff as they inched into the strong current.

"It's col', Gabe," she said. She gasped and clutched him more tightly when her foot slipped on a rock and the fast water splashed up her legs. "It 'bout ter push me over."

"Jist take it slow hyar," he said, reassuringly. "Ever'thin' be awright."

Hester stumbled and her knee sank into the water. Her grip turned into a death clutch on Gabe's hand as she babbled, "He'p me."

The giant Negro hoisted on her hand, weaving at the pull of the current as he struggled to keep his footing. The two felt around on the bottom, sliding their feet into crevices for stronger footholds as they crept farther out into the flow. A swirling current around a large midstream rock undid the girl. Her advancing shoe found nothing where the irregular bottom should have offered a foothold. Hester screeched wildly and her unbalanced body went into the stream. The sodden weight of the massive roll of cloth around her middle tore her from Gabe's grasp. She bounced off his legs as her body rolled downstream, her wild screams drowning out the night sounds each time her head came up. Challenging shouts arose from the patrol at the ford below, up in arms at the commotion of the fugitives.

Gabe abandoned his staff and threw himself into the fast moving water, rapidly overtaking the tumbling girl. He got to her before the whitewater constrictions and braced himself against a large rock. The pull of the current taxed the great strength of the giant but he dragged her massive weight closer to the bank where a tree overhung the flow. His grasp on the branches and grunting struggle delivered them into a quiet eddy and shallow water. The two lay there gasping while they recovered their breath and Gabe calmed Hester's hysteria.

"Gwine be awright, Hester," he said, reassuring her. "We 'cross now." He listened a moment. "Got ter git. Dose sojers be atter us right quick."

The alarm of the soldiers had turned into a series of shouts. At least two men answered back and forth as they hunted upstream from their picket point.

"You hear 'em, Hester?" Gabe said. "Dey's scairt." He chuckled as he soothed the girl. "Dey don' like de night an' dey's comin' on mighty slow."

He picked up the girl when she did not rise to follow him. Heading straight away from the river, the giant rapidly threaded the large trees of the rising ground. By the time they had reached the ridge, the shouts of the pickets had faded to distant cries and echoes. Gabe stopped and put down the girl.

"Tek off yer clothes an' we wring 'em out," he said.

He stripped without waiting on her. Water spattered the ground as his strong grip and twists of his garments reduced them to dampness. Hester simply watched while he donned his clothes, and made no move to undress. She had shaken out the great roll at her waist by the time he finished, and was smoothing the folds down to her ankles. "Tek it off, girl," Gabe said. "Got ter git de water outen dat dress. It heavy. Wear you out if you don'."

"I won't!" Hester said. She cursed him, her explosive refusal reinforced by turning her back. The girl was swearing under her breath when he seized her and silenced her tirade with a choking hand.

"Don' you holler," he said, as he shook her. "Dose rebs be right atter us."

Gabe held the struggling figure while he stripped off her clothes. Tossing her aside, he twisted the sodden dress until no water dripped. She hit him with a stick as he finished the task, a dark, angry form muttering imprecations and wildly flailing at him. He yanked the stick from her hand and threw the dress back at her.

"Shet up!" he ordered.

But the girl kept up her complaining whine. The giant's hard slap to her face shut her mouth and knocked her down. Hester's curses turned into whimpers as she crouched at his feet and made amends.

"I'se sorry, Gabe," she whispered, contritely. "I put on

de dress."

They fled on west through the night, striking the main trace to Traveler's Rest and Toccoa Falls in the early morning. Their sneak around the few buildings of the small settlements evaded the dogs that barked at their passage, and one suspicious owner investigating with his weapon. Dark faded as they passed the falls and went on toward the trace to Clarke's and Demorest's, restricted to paralleling the road because of the rugged hills. Gabe headed into the nearest thicket when dawn broke and the sun's first rays lighted the tops of the mountains.

"Got ter hole up," he said. "T'night see if we kin fin' de best way west ter Hannibal."

Hester dispiritedly slumped to the ground. She sat with her arms wrapped about her knees while Gabe gathered up a pile of leaves. "You got any Granny's vittles left?" she asked. "I'se hongry."

Gabe upended his possibles sack and dumped out its cargo. The last of the bacon and sweet potatoes made a small pile before her but the pone was a soggy mass of crumbs. They ate it all and went to ground, hiding in the thick patch of woods for the day to sleep and rest up.

"Quit it, Pa," Jared said. His son's irritated protest simply made his father madder.

Minns cursed the boy as he led his limping horse. Jared walked his own mount behind and Old Blue investigated the surrounding trees. Athey spit out his chaw, then washed out his mouth with a swig from his canteen before swallowing a draft. His bitter denunciation continued as they followed the well-worn lane.

"Goddamn it, boy. If you'd tied the picket rope tight we wouldn't had to chase that fool horse clear back 'most to Turner's."

Jared protested. "It was that Old Blue, Pa," he said, defensively. "You ain't got no cause to blame it on me." The boy's aggrieved pleading did nothing to soften the angry glances from Minns. "You know it war Blue done it yet you keep fussin' at me. He chewed that rawhide where the salt was."

"Don't matter," Minns said, irritably. "Here 'tis 'most noonin' an' we still 'round Clarke's." He looked ahead along the winding forest lane, its ruts glistening with fresh mud. "Where the hell's that blacksmith, anyhow."

"Man back in the village said he's down the road a good mile, Pa. We ain't there yet."

Minns' grumbling continued around the next bend, the heavy forest opening into a clearing with a house and barn. A cow cropping grass was visible in the far end of the pasture. Two roosters crowed in the opening beyond the barn and a few hens scratched industriously in the dirt. The rider's clinking approach was challenged by a nondescript hound, its barks and growls accompanying its rush from under the house. The dog circled them as it advanced, while Minns readied his rifle and Old Blue ran forward with his hackles up.

Jake came around the side of the barn and walked briskly toward the travelers. "Back, Pete," he yelled. Ignoring his owner, Pete barked furiously and rushed them again. Jake's thrown stick and a "Git back, damn it!" spawned a yelp and a retreat as the missile hit. The dog ran back under the house, but continued to growl at the hunters from the safety of his hideout. Minns led his horse to a halt a few feet from the farmer, leaving distance between them while he solemnized his greetings.

"Howdy," Minns said, holding up his hand in the universal peace sign. "You the blacksmith they tol' us 'bout at the village?"

"Yep, an' a howdy to yuh. I'm Jake."

"Athey Minns," the hunter replied. He motioned toward the others. "My son Jared an' his dog, Old Blue."

Jake walked around Blacky and stopped at the right foreleg. He forced the horse to take a step and observed the limp before he bobbed his head as if satisfied. "He's got a bad lamin'," he told Minns. "Watched'ya comin' up the lane."

"Kin you shoe Blacky quick?" Minns asked. He shifted his chaw and spat, wiping off the dribble with the back of his hand. "I got ter git on atter some 'scapes."

Jake nodded and took the bridle, leading the limping horse to the blacksmith shop. He bent over and raised the offending foreleg between his thighs, then clamped it there while he inspected the hoof. Picking at it with his tools, he whistled in amazement and beckoned to Minns. "Looky here," he said.

Minns crouched down beside the blacksmith. He swore when he saw the split in the bottom of the hoof and the loose shoe.

Jake released the leg and stood up. Blacky snorted and limped away a step. The blacksmith's hand stroked the horse's neck as he gentled him and said, "This hawse ain't goin' nowhere, Minns. Not 'til that hoof grows out some."

"Can't fix the shoe across the split?"

"Nope. I can shoe him but he'll still be lame. Needs to have that shoe off, then feed up an' rest a few months in a soft pasture while the hoof grows out."

Minns swore. "Can't stop here, God damn it. We got ter git on."

"Not on that hawse, ye ain't."

"You got one I could borry er trade?"

Jake laughed, then lied about his horse hid in the far pasture. "Ain't no hawse nowhere 'round here." Bitterness crept into his recital when he gave the reason. "Them damned troopers took 'em all 'bout time the crops was in. Had the best mule 'round. They took him too."

Minns' earsplitting oaths alarmed Jessie Mae inside the house. The door slammed behind her as she hurried down the steps from the stoop. She finished wiping the water from her hands just as she stopped before them. Her stained, wet apron hung limp and added to her disheveled appearance as she worriedly asked, "What in heaven's name is wrong, Jake?"

"Jest a lame hawse that can't be rid, Jessie Mae." He introduced the Minnses and gestured to the hound. Minns' silence did not conceal his working face, muttering taking the place of his curses as he led Blacky away a few steps and watched the limp.

Old Blue snuffled his way into the barn as they spoke. His sniffs led him next to the house and then to the space under the corncrib. The hound's tail wagged as his nose worked, intent on some lingering scent still hanging in the

air after the night's light showers. Blue let out a little yelp as
he crawled under the corncrib. His tail stuck out of the gap
in the stone foundation and flopped back and forth furiously as he squeezed in farther and uttered little yips.

"What's Blue after, Jared?" Minns asked.

"Probably an ol' coon, Pa, been stealin' from the crib."

"Warn't no coon," Jake said. He left the two horses in
front of the blacksmith shop and walked over to the nearby
crib with the Minnses. Sight of the few bushels of corn inside
raised his ire. He swore feelingly and told them of the
robbery. "It war them army foragers," he said sourly. "They
done took most all the corn."

Another yelp from Blue and a wiggling tail and Jared
fell to his knees beside the vent. He pulled the dog back out
of the opening under the crib. When the hound's head
emerged Blue had a piece of cloth clamped in his jaws, a
scrap of homespun. Jessie Mae's hand flew to her mouth,
her involuntary shiver unnoticed by the men ahead of her.

Jared wrestled with the wriggling hound and excitedly
shouted, "No coon done wore that, Pa!"

"Yer right, boy," Minns said.

The hunter pulled the scrap from the dog's mouth and
smelled it, its rank odor pungent even to the others. Minns
looked suspiciously at Jake and Jessie Mae and he cradled
his rifle. His face slowly transformed as his scar grew redder
and his mouth turned grim. Swinging up his weapon, he
pointed the cocked piece at the farmer.

"Now tell me who was hidin' hyar an' don't you lie to
me."

Jessie Mae ran in front of Jake and exposed her body
to the weapon. Her cries of fear and protest belabored Minns
as she seized the muzzle and pushed it to one side. Holding
onto the barrel, she contemptuously discounted the escapees. "It warn't nothin' but two ol' niggers runnin' nawth."

The blacksmith cursed and stepped from his shelter
behind his wife. He yanked her back out of the way, then
slapped her while telling her to mind. Jessie Mae shrank
from her angry husband, her hands fluttering up to ward off
more blows. But Jake turned from her and shook his fist at
Minns. "You ain't got no call to fuss us like this," he said

resentfully. "Ner cause my wife no trouble. You put down that rifle an' I whip yuh good."

"Shet up," Minns vehemently replied. His scar bulged and reddened, his contorted, murderous face frightening the farmer as the hunter got madder. Jake pushed Jessie Mae farther behind him when the infuriated Minns again threatened them with the rifle. The hunter reached out and poked Jake's belly with the muzzle and yelled, "Who were they, man?"

Jessie Mae held up her hands in supplication and Jake backed down, his "Jest two niggers," gasped out in a weak, strangling whine. "Come through day 'fore yestiday," he said as he anxiously eyed the rifle. "Jessie Mae told me 'bout 'em. Traded some eggs fer the bear skin over thar on the barn."

"What'd they look like?" Minns' menace increased as he struggled to speak, becoming almost inarticulate from rage and his tension. He aligned his rifle and leveled it with the blacksmith's heart, its muzzle at point-blank range. Jared backed up a few steps, his weapon ready.

Jessie Mae's tears flowed as she hurried in between Minns and Jake and screamed, "No! No! Don't hurt us!" Her nervous hands wrung her apron into knots and her body shook. Thin streams of water trickled down her cheeks.

"They was one big Negro," she explained, "an' a mulatto with curly, dark brown hair an' light colored eyes. They had the bear skin an' traded fer eggs. Didn't say much. Headin' nawth to'ard Turner's seemed like, from directions they asked."

Jared danced with excitement. "It be them, Pa," he said exultantly. "Old Blue done cotched 'em."

At the boy's exclamation, the tension slacked and all eyes shifted to the surroundings in a search for the dog. He was nowhere to be seen, his tracking long since gone from the farmyard. Minns' stentorian voice called out, "Blue! Blue!" A yodel followed a small yelp from edge of the forest to the west. Another yelp and a flash of spotted fur fixed his path through the trees.

"We got to settle here," Jared said. "Blue's cold trailin' 'em, Pa. He ain't goin'a wait."

Minns' conciliatory tone smoothed over the difficulties with the farmers. "I ain't meanin' you no harm," he said, "an' I'm right sorry fer the ruckus. But they done kilt my boy, Jeremy." His face softened at Jessie Mae's cry of compassion. "It's why I'm so sot on catchin' 'em, Ma'am. We buried him down to Greenwood an' been chasin' the two ever since."

"Well, you ain't chasin' 'em no more on that horse," Jake said. He waved to the forest to the west. "If you want to git after 'em in that tangle, you go on foot. Ain't no hawse git through that, once the old road runs out over to'ard the Tesnatee."

A shiny gold piece paid for the horses' care and the Minnses' sundries, and ended the rancor. Its weight as he hefted it mollified the blacksmith's hard- feelings. He shook to settle the agreement, then filled the Minns' sacks full of food and threw in new powder for their horns. The hunters hastily gulped down a big bait of dinner from Jessie Mae's table, depleting her store of meat. But the woman insisted on salving and rebandaging Jared's rapidly healing hand before she would let them go, her compassion and sympathetic clucks not lost on the boy. He thanked her in embarrassed awkwardness when they left the house.

The farmers kept a close watch while the Minnses quartered the pasture into the big woods. A long bugle echoed faintly from the far side of the hill, a challenge Pete answered with barks.

"Good riddance," the woman murmured.

"An' maybe we keep the horses if they don't come back," Jake added.

Jessie Mae smiled and tossed her head, then sidled into the curve of his waiting arm. The two were laughing when they re-entered the house and Pete sought his bed underneath.

Minns and Jared paused at a soft place in the woods road, its message clear. Stamped into the marshy ground of the seep were footprints of man and dog, set out by white eggshell that sparkled in the sun's rays. Quiet reigned when they chased on west at a half-run, pursuing Old Blue, the glade soon filled with the renewed cries of the forest lookouts.

Judah shifted in his crouch and squinted up the trace. His eyes scanned the bordering slopes, checking the few men he could see. "We better skedaddle," he told Rufus. "Got ter git back up to'ard the village at Mount Yonah. They sure ain't come on down and Bell said that Lieutenant rode west. Could'a cotched 'em."

"Sun's pretty high, awright," Rufus said. "But ain't heard no shootin'. Don' know where Claude an' Hannibal got to."

The two men hid in the brush at the side of the trace from Mount Yonah to Gainesville. A strong breeze whistled through the shallow pass. It rustled the brush into a clatter and masked the sound of their low talk.

They had questioned the boy closely when he sought them out the previous day, walking openly and loudly shouting their names. Rufus seized him as he brushed a clump, then dragged his squirming body into cover, the boy's squall choked off by a strong hand clamped over his mouth. Bell gave them the message from his shoemaker father and repeated the news from Jessie Mae about Claude. He also told them of Luke's killing before the small reb patrol galloped west.

Rufus had shaken his head, dismissing the news of Luke's execution. "He he'ped de rebs agin us at de ford. Deserved hangin'."

Bell had left soon after, quickly sent away on his return journey. "Git, boy," Rufus told him. "Don't want you 'round if de sojers come."

Their uncertainty in the morning daylight ended with Rufus' decision. "Got ter call de men in if we ter move," he said.

Judah raised a cow horn hanging from a strap and sent two short notes pealing out over the surrounding peaks. A few of the eleven men came in from closeby stands, but another blast was needed and a half-hour wait went by before the rest joined from their scattered hideouts. The early arrivals grumbled and yawned as they lounged in the brake, and gnawed on sweet potatoes while they waited on the stragglers.

"Goin' back up de trace," Rufus told them, once they were tightly bunched. "Ain't heard nothin' from Claude. An' Hartsill comin' west, but he ain't got but maybe four men an' dat Sergeant Gill wid 'im."

Judah smiled grimly and his fist clenched. "We kin kill 'em all," he said, "fo' headin' nawth."

Jubilation filled the air as the men cheered and laughed. Their spirits lifted by the news and their wait of indecision over, the coffle formed a quick line that headed out parallel to the trace. Only at narrow places or where a slide or cutbank forced them into the trace did they expose themselves. Judah scouted a quarter mile ahead, instructed to fall back if any danger threatened.

Claude slid down the bank to the road, its surface slick from the massive mat of pine needles. Hannibal followed, once the planter called out an all clear. The trace to the south was not occupied but its surface contained heavy rutting and the tracks of many men.

"Been a passel o' men by here," Hannibal said. "Maybe more follow. What we do now, Claude?"

"We got to move along it closeby. Give us a chance to skedaddle into the deep woods if others come."

"Gittin' skeered, Claude." Uneasy, Hannibal shivered and fixed his eyes on the road behind them. "Dey's too many rebs. Dey 'most ketched us back up dere where we was tryin' ter circle de town. Dat ball whistle right by."

"I heard it," the planter said, scornfully. "It wasn't even close. He turned his head and cocked it toward the trees. Ain't no problem near, Claude thought. But his heart beat faster at the Negro's fear. He concentrated on the forest sounds, particularly the birds, and watched for any movement. His rigid, alert stance relaxed when small birds called nearby. An ass-up's knocking peck and the rattle of falling bark drew his attention to a dead oak. The active little bird was girdling the tree, looking for food. Free, Claude thought, but always driven and on guard, just like us. He shrugged and laughed when he turned to Hannibal. "That picket was shootin' at me, not you. He missed us, so you ain't got no call to worry. We goin'a go on south like Jessie Mae said. Get to

Blackshear's an' Granny Pearl."

"Feel powerful bad," the Negro retorted. His downcast face exuded gloom and his shoulders sagged as he continued his doleful grumbling. "Somethin' bad gonna happen."

"Will you hush!" Claude said, exasperated. He shook his forefinger at the Negro. "I don't want no more o' that talk. Now you come on."

Claude angled back into the woods with Hannibal behind him. He struck out to the south along the trace, going far enough from the road to end up among the big trees where there was little brush. They had hiked about two miles in their southerly swing around the town and were well below it when the road crossed a small creek, its bed winding around a steep bank with a meager, grown up bottom to the east. Claude lay on a slope as he looked over the high hill facing them, the latter's steepness a daunting one to assay. Needs a big circle if we don't climb it, he thought. Be pretty tired. He took his time, evaluating the slope, then the bottom, its heavy cover offering a possible crawl. Hannibal lay on the ground on his back while Claude planned their travel. A mournful sigh escaped the Negro as he rolled over toward the planter.

"Ain't no good Claude. I jist know de debbil got us. We gonna hang when dey ketch us."

Claude's exhaustion and strain could not stand the fatalistic prediction of the servant. He lost his temper and pounded on the ground with his fist, exploding with, "Shut up, God damn it! I don't want no more o' that talk." But Hannibal's gloomy, terrified face reproached him, and silently beseeched him for help as the man trembled and sweat ran down his cheeks. Doubt assailed the planter, but doubt that he cast aside. He suppressed the terror of the moment to pause and gently reassure the loyal Negro. "We're goin'a make it to Blackshear's. Now help me figure how to go."

With a task to take his mind off the dangers, Hannibal perked up and shifted to Claude's side. After peering at the steep hill and the flat, he chose the bottom. His advice was gratifying to the planter, and confirmed the latter's own thoughts.

"If we go 'roun', Claude," Hannibal said, "it take a long time. Better ter put into de bottom over dere." He pointed out a hole between two large bushes. "We kin hide in all dat brush and crawl across ter de woods."

"Just what I was figurin'," the planter replied. "We have to chance it."

They stole down the slope to the edge of the bottom, hiding behind trees as they scooted from one to another. Where the brush started, dried stalks of goldenrod and brambles cluttered the edge and reinforced the cover. Small trees and bushes had invaded the fertile field, irregularity of the growth offering invisibility to the fugitives. Claude led the crawl and stuck close to the base of bushes in his attempt to be quiet. He was grateful for the wind. It swirled in the valley and whipped the bushes together. They rattled and shook, their natural movement hiding the travel of the fugitives.

Claude left the brush at a great oak, its trunk down and root fan sticking into the air. It was fine cover, a place to hide while he reconnoitered their advance. He crouched behind the six foot thick trunk and scanned the timbered slope until Hannibal joined him.

"We'll cut up the hill from here," he said. "You ready?"

At the Negro's nod, Claude stepped around the root fan to head uphill. A pistol barrel stuck him in the stomach, and a sharp, "Hands up!" demanded instant obedience.

The planter tensed and threw up his arms as his scalp prickled and a tremor ran up and down his backbone. Instant sweat dotted his face and dampened his armpits. He grew deathly afraid as Hannibal's premonition rang in his memory.

Petrified with fear, Claude could only wait as another trooper ran up behind Hannibal from the other end of the fan. His leveled rifle halted the Negro's surge toward the planter. The two prisoners marched around the obstruction under the unkind prodding of the troopers, threats and kicks spurring them on. A hundred yards of weaving through the trees took them to a clearing. Claude's body jerked at the sight of the Lieutenant talking to the Sergeant. Hartsill puffed at his cigar and waited silently at attention until they were marched to a stop before him. A tendril of smoke trailed from the stogy clamped in his jaw. Throwing away the butt, he struck Claude full in the face with his palm. The hard blow staggered the fugitive and its loud slap froze both the troopers and the birds into silence.

Claude blew up in unreasoning wrath at the deliberate insult. It and the wearing terror of the long escape drove him beyond any semblance of reasoned thought or action, and tore away his inhibitions. His desperation produced an uncontrollable rage that overcame caution. He swarmed all over the Lieutenant, his roundhouse bludgeoning knocking Hartsill to the ground. The planter fell on top of the rebel officer. He was shouting curses as he rained down blows and sought Hartsill's throat. "You God damned rebel bastard," he swore. "I'll kill yuh!"

"Don't kill him!" Hartsill yelled as they struggled. His cry to Gill stopped the trooper's shot. The Sergeant had pulled his pistol when Claude attacked. Gill repeatedly aimed it and raised the barrel as the fighting men rolled over and over and struck each other.

A pair of troopers held their rifles on Hannibal. The Negro clenched his fists and cursed. His shuffling feet and trembling body eased toward the fighting men as he warily eyed his captors.

"Don't'cha try it, nigger," one guard cautioned. He deliberately stepped back and aligned his rifle with Hannibal's heart. The other at the side also took aim. Hartsill's blows and curses drew their attention back to the fight.

"Get him off me," Hartsill said. "We're goin'a hang this nigger."

At Gill's command, the other two men of the patrol jumped on Claude's back and struck him over the head with their pistol barrels. His limp body rolled off the Lieutenant and lay unconscious as Hartsill rose to his feet and staggered to the nearby creek. Dunking his head in the cold water, the officer washed the blood off his face, its bruises and a swelling eye mementos when he returned to the troop.

"Haul him up," he said, when Claude came to and groaned. The planter was holding his head in his hands and trying to rise when the troopers yanked him to his feet. He almost fainted from their rough, forceful manhandling. It wracked him and sent additional shooting pains through his bad shoulder.

The planter swayed and rubbed his sore head while he faced the angry officer. Hartsill's face was set in a cruel scowl as he daubed the blood from his split lips and sucked on the injury. They locked eyes, two hard men taking the measure of each other, warriors. But it did not change Hartsill's order. His mouth compressed into a bloody slit as he spat it out. "Fifty lashes each, then hang 'em."

Claude thrust the troopers away from him and jabbed his finger at the rebel officer's chest. "You can't do this," he protested.

"I don't listen to no nigger," Hartsill contemptuously replied. He threatened Claude with his pistol, while his troopers seized the prisoner and pinioned his arms.

Claude struggled against the men, so enraged that his voice quavered as he identified himself. "I'm a Union officer, Lieutenant. Lieutenant Claude Shaw, 7th Ohio Cavalry. I'm a prisoner of war, not a renegade."

Hartsill's fury increased as he railed at the prisoner. "A nigger officer? I heard o' such. We got an order from old Jeff Davis himself on Yankee niggers. You're condemned."

"No!" Claude frantically shouted. "I'm a white man, Lieutenant, died black with walnuts." But his confidence failed him at Hartsill's unyielding scowl and his fright increased. He reached out a sweating, imploring hand and said, "I'm a prisoner of war, man. You can't do this."

The reb was unyielding as he pronounced judgment. "You're a nigger in color and with a nigger, so you'll be hung as a nigger."

Claude wrenched himself free of his captors and stiffened into an erect, military stance, putting his fears behind him. His face grew cold and hard as he straightened his backbone and braced himself. He accepted his fate. No reasoning could change the reb. His death would occur in an inglorious way, but his passing in war would be met with the dignity and bravery of an officer of the 7th Ohio. He would protest to the end but he would not grovel.

"You're a man without honor, Hartsill," he said quietly. His soldierly bearing matched that of the reb and his courteous demeanor mocked the Confederate. "Not like the friends I have in the South, Lieutenant. Do you hate me so much that you would sacrifice the principles of a Confederate officer and gentleman?"

Hartsill swelled up and turned red. "Don't talk to me of honor, Shaw. You damned Yankees killed all my family and I'm hanging you."

A feeling of peace entered Claude's soul. His life was nearing an end but he faced his death with courage. It was with sadness that he said, "Oh Lord, forgive them, for they know not what they do." Some of the rebel troopers started at Claude's prayer and two glanced at each other and muttered.

But Hartsill, pitiless, nodded to Gill who called out, "Tie 'em up, boys and git the whip."

The troopers hustled to obey the Sergeant. They bound the two fugitives tightly to separate trees, the prisoners' backs bent down to receive the lashes of the men. Gill picked the biggest trooper to whip him, Claude could see, a large man who stripped off his impediments before he flicked the whip out to its full length to try it. The officer's memory ran riot as he prepared his soul for the fifty lashes. He was amazed that his thoughts turned to Hannibal and the servant's rescue from his abusive owner. Claude well remembered tearing the whip from the man's hand. Now he was under the whip, just like the slaves. It would be a fitting revenge, he thought. Him, a planter, now passing as a Negro, getting whipped and hung. And Letty would never even know. His children with no father, a man in an unknown grave in Georgia. Self-pity overcame him and he wept in impotent fury, straining at his bonds. His grief and outrage exploded into a searing strike across his bent back, the red pain electrifying all his muscles.

"Stop! Stop!" he roared angrily. "I'm a Union officer!" His demands went unheeded and the whip descended in a second, even more forceful blow.

Maddened, Claude's protesting scream echoed from hill to hill, his tortured face turned to the soldier as the man flipped the leather braid before the next blow. The trooper laughed at his victim and his arm went back for another strike.

Boom!

The deep-voiced gunshot rang through the trees. A piece of the trooper's skull flew out into the forest, blood and hair spattering over the face of the watching planter. The man crumpled like a wet towbag. His body slumped into a quivering heap, the air expelled through his throat in a rasping rattle.

Yells and musket shots followed, with screams and curses from Hartsill's men. Men ran by Claude from the forest and interposed themselves between the fugitives and the rebels.

"Git 'em alive if you kin," Rufus hollered, taking up a position by Claude.

The redhead's knife made a quick slash at the tight cords and released the planter before he moved on to Hannibal. The freed men coalesced behind a big tree while the fighting proceeded to its grisly end. Claude shuddered at the sight of the down trooper still clutching his whip. Blood and brains had run out of the opened skull, its red and gray mixture already attracting a still mobile bluebottle fly.

When the shots stopped, Rufus waved to his men and bellowed, "Bring 'em over here."

A group of milling Negroes restrained two struggling figures, Hartsill's and Gill's curses damning them to hell. The group ignored the dead men on the ground and dragged the rebs toward Rufus. Claude counted seven bodies lying still and silent, and two men who hobbled along behind the group. Rufus' men had suffered, he thought, and for him. A flush of warmth rushed over him, his mind on yet another rescue by the big man and his loyal friends. Truly they were his friends, he thought. He was black on the outside, just as they. But they had souls just as white as he.

Hartsill was disdainful as he stood before Rufus, every bit the prideful Southerner. He grasped his left arm tightly and blood dripped from his fingers. But he sought no help from them even as he berated the Negroes and Claude and rasped out curses. Gill swayed and clutched his side, a light, bloody froth bubbling from his mouth. He gasped as he breathed, but swore at them while he tottered and fought, still contesting the strong grips of his captors.

"You got anything to say, Hartsill?" Rufus asked. His brusk tone and cold eyes stopped the Lieutenant's cursing.

The officer spit in the slave's face. He laughed when Rufus wiped off the gob and rubbed it into the prisoner's coat. "You're goin'a kill me, nigger, so go ahead. No use waitin'."

Spying Claude and Hannibal behind the Negroes, Hartsill shook his bloody fist at the officer. "Let the nigger Yankee pull the rope," he said scornfully. "He's the murderin' kind."

Rufus hit Hartsill hard in the mouth. The blow staggerd the officer and shut him up. He spit out teeth and cleared the blood from his throat and a red stream ran down his chin whiskers. At Rufus' gesture, the slaves quickly cinched tight nooses around the prisoner's necks. Hartsill laughed at them when they cast the loose ends at branches, taking several tries to get the ropes right. But Gill pleaded for mercy.

"I ain't done nothin' boys," he said. "Jest doin' fer the Lieutenant what he tells me."

Hartsill reproved the man, but was unable with commands or curses to stop Gill's grovelling. He quit when Gill started crying and said, contemptuously, "Get your backbone up, Gill. They're goin'a hang us, so act like a man."

Claude had to admire the Confederate officer's bravery and rallying of Gill. In extremity, with his life at an end, the reb faced hanging with equanimity and courage. The planter interceded with Rufus.

"Tie their hands an' feet, Rufus, an' drop 'em from a horse. Don't just haul 'em up an' let 'em choke."

Rufus ignored him and beckoned to Judah. The Negro driver approached Gill and pushed his face close to that of the sweating Sergeant. He had a rawhide in his hand, its strands hanging from a noose in the middle. Gill stirred uneasily, his eyes on the noose as Judah swung it back and forth. When it's motion stopped, his eyes shifted to face the intense, silent gaze of the Negro.

"You 'member all de gals, Sergeant?" Judah asked politely. "Whole country know 'bout yer little gals."

The Negro's voice was so soft, Claude had to move closer to hear. He sensed something monumental was happening.

Gill shrank back in fear and strained against the noose. He threw up his hands, saying, defensively, "Ain't done nothin' to no gals."

"You liked 'em young, didn't yuh, Sergeant?" Judah said. He remorselessly attacked when Gill shook his head. "Beat 'em hard atter yer pleasured yerself wid 'em."

"I didn't hurt nobody," Gill screamed. His frantic, fearfilled squall and jerking against the rope caused the men to haul him up to his tiptoes. They strangled him until he choked before letting him down again.

They're playing with him like a cat in the barn with a mouse, Claude thought. He was sickened with the tormenting, but fascinated by it, unable to look away.

Judah went on, his calm voice growing stronger as his denunciation searched for a climax. "Two of dem little gals my kin, Sergeant. You kilt 'em wid yer beatin's, like so many others."

Gill frantically flopped about, given just enough rope to stand flat-footed but ringed with men to prevent escape. A bloody dribble ran down his chin and little bubbles foamed about his lips.

"Do you git it now, Sergeant?" Judah asked. He was back to his softness, a softness covering steel. "I gwine mek sure you don' never pleasure no other little gal."

He cut the Sergeant's suspenders and loosened his belt, then pulled down Gill's pants. The stripped garment dropped down around the prisoner's feet and exposed Gill's white legs and privates to the cool air. Gill crossed his legs as the chill struck, his attempt to shield himself unsuccessful in defending his seed pods and goad. The Sergeant's tortured cry, "No! No! Don't cut me!" degenerated into sobbing as Judah seized his privates and yanked them forward.

Slipping the rawhide noose around the members, Judah pulled it tight at the body. Its stricture evoked terrified screams from Gill. "No! No! Don't!" His violent struggles against the noose tightened the rope on his neck. The hangman's loop soon choked him into submission. Exhausted, Gill sagged back into a trembling, gasping hulk.

The implacable Judah pulled the rawhide hard and Gill's crotch followed as he frantically tried to ease the hurt. He screamed when Judah's knife pulled upward through the flesh, one hard, flowing stroke doing the emasculation and deflagellation. The Sergeant's hands flew to the site, now only an open wound with the blood spurting.

"Dey here, Gill," Judah said. The Negro swung the rawhide before the Sergeant's eyes. Its pendulous, ghastly cargo dripped blood.

An unearthly howl of anguish rose out of the depths of the tortured man. He screamed again and again, his bloody hands rising up to his face and hiding his eyes. At a motion from Judah, the men swung him up and tied off the rope. Strangling from the noose, Gill tried to climb the thin strand, unable because of the slippery blood on his hands. His thrashing grew weaker as his face purpled and his eyes protruded, Judah and the coffle impassive to his struggles. Shuddering was followed by limpness, the only sounds the drip, drip, drip of the blood onto the leaves below. Its red pool rested beside the rawhide and its noosed flesh. Claude stared in horror during the execution, unable to do other than tremble. He was fascinated by the statuesque slaves, their faces hard and grim, triumphant.

Hartsill's strangled query broke their spell. "You goin'a do me the same?" he croaked through his air-starved throat. "It's not fittin'."

"No, Lieutenant, we ain't," Rufus replied.

His denial was followed instantly with, "Swing him up, boys."

Hartsill, off the ground two feet, maintained a rigid body, hands at his sides and boots together until lack of air destroyed his will and produced unreasoning panic. He commenced dancing in the air and clawing at his neck, trying to get his fingers under the noose. His struggles ended just like Gill's, with jumping-jack motions that subsided into shuddering and trembling before the body turned into a limp mass of flesh.

Rufus fired a shot into each when both troopers quit moving. His men ignored the swinging bodies and bunched around him. Judah acted as spokesman while he cleaned his knife blade on Hartsill's pantsleg.

"What we do now?" he asked.

"Git ter de horses, boys," Rufus said. "Best Claude an' Hannibal go on alone like dey planned. Horses he'p 'em git away quick. We move on nawth."

He sent three wounded men to Demorest's and Granny Ella, their mounts' hoofbeats rapidly fading in the forest. Claude and Hannibal left Rufus and the few surviving Negroes on foot and headed south on the remaining horses. The two groups of ragged men had an emotional parting before the breakup. Claude embraced each man and wrung Rufus' hand while he reiterated his blood debt, unconsciously falling into the slaves' vernacular in his thanks.

"You pertec' us agin, Rufus, you an' yer frens. You all come on in ter Greenbottom. I he'p yuh all."

Claude and Hannibal rode the horses to exhaustion through the day, balls from one picket post wailing by their heads when they ignored the challenge and galloped past. They abandoned the mounts in a pasture east of Gaines and went on south through the countryside afoot. It was dark when Hannibal sought out Granny Pearl at Blackshear's.

"You Granny Pearl?" he asked.

The olive skin glistened on the fat face that peeped around the door frame of the cabin, firelight reflecting off its shiny cheeks. Suspicion clouded the woman's searching inspection of the fugitive.

"Who want ter know? she said.

"I'se Hannibal," he told her. "I'se got a Yankee officer wid me. We runnin' an' come on from Jessie Mae up ter Clarke's. She say you he'p."

The old woman threw the door open half-way. "Git in here," she said. When Hannibal sidled through the cracked opening, she asked, "Whar's de fren?"

"Hid in de trees."

"Git 'im in de cabin."

The door slammed behind Claude a moment later. He felt safe as the two aimed for the crackling fire and its comforting warmth. The fat, dumpy woman fed them stew while they talked, its steaming body thickened with a little meat and many potatoes and turnips. She topped it off with a dip of honey spread on small pieces of pone.

"Ain't got much corn now," she said. "Too many movin', what wid de militia an' deserters 'roun', an' de Yankees drivin' dose people outen 'lanta. Deys all 'bout et up de country."

Hannibal stretched, then yawned with a great, gasping intake, the food and hot fire exacting their toll. "What'cher do wid us, Granny?" he asked. "We powerful need ter sleep an' den head on to'ard Dalton."

The old woman laughed. "Jist hide yuh fer ternight," she said, "den pass yuh on up de way."

Granny slid a crude bed aside and picked up some sacks from the floor. They gathered around her when firelight exposed a three foot square of discolored dirt. She fell to her knees and brushed away the surface, revealing a planked cover. When Hannibal lifted the wooden slab, a dark entrance appeared, a hole both uninviting and with spiderwebs across the opening.

"Dishere ol' cabin first one 'roun' back in Injun times," Granny told them. "De tunnel lead out ter a well fer 'scapin'. Ain't been used in long time. Tek some sacks fer sleepin' an' git on down dere."

"Den what, Granny?" Hannibal asked.

"I calls you early. Git'cher over ter Coal Mountain an' de preacher. He carry yuh by Nelson's er maybe even up by de white stone place."

She ignored Hannibal's further questions. Instead, Granny ordered them down into the tunnel. Claude went ahead. He cursed the everpresent spiderwebs as he brushed them from his face.

Hester and Gabe waited at the side of the path to the outhouse, not hiding but openly in the light near the cabin. They singled out the old woman when she came back from her nightly relief.

Hester stepped in front of her and said, "Granny Ella?"

"Yes chile?" Granny calmly replied, as if strangers were expected. "Who you?"

"I'se Hester, Granny. De others tol' me you be by soon if we wait. Granny Esther over to Calhoun's say you he'p us. We runnin'."

The rail-thin woman motioned with her stick, tapping their legs with its tip. "Foller me an' be quiet," she said in a low voice.

Ensconced safely in the sick cabin, the hospital of the plantation, Gabe and Hester rested on pallets next to the several sleeping occupants. Granny Ella brought them cold johnnycake for supper. She brushed off a few ashes still sticking to the bottom before she smeared on a small dab of honey. As they ate, she cautioned them to stay with the sick.

Gabe shook his head and said, "Don' like dat, Granny."

"Best place ter hide right now," Granny Ella replied. "We got de pox in here." She chuckled. "Ain't nobody gwine come 'round de cabin wid de pox inside. Dey don' know de men 'bout up an' 'roun'. Dey cured. Can't hurt nobody."

She left them in the cabin full of snoring patients. Gabe swore, quietly complaining, until Hester slapped him and he settled down. But she heard him mumbling even as he slept.

Chapter 20

Granny Pearl

---

*November 20, 1864. Coal Mountain, Geor-
gia. Temperature 68\46. Possible squalls
and heavy showers during the night. Gusty,
changeable winds to 20 knots. Moon dark
except for a sliver, setting after midnight.*

The Minnses had camped near the Tesnatee River the previous night, finally worn down from rapid travel. Their fire lay in a secluded cove northwest of the town of Mount Yonah, after Old Blue's cold trailing took them to the turnaround in Claude's track. A single footprint and a knee impression in the mud revealed the watering place of the fugitives at the river. With dusk coming on fast and the old dog submerged in the shallows, Minns squatted back up the bank, his jaw working as he chewed and spit and brooded. The water was high and roily, not a crossing place for man nor beast. Jared tossed in a stick, which rode downstream at a rapid pace.

"They went south, Pa," Jared said. "Too deep to cross here jest now."

"I 'spec' so, boy," Minns said. "Old Blue cut their track if we quarter 'cross toward Mount Yonah in the mawnin'. We git back up here in a good thicket and camp ternight." Minns looked up at the sky. "Don't feel like it's goin'a rain agin but be col' 'thout a fire an' half-face."

A small deer had bounded out during their search for

a protected night camp, the two rifles slaying it instantly. Gorged full of venison and liver on top of Jessie Mae's fixings, the Minns denned up in a hastily made half-face that deflected the night's showers.

Hot roasted meat on top of a good sleep enlivened them the next morning. They trailed out an hour after sunup with Old Blue casting ahead. The hunters struck back southeast at a fast walk, on a beeline toward the little village they had passed the day before. Their long strides ate up the miles to Mt. Yonah. Old Blue didn't strike during their approach, but in a damp field past the town, the hound yelped and swung south, his keen nose and steady pace taking him to Claude.

Its globe barely showed above the hazy horizon as rays of the morning sun shined dimly through a hole in the east wall of the sick cabin at Granny Ella's. A crude opening covered with oiled cloth, the window allowed the night's darkness to grade into a distinguishable gray. Yawns and creaks rose from the awakening men as the light intruded and they faced the new day. Remnants of the night's shower dripped from the eaves, the drops exploding into little plopping splashes as they struck the ground.

Gabe gestured to the other two pallets in one end of the hut as he knelt beside the one nearest to him. "Yer all Rufus' men?" he asked.

The bearded patient sighed and raised his head off a doubled-up coat serving as a pillow. "Yep. I'se Sim. Seed yuh at de thicket."

Gabe pulled thoughtfully at his beard as he searched the man's face, then said, nodding, "I 'member yuh now. Why you men here?"

"I'se shot yestiday in de fuss o'er ter de west by de ribber."

The giant Negro scratched his head and squatted down by the pallet of the injured man. The wounded Sim had stuck his left leg out from under a blanket. Its lower calf showed a large, crusted hole. With drops running down his brow from his intense sweating, Sim threw off the rest of the cover and tore off his shirt.

"Burnin' up," he said. His feverish eyes locked with the giant's. "Water. Got ter hab water."

Gabe called to Hester to bring the pail. The wounded man swilled down three dippers full, his greedy mouth leaking little streams in his haste to fill his belly. Hester set the pail aside when Sim gave up the dipper and wiped his mouth with the back of his hand. She moved away toward the fire but Gabe motioned her to stay. His questions enlightened them both.

"What happen in de fuss?"

"We come on dat Lieutenant, de one from Anderson dat allus chasin' us over'n de thicket." Sim searched his mind, his words stopped while he tried to recollect. Seeing the furrowed brow, Gabe prompted him.

"You ain't meanin' Hartsill, are yuh?"

"Dat him. An' de Sergeant, dat Gill." His curses consigned Gill to hell before he electrified them with the rest of his news. "Dey had de Yankee officer an' Hannibal tied to a tree, whuppin' 'em."

Hester cried out and her hands flew to her mouth. She knelt beside the pallet, trembling and silent. The giant eased forward and helped the patient to sit up and to take another drink, while the girl poured some of the water on her bandanna and wiped his forehead and face. His look of gratitude thanked them as Hester burst into tears.

"What happen' to Hannibal?" she said. Her sobs rose into a scream, her voice cracking. "He kilt?"

When Sim shook his head, her face lighted up and she hugged him. Hester fussed over the Negro, trying to help while he moved his injured leg. But he pushed her away and reached down with his own hands to reposition the member. After he was satisfied, he turned to them, and his sweating face broke into a smile.

"Rufus set us watchin' fer de 'scapes," he said. "We snuck in on de rebs atter dey took 'em. Kilt all 'cept Gill an' dat Lieutenant. Rufus hung 'em up."

Gabe nodded and said, "I 'spect dat o' Rufus. He hate dat reb, what he do to us niggers." His raspy voice turned angry. "He mean. An' ol' Gill kilt all dose gals. He need de rope."

Sim chuckled as he told them the juicy part. "Judah done cut dat Gill a'fo' dey hang 'im up. Jist like a boar shoat." His laugh turned into side shattering, gleeful chortling. "He squall good."

Great bellows burst from Gabe as he hoorawed. His giant body shook and he slapped his hands together in thunderous claps. "Cut 'im, did he? Dat ol' Gill musta hollered some."

"Screamin' loud 'nuff," Sim said, laughing, "ter kerry ter de thicket." He wiped his eyes and his face screwed up into a wicked grin as he moved closer to whisper to Gabe. "Judah don' jist take de nuts, he cut off de rod."

The two howled together, their merriment drawing curses from the sick patients in the cabin. Rufus' other two men joined in the celebration when Sim retold the story.

Hester fidgeted and her hands fluttered before her breast while the gruesome tale unfolded. Unmoved by the jollity and driven by her fears, she was powerless to keep still any longer.

"Where's Hannibal?" she asked.

"Dey gwine on down de road on hawses," Sim said. "Heard 'em tell Rufus dey gwine ter Blackshear's, er some place like dat, den on west."

"Dey's two days ahead o' us, Hester," Gabe said, "an' dey's safe." His quiet assertion settled the girl and her body lost its strained tenseness. The talk died down into casual jawing. The men gossiped and smoked while the girl took water to all the patients and Gabe visited with the other two men of the coffle.

Only a few minutes later Granny Ella entered the cabin, followed by a short, stockily-built girl carrying a steaming, cast-iron pot. Granny nudged her helper after the container was safely on the floor. The sturdy girl ran to a shelf as the old woman called to the men.

"Fannie atter de bowls an' spoons. Git yer brekfis'."

Gabe ate three large bowls of the stew, his huge bulk absorbing the tasty collection of vegetables, thickening, cornmeal and bits of meat. He belched and rubbed his stomach when he surrendered the empty bowl to Fannie.

"Gittin' ga'nt from all dis runnin', Granny," he said. He

sighed and his face turned somber. "Miss all dose regular fixin's Aunty Emma gib us over ter de thicket. She fed us right good."

At the mention of Emma's name, Granny's grave face dissolved into tears. "Ain't no mo'," she said, sobbing. "De word come from Calhoun's yestiday. She done kilt by dose sojers fo' dey come over here, de ones dat Rufus took."

Gabe's mouth fell open in dismay. "Aunty Emma kilt?" He could not contain his rage. He swore great oaths as he strode to and fro, an aroused lion of a man whose body could not rest, one who shook as he paced in the cage of a cabin, a revengeful man who repeatedly struck one fist into his other palm, damaging himself as he would damage the killers he maligned.

"Don' need ter fret," Granny said. "Sim an' de others done kilt de officer an' all de men." Sim nodded and Granny's voice soared triumphantly. "Dey finished!"

"Good riddance," Hester echoed. She scraped her bowl absentmindedly, her brows knitted in thought, until Fannie took it and the wooden spoon. The girl's interruption woke Hester from her trance.

"Where we go now, Granny?" she asked.

"You he'ps me wid de sick," Granny said, "den Gabe an' me talks wid yuh."

Granny sent Fannie off to wash the bowls and spoons and take back the kettle while she turned to the sick. Her gentle old hands and homespun medications joined with her advice as she bathed each in loving care and a soothing patter. "You gwine git well," she told each of the invalids. But she also warned them. "Don' say nothin' 'bout Gabe er Hester, er I'se put de hex on yer."

Once her doctoring was finished, Granny led the fugitives to the outhouse. A tumbledown, roughsawed, board shack waited on them. Fannie lurked outside at the turn of the path to order away any intruders. They sat on the threeholer while the old woman talked, the basket of corncobs for cleansing kicked to one side, out of the way of their feet.

Hester wrinkled her nose in disgust at the rank smell of decay. "Dishere ol' place purty bad," she said.

"Ain't nobody gwine bother us here, Hester," Granny replied. "De Massa build it fer de sick an' de rest scairt ter come in. Fraid o' de pox. Don' know dey ain't no danger. But we safe ter talk."

Hester's mind was on Hannibal, not the outhouse. "What Claude an' Hannibal do now, Granny?"

"Granny Pearl send 'em up de road ter Coal Mountain an' Nelson's from Blackshear's. She got ways."

"Where's Nelson's?"

"De tavern two days west, 'cordin' ter my gran'son, Cleve. He take yuh bof dere. Been dere lots an' knows de trails. I'se sent fer 'im."

"It de right place?" Gabe asked, as he thrust his way into the women's talk.

"Maybe you fin' Claude an' Hannibal dere," Granny said. "Dey gwine tek 'bout two days ter git ter Nelson's."

The old woman sat on her hole, the outhouse quiet except for Gabe's rumbling belly. Granny's ruminations ended with a muttered, "Dat's de way." Her bright eyes gleamed as she told them the rest of her plan. "You bof head on over to'ard Dalton wid a guide. De Yankees allus dere but de Gen'ril, dat Sherman, he gone down country from 'lanta. 'ceptin' ter Dalton, ain't no way ter jine de Yankees now t'hout gittin' ketched."

Gabe's belly growled louder. "Need ter use de outhouse, Granny," he said, anxiously.

The two women fled when he undid his pants and added to the stink of the threeholer. He found them at the bend in the path a few minutes later. They were accompanied by a rail-thin boy, coal black and as tall as he. The young man stepped forward, his thinness and unfolding similar to a lanky praying mantis. Though just a sliver compared to the giant's bulky mass, he looked Gabe straight in the eyes, unafraid.

"Dishere's Cleve," Granny said. "He my grandson." The old woman's love and pride were evident in her tone and she patted him on the back as she spoke.

He put his arm around her and squeezed hard, then planted a sloppy, smacking kiss on her cheek. Swinging her feet off the ground, he whirled her in a circle. "You knows right, Granny. I'se yer boy."

"Go 'long," she exclaimed, and playfully pushed at him. "You's jist like yer daddy, charmin' all de gals." She straightened her dress and fussed at him a little more when he set her down. But her face crinkled in a smile as she tersely ordered him onto the journey.

"Tek Gabe an' Hester ter Aunty Mittie over ter Nelson's. Hide 'em 'long de trail an' see dey git fed good on de way. You knows whar."

The boy asked, "Any chasin' 'em now?"

"No. De sojers got kilt over near de ribber yestiday. Dey's jist de militia an' de trash in de woods ter bother 'bout." Her gaze rested briefly on the rounded curves of the delectable girl. "Don' want no trash ter git Hester."

The girl's sharp intake of breath and shrinking away brought Gabe to her side. He placed his arms around her and squeezed her tight. A few soothing pats and strokes of her head stopped her shuddering. "Dey ain't goin'a touch yer," he said, "not so long as I'se wid yuh."

Granny looked about. "Fannie?" she called. "Where you hidin'?"

The young girl ran up to the group with a possibles sack on a strap and three blankets. Cleve took the sack for his shoulder and one of the blankets. He handed the others to Gabe and Hester.

"Gwine rain some more, 'ccordin' ter my bones," Granny said. She shivered and drew her shawl more tightly about her shoulders. The wind whistled in the trees, its rustling adding to the threat of the lowering clouds. "You need de blankets fer coats, and shelterin' in de night."

With his blanket fastened over his shoulder and his sack hanging, Cleve girded up his belt. He stalked about restlessly while Gabe adjusted Hester's load. When the giant stepped away, Cleve grabbed his arm and impatiently shook it. "You ready?" he asked. "We got ter lope on out if we gwine mek 'lonega t'day."

Hester flew into the outhouse, then ran to Granny's side when she emerged. She and Gabe hugged Fannie and the old woman, their thanks expressed in tight embraces.

Drops fell in a light shower as the fugitives followed

Cleve to the west. Granny Ella and Fannie waited on the path even though spattered with intermittent raindrops. The old woman waved to Hester when the girl turned and her bandanna flashed, just before she passed out of sight.

Claude and Hannibal waited in the near blackness of the tunnel, a small candle-end casting dark shadows from its smoky, yellow flame. Hannibal fumbled in his sack but its flatness yielded only a few nuts to crunch on. At the well end of the tunnel, dull daylight showed.

"Don' look like no sun t'day, Claude," Hannibal said.

"Goin'a rain more, from all the clouds yestiday," the planter replied. "You heard the patterin' last night." His tongue slurred into the slave's patois. "We need ter git on, if Granny jist let us out. She waitin' mighty long."

As if to answer the planter's complaint, the board cover rattled and dust sifted down into the tunnel from the cabin floor. Granny Pearl inspected their dirty, eager faces framed in the opening, then beckoned them up but with her finger across her lips. They stole into the cabin and headed straight to the smells of the pot bubbling in the warm fireplace. But Claude ran to the cabin door at the sound of a loud commotion outside. A hubbub of yells, curses, and crying filled the air. Peeping from the opening, Claude saw a gathering of women and children, a restless group milling about. Most had bundles in their hands; even the little children carried some small possessions.

The throng mystified the planter. His questioning face turned to the old woman. "What's happening, Granny?

"Dey's gwine to de free lan'," she answered. "Ain't no vittles much since de Gin'ral burn 'lanta an' de people come outen it. Too many militia grabbin' de feed." Her voice resonated, its tone exultant. "De slaves know Linckum done free 'em. De Yankees tol' all de folks dey's free. Dey's gwine ter Tennessee."

"How? They goin'a hoof it? It's a long way."

"Don' matter, dey's gwine on. You bof walk wid 'em, fur as de preacher."

Hannibal stuck his head over Claude's shoulder while they both watched the boisterous crowd. But the Negro retreated after only a cursory view and sought the fireplace. "Dey ain't gonna git far," he said. "Dey jist wear out on de trail, all dose little chil'ren."

New, angry outcries arose from the multitude. Something in the hubbub drew Granny to the door like a magnet and she wiggled by Claude. "It's Miz April," Granny whispered, after a brief glance. The approaching white woman had a gray, knitted shawl over her shoulders, a knit as colorless as her gray-streaked hair and pinched face. Its folds were pulled tight against the chill and the tasseled ends flopped in the breeze. Granny spat in disdain. "She de Missus o' de big house. Her an' Massa Jack own de lot o' 'em 'til dey's free."

"They the Blackshears?" Claude asked.

"No," Granny replied. "Dey name's Guyton. Ain't no kin o' de Blackshear de place named atter way bek."

Tall and angular, the woman entered the middle of the crowd, her head bare and her loosely-tied hair flying in the gusts. Her sweeping skirts tattered and the bodice frayed, she was as bedraggled as the south, Claude thought. Just another reb gone to seed with their cause. Slavery was done and they didn't know it yet.

The woman cried and shouted at the same time. "Don't leave me," she begged. "You belong here. Marse Jack done give you a good cabin an' vittles." Tears flowed and her cries grew sorrowful, much like a petulant child. "I need yuh."

A bulky Negress with a small child clinging to her skirt slapped April hard. "Git 'long wid yer," she said. "We's free. We's leavin'."

The others added to the insult by spitting on their mistress, little children running in with bravado and spitting, then dashing behind their mothers.

Miz April's surprised face whitened in shock and she convulsively uttered a sharp, "Oh! Oh!" Fear replaced her melancholy and she hastily backed away. She blubbered as she forced a passage through the women and escaped. Her sobs increased to screams as she wiped her face with her shawl and ran for the big house.

Mouth-watering aromas and the sound of Granny ladling up some stew seduced Claude and he abandoned the door. The planter riveted his attention on the food and joined Hannibal at the fireplace. The hungry men scraped their bowls clean, and emptied a refill soon after. A piece of pone and honey repeated their sweetening of the preceding night. Belches and belly rumbles added their chords to the crackling of the fire.

"Mighty satisfying," Claude said.

Hannibal shook his head and mumbled while he reached for another bit of pone. "We powerful grateful, Granny," he said, munching away. "Now what'cher do ter he'p us over ter de preacher? Me an' Claude don' look like no women." He laughed at his little joke.

The old woman grinned and said, "Gwine make bof of yer inter gals."

Hauling out two large dresses from great piles cluttering wall pegs, she held them against Hannibal and appraised the fit. "Dese was Miz Louisa's," she said, "de cousin o' Miz April. She so fat she can't walk, jist like a big, ol' brood sow."

Hannibal backed away and his mouth opened to protest. She whacked him hard in the face with a fold of cloth. "Be still!" she impatiently ordered. "Dey fit over yer clothes. But you's got ter shave fust an' git rid o' dem guns."

They abandoned their rifles in a corner, then reloaded the revolvers Rufus had given them. Claude drew and replaced the charge in his derringer. Its heavy ball would be better at close range, he knew. With pistols in their belts and the derringer in the planter's pocket, the men were formidable antagonists. Claude took the time to be shaved bare all over his head and to renew the stain on each of his worn places. After the few minutes for shaving and Claude's dyeing, the fugitives were ready for the costumes.

Granny Pearl screamed with laughter when the now smooth-faced men tried to don the dresses over their coats, their efforts helped by two women called into the cabin. Shaking out all the folds of the faded, ruffled skirts and adjusting of the bodices converted the men into a fat woman and an extra tall, bulky one. Claude was dumpy but Hannibal's legs showed at the bottom; his skirt cleared the ground a full half a foot. With splits at the side to add easy access to their weapons, simple mufflers and bandannas completed their camouflage and hid the differences of their heads and faces. Granny and her two assistants paraded around them when done, inspecting the new women for the group.

"Dey look awright ter me," one said.

The woman snickered, unable to prevent her mirth from growing into a bodyshaking chuckling. Her glee sent Granny and the other Negress into gales of laughter. Hannibal's injured rejoinder brought more laughter and humorous gibes from the women.

"Don' recken you's got ter fun us," he said, plaintively.

"We leavin' now, Granny?" Claude asked, ignoring the quips.

The old Negress silenced the giggling women with a wave. "You go 'long wid Henrietta here," — she pointed to the fatter Negress —, "an' Delcy." The two women smiled and tossed their heads at the introduction. "Dey de leaders an' dey do de talkin'. You understan' dat?"

"But we's ..." Hannibal started to say.

Granny slapped him stingingly and screeched, "You listen ter me!" Her fierce voice and piercing eyes cowed the big Negro. "Yer'e men. De women got ter hide bof o' yer in de middle. De only safe way ter do it be if you keeps quiet. You unnerstan'?"

"I ain't talkin'," Granny," Hannibal replied. "No talkin'," he repeated.

"We do what they say, Granny," Claude said. He grasped Hannibal's arm and squeezed it while his gaze locked with the other man's. "Just listen to them," he said to the Negro. "We got to go with the women."

"Keep in de middle o' all de chil'ren," Granny said. "Henrietta walk in front. She de biggest an' de most mouf to sass back wid if you cross de militia er any trash. Now y'all git."

Granny's resolute figure filled the cabin door while she watched the laughing group depart down the lane. Children skipped ahead, playing, as the travelers braced against the damp wind with its intermittent, spattering raindrops. Granny's parting shout conveyed all the desire of her heart.

"Git ter de free lan'!"

Wheeling vultures circled miles to the south as their
numbers increased before the feast. The big birds sailed
back and forth, their wings flashing upwards and down-
wards as the gusts buffeted them. While the carrion birds
gathered, Old Blue worked the track of the fugitives' scent.
His doubling back and occasional yelps signalled his slow
unravelling of the mystery of the spot where Claude and
Hannibal had milled around at a crosstrail. Blue's wagging
tail finally pointed north, his yelp intense when he struck
out to the south at a renewed clip, the Minnses close behind.
    "Most likely find 'em dead, Pa," Jared said. He pointed
with his rifle as he paralleled his father's lope. "Those
buzzards high now but fixin' to light on somethin'."
    "Yep," Minns replied. He spit, the brown stream mark-
ing the black bark of an oak. "If they's there, we kin head
back to the homeplace."
    Minns and Jared followed Blue through the timber
bordering the south trace where thick leaf falls made for soft
footing. Old Blue snuffled his way easily through the wide
aisles of the stately trees. Rain had wetted and softened the
duff. Its mouldy smell rose in the damp air and their footfalls
were virtually silent. The water had washed out some of the
scent, leaving Blue with a faint trail, but the old dog's nose
took them relentlessly toward the fugitives.
    By midmorning, with the clouds lifted slightly and the
showers ceased, the hunters broke out into the meadow
near the killing ground. When they started across, with
Blue racing ahead and bugling repeatedly, swirling winds
brought them the smell of death. Two buzzards lifted from
a nearby snag and flew off as the dog ran beneath them.
Blue's excitement and barks increased and his tail took on
a frenzied beat.
    "Got some killin' here," Minns said.
    He hurried ahead, with Jared running behind. They
burst onto the battle site an instant later, the swelling
bodies sprawled obscenely in the glade. Two figures hung
from limbs in the forest, swaying in the gusts, while Old
Blue raced around the site with the Minnses in pursuit. He

bugled in a frantic medley as he cast about in the glade, then ran down to the edge of the bottom. His yelping stopped at a grassy spot near the trace. Flopping into the stream beyond, the old dog lapped water and rolled before his exit and shaking. He trotted up to Jared and looked at the hunter as if to say, "My job's done."

"Blue says they's here, Pa," Jared said. "We better look at the two on the ropes."

"Yer right, boy. Let's git on up thar."

A few yards up the hillside beyond the meadow they faced a grim discovery.

"God almighty!" Minns exclaimed. "It's Hartsill."

"Gill too, Pa," Jared said, from his stand by the other tree. He leaned over and inspected the noosed object below Gill's feet. The boy threw up as he turned away from the sight and staggered to a nearby tree, clutching its bark.

Minns laughed when he glimpsed the missing crotch and the parts on the ground. "Looks like somebody had it in fer ol' Gill."

The hunter swung about, his face puzzled. "Where are they, Blue?" He sicked the old dog onto the trail, encouraging him with gestures and oaths. Blue just cavorted and wagged his tail. He had no interest in the scent but lay down on the soft mat with his tongue out and dripping.

They were casting about the battlefield when a weak voice called, "Water! Water!"

A body under a pine sapling waved a hand at the hunters. Minns put his canteen to the soldier's lips in seconds but the water dribbled out of his slack mouth. The hunter raised the wounded man's head to help. The trooper's shirt was matted with dried blood and two holes showed in the right side of his chest. A great sigh escaped him when he took his lips away from the canteen.

"What happened here?" Minns asked. He gave the man another sip.

"Rufus," came the weak reply. "'scapes from the thicket. Had men. Kilt us all."

Jared pointed to several bodies nearby. "They's niggers, Pa. Rest are white men."

"More water."

Minns tilted the canteen, then passed the empty vessel to Jared to fill at the creek. The boy squatted down beside his father when he came back. Minns prodded the injured man.

"The Yankee officer an' Hannibal. They here?"

The trooper looked up at the hunter, his concentration fading as his weakness increased. Minns splashed water over the man's face and shook his limp form into consciousness.

"The Yankee, man! Was he here?"

"Gone to Blackshear on hosses," came the whisper, so faint Minns bent over for the rest. "South. Told Rufus they's headin' fer Dalton after."

Closed eyes and shallow breaths answered Minns' next question, the pallid gray visage of the unconscious man peacefully uncomprehending. "He ain't fer long, boy," Minns said. The hunter eased the man's head to the ground. He straightened him onto his back and crossed his hands on his breast before rising and reclaiming his rifle.

"Do we leave 'em here, Pa?" Jared asked. "Hardly seems fitten."

Minns shrugged and shook his head. "No way to bury 'em, boy. We'll tell the next militia we cross. They kin do the diggin'." His searching eyes surveyed the creek and the western forest. "We be goin' on west," he said, as he checked his belt and moccasins. "Cut that Yankee's trail when they swing back nawth to'ard Dalton. Got to be militia over yonder give us direction."

Jared called to Blue and strode away from the carnage. The hunters stopped at the creek to fill their canteens, then forded it at a downed log. Blue swam it easily, coming out at a patch of sage grass. The old hound deposited his usual shower on the bank before he followed them into the forest.

Henrietta's group of slaves crossed the Chattahoochee River on a relic of a ferry, a ramshackle set of logs tied together. Though the craft was makeshift, the advice of the Negro operating it was not. The garrulous old man gave them critical trail hints as well as encouragement. Angling around to the north after landing, Henrietta and the other women gabbled away and enjoyed their freedom as the miles of the trace went by. Their happiness crumbled into fear at a timbered bend.

"Halt!" a voice thundered out of the forest.

Children screamed and clustered about the women. They sobbed wildly and clutched the skirts of the Negresses, trying to hide behind them when three armed white men ran down into the trail. The intruders' rifle barrels swung back and forth to intimidate the Negroes while the men spread out to cover all sides at the ambush site.

"What you want?" Henrietta screeched. Her shrill cries flayed the ragged men with abusive oaths.

Ignoring her demand and her curses, the three circled the Negroes and pointed them like a bird dog. The children howled and the slaves crowded together, their fearful faces turned outward as the men herded them into a tight group. Henrietta and Delcy bombarded the bandits with invective until the men stopped prowling and the antagonists faced each other.

A smaller man stepped toward a large, rawboned figure, the latter's dirty face shadowed by a shock of long, blonde hair that flared out below a dusty, black derby.

"Ain't likely they's got much, Snipes," the small man said. "They's jest more o' them 'scapes headin' fer the Yankees."

"Don't know 'til we search 'em, Willie," Snipes answered. He motioned to Willie to move farther around the party and cover the side next to the trees. "Could be they's carryin' a little gol' like that last bunch. The niggers stealin' ever'thin' they kin carry off."

"Yer right, Snipes," the third man said. His scornful cry from the other side of the covey backed up the leader. "We done got all that siller last month. Made a nice pile."

The Negroes milled about, the women caressing the children, bending to hug and quiet them.

"Looky at that big'un, Ted," Willie hollered. "We take turns at her."

"Strip off!" Shipes shouted.

His order and prodding rifle barrel galvanized Claude into action. He sidled up to Hannibal and whispered. "Git on over to Willie. I kill Snipes an' you Willie. Then we both fire at the other one." At Hannibal's slight nod, he added, "When I holler."

Hannibal stuck his hand under his dress and eased through the frightened children. Their weaving in and out and crying was disconcerting to the bandits. Snipes yelled and threatened, but his shouts and waving arms only increased the tumult and anxious wails of the group. The confusion let Claude whisper to Henrietta without being noticed. She screamed hysterically at the bandit after the planter had inched away a step or two and had started comforting some children.

"Don' you hurt de chil'ren!" she cried out. "I tells 'bout de gol'! I tells!"

The three men drew in closer at her sobbing hysterics, Snipes within a few feet of Claude, and Willie close to Hannibal.

"Where's the coin, nigger?" Snipes asked.

He pushed through the wailing children next to Henrietta, bumping them aside. Willie dropped his rifle barrel as his eager gaze searched the face of the crying woman. He crept nearer, his attention focused on Henrietta rather than the others.

Snipes first intimation that anything was wrong was of Henrietta seizing his coat and Claude's revolver blasting its ball into his left eye. Blood and brains splattered from the back of his head when the ball tore out, his conscious craving for their meager belongings erased in an instant. Willie suffered the same fate at Claude's shout, the report of Hannibal's pistol following as an echo to the crack of the planter's gun. Willie dropped like a stone and left a clear shot at Ted, across the covey.

That worthy reacted instantly and swung up his rifle. He fired at Claude without aiming, just as soon as it was level. The ball whistled by the planter but tugged at Henrietta's bandanna. Shreds of cloth sifted down as she screamed. Clapping her hand to the side of her head, she shouted, "I'se kilt! I'se kilt!", and fell over in a dead faint.

With the other outlaws down, Ted abandoned the hold-up and fled toward the forest, fumbling at his powder horn in a vain attempt to reload as he escaped. He was twenty yards away when the two fugitives took careful aim at the fleeing man and fired together. Puffs of dirt spurted from the back of his coat when the two pistols cracked and his body crashed to the ground with a thud. Loud gasping noises followed. Ted's battered figure thrust itself up and crawled along the ground on its hands and knees, dribbling bright red blood. The wounded man scrambled for the obscurity of the forest, but his last gasping breaths and escape were finished by a ball from the avenging Hannibal.

"Reload all those rifles!" Claude shouted.

His cry galvanized Hannibal into furious action, while the planter tended Henrietta. He tugged at her large bulk and helped her sit up. But she ignored his attempts to raise her to her feet. Her fingers were busy exploring her bleeding ear. Little sorrowing sobs and sniffles bubbled out and were interspersed with self-pitying curses. Claude pushed her hand away and examined the perforation in the cartilage, a neat round puncture. He chuckled as he stanched it with a cloth.

"You got a nice hole for jewelry now, Henrietta. Musta been a small caliber. It's pretty round."

Henrietta felt up the side of her cheek and wiped off the slimy mass of clotting blood that stained her brown skin. She fingered the ear and tenderly explored the oozing hole. Its bleeding was about stopped from Claude's pressure. A grimace and a small "Oh!" followed when she stuck the end of her little finger in the puncture and rubbed it around. Fumbling about in a pocket, the woman pulled out a velvety brown tobacco leaf and rolled it up.

"Git me a willow shoot," she said. "A small one, Claude, big'ern de hole."

He ran to a nearby trickle with its willow thicket and cut a sucker, stripping its soft bark on the way back. Henrietta re-rolled the tobacco leaf around the stick and forced it through her new ear hole. A search through her possibles sack turned out a small fraction of a broken mirror. One look enamored the woman. She preened and swung her head from side to side as she inspected the stick and her ear.

"Looky dere, Delcy," she said, proudly. "I'se got a place

ter hang all dose fancies we took from Miz April. Soon's it heal up."

Claude chuckled. Henrietta had turned the injury into a beauty spot, to be used for jewelry. His delight ended when Delcy jerked his sleeve.

"Need one o' dose too, Claude," Delcy said. Her stormy face and pouting lips augured trouble. "You shoot me too?"

"No!" he said, testily. "And neither will Hannibal."

Delcy flounced off into the crowd of still crying children, her imprecations consigning Claude to hell. A little girl diverted her. The child grasped at her dress until the sympathetic woman took the girl into her arms and soothed away the fright. Claude dragged Snipes' body from the cluster as the group of Negroes drifted away from the dead men. He took Snipes well into the woods, hiding the other two bodies with their leader before he joined Hannibal. The Negro had collected all the weapons at the side of the trace, reloaded them, and had assembled both the powder horns and cartridge boxes. But he also had found something else on Snipes, a few small gold and silver coins. Claude seized them, murmuring to the slave. At Hannibal's agreement, he called up the women.

"Henrietta, Delcy, the rest o' you, come here."

The women and children gathered around the men, their alarm settled back into a calm readiness to move. Claude slipped some of the coins into his pocket and held up the rest for the Negroes to see.

"They had a few coins that'll he'p yuh," he told them. "Hannibal gives 'em all to yuh, one to each woman and then the rest, half to Delcy an' half to Henrietta."

The women squealed in delight. Shiny coins glinted in their palms as they admired them and showed them to the children. Claude interrupted their chattering.

"We got to move on now, Henrietta. You know where to go, don't yuh?"

"De big ol' barn in de fiel' dis side o' de Nelson trace," she replied. "Dey's allus boys 'round dere hidin', waitin' ter he'p runaways, 'ccordin' ter Granny. Dey take us nawth."

Another hour of shuffling travel finished the children, worn out as they were from a hard day's journey. The women

fed them a little pone and bacon before the sleepy youngsters sought the remnant hay of the barn. A brief inspection
told Claude the structure was unused. No fresh animal
droppings lay around and all harness and tools were
missing. Full dark found the fugitives scattered about in
clusters of women and children, only snores disturbing the
night.

Giggling and rustles woke Claude in the great dark of
midnight. Wind sighed in the trees but faint starlight
showed, presaging a fair day. He rose quietly and sound-
lessly crept to the door of a stall holding the culprits, his
pistol ready. A female whisper stopped him.

"Don' push so hard, Hannibal." It was Henrietta's voice,
disembodied in the blackness. Thrusts and gasps followed,
the two not quiet in their coupling.

Delcy's complaining whine came out of the dark. "Don'
yer use 'im all up," she said angrily. "He ain't no good ter me
den." A sharp slap reinforced her objection, Henrietta's
curses at Delcy interspersed with her giggles.

Claude chuckled as he stole back to his hay and settled
in, his tired body resuming its sleep.

"It's dem, Gabe," Hester said, apprehensively.
"Who, Hester?"
The girl pointed out the two buckskin clad figures and
the trailing dog. "Dem Minns, dat's who."
The three travelers lay on a slope overlooking part of
Dahlonega and the government mint. The monumental
building stood out in a scattered collection of frame structures. They had forded the Chestatee east of Auraria and
had come back up the stream to find the crossroad and the
trace going west. Drenched from the turbulent water,
progress had been slow, even after the Negroes had wrung
out their clothes. Over her protests, Gabe again had insisted
on stripping Hester, with Cleve helping to hold the squirming woman. But even the damp clothes rubbed and irritated, and slowed their advance to the town. The evening
sun sent a few sunbeams through heavy, fast-traveling
clouds as the fugitives surreptitiously watched the Minnses.

Striking glints on suspended water droplets, the rays were welcomed after the rain on the trail.

The men's motionless figures bracketed the girl, her trembling and fluttering hands finally bringing Gabe's reassurance. "Dey don' hurt yuh here, gal. We wait 'til we sees what dey do. Den Cleve take us to his fren.'"

"Gabe right, Hester," Cleve added. "We be dere atter dark an' stay t'night. Ain't nothin' ter bother yer head 'bout."

Jared and Athey Minns entered several buildings as they watched, while Old Blue lay in the dust and waited. The men's walk became brisker as they circled through the town in their search. Minns gestured to the west along the Dawson road when they last bunched in sight of the fugitives. He harangued the boy with violent arm waving, but his argument with his son was unintelligible to them. Prodding Blue off a snuffling run in a piece of tall grass, Minns headed west out of town, followed by his boy. Their rapid gait on the trace soon took them from the view of the fugitives.

Another hour passed before Cleve moved and led them to his friend, their refuge in a cabin two miles west of town. It was well after black dark before they were fed and bedded down.

"Don' tell yuh who we wid or where, in case yer took," Cleve replied, in answer to Hester's query. "Best you don' know."

"We move on atter daylight," he added. "Git away from de cabin soon's we know 'bout dose Minns."

"It's a good place, Pa," Jared said. The boy fell to the ground and spread out his arms and legs on the thick carpet of pine needles. He groaned and stretched, rubbing his legs after he sat up. "Tired, Pa, an' I hurt. We orta give this up. We ain't goin'a ketch that Yankee."

Minns swore and his scar blossomed. "Shet up, boy!" he said. "We keep goin' 'til we find 'im, him an' that nigger."

He rapidly made camp and his fire and roasted venison filled Jared with more cheer. Once he was fed, the boy wiggled his fingers and made a fist, then rebandaged his injured knuckles.

Minns reached for his son's hand and gently felt of it, saying, "Any more pain, boy?"

"No, Pa," Jared replied. "The crust is dry and they ain't no more ache." He opened and closed his hand. "'bout time to leave off the bandage. Maybe one more day."

His father nodded and moved closer to the fire. Old Blue snored with his back to the blaze when Jared commenced his refrain. But Minns stared into the flames in thought, his jaw working his cud. Night damp had settled before he tossed away his chaw and sought the mat of pine needles. Soon his snores were added to the rest.

CHAPTER 21

The Right Reverend Rodney Duckworth

November 21, 1864. Nelson, Georgia. Temperature 61\40. Sunny and cool. Winds to 10 knots from the west. Moon almost dark.

Henrietta and Delcy stuffed food into Hannibal's mouth, tidbits from the Negroes' meager store of provisions, robbing the group shamelessly to fatten up the object of their desires. He basked in their attention at the morning meal and eagerly accepted their seductive invitations. His hands strayed over their curves one by one, their ample bottoms well displayed next to his crouch by the fire. Claude cooked his own bacon at some coals nearby. The planter's sidelong glances and amused chuckle followed Hannibal's progress with the women.

"We need to move on, Hannibal," Claude said. "You 'bout ready?"

The planter's query went unheeded, the Negro jollying Henrietta as Claude spoke. They made a fine threesome, he thought, two strong women, each wanting the man, and Hannibal basking in their desire. The Negro would most likely take them to the stall again before he'd be ready to move. As if the planter were clairvoyant, Delcy pulled Hannibal to his feet and led him toward the barn. Henrietta swore at Delcy's giggles and cuddles, but ran along close behind when the three entered the structure. The other Negresses shooed away the curious children. Their shouts and play diverted the youngsters' attention from the amorous women and Hannibal's willing help.

Brisk winds driving them, clouds scudded by the sun, its orange, shining ball well up in the eastern sky. Prospects for a fair day pleased the planter, its coolness well suited to a hard hike. He rechecked the rifles and his pistols and honed his knife, glancing at the barn now and then in anticipation. But the sun was another hour high and his irritation boiling over into curses before the laughing trio came out of the structure. Hannibal wiped the sweat from his face as he walked and pulled his soaked shirt away from his heaving chest. Dunking his head repeatedly into the log watering trough, he splashed the cold water over his upper body, then rinsed out his shirt and twisted out the moisture.

"Ready ter go now, Claude," he said, while he donned the damp shirt. He sat down with a tired sigh. "Dey 'bout tuckered me."

The planter laughed. "You took long enough," he said, as he eyed the women. Henrietta and Delcy chattered nearby and bragged about Hannibal. "Don't know how you did both of 'em in one night."

"Dey's powerful eager, Claude. Dey men's long gone and dey hot fer pleasurin'. Don' need much."

"Well let's get on up the road and find the church."

Wails followed them when they abandoned the company of the Negroes and headed toward Coal Mountain. Henrietta and Delcy besieged Hannibal with plucks at his clothes, coy looks and suggestive gestures. Seductively inviting him into the barn, they cast their nets and tried to lure him from Claude's side. The servant left them slowly, looking back, until Claude swore at him and he ran to catch up. Each of the men had discarded his dress and bandanna, for the planter was aiming to make a rapid hike to the church.

"Come back, Hannibal," Delcy trilled after him in a sweet, melodious voice. "Come back to us."

Henrietta's lament followed Delcy's invitation, and Hannibal's rejection when he hurried after Claude. Both of the women made one last rush after the hustling men but were soon outdistanced. The fugitives turned for a final look and wave where the trace angled east, only to see the women sidling up to a tall, young stranger.

"Dat's one o' de boys Granny tol' 'bout, Claude," Hannibal said. "De ones take 'em to de free lan'."

"He looks big enough for guidin' but don't know how he'll take to those two women."

Hannibal chuckled. "He got good time comin'." A moment later he guffawed. "Dat Delcy, she all over yer kissin' and Henrietta jist as good. Dey somethin'."

The two glanced at each other and smiled, their understanding and delight breaking out into broad, silent grins. Hannibal stepped off like a conqueror when he resumed the trail and took the lead a few yards ahead.

It was only a short hike before the outline of the first house in the village showed through the trees. They had smelled its chimney smoke down the trail and silently stole up to the clearing. Circling the tiny crossroads settlement, they went far east to avoid the barking dogs, then swung back to a spire in an open glade. The church was empty, its coldness evidence that the structure had not been used recently. In the back were the usual outhouses, placed at opposite corners of the church plot, with the peaceful, shaded graveyard in between. Many fresh, yellow-brown mounds brought the war home to the fugitives as they picked their way through the trees.

Claude paused and leaned on his rifle while he inspected the remnants of the carnage. He shook his head, saddened by the sight. "They's been some bad killin' o' these folks," he said. "Ain't long back, Hannibal."

The Negro nodded and scraped one of the mounds with his foot. Its soil was loose, easily disturbed. "Fresh," he said, tamping back the scar with his shoe. "Fight have ter be right near, Claude, fer all dese ter be buried in dis yard. Got ter put de body in de groun' right quick, so dey's kilt hereabouts."

The planter picked up his rifle and cradled it across the crook of his left arm. He stepped out to the path by the church. "We'll go on up the road," he said, "just like Jessie

Mae told us."

"What we do den?"

"Sing Rock of Ages to find the preacher. Start when we get close to the next hill up ahead."

"Den I'se leadin'," Hannibal said, firmly. He strode about ten yards in front of Claude, his rifle at the ready.

A half hour later, their cracked voices commenced the hymn.

"Rock of ages, cleft for me,
Let me hide myself in Thee,
Let the water and Thy blood,
From Thy wounded side that flowed,
Be of sin the double cure,
Save from wrath and make me pure."

Another mile of hard going added to their doubts that the preacher ever could be found.

"He ain't 'round here, Claude," Hannibal said.

"We'll try it once more," the planter replied. "Jessie Mae said it'd get 'im for sure."

"Save from wrath," came out in loud, startled yells as the bushes rustled and a man stepped into the trace ahead of them. They cocked and aimed their rifles in an instant, but the terrified cry of the intruder gave them pause.

"Don't shoot, boys!" he shouted. Taking advantage of their indecision, the man waved his arms and darted back into the brush.

Claude sang out, "If you're Preacher Duckworth, we're lookin' for help." His bellow reverberated through the forest, a dangerous alarm he instantly regretted. He and Hannibal rotated anxiously and eyed the brush while they waited on the preacher.

After a minute of total silence, only the birds resumed their calls, but then the bushes waved and the man walked out into the trace. He paced slowly toward them with his hands in the air. "I'm the Reverend," he said, "Rodney Duckworth."

His precise English intrigued Claude. But it was the preacher's appearance that baffled him and struck him speechless. And Hannibal stood with his mouth agape at the caricature of a man, so different from poor white dress.

The tall, gangly preacher had on shiny but scuffed black boots, wrinkled, dark-gray pants and a frayed, black frock coat, all in the middle of a wilderness. A frilled white shirt and flowing red neckpiece projected from his bosom and a high, glistening beaver covered his head. His florid complexion was overshadowed by a noble, hooked nose that projected well beyond slim, colorless lips. Bat ears, accentuated by bushy gray sideburns along the hollows of gaunt cheeks, contrasted with his complexion, the latter evidencing a rounder's life.

His stop before Claude and his active hands brought another shock. When the preacher removed his hat and wiped the sweat from his face with a bandanna, his head shined in the sunlight, its slick white pate surrounded by a border of scant hair. The luxuriant, bushy sideburns, sticking straight out, framed a hawk face that broke into a beautific smile, one of warmth and comfort.

Claude gaped at the transformation when a soft, assured voice asked, "How can I assist you, son?"

"Jessie Mae, over to Clarke's, told us you'd help us on up the road, Reverend." The preacher appraised them, his silence leading Claude to explain. "We need to reach Dalton to escape the rebs."

Duckworth's reaction surprised the planter. "You use fine words, young man. It's a credit to your schooling."

Claude smiled and bowed his head. "I thank you, sir," he said. "Now, can you help us?"

"Who are you?"

"Lieutenant Claude Shaw, 7th Ohio, and Hannibal Shaw, my friend. We escaped at Columbia."

Duckworth's quizzical grin led Claude to settle his uncertainty. "I'm dyed black with walnut dye, Reverend. It's safer that way, since I can pass as a Negro."

The Reverend bobbed his head up and down. "Two others like you came through months ago. From a Granny Mandy I think, at Columbia."

"She de one," Hannibal said, his chuckles bubbling out. "She dye Claude."

Duckworth slapped his thigh and burst into laughter, finally suppressing it to a soft snigger. "It surely does fool the rebs."

A noise back down the trail cut off his talk. Duckworth whipped around in alarm while the fugitives aimed their rifles. His body tensing as if ready to run, the preacher scanned the trace and brush.

"You've not been followed, Lieutenant?" he asked.

"We may have two man hunters after us," Claude replied, "the Minns from Columbia."

The Reverend's mouth settled back into a grim line and his face twisted in agony. "I met Minns once over at Demorest's," he said mournfully. "He was hanging a man. I tried to stop him to pray. He just laughed."

"Dat's de Minnses, Reverend," Hannibal said, then, emphatically, "Dey mean."

Duckworth turned toward the bushes when a deer showed in the trail below them. "Come along," he said, beckoning them to follow. "We'll go on over to my cabin. I'll soon have us on the road west."

"Us?" Claude asked. His question brought a surprising answer.

"I do all the escapes myself. The rebs hate to interfere with a man of the cloth."

An hour of subtle trails convinced the planter of the preacher's canniness. He wove through the maze of forest on a gradual circle to the west, always treading softly and with confidence. The astonished planter followed, with Hannibal shaking his head at the easy, yet hidden passage into wild country. Breakout onto an overgrown forest road led to better footing and faster travel. A quick hike to a clearing followed, one smelling of smoke. Its tiny, almost invisible cabin rested in a thicket of small trees that backed up against the steep face of a hillside. The preacher waved at the few Negroes who shouted greetings and loped toward them. A black hearse stood near the cabin, with two horses on picket ropes in the meager pasture.

"We'll eat and rest first," Duckworth told the fugitives. "Then we'll lay you out in the coffins."

The noon sun reflected off the pool in the creek, its gurgling, slow travel to the southeast obstructing the passage of the man hunters. Old Blue ran down the bank and jumped in with a splash. Underwater only an instant, he popped up and swam to the other side. When the men did not join him, he flung himself eagerly into the water and paddled across to the bank beside them. Jared shied away and swore at the shower when Blue shook water off his dripping coat. The old hound sniffed the breeze, hesitating as he explored a vagary of scent. Unmoved, he padded to the creek and stuck his muzzle down and drank, his protruding tongue making little slurping sounds. Minns and Jared knelt upstream and palmed up the clear water, its coldness refreshing to the travelers.

"Recken we be halfway to Tate, Pa," Jared said, "from what that man tol' us back at the tavern at Dawson's."

"Have to be, boy." Minns pointed at the monumental peak to the northwest. "That big ol' mountain's starin' at us. He said we'd find Oglethorpe to the nawth an' it ain't much more'n five mile off."

"We stop fer grub, Pa?"

Minns sighed and stretched. "Could rest a spell. Up an' down them hills an' that spill over thet bank got me hurtin' some."

"You hurtin', Pa?" Jared laughed, but his chuckling instantly ceased under his father's angry glance. With a sly look, his barbs continued. "First time ever heard you say you're hurtin', Pa. Ain't like yuh."

"We been out too long this time," Minns said. He sighed and shook himself, grumbling about the cold. "Need a hot fire in the cabin an' some o' them stillin's. They'd warm my bones."

"Give it up, Pa. Let's git on back down to Columbia."

Minns scar commenced its fiery rise into prominence as he shook his head. "Fetch some wood fer a fire," he said sharply. His angry command drove the boy into a scrambling retreat to avoid a blow. The hunter watched as Jared kindled the blaze and searched his possibles sack. "Goin'a eat," Minns said, "then head on west over to Tate. Maybe we hear there 'bout them bastards coming through."

"You fixin' to stop at Tate, Pa?"

"Nope. That tavern keeper at Dahlonega said Josh

Terrell over there's the one to see. He ain't s'posed to be more'n a mile beyond Tate's workin's."

Speared venison chunks soon sizzled over the flames. The boy busied himself with the chores around the fire, feeding dry sticks into the blaze and cooking the meat. He pushed a few chestnuts into the ashes at the side and covered several mud-coated potatoes with hot coals. It was a small fire but a blazing one, for the dry wood from an ancient blowdown burned furiously. Both Minns and Old Blue sought its heat, Minns with his left leg stretched close before the blaze and Old Blue on his side, his wet back steaming. Jared fed them the meat and nuts first and filled all to fullness. They rested there while they waited for the potatoes to bake. The mealy, orange sweets went down with relish an hour later. A cool drink from the creek finished the meal and the welcome rest.

When he headed downstream, Minns' sharp intake of breath turned into a curse. "God damn that leg," he said. "It's got to act up right when we gittin' close. I kin feel that Yankee."

"That limp jest goin'a git worse, Pa," Jared said, reproachfully. "You ain't been tendin' it." His patience broke and he shouted at Minns, "Give it up, Pa!"

Splat! Thunk! Minns' slap was followed by a fist in Jared's face and the hunter's slurred curses. "Goddamn yuh, boy! We ain't goin'a do it, you hear. You jest shut yer damned mouth. That Yankee kilt Jeremy an' I ain't goin'a rest 'til he be dead."

"But, Pa —"

Minns knocked him down and put his rifle muzzle on the boy's chest, then cocked his piece. Jared's frightened eyes looked up at his father.

"Don't shoot me, Pa," he pleaded, his voice quavering. "I won't say no more 'bout it." Tears ran down his cheeks and he lay still, his face white. He watched apprehensively while the muzzle alternately withdrew and then poked him in the chest.

The hunter's congested face formed a fearsome backdrop for the jagged scar, but its crimson swelling gradually subsided into its normal whitish line as Minns' rage cooled.

Finally he withdrew the rifle and motioned the boy erect, but he kept the muzzle aimed squarely at Jared's middle. Minns' soft, strangling voice was barely audible, issuing as it did through his clenched teeth.

"You buck me one more time, boy, an' I leave yuh fer the buzzards. You ain't no Minns lessen yuh even the score fer yer brother."

Jared ignored the threat and smoothed over the fuss. "Let's go, Pa," he said submissively. "We git on after those 'scapes."

Travel downstream proceeded slowly, with Blue sweeping the ground ahead and to the sides. The old dog snuffled and snorted at an occasional hole but always went on, never striking. Minns' slight limp was no impediment to their progress but he took special care of his footing, evading debris and other than flat steps. A half-mile walk ended at a fine ford where the creek spread shallowly over some gravelly bottom. They did not stop but splashed across to the other side. Old Blue sprawled in the shallows and lapped water while the men forged on. He loped ahead of the walkers a few minutes later, his bony ribs sticking out.

"Gotta stuff more fat inter Old Blue, Pa," Jared said. "Looky at them ribs o' his. Ol' dog's right poor."

"Keep yer eyes sharp fer a deer an' we feed 'im up ternight," Minns said. "Better if we could find a fat hog. That'd do us."

The cool weather invigorated them as they swung along on the trace toward Tate that easy afternoon. The road wound through the hills guarding Mount Oglethorpe, the latter's majestic bulk diverting the trace wide around it. When the sun had shifted well west, Minns paused for a drink at a spring and a renewal of his chaw. He groaned as he sank onto a log beside Jared, but his temper was easy, friendly to the boy.

"That ol' mountain 'most behind us," he said, happily. He clapped his son on the back. "I ain't mad at yuh, boy. But it shore rankles me we can't find that Yankee. Ain't nobody we seen on the trace know nothin'."

"We'll git 'im, Pa. Him an' that nigger."

"Look fer somethin' we kin use fer vittles, boy, case we

don't git ter Terrell's."

Jared nodded and trotted up the trace, well in advance of his father. A large grove of hardwood trees covered the next ridge. He heard the gobble off the trail before he was close to the the crest of the hill. Easing along slowly with his rifle ready, he stole into the deep forest, slinking from tree to tree, with Old Blue close behind him. The trailing Minns hurried to join up when the calls grew numerous. His heavy breathing whistled in his throat when he paused beside his son.

"Keerful," Jared whispered. "We kill us two if we's quiet."

They had frozen into stands behind a large oak when the turkey flock rattled the leaves. A flash of barred feathers showed through the hardwoods. The birds were coming right toward them, scratching up the duff and pecking at the turned nuts.

"Ready, Pa?" Jared asked, when he had a good bead on a turkey.

"Yes, boy."

The two rifles spoke as one. Two gobblers flopped and thrashed about in their deaththroes, beating their wings futilely. They did not hear their flock go thundering up through the trees as the rest scattered.

Consumption of the soft, raw livers refreshed the two hunters. Old Blue greedily swallowed pieces of the hearts and gizzards, tough meats but full of energy. He belched and wagged his tail and grinned, then begged for more, but Minns drove him off with a curse. The hound ran on ahead without waiting while the two men slung their possibles sacks and picked up the birds. Minns swung the heavy body of one gutted turkey onto his back, its feet tied with rawhide in a loose loop. Drawing the thong over his shoulders, he fastened the leather to his belt to leave his hands and rifle free. "We'll take the birds to Terrell," he said. "He hates the Yankees an' niggers bad 'ccordin' to that taverner. Maybe he heerd o' them 'scapes."

Jared nodded and hustled after the dog, his father limping along behind. Heavily burdened, they headed for Terrell's at a slow pace as the heat from the afternoon's sun grew weaker and the wind cooled.

Gabe and Hester had followed Cleve out of their sheltered cabin west of Dahlonega in early morning, after word had come from runners that the trail to Dawson's was clear of the Minnses. Cleve led them away from his refuge at a fast lope, the turnoff to Nelson's trace gained by the time the sun reached its nooning. They had passed few travelers on the road, the fugitives striking into the woods when any were seen ahead. One family in a buggy shouted at them when surprised at a sharp turn, a good ambush site where the road curved around a steep face with thick trees. The man pulled up hastily and ran into the forest behind them. He fired a pistol several times, but its balls whistled by without effect. The encounter frightened them off the trail for another mile before they crept back and waited, only re-entering when Cleve decided the way was empty. Farther along, a pleasant glade and spring lay a half mile off the crossing to Nelson's. Cleve's smile welcomed them to his small stopping place, a hidden park in the wilderness.

"It be safe an' quiet," he said, reassuring them. "Ain't nobody come dis far off de trace."

Gabe gathered small, brittle twigs while Cleve took Hester to a sheltered trickle of water out of a tiny pool. The lovely, round spring was overgrown with cress and bordered by green moss.

"De water col' an' good, Hester," Cleve said, after he dipped up a handful and noisily swallowed it. "Leave you here while we light de fire."

She made her simple ablutions at the spring, her few minutes in the quiet, peaceful forest satisfying to the girl. "Take keer o' Hannibal," she prayed, while she knelt at the water. "We git ter de free lan'."

A tiny, hot fire blazed when she returned. Little smoke trailed up from the dry wood Gabe had searched out. Spitted bacon sizzled and dripped grease into the flames. Cleve spread a small cloth on a nearby level spot and placed some pone, cold, boiled sweet potatoes and apples on the sheet. The boy hummed a spiritual as he worked, now and then breaking into song. With the food laid out, he placed a knife by the potatoes, then joined Gabe at the fire.

"Ain't much," he said, "but good. We got plenty ter last 'til Nelson's."

"How fur, Cleve?" Gabe asked from his squat by the fire. He turned the sticks of meat. The strips of pork answered by showering drops of flaring grease into the flames.

"Bout fifteen more mile an' two mo' ribbers." Cleve's praying mantis frame stretched and his joints popped. "Ain't bad travelin' if we don' cross too many movin' on de trace. Hills ain't so big. Make it easy by dark."

"Who we see dere?" Hester asked. The girl stood beside the lanky youth, her turned-up face at his chest.

He patted her head and shoulder. "Probably Aunty Mittie. She smart. An' she he'p yer."

"She know where Hannibal be?"

The boy silently pondered the question. Her jig of his sleeve and impatient face prodded him to reply.

"She know," he said, "if he come over from Blackshear's." Cleve shook off her restraining hand and pulled up all the sticks, then rested them on the leaves next to the cloth. He sat down and patted together a pile of leaves next to him, and urged her to join him. Offering her a stick of meat, he said, "We eat, we git dere faster."

Their simple dinner done, they headed down the trace toward Nelson's Tavern. Hester's complaints increased as the sun fell in the sky and the wind grew colder. Its sharpness became more biting as the day wore on toward dusk. They had been delayed at another crossroads for almost an hour by the passage of a small body of troops, a grousing, straggling line that slowly headed north.

"Gwine jine de rebs up in Tennessee," Cleve told them. He spat contemptuously as the soldiers filed past the junction. His whispered remarks continued as they lay in the thicket of the hillside. "Dey all leavin' dis side o' 'lanta goin' ter de nawth. Ol' Hood over in Alabama and de Yankees cut 'em off. Dese goin' up west o' de big mountain."

It was half-dark when Cleve led them to a short row of cabins. Afterglows of light in the west shined orange and purple in the sky and firelight showed through oiled openings in cabin walls. An acrid scent of wood smoke blanketed the cluster of huts and the cries of happy, playing children pealed out, silenced when they discovered the approaching party. The runaways collected children like the Pied Piper as they walked along the quarters. Their passage stopped at a larger cabin in the center of the row, one with at least two rooms.

"Aunt Mittie here," Cleve told them and pounded on the door. "We see if she he'p."

A frightened, low voice and shuffling could be heard behind the panel. Whispering inside the cabin increased as the door bar slammed down tight. A faint, "Who dere?" barely reached them.

Cleve pounded again. "It's Cleve, Aunty. From Granny Ella up ter Demorest's."

The bar scraped when it rose from its slots and the door swung back a few inches. A wizened, wrinkled face peered through the opening, a great spray of wild, reddish-gray hair offsetting freckled, amber skin. Beads hung from the woman's ears and two copperish circles surrounded her neck. The short, fat figure was enclosed in a sack, shapeless and untied at the waist.

"See, Aunty," Cleve said, pushing forward. "It's me an' my frens." He leaned toward the Negress and whispered so no one could hear inside the cabin. "Dey's 'scapes an' need he'p."

Aunty Mittie swung the door wide and shooed off the small children as she ushered the fugitives into her cabin. She slammed the door closed with a bang behind them and dropped the bar. It was then that the women came out of the shadows of the other room and two small faces peeked around the frame of the inner door.

"Dishere's Henrietta an' dis Delcy," Aunty said. "Dey come in by wagon." She looked hard at Cleve's party, her suspicion evident in her tone. "Who dey?"

"Hester an' Gabe from over past Calhoun's, Aunty. Aimin' fer Dalton."

Enticing smells from the steaming pot on the hook at the fireplace drew them all together. The women chattered away as they helped Aunty ready the food, while the men sat on stools and leaned against the cabin walls and just looked on. Satisfying the children and all the hungry travelers almost emptied the pot, its vacant maw replenished with Aunty's peeled potatoes and turnips. A few dried peppers and onions added to the spicy atmosphere of the cabin. Cleve tossed in the last of his bacon, its meat and grease increasing the fragrance of the new batch of stew. The pungent air thickened with vapors from the steaming pot and redolent travelers, little able to wash. Heat and the stifling, moist air soon made everyone relax and sweat; subversion by the warm cabin increased the lassitude engendered by full bellies. Languor and cosy camaraderie overcame the Negroes' fears and inhibitions. Aunty Mittie and the fugitives gossiped away the evening while the children slept.

Bump, bump, bump. Duckworth's hearse entered another stretch of ruts and rocks on the road. The wagon's large wheels rode up over the projecting clumps of mud and cobbles, then fell into holes in the trace, wracking the vehicle violently as it bounced along. Claude rocked back and forth in his coffin, enduring the painful knocks and the din of the creaking travel. Dim light filtered through the air holes in the bottom planking. He swore silently as the coffin thumped him during the hearse's side to side lurches and added to his sore spots from their long flight. God damned poor way to escape, he thought, hid in a damned coffin. And all the while a jackleg preacher up on the seat spouting gospel to passersby, while his man clucked to the team and reined them along the trace. But he had to admit it was a slippery way to get them past the rebs. Posing as dead killed near Atlanta, veterans going to the family burying plot up near Jasper and the white stone.

The arm had been almost too much. He had to admit, though, that loading a stinking piece of blown up reb into the rough-pine casket was a master stroke. The stink was so bad that no militia would dare open the coffin. His smelled worse than the one put in Hannibal's box. Claude had protested when Duckworth ordered him into the coffin. The wide-bodied, black hearse waiting to carry them chilled his heart and gave him the shudders. Its glass sides let all inspect the contents of the vehicle. And when the preacher took the wrapped bundle and tossed it into Claude's coffin, he had nearly fainted from the smell. Hannibal had rolled his eyes and said a prayer, then clamped his eyes shut and held his nose. His own protests had erupted in vain.

"The Lord will provide, Claude," Duckworth had told him. The preacher's angelic smile as he quoted the scriptures shamed the angry planter into silence and a grudging forgiveness. Folding his hands over his heart, Duckworth grinned, his pious mien offsetting his humor. "These are for you and Hannibal to scare off the rebs. Now lie flat while we seal you in."

Claude's fear of the coffin tormented him as the journey grew long and he tired from the continuous buffeting. Plank and psychic prisons confined him and drove him into a state of almost unbearable anxiety. Trapped within the coffin's darkness, he could do nothing but wait, while his mind feverishly invented disasters, ones in which he would suffer. Hoofbeats and a loud challenge resurrected his sanity when he was near breaking, almost ready to shout out for freedom. He reckoned it was late afternoon, and that they must be near Nelson's, from the rapid advance of the team over all those bumps and turns. But the abrupt, chilling command came as a frightening shock.

"Hold up!" a voice shouted.

"Whoa!" Duckworth's helper sawed on the reins and pushed on the foot-brake lever. Brakes shrieked as the hearse creaked to a stop.

A small patrol cantered out of the trees, its Sergeant with his pistol drawn. Three troopers surrounded the hearse at his command, standing easy with the horses but with rifles at the ready.

"Who air yuh?" the Sergeant asked.

Duckworth stood and tipped his hat. "Reverend Rodney Duckworth, sir. And whom am I addressing?"

The preacher was ever formal, Claude realized, as he listened. Duckworth used a deliberately cultivated pose to confound his challengers. And each time he delivered his message with calm confidence. It had been so up the trace with the passersby. His greetings and banter were ever reasoned and always closed with a biblical reference. The planter lay there waiting on the answer, hardly breathing and very quiet, hoping Hannibal would do the same. A curse and gentling of a horse preceded the trooper's answer.

"Hopkins, preacher. Sergeant Hopkins, with the Army of the Tennessee."

The preacher folded his hands and gazed at the troopers with a benign look. "May the Lord bless you and keep you, Sergeant, you and your worthy men. The Confederacy can be proud of you doing your duty." His voice took on a biting edge. "Now what do you want?"

"We're ketchin' stragglers, Reverend. Lot's been desertin', now that Atlanta's taken. The Lieutenant's over to the other trace while we git this side. Need to look to see what yer carryin'."

Duckworth played the indignant preacher and protested vehemently. "You can't do that! These men died in the fighting three days ago. It'd be an abomination if you went rustling through their caskets."

The Sergeant was humble but firm. "Got to see, Reverend. Have your man open the back."

Claude could hear the dismount of several men and their reluctant steps as they gathered at the rear of the hearse. When the back door was opened, explosive curses burst from the Sergeant, castigating Duckworth.

"Jesus Christ, preacher! Why the God damned hell didn't you tell me they was ripe!"

Duckworth's calm tone held to his usual soothing verse. "Never take the name of the Lord, thy God in vain, son. Do you remember your Commandments?"

"Damn it, preacher. I ain't goin'a interfere in the Lord's business, but you didn't have no call to do that." The Sergeant's mournful voice dropped to a near sob and his body trembled. "I don't need no more stinkin' bodies to look on. Done seen too many a'ready. Why'n't you tell me?"

"I told you they were killed three days ago. I don't lie, so you should have known. Now may we go on?"

Creaking leather and stamping of horses' hooves told the fugitives that the troopers were mounted and ready to move out.

The Sergeant's voice was full of gloom when he passed them on. "Bury 'em deep, Reverend," he said sadly. "An' say a prayer fer me. I done had enough family put under in this war. Time it come to an end so's we kin all go home."

"The Lord says, 'I am the resurrection and the light. Whosoever believeth in me shall never die.'"

"You're right, Reverend. I say my prayers."

Duckworth called out to them as the patrol walked its horses away from the hearse. "Keep the Lord with you, Sergeant, you and your men, and you'll make it home."

The hearse's driver stayed on the ground to check the harness until the troopers passed out of sight. Mounting to the seat, he started the team off at Duckworth's nod, his clucks and flipping reins goading the horses into a fast walk.

"We'll be at Nelson's soon and stop for the night," Duckworth said loudly.

Claude sighed in relief at the preacher's welcome news, a promise to release him from the unsettling prison. But urgent necessity overcame his feelings of deliverance from fear. He rolled over in the coffin and fumbled at his belt, no longer able to withhold his need. A stream of water ran out of one of the holes in the bottom of the coffin. Its dribbling passage was accompanied by a relieved, "Ah!"; its loss at once restored his comfort while it added to the muddy spots on the trace.

Stars glistened in the black sky when they hauled up behind the barn at Nelson's. Duckworth's driver slid the coffins onto the dirt on greased plank skids pulled from the hearse. Rolled over, the perforated, hinged bottoms readily came free. Hannibal stood in his coffin and stretched. But Claude jumped out and hopped around, his relaxing contortions accompanied by mumbles about the trip. The fugitives rapidly cleared the stink from their clothes by flailing their arms and beating the cloth.

"Damn!" Claude exclaimed as he took deep breaths of the fresh, windy air. "Didn't know how hard it'd be." He kicked the confining wooden box and laughed at its reverberation. "Coffin's pretty small, Reverend. Think I'll use a big one when I go."

"Don't think of it, son," Duckworth replied. "'There is a time for all things,' is part of our religion. The spirit goes to the Father. The lump of clay needs no fancy box."

"I'se needin' stew, preacher, not no box," Hannibal said. He turned up his nose and sniffed the night breeze. "I smells stew over ter de row dere."

The preacher ignored Hannibal and said, "You find Aunty Mittie, Lieutenant. Go to the double cabin."

"Then what, Reverend?"

"Stay hidden with her all night. I'll be at the big house. I'll see you early, so be ready before the sun is up."

Picking up a worn leather valise, the Reverend walked up the lane toward a big house in a grove of trees, while Claude and Hannibal went toward the cabins. A group of children led them to the door of the larger place, then pounded on the planks with their small fists and called for Aunty Mittie. Hannibal rushed into the cabin when the door cracked and the firelight showed, and made straight for the fireplace and its fragrant pot. Claude edged in behind him, disturbed by the large crowd that hung back from the opening. Silence gave way to shrieks of welcome as Henrietta, Delcy and Hester all ran to Hannibal and threw their arms around him.

Gabe's cheerful face looked out over the surging women surrounding Hannibal. "Howdy, Claude," he said to the amazed planter. Claude stood transfixed, his open mouth speechless, as the giant and Aunty Mittie beckoned to him to join them at the fire.

"They's not gone by here yet, Minns," Terrell said.

His assurance did not satisfy the famished hunter, burdened as Minns was with the scent of the steaming bowl of food before him. Jared fed noisily at the table, Terrell's wife impassive by the kettle at the fireplace. Minns put down his spoon and bowie.

"You got a spy?" he asked.

Terrell's self-satisfied smile turned into a smirk. "Whole bunch owes me 'round here. They goin'a tell me if any escapes 'round the village."

"They gotta go through Tate?"

"No," Terrell replied. "They kin cut over to Nelson's Tavern an' circle 'round on the south trace. Most likely they's passin' by there. Plenty of hands to hide 'em at the works." He reassured Minns when the latter frowned. "I'll hear if they do, Athey. We git word on 'em by mawnin'."

"You have a place we kin lay up? I kin pay fer the keep."

Terrell dismissed the offer with a shake of his head and a hand raised in denial. He stirred his stew, then spooned up a new portion ready to eat. "Ain't no need," he said. "Them turkeys you give us more'n pay. My old lady feed yuh tonight an' in the mawnin'." He took a sip of stew and a bite of bread. His words came out mushy as he chewed, like the dribbles from the sides of his mouth. "You can sleep in the barn. There's good, sweet hay." He waggled his empty spoon at Minns, soup from its edge dripping onto the table. "But no smokin'. Don't want no fire."

Minns picked up his pouch of chewing leaves and held it out. "Ain't never took it up. We chaw, Josh."

Terrell motioned to his wife to refill Jared's empty bowl while Minns attacked his own with the large spoon, spearing pieces of meat with his bowie. The two hunters ate the spiced stew and pone to bursting, the meal's bulk washed down by cool milk. Terrell and the woman watched them feast, her silence broken only by a chuckle when Jared belched and pushed his chair back, then wiped his mouth with the back of his hand.

"Mighty good, Ma'am," he said with a little grin.

The woman smiled at the compliment. Her creased, sweaty face softened, its worn, angular lines transforming into the softer curves of its youthful, smooth beauty, revealing, in that one unguarded moment, what age and Terrell's husbanding had destroyed.

Whining and yelps at the plank door of the house were followed by scratching sounds.

"Shet up, Blue!" Jared yelled. His angry voice quieted the dog's scratching, but the hound's whine continued. The boy picked up his bowl and held it out to the woman. "If you'd fill the bowl heapin' full, Ma'am, I'll feed Old Blue. Mighty hungry old dog an' gittin' thin."

She fished some large chunks of meat out of the pot as

she ladled the stew, then added cornbread on top of the full bowl. Jared carried it gingerly to the door and went outside, but not without difficulty. Old Blue crowded his legs and jumped around him, almost upsetting his balance, until he put the steaming dish in front of the animal. The hound made short work of the hot feed, lapping up spilled drops as he pushed and rattled the empty bowl on the stone at the stoop. Jared tossed him another piece of pone when he sat on his haunches and begged a handout with wet, open jaws and a wagging tail. But Blue gobbled down only one. He nosed a second that the boy offered, then stalked off, leaving the cornbread lying in the dirt.

The old dog visited a nearby tree and then lay down without eating the remaining cornbread. Jared laughed and said, "Guess yer full. Ain't like yuh to turn down pone."

Inside, Minns was taking his leave for the night. When the boy entered, the hunter tossed him a pair of apples, their hard, red fullness promising tart, juicy bites. Minns' pockets bulged from several others. Terrell accompanied them to the barn while his wife watched from the door, its light an invitation to warmth and plenty.

"They's water at the side o' the barn," Terrell said, "case you need it." He pointed to a shine in the starlight, its reflected rays a ready beacon. "Never failin' spring an' pool outen the hill."

Climbing the ladder to the hayloft, the farmer threw down several forkfuls which Minns arranged into a pile. Old Blue didn't wait. He flopped into the middle of the fragrant hay until the hunter kicked him out with a curse and tested its softness. Terrell tossed down more hay until the travelers were satisfied. The farmer grumbled and favored his right leg as he sought the rungs of the ladder. "Ain't been right since that Yank minie ball," he told them, once he was back on the floor of the barn.

"Glad it ain't no worse, Josh," Minns said, sympathetically. He felt of the hay and spread out the pile. "We be jest fine here. An' I'm beholdin' to yuh fer the help."

Terrell shrugged and said, "Glad to git back at them Yanks anytime. Bastards all need killin'." He paused before stomping out the door. "Call you early, Athey. Git you after them niggers once yer fed good."

Minns nodded and leaned his rifle against the rails of a nearby stall. As Terrell left the barn, the hunter sank into the sweet hay, groaning a little and mumbling to Jared. He snored almost before he finished shaping a hollow in the mound of sweet grass.

When the men were well bedded down and Terrell back in his house, Old Blue crept up to the snorers and fitted himself into the curve of Jared's leg. The boy sighed in his sleep and patted him; the old dog's tail thumped out his answer.

Chapter 22

Aunty Mittie

November 22, 1864. Talking Rock, Georgia. Temperature 58\39. Partly cloudy and cold with possibly intermittent light showers. Strong northerly winds to 20 knot gusts. Moon dark.

"Git up, Claude," Aunty Mittie said.

The planter gasped and jumped to his feet at the kick in his side. He swung his head wildly about as his eyes searched the cabin. Only Aunty Mittie faced him, a frightened old woman who paled under the threat from his derringer. Claude uncocked and pocketed it in one easy motion. His chagrin ended in a wry smile and an apology.

"Those Minns got me mighty touchy, Aunty. Don't mean to cause you no trouble, flyin' off like that."

She gurgled, unable to speak until she had cleared her throat and her ashen face had flushed with blood. A trembling palsy of her fingers escalated into spasmodic jerking of her body and limbs. The planter grabbed her when she started to fall.

"Got de trembles, Claude," she said. "Dey bad if I'se scairt sudden like. Can't hardly git 'roun' in de cabin sometimes."

He helped her to her chair in front of the fireplace. The fire was blazing hot and its brisk flames worked on some new logs. As he warmed himself, Gabe came in with an armload of billets and threw them onto a pile at the side of the chimney.

"Gwine be a cold day," Gabe told them. "Maybe rain too, wid lot o' wind." The giant backed up to the fire and warmed his seat and his hands at the same time.

A crash startled them and Claude jumped out with his derringer ready. But it was only the wind driving the door open with a shuddering bang when it struck the cabin wall. Duckworth came right behind with his hat clutched in his hand and white pate shining. His driver wrestled the door closed against the cold, gusty breezes while the preacher sidled up to the warmth.

"It's time to go, Claude," Duckworth said. He held out his hands to the fire and washed them in the heat. "Cold, but the sun's up, bright. It'll treat us to another of God's glorious days."

The planter shivered and moved closer to the hearth, saying, "Feels cold, Reverend, and like rain."

"No, Claude," the preacher replied. "Praise the Lord this day, for his messengers, the cold and wind, restore us from our laziness. The righteous will rejoice."

Duckworth's glance around the cabin stirred Gabe into a fast slide into the other room. His rousting calls soon turned out Hannibal and the three women, followed by Aunty's two grandchildren. Claude stepped away and made room as they all approached the fire, their yawns and rubbed eyes giving way to grumbles. He wondered which woman Hannibal had bedded as they clustered about the big Negro. Each hung onto his clothes and arms and murmured endearments.

Claude covered his grinning mouth with his hand, chuckling at the sight of the possessive women. It had been a surprise to the fugitives that Henrietta and Delcy had abandoned the runaway Negroes to follow Hannibal. Their desire and possessiveness had complicated his promise to Hester. The night before had brought an hour of shouting and catfighting as the three women argued about who owned the man. Sheepishly, but wisely staying silent, Hannibal ate his bowls of stew while they fussed at each other. Aunty Mittie finally had gotten tired of the raucous commotion. The old Negress had jerked the arms of Henrietta and Delcy alike, and had flailed them with her sharp tongue.

"De two o' yuh ain't got no claim ter Hannibal," she said. "He be Hester's man so's you jist let him be."

Her decree had stopped Henrietta's and Delcy's overt cuddling to the Negro. And Hester's triumphant look as she clung to Hannibal imitated that of the cat that got the mouse. But now they were back in the early morning, chasing Hannibal as hard as ever. Aunty's stick raised welts on their backs when she shooed them off.

"Git away from de man!" she said, crossly. Her irritation increased and she struck each of them again. "I tol' yuh he's Hester's. You bof git!"

"Don't know why she so good," Delcy complained.

"Hester gwine wid Hannibal ter de free lan' an' be his woman," Aunty replied. "Man don' need but one woman, so you leave him be."

Duckworth pushed Aunty behind him as he faced the two angry women and smoothed over the troubles.

"You can go with me," he said soothingly. "I know many honorable men who'll be happy to have you."

Henrietta's face brightened and Delcy grabbed the Reverend's hand.

"Where, Reverend?" she asked. "Dey close?"

"Yes, Delcy. They're waiting for you back at Coal Mountain." He prodded them into action. "Now eat quickly so we can get on the road. We need to pass Claude and Hannibal beyond the white stone today."

Aunty Mittie distracted them from Hannibal by reminding them of their bellies. "Delcy," she said, "you dish up de stew. Henrietta he'p. I'se got ter talk ter de Reverend 'bout de trail."

Claude and Gabe joined the plotters when they moved to one side, while the others gathered around the pot on the hearth and attacked the stew. Slurping sounds from the feeding children accompanied Aunty's astounding news.

"Word done come, Reverend, dat de Minns wid Terrell over to Tate. You can't move Claude in de wagon. He got ter go 'round on de south road."

"The Lord will provide," Duckworth piously proclaimed.

"De Lord he'p dose dat he'p demselves, Reverend," Aunty said. Her lined face tightened and her lips curled in a sneer. A mask of hate converted the amiable woman into a dragon. "I'se got plan fer dat Terrell. He hate niggers an' I'se hurt him ever chance I git. He 'bout at de end o' his rope."

Claude's spirits had dropped at the news of the implacable Minns, and his day turned gloomy. The man hunters intended to hound him to his grave. Only one way remained to settle the matter, kill them before they killed him. His soul revolted at killing another man, more dead on top of all those he had fired at in battle. Then the two boys. His heart flip-flopped in pain at the remembrance of the blood and the young bodies. Claude suddenly felt sick, but he pinched himself hard and gulped down the nausea. Unbidden, the Minnses returned to his thoughts. In his heart he knew it was necessary. Just go ahead and kill them, he concluded, his decision to act finally made. It was a watershed for him, a man doing what could not be evaded in order to save his own life. His reverie took him away from the talk of the plotters. Suddenly conscious of his name being bandied about, he bent toward them, intent on their plans.

"We put Henrietta an' Delcy in de coffins," Aunty said. "Dey ain't got no chil'ren o' dey own wid 'em. Claude and' de rest go wid Cleve ter Miss Mary up at Blaine's. Dey think she reb but dat young gal he'p de 'scapes ever'time I send 'em."

"You think she can get them through?" Duckworth asked. He left off his biblical quote in his unthinking hurry.

Aunt Mittie's confident voice joined her vigorous nod. "Sho' kin. Tek 'em on to Granny Eva at de Old Town over on de Coosy Ribber. Dey close ter Dalton, dey gits dere. Eva got ways ter he'p."

The old woman nudged Gabe and pointed to the wall. "Hand me de horn," she said.

Gabe reached for the supporting leather strap and held it out to her. The curved ox horn had been carved into a hunting horn, its tip rounded into a mouthpiece. Scrollwork and hunting scenes decorated its polished surface. Massive striations of black and ivory color blended well with the rawhide strap, a magnificent utility horn to call up dogs or men. Claude was fascinated with the piece, its shape so reminiscent of ones he had used while fox hunting. But its purpose was a puzzle to the Reverend.

"What's that for, Aunty?" he asked.

Aunty's jaw set and her face tightened. Wrinkles formed little spiderwebs at the corners of her eyes. "You ain't never needed he'p a'fo', Reverend," she said grimly. "You needs it on dishere trip an' de horn git it fer yuh."

"You think Terrell will attack me?"

"Not dat Terrell," Aunty replied, contemptuously. Her leathery face crinkled into a scornful grimace. "He got no stomach fer killin'. But dose Minns stop yer at de tight stretch by de talkin' rock place. You 'member de trail, Reverend?"

Duckworth put his forefinger to his right cheek and thought for a moment. "Right where the trace necks down and goes by the deep place in the creek?" he said, waving his finger like he was drawing lines on a map, "and then on into the meadow?"

Aunty nodded. "Dat de place, Reverend. De Minns stop yer right dere in de meadow atter de steep bluff. When dey do, git old Covey here ter blow de horn like dis."

Putting the mouthpiece to her lips she blew two short notes, then a long blast. Even with the little breath of the old woman, the horn awakened with rolling, musical notes. Its loud, compelling peals resounded in the cabin; awed silence followed. Hannibal came over at the blast, leaving the women to clean up the mess and to replenish the vegetables and water in the pot.

The Reverend turned to his driver and asked, "Can you do that Covey?"

"Sho' kin, Reverend," the driver replied. "Done blowed de fox horn passel o' times." He reached for the horn and hung the strap around his neck. Blowing softly, he repeated the notes.

"'member, Reverend," Aunty Mittie said, waggling her finger in his face. "Soon's you see dem Minns, blow de horn. De men come runnin' ter he'p."

Duckworth was mystified, Claude could see. He didn't

seem to understand that Aunty Mittie could protect him against the Minnses.

"What men?" Duckworth asked.

"'scapes, Reverend. Hid out. Dey got knives an' dey settle de Minns if you want."

Duckworth shuddered. "The Scriptures say, `Thou shalt not kill,' Aunty. I couldn't do that."

The old woman's face flushed and grew grim; its skin tightened into leather stretched over magnificent cheekbones. Regal in her flashing eyes and suddenly expanded appearance, she fluffed up just like an aggressive chicken asserting its dominance, except this time the blood of African Ashanti kings came through when she flung the gauntlet at him.

"You give de order, Reverend," she said coldly. "De boys do de killin' fer yuh."

He shook his head in defiance. "I'll kill no one," Aunty, nor order their deaths. The Lord will take care of us."

Old Covey fondled the horn as he stood behind the preacher. Claude watched the Negro, thrilled at his reaction to the old woman's offer. Covey's face followed Aunty intently as she pronounced sentence on the Minnses. It was as if Aunty had transferred authority to him, not the Reverend, Claude saw. Subtle, but the understanding flashed between them in their stares, Aunty giving Covey his instructions and her order. He'll try to kill the Minns, Claude thought, as he listened and searched the Negroes' faces. Don't matter what the Reverend does, Covey'll see to the Minns.

The parties separated after Gabe and Hannibal helped Henrietta and Delcy into the coffins and loaded the boxes into the hearse. Their lamentations and tears at parting from Hannibal had changed to curses when they smelled the long dead rebel parts. The preacher and Aunty had talked the women into the coffins, with the old woman's final order delivered in a threatening tone.

"Don' you mek no noise, you hear?"

Muffled curses answered her but the complaints soon subsided into silence.

Claude enveloped the Reverend's right hand in both of

his and pumped it gently as he looked him straight in the eye. "I thank you for the help, Reverend," he said softly. "And I wish you well." His warning followed. "Be careful of those Minns. They're killers."

Duckworth shrugged off the thanks and the danger. "Luke said, `we have done that which was our duty to do.' Don't you worry about the Minns. The Lord will provide."

Climbing up on the seat next to Covey, he waved goodbye. The confined women remained quiet when the hearse started out of the lane, though the wagon's creaks and jolts disturbed the peace of the morning. Covey sang as he flipped the reins to spur on the team. The Reverend joined him in the clean, morning air, their old time and well remembered verses carrying away in the wind.

"Say, brothers, will you meet me,
Say, brothers, will you meet me,
Say, brothers, will you meet me,
On Canaan's happy shore?"

Claude marveled at the cheerful Reverend and his faithful follower. Covey always in the background, a silent servant, ever there and ready to assist. The Reverend, with his unshaken faith in good works, helping any who came by. He could only wish them a safe journey and pray, "Oh God, protect them," as they rode away.

Aunty Mittie jolted him back to his need to leave. "Cleve take yer over by Miss Mary's," she said. "You's got ter move quick."

Gathering up Hester and a sack of potatoes from the cabin, Claude hurried back to Aunty's side. Cleve was bent over her, listening, as she grasped his wrist and issued her instructions. Claude heard only part, but paid close attention not only to her wise counsel but also to her directions. Finished, she sent Cleve off to the trace. They all jumped at her orders, Claude realized, as he trailed his rifle and trotted after the guide. She's a powerful woman, he thought. Got 'em all under her thumb. Except the Reverend. He chuckled at the thought of the man, then realized his neglect. Calling to Cleve to stop, he ran back to the woman in the cabin doorway.

"I thanks yuh, Aunty," he said, humbly. "You saved us

all an' I'm in yer debt." Grabbing her by the body, he squeezed her tight and raised her heavy bulk off the ground before planting a big kiss on her cheek. "I'll be back atter the war to he'p yuh like you've he'ped me."

Fussing camouflaged her delighted smile when he set her down. Her hands flew up to her hair and then hid her face. "Go 'long, wid yer, boy," she whispered, crying. "Git on up ter de free lan'."

She waved goodby when they passed the point of woods at the turnoff. His last vision was of another protective woman, a squat, fat figure at the door of a decrepit cabin, with her two grandchildren clinging to her skirts.

Minns dunked his head in the cold spring water, blowing bubbles and rubbing his face and beard vigorously. He flung drops around like Old Blue when he emerged and tossed his mane, then wiped off loose droplets with his hands to finish his wash. The scent of frying bacon drifted down from Terrell's farmhouse and accentuated his hunger. He sniffed the breeze and then went back to the barn, emerging with the rifles. Jared had followed his father to the outhouse and then to the spring after Terrell had waked them a few minutes before. Old Blue had made his usual morning run at the trees around the farmstead, first to snuffle and then to deposit his markers. A few local dogs answered his challenging barks. Terrell's dog stiff-legged around the alert Blue, both their hackles raised, until a truce was established.

Jared combed his fingers through his hair and shook off the cold water. "That bacon smells good, Pa," he said. He scooped up a few palmsfull from the pool, relishing its fresh taste. "Good to drink some water ain't got mud in it."

"We check the guns first," Minns reminded him, "then git to the grub an' Terrell. Hope his woman's made some pone and bacon to take with us."

Yellowish rays of the sun penetrated a high haze but were bright enough to cast shadows of fast moving clouds. A few minutes in the cold, early light satisfied Minns, his weapons receiving more attention than his person. His greasy buckskins showed the residues of weeks of chase, their surfaces blackened from camp smoke and the dirt that joined the grease he had wiped onto the leather. Not much better than his father, Jared's figure added to their imitation of the animals they hunted, creatures of the forest and not of towns or Terrell's.

The door creaked when they entered the house. Terrell sat at the table, munching on a slab of pone. He motioned them to stools at the side of the well-stocked surface. It already held greasy bacon in a wooden bowl and fried eggs on trenchers at their places. When their stools screeched on the floor as they bellied up to the food, Terrell's wife picked up a skillet at the fire and knocked its circle of browned pone onto the table. She broke the hot bread in half and added the pieces to the eggs on the trenchers, then pried beeswax from the top of a small, earthenware jar. The crock went on the table between between the two hunters.

"It be good honey," she said defensively, eying her husband. The woman held out a wooden spoon but her nervous hand dropped it on the table. She shrank back involuntarily as if expecting a blow.

Minns smiled when he picked up the utensil, though his scar twisted his cheek grotesquely. "'preciate it, Ma'am," he said politely.

The woman's worn face relaxed and her tension gave way to an answering grin. Wiping her hands on her apron, she turned back to the hearth and cracked another skillet full of eggs. Their sizzle and scent were ignored by the Minnses as they attacked the food before them.

When they had eaten to sufficiency and the complimentary belches, Jared took a big bait out to Old Blue. Terrell smoked his pipe and stared at Minns, saying nothing, his message unfathomable. The hunter eyed Terrell speculatively, meeting his silent stare, before he opened the purse at his belt. He searched through some clinking pieces, then recovered a small gold coin and gave it to the woman. She gasped in delight and turned its yellow surfaces back and forth to the firelight. The polished faces sparkled and entranced her. But Terrell glowered at the far end of the table.

"Don't need no pay, Minns," he growled. "Yer boy an'

you my guestes."

Minns' shrewd glance took in Terrell's fury at the infringement on his hospitality and his jealousy about a gift to his woman. The present transcended the bounds of the man's castle, everything within under his ownership and control. The hunter's contrite apology glossed over his transgression. "Ain't meanin' no harm, Josh. Jest that we be grateful fer the fine food, an' your good woman he'ped us. Give her a piddlin' present." His polite genuflection continued. "If you don't mind o' course?"

Mollified by the plea, Terrell nodded assent to the woman. Her face had frozen with fright when Terrell's sharp voice disapproved of the gift. She smiled at the reprieve, and slipped the coin into a pocket in her sweater.

"Now which way you think we should take to cut the trail o' those 'scapes?" Minns asked.

Terrell puffed up, then leaned forward to give the hunter the report of his spies. "They's travelin' with Reverend Duckworth, hid in coffins."

"No!" Minns exclaimed, his face a mask of unbelief. "In coffins?" As Terrell's head bobbed up and down, he added, "Reverend Duckworth? The one over to Coal Mountain?"

"Yep," Terrell replied. "He's jest a jackleg preacher. Goes 'roun' preaching hellfire an' damnation. Lot's o' brimstone, too." He laughed derisively. "Got hisself a black hearse bigger'n a farm wagon so's he can carry more'n one. Buries folks and reads over 'em. 'ceptin this time he's got the scapes hid in the wagon, takin' 'em to'ard the white stone."

"How you know that?"

Terrell ignored Minns' question. "You git on up the trace fast as you kin," he emphasized, "'til you come to the talking rock place where the old Injun town was." He leaned farther over the table toward Minns, his gleaming eyes intent. "You can't miss it, Athey. The trace runs right 'round the big bluff beyond and the creek cuts the way down to one wagon."

Minns nodded thoughtfully and asked, "How fur a piece is it?" He absentmindedly picked up another chunk of pone and nibbled on it after adding some honey.

"bout ten mile," Terrell replied. "They stayed over 'roun'

Nelson's last night. Got long way to git there, cuttin' up from the south." He paused and looked thoughtfully at Athey's high, coppery cheekbones and black hair. "Injun 'em from the brush jest like those old Cherokees uster. Kill the preacher first. He ain't nothin' but trouble 'roun' these parts."

"Don't hold with killin' men o' God," Minns said. "It don' seem right."

Terrell spat out his warning in a slighting tone. "You don't shoot 'im first, he fox yuh."

Minns pondered the comment while he picked at a few remnants on his trencher. He waved away more pone offered by the woman. Terrell watched him in silence, leaving the hunter to sort out his thoughts. Terrell's wife had come over with two large pones for their possibles sacks and a slab of uncooked bacon before Minns passed sentence.

"We kill him fer yuh. Can't have no preacher gittin' in the way o' settlin' with that Yankee."

With their possibles sacks enriched with the food from the hearth and swollen with a dozen apples each, Minns and Jared took their leave of Terrell. He smiled when they struck out on the trace to the west at a fast pace, pleased that the Minnses would remove an old annoyance. Old Blue was running in his usual circle to the fore when they disappeared from view.

Terrell laughed. "Goddamn yuh, Duckworth," he said triumphantly, "you won't be botherin' me no more."

His approach to his kneeling wife was stealthy. The woman started up fearfully from the kitchen hearth when she heard the scrape of his shoe beside her. Glaring at her in silence, he held out his hand, its demanding surface in front of her eyes. She placed the shining, yellow coin in his palm, her lined face distraught and her eyes misting into tears as he put it in his purse.

Cleve avoided Tate. He ran them quickly up the south trail into the heavy timber that covered the steep hills to the west. Once on the ridgeline, he followed the high ground, descending into saddles between the peaks, but keeping out of sight. His gait, with his spindly, grasshopper legs, made the rest trot to keep up as they sweated up and down the slopes. Hester lagged at the tail of the column; the men stopped occasionally to let her catch them. They had already drunk at one spring when she trotted into the group of resting fugitives and flung herself down by the pool. After a moment of gasping rest, she rolled over and rose to her knees. Her bosom heaved while she washed away the sweat beading her dripping face and then rejoined them on the ground.

A little delay and rest revived the girl. She sat up and sighed after her cleansing and recovery and took in some sharp, deep breaths. "It's col'," she said, shivering in the wind, "but I burnin' up wid de runnin'. You got ter git on dis fast, Cleve?"

"Right fur piece yet ter Blaine's," he said. "Miss Mary knows yer comin'. Aunty send a boy soon's I tell 'er 'bout yuh. She be waitin'."

"Take it slower, Cleve," Claude cautioned. His sympathy for the girl hid the ache in his calf from the nearly healed bayonet wound. He wasn't limping yet but his leg cramped bad on the upslopes.

Cleve's unsmiling face maintained its smooth composure as he glanced from one fugitive to another and presented his ultimatum. "You want ter git ter Blaine's, den hurry atter me. I bring yer dere t'day, an' safe."

A few minutes more rest for the girl were all he'd allow. She sweated and cursed when he left at his half-trot, but followed the trailing Gabe, his offer to carry her refused.

Three hours of hard travel took the fugitives well to the northwest, their winding path difficult and tiring. They were delayed by another meager detail of soldiers at a place where a small creek cut the trace west. Bushes hid them while they surreptitiously watched the crossing. The sloppily marching men splashed right through without slowing. Their wet shoes picked up gluey masses of dirt on the other side and added to the soldiers' burdens. The fugitives could hear the curses, but the line never faltered.

"We got ter ford de crick fo' turning west," Cleve whispered. "Soon's dey's past."

Hester dozed while they waited, with Gabe's coat covering her. The fugitives dallied until long after the soldiers' noises had died away. Birds were calling, giving an all clear, when they finally descended to the creek. Cleve dashed to the other side, his feet throwing sprays of water. He avoided the sticky mud of the far trail and rapidly disappeared into the trees and brush on the next upslope. Except for Hester, the others rushed across behind him. Gabe carried the reluctant girl through the cold water but she fought clear on the other side and pushed him away. She hesitated, fussing, until the racket of the travelers was very faint, then straightened her dress and ran after the others. Another mountain slope and crest to the west tired them as they hurried on. Their journey took them to its heights. It was open, covered by old burn that allowed a magnificent view of the western lands. Cleve pointed out the stream at the foot.

"Dat de east branch o' de Talkin' Rock Crick. We go down dere and cross. Den Blaine's ain't too fur."

He slid and slipped down the slope as he led them through the forest to the bottom. They halted in a clear space on the creek bank and waited on the tiring Hester. She had just joined them when a hunting dog bugled far away to the south, its yelps carrying across the tops. Hester started and sought Hannibal's protective arm.

"Dat sound like de Minns' dog," she said, her body shaking. "It Old Blue! He atter us."

"Can't be, Hester," Hannibal said. He hugged her close. "De Minns gone west from Tate's an' ain't nowheres 'roun' here. Dat jist some ol' dog runnin' a deer."

Hannibal's explanation failed to calm her shivering fear, a dismay that broke out into sniffles and laments. The girl's crying fit and wails of doom infected Cleve. He was unable to be still, pacing to and fro as his agitation increased. But though his body trembled and his brow furrowed in doubt, his decision was sharp and clear.

"Git in de crick and wade down 'bout a mile," he told them. "Don't grab nothin' from de bank. Den Gabe carry Claude, an' Hannibal tote Hester on t'other bank. We slide on over ter de trail ter Blaine's fo' dey put down. Fox dat ol' dog if he come atter dis chile."

"You done dis a'fo', Cleve?" Hannibal asked. He held the girl against him and stroked her back.

"Twicet de dogs atter me when I come thoo. De ribber an' carryin' throwed 'em off bof times."

The fugitives felt along the irregular bottom as they worked their way in a straggling line. Hester had tied her skirts up about her bosom, so the cold water on her bare skin offset her heat from the hard work. Cleve took his time in the current, making sure of his footing, and his sharp eyes missed nothing. Attuned to the forest, the men listened to the chirps from the small birds while they waded the stream and the two fugitives were carried in the portage. The pale sun lay well down in the sky when they turned into the trace leading past Blaine's. Cleve's slow stalk, once they were headed for Miss Mary's, covered the easy slopes in another hour. They only had to hide once, when hoofbeats in the road drove them into the brush before the rider flashed by.

"That was a Yankee!" Claude burst out.

His belated recognition came too late, as the trooper galloped around a bend in the road and was hidden from them. His hoofbeats rapidly receded into the distance. Cleve tackled the planter to keep him from dashing into the road and grabbed at the open mouth ready to shout after the man. When the skinny guide had trouble holding the thrashing planter, Gabe jumped on Claude's back, pinioned him, and drove his face down into the leaves.

"Jist a reb wid some Yankee kit, Claude," Cleve whispered. "De sojers been doin' dis 'cause dey can't git nothin' from de rebs. De Yankee uniform warm."

"You gwine be quiet?" Gabe asked. The giant's rasping rumble in the Claude's ear was answered by the planter's struggling upheaval. Unable to throw them off, he finally gave in and wiggled his head in agreement.

Another mile of cautious woods' travel, hidden from the road, led them to a narrow lane, the way overshadowed by a small ridge that sheltered a lush valley. Except for the thick, still green pasture, which held a few milk cows, the fields were covered with the stubble left from harvesting. A two story house sat well back in a grove of large trees that bordered the pasture. The lane ended at the dwelling's inviting porch, which faced a large grassed lot running down to a barn next to the pasture fence. No cabins graced the side of the clearing but a corncrib and spring house were handy to both structures.

"Ain't no slaves here," Cleve told them. The guide's laconic comment confirmed Claude's own conclusion.

The fugitives moved stealthily along the toe of the forested slope to approach the open ground, slinking from cover to cover in their caution. Cleve lay down behind some brush at the edge, his limber-jack frame stretching out and joining the skinny limbs of the bushes. The other fugitives ranged beside him, while the planter and Hannibal checked their pieces and readied for any trouble.

Late afternoon sunlight broke through the clouds over the western ridge that shaded the magnificent hollow. Weak, yellowish rays bathed the farm but brought no warmth to the fugitives. Shadow patterns changed rapidly as the clouds scooted by and sunbeams marched over the grass and porch.

"Mighty pretty place, Cleve," Claude said, admiringly. He grunted approvingly as his practiced eyes took in the well kept nature of the buildings and the look of order about the place. "These people are farmers."

"Dey ain't no plantation owners, Claude, dat's fer sure. Do dey own work and work harder'n any fiel' han'."

"That pasture usually have the high grass this late?"

"It's warm in dishere holler, Claude. Hol' de good grass 'most ter de bad col'."

Their attention shifted from the pasture when a figure walked around a corner of the barn. It was dressed in pants but rolled its hips like a woman and wore a head scarf. The small woman carried a wooden pail in one hand and swung it back and forth as if empty. She stopped at the corncrib and hung the bucket from a peg. One or two pigs disturbed the peaceful scene, squealing in noisy competition behind the barn.

"Dat's Miss Mary," Cleve said. He fished a short stick from a pocket and put it to his lips.

Cleve's willow whistle trilled its reedy call over the flat, an alarm in the midst of the bird calls. The woman instantly halted. She glanced furtively about, her tense body and raised head imitating the deer alerted at the far end of the pasture. The two relaxed together when no danger threatened. Mary went into the house, emerging a few minutes later with a pair of gloves. She picked up an axe and a bucksaw at a chopping block, its surroundings void of billets, and headed for their part of the woods.

"Ain't nobody ter home but her an' her grandpa," Cleve said, admiringly. "Dat girl do ever'thin', Claude. Wood choppin', farmin', huntin' meat, an' she feed good."

He glanced at the planter and poked him. "She make de best woman you could hev, Claude, if you tek 'er 'long."

The planter laughed, tickled that Cleve was matchmaking. And for a white woman to boot. In the middle of their escape, he mused, amazed that the youth would think such thoughts while they were on the run. Danger threatened and their journey was uncertain, but here Cleve was, planning the future of his friends. The Negro could only be confident that they would make it to the free land.

Claude's good humor and affection erased for a moment his thoughts of cold and danger. He whispered to Cleve as the guide waited for the rapidly approaching woman. "A'ready got a wife an' chil'ren, Cleve. Don' need no mo'."

Mary entered the woods, calling softly for them to stay hidden. She began her wood-chopping on a small, downed maple tree, first stripping the branches with her axe. Chips flew as she worked up the severed branches into firewood, the pieces chunked onto her growing pile. Patter filled the spaces between chops. Her calm, unhurried recital led them through her plans to move the party to the old Peak Casler place, at Old Town on the Coosawattee River. There they would have Granny Eva's protection. By dusk she had piled up a large stack of billets, and had finished her soliloquy. Picking up an armload of firewood, she went for the house.

The fugitives crept into the barn when dusk had given way to intermittent starlight. Black dark did not keep Cleve from the cows. He brought them up to the trough and watered the animals before he separated the milk cow and tied her off in the barn. Claude searched out the girl's pail, then washed it at the trough and handed it to Hannibal. The Negro milked out the fresh cow in minutes, his pail brimming with the creamy liquid. Its surface showed palely against the small light from the stars, the fugitives black blobs around the steaming milk.

"Miss Mary tell us ter drink it all," Cleve said, "so we share turns. Claude, he go first."

The planter got out his small pot and ladled up a brimming portion. It touched him that Cleve, a slave, had chosen him, the white man, to go first. Deferring to his scruples about eating out of the same container as a Negro? He started to put the measure to his lips and was revolted at the thought. These were his friends, risking everything for him, equal in every way. Ashamed, he turned to Cleve and held out the milk. "We share alike, Cleve. You get to go first, then the rest, and I'll be last."

The warm milk disappeared down their gullets in successive gulps, each with a quart of the rich liquid to tide over grumbling stomachs until Mary could get them some bacon or pone. Groans and sighs of pleasure filled the barn as the fugitives sank onto soft mats of fragrant hay. Claude washed the bucket and Cleve turned out the cow, their final chores before they sought their rest. Snores drowned out the movements from the stabled horse, the long day of hiking taking its toll.

"Where the hell are they, Pa?" Jared impatiently asked.

The boy moved restlessly in his cover overlooking the meadow, his apple core tossed aside to join the others nearby. Late afternoon sunlight showed through the brush cover and mottled his buckskins while he stretched and wiped his mouth. Old Blue lay on his back beside him, his legs sprawled out. Alerted by the boy's irritation, the old dog turned over and ambled down to the creek on the other side of the trace. He jumped into the water and lapped up a dollop before racing out and shaking himself.

"God damn yuh, Blue!" Minns yelled, waving his arms. "Git back here!"

Minns' rise and shouted invective exposed him just as the hearse came around the sharp bank on the other side of the spacious flat.

Covey sawed on the reins and shouted "Whoa!, Whoa!" as he pulled the hearse to a screeching stop. Duckworth and the driver cringed at the hunters Aunty Mittie had warned about. The Negro instantly dropped the reins and swung up his horn. "Toot! Toot! Tooooooooooooooooooot!" Covey's three loud blasts from the fox horn rang through the meadow and echoed over the surrounding hills. He was turning the team in a tight circle when Duckworth grasped his arm.

"Stop here, Covey," the preacher said. "They will not harm us."

Still raging at the dog, Minns shot out of the timber on a dead run as he headed straight for the hearse. Jared cocked his rifle and followed to back up his father. A half minute of pounding steps delivered them to the two sides of the hearse, where they circled in close. The hunters pointed their rifles directly at the two men.

"Whar the hell you been?" Minns' said, irritably. His hoarse croak continued. "We been a'waitin' fer yuh most all day."

"Who might you be, sir?" Duckworth said, very formally. "And why do you wait for us?"

The preacher's icy politeness and refusal to acknowledge him infuriated Minns. "Goddamn yuh, Reverend!" he said angrily. "We done met afore an' you know it. I be Athey Minns."

Duckworth smiled, ignoring the profanity and the anger. His angelic tone continued. "So what do you want, sir?"

"I mean to have them 'scapes you got in the wagon. Now git down from thar."

Duckworth placed his hand on Covey's leg and shook his head in disapproval when the Negro started to step over the side. With all the dignity of his costume and his office, he sat straighter and refused.

"I'm the Reverend Rodney Duckworth, Minns, taking two bodies for burial. The Lord said, 'When thy days be fulfilled, thou shall sleep with thy fathers.' Now step aside, sir, and let us pass to the last resting place for these men."

"If you don't step down this minute, Duckworth, we rest the both o' yuh right here."

The preacher looked along the sights of the unwavering rifle barrel, gazing at the fierce eye of the hunter that capped the ominous, black hole of the muzzle. He sighed and swung over the edge of the cockpit, on the ground before Minns in two steps that shook the hearse. Jared took Covey prisoner at Minns' shout and marched him to the back of the wagon on the other side.

"Now open 'er up," Minns said, gesturing with his rifle.

Duckworth straightened his clothes and faced the hunter resolutely, his face set and determined. "I protest, Minns," he said. "This is desecration. The Lord, thy God, says, —"

Minns jammed his rifle butt into the preacher's chin and knocked him down. A gout of blood spurted, Duckworth spraying it around as he rolled on the ground and moaned. Covey whipped out a bandanna and ran to the preacher. The servant dropped to his knees beside the injured man and daubed at the blood. He spouted angry curses until Minns kicked him in the mouth. But the Negro ignored his own hurts and stopped the preacher's bleeding in seconds with the bandanna and compression of his hand. Covey spat out a tooth and gob of blood while he helped the half-conscious Duckworth to stand.

"It jist a cut, Reverend," Covey told him. He held the swaying preacher erect while the bloodied man regained his senses and faced the hunter.

Duckworth's weakened voice protested the intrusion rather than their injuries. "Don't do this, Minns," he said. "The Lord said, 'Vengeance is mine, I will repay.' He'll not countenance your interference."

Minns laughed. "I take my chances, preacher. Now open the hearse."

The stink of long dead parts rolled out of the opened rear door of the vehicle. It drove Jared away from the group, his retching immobilizing him for a moment. Minns cursed in shocked disbelief, then stepped back and covered his nose. His surprised face twisted uncertainly and his rifle hung from his hand.

"I told you they're dead bodies, Minns," Duckworth said. His weak voice was triumphant. "Now let us bury them in peace."

Old Blue's growled and his hackles rose as he pointed the approaching Negroes.

"Look out, Pa!" Jared screamed in alarm. He frantically danced about and waved at the rushing men encircling the hearse. "We got ter run!" The boy dashed to one side where he had a free aim at the intruders.

Eight trotting Negroes were close around the group at the hearse when Jared shouted his warning to Minns. Two more were advancing from the trees. Moving in swiftly and silently, one of the leaders held a cavalry saber and the others had knives. Minns cursed as he leveled his rifle against the peril.

Bang! The man with the sword dropped, blood flying from his face.

Crack! Jared's rifle ball took down the man next to the first, his body crumpling into the dirt.

"Run, Pa!" Jared shouted, as he abandoned the hearse and fled north on the trace. He was running as hard as he could when he shot down a second pursuer. The Negro had cut across to intercept, but fell inertly when Jared emptied his pistol into the man's body.

Old Blue's frantic barking accompanied his dashes as he rushed about and worried the attackers. Treating them like a bear, he assaulted them with ferocious growls and flashing teeth, lunging in and out and biting at their legs. He scared them off long enough for Minns to escape the ring through the gap. The man hunter fled after the speeding boy with long, jumping steps. Only one of the Negroes pursued, a tall, gangling man, while the others milled around the hearse, herded in by the fierceness of the dog.

Covey's piercing screech of, "Kill! Kill! Kill!" rose above Blue's frenzied barking. The driver reached for a dead man's knife while Duckworth sat at a wagon wheel and held his head.

Minns stopped at the edge of the field when he heard the thundering steps behind him and the chilling cry from the hearse. He pulled his pistol as he turned. Leveling it at the pursuing man, the hunter took some deep breaths to calm himself. The weapon's menace did not fend off the onrushing Negro, his knife held low and ahead as he closed. Minns waited until point-blank range before he fired, so close that the heavy bullet burst clear through the man's chest. The body dropped like a limp ragdoll and slid to the hunter's feet, its outstretched knife slicing Minns' moccasin and bloodying his left foot. Only a few red drops flew when he shook the member, the wound slight and ignored.

Reloading his rifle, Minns' hands automatically went through the long-familiar movements while he searched for Blue. The dog was still harassing the Negroes, barking, biting, and evading their attempts to catch him. His diversion and threat kept them corralled in a tight group while they swiped at him with the sword.

"Blue!" Minns yelled. "Blue! Come on, Blue!"

The dog broke off his attack and raced to join the hunter. Blue's body was stretched out and his tail extended to its limit.

"Kill! Kill! Kill!" Covey shouted. His call to arms carried a menace, a chilling threat to the waiting Minns, and decided the Negroes on pursuit. A group of men separated from those milling at the hearse and ran toward the hunter.

Blue easily distanced the compact body of Negroes following behind, their slower trot aimed at a long but purposeful chase. His master finished reloading his rifle and pistol while the dog came up. The hound's tongue was hanging out by the time he was in the trees and settled down nearby. Gauging the distance to the oncoming men, Minns took a fighting stance.

"They's close enough, Blue," he said.

The hunter swept the rifle up to his shoulder in one graceful, flowing motion. Only a moment was needed for aiming before he fired and another Negro dropped. The last four men neither stopped nor cried out, their silence and purposeful advance unnerving.

Minns fled at once, hesitating only long enough to kick at the resting dog as he went by. "Git, Blue," he hollered. "Jared be a'waitin' fer us."

The two ran along the trace, a good, open path with a straight shot that increased their chances of escape. But the rutted road held dangers for falling. Minns soon shifted over to the side and paralleled the trace in the easier footing of the open forest.

They had raced a good mile when Jared stepped out and halted the two. Minns mopped his sweaty brow while Old Blue steamed, his tongue far out and dripping. The hound cast about, snuffling, and drifted away from the trail. He splashed in the creek when he found it, cooling out before he rejoined the hunters.

Jared eyed the back trail uneasily and worriedly shifted from one foot to the other. His voice trembled as he hitched up his belt and possibles sack. "We got to run on quick, Pa," he said. "I can hear 'em comin' an' Old Blue don't like it."

The dog trotted back down the trail a few steps. As if to answer his growling unease, the party of Negroes appeared about a half-mile off. As before, the men were advancing at a slow, energy-conserving trot. A howl broke from the Negroes when they sighted the man hunters, an eerie, ululating that raised Blue's hackles. But it intimidated him into a growling retreat, his tail down as he slunk behind the hunters.

"I'm scairt, Pa," Jared said. His nervous face worked and his body trembled. "Blue's scairt too. Those niggers air different. They mean to kill us."

Minns' calm voice showed no emotion but his scar commenced its reddening rise. "We jest lose 'em, boy," he said. "If we don' and they follow us termorrer, we kill 'em all. Ain't but four o' 'em and we got four shots."

"Got to be a good ambush, Pa," Jared said. "They scare me."

Minns took a last look at the Negroes and said, "Git on up the trace, boy. It's comin' on dark soon an' they can't foller us in the black dark."

Splashes of light from the setting sun were fading into dusk when Minns girded up his belt and they ran on north. The hunter kept up a fast pace and the noise from their outdistanced pursuers slowly disappeared into the night sounds of the forest. He kept the party on the trail through the darkness, not stopping for another five miles. In a rough area with a large creek, Minns cut off the trail and headed upstream. They bedded down in a thicket of young pines blanketing an old burn scar, the ground soft from a multitude of needles for mats, and with fronds for cover. The hunters went to ground as quietly as possible, well away from the rushing stream and its noise. In the silence of the forest, Minns tied Old Blue down slope, the dog's nose their best alarm against attackers.

"Cass!" Terrell shouted. "Where are yuh, boy?"

The farmer walked toward the barn in the early darkness, his boots clumping from the heavy load of his burly frame. A whistling wind carried the scent of pone from the circle in his hand.

"Here, boy, here," he called. Only the sighing wind answered. He spit and cursed. "Where are yuh, God damn it?"

Next to the barn a shadow moved in the gloom and separated from the limp body of the dog. It flitted along the barn wall and crossed to the trunk of the large oak in the barnyard.

Terrell whistled and called while he sauntered down the slope toward the stable. His cries for the dog degenerated into an irritated grumble. "Probably off chasin' that bitch down to the blacksmith's," he muttered. "Damned dog ain't got no sense." His stentorian, "Cass!" brought no response. Terrell's bellow came just as he passed the tree.

The movement and a slight scrape surprised him. But they did not give enough warning for him to escape the muscular arm that encircled his throat. He strangled and wrestled with the arm as a long knife repeatedly jabbed him deep in the belly, tearing upward into his stomach with each thrust.

CHAPTER 23

Miss Mary

November 23, 1864. Carters, Georgia. Temperature 53\33. Possible frost in sheltered, quiet pockets in the the valleys. Partly cloudy and cold. Winds northwest to 12 knots. New moon.

The horse stamped at the faint sound of footsteps approaching the barn, bumping the rails of its stall in its nervous shuffle. Hay rustled under its hooves and timber joints creaked from the strains. But the slumbering fugitives slept on in their tired unconsciousness.

"Cleve?" Mary called out softly. "Where are yuh, Cleve?"

Her girlish voice scared them into wakefulness when its disembodied tones floated into the blackness of the barn. Gray gloom framed her dark figure in the outline of the large door, the opening visible from the faint starlight and the shining of the sliver of new moon.

Hannibal hustled to her side and said, "Time ter go, Missie?"

"There's four hours 'til dawn," she replied. "Cleve ready?"

Cleve materialized from one of the stalls. "I'se here, Miss Mary," he said. The boy yawned and stretched and popped his joints. His lanky frame folded and jerked as he slapped at his clothes and brushed off the bits of straw.

A tantalizing aroma drew the rest to the girl. Her busy hands parcelled out the slabs of roast pork and pone, the unusual meat a welcome change from the fat bacon of earlier feasts. The tattered group demolished the food, its solid bulk washed down by warm milk from a quick, early morning milking of the cow. Gathered in the dark, she could not see their shivering in the cold wind blowing through the open-ended barn, nor their anxious eyes nor wild appearance, travel stained as they were by all the days on the trails.

It was Cleve who expressed the fears of the others, offhand in his approach but with a guile that skirted around Claude's thoughts of a betrayal. "Saw a reb on de trace comin' in, Missie," the boy said. "Dey 'bout?"

Mary fidgeted before answering. Her apparent unwillingness to reveal a confidence disturbed Claude. But he was relieved when her basic honesty compelled a grudging revelation of the truth, and of her status in the area. "That was Lieutenant Garrity," she said, "from the troop campin' over toward Adamsville. It's 'bout ten mile west. The officers come by near ever'day for visitin'."

She hesitated a moment and her cheerful tone turned somber. "They're courtin' me all the time. Patrick asked me to marry 'im but I won't accept 'til this war is over."

The girl sighed mournfully, her sadness almost at the state of tears. She wrung her hands together, her bitter outrage cutting to the futility of the conflict. "We're about beat but Jeff Davis can't see it yet. Lots o' the boys just goin' home anyways. They're done with fightin'."

Hannibal's concerned, "We got ter pass any pickets?" diverted her to the predicament of the fugitives.

"Over at the big branch o' the Coosy," she replied. "But they ain't none on Talking Rock Creek. We cross both, the creek twice. It's pretty windin'." She paused. "The river's 'bout nine or ten miles from here, the roundabout way we go. The Army's got a detail there to guard the bridge."

The big Negro persisted in picking at the maze of the escape route. "Where we cross, Missie?" he asked.

"There's a good sized gully at the bridge," she said. "You circle and cross maybe a thousand feet upstream. The river widens into a broad, shallow riffle, easy to ford if you're careful on the rocks." Her voice sharpened. "But be quiet about it."

"How we gwine from here, Missie?" Hannibal said. His assertive voice turned troubled, his uncertainty penetrating the gloom as he continued to tiptoe his way through the labyrinth of the problem. "If Cleve losted, we have ter rustle on 'thout 'im."

"You stay 'bout fifty paces behind me. Run into the forest if I'm stopped or anyone passes."

Hannibal persisted in worrying the riddle like a dog with a bone. "Den what?" he said. "We strike out 'roun' de rebs?" The Negro shuffled closer, intent on the girl's reply.

His questions mirrored Claude's worries. He had been less than satisfied with the almost grudging way that the girl parcelled out the information. But perhaps she just was being cautious, he thought, in case they were captured.

"When I canter onto the bridge," she said, "you go on up the river and cross. I'll wait for you 'bout a mile on past."

Mary was silent for a moment and then presented her last instructions to the attentive fugitives. "If I get taken, swing way clear and keep quiet. You can come back to the road and move along it to the Peak Casler place at Old Town. Granny Eva'll help you on up to Dalton. There's only one main trace north past the junction there. It goes all the way to Spring Place and then up to Tennessee."

Hannibal saddled her mare and led it from the barn, while the others drifted into the darkness for relief and a last drink at the cow trough. The servant held Mary's foot when she mounted the mare, its fractious jockeying keeping the girl busy gentling the beast. When its small bucking spasm was done, she chirked at her mount and turned it into the lane at a fast walk. The fugitives followed in a file behind. But they had to trot to keep the mare in hearing distance. When the girl paused a mile down the road, Hannibal ran up to her, his puffing interspersed with protests.

"Can't hardly foller yuh, Missie, wid dat fast hawse. Dishere chile 'bout tuckered out an' Hester, she beat."

Mary chuckled as her horse pranced about. She pulled on the reins and caressed the mare as she soothed and quieted her.

"Bess ain't been run in a good while," she said. The girl laughed in a pleased way as she stroked the mare's mane and patted her neck. "She's got fat and sassy. But she'll settle down directly."

The miles to the bridge took them through woods and ravines. They forded small rivulets and the big creek on the way, their wet feet aching from the cold water and pinching leather as it dried. Instead of staying on the main trace, Mary led them on back trails, overgrown at times such that she had to force her horse through the bordering brush. The way was arduous, with steep slopes and sliding places that demanded slow travel of the mount. Hannibal's complaint disappeared when the ground was so rough that the fugitives could easily keep up with the horse. The young woman paused on the main trace less than half a mile from the bridge, glowing campfires of the rebels visible in the gloom of the early morning. Claude stood stock still and listened as his eyes searched the dark and he evaluated the threat. The rebs were camped in a flat on the far bank and apparently were asleep, since he could neither see nor hear any morning activity. And no fires showed on the side of their sneak past the pickets. Grouping at the stirrup of the girl, they listened to her helpful orders.

"Close in behind me as I canter onto the bridge. I'll have Bess prancing to make a lot of racket. You slip into the woods on the right. The riffle's not far, but don't go on past it after you cross, not 'til I cough or fire my pistol."

While they trotted behind her and then moved into the shelter of the big trees, Mary kicked Bess in the sides to spur her on and cantered toward the bridge. The rapid hoofbeats as she neared the structure brought an immediate challenge from the pickets.

"Who goes there?" one shouted. His rifle lock clicked as he cocked it.

Her reply boomed out in the darkness. "It's Mary, boys! Hold your fire!"

The girl drove Bess onto the timbered bridge at a canter. Its loose wooden surface bounced up and down and clattered from the impacts of the steel-shod hooves. Mary sawed on the reins and cried out, "Whoa! Whoa!" Bess pranced about, excited by the pickets and incited by her rider. The horse's hooves struck and vibrated a board at every step, her stamping controlled by the girl to create a maximum commotion.

A picket ran up to the horse and hauled it down with a hard pull on the halter. The skittish animal swung him about under the girl's furtive kicks. Lifted off his feet, the man's curses increased as he tried to subdue the spurred horse. But Mary tightened the reins and the pain of the bit forced Bess's head back. The mare reared up and then bucked as the rider continued her surreptitious kicking. Bess's forced dance pounded the loose bridge planks. Their solid drumming and the girl's loud, "Whoa, Bess; settle down," made a racket that no patrol could ignore. The other picket ran to assist just as the thunderous uproar begat turmoil in the camp.

"Turn out!" a voice shouted from the tents. "Turn out, God damn it!"

Lieutenant Garrity ran from his tent and down the slope to the bridge. The officer was roaring orders and buttoning his shirt as he approached. Men streamed from the tents as the noise intensified, yelling and curses forcing them out. One thing was constant, Claude saw. Each man had his weapon, though he might only have on his drawers, or pants with one suspender over his shoulder.

Claude lay on a slight bank and inspected the military scene with an amused detachment. Entranced by the pandemonium and the attempts of the rebel officer to get the confusion under control, he irritably brushed off the Negro's hand when Hannibal pulled at his coat.

"Leave me be," he said.

The servant grasped Claude's arm and yanked, his summons urgent. "We got ter hurry on up ter de riffle now, Claude. Can't wait no mo'."

Hannibal's jerk twinged Claude's injured shoulder, its pain penetrating the planter's detachment. With his mind finally awake to the danger of delay, he meekly followed the Negro through the dark. Hannibal's way was not visible to the stumbling, clumsy planter until his eyes adjusted again to the blackness.

Claude swore when he realized his mistake. "Goddamn," he said, shaking his head in disgust, "I was gazin' into the fires like a fresh caught private."

The file of fugitives found a path up the stream, a game trail that led along the bank and forked at the riffle. While they sought the ford, the commotion at the bridge died down to low voices and an occasional stamp from Bess that rattled the boards. But the conversation was unintelligible murmuring until the fugitives crossed to the other side and descended the river close enough to distinguish words. The coughs started while they watched the crowd on the bridge.

"You all right, Mary?" Garrity asked.

The girl's sobs carried easily to the fugitives, hid in the brush next to the gurgle of the river.

"Got to ride on, Patrick," Mary said. Funneled up the ravine to Claude and the rest, her words were clear and followed her plan. "Already stayed here too long to visit with you an' the boys." She sniffed and blew her nose. "Grandpa havin' those spells right regular, now. Onliest thing that helps is that tonic from Granny Eva over to Old Town. He drunk the last 'bout midnight."

Garrity bent over the girl and took her arm. "I'll send a trooper with you," he said, worriedly. "Lots o' stragglers an' deserters roamin' about."

"It ain't necessary," she replied. "I got my pistol here."

Gabe moved his great bulk, his step unfortunate. A loud crack from a broken branch channeled down the ravine to the bridge, cold causing its break to resound like a pistol shot. The sharp explosion contrasted with the steady sighing of the wind in the trees.

"Who goes there?" a picket challenged.

The demand was followed by the crack of Mary's pistol. Twigs fell but its ball passed harmlessly by the watching group. Cocking of pieces and some kneeling men aiming rifles frightened Claude more than the pistol shot and spurred him to flee.

The party already had run ahead of him on the western slope. Their passage rattled the thick layer of crisp leaves, a revealing telltale. Claude snorted like a buck and shook a bush. His fear urged him to leave but he forced himself to stand and listen to the patrol and to the delaying tactics of Mary.

"Ain't nothin' but them deer, Lieutenant," a voice said disgustedly. "It's them we seen crossin' 'bout dark, sir."

"You recken so, Sergeant?" Garrity asked.

"I seen 'em myself, sir. They's feedin' in the old pasture down the road. Plenty o' browse. Comin' back across the river now to yard-up in that thornapple thicket. We git one er two fer the boys, soon's daylight."

"They were there, Patrick, when I came by," Mary volunteered. "Bess scared 'em into movin'."

With the patrol diverted, Claude picked his way up the slope to the west. He and the other fugitives stopped at the ridge and waited on the girl. They resumed their slow travel through the gloom of the woods when they heard Bess's hoofbeats on the planks and then thuds as the horse's hooves plowed into the soft surface of the trace. Mary slowed the mare to a walk a mile beyond and waited at a densely wooded bend until they came up to her. In the east, the sky lightened and stars faded in the deepening glow from the rising sun.

Minns and Jared struck out east of the pine thicket at a strenuous trot, their cold bodies warming up quickly. Old Blue's lank figure swept the forest ahead of them. His nose searched out the scent trails flitting by on the cold wind, little warmed by the feeble rays of the early morning sun. Gusts made the trees pop and leaves were swirling in the open places when they stopped on a small bench with a spring.

"Any pone er meat left, Pa?" Jared asked. "Er an apple? I done et most ever'thin' last night an' give the rest to Blue. He's 'bout to starve."

Minns fumbled around in his possibles sack but his fingers recovered only a small piece of pone which he tossed to Jared. Blue jumped and caught it in the air when the boy lofted it to him. The dog's voracious mouth swallowed the morsel in one quick gulp. Blue sat on his haunches and wagged his tail. His grin widened and his tongue hung out while he waited expectantly for another donation. Minns knelt and turned his sack upside down. It was empty except for necessaries such as flint and steel and extra rifle balls.

He chuckled as he reassembled his kit.

"Nothin' more in my poke, boy," he said. "We sure are a poor set o' hunters." He laughed aloud, the ruinous state of their persons and kits seeming to tickle him, their long quest not dismaying him at all. "We got to find a farm er the soldiers to git supplies an' then slide on after that Shaw."

"Could git a deer, Pa," Jared said, hopefully.

Minns shook his head and said, "No, boy. Don't seem to be no deer 'roun' here. Powerful skeerce. Ain't seed a track yet this mawnin'."

A breeze stirred the treetops, a gust that whistled by in a sighing, mournful dirge. It startled the boy, who shivered and turned up his collar. Jared looked back along their trail, then shuddered as he moved over closer to his father. He fidgeted nervously and readied his piece, then reopened his earlier argument, repeating his worry about the pursuing Negroes.

"You recken them niggers still comin'?" he asked.

Minns exploded in anger and contempt. "You still thinkin' on them bastards?" He spit, his disgust mirrored in his face. "They ain't even near us, so you jest shet yer mouth 'bout them niggers."

The boy argued back, but his voice trembled. "I won't, Pa," he said. "They's huntin' us. I jest know it." Jared struck his breast with his fist, his face gloomy and downcast. "My heart done tol' me, Pa. They be waitin' fer us down the road."

Minns scarred face tightened and his lips curled as his keen eyes took in the fright of his son. "Yer puzzlin' on it that way, boy," he said, "it makes you run. Ain't no Minns never done that."

"We best git 'em first, Pa, er they'll kill us."

Jared's earnest plea, doleful in its predictions, led to a subtle change in his father. Minns looked about sharply and cradled his rifle, ready for instant action. He fingered the pistol in and out of his belt loop and checked his sheath knife. The boy imitated his father's movements to prepare for a fight. He had observed the older man's habits many times in the years of hunting men and game. Jared's face brightened, knowing that Minns was ready for action and his mind was made up. He would settle with the Negroes before they chased Shaw farther.

The hunter's confidence allayed the boy's fears. "We jest ease back down to the trace," Minns said quietly. "Kill them niggers if they's still comin' on an' then head over to the main road to'ard Old Town. Terrell said those 'scapes most likely pass there."

Calling to Blue, Minns took the lead and struck downhill toward the creek. His trot devoured the distance back to the trace, while Old Blue explored the forest ahead to flush out any scent. About a mile down the trail, the dog held back and sought Minns' side. His nose was twitching and his hackles starting up as they stole along, careful of noise and alert to any change in the forest sounds. Minns kept Blue close, silencing him and urging on the faithful hound. He motioned Jared to one side of the trail while he took the other and padded forward. Each cocked and half- raised his rifle as they trod softly toward the sharp turn ahead at the bend in the bordering creek. A thicket of brush faced them at a cutbank, a perfect place for an ambush. They were less than fifty feet away when Blue crouched and growled. His tail twitched back and forth in a nervous beat.

"Oooo! Oooo! Ooooooooo! Ooo!"

Bloodcurdling ululations and screeches burst from the four Negroes that exploded out of the cover at the two sides of the constricted passage. The attackers rushed the hunters with large knives raised. Too close for aiming, the Minns pointed their rifles and fired at running bodies. At the shot, two men collapsed into the churned ground of the trail. Minns drew his pistol and killed another man in a second, but Jared's pistol misfired. The boy shrieked for help and fled from the Negro closing him at a run.

Off like a shot at Jared's screams, Blue bit the Negro in the leg. The old dog staggered the vengeful man just when he overtook the boy and sliced at his head with a roundhouse swing. Blood spurted from a cut on Jared's head, but his wildly rotating body evaded other wide swipes with the massive blade.

Blue's ferocious growls accompanied his gnawing on the Negro's leg. The dog's tenacious grip and pulling kept the man just inching along the trail and off balance. His hold on the frantic Jared weakened as the boy struggled. Only a fragment of Jared's sleeve remained when the screaming boy tore loose from the Negro's grasp. Minns barreled into the ambusher an instant later and hurled him into a tree. The shock of the collision knocked them both down, with Blue boring in on the Negro's body. Minns missed when he grabbed for the man's knife-hand as they fell and bounced on the ground, unable either to conquer the man quickly or to get the blade. But he clasped the Negro closely to avoid the slashes and pounded the man's groin with his knee while one hand sought the knife.

The Negro screamed in pain under Minns' relentless attack and wrenched himself out of the hunter's bearhug. Escaping, he took a wild swing as Minns rolled away. Then he rose up fighting, a maddened man who slashed violently with the knife, aiming at man or beast. His whistling blade found but one target, and amputated half a foot of the dog's tail. Old Blue let go of the Negro's leg and yelped, then howled as he separated from the fight. He abandoned the struggling men and slunk off after Jared, stopping in an open place to lick his bleeding stump. His whimpering and howls joined the murderous cacophony of the fighting men.

Minns was implacable as he engaged in the rough and tumble fight. The Negro got no second chance to slice or stab when the men came together and fell to the ground. Minns' iron grip on his wrist pinned his knife-hand. The man hunter, his life spent in the savagery of the forest and in tiffs with argumentative tavern brawlers, kneed the ambusher in the groin, a hard, mashing thrust. Once, twice, his blow fell, the Negro's screams of pain followed by weakening resistance. But Minns, cursing and destructive, could not just cow his opponent. He smashed his forehead into the Negro's nose. Its shape flattened forever and red streams rushed forth, followed by a squall of pain. Gasping and strangling noises soon intruded; lack of air forced the fighter into frantic struggles to clear his blood-clogged nose and throat.

Muscle fought against muscle, the grunting, rangy hunter against the bulky Negro. Slowly, the straining men rolled over until Minns pinned the man to the ground, the latter's clenched knife far from his body. Minns' visage took on an evil hue with his scar flaming bright red. His face dripped sweat on that of the Negro's, inches away as he stared intimidatingly into the man's eyes. Lying on his back, Minns' opponent was drowning in his own blood, lunging and frantic to gasp more air.

The hunter's hate spewed forth when he had the man beaten. "So you'd kill my boy, would yuh, you nigger bastard. Yer goin'a feel the knife you was givin' 'im."

Minns forced his own bowie down against the man's left arm near the shoulder. With the point in place, the hunter thrust and thrust, overcoming the Negro's straining and his slipping hand. The knife severed the biceps cleanly. Minns rotated the blade against the weakening arm to cut the muscles away from the bone while the man screamed in pain. The hunter finished the job with a stab in the shoulder. The beaten man's left arm fell limply to the dirt while he whimpered and tried to clear his throat of the choking blood.

Veins bulged on the hunter's forehead as he stared into the terror stricken eyes of the fallen man. Minns' sweating, twisted face and grim lips added to the malevolent distortion from the red scar. Tossing aside his own bowie, he wrestled the man's blade from his hand and held it aloft.

"See it, you bastard?" he spat out. "It's your'n an' now you git it back."

Raising the huge knife to arms-length, Minns drove it into the man's face, right down through his mouth and throat and into the backbone. The Negro bucked and gagged at the thrust, gurgling as air rushed out in a throaty rumble. A flood of red blood spewed up around the projecting handle of the blade, its forceful spray added to the great pool collecting in the trail. Minns rose and kicked the quivering Negro, his knife ready during the few seconds that the body's tremors continued. The hunter stared at the man's face while he brushed the dirt off his buckskins and took great gasps of air, intent on the dying man until the Negro's eyes filmed over and life fled. So intent that his animal wariness missed his son's return. Minns leaped away in alarm at a touch on his sleeve, then swung around in a fighting crouch until he saw the boy.

"They's one still alive, Pa," Jared said.

He had a bloody bandanna tied about his head. Streaks of red stained his arms and buckskin coat. Jared commenced reloading his rifle while Blue lay nearby and licked the stub of his tail. Its red end dripped when he took away his tongue. The old dog bounded up and wagged the stub when Minns jumped to Jared's side and reached for his son's wounded head.

"You hurt, boy?" he said huskily.

Jared shrugged. "Ain't much, Pa," he said. "Cut a little gash along the side. I done washed it off and used the cloth."

He shied away from his father's probing hands. "I be a'right, Pa. Ain't bleedin' no more."

"What about Blue?"

"He ain't hurt bad. Little ol' end o' his tail gone, that's all."

Minns ignored the dog while he washed off the blood from the Negro. Picking up his own weapons, he strode about and examined all the bodies. His next actions were very deliberate. He and Jared reloaded all the weapons and cleaned their knives before they faced the problem of the wounded man.

The fallen Negro had tried desperately to escape from them, digging his fingers into the dirt to drag along his lifeless legs. He was only a few feet from the bushes, still laying down a blood trail, when Minns seized his arm and turned him over onto his back. The wounded man's eyes bulged in fright.

"No, Massa!" he cried, raising his arms protectively. "No! Don' kill me!"

Minns poked him with his rifle muzzle. "Like ter kill us, would yuh?"

Froth bubbled at the corners of the man's mouth and terror filled his voice with faint, trembling warbles. "Don', Massa!" he begged.

Minns laughed and shot him through the mouth. His blood choked off his entreaties as he died.

Jared bent over and retched but little came up except yellow bile. He staggered over to a tree and leaned against it. Sobbing and distraught, he again challenged his father.

"Can't we give it up, Pa?" he pleaded. "We ain't doin' nothin' but killin' an' we ain't ketchin' that Shaw. He's done gone, Pa."

Minns' prolonged quiet fascinated the boy, the hunter's mesmerization with the Negro dead so unlike him, a fatalist who instantly accepted tragedy, and went on. Jared sobbed as he sidled close to his father's side, near enough for a feeling of protection, a feeling of warmth, a feeling of oneness. He hesitantly reached out his hand but drew it back, not daring to touch his father's rigid body. Minns stared long at the dead men in a trance-like oblivion, unheeding of his son's need, a meditation where his face went through the fury of anger and on into peace, his scar alternately reddening and paling. But he made no sound until he suddenly wrenched himself around and grasped Jared and bearhugged him.

His voice was at once soft and gentle, yet hard as iron. "Kill onliest those that need it, boy," he said. "An' that Shaw do need killin' fer Jeremy. If you want to go on back, you git." His tone hardened. "I'm after Shaw 'til I kill 'im."

"Or he kills you, Pa," Jared sobbed. "I couldn't bear that."

Minns held his crying son, a young man, big and strong in body but driven to exhaustion by the chase and the fights. They stayed there for an hour while the two talked and Jared regained his composure, and renewed his resolve to go with his implacable father.

Mary held Bess in check at the crossroads while the fugitives straggled up. The hours of hard, tiring travel had removed the fractiousness from the horse and she stood with nothing more than light reining and pats and soothing commands from her rider. Claude and the fugitives lined up at the side of the road, he and Hannibal at Mary's stirrup to receive her next instructions. Cleve was nearby, adjusting the strap on his possibles sack. The girl rose in her stirrups for a better look around. She searched the forest and made a sweep of the roads, then settled into her saddle and looked at Claude.

"Cleve's leavin'," she said.

Her sudden announcement stunned the planter. "Why?" he asked.

The praying mantis flexed his spindly frame and extremities. "You don't need me no mo', Claude. I'se cuttin' back 'cross thoo Ellijay an' 'lonega. Dat's de short way."

"Cleve's right," Mary said. She leaned over to grasp the proffered hand of the lanky youth. "He has to hurry on back to Demorest's for the next bunch comin' through."

Claude's concern must have shown in his face, for she tried to calm his fears. "Don't worry, Claude. I'll lead you to Granny Eva."

"How far is it?" he asked.

"Only 'bout another mile. We take the lane there at the broken off oak."

The well marked entrance lay only a few rods away where a lightning devastated monarch made the turnoff unmistakable. Trees had been set in rows on each side of the lane, grown now into imposing sentinels. The orderly landscaping distinguished its path from the native growth at the sides. Double lines of towering oaks marched down the western slope to the manse and outbuildings hidden in the trees beyond.

Cleve readied himself for his journey by receiving all the food scraps the others could resurrect from their sacks, a scant addition to his meager possessions. He accepted their homage artlessly, passing off the importance of his help with a, "Twarn't nothin'," and a dignified smile. The planter, overcome with emotion, was unable to let Cleve part with just the simple thanks of the others and the kiss from Hester. Gulping and near tears, Claude grasped the youth and hugged him tight. His voice almost failed him as he bid goodbye to the cheerful, helpful stripling.

"You risked yer life fer me, Cleve, an' I be grateful. I he'p yuh if I kin, once't we git ter de free lan'."

He didn't realize he had spoken in the dialect of the slave until he stepped back, tears in his eyes. A surge of trembling ran through his body when he thought of all the help on the trail. Now Cleve was leaving, perhaps forever. The gangly boy ran down the eastern trace, waving goodbye and with a last shout. He and I ain't no different, Claude thought. We're both men, an' just want freedom. And by the living God, the Negroes shall have it.

They all stood in silence until the boy disappeared, no one inclined to disturb the moment of comradeship and regret. Finally Mary clucked to Bess and motioned them on, her "Keep quiet," her only caution.

She took them into a side trail that angled away from the lane, its path overgrown and hidden after its entry into a small ravine. A trickle of a creek fell from one small, green-bordered pool to another, cool water that refreshed them as they traveled on. Willows shadowed the flow all along the length of the tiny stream and gave them cover.

Mary stopped a half-mile in and dismounted, tying off Bess at a green patch of grass. The horse fell to cropping the lush growth, its feeding sounds of little danger to the fugitives. The girl motioned them to follow and stole along quietly for a few rods, then squatted down next to a cleared area bordered by a worn track. Buildings and pasture stretched below her and smoke from a few cabins to the right hung in the wind, acrid and irritating.

"The backhouse is just down the path," she said. "Be someone 'long directly an' we find Granny Eva."

She had hardly spoken when a little Negro girl skipped along the path and headed toward the cabins. Gabe seized the child at Mary's nod. He brought the struggling victim to earth at her feet, his hand choking off any scream. Mary bent toward the small-boned face and signalled silence with a "Shhh," and a finger over her lips. When the child still wriggled, she stroked the girl's head and soothed her.

"Hush," she said. "We won't hurt you. We want Granny Eva."

Big eyes rolled around and took in the Negroes and the young woman's friendly smile. The child's struggles ceased and she relaxed in Gabe's grip. He eased his hand away from the girl's face and stood her upright, then gently patted her head.

"You're Rosemary, ain't you?" Mary asked. "Granny's granddaughter?"

The little head nodded, affirming the guide's judgement. Silent as the grave, the girl made no effort to escape or to protest.

"Go get Granny Eva," Mary said. "Tell her Mary's here in the ravine."

With a nudge on her bottom, the girl scooted up the path and headed for the end cabin.

The planter shifted restlessly as he watched the child depart. "Aren't you afraid of her telling?" he asked.

"No, Claude," Mary said with a grin. "Rosemary and I met two-three times before. She always gets a present."

The guide pulled several pieces of sticky taffy from her bulging pocket. She passed one to each of the fugitives and kept the remainder for the messenger. Their stuck jaws rapidly confirmed the chewiness of the lumps.

Granny Eva sauntered down the path soon after Rosemary disappeared in the cabin door, her remarkable appearance striking them dumb. Tall, erect, big boned, Granny's ebony skin set off a smooth, round, moonlike face. With at least three hundred pounds on her huge frame, and swinging a massive, knobbed, straight cane, she approached like a fat, upright bear, larger than most men.

"Now, dat's somethin'!" Gabe gasped. His cry of delight cut through the amazed silence. "Dat some woman!" The giant's great bulk of a body rose to its full majesty so he could better see Granny approach.

Mary pulled him down and warned him off. "Men don't fool with Granny, Gabe. She's smart and she can beat most ever'one with that stick. An' she does conjurin'. The men 'round here are afraid of 'er."

Gabe laughed. "Don' matter, Missie. I'se jist lookin'."

The imposing old woman turned through the opening in the screening brush, with Rosemary edging ahead of her flowing skirts. Mary handed over a cluster of cemented taffy pieces, then put a few more on the sticky pile in the girl's outstretched hand. The child pried one loose and stuffed it in her mouth. She clutched the others tightly in her grip and wandered off to one side. Her jaws worked against the tough candy while the fugitives waited on Mary and Granny Eva, the two squatted down together.

"Got some 'scapes, Mary?" Granny asked.

"These four, Granny," the girl answered. "One here, Claude," Mary pointed him out and he nodded to the giantess, "is a Yankee officer. The others are Hannibal, Gabe and Hester."

Granny peered at Claude, her dark eyes exploring every part of his bedraggled appearance and brown face. Claude sensed the camaraderie of the women, an unusual bond. The Negro was using Mary's first name rather than Miss Mary and was treating her as an equal. He stared Granny straight in the eyes, eyes both shrewd and unflinchingly direct.

"We need your help, Granny," he said, "to get back to the Yankees at Dalton. And we got hunters after us, the Minns from over to Columbia."

"Heard o' de Minns," Granny said. "Dey ain't no good." She waved her massive stick and contemptuously dismissed them. "Dey git kilt if dey comes hereabout."

"Dey's got Old Blue, Granny," Hester said worriedly. "He 'bout de best trackin' dog 'roun' dose parts."

"We seen dogs a'fo'," Granny replied. A growling, "Arrr," rumbled from the old woman's throat as she gestured disdainfully and dismissed the difficulty. "We fix him too, 'long wid de Minns."

"Hesh," she said, when Hester again opened her mouth, and Gabe pushed forward. His question died in his throat at the warning look of the giantess and her raised club. Turning back to Claude, Granny asked, "Why you black?"

"Walnut stain from Granny Mandy over to Columbia," Claude said. "She he'ped me git away."

Granny rocked back on her heels, stifling a laugh as she almost overturned. Her wide mouth broke into a grin and exposed even white teeth in beautiful contrast to the ebony face. Huge copper rings hung from extended lobes of large ears and a red turban rested on her head. Claude had never seen such an imposing figure, marred only by a cast in one eye. She probably uses it to cast the evil eye on any that crosses her, he thought.

"Rosemary, chile?" Granny called out. "Where is you, chile?"

The old woman felt around behind her massive buttocks when the girl stirred. Rosemary crept past her granny's bulk and into the protecting crook of the woman's arm and fat hand. Her jaws worked on the taffy as she looked up impassively.

"Git on back ter de cabin an' fetch de pepper gourd," Granny said.

Rosemary scurried off, her short, skinny legs pumping. A large gourd filled the circle of her arms when she returned a minute later. Granny pulled the stopper and drifted out a sample by jostling the gourd into the breeze. Their burning eyes and noses and explosive sneezes set her to laughing.

"See what we got fer de Minns an' dey dog?" she said. "Ain't no houn' git past dat."

Claude had to agree. It pained him just to look through the mists of his crying eyes and he sneezed repeatedly. Desperate, he imitated the frantic purges of the other victims and splashed up water from a pool. The treatment did little good at first but gradually cleared the pepper when he dunked his entire head. Mary and Granny waited imperturbably until the fugitives regained some semblance of comfort. Hannibal and Gabe mumbled their discontent and Hester sobbed her protests.

"Shet up!" the old woman said. She threatened them with her stick, her face a thundercloud. "I'se tryin' ter sho' yer de way ter 'scape. Now you pay me some mind."

Her arrangements with Mary astounded Claude. Taking his knife, Granny cut off a foot of pants leg from each man and a great swathe of hemline from Hester. She tied the bundle of cloth with a rawhide, then gave it to their guide, along with a little pouch of the powdery red pepper. Granny chattered away all the while about the arrangements to fool the Minnses.

"Do like allus," she said to Mary. "Scatter de pepper in de lane clean out inter de trace ter drive off de dog. Drag de clo'es in de dirt 'bout two mile 'long de trace to'ard Cartecay's, clear over ter de big water."

Claude interrupted. "Why you doin' that?"

Mary's and Granny's pained expressions at his lack of understanding were broken by the girl's careful explanation.

"Ever'time they's a dog, we drag the clothes to the branch o' the river crossin' the trace to Cartecay. Leave plenty o' scent on both sides o' the water. The trace goes East, but they'll think you're wadin' up or down a bit to throw 'em off before you cut the Talkin' Rock road and head back north through Ellijay."

"They don't catch onto the trick?" Claude's asked. His suspicion was allayed by the girl.

"Worked before with two parties," she said confidently. "Delay 'em while they try to puzzle out the false trail an' which way you went. By then Granny'll have you fixed."

She's treating me like an ignorant kid, Claude thought, irritated at the condescension in Mary's voice. His reason prevailed when he reviewed the plan. The girl and Granny had done this before. They knew how man hunters thought. And that stroke with the red pepper and the scent trail was good. His doubts vanished, his troubled face clearing and his good humor restored as he pursued his fate.

"What happens to us, Granny?" he asked.

"Git Mary off, den we send yuh ter de hidin' place."

Mary smiled and accepted their grateful homage as they hugged and thanked her. Claude helped her mount, his hands locked under her foot. She put Bess to the ravine with a wave, the horse's sides rounder from the lush grass.

When she was gone, Granny felt behind her and said, "Rosemary?"

The child scrambled around the bulging woman and stood before her granny. She sucked on the taffy, her big eyes shining, searching the old woman's face while she waited on another errand. Granny held the girl's arm firmly and stared unblinkingly into the child's eyes.

"You keep 'em out o' sight, you hear?"

The girl nodded, attentive to her granny. She made a little sucking gurgle as she finished with the lump of taffy and swallowed down the remnant. Unperturbed, she popped in another, almost as if bored with an action repeated many times.

"Take 'em roun' behint de barn," Granny said, "dèn 'long de growed up strip." She shook the little girl gently. "Unnerstan'?" At the girl's nod, she continued. "Den down ter de ribber at de hid-out flatboat. Keep in de thickets ever'time you kin."

Claude wondered when she would get around to them. He didn't have long to wait. Granny switched to the fugitives when she had the girl's understanding.

"Take de flatboat and drap down de ribber 'bout half a mile past de big bend," she said, her severe tone brooking no argument. "Put inter de little cove on de other side. Dere's a gravel bar dere wid thick bresh 'bove it." She raised her stick and threatened the planter when he made as if to interrupt. "Slide de boat behint de bresh," she said, "an' kiver it good. Den git on west up ter de flat an' hide in de barn dere."

Hannibal's stomach growled and he rumbled, "Kin we git some grub, Granny?"

He put his hand on her arm and Gabe joined him at her side, pushing Rosemary away. The child let out a squall and darted behind Granny's voluminous skirts. The woman raised her club and struck the big man on the shoulder.

"Don' you tetch Rosemary!" she thundered.

Gabe cursed and rubbed his upper arm, shying away from her raised stick. "Ain't no need o' dat, Granny," he said, aggrieved.

"Ain't nobody hurt Rosemary," she said, combatively. "You keep yer han's off dat chile." Her fierce eyes challenged Gabe but the big Negro backed farther away, intimidated by her threatening club, its knob poised for another blow. His hand was busy massaging his sore muscles.

Claude's stomach grumbled loudly and reminded her of their hunger. "Dey's a barrel o' taters and onions in de barn," she said. "An' dey's hickory an' walnuts 'roun' in de woods. Maybe some chinkapins too. Feed quick an' keep outen sight 'til I sees yuh ternight."

Rosemary grasped Claude's hand when Granny slipped out of the brush and headed for her cabin. The child pulled him beside her as she guided them to a second path through the overgrown ravine. It passed successively behind the barn and beyond into a dense thornapple thicket, impenetrable to the uninformed and thick enough to hide their passage to the river.

"Old Blue really got 'em this time, Pa," Jared said.

The hound raced down the trace toward Cartecay. Scent from the dragged clothes matched his imprint and signalled a clear message. He yelped every few steps, little melodius barks that were interrupted by a long bugle whenever he hit a particularly strong deposit in the soft, damp roadbed.

Minns stopped in the rutted surface and inspected it closely, then called in the boy and the dog. Blue gave up his run with reluctance, only leaving the hot scent trail when the hunter's curses cowed him. But he evaded Minns and slunk back behind Jared.

"Ain't right, boy," Minns said, his face troubled. "Ain't no reason they be goin' East."

"Maybe they's strikin' roundabout, goin' past the cricks an' farms, Pa. Old Injun trails all through here. Them Cherokees left plenty."

"You think we orta go on?"

"Sure, Pa. Seems like they's lookin' to sidle on nawth up the trails 'long the rivers. Too many people are movin' on that main trace past the Old Town. Git caught if they use it."

Minns wrinkled face and twisting scar mirrored his lack of conviction. "I don' know. They done got clean over to the Coosy 'thout us ketchin' 'em."

"Go on, Pa," Jared said. "Put Old Blue to it."

The hunter called to the dog and struck east. Old Blue lined out at a run on the hot trail. His yelps and bugles soon left them behind, their hurrying delayed by Minns' limp. Jared fell back beside his father.

"That foot hurtin' you bad, Pa?" he asked.

"Ain't much," Minns said. "It's achin' some where that damn nigger's knife cut me. Git it into the cold water when we strike the next crick an' it'll be a'right."

Blue was cooling out when they reached the big stream, his body submerged in the cold water as he lapped up a few mouthfuls. Minns splashed his bare foot into the water beside the dog after he fingered and inspected the wound. The swelling around the cut was reddened and hot to the touch. An hour of soaking produced a better appearance and increased Minns' eagerness to move. Urging on the dog, he and Jared explored both sides of the ford. Try as he might, Old Blue could turn up no trail. The hot scent vanished completely at the water's edge.

Minns' exasperation boiled over at the failure. His curse and kick at the dog sent Blue yelping into the bushes. The old hound stretched out in a protecting clump with his head down flat, a hideout where he could watch the men with a wary eye while he rested.

Jared sighed, his face downcast. "We ain't never goin'a find 'em in a chase, Pa" he said. "We best git ahead of 'em, on up to the Dalton road, then ambush 'em when they come by."

His father's mood brightened and his shoulders straightened as he laughed and clapped the boy on the shoulder. "Ye'll make a hunter yet," he said.

They struck north on the old Indian trail on the west side of the river, crossing the smaller creeks that headed into the mountains. Their journey gradually bent northwest toward Spring Place and the turnoff to Dalton.

CHAPTER 24

Granny Eva

November 24, 1864. Spring Place, Georgia. Temperature 62\35. Sunny and cold, possible frost in quiet, cold spots in the valleys. Mild, easterly winds to 10 knots during the day. A new moon almost all night, a slight silver crescent.

Voices woke the fugitives in their burrows, hollows under redolent tobacco leaves piled in a corner of the barn. It lay at the border between field and woods, a building with a high center bay and "A" roof flanked by two narrow sheds along the sides. Night enfolded the travelers in their alarm, a sliver of new moon and starlight outlining trees and two moving shapes when they peered out. Full dark had followed a colorful sky at sundown. Their long day of hiding, after meeting Granny in the morning, was now interrupted by intruders. Claude and Hannibal knelt and cocked their pieces. The hidden group shivered in the cold night wind while the figures approached the barn.

It was Hester who allayed their fears. "Dey's niggers talkin'," she said. "Ain't no harm from dem folks."

"Ter git us on de road, maybe?" Hannibal said, and uncocked his rifle. "Recken Granny send us de guide?" He still kept his weapon pointed and ready, his vigilant crouch primed to react to possible danger.

Claude's sharp, "Shut up!" silenced them. "We wait an'

see what they do," he added.

The fugitives had drifted down river in the leaky flat-boat, the craft tilting and turning from Claude's and Gabe's shifts and powerful thrusts with the paddles. Hester had picked up her feet in distaste out of the sloshing water and mud on the bottom. But her complaints stopped when Hannibal hoisted her in his arms and protected her clinging body. Their last view of Rosemary was of her waving from the landing, until the rushing current carried them out of sight around a steep bank. The little girl's jaws never quit working on the candy while she led them to the boat, and her farewell was mumbled out through dripping juice. A hug from each had sufficed for thanks, all except for Gabe, who would not touch the child. He grimaced and grumbled while he rubbed his arm.

"Ain't gwine let dat Granny pound on me no mo'," he said. He winced at a particular sore spot he was fingering. "She good wid dat club."

They had found the barn empty except for hundreds of sticks of curing tobacco in the high bay, and an old wagon underneath. Workbenches at the sides of the sheds carried the odor of tobacco and shreds of hands tied in earlier processing. The entire barn smelled of tobacco, its purpose the curing and stripping and preparing cured leaves for sale.

Granny's barrel with the potatoes and onions fed the fugitives through the day and into the night. Walnuts added a little variety to their fare but chinkapins were scarce, hard to come by, though trees abounded. Telltale scratchings in the woods identified the culprits, wild turkeys that had fed on the nuts. Searches turned up only a hatful, rich in flavor but few for their wants.

Sleep had come easily in the quiet barn, what with full bellies and redolent beds. Tobacco leaves, from sticks of tobacco thrown down for soft mats and others for covering, offered a fragrant change from tree leaves or pine needles. The forest, sighing under the easterly winds, protected the barn from being too cold, and their corner and the tobacco leaves kept them very warm. The day had passed slowly

while they rested and recovered from their hurts, and
wondered in their low-voiced banter what Granny had in
store for them. Restless as the dusk gave way to night, the
fugitives finally ventured out, returning to the barn as their
refuge. Now the intruders interrupted them and threatened
their peaceful stay.

"Hands up!" Claude said, when the man was near
enough.

He stuck his rifle barrel into the belly of the first shape
entering the barn. The man's breath escaped in a great
"Woosh!" as he doubled over from the hard thrust. Hannibal
grasped the intruder from behind and choked him further,
even as the man labored for air. But the Negro found he had
seized a powerful figure, a bulky man who struggled fiercely
against the fugitive's throttling hold. The captive swung
Hannibal around and wrestled both men upright in an
attempt to free himself. The second intruder thrashed about
in Gabe's vice-like grip, his strangling shouts reduced to
wheezing and gasps when he could free his windpipe.

When the first man still struggled, Claude jabbed the
rifle barrel in hard against the captive's ribs. His blow drew
a cry of hurt and a gurgling protest, followed by even more
frantic writhing. Claude jabbed him twice more and angrily
threatened him. "Be still, damn yuh, or I'll shoot."

Held tight, the man in Hannibal's grasp collapsed at the
planter's threat and pokes with the barrel. Nearby, Gabe
had subdued his victim. The giant carried the weakly
struggling figure over close to Claude, the man's dragging
toes making little scraping sounds. But the planter ignored
the two Negroes. Instead, he leaned over close to the man
pinioned by Hannibal, trying to see into his eyes in the
darkness.

"Who are yuh?" he asked.

Hannibal let up on his trembling captive long enough
for the man to gasp out, "I'se Douglass. He Lester."

"You be quiet, we turn you loose. You understand?"

Claude's menace produced nods and shakes and gasped
agreement from both. The planter backed off, his rifle
pointed but not jabbing Douglass when he ordered their

release.

"Turn 'em loose," he said. "If they run or shout out, kill 'em."

"Ain't gwine run," Douglass said indignantly. He took several deep breaths and cleared his throat. "Granny Eva send us. She tell us de niggers "go see Jenny ternight" at dishere barn. De others comin' too an' she be here directly." He spat in front of Claude, still outraged. "Ain't no reason ter beat us."

Hester's joyous lilt celebrated the messenger's announcement. "Dey's goin'a be a dance? We's have fun 'stead o' all dat runnin'?"

"From all 'roun'," Douglass replied. His resonant voice took on an air of importance. "I'se got de best fiddle, banjo an' bones comin'. Spread de word fer Granny. Dey all be here directly."

Hester sang as she danced along the floor of the barn, catching onto the wagon as she swung gracefully around its end. Her sweet, musical voice presaged the foot stomping to come but her tune carried the hazard and invitation of their escape in their valleys of challenge.

"My sister, don't you want to get religion?
Go down in the lonesome valley,
Go down in the lonesome valley,
Go down in the lonesome valley, my Lord,
To meet my Jesus there."

Her verse and melody converted the Negroes into a chorus as Hester's first recital rose in crescendo to a second and was joined by the men. Louder and stronger choruses of the song rolled out in increasing volume, the singers keeping time with their feet at first, them clapping with their hands. Hester shifted to an open space and danced about, her skipping feet in time with the rhythm. Little by little all the Negroes were shuffling, jerking, clapping and singing at the tops of their voices. Claude laid aside his rifle and unsuccessfully joined in. His off-key croak cracked the sweet melody of the celebrating slaves.

The sound of several persons approaching broke into the beat of their jubilee and stopped the revelry. Hannibal and Claude cocked their pieces and covered the entrance from their crouches behind posts. Cautious footfalls and laughing collisions accompanied the dark figures that drifted in. Granny's massive bulk and her distinctive turban towered over the others. Her familiar voice reassured the fugitives hid in the darkness of the barn.

"Claude?" she said, anxiously. "You dere?"

"I'm here, Granny," he instantly replied. "And all the others."

A match scratched and a candle flamed. The faint light at Granny's hand revealed her and several women and men. Two of the latter held a guitar and a banjo.

"Git de candles lit, Douglass," Granny said.

Douglass leaped to do her bidding. A few moments later, several candles rested on shelves on the posts. Their yellow, smoky flames lit up the center bay of the barn and an increasing crowd of men and women as others joined the group. Granny was the center of attention, her height surpassing all except Gabe. And everyone waited on her command, Claude noticed.

"Move out de wagon an' clear de flo'," she ordered. "Lester, you start de fire an' git de poles an' de pot."

The Negroes scurried off, the men moving the wagon out of the barn, the women cleaning the floor of anything that would vex the dancers. A huge fire soon flamed on the west side of the entrance. Sparks flew downwind, away from the structure and its valuable tobacco. A tripod of large saplings held a cast-iron rendering pot over the fire. Its huge belly soon received a charge of water and ground corn, mush cooking for the feast to follow. Nearby, a man set down a covered crock and protected it from passersby. Claude drifted over, curious about its contents.

"It's bee honey," the Negro told him. "Add it when de mush cooked."

The planter dipped in a finger to taste the honey, then circulated back through the happy throng of men and women. Their chattering and laughter cheered him and cured him of the gloom he had felt earlier in the day. Infectious optimism of the Negroes in the face of their oppression had continually buoyed him on his journey. All along his escape he had found their spirits unconquered, willing to sacrifice to get to the free land, and willing to help him. Now he was here, ready to enjoy a carefree moment with them, an escape from his trials and their oppression. His pity for himself evaporated under the happiness of the truly persecuted, their lot to survive until liberated from a conquered Confederacy. Claude leaned against a post in the barn and watched the happy revelers mark off a rectangle and bring over some stools and benches from the sheds. The guitar and banjo players took their seats and tuned up while the bones man rattled out a few trial clacks. Claude sensed the woman before he heard her question.

"Ain' got no 'oman?" she whispered, her lips close to his ear.

The languid but bold eyes of a buxom young Negress faced his when he swung around. A bright red ribbon splashed across her forehead and a shiny green sash emboldened a trim waist, overhang accentuating her ample bosom. She moved closer to him and grasped his coat, then inched her bosom into his body. He smelled her musk, her odor at once compelling and repelling. Unbidden, his desire rose, the nearness of the willing woman weakening his will and his vows. The musical instruments and the caller saved him from her advances. Their medley of notes and commands attracted her like a bee to a flower. Abandoning Claude, she rushed into the square with the rest of the young women and faced the line of men. They formed up for a calling of the figures, the first dance of the night's fun.

Guitar and banjo swung into a fast beat. The bones picked up the rhythm as the men and women went to the east, then to the west, and followed by circling about in couples. Hannibal swung Hester off the floor when they rotated, her laughter rising above the din from the others.

Claude's excitement grew as he looked on from his stance by the post. The sensuality of the dance goaded him beyond restraint. Setting aside his rifle, he jumped into the line, and joined in for the circling with his arm around a trim waist. The planter twirled and stamped and stretched, boisterous at the climax of foot-slapping against the dirt floor. He was winded and laughing when he came to a stop opposite Granny on her stool.

Claude bowed to the woman and held out his hand.
"Will you dance with me, Granny?"

Her teeth flashed white in a broad, ebony smile. Chuckling, she fended him off while she beckoned to Gabe. "You
stay wid Emily, Claude. Gabe de onliest one big enough ter
pleasure me."

Thunderstruck, Claude stood in silent wonder as the
implication sank into his consciousness. The waiting Emily
slipped her hand around his elbow and snuggled in close.
She hugged him while he stared open-mouthed at Granny.
The giantess grinned and winked at him and pranced off
with Gabe. When she entered the quadrangle, her massive
bulk took on a sensuous shaking.

"Pleasure her?" Claude asked Emily, mystified. "What'd
she mean?"

"He an' she gwine take dey time in de 'baccy leaves over
in de shed, Claude, soon's dey's ready. Granny ain't got no
man no mo'. She pleasure wid ones comin' thoo dat strike
her fancy." She looked up at him speculatively, a twinkle in
her eye and droll grin challenging him. "Kin do de same if
you want."

Wild thoughts ran through his mind and sweat beaded
his face. Overcome by the smell of the woman, he crowded
his body against hers, conquered by his desire and his need.
But even as he surrendered to his lust, a last shred of honor
picked at him. His cry when he jumped back was one of
desperation and escape. "Let's get to the dancin'."

Emily laughed as he stripped off his coat and took her
hand. They whirled and twirled through the hours of steps
and jumps and stamps, the incessant rhythm of the strings
and the clacks of the bones raising a fever in him. The odor
of the woman added to his sweating and did nothing to
relieve his torment, torn as he was between the passion of
his body and the chains of his mind. While he thought of
Letty off in Virginia, his body rubbed against the soft,
cushiony delights of the Negress, her purveyance of her
lustiness forced at every touching, with every reel filled with
her suggestive invitation. A particularly lewd embrace and
her orgiastic kiss snapped his last scruples. He took Emily's
hand in his and started for the door with the laughing

woman. She skipped in front of him, tossing her head and pulling him to the side. Desire vacuumed his mind of doubts. He clasped her moist fingers tightly and ran with her, following her invitation into the warm darkness of the shed rather than the mind-clearing cold of the night air.

A faintly paling sky ended the merrymaking and a last gathering at the remains of the mush pot. It had been set off the fire when the honey was stirred in. The revelers had eaten of the food when hungry, dashing out between dances. Slices of a stolen ham added to the appetizing taste of the sweet mush. Baked onions and potatoes filled out the feast, hot, tasty vegetables resurrected from the ash beds of the fire. Sleepy Negroes drifted off to the leaf beds in the sheds as the morning star rose in the sky, its clearness a harbinger of a fine day.

Granny was back on her stool when Claude joined her. She smiled at him, fresh and cool and awake, amazing him with her stamina. He was tired! And his lined face showed the exhaustion he felt after a night of revelry and passion.

"Soon be time fer you ter leave, Claude," she said. "I needs ter talk ter Hannibal an' Gabe. An' Hester if she be about."

His vernacular came out automatically. "I'se git 'em, Granny."

The group soon stood before her, knuckling their eyes and yawning as they stretched. But their grumbles at his impatient spurring goaded him into explosive anger, and a return to his military bearing with its demanding discipline.

"Shut up!" he ordered. "Granny's fixin' to help us and we've got to listen."

"You sleep 'til de sun up half," Granny said, "den slip on up de trace to'ard Chief Vann's. It de onliest way ter git dere quick." Her warning was deadly serious. "Jist watch fer dem secesh boys. Git off an' hide if dey come 'long. Dey bad."

She objected to their rifles. "Got ter leave dose," she insisted, over their protests. "De secesh militia kill ever' nigger dey fin' wid a gun. You got any others?"

Claude and Hannibal pulled out their hand guns and showed them to her. Claude's derringer was easily hidden in his pocket and his revolver hung by a loop behind his thigh. Hannibal's weapon was another matter. He holstered Snipes' horse pistol in a belt loop in front. Its large grip and bulky cylinder made a noticeable bulge in his coat when the lapels were closed. Granny clucked in dismay.

"You got ter carry dat behint, Hannibal, if you don' want ter leave it. De seceshers shoot yuh fust off, soon's dey see dat."

He shifted the loop behind his hip, its new location hidden by his coat and satisfying to the woman.

"Where do we aim for, Granny?" Claude asked. He brushed off the floor in front of her stool and handed her a splinter. "How far before we get to the Dalton trace?"

She sketched in the roads to the surrounding towns, with the barn a hole in the dirt and the river a scratch meandering past. "Swing 'roun' de edge o' de woods here at de barn," she said, "'til you strike de ribber. Go bek 'cross in de skiff dere an' aim to'ard de mountains. It ain't fur on 'til you cut de nawth trace." She marked the map with a swipe. "Be 'bout ten mile on nawth ter de crossin o' de big Holly Crick branch o' de Saugy. It heads up way east of Spring Place and de Injun house, Chief Vann's. You don' want ter foller it."

"Where then?" Claude asked, impatiently, when she hesitated. Her silence grated on him. The planter stuck his splinter into the map in several places and eyed her. "Here? Here?"

"Be still, Granny answered, and slapped his hand lightly with her stick. "I tells yer if you ain't so testy."

Gabe chuckled and clapped him on the back. "She some woman," he said.

Claude laughed at his own restlessness, at his urgent desire to be gone. His ashamed face mollified the helpful woman.

"Cut 'cross nawthwest ter de Dalton road from dat Holly Crick fordin'," she said. "It ain't too fur up. You's on de last piece den. You git bek safe if you kin ford de Saugy branches ter de nawth, an' 'scape de secesh pickets 'roun' de town."

"Are there many?" Claude asked.

"Dey's allus skirmishin' dere," she said. "De rifles

bangin' and den de cannon some." She waved her cudgel at him. "You be keerful."

He nodded, then glanced around the barn. All the strange Negroes had disappeared after they stored the poles and the cleaned pot. Emily stared back at him from her slouch by a post and Douglass and Lester waited behind her.

"They goin' with us?" Claude asked.

Granny shook her head. "No, Claude. Sent all de others out in fo's like yo'uns. Douglass an' his frens de bait ter fox de Minns wid if dey still pokin' 'roun'."

At her beckoning, the three slaves came into the candle light. Douglass carried a wooden pail full of a dark brown, evil looking mess. A strong odor of cured tobacco enveloped them when he set down the bucket. Without another word from Granny, the two men took off their pants and shoes and Emily shed her dress and shoes.

Claude stared at the half-naked Negroes in disbelief. His mind could not fathom Granny's intentions until she tapped his legs with the thin end of her cane and flicked the bottom of his pantsleg.

"You an' Hannibal take yer pants an' shoes off. An' Hester too."

Hester's protests earned her a whack with the knob end of Granny's cane and a sharp reprimand. "Don't you talk back ter me. I beat yuh good." Her threat cowed the girl into silence.

Two piles of clothes separated the lines of stripped Negroes. Picking up the outfits from Hannibal and Claude, Douglass and Lester quickly covered their nude extremities, while Emily did the same with Hester's garments. The dress stretched and a seam split over her bulging upper body, Hester's curves inadequate to satisfy those of the buxom woman. Claude was mesmerized by the display, unable to forget the night's pleasure until Hannibal interrupted.

"What dey gwine do now, Granny?" Hannibal said.

The woman shook her stick at him. "Wait," she commanded. Queenlike in erect bearing, she sat impassively on her stool.

Emily squatted and set to work. Dipping the remaining clothes and shoes into the pail, she soused them thoroughly with the tobacco mixture. While Douglass and Lester wrung out the pants and dress into another container, Emily called the fugitives to the tobacco bucket, one by one.

Claude stepped up to the kneeling woman, his nakedness embarrassing to him. His thoughts went back to the night before and her seductive subversion. But her eyes this morning were clear of guile and stared into his unflinchingly. Her hands were swift and thorough when she prepared him for the tobacco scented clothes.

"Git yer foot in de bucket, Claude," she said.

The cold mixture squished around his foot and wiggled toes. Emily applied a full coating of the tobacco to above each knee. His legs done, Hannibal and Hester followed and received the bath. The fugitives donned the wet clothes and shoes when finished at the bucket. As he did so, Claude's legs prickled and he pulled at his pants.

"It de pepper, Claude," Granny said. "Terbaccer keep de dog away. He smell it 'stead o' you. De pepper drive 'im off if he git close."

"You gwine git me too, Emily?" Gabe asked.

"Sho' nuff," she said, and tapped the side of the bucket. Emily, impatient, repeated her gesture when he delayed putting his foot in the mess, then flayed his reluctance.

"Git over here, Gabe," she angrily ordered. "Tek off yer shoes and step in, if you don' shed de pants."

He dipped his feet and pants together. Emily sloshed the liquid up his clad legs to wet them above the knee. But his shoes were too large for the bucket, their coating done by splashing.

"Dat orta do," Emily said, when she was finished and stood up.

Douglass picked up the pails and walked toward the shed while the buxom woman gathered a fold of Hester's dress and wiped off her hands. The strained cloth of her bodice split when she stretched and inhaled a deep breath. She gasped as her full bosom spilled out of the skin-tight dress. Covering herself with her hands, she ran out into the cool of the early morning.

"Damn!" Claude said. His disappointed face expressed his embarrassment. "We didn't even thank her." He started after the woman, only to be called back by Granny.

"Ain't no need, Claude. She know you 'preciate de he'p." Her eyes twinkled and she laughed. "An' de fun."

Douglass and Lester disappeared from the barn while Claude was listening to Granny. He didn't realize they were gone until she revealed her plan.

"Dey gwine head up ter Spring Place an' de Dalton road fastes' dey kin git dere. Den try ter circle 'roun' an' leave good scent nawth to'ard Tennessee. If de Minns' dawg strike der trail ter de mountains, de Minns ain't gwine trouble yuh no mo'."

"Dat sho' good," Hannibal said feelingly. The Negro's approval of the diversion was accompanied by grunts and nods from Gabe, the giant's head bobbing up and down.

Claude's silence covered his relief and gratitude to the amazing Granny. Not only had she fed them and given them solace and pleasure, she had mounted an offensive against the talents of his most feared pursuer, Old Blue. For the dog was the key to their downfall, he thought, if they were to cross with the Minns. He refused to dwell on fighting the man hunters, the fugitives' combined strength more than enough, unless the hunters fired from ambush. The planter recalled the men like Minns that he had met in the mountains of Virginia. They'd try for the upper hand, he knew, letting him know who did the killing before they fired the fatal shots. Particularly Minns. The hunter's compulsion to avenge his son's death would increase his desire to inflict pain before he killed them. But if he and Hannibal and Gabe could close the Minns without being wounded, they'd kill all the hunters and be done with them forever. His reverie was broken by Granny rising from her stool.

"I'se ready ter go," she said.

He could not let her leave unrewarded or unsung. Claude gave Granny the last two small gold pieces from Snipes' purse and hugged and kissed her. Her eyes widened at the gift, then brimmed with tears. She clutched the shiny gold as she sat back down and sobbed, rocking back and forth on her stool. Gabe knelt and put his arm around the weeping woman. He soothed her with whispers and hugs and gentle strokes of his huge hands. She was calm when he took her out of the barn, his arm around her shoulders. The giant returned an hour later bearing a simple message.

"She pray fer us." He shook his head, his face very solemn. "She say it mighty dangerous, dishere stretch, so be keerful."

"You took her back to her cabin?" the planter asked.

"Sho' did, Claude. She safe."

The sun had burned off all the worst chill when they rolled out of the tobacco leaves and struck to the north around the woodlot. Gabe scouted fifty paces ahead to alert them to any danger and Claude watched the rear. They passed the river and arrived at the trace after a mile of windy, cool travel with no intruders. The northern road penetrated dense forest interspersed with fields. Gently rolling hills filled the valley, with massive mountains bordering the eastern foothills. Their wary travel followed a path through terrain easy to hide in if need arose.

Minns' sweep with Old Blue carried them all the way north past Spring Place, then a few miles east of Chief Vann's house on the road to Ellijay. The hound showed no interest on any of the trails so they cattycornered back over to the north trace.

Jared protested the hard going around the creeks and steep sides when he slipped and fell as they cut across. "They ain't goin'a be on the mountains, Pa," he said. "Not after all these weeks o' travelin'. They'll be limpin' jest like you an' stayin' 'roun' the trails."

His father bristled. "I ain't hurtin', boy," he said huffily. "Jest that the cut that damned nigger gimme swole up my foot some. Binds the moccasin."

"Well we orta stop so's you kin soak it agin'. The cold water he'ped yuh last time."

Minns paused at the next tiny run where he bared his foot and stuck it in the cold water. The arch was puffed out, its swelling marked by a red gash and reddened streaks along the side of the foot. The hunter sighed in relief as the gurgling bath massaged the member. A short immersion left a shrunken, white foot, its spray of reddened skin diminished but not eliminated.

They made their foray north a brief one when Old Blue's nose found nothing of interest except a spikehorn buck. Stuffed with its liver and venison at the nooning, the old dog's bulging belly hung grotesquely below a rack of emaciated ribs. Jared laughed at the sight of the hound scrambling about, trying to cram down another bite of the scattered fragments.

"Old Blue 'bout full, Pa, but he's still tryin'."

Minns' jaw worked on his tobacco after his bait of deermeat, mingling the leaves into a juicy, round chaw. He sprawled on the soft bed of duff, his body up on his elbows as he watched the dog and boy. A shadow crossed his face when he surveyed their decrepit outfits, and the wornout dog and his hurting foot. Jared's thin body and clothes mocked him. White skin showed through holes in his son's leathers. More importantly, the boy's and his moccasins were ragged and were patched with inner pads of green hide. They made for uneasy footing while running, and invited more falls. Try as they might, the planter was as elusive as ever and the pursuers were no closer to killing him, or so Minns believed. He did not realize that he now was ahead of the fugitives, now in a position to wait for them to cross to his path. Jared's desire to give up the chase intruded into Minns' gloomy assessment and magnified the loss of will caused by the aching pain in his foot. The burden of his failures and the hunters' hurts crumbled Minns' resolve for vengeance and reinforced his decision.

"We give it two more days, boy," he said. "If we can't take 'em by then we're goin' on home."

Jared's surprised face transformed into a smile of hope and joy. "It be right, Pa," he said, jubilantly. "Even Old Blue 'bout tuckered out an' they's gone agin'. We ain't goin'a find 'em 'ceptin' by luck."

"When we git back above Spring Place we orta let Blue make another swing," Minns said, reflectively. "If he don't find nothin' we kin ease to the west along the Dalton trace. Talk to the first militia we cross."

Jared cinched up his belt and put some cooked deer

meat into his possibles sack. He swung an unskinned deer leg on a thong over his shoulder, his tread springy and his whistle cheerful as he cradled his rifle and faced his father. Old Blue picked up the last bit of meat and gulped it down; his stub tail wagged as he joined the boy.

"Won't take long to find the militia, Pa," Jared said. "Jest over to'ard Dalton four, five mile, I 'spect."

Minns stepped out with less of a limp, his shoulders up and square now that the decision was made. It was late afternoon when they were challenged by the pickets at the Coyehuttee, a west branch of the Conasauga. Their Sergeant gave the hunters his wisdom on intercepting runaways, acquired from months of experience with Negroes trying to cross to Dalton along the trace from the east.

"Send all we ketch on back ter the camp," was his final comment.

Minns grasped the man's arm, his voice rising. "Where's that?"

"You come right by it 'bout a mile back."

"That place?" Minns said, disappointedly. "Warn't nothin' but some ol' broke down niggers and a few militia. Is that all you ketch?"

The Sergeant nodded. "'bout right, Minns," he said. "Ain't many niggers hereabouts. Mostly Union folks farmin' that don't hold with slavin'. The young nigger bucks and the fillies 'scaped long since." He let out a half-hearted, rueful laugh as he winked. "Ain't even no use goin' pleasurin' no mo'. Ain't ketchin' no women worth havin'."

"Where do they try to cross? We want to ambush a bunch."

"Go back 'bout two mile," the Sergeant said. "The old road bears off to the nawthwest. Git on up it an' cross at the riffle into the cornfield in the bottom." He spit at a nearby stob and wiped off the dribble. "Over on the west side o' the corn, the path cuts up a wooded holler. They ain't much hills, jest rounded knobs. You kin take a stand at the saddle. They's real good cover."

Minns, intent on the Sergeant's descriptions as he absorbed the advice, asked a few questions about the bushwhack site. He shook the soldier's hand warmly when he fully understood the man's suggestions.

"We thank yuh, Sergeant," he said, appreciatively. "We got good reason fer findin' a 'scaped Yankee an' his niggers. They kilt my boy."

"Ye ain't takin' no prisoners?"

He laughed at Minns' angry gesture and reddening scar. "Git 'em all," he said. "Can't have no niggers killin' white folks."

When they were a few rods off on their return to the fork, he yelled, "We back yuh up here if they come by."

It took two hours to get to the ambush site. A fine, dense thicket lying close to the ground shielded them from the wind and concealed them from their intended victims. They made a roaring fire against a cut bank behind their stand and fed hugely on roasted deer meat. Scraping away the coals after the fire burned down, the two hunters slept on the warm earth, Old Blue curled in the hollow of Jared's bent knees.

Gabe led the group when the fugitives forded Holly Creek, the east branch of the Saugy. Its flow was higher than Granny had told them, also cloudy, as if an earlier rainstorm in the mountains had carried down some silt. They discovered a few holes in the swirling flow of their passage point, their water depths requiring an exploring foot or poking staff before they walked on. Hester's half-scream when she went under in one was choked off by Hannibal's rescue. Claude followed with a submerged bath when he stumbled and fell. Dripping and banged about, the fugitives came ashore at a clump of green holly trees. Their ford lay a mile downstream of the Rock Creek flow and west of the latter's crossing on the north road from Old Town. The sight of wagons and people on the trace there had discouraged them from a nearby passage of the tributary creeks. An upstream circle had appeared to be undesirable, since they would have had to expose themselves to the road traffic when they hiked toward the mountains. Thus, it was well after midday before they waded the branch, below the junction of Rock Creek with Holly Creek.

Claude gasped and choked from some strangling water

that intruded on his breathing. Hacking and coughing, he
spat out the offending material and slumped onto a downed
log. "That was a caution," he said. He breathed deeply, then
spit out additional phlegm as more coughing cleared his
throat. "We'll stay here a bit, 'til we get rested."

Gabe left the other Negroes and squatted beside the
planter. "Granny say ter cut over onter de Dalton trace,
Claude. How we goin'?"

"Quarterin' the sun, Gabe," he replied, and pointed to
the northwest. "Shouldn't be more'n four or five mile."

When they moved, the planter sent the big man ahead
on the track. Gabe struck straight across country, through
the narrow valleys and over the rounded, forested hills. But
all the climbing and skidding down the slopes to avoid farms
tuckered out the men and reduced Hester to tears. Hannibal
pulled her up slopes and carried the failing girl much of the
way. Hester protested the final stretch of the forced march
when she fell over some roots and slid down a steep bank.
She flounced to a log and sat down, rubbing her elbow while
she blubbered. Hannibal's soothing couldn't quiet her.

"Ain't got no reason ter run on so fast," she sobbed.
"Why can't we rest some? I ain't goin' no mo' t'day."

Shouts and rapid hoofbeats in the bottom below scared
them into statues, poised in uncertainty. Rifle shots cracked
down the slope, sharp snaps that were joined by the heavier
booms of shotguns sprinkling death. Pellets sprayed through
the limbs above the fugitives, creating little chopping noises,
and a few twigs dropped around them. They went to ground,
collapsing behind trunks and logs. Fearsome cries increased at the fighting ground, an invisible battle of shots,
yells, screams of mortal anguish, metallic sword clashes
and horses crashing together.

"Got a cavalry skirmish goin'," Claude said, as he slid
along the line of hidden Negroes. "Keep down 'til they're
done."

Hester sobbed and trembled and squeezed closer to the
planter, prone behind her log. He patted her back and
soothed the girl. "You'll be all right," he said. "Just be quiet."

Unseen horses smashed through the small growth
below them. Breaking saplings added their splintering

cracks to the din. But the firing slackened with the retreat of the fleeing body of riders. Their yells diminished as they returned a few scattered shots and dashed off to the north. The other troopers stayed in the valley and bunched. Claude trembled in relief when "Dismount!" stopped the troop and leather creaked. The metallic shriek of sabers being sheathed and moans from wounded men replaced the blasts of weapons. A horse's anguished screaming raised hackles on Claude's neck as he cautiously tried to see through the cover. One gunshot silenced the horse but not the wails of the wounded.

"They'll be gone soon," Claude said in a low voice. He raised his head cautiously and craned for a look at the force still in the valley. "Be real quiet. Can't tell if they're rebs an' can't take the chance o' sightin' 'em neither. They'd shoot first if we come on 'em while they're fevered up."

More creaking and moans followed a few commands, the words unintelligible to the hidden fugitives. Movement of the force to the north was slow, the sounds of walking horses gradually fading away. The sun had fallen well toward the horizon before Claude led them into the valley. Its flat, cropped fields and narrow, country road bordered a small, brushy creek, grown up with the usual willows.

Hester shrieked and hid her face at the torn bodies and the gouts of blood, the victims of gunshots or sword cuts sprawled over the field. Eight bodies lay on the ground, all clad in the nondescript outfits of the Confederates. The troopers, grotesque in death, were flanked by the carcasses of three horses. A buzzard circled over while they picked their way through the dead. The scavenger's presence was a shuddering reminder of the death that lay around them.

Claude looked about in dismay. They had been only a few yards from a Union cavalry patrol, with rescue in their hands. His gorge rose at the missed opportunity. But that damned skirmish had prevented it, he told himself. He did not regret not approaching the patrol after the battle. His fights in the war convinced him of the rightness of his caution. They would have killed his band without waiting, he realized, men on edge and with comrades down.

He knelt at a body on its back, the peaceful expression

on the reb's face surprising him. The man's hands held a
bible and were folded over his breast and the bloody hole
centering it. Lived long enough to pray, Claude thought. Or
was laid out by an enemy trooper before he left. Strange
camaraderie happened on the field. He once had helped a
rebel officer, the man's last wish scrupulously obeyed. He
had hoped someone would do the same for him while he
arranged the officer's limbs. Now here was a cavalryman, an
enemy, laid out with his bible. Claude crossed himself and
bowed his head as he recited the Lord's Prayer. He was still
kneeling when Gabe called to him.

"Dey's one here still breathin', Claude."

Gabe's crashing steps broke down the splintery willows
enough to reveal the wounded man. A pistol clicked empty
as the man cocked and triggered it. He threw it down in
resignation when Gabe nudged him with his foot, the reb
falling onto his back. One thigh dripped red when it stretched
out, its pantsleg soaked to the shoe.

A youthful, drawn face pleaded with Claude when the
planter bent over him. "He'p me! Please he'p me!" His lined,
graying visage brought a new sadness to the planter, its
shade a companion to a mortal wound. The boy's hand
grasped Claude's coat in a clutch of desperation. His grasping message reinforced the pleading in his eyes. "He'p me,"
he whispered.

God almighty, Claude thought, another boy. Wouldn't
it ever end? Tears ran down his cheeks at the sight of the
wounded man. His turmoil ended with another call for help,
an imploring whisper that implied doom and conquered his
soul. It's pathos galvanized his resolve and spurred him into
rapid action. Jerking out his knife, he slashed at the pants
and quickly freed the leg. Removal of the bloody covering
exposed the massive wound in the inner thigh. A splash
from the creek water cleaned the leg and revealed a tear
across the muscles, still flowing blood. The planter seized
Hester's bandanna and held out his hand to Gabe.

"Got any o' your chewin' leaf left?" he asked.

Claude stopped the bleeding by compressing the fresh
tobacco leaves tight against the wound. "Let's get him over
there," he said. With all hoisting, they moved the man to a

grassy spot next to the creek.

"Water, water," the boy whispered. Light-headed, he mumbled unintelligibly until they brought the cold water. But after they dashed some on his face and he gulped down a large measure, its impact restored him. Claude bent down close to the wounded man's lips to hear his faint murmur.

"Git me home," he said weakly. "Ain't but 'bout two mile. Wood Stephens' place."

"Where's that?" Claude asked.

"Nawth." The wounded man raised his quivering arm a bit and pointed with a forefinger. "Cut 'roun' the hill there. I show yuh."

"Any wagon an' team hereabout that we can get?"

"Army took all o' 'em. Have to carry me if you he'p."

His pleading face tugged at Claude's heart and erased any idea of leaving the youth. Seizing a bloody saber lying by a dead man, Claude told Hannibal to follow and ran for the slope.

Two saplings made rails for a stretcher. The Negroes picked up the bodies of the downed troopers with distaste, reluctantly stripping several under Claude's insistent prodding. Coats slipped on the poles and lashed tight completed the makeshift carrier. They loaded the man onto the stretcher and covered him against the cold day. Gabe and Hannibal took up the handles for the first leg of the trip, while Claude led the way and Hester walked beside the soldier.

Stepped off at a slow pace to avoid causing the boy more injury, the journey consumed almost two hours. And Claude, cautious, was always on the alert against trouble. He steadily picked out the way, detouring around scattered farmhouses and keeping to the valleys as much as possible. They climbed the forested slopes only when cover was scarce. It took all four of them to manhandle the stretcher across steep places, inclines where Claude exhorted the others and comforted Stephens when he cried out from the pain of sudden knocks. The sun was still an hour over the western tree line when the boy raised his head and smiled. A two story, unpainted house lay before them, a homestead framed against a background of barns and empty pastures.

"There it be," he said, gratefully, "home. Mama, she be

waitin'." His happiness warmed Claude's heart and he
stroked the boy's brow. Stephens showed more strength
and he struggled for a better look, his spirits bright. But the
trooper fell back, exhausted, sweat beading his forehead.

When they turned into the lane, a stocky, muscular
man rushed out with a rifle and thrust it at them, shouting,
"Git! Git! You bastards ain't stealin' nothin' here."

The threat of the rifle stopped them, its barrel squarely
aimed at Claude. Behind the farmer, white faces appeared
at the windows and a woman came around the side of the
house. Marching up to the rifleman, she pushed the barrel
aside and remonstrated with him.

"They ain't botherin' nothin', Wood. They got a hurt
man."

The wounded soldier raised his head from the pallet
and cried out as loudly as he could, "Mama! Mama!"

Even with the weakness and the distance, the woman
recognized her son's plea. She ran to the stretcher, falling
to her knees and crying when she saw the ashen face of her
boy. "Wood!" she screamed. "It's Clarke!"

She ran her hands over his face while he smiled and
relaxed back against the pallet, now on the ground. Her
tears and kisses intermingled as she loved him, uttering
endearments amid her tears. Wood ran up and knelt beside
the stretcher, then reached out cautiously and took his
son's hand. His apologetic face glanced once at Claude
before he turned to the covers. When he stripped off the
layers, the farmer blanched at the bloody leg and the woman
fainted dead away.

"We get him into the house," Claude said, "I can help
him."

Wood looked from his son to his unconscious wife, then
to Claude. "I'll take her," he said. "You fetch the stretcher."

A few minutes later, Clarke was stripped and rested in
his own bed. He sighed, his voice stronger and his color
slightly better. "It's warm, Mama. An' so soft."

Wood yanked him back when Claude started to unwrap
the bandage. His hard voice was stern and uncompromising
as he asked, "Who are yuh?"

It was not a time for lying, Claude told himself, but a

time to rely on the man's debt to them for their rescue of his son. He stood at attention and stared unflinchingly into the man's eyes.

"Lieutenant Claude Shaw, 7th Ohio Cavalry, headin' for Dalton. I had a wound and can help the boy."

Only one conclusion was possible for the reb, an escaped prisoner and running Negroes. His weathered face twisted in rage, then softened into acceptance as his son moaned and his wife's tear-stained face implored him for help. She grasped Claude's hand and pulled him down to the bed while Wood acquiesced by his motionless silence.

Claude undid the wound, now just oozing small drops. Calling for a pan and hot water, he bathed the leg and washed out the ragged tear. Then he treated it as Granny Esther did at Calhoun's, flushing the depths with raw whiskey from Wood's ready jug. Clarke jerked and groaned at the burning. Sweat dripped from his face while he endured the flaming hurt. The planter finished the treatment by filling the gash with a salve of mixed honey and bear grease from the mother's larder. Loose wrapping with white cotton strips completed the doctoring. Claude's advice to Clarke's mother was brief.

"He's got to rest and feed up good. When I was wounded, heat helped, so keep him warm."

The mother could not speak through her sobs; she just nodded her head and leaned against the officer. Hugging him until she regained her composure, she went to her husband.

"Help 'em, Wood," she said, crying. "You hated the Yankees since they kilt Chub. Claude's paid yuh back."

Wood was a grim, hard mountaineer, but it took only a minute or two, like ages to Claude, before his stern face crumbled and he surrendered to his wife's entreaty. He motioned to the officer and led him onto the porch, where he gathered Claude and the Negroes into a tight band. Wood choked up and a tear trickled down his leathery cheek. "We be grateful to yer fer savin' our last son," he said. He wiped his eyes with a callused hand and gave his word. "We'll feed yuh and you kin sleep in the barn. Termorrer I'll set you on the road to Dalton."

CHAPTER 25

Hester and Gabe

November 25, 1864. Coyehuttee Creek (West Branch, Conasauga River), East of Dalton, Georgia. Temperature 64\36. Sunny and cold. Winds variable to 12 knots. Moon almost entire night, a silver crescent waxing in first quarter.

"He's better, Claude," Belle Stephens said. Belle's nervous hands belied her whisper. Her fingers twisted her apron into wrinkles while she waited at the bedside.

Clarke looked up from his sick bed, his eyes bright and clear and roses in his thin cheeks. He was washed and clean. His glistening blonde hair, brushed back in wavy splendor, complemented his fair complexion and pale blue eyes. The restored boy grasped Claude's hand when the planter knelt beside him. He stroked it gently, then took it to his lips and kissed it and mumbled his thanks.

His mother gasped and her hands flew to her mouth when Claude unwrapped the boy's injured leg. Wood bent behind the planter, intent on the wound, while his wife turned away crying. The gash was crusted over, with the leg swelled around the ragged edges but not angry. The planter smiled and uttered a little cluck of satisfaction.

"Looks like he'll be all right," Claude told them. "No fever and the leg's not showin' any poison. Ain't no red streaks."

A mother's relieved, grateful prayer filled the room as Belle raised her hands to the ceiling and gave thanks. "Praise be to the Lord!" Wood Stephens added. Tears splashed the coverlet when Belle fell to her knees and pressed Clarke's head to her bosom. She covered his face with kisses while she stroked his hair and mixed incoherent endearments with prayers of joy and thanks. Her paroxysm finally ceased, crying replaced by concern for the wound and the success of Claude's doctoring. Withdrawing, wringing her apron into submission as she waited, Belle gave up her boy to the planter's full attention.

Claude added more salve to the crusting and wrapped the injury in a new piece of white cotton. When he was done with his ministrations, he patted Clarke's cheek and took the youth's hands in his own, his face gloomy.

"You remind me of my little son up in Virginia," he said. His melancholy produced a saddened, regretful mien and doleful tone. "We done killed too many boys in this war, Clarke. Don't you go back, even if the leg heals good. Stay with your folks; the fightin's 'bout over."

Wood started at Claude's confession and counsel, his arm gathering in his sagging wife. She leaned against him, content to watch the recovering boy and the sympathetic planter. The two veterans peered fixedly into each other's eyes, two warriors escaped from the killing. Enemies only in their allegiance, friends in their extremity, Clarke with his wound and Claude with his escape faced the future with uncertainty. But their silent communing cemented their mutual understanding and respect.

A tear ran down Clarke's cheek and he turned to his father. "He'p 'em, Pa," he asked. "They's jest like us." The boy's weak summons drew his father to his side. His mother brushed back his locks as Clarke's compelling grip on his father's arm pulled the man closer. "He'p 'em!"

"I'll do that an' more, boy," Wood said, emphatically. "I promise." He patted his son's hands and adjusted his covers. "Now you eat what yer Mama brings yuh an' git back to sleep. You'll be well directly."

Clarke nodded and relaxed on the bed, settling into the soft covers with a grateful sigh.

Back in the kitchen, Belle Stephens became a whirl-wind of activity. She bustled about while she and her daughter rattled pots and pans and prepared for the multitude. Belle sent in a bowl of well-sweetened mush and milk for the invalid. His sister tended to Clarke while the mother readied to serve the two men seated by the puncheon table.

"My friends need breakfast too, Wood," Claude said, very polite when he reminded the farmer of the three Negroes. Hester and the men waited in a group at the foot of the steps to the porch. Gabe stamped about in the brisk morning and flailed his arms against the cold, while Hannibal clutched Hester close to his body and shielded her from the biting wind. "I'm black from the walnut dye I told you 'bout but they's Negroes."

Stephens bridled and his voice hardened. "I ain't never fed no niggers in the house, Claude."

"They're my friends, Wood. They set me free and they saved my life." Digging into the countryman's honor about debts, he added, "And Clarke's life too."

The farmer stirred under the barb, its implications penetrating into his conscious thought. To the mountain-eer, honor fell above life itself. The fugitives had saved his son and his honor rose to acknowledge his debt.

"Set the plates, Belle," he said, "'stead o' the trenchers. We got guestes to feed."

Belle rummaged about on a shelf and produced three more chipped china plates while Wood ushered the Negroes into the warm kitchen. Six thankful souls gathered around the table, delicious aromas rising from the sliced meat, eggs and pone. Sweet potatoes steamed in a pile in the middle. The chickory coffee was hot, if not like the real bean, and plentiful and odorous. Belle said the grace while they bowed their heads.

"Our Father, bless our son and these travelers that saved his life. Protect all of them; take them safely through the wilderness of their lives. And bless this food to our bodies and us to thy service. Amen."

A chorus of amens added to the woman's blessing before the group, Negro and white alike, attacked the appetizing food, old prejudices forever set aside.

Minns scouted the ambush site in the early morning while Jared watched the trail. The hunter's ramblings took him west along the overgrown track to a large, wooded ravine. Its shallow, rounded gash led him even farther to the west, toward Dalton and its occupiers when he followed its seeping bottom. Always careful of his footing, Minns avoided the marshy spots with their rank grass and boggy traps for the unwary step. A Yankee camp lay on the rolling, western farmland and forest and scattered through the outskirts of the town. The Union Army's innumerable tents shined in the morning sun. Wide fields separated the rounded hillocks, and infantry works were visible on both sides of the fallow field separating the forces. But Minns found only one rebel soldier at the junction of the ravine and the fallow field, a young man nervous at the intrusion when Minns and Blue stole into his firing pit.

"You 'lone, boy?" Minns asked.

"Who are yuh?" the youth said nervously. Not more than fifteen, the picket's uncertain gaze trembled before Minns, but not before he cocked and pointed his rifle.

When Minns struck aside the barrel, the boy's tightened finger fired the weapon into the bank. The hunter laughed and seized him, pinning the youth's arms as he struggled and screamed his protests. Commands and cocking noises carried across from the Yankee pits and a holler challenged them.

"Hey, Johnny, what'cher doin'?"

Minns shouted back. "Go to hell, Yank. This here's a private tussle."

Laughter followed from the Yankees and their pits subsided into silence.

"Be quiet," Minns said. "I ain't goin'a hurt yuh."

His victim cowed into submission, Minns surveyed the line of pits. Old Blue lay crouched on the cool dirt, threatening the sentinel into immobility while the hunter peered about. Minns turned back to the picket after a cautious squint at the Yankee positions.

"Any more our boys 'round?" he asked.

"Jest me in this stretch," the reb replied. "Only one o' us

'bout ever' half mile, now Hood's gone up ter Tennessee an'
Sherman left 'lanta. Don't do no fightin' much, jest watchin'
an' snipin'."

Minns nodded. He left as abruptly as he came, stealing
back through the heavy brush at the end of the ravine. The
dog was gone when the sentinel turned around. He seized
his rifle with trembling fingers and fumblingly reloaded
while he cursed the hunter.

Minns and Old Blue made plenty of noise when they
came up on Jared, the boy still in his ambush at the saddle.
They crouched beside him for a moment before moving over
to Athey's own stand.

"You seen er heard anythin', boy?" Minns asked.

"Ain't nothin' stirrin', Pa," Jared replied. He shivered in
the wind whipping through the trees. "Purty cold. Need
more o' that fire."

Minns shook his head. "Can't trust the smoke. Jest
cover up with bresh."

"How long, Pa?"

"We stay right here 'nother day. If they don't come we
git on back like I said."

Minns chewed on remnants of cooked deer meat from
his possibles sack when he was settled in his stand. He had
cut more brush and added it to the natural growth, dense
enough also to give him cover from the biting wind. Old Blue
squeezed into the stand with him and curled up around his
feet. The dog's heat warmed Minns while they waited on
their quarry, but the animal's snores disturbed the quiet of
the forest until the hunter slapped him into consciousness
and silent watchfulness.

Wood Stephens' bulky frame slid back down the bank,
his worried face transferring his fears to the planter.

"They's a set o' pickets at the bridge," he said. "Ain't like
'em." His lips compressed into a grim slit and his face
creased with worry lines. "Somethin' bad fixin' to happen.
We gotta go back 'round to the old road."

"Can't go south?" Claude asked. "River looks better fer
crossin'."

"No," Wood replied, shaking his head. "They's a bad

ford an' too many farms. Our boys er thick that way. They ketch yuh right fast."

The Negroes lay prone behind some trees as Claude and Wood stole back from their lookout. The guide's low-voiced warning kept them silent and still, a caution they heeded while their wide eyes followed the planter. He whispered to Wood as he pointed upstream.

"Can we swing around to the north, say up five mile?"

"Too rough to git through, ground and the water. Lot's took there an' some hurt. Best way is to circle to the wye, then foller the old road."

"How far?"

"Mile er so. We jest slip back through the woods and skirt 'roun' the nigger camp. Take maybe an hour." Wood looked up at the sun and the fast moving clouds. "Ain't more'n noon so's you should git to Dalton 'fore dark."

The overgrown wye showed no evidence of the Minnses' soft moccasins when the men arrived at the junction. Wood led them in until they were well screened from the main road, and halted in a small clearing. He gathered them in close to give them his final directions.

"Rest be easy," he said confidently. "Jest foller the trail after you cross the river. They's a good ford and the river ain't too high."

"Any place to hide quick on the other side?" Claude asked.

"The standing corn in the bottom 'll give you cover to the trees," Wood replied. "It ain't been shocked yet."

"Road go on west to Dalton?"

"Trail heads up to a saddle 'tween two small hills, then leads west inter a ravine with good cover. It drops down to the pickets at a fallow field. You have to git by them on yer own."

"Many hereabouts?"

"Most likely only one, Claude. Our Georgia boys mostly gone after that Sherman bastard."

Two strong, uncompromising men faced each other in the shaded midday light, a Rebel and a Yankee. But the common bond of the wounded boy and the help of each to the other bound them together, even beyond sharing salt.

Wood broke the silence of their face-off, squirming uncom-
fortably in his awkward attempt to express his gratitude.

"I be grateful, Claude. An' fer Belle too."

The planter sighed and his eyes grew misty. He trembled
as he made his vow. "I'll kill no more boys in this war, Wood.
Your boy is the last one hurt I want to see. We thank you and
Belle for your help."

Hannibal and Gabe echoed Claude's gratitude. But
Hester stole silently up to the farmer, instead, and gave him
a hug and a kiss. Her tribute brought a smile to his
weathered face and an unbegrudging acceptance of equality.

"Ain't no reason we all can't leave in peace, Claude.
You, me, the niggers." Wood's lined features softened when
he searched the faces of the quiet fugitives. "Ain't no reason
we all can't be free."

A friendly wave in parting and they soon were hidden
from each other, Claude and his companions on the trail to
the river. The riffle wet them above their knees and soaked
the men's pants to the waist but provided a safe footing.
Hester giggled as she tied her skirt up around her middle,
her legs bare to the chill water. She carried her shoes and
this time waded the stream without falling. But the cold
wind and wet extremities forced them into sheltering growth
on the west bank, a dense stand of willows and grass. They
wrung out their clothes and dried off, shivering until they
warmed up, and Hannibal used the last of the walnut dye
on Claude's light spots.

Meat and pan bread from their possibles sacks graced
a small cloth on the ground as they rested on the duff. The
sight and aroma of the Negroes' food prodded Claude's
stomach into growling twists. He picked out a few aromatic
pieces from the ample store forced on them by the grateful
Belle. Rest added strength to their lift from the feeding,
remnants either stuffed down full gullets or cached in the
sacks.

Claude chuckled at the sight of them saving scraps.
"Recken we got plenty this time, Hannibal," he said.

"Dat Miz Belle mighty good ter us," Hannibal replied.
He swallowed down one last piece of meat. "She right

grateful 'bout de boy."

The planter nodded. "She's to write me 'bout Clarke. He'll be up and around directly."

Obscurity in the cornfield gave way to a wide path through the forest, the clearings grown up with bushes. The thick brush along the formerly well-opened trail bothered Claude as they penetrated the regrown wilderness. Somehow it seemed forbidding, a somber tunnel that cast a dark veil over his thoughts, and added to the menacing shadows formed as the clouds cast the forest into gloom. The bordering trees' heavy canopy with its remnant leaves shielded out some of the direct light among their trunks. Flickering rays penetrated the cover through openings created by the wind in the tops. They made little, dancing flecks of light on the leaves. A dance of death, Claude thought, and shuddered. His dread increased as he reflected on their plight and the pickets at the edge of Dalton. We'll find a way, he told himself impatiently. After this far, to fail? He rejected the frightening idea, angry with his lack of confidence as he faced the unknown.

As usual, Gabe had led off when they stole on, their footsteps light as though they expected no trouble. Claude and Hannibal bunched at a widened place, just below the easier grade of the shallow, rounded saddle.

"I'll spell Gabe, Claude," Hannibal said. "He done broke back 'nough bushes fer us ter git through."

The silent planter was intent on the forest sounds and just waved him ahead. Hannibal brushed by and rushed to catch the giant. The fugitives had come out onto the slightly sloping ground of the saddle and were almost together when Gabe stopped and pointed to a seep in the ground.

His bellow, "Dere's a dog track!" would have awakened the dead.

Old Blue snarled and launched himself from the stand, his attack destroying Minns' surprise.

Hester shrieked in terror. "It's Blue!" she screamed hysterically. "De Minns here!" Her body shaking, she sank to the ground.

Gabe charged even as the dog growled and jumped for him. The giant kicked the hound aside as he aimed for the

Minnses' hideout. Minns and Jared had made a cardinal error, setting up their stand too close to the killing field for an aimed shot. Taken unawares by the dog's attack and unable to murder the fugitives one by one from hidden rests, Blue cost them their chance at stealth and surprise. Minns jumped out and swung his rifle at Hannibal, firing while in mid-stride. The Negro dropped like a dead-shot bird. Gabe took Jared's blast in the side but the blow from the tiny ball brought only a grunt and did not stop his assault. His eyes fastened on the boy and he charged in, Old Blue barking and snapping around his legs. The Negro tripped over the dog and fell at Jared's feet, but pulled the boy down with him when he toppled over.

Pandemonium ruled the fight, with the warriors in frantic motion. Shouts and curses relieved their tensions as most men did in battle charges. Only Hester was still, her head bowed over the fallen Hannibal as she cried hysterically. Red streams of blood ran down her arms when she raised her imploring hands to the heavens. At the sight, her horrified face gradually twisted into one of rage and hate. She crouched by Hannibal and watched the fighting men, her body tensing into that of a lioness ready to spring. Her eyes fixed on Minns, her pursuer and tormentor, a demon now trying to kill them all. Creeping forward close to the ground, she went by a blasted yellow pine, a majestic tree with a top reduced to splinters by lightning. Her gaze diverted from Minns when she fell over the debris and painfully landed on a pile of stickery fragments. A four foot splinter with a massive knot in the big end stuck out of the tangle. Hester seized the club and raised it, ignoring the stickery edges and tearing barbs that savaged her hands. With the weapon poised, she again resumed her crouching stalk of Minns, her eyes focused on him like a snake's on a bird.

Claude had drawn his derringer with its large, heavy ball, instead of the lighter revolver, as soon as the dog attacked. He rushed in for a close shot when Minns pointed his rifle and fired at Hannibal. Claude's derringer was good only for action at a few feet, mostly across poker tables, so he aimed to close the hunter's body. Minns gyrated after his shot and dropped his rifle when the planter rushed him, then pulled his own pistol. But the planter was faster, firing just as the hunter squeezed the trigger.

They both missed their body shots, but the planter's earlier ball struck Minns' pistol hand and mangled it into uselessness. The man hunter stared in shock at the spurting blood and dangling fingers, one hanging by a thread of skin. He did not see Claude lying next to an oak trunk, half-conscious and vulnerable. The hunter's preoccupation with his hurting, bleeding hand overwhelmed him and diverted him from the planter.

Claude's right leg had deserted him at Minns' shot. The boom of the weapon was followed by a great blow which struck his foot and jerked it around. Its yank, added to his jump toward Minns, turned him on his back. He came down on the hard ground against a dense, knobby oak root, the loss of breath and heavy blow to his head knocking him unconscious. There was an instant of senselessness, then he lay prone, only half- conscious. His head ached and his eyes were unable to focus clearly when he could see Minns. Something nagged at him as he lay there, his conscious thought almost as if at peace with himself, detached from his body. He marveled at the bloody hunter's swearing and Minns' fumbling tries to wrap his hand in a piece of cloth. Claude's mind told him to move but his senses were unable to force his muscles to act. Alarms ran through his thoughts. He'll kill me if I lie here! Conscious warnings intensified as he tremblingly recovered and sat up. Unable to keep his equilibrium in a dizzy whirl of seeing double, Claude rolled over onto his hands and knees and crawled away from Minns just as screams erupted down the slope.

"Pa! Pa! He'p me!"

Jared's terrified cries were followed by a gunshot and a bellow from Gabe. Blue's ferocious growls added to the thrashing of the fighters hidden behind Jared's stand, the boy running away and hollering when he got free. Gabe crashed through the brush in pursuit. Blue's barks and growls followed the din of the retreating fight as it moved down the hill.

Minns was as if deaf, his preoccupation with his hand

continuing as he lingered in the glade. He made no move to reload his weapons but stood stunned, rooted in place, while his mumbling sorted out the disastrous wreckage of his plans.

"Jeremy kilt. Jared goin'a be kilt. Ain't got no hand kin use."

His paralyzing shock turned into a tiger's roar of hate and vengeance and a thrusting, bloody hand flinging red drops. "I'll kill that damned Shaw!"

Looking about in fierce concentration, he spied Claude creeping away, unable to rise. Minns pulled his knife with his left hand and grasped it in an edge-up position. He ran toward Claude just as Hester screamed her hate.

"Fer you, Minns!" she shouted. The enraged girl sprang in with her knobby club and struck him on the blind side of his head. Her glancing, roundhouse swing gashed his left cheek and knocked him down. Minns' knife flew off into the leaves and blood spattered his scar. But Hester's blow, which diverted him from Claude, only infuriated the hunter rather than subdued him.

"You God damned nigger bitch!" he yelled when he bounced up. Minns went for the girl, his fierce eye fixing on her. "I kill yuh after I do fer Shaw!" He seized her club and jerked the girl into his grasp. His good hand reduced Hester into a beaten heap in a few blows, her club under her.

Minns scuffed around in the leaves, flinging them about in his frantic effort to find his lost knife. He stumbled over his rifle in his circles. Its shining metal sparked a wild gleam in his eyes and his promise when he picked it up. "I shoot the bastard," he said. Maddened, he laughed hysterically and shouted out, "You hear me, Shaw? I shoot yuh."

Cradling his rifle in his right arm, he tried to load it left-handed. His first try with the powder horn spilled powder over the edge of the measure and blood wet the charge, ruining it. He gave up after another unfortunate attempt and poured powder directly into the barrel from the horn. When Minns rummaged in his pouch for a ball, he dropped several from his trembling fingers before taking one into his mouth. The hunter's incoherent mumbling increased and a tick twitched his scar. Unable to find a patch, he wet the ball

with a bit of chaw and dropped it into the end of the barrel.
Hard ramming seated it and his awkward thrusts with a cap
finally armed the weapon.

An anguished scream down the slope froze Minns like
a deer poised for flight. His head up and intent on the forest
sounds, he heard only deep silence. It marked the end of
Jared's battle, mournful howls from Old Blue sounding a
dirge for the boy. The hunter shook himself and turned to
Claude. His menacing scowl was accompanied by a string
of rambling curses while he catfooted toward the crawling
figure.

"Goin'a kill yuh, Shaw. Goin'a kill yuh."

Claude turned over onto his back and inched along in
the leaves as Minns approached. He was still seeing double
and weak from his fall and could not seem to orient himself.
His mind told him to flee and his legs refused, and all the
while his fears grew. The sweating planter groped for his
knife as Minns got closer, the man hunter advancing to
point-blank range.

Forgotten by Minns in his anger, Hester kept her eyes
fixed on his buckskin-clad back as she stole along behind
him. She had picked up the club absentmindedly when she
rose from Minns' beating, ignoring the hurtful edges. Her
reverse clutch unknowingly converted the splinter into a
cruel spear with ragged edges. The heart pine, full of resin,
was sharp and hard as stone. Hester's stalk, in time with
Minns' staggering walk, took her just to the rear of the
hunter. He was cocking the rifle when she screamed exultantly and ran forward, jamming the sharp end in under his
ribs on the left. The unforgiving point went clear through the
man, the splinter's jagged edges tearing and rending, until
the reddened tip stuck out a foot in front of his belt. Minns'
rifle fired when the pitiless girl struck him and its ball,
unaimed, flew off harmlessly into the trees. Hester gave him
no mercy. She jammed herself against the base of the spear
and forced it in farther, even as her hands turned red from
the stickery edges.

The hunter screamed in anguish when the splinter
ripped through him, and tore himself from the girl's grasp.
His wounded, tormented face worked in agonizing contrac-

tions while he careened off; then he turned back toward the vengeful Negress with his rifle clubbed in defense. But Minns dropped the weapon and sought the splinter when she made no move. Groaning, he grasped the bloody spike sticking from his stomach and pushed on it, without avail. Hester laughed triumphantly at the staggering Minns, savoring his agony and mortal wound.

"Got to git this thing out," he muttered. "Ain't finished yet, ol' hawse."

Minns' bleeding hands and belly dripped blood along his legs as he clutched the spike. He howled when he reached behind him and tried to dislodge the splinter while he pushed on the point. But the rough wood stayed firmly in place, anchored by its serrated edges. Minns' anguished moans degraded into whimpers as he headed off toward an old stump.

Hester did not follow the hunter but knelt at Claude's side and slid out his bowie. Her frame resumed its catlike rigidity and crouch as she commenced another stalk, her eyes glued on Minns' search.

A stand of saplings had sprouted from the old stump near the trail. A deformed pair had grown together, leaving their crossing in a compressed vee. It was there that Minns found his help. Backing up to the vee, the hunter forced the spear down into it and wedged the knot. The splinter tore at his middle while he tested its tightness, and his groans came rapidly when he forced himself to pull toward the sharp end. Its agonizing hurt was so compelling, so shattering, that he missed Hester's stalk, her menace escaping his notice during his concentration on the spear. She stole slowly, stealthily toward him, picking her way quietly through the fallen leaves. Hester held her right arm out rigidly, its hand clasping Claude's knife. Blade out in front, edge up, the long bowie at the end of her arm was a phallic symbol of revenge.

Minns had about escaped the spear when Hester seized his beard and jerked his head up. He flinched at the sight of the girl's passionate hate and the rigid knife, and his eye flashed terror. "No! No!" he cried. Spittle dribbled onto his beard as he begged. "No! No!"

The knife drove upward into his pelvis even as he pleaded and his rising under Hester's thrust propelled him back onto the spear. Again she thrust. And again. Her arm and knife dripped bright red when she stepped back from the monstrous thing impaled on the spear.

Scarred from past battles, wounded in the face and hand and speared in the middle, the mortal knife wounds reduced Minns to unintelligible mumbling and ineffectual gropings as his life ebbed away. He sank into twitching, his buckskin-clad figure forming a scarecrow in death. The girl lifted up his head and inspected the one lifeless eye and drooling mouth. Minns' tongue dripped blood and spittle as it hung out. The thick red serum dangled in strings from his beard, their long teardrops breaking off and renewing as they fell and spotted the leaves. Hester spit in Minns' face, her last slash to his right cheek leaving him with a wound to match his scar.

Claude sat up and motioned toward Hannibal when Hester slid the bloody knife back into his sheath. "Help me," he said.

The girl pulled the planter erect and braced him when he walked in his dizzy, tottering journey to Hannibal's prone figure. Claude collapsed down beside his friend in fear, the body still prone just as it fell. His, "Thank God!", when Hannibal's chest heaved up and down, gave way to weeping. The trembling Hester fell onto the unconscious man and added her tears, her endearments and caresses interspersed with kisses.

A roaring fire at their camp warmed the fugitives against the cool night, the cheering blaze centered in a rounded dent in the earth. The well-matted surface lay down the slope from the saddle and held a small spring below. Heavy growth around the water and the rolling ground screened them from intruders and broke the force of the winds. Hester and the planter had dragged Hannibal to the camp after inspecting his wound, but quit on a search for Gabe, unable to continue. Hannibal lay inert while Hester crooned over him, the three injured fugitives resting for the night.

Minns' rifle ball had struck Hannibal's left cheekbone and shattered it. But the dense, rounded surface had deflected the missile along the facial bone at the side of his head. Its slashing travel had left a long gash that bled all over the Negro's jaw and neck. The wound ended in a lump under the skin behind Hannibal's left ear.

After they camped, Claude cut into the skin to remove the pellet. When the mashed lead dropped out into his palm, its lightness told him why Hannibal was still alive.

"Look, Hester," he said, as he rotated the mass before her. "Its a small rifle ball. If it'd been a minie, it would'a killed him. Minns' huntin' rifle helped us."

They knelt while Claude prayed his thanks and for his friend's recovery, and Hester chanted to her Lord.

Claude tried to control his shaking while he sat before the fire, reliving the fight and its gruesome end. His vision gradually had returned but a monumental headache bedeviled him and his neck hurt. Chewing on a piece of Belle's meat, he shivered in fear when a howl rang out up by Minns' body. His derringer appeared as if by magic.

Hester put her hand on his pistol and grasped it tight. Her calm voice soothed him. "Old Blue's hurtin', Claude," she said. "He don' have no master no more."

A whine and glinting eyes scared them a few minutes later. The old dog lay in the shadows of the night, his crouch just outside their camp. He whined again and wagged his stump. When Claude held out a piece of cornbread, its odor was irresistible. The dog's ribbed body inched along the ground until he could seize it. That piece disappeared in one fast gulp and he took another with a snap. Claude fed the old hound to fullness, then stroked his head and back, scratching behind his ears and cooing to him. Old Blue stretched out along the planter's frame when the two drifted off to sleep in the welcome warmth of the fire.

CHAPTER 26

Hannibal

November 26, 1864. Dalton, Georgia. Temperature 62\33, fair and cool. Northwest winds, gusting to 15 knots during the day. Crescent moon rising about sundown, waxing in the first quarter.

Thunk! Thunk! The heavy pounding interrupted the rat-tat-tat of a nearby woodpecker and the chirps of the smaller woodland birds. Thunk! Claude stood on one foot in the thick leaves as he swung his arm, his right foot resting on his left shoe. Toes protruded from his holey sock. Overbalanced, he almost fell when he struck the tree again with his shoe heel. His pounding against the hard bark drove the chunk of leather back onto the nails.

Hester's soft voice interrupted the planter's fixation with the shoe. "Dat 'bout done, Claude? De shoe 'bout mended?"

Claude shook his head in disgust. "The nails keep comin' through the heel where Minns' pistol ball centered it." He sighed and shuddered, a chill running through him. "Sure knocked me upside down, Hester."

She nodded and went back to her task of picking splinters from her damaged hands, her eyes and a knife point busy. The young woman basked in the warmth of the fire while she waited on the men and tended to her hurts. Her face was placid but puffed and scratched from the fight

with Minns. Hannibal drank noisily at the spring below,
then dunked his head in the cold pool and flung drops
everywhere when he emerged, blowing. The girl already was
clean. She had rinsed out her bloody dress and washed her
body before the men were up. Only the splinters and bruises
remained.

When Claude pounded his shoeheel again, she put
away her blade and joined him. "You got ter fin' Gabe," she
said. "He dead most likely. Tek his shoes an' stuff 'em wid
grass."

At the girl's practical suggestion, Claude put bark over
some offending nails inside and tied the ruined shoe on
loosely. He grimaced when he hobbled about to try it.

"Ain't bad," he said. "Only a few sticks. Soon as
Hannibal's ready we'll go after Gabe."

They warmed at the fire while Hannibal washed out his
shirt. Bloody seepage from the spring water discolored the
tiny trickle down the slope until the garment was clean.
When it was wrung out, he splashed at the spring until he
and his other clothes were free of the caked blood from the
fight. Hannibal's eyes were clear when he joined them and
fell to on the remnants of Belle's largess. At the meat's
appearance, Old Blue sniffed and abandoned the stump he
was investigating. He crouched at Claude's side and eyed
the food and Hannibal's gorging. His whine pried a piece of
meat out of the Negro. The hound caught it in the air and
gulped down the offering.

Claude stroked the old dog and felt of his ribs. "Blue's
sure poor," he said. "Those Minns didn't feed him right."
Taking pity on the hound, he rummaged up some more
pieces of pan bread from his sack. Blue greedily swallowed
them all, his stub tail wagging at the gift and the planter's
pat on the head. But his eyes never left Hannibal and the
meat. His shameless begging finally coaxed out another
large gift. Claude roared with laughter and said, "He's good
at beggin'."

Hannibal chuckled as he put away his sack and wiped
his mouth on his sleeve. "Dat ol' dog gonna make yuh one
fine fox houn' up ter Greenbottom."

"Your head all right now?" Claude said.

The Negro gingerly fingered his wounds. "Powerful pained," he said, "but I git dere. Dat Minns 'bout finished dishere chile."

Hester shuddered and grabbed him around the body. She hugged him fiercely and kissed him. "You ain't goin'a leave me, boy. Yer bone too hard fer de ball. De Lord done look over us bof."

Claude moved his own head sideways and his neck grabbed him. Then his headache added to his misery. But at least his pains were much better, he thought. Hester's hot clay, baked into a brick in the fire, had felt wonderful when she wrapped it against his neck and weakened shoulder. Two treatments and he could function. We'll all be well, he told himself, after a big rest in Dalton. The thought spurred him to action.

"You ready, Hannibal?" he asked.

The servant nodded and swung out toward the trail with a firm step. Hester and Blue fell in behind him. Claude brought up the rear while they climbed the slight slope to the fighting ground. When they sighted Minns, Hester ran into Hannibal's arms, hiding her face against him while Claude searched the site. She would not go near Minns, a buckskin clad scarecrow impaled on the spike. But Blue sniffed the hunter's body, then howled, his hackles rising. The hound backed away and crouched in some soft leaves, but his eyes were alert and followed the fugitives as they moved about.

Claude stumbled over Minns' rifle as he circled the body. Its brass and silver trim flashed in the sun when he picked it up. The rifle's long barrel gleamed with oil, the metal's blackness contrasting with the beautiful, tiger-striped, curly maple stock. Claude rubbed his hands along the polished wood and barrel and examined the sights, then hefted the weapon and tried its balance.

"Mighty fine rifle," he told them. "I'll keep this one."

He whistled in amazement at the maker's mark on the lock, an engraving with fancy curlicues that enclosed a name and date. "It's a Fordney, Hannibal, from Lancaster. He was one of the best." Claude rotated the piece and admired the furniture, and the smoothly curved stock that added to the beauty of the long gun. He checked the bore, good rifling showing at the end, and held it up for the Negro's inspection.

"See?" Claude said. "It's probably 36 caliber or there-abouts. Saved yuh, bein' so small. Good for squirrels or deer, either one." He swept the rifle up level and sighted quickly on an oak knot. The piece fit naturally in the curve of his shoulder, instantly aligned. "Old Minns knew his guns," he said, admiringly.

A search of the dead man turned up only five lead balls and a few caps. Claude took them and the carved powder horn, his trophies from the victory. A fat leather purse hung from Minns' belt. Curious, he dumped it out. Clinking and the sparkle of yellow gold followed, the disgorged coins building an impressive mound in his palm.

He held them out to the girl. "They're yours, Hester," he said. "You killed him."

Hester shuddered and drew back. "Don't want nothin' o' Minns."

"I'll save 'em for you and Hannibal," Claude said. The refilled purse went into his coat pocket, along with the lead balls and caps.

Minns hung where he died, an apparition to frighten anyone on the trail. Claude paused before leaving and said a prayer over his foe. "You tried to kill us, Minns," he said at the end, "but may God let you rest in peace."

Jared's rifle lay down the grade where he and Gabe had first fought. The bent barrel and broken stock attested to the ferocity of the blow it had rendered. Drops of reddish brown blood and scattered leaves led them to Gabe and Jared at the foot of the slope. Gabe's huge frame blanketed the broken body of the boy. Jared's back and neck were bent out at odd angles over the log where the Negro had destroyed him. Bloody stains at his mouth and nose marred the contorted face and the protruding tongue. His pistol was missing but his knife was buried to the hilt under Gabe's left arm, the hunter and the hunted locked together in death.

Old Blue sniffed once at the dead boy and howled, an eerie, mournful note that caused shivers to rush up and down Claude's spine. The hound cast about restlessly as if lost, running in and snuffling at the body and whimpering. Claude felt for the old dog, his boy dead, a friend so different from Minns. The planter called in the dog and petted him until the animal crouched and lay still.

Hester had wasted no time. She undid the thongs of Gabe's shoes and yanked them off as soon as they found the dead men. Her search for sweet grass took her down to a cleared field. Claude pulled on the enormous leathers when she brought them back, pushing his toes through the soft grass the girl had stuffed in them. The big shoes flopped when he walked but cushioned his feet against hurt.

Hester held a few more wisps of grass, while she watched him clump around in the leaves. "Dey all right, Claude?" she asked.

"They'll work just fine," he told her. His head swung about, sighting the dog but not the Negro. "Where's Hannibal?"

"Last heard him on down de slope."

Hannibal's halloos in answer to Claude's yell guided them to his side. The Negro motioned to the deep hole by the fanned, upright roots of a windfall. "Good fer Gabe, Claude. We bury 'im an' say de blessin'."

"We'll put 'em both in together. The boy needs some words too."

A quarter hour of sweating, grunting labor sufficed to move the bodies into the hole. Working with their bowies, the men scraped down a thin blanket of earth and cloaked the warriors forever. Deadfall limbs tossed on the meager layer added a secure cover under the trees. A dirge for the fallen sounded among the clattering branches of their tops, mournful chords composed by a brisk wind. Claude sighed in pity at their reminder, pity at the sacrifice of two strong, young men. The grave would be lost in the woods, never to be discovered. It at least ought to be marked, he thought. He made a rude cross of two sticks before scrambling up to the edge for the prayer.

The officer stood with bowed head while he composed himself. It's them and not me, he thought sadly. Gabe saved our lives when he charged the hunters and hurried them. And lost his life in the end. Regret deepened into gloom as he recalled the ever-willing giant and his help. Surviving a battle so often depended on luck. He was lost in his personal reflection, and dejection over Gabe's death, when Hannibal punched him in the arm.

"Got ter move, Claude," he said. "Pass de pickets t'day so don' want ter git ketched here moonin'."

Composing himself, Claude raised his right arm in benediction and made the sign of the cross. "Dear Lord," he said. "We consign to you the souls of Gabe, a fine friend who laid down his life for us, and the Minns boy, who was faithful to his father and to his trust. It is for you to judge them. We ask that you be merciful and take them to your bosom into eternal rest. Amen."

"Amen, Amen," quickly followed from the two Negroes.

Hester turned immediately from the grave, leaving the men to follow. Old Blue pawed at the new earth and whined before he chased along behind her. He and Hannibal soon took the point while they walked back to the saddle. But Claude could only lumber along after the Negroes in Gabe's great shoes. Even with grass inside to cushion the shocks, they pinched and flopped and his feet slid about. He cursed them roundly as he tried to tread softly, and failed.

The young woman shuddered and averted her eyes when they passed the spike with its impaled body. Old Blue snuffled once at Minns, then ran in close to the planter while they hustled along the trail. They crossed the saddle and dropped down into the ravine beyond in just a few minutes of scouting, and soon spied the open field and the infantry works. Claude put Hannibal and Hester behind a thicket of willows at a seep, leaving Blue clutched tightly by the big Negro, while he cautiously reconnoitered the ground. He had gone only a few feet when tobacco smoke drifted by. A crawl placed him behind the single picket, a boy who watched the Yankees only intermittently while he puffed on his pipe. A set of logs protected the rebel soldier, a thin slit between two allowing unobserved glances at the enemy works. Claude shivered and felt like throwing up as the enormity of his ill-luck overwhelmed him, and his face sank down onto the weedy ground.

"God almighty," he whispered, "another boy! Do I have

to kill him too?" His mind reeled from the implication as his revulsion almost overcame his peril.

Trembling and morbid premonitions gave way to reason while Claude inspected the approach to the infantry post. It was impossible to get into the pit without noise, he told himself. The bushes provided good cover but his flapping shoes would make too much racket. He waited patiently, not ready to force a fight. With all the movement he could see on the other side of the field, it seemed that an opportunity should present itself. It surprised him when it came. Shouts from the Yankee dugout echoed crisply in the cold air and stirred up the picket.

"Hey, Johnny, you got any 'baccy?"

"Plenty, Yank, but I got ter go git it. Trade ternight fer bacon?"

"Done. First moonlight we hold our fire."

The boy picked up his rifle and cautiously inched back out of the pit before casting up the trail. Claude stepped into the path beside him when the picket passed his hiding place. Seizing the rifle, he pushed the derringer into the boy's face. "I'll kill you if you move, boy," he threatened. "Gimme the rifle."

Frozen into a statue by the menace in the planter's voice and the hard prod of the derringer under his chin, the picket instantly released the rifle. His rigor gave way to trembling and sobbing when Claude tossed the rifle aside and relieved him of his knife. Swung around to front the planter, the picket's terrified face and tears broke down into pleading sobs. "Don't kill me," he said, "don't kill me."

"How old are you, boy?" Claude asked.

"'bout fifteen."

A pang ran through Claude. Fifteen! And a rifleman, not a drummer boy. Killing and being killed and for no good reason now that the rebs were beat. But old Jeff Davis couldn't see it yet, according to Mary. The planter waved the boy on up the trail. The youth scrambled ahead, eager to do Claude's bidding. Hannibal was crouched when they arrived at the Negro's hideout, his knife ready for intruders. A few seconds sufficed for him to bind the boy's hands and to thrust him into a submissive squat. Blue's sniffs at the boy

frightened the youth, his body inching away as he talked to
the hound to make friends.

Hester's troubled frown switched from the captive to
the planter. "How we git on ter de Yankees, Claude?"

Claude reassured her. "They's only a little field down
there, Hester, with thistles and cockleburrs. We wave a
white flag and march him across with us as a prisoner."

The girl's hands worried her dress and her voice quivered. "Dey ain't goin'a shoot us?"

"Not if we call out. You'll see."

Claude's relief at their imminent escape was overcome
by the prolonged strain of his tense wariness. He had been
on edge for too long. Exhaustion, fear, debilitation, anxiety,
all overloaded his whole being. Dizzy and uncoordinated,
his heart pounded as his anxiety conquered him and led to
the crumbling of his being into chaos. His breakdown
progressed into a crashing descent into physical and psychic collapse, his nervous control finally overwhelmed. His
body quivered, first slightly, then uncontrollably as he tried
to gather himself for the final journey. Hester eased him
onto the ground when he fell over, unable to talk. His mouth
drooled and his shudders rolled over him in waves from top
to bottom, much like shivering due to chills. But his
breakdown lingered only a few minutes, then passed on like
a rushing cloud. When his fit left him, he felt shaken and
exhausted from the nervous discharge, but resigned to the
next challenge and anxious to be gone. Careful, he told
himself, there's still the field to cross. Don't want no accident.

The rifle pit was crowded when they slithered in past
the screening bush and logs. Dug for two men, it now held
four, with Blue crouched behind the bushes outside. Claude
eased his eyes up to the firing slit to observe the Yankees.
His movement in front of the opening brought a shot from
across the field. A ball plunked into the log not far from his
head and jarred down a trickle of dirt. He jerked down in
fright as the reb laughed.

"They kill yuh if you ain't keerful," the boy warned.
"Been three men kilt right'chere."

Claude's heart beat a tattoo while he sat in the dirt and

tried to calm himself. "Got to signal 'em," he announced. His questioning face looked at each. "We need somethin' white for a flag."

Hester giggled nervously and raised her dress. "We ain' got nothin'," she said. "Me an' Hannibal don't wear no under clo'es."

The officer's eyes focused on the boy. "What you got on?" he asked. "Your mama make you wear drawers, boy?"

Hannibal stripped the picket's pants over the boy's struggles. The search turned up a pair of dirty, gray drawers, long unwashed. Hannibal fastened them to the reb's rifle barrel and waved it about.

Claude sighed. "Ain't white," he said, "but it'll have to do. Crawl out to the side and wave it without showin' yourself."

Two cracks and a shout answered the exposure of the flag. The Yankees had fired at the first movement, but apologized a moment later with a contrite yell.

"Ain't meanin' to shoot yer flag, reb. What'cher want?"

Claude's stentorian bawl left no room for question. "Don't shoot! This is Lieutenant Shaw, 7th Ohio, escaped prisoner. We're comin' out."

Pandemonium erupted in the works across the field, shouts for the Sergeant of the Guard echoing back. Claude risked a glance through the rifle slit, just in time to see more rifle barrels sliding out toward his waving flag. The Yankees were getting ready. It scared him and he prayed aloud. "Oh, God, don't kill us now. See us safely through the wilderness." But there was nothing to be done but to surrender, he knew, and to march across the field. Once more he glanced through the slit, then squatted with the others and issued his orders.

"The reb goes first," he said crisply. "He takes the bullets if they shoot right off." Claude's derringer subdued the picket's protest as he continued. "Hester follows behind if they don't. Hannibal next and I come last. Blue stays close with me. Keep your hands way up in the air."

His bellow carried across the field, unmistakably loud and clear. "This is Lieutenant Shaw, 7th Ohio. Hold your fire! Hold your fire! We're comin' across the field, four of us."

"Come on out!" a Yankee yelled back.

They moved fast at the reply. Hannibal pushed the reb out of the side of the pit. The frightened boy jumped up and threw his hands above his head, shouting, "Don't shoot!" He stepped off smartly into the thistles, aiming straight for the waiting men and their menacing rifles. Hester and Hannibal followed, Hannibal still waving the drawers. Claude's rifle hung barrel down from his hand when he brought up the rear with the dog. Old Blue rubbed his leg and stayed in close as they threaded their way through the thistles.

The Yankee rifle barrels steadied and aimed as the fugitives advanced. "Keep comin', reb," hidden voices called. "Keep comin'."

Claude's heartbeat about overwhelmed him as he hurried toward the other side. The skin on his back crawled in fear and the hairs rose on the nape of his neck. Perspiration drenched him and streams of sweat ran down his sides. Was there a rebel sniper to pick him off? He couldn't keep gloom out of his thoughts. His legs hurried but his mind raced far ahead, morbid thought tripping him up with disasters even as he drew ever closer to safety.

Hands reached out and seized the boy when he tumbled over the parapet, and instantly dragged him out of sight. Hester and Hannibal followed, disappearing behind the fortification. When Claude reached the head logs, he jumped over, only to be beset by three men who spread-eagled him while their Corporal put a pistol to his head. He froze, his caution keeping him from struggling while he screamed in protest.

"God damn you! I'm Lieutenant Shaw, 7th Ohio. Let me up."

The men atop him laughed and kept him pinioned, while the Corporal shouted out a report. "Ain't nothin' but three ol' contrabands, Sarge. An' one reb. Got a dawg too."

Blue growled and circled the captors, his hackles up, but curses and kicks drove him off. He crouched, his stub tail straight up, but his ominous growling gradually diminished to a vigilant silence when the prisoner's struggles subsided.

The Corporal spit to clear his mouth, then shouted to

his invisible commander. "What'cher want us ter do, Sarge?"

A disembodied, irritated yell replied, "Haul 'em 'round here."

The detail dragged Claude and the fugitives back from the line to a fire shielded by a log cabin. An odor of strong coffee assailed the planter as he approached, powerful, permeating, awakening long dormant desires. Intense longing made his mouth water as soon as he saw the pot. But his eyes shifted to the Sergeant when a soldier yanked his bad shoulder and they were stood up before the man. Other men ringed them with rifles and fixed bayonets. Hester and Hannibal eyed the cold steel and clustered together. Mute in their timidity and terror, they looked to the planter for succor. Even Old Blue was cowed and crept in close to Claude. His growling rumbled and his hackles were up, but his tail was down when he sought protection behind Claude's legs.

The Sergeant left them no hope. His insulting gaze took in the curves of the girl while he drank from a tin cup and tossed the dregs into the fire. Satisfied with his inspection, he growled at them. "What's the hell's this about the 7th Ohio?"

"You dumb, Sergeant?" Claude asked. His icy tone and erect stance cut through the fog of the man's misunderstanding. "Come to attention when you address a superior officer."

The soldiers stirred and muttered. Dark looks of anger clouded their faces and they took a stance for thrusting bayonets.

Uncertainty flitted across the Sergeant's face and his voice changed from overbearing to just disrespectful. "Ain't never seen no nigger officer."

Claude snorted in disgust. "I'm dyed with walnut hulls, God damn you. I'm as white as you are. Now order your men to put down those rifles."

A few men laughed derisively but the others grinned and dropped their muzzles toward the ground, even before the Sergeant told the soldiers to stand easy. Truculent and unconvinced, the Sergeant fidgeted, then scowled and insulted Claude.

"You may be a Lieutenant," he said, omitting the "sir," "but yer black an' I ain't takin' yer word fer it. We're goin'a go see the Colonel."

"I want my rifle back," Claude insisted. "I took it in battle over by the river. It's my property."

"You git it if the Colonel says. Now march!"

The Sergeant told off a detail to guard the prisoners and carry the confiscated weapons, then escorted them into the Union camp. After a brisk march of no more than a thousand or so paces, they advanced on a large, snowy-white tent that overshadowed a row. A few lounging officers straggled up to see the fun, joining a mystified group of hangers-on.

Lt.Colonel Daniel Wills came out into the sunlight when he heard the commotion of the detail and the gossip of the chattering onlookers. A tall, potbellied man, he had to stoop to clear the flap of his tent. The Colonel adjusted his campaign hat as soon as outside, stroking its feather into prominence. He took his usual position on the parade ground before his tent and stood at attention, smoking a stogy, with his adjutant at his side. The Sergeant marched the three prisoners to a stop before him with a flourish of commands. Fine dirt flew up in little sprays from their shuffling feet, particularly as Claude's shoes flopped and scraped. When halted in front of the Colonel, the planter forced his injured shoulder back and stiffened his spine. His hurt neck throbbed when he straightened up to erect attention. Hannibal supported Hester a step to the side.

Wills stuck out his jaw belligerently in his usual pique. A tendril of smoke rose from the cigar in his fingers as he brusquely questioned the Sergeant. "Why the sam hill did you bring those Negroes here, Kinsley?"

The Colonel was in a quandary, the Sergeant could see. He trembled at the thought of Will's choler and explosive temper, a harsh man when aroused. Kinsley had faced the Colonel's wrath before, suffering castigations he didn't want to have repeated. He was as brief as he could manage.

"They come inter one o' the fallow field pickets, sir. Brought a reb prisoner with 'em." He pointed to Claude. "This one claims he's a Yankee officer. Hell, he's too black fer that."

The assembled group tittered and the guard detail laughed aloud. Claude opened his mouth but "Sir" was all he got out before he was whacked in the back by the Sergeant. "Be quiet 'til the Colonel speaks to yuh."

Perverse, ignoring Claude when his eyes lighted on Hester and her curves, Wills motioned the two Negroes forward. He waved at Hannibal with his cigar. "Who the hell are you? And who's the woman?"

Surprised by the officer's switch but always seeking favor, Kinsley prodded the Negro to answer. Hannibal could only stand there mute. His big frame quivered and his face contorted while he held the swooning Hester.

Claude clasped Hannibal's trembling arm and reassured him. "Easy, Hannibal, easy," he said. "It'll be all right. Just rest easy."

Wills' temper boiled over at the interference. "Seize him!" he ordered. His men pinioned Claude, twisting his bad shoulder until he groaned and was close to fainting from the pain.

Will's choleric face and bulbous, veined nose flamed red as he berated Claude. "God damn it," he said, fuming. "You keep quiet, damn your hide, 'til I ask you."

Hannibal's shouts, "No! No! Turn 'im loose!" stopped Wills' tirade. The Colonel stood with his mouth agape at the Negro's protest and immediate attack. Berserk, Hannibal dropped Hester and wrested the restraining arms off Claude, throwing the men aside with superhuman strength. He faced the bayonets ringing him, once the planter was free, then stood between Claude and the blades like a caged lion, defiant and uncowed. "Leave 'im be," he said emphatically. "He be a Linckum sojer, hurt bad by de rebs."

The Negro's blazing eyes and crouch, his head swinging from side to side as he watched for an attack, struck silence into the crowd and froze the detail into immobility. Blue growled from his post beside Hannibal. His hackles stood straight up and his bared canines threatened violence.

Wills chuckled as he took in the amazing defense. His mercurial temper crumbled and his body relaxed. "Ease off, boys," he said, between puffs on his cigar. "Maybe we'd better listen."

The Colonel's astonishing command brought down the threatening bayonets. His men backed away at the Sergeant's gesture.

Hannibal eased around in front of Claude, who was holding his arm, his damaged shoulder hunched up. The Negro's quiet dignity when he faced the Colonel silenced all the onlookers. He stood with the confidence and erectness of a warrior who had killed, a heritage from his far-ago ancestors in Africa who judged fearless men. All could see that here was a warrior, unmasked finally, escaped from the degrading subservience of slavery, a dignified ambassador for his friend.

"I'se Hannibal," the Negro declared. "He Claude. He a sojer in de Linckum army. We 'scape from de camp down by Columbia."

"You escaped?" Wills said.

"Yassah, Colonel. Bout fo' weeks back. We done walked all de way. Granny Mandy down ter Columbia done dye Claude black fer de niggers ter git him thoo de rebs."

Kinsley's detail began chuckling and grounded their rifle butts. The men stood easy, resting on their weapons. All the tension slipped away, the laughing hangers-on intent on the next development, a tale to be told around the campfires. Wills shifted his gaze to Claude and his features broke into a smile. Then a chuckle welled up as he pulled on his cigar, his puffs of smoke flying away on the wind. He sniffed at the fugitives' odor and wrinkled his nose, but his distaste at their tattered, unwashed appearance was overcome at last by the necessities of military protocol. Facing Claude at stiff attention, he asked for his due.

"Report!"

Drawing up his dirty, thistle-covered figure to the best erectness his aching body would allow, Claude introduced his companions.

"Hannibal Shaw, a free man and my friend. Hester Pickens, his intended wife. They saved my life."

He saluted Wills in grave silence, then waited until the Colonel formally returned it before he spoke.

"Lieutenant Claude Shaw, sir, L Company, 7th Ohio

Cavalry. Reporting for duty."

THE END

Epilog

Captain James Claudius Shaw, 7th Ohio Volunteer Cavalry, was born February 22, 1827 and died February 13, 1894. He was my Great Grandfather.

A well-to-do merchant along the Ohio River, in the area that includes Crown City, Ohio and Cabell County, West Virginia, he had conflicting interests pulling at him when the Civil War erupted. Grandpa was a slaveholder, yet went with the Union. He was 35 when he volunteered in August, 1862, leaving Grandma Lutetia and children. Claude Shaw believed in the Union, rejected the Southern secession, and served and fought with Ohio troops. Although a Union man, he took a Negro slave with him as a body servant, no small dichotomy!

With three horses shot out from under him in different battles, Grandpa Shaw finally was seriously wounded and captured on November 6, 1863 at Rogersville, Tennessee. He sent his body servant home to tell Grandma that he was alive, the man faithfully returning to assist him during his confinement.

The two experienced the rigors of several Confederate prisons. Progressing successively through prisoner of war camps in Virginia, at Lynchburg, Libby Prison in Richmond, and Danville, the two men later were sent to Macon, Georgia, and ended up in the final camp at Columbia, S.C. Using $50.00 in gold obtained through a Charleston, S.C. friend, Claude Shaw bribed a Camp Sorghum guard on November 1, 1864 and escaped. In the ensuing days of November, not a time to sojourn in the open without gear, he and his body servant, with no arms and little kit, evaded capture and escaped through the Confederate hostiles, arriving back at the Union lines at Dalton, Georgia on November 27, 1864. Twenty six days and about 300 miles in the cold wilderness!

Grandpa Shaw left no written record of his travail, only family tales of his wounding, capture, and escape by bribing a guard with gold. His military record documents the capture, imprisonment sites, and escape. A copy of a canceled bank draft in the family's possession certifies to the gold. The original is part of the collection at an Ohio museum.

It is inconceivable that Grandpa Shaw could have escaped without the willing help of his body servant and that of the indigenous Negro population through South Carolina and Georgia, help that was life-threatening to all participants. The underground railroad was a fact. That escaped slaves and other men, deserters, bandits, draft evaders, lived in the woods and were not captured is a fact. That Union personnel walked out through the Confederates, with Negro help, is documented in the literature of the war. What is not known is the extent of Negro participation in Grandpa's escape, yet they must have played a major part in its success and I am humbly grateful.

Various historic sites mentioned existed in 1864. These include Greenbottom, a major flat along the Ohio River, Chief Vann House and the Calhoun plantation, along with the Camp Sorghum prison and most of the towns, and the earlier Revolutionary War revetments at Ninety Six. The Shaw manor house, "Greenbottom," is fictional. Except for Claude Shaw as an adaptation of my grandfather's name, and Letty for my Grandmother, and a few historical names, such as Jefferson Davis, Lee, Hood, Hardee, and Garrard, all the other persons' names in the tale are fictional, along with their characters. Shaw's escape on November 1, 1864, the bribing with gold, Sherman at Atlanta, and Hood's entry into Tennessee are historical, as are the verses. All other events and actions are fictional. This is a novel about a real prisoner of war escape from the Confederates, with participants experiencing fictional, though realistic, problems along the way. Only the end points of the escape and method(hiking through the hostiles) are known for sure.

Grandpa Shaw's body servant performed in exemplary fashion in his service, from family lore. His name, like so many other unsung heroes, is lost to history. He was, in brutal fact, a slave, yet he was extremely loyal to his master. It seemed only fitting to give him the name of a dedicated conqueror with strength, courage, grit, ingenuity, savvy and determination, a man conquering long odds, one with immense stature in history, for he must have had much the same attributes. Accordingly, I have named him Hannibal.

Waldron M. McLellon
Fern Park, Florida
March 1, 1994

ABOUT THE AUTHOR

Waldron Murrill McLellon

Photo by Doug Seibert,
Esquire Photographers, Inc.

With four Civil War Grandpas, all of whom survived, Mac McLellon grew up with a lifelong interest in the conflict. He knew two of these Grandpas as a youth, one a Confederate, the other a Union veteran. Many tales in the family supplemented his Grandpas' military records.

A naval officer who later was a university faculty member, Mac McLellon published widely in the professional literature. After academic retirement, he concentrated on poetry and fiction, rather than professional engineering topics. *Leather and Soul* is his recreation of one Civil War Grandpa's unusual ordeals.

Leather and Soul
—A Civil War Odyssey—
From Bondage to Freedom
A Passage of Body and Soul

by

Waldron Murrill McLellon

For additional copies of *Leather and Soul*, telephone TOLL FREE 1-800-444-2524. Credit Card orders accepted.

To order *Leather and Soul* direct from the publisher, send your check or money order for $16.95, plus $3.75 shipping and handling, total $20.70 postpaid, to Butternut Press, Publishers, 1913 Winnebago Trail, Fern Park, FL 32730-3015. Florida residents send $21.89 postpaid, which covers price of book, sales tax, and shipping and handling. When ordering more than one copy, add $1.50 shipping and handling for each additional book ordered.

For *quantity purchases*, telephone Butternut Press, Publishers, (407) 339-9244, or write to Butternut Press, Publishers, 1913 Winnebago Trail, Fern Park, FL 32730-3015.